# THE
# LAST LIES
## OF
# ARDOR BENN

KINGDOM OF GRIT: BOOK THREE

# TYLER WHITESIDES

orbit

**www.orbitbooks.net**

F123716u9

ORBIT

First published in Great Britain in 2020 by Orbit

1 3 5 7 9 10 8 6 4 2

Copyright © 2020 by Tyler Whitesides

Map by Serena Malyon

Excerpt of by *The Rage of Dragons* by Evan Winter
Copyright © 2019 by Evan Winter

The moral right of the author has been asserted.

*All characters and events in this publication, other than those
clearly in the public domain, are fictitious and any resemblance
to real persons, living or dead, is purely coincidental.*

All rights reserved.
No part of this publication may be reproduced, stored in a
retrieval system, or transmitted, in any form or by any means, without
the prior permission in writing of the publisher, nor be otherwise circulated
in any form of binding or cover other than that in which it is published
and without a similar condition including this condition being
imposed on the subsequent purchaser.

A CIP catalogue record for this book
is available from the British Library.

ISBN 978-0-356-51103-0

Typeset in Baskerville by M Rules
Printed and bound in Great Britain by Clays Ltd, Elcograf S.p.A.

Papers used by Orbit are from well-managed forests
and other responsible sources.

MIX
Paper from
responsible sources
FSC® C104740

Orbit
An imprint of
Little, Brown Book Group
Carmelite House
50 Victoria Embankment
London EC4Y 0DZ

An Hachette UK Company
www.hachette.co.uk

www.orbitbooks.net

*To Dean and Wally*

STRIND

Leigh

DRONODAN

INTERISLAND WATERS

Marow

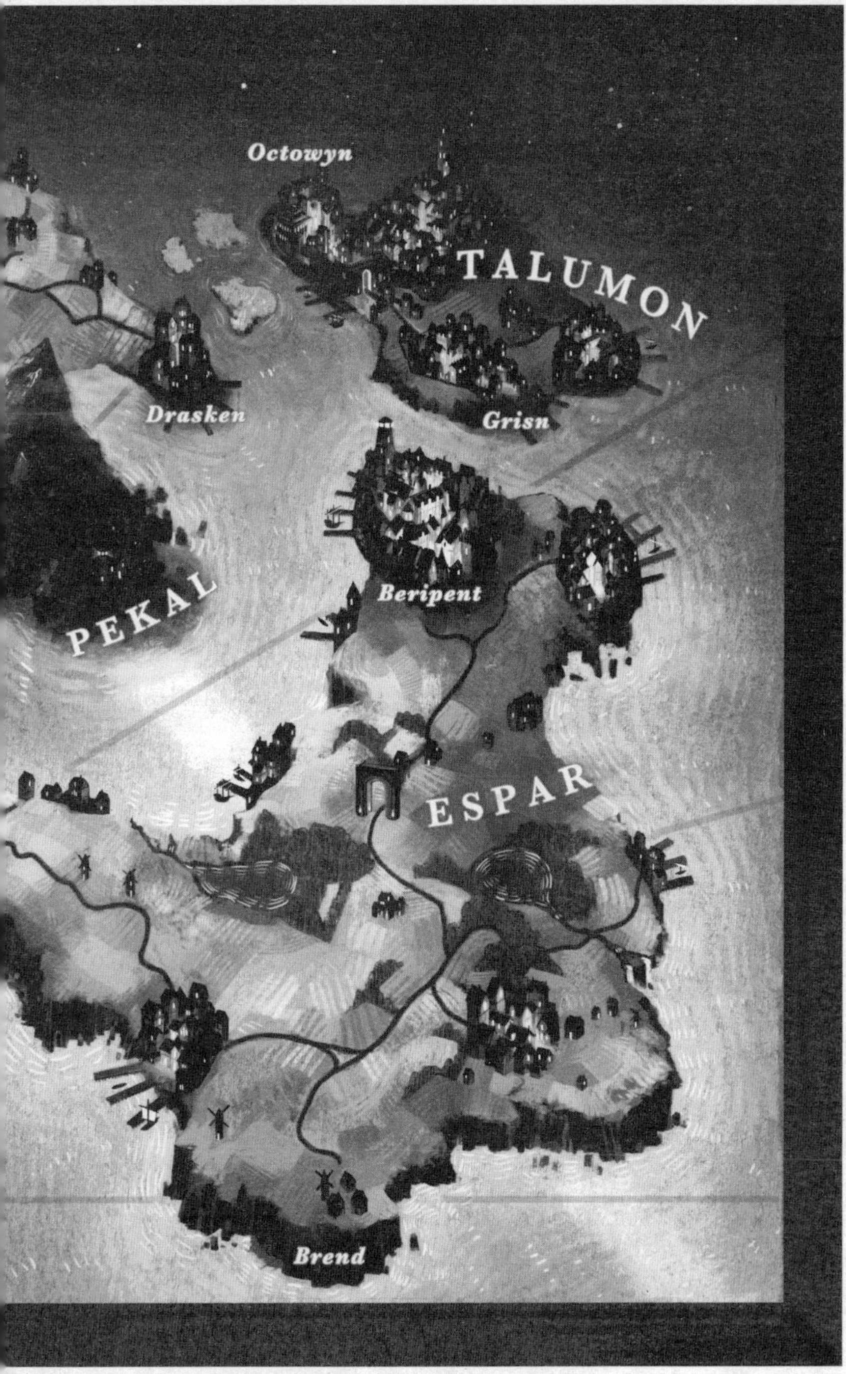
Octowyn
TALUMON
Drasken
Grisn
Beripent
PEKAL
ESPAR
Brend

# PART I

———————

Life should ever point us to the Homeland, though each day is not without its mighty tribulations. Though we struggle in a line, the circle saves, and the sphere governs all.

—Wayfarist Voyage, *vol. 3*

That great red eye foretells with clarity, recalls with wisdom, and perceives the present as in one still moment.

—*Ancient Agrodite poem*

# CHAPTER

# 1

Ardor Benn stumbled on the hem of his sea-green Islehood robes. Well, wasn't *that* befitting? He might have chuckled to himself, if there hadn't been so many people watching.

The Char was as bustling as usual, though the day carried a chill uncommon to summer. A reminder that, although it was the Third Cycle, spring wasn't a distant memory.

Still, Ard wasn't cold. In fact, he probably would have been comfortable wearing nothing beneath his Islehood robes. But he'd learned pretty quickly that free-flying was frowned upon in the Mooring. And now things were awkward with Isless Shora, and Isle Ton couldn't look him in the face, and he'd earned his second visit to Cove 1 for remediation from the Prime Isle...Anyway, today proved it was a lesson well learned, since Ard needed a belt beneath his robes to strap on his holsters.

There was a crowd waiting at Oriar's Square—mostly working class Landers who'd caught wind of today's showdown and wanted to see it unfold for themselves. They parted as Ard approached, a few holding up pendants of the Wayfarist anchor to show their support. Nice to know he had the blessing of the crowd, but he didn't let it lull him into false security. If this went like last time, the crowd would just end up getting in the way.

*It'll go better than last time*, Ard tried to convince himself, scanning the mossy flagstone pavers in the center of the square. He was supposed to stand on the one shaped like a tricorn hat. Really, Raek? All the stones were roughly triangular.

"I said, come alone," Dalfa Rhed called, cutting through the row of onlookers. She was a wiry woman who barely reached Ard's shoulder. One of her front teeth was missing, and she spit through the black hole of its absence.

"I am alone," Ard reassured her.

Dalfa pointed at the throng surrounding them. There must have been fifty people already. "What's all this?"

"Citizens of Beripent, enjoying a summer's afternoon," Ard answered. "You can't have expected me to close the Char. I'm only a humble Isle."

"Cut the slag," she said. "You're Ardor Benn. Criminal ruse artist."

"Reformed," Ard said. He wasn't trying to hide his past. "Or at the very least, _retired_."

This earned him a chuckle from the crowd. Little comments like that only helped to build the image he was developing. There was a reason Ard had a waiting list of people who wanted to see him for spiritual guidance at the Mooring. Holy Isle Ardor Benn was something of a novelty—a legendary criminal turned pious.

"I got your request to meet." Ard held out his arms, the wide robe sleeves hanging like curtains. "What can I do for you?"

Instead of answering him directly, Dalfa turned to the crowd. "This man defiles the Islehood robes with his Settled lies! Five years ago, he gained access to my chateau in northern Strind, posing as a nobleman looking to expand his interests."

"That's a little vague," Ard cut in. "What was I doing, exactly?"

Dalfa spit again, glaring at him. "It slips my memory."

Ard sighed. She was too smart to confess to counterfeiting Ashings in front of a crowd. There might be Regulators observing the exchange from the peripheries.

"The point is," Dalfa continued, "while I thought we were

engaged in honest business, Ardor Benn was actually plotting to rob me!"

Ard could see that her punchline didn't land with the impact she'd hoped. The crowd hardly seemed surprised. Most of them had probably read about worse in the official Letters of Apology that Ardor Benn had written after the queen had pardoned him.

It was by no means a complete summary of his decade of rusing. Many of his targets had been other criminals who Ard had decided would rather not be apologized to, for fear of drawing the Reggies' attention. Really, he was doing them a favor by keeping quiet.

But he'd worked hard on the letters he had written, choosing words that technically apologized for his crimes, but never for his cleverness in committing them.

"He left my chateau," continued Dalfa in what seemed to be a more calculated attempt to shock the onlookers, "went directly to the public treasury, and withdrew a thousand Ashings in my name!"

This *did* earn a reaction. Because, well, a *thousand* Ashings. That sum was far more than these citizens would see in a year.

"Don't let it shake your trust in the public treasuries," Ard assured the throng. "A withdrawal requires all kinds of paperwork, two signatures authenticated against the ones in the treasury's books, a wax seal with a notary's signet stamp..."

"Then how'd you do it?" someone called from the crowd.

Ard scratched his head. "I don't recall. Dalfa?"

Her face was twisted into an ugly sneer, and he knew he'd pushed her too far to admit it now.

"Oh, that's right!" Ard said in mock recollection. "You signed the paperwork and had a notary present for the seal—"

"I thought I was signing something else," Dalfa yelled.

Ard smiled at the onlookers. "And that, my friends, is why it's always important to read the fine scribing."

The cocking sound of a Slagstone gun hammer returned Ard's attention to Dalfa. She had a Roller leveled at his chest, not a drib of amusement on her face. Ard, too, felt suddenly less amused. The public setting was supposed to avoid all this threatening and gun-pointing.

Ard held up his hands, a somber look on his face and his tone to match. "You can read my apology in the official letter I addressed to you," he said slowly. He certainly wasn't going to apologize *again*.

"I don't care about your apology," Dalfa said, waving the Roller. The wiser citizens in the crowd were repositioning themselves to avoid the line of fire. "I want my Ashings back."

"I paid you in full," Ard said. Sparks, this was shaping up to be *just* like last time. That was what happened when old enemies learned of his official pardon. The little rats were hungry to exploit the fact that the legendary Ardor Benn had gone clean.

"I paid you *all* back," he insisted. *Well, everyone mentioned in the Letters of Apology, at least.* "Do you really think the Islehood would let someone with criminal debts join their—"

"You're not part of the Islehood!" Dalfa bellowed. "You're a ruse artist. And this"—she gestured at his holy attire—"is nothing but an elaborate ruse for reasons only Homeland knows."

"Come on, Dalfa. Have a little faith." He might still be able to diffuse the situation. "You know my old reputation. I was a busy criminal. Would I really sit in the Mooring for over a year with nothing to show for it?"

"I know you to be patient, too," she said, not lowering the gun, "if the payout is big enough."

"Are you aware of my agreement with Her Majesty?" Ard asked. It would be good for the people to hear it, too.

"Queen Abeth Agaul employed *you*—a known criminal—to find her missing son and heir to the crown," Dalfa said.

"Which I did," answered Ard. Never mind that the poor lad had promptly been shot on his brand-new throne.

"Whatever deal she offered you after that was clearly swayed by Her Majesty's feelings of gratitude for what you'd done."

"Questioning our crusader monarch is grounds for treason," Ard said. "Queen Abeth has accomplished more good in two years than many kings and queens do in a lifetime."

The crowd murmured its approval. Queen Abeth had always been well loved, even as an expatriate of Termain's Archkingdom. She was the woman who seemed to have endured it all—the assassination of her husband and son, the exiling from a kingdom she had been groomed to rule, her own supposed assassination in the streets of Beripent. Abeth Ostel Agaul had risen through it all.

Ard hadn't been one bit surprised when the new Prime Isle had decided to instate her as a crusader monarch. Like King Pethredote had been, Abeth was a placeholder ruler, not allowed to marry or produce an heir, working closely with the Prime Isle to establish stability across the islands until a decision could be reached about a new ruling bloodline.

"As payment for my services," Ard explained, "the good queen pardoned my crimes on the condition that I don't commit another. I made my apologies, paid my restitutions... Why would I jeopardize this arrangement just to slight you?"

"And if the pardoning wasn't enough," said Dalfa, "I heard the queen paid you a pretty Ashing, to boot."

It was true. And Dalfa Rhed was the third person to try to take advantage of this. Never mind that Ard had already paid her back. Now that he was wealthy and lawful, it gave her the perfect opportunity to leverage his new reputation for *more* Ashings.

"So how about you do the right thing?" Dalfa said. "Prove your honesty to these people and pay up." She finally holstered her gun, probably realizing how much it looked like she was threatening him.

"I'd be happy to produce proof of my payment," Ard said. "The receipts are in my cubby at the Mooring."

They were actually under his bed in his apartment in the Northern Quarter. He didn't keep anything of true value in his Mooring cubby. Too many Holy Isles disagreed with his admittance into the Islehood. There was no telling what lengths they'd take to get him expelled.

"Receipts that you could easily forge or falsify," Dalfa said. "As you've already proven."

Ard shrugged. "Well, I'm not paying you twice. If you're determined to investigate this further, perhaps you should contact a private inspector. I'd happily refer you to one I've used in the past..."

"Anyone will do the right thing if a Regulator is twisting their arm," said Dalfa. "But this is a matter of character."

"Yours, or mine?" Ard asked.

Half a dozen fellows suddenly appeared through the crowd, taking up positions behind Dalfa Rhed. Had they been there a moment ago? Surely, Ard would have noticed such ugly-looking sons of guns. They seemed happy to show off the Rollers on their hips, and one went so far as to crack his beefy knuckles.

"Hey, now." Ard held out his hands. "I know northern Strind is still a bit of a wild frontier, but you're in Beripent now. We take our laws seriously."

"We know the laws," said Dalfa. "And it's well within our rights to haul a suspicious character to the nearest Reggie Outpost."

That threat was barely even veiled. He wouldn't make it to the Outpost. Once Dalfa's thugs had him away from the crowd, it would be lights-out for good.

"Suspicious character?" Ard glanced down at the flagstone pavers. Aha! That one looked a bit like a tricorn hat. He took a large step sideways, positioning himself in the middle of the flat stone with his feet at shoulder width, knees slightly bent.

"I don't believe it's lawful for a Holy Isle to carry guns concealed beneath his robes," said Dalfa, pointing at his midsection.

"Who says I'm wearing anything under this?" Ard slipped his hand into the pocket of his robes, fingers wrapping around a cool glass vial.

"Sparks, I hope I don't find out," she answered. "I'll let the Regulators sort that out once we get you to the Outpost." Dalfa raised her hands and the six muscled men lumbered forward.

Showtime.

Ard dropped to his knee on the paver, pulling his fist from his pocket and smashing the vial of Ignition Grit against the flat rock beneath him. The chip of Slagstone inside the vial sparked on impact, consuming the green liquid solution in a short-lived detonation cloud.

The Ignition Grit did its job as calculated. The brief cloud detonated the loose Void Grit that Raek had placed beneath the triangular paver. The result was a rush of wind that propelled the flat rock straight into the air like a flying platform. There was only one problem.

Ardor Benn was kneeling on the wrong stone.

He fell sideways, bits of loose rock and soil pelting him in the face as the stone paver in front of him soared up. He cursed as his ride went skyward without him, but the sudden eruption had still been enough to knock back the goons and disperse the crowd of innocent citizens.

Ard's original overwrought escape plan was shot. He was supposed to have ridden the paver into the sky, grabbing a thick rope that Raek had strung between two treetops directly overhead. He could have hung there for a moment like fresh laundry on a line, before cutting the rope so he could swing out of Oriar's Square like a swashbuckler.

Well, now it was time to improvise.

Ard sprang to his feet, yanking up the front of his robes unceremoniously and drawing his twin Rollers. The Prime Isle would give him another reprimand for this, but it wouldn't be serious. Ard knew Olstad Trable secretly enjoyed having a celebrity in the Islehood.

The nearest thug lunged at him, a knife in one hand and a

Singler in the other. Ard baited him forward. One step. Two steps. Okay, that was far enough. This meathead clearly didn't spend much time thinking, since he'd forgotten one of the world's most basic truths—Things that go up typically come down.

The flat paver stone took him straight over the head with a crunching sound that made Ard's stomach turn. How was that for a tricorn hat? Oh, things were as bad as they could get now, with a dead man between him and Dalfa. One of the other men cracked off a shot, but the ball went wide. Retreating across the Square, Ard shot twice in response. He intentionally aimed low, letting the Roller balls chip the stone ground with hopes of deterring his enemies from chasing. He really didn't want to shoot anyone. Prime Isle Trable would have a hard time justifying that.

Flames! His escape route was cut off by the sudden arrival of two more thugs—women who were clearly on Dalfa Rhed's side. If he wanted to get to an open pathway out of Oriar's Square, he'd have to sprint through a maelstrom of Roller balls.

Ard's glance turned to the ruins of the Old Palace Steps. Just over four years ago, he'd saved all of humankind on those steps. Maybe they'd show him some kindness now.

He leapt the chain that cordoned off the historic site. His robe caught and he fell flat on his face, another gun ball missing him, perhaps thanks to his clumsiness. Maybe these robes *were* good for something!

He scampered forward, getting his feet under him as he ascended the stone steps. Was this the stair where he'd become a Paladin Visitant, crouched in shadow while Grotenisk the Destroyer breathed centuries-old fire to fertilize the bull dragon egg?

There wasn't much time for sentimentality now. Ard had no plan. He was simply trying to gain the high ground. That was always the tactical advantage, right?

Whatever he was doing, it seemed to be working. Halfway up the steps, his enemies stopped shooting at him. Dalfa Rhed was reckless to open fire in the Char, but her team wasn't foolish enough to put divots into a historical monument like the Old Palace Steps.

Ard was far from safe, though. One of the women and two of the men were stepping over the cordon chain, thin swords brandished. If only there was some way off this ruined stairway to nowhere...

A rope!

Almost like a gift from the Homeland, Ard saw a rope dangling from the tall oak that framed the steps to the right. Glancing up, he saw that it was Raek's original escape rope, conveniently severed so the cut end draped across the crumbling landing at the top of the stairs.

Perfect! A way out, and *still* a chance to look undeniably heroic. Ard holstered both Rollers and sprinted the final steps, catching the limp rope in both hands and leaping from the landing. He swung in a wide arc, his momentum and the significant length of his rope looping him around the side of the Old Palace Steps.

He was spinning in a madly dizzying fashion, but he still managed to glimpse the looks on the faces of his pursuers. They stared in obvious awe at his reckless acrobatics, swords gripped loosely.

Now, if only he knew how to get down.

Just then, the knot in the tree must have failed, dropping him to the stone pavers just yards from Dalfa. He didn't land gracefully, his Islehood robes tearing as he rolled painfully across the ground. Dalfa opened fire, but the ball from her Roller pinged harmlessly off a transparent Barrier cloud that had suddenly formed between them.

A rough hand seized Ard by the back of the neck and yanked him to his feet.

"Why can't you just escape like a normal person?" Raekon Dorrel asked, pointing his crossbow into the Square and sending a bolt through the leg of Dalfa's nearest man.

"How do normal people escape?" Ard asked, starting down the open path through the Char.

"On foot," Raek replied, reloading as he followed. "Not swinging across Oriar's Square like a windblown sailor."

"That was improvising," Ard said. "I was supposed to fly up on that paver."

"See? Not normal."

"Tricorn hat?" Ard spit. "That stone looked more like a croissant."

"I didn't think of a croissant," said Raek. "That's good."

"Not helpful now." Ard glanced over his shoulder to see that Dalfa and her thugs had not been slowed by Raek's Barrier cloud. Seven of them. Following at a dead sprint.

"If you're going to be so picky about the shape of the rock, you should have come with me when I was setting things up last night," Raek said.

"I had a man in my Cove pouring his heart out," said Ard. "I couldn't ask him to wrap it up so I could set up for tomorrow's showdown. I trusted you to take care of it."

"Well, I had my doubts about the flying-paver-plan from the beginning," Raek said. "Running was always a better idea."

Although winded from his sprint, Ard found enough breath to scoff. "Not nearly exciting enough. *Cowards* run. Reformed-ruse-artists-turned-Holy-Isles fly out of a conflict on a flat rock."

"Sometimes I wonder if you actually hear the words that come out of your mouth."

"Your rope didn't hold, by the way," said Ard. "I'm questioning your knots."

"The rope didn't hold because I untied it when I saw you flailing helplessly ten feet above the ground," said Raek.

"I mean before that," Ard said. "The other end must've come untied because I found it draped across the landing at the top of the steps."

"Yeah," Raek said. "You're welcome for that, too."

Ard slowed, pointing ahead. The path was clear of citizens—they knew how to scurry when trouble erupted in the Char—but a handful of blue uniformed Regulators were making directly for them. "About time they showed up!"

At his side, Raek cursed. "Since when are we *happy* to see Reggies coming toward us?"

"Dalfa started this trouble," Ard said. "She and her crew won't stick around to answer questions." He glanced back. "See?" Sure enough, their enemies were darting off the path into the lush foliage of the Char.

When he turned back, Raek had moved over to one of the historical ruins on the side of the pathway. It was one of the better-preserved structures from Old Beripent. There was a crumbled second story, but the first floor looked well intact.

"Lose the robe!" Raek called as he ripped open the mossy wooden door of the ruined building.

"What?" Ard cried.

"Trust me," said Raek. "You're going to want deniability."

Ard grimaced. Dalfa hadn't made up the law about concealing firearms beneath an Islehood robe. He stepped off the path and pulled the dirty sea-green fabric over his head. Ditching it under some ferns, he stepped back onto the path, heart pounding to see how close the Reggies were.

"Come on!" Raek shouted, peeking his head out from the doorway of the ruins. It seemed like a terrible idea to corner themselves in a run-down building while the Regulators could clearly see them enter. But he couldn't leave Raek.

Sprinting across the path, Ard ducked through the doorway and his partner slammed the old wooden door shut.

"Trespassing on historic ruins in the Char is punishable with jail time, *and* a fine," Ard hissed through the sudden darkness. The building was windowless, but sunshine leaked through the worn doorframe, casting thin lines of light filled with dancing particles of dust.

"Tell that to the guy who just jumped off the Old Palace Steps." Raek took a Grit pot from his belt and threw it against the door. The Slagstone sparked when the clay shattered and a dome of Barrier Grit effectively sealed off the door.

"This is a bad idea." Ard glanced around. The room was bigger than he'd expected. Maybe fifty feet long, but only half as wide. "I could have talked my way out of it. We're the good guys now. We've got nothing to hide."

Now it was Raek's turn to scoff. "I'm literally hiding *so* much in my pack right now," he said, shrugging out of it.

Ard held his breath, then decided to ask it. "Heg?" He knew his friend had been using it again—detonating Compounded Health Grit directly into that pipe in his chest. Since their confrontation on Pekal two years ago, Ard couldn't count how many times his friend had gone clean.

Or how many times he'd relapsed.

"I've got vials of liquid Grit in here that the Greater Chain doesn't even know exists," Raek said, artfully dodging the question.

The rickety wooden door thundered under the pounding of fists. "Open up!" cried a Regulator's voice. "In the name of the crusader monarch! Open this door at once and surrender yourselves!"

"They're just going to blow their way in," Ard whispered.

Raek shook his head. "And destroy one of the Char's historic buildings?"

Ard tilted his head to catch a woman's voice making a report. "We've swept the building, sir. This door is the only way in or out."

"Very well," came the reply. "They're not going anywhere. We'll station ourselves here and starve them out if we have to."

Ard turned to Raek, exhaling sharply. "Bury your pack," he whispered. "I'll go out there and—"

"One crime," Raek cut him off. "All they have to do is find us guilty of *one* crime."

Ard understood the stakes. If he violated the terms of agreement with Queen Abeth, she would revoke the pardon and it would be back to his old lifestyle.

"We can't risk it yet," Raek said. "Not until you get what we need from the Islehood."

Right. Finding out where the Islehood stored its growing collection of dragon shell fragments was the entire point of this plan. With the little bull dragon finally mature enough to fertilize the eggs, there had been a huge influx of shell. In keeping with tradition, the Islehood had complete control over it, safeguarding the broken fragments until they could be processed into Visitant Grit.

It actually hadn't been hard to figure out where the Islehood was storing it. Ard had learned the location two cycles ago.

The hard part was deciding not to tell Raek.

"And when we *do* lose the queen's pardon—hopefully soon," Raek went on, "I expect to be doing something a lot more impressive than *trespassing*."

"How do we get out of here, then?" Ard whispered. "They said they could starve us out. And I'm already hungry!"

"Relax." Raek dug into his pack. "We don't have to go out the door."

"Blast Grit?" Ard said hesitantly. "You're going to blow a hole in the wall—"

"That could bring the whole place down on our heads," Raek cut him off, holding up a pair of thick, elbow-length gloves. A grin split his scarred face. "I think it's time to give these another try."

"The gauntlets. Are you serious?" Ard retorted. "Didn't you break every one of your fingers last time?"

"Only nine," said Raek. "My left pinky was spared. And anyway, I've made some improvements." He pulled another Grit pot from his belt and tossed it to Ard. "Detonate this against the far wall, will you?"

Ard glanced at the clay ball, a white spot painted on one side. "What is it?"

"Silence Grit," Raek replied, tugging on one of the bulky gauntlets.

Ard crossed to the back of the long room and pitched the pot against the stone wall. He was standing within the radius when the cloud formed and everything went absolutely silent. He breathed in the quiet for a brief moment, trying to feel the Urgings from the Homeland that he'd spent the last year preaching about.

There was nothing. He felt no guidance beyond the cleverness of his own intellect. And he had felt nothing since the night of Gloristar's marvelous transfiguration. She had claimed to *be* the Homeland. And if that were true, perhaps it explained why Ard had felt nothing since. He had seen the Homeland with his own eyes. He had seen her fall from the Old Post Lighthouse, swallowed into the depths of the sea.

And in the two years since her death, he had felt no Urgings.

Ard turned to find Raek fully geared up. In each gloved hand he held an iron rod about a foot long. Both ends of the rods had been flattened like the head of a nail.

"That's your improvement?" Ard asked, stepping out of the Silence cloud.

"And I sewed the rods to the palms of the gloves so they won't slip," he said out of the corner of his mouth. The other side of his lips were busy clenching two small blue vials like cigars. As Ard watched, Raek carefully spit a vial into each of his palms, the glass clinking as it rested against the iron bars.

"I see how convenient these would be in a hurry," Ard said sarcastically.

"They're a work in progress," replied Raek. "Ready?"

Without waiting for Ard's affirmation, Raek closed both of his fists, shattering the vials against the metal rods. Two spherical Grit clouds sprang up, encompassing Raek's hands entirely, closing tightly around his padded forearms. They shimmered. Vaporous, transparent. Both no larger than his head.

Grunting in satisfaction, Raek bumped his fists together. The impenetrable Containment cloud was one of the late Portsend Wal's creations—as durable as a Barrier cloud, but lightweight and movable.

The hard shell of the Containment clouds had formed around the bars Raek was holding, giving him a convenient handle through the center of the detonation.

"The newly flattened ends should keep the rods in place," Raek explained. That had been the problem last time. His handlebars had shifted sideways so they were no longer supported through the center of the clouds. When he had punched, his fist had slid forward inside the sphere, slamming his knuckles against the inside of the Containment shell.

Raek bellowed, dashing a few steps to pound both protected fists against the Barrier cloud that sealed the door. The force rattled the hinges, and the old wood trembled.

"Umm…" Ard said. "Did I detonate that Silence Grit in the wrong place?"

"Nah," said Raek, turning away from the Barrier cloud. He lowered his voice. "I just needed to make a little ruckus at the front door so they think we're focused on getting out that way. With a little bit of luck, we won't have anyone stationed around back."

Ard followed his large friend to the Silence cloud on the other side of the building.

"You might want to shield your eyes." Raek said loudly, now that no one could overhear them. He drew back his arm and punched the wall with his armored fist. The huge muscles on his bare arm rippled, and Ard saw the mortar crack all the way around the big stone he'd struck. Loose bits chipped and flew, and Ard was grateful that he'd raised his hand to protect his face.

Well, a couple more blows like that and they'd have a genuine hole!

Raek punched again, this time lower on the block. Then he

delivered three more hits in rapid succession with alternating fists. The large stone block was more than halfway free, ready to tumble outside with just a few more strikes. Its vacancy would leave a hole large enough for the two men to climb through.

Raek grinned, drawing back his fist once more, but Ard caught his arm. Something had fallen to the floor at Raek's feet, dislodged from the wall and lying amid the loose debris.

A folded piece of parchment.

Ard stooped and picked it up, shaking off the dust. Raek shrugged in disinterest and punched the stone block again. Unfolding the parchment, Ard felt his breath sucked away by its simple message.

*Ardor Benn—Tofar's Salts. 8th of 3rd. Noon. Ask to see the Be'Igoth.*

Ard looked up sharply, half expecting to see someone lurking in the shadows of the old room. His pulse was racing every bit as fast as when he'd been swinging through Oriar's Square. A note addressed to him. *Here?* And the eighth day of the Third Cycle... That was only three days from now. How was this even possible?

"Raek," Ard whispered, but his friend didn't pause, slugging the wall a final time. The big stone block finally sloughed outward, a square beam of light cutting through the dim room.

"Someone might have heard that," Raek said, since the block had fallen outside the radius of their Silence cloud. "Ard?"

He was a statue, staring at the paper in his hands, turning it over in the new light as if additional words might appear.

"Ard!" Raek snapped. "Let's go."

He swallowed against the cryptic message he'd just read, wadding the parchment in his hand and climbing through the hole in the wall. Raek followed, blowing on his gauntlets as if they were smoking from the action.

"Raek." Ard tried to show him the piece of parchment. "This fell out of the wall—"

"Save it," Raek cut him off, holding up a Grit-covered fist, a worried look on his face. Just then, Ard saw one of the Regulators moving along the side of the ruins. At the sight of them, he let out a shrill cry.

"It's time to escape like a normal person," Raek muttered, clapping Ard on the back with his orb fist. "Run!"

~

*You deserve the truth, so I'll do my best to lay it all out for you. Consider this my glass mind. No tricks. No lies. All my barest intentions made plain even to the simplest of human minds.*

# CHAPTER

# 2

The body in the handcart was heavy, but that wasn't what caused Quarrah to stop for another break. Fear was what was slowing her down. Fear that the Moonsick figure sealed inside the long wooden box might leap up at any moment and start tearing into the arrogant Talumonian citizens that strutted these streets.

Ugh. Talumon was such a haughty island. Quarrah didn't particularly enjoy being here, but it was nice to have employment options on all the islands, now that the war had ended. She'd done some of her best work on Talumon in the past. Jobs seemed to line themselves up, clustered together like the endless towns and cities that populated this island.

But she definitely preferred Beripent to this self-important place. There was a dirty hardiness to Beripent's streets, where the cramped neighborhoods encouraged people to keep their heads down and mind their own business.

Quarrah continued forward, mindful of the storm clouds overhead and the wind that whipped her sand-colored hair. Good. The rain would give her an excuse to stay at Lord Dulith's manor and find out what kind of "cure" he was talking about.

"Best find shelter, young lady," called an old man, checking the knots on the canopy covering his front porch.

See...much too nosy for Quarrah Khai's liking. She didn't reply, knowing that if she engaged him, the next thing out of his mouth would probably be, "What's in the box?"

She'd already answered that half a dozen times after smuggling it past harbor security—"Delivery for Lord Dulith." But the shape of the box was a telltale coffin, and the Talumonians were gossipy enough that she'd had to offer *some* explanation. She'd settled on a shipment of Fielders, and the lie seemed to satisfy the passive curiosity around her.

Dulith's manor was old and stately, red stone walls rising three stories. Quarrah had scouted it well before approaching. There was an east and a west wing, servants' quarters, and a comfortable, open-air courtyard, ideal for entertaining if the weather was cooperating.

The rest of the property was nothing extravagant, with a graveled walkway leading to the front steps. A small stream meandered across the east side, diverted into a manmade lagoon, where refuse could be dumped through chutes from the east wing. Flowering bushes and a few stout trees were the only real hope for concealment on the grounds.

As simple as the manor was, its primary resident was much less so. Like all the wealthy nobles, Lord Dulith had the time and the means to pursue any number of interests. And while many squandered their fortunes on collecting useless furniture or gambling, this particular man was an aspiring healer. At first, Quarrah had guessed he was a Hegger. If he obtained the proper licensure to practice healing, it would be that much easier to get access to Health Grit.

But her opinion had changed the moment she'd met him.

Quarrah stopped her cart at the edge of Lord Dulith's property. Letting go of the handle, she reached into her Grit belt, withdrawing a small glass vial full of orange liquid. Carefully, she pried up the corner of the coffin's lid. At once, a misty Grit cloud escaped its confinement. It billowed around her hand, creating a spherical dome, which made it immovable.

She gagged at the stench that wafted from the long box. It was an odor ripe with awful memories of every Moonsick encounter she'd faced—including the most recent capture of this poor soul.

Holding her breath, she slipped the vial inside the coffin, propping it on a block of wood she had nailed inside to serve as a makeshift shelf. Then she slammed the cover shut, hearing the glass crunch against the lid, containing the detonation inside.

Quarrah stepped back, examining her work. It was a poor woman's excuse for a Drift crate, but hauling one of those around surely would have led the Reggies to stop and search her load.

The cloud of Stasis Grit would keep the Moonsick man contained in a state of unconsciousness. Even his ragged breathing and heartbeat would be suspended—assuming the creature's heart actually still beat at all. Despite all her encounters with Moonsick Blood-eyes, Quarrah still understood very little about them. Irrationally violent, their voices stolen, blinded by bloodstained eyes...It was a terminal condition. Only one person had ever survived Moonsickness, and Quarrah wouldn't have called it a cure. Prime Isless Gloristar had transformed into something altogether different.

Quarrah picked up the cart's handles, satisfied that the fresh Stasis cloud had been fully contained inside the coffin. She trundled up the gravel path toward the manor as the first raindrops fell.

F12371649

By the time she'd reached the bottom step, a well-dressed servant and four muscular laborers were waiting for her, the group framed by massive pillars that supported the front porch.

"Quarrah Khai," the servant greeted her. "Lord Dulith awaits you in his study." He gestured into the house. "Right this way."

"I really shouldn't leave this unattended," Quarrah replied, jabbing a thumb at the long box. "It's kind of a time-sensitive delivery."

She didn't mention that they had less than ten minutes before the package would wake up and start killing people. Honestly, she didn't know how much information the manor staff knew about their master hiring a criminal. Quarrah's contacts in Talumon said they'd never known Lord Dulith to go outside the law before.

"Lord Dulith understands that the goods are volatile," replied the servant. "These men will make sure the package gets where it needs to be."

Normally, she'd be happy to hand it over, get paid, and disappear. But something was different about this job. At the risk of seeming like Ardor Benn, Quarrah had an itch to know more about her employer's plans. This man had quietly claimed to have a cure for Moonsickness. She certainly didn't believe it was true. But what if he'd found something he didn't fully understand?

What if he'd found Metamorphosis Grit?

As the broad-shouldered laborers surrounded the handcart, Quarrah followed the servant into the manor. It was quiet and dry inside, the wall sconces lit with little orbs of Light Grit to combat the early dusk brought on by the storm.

The servant led her down the wide corridor and introduced her at the doorway to the study. Lord Dulith stood from the soft chair where he'd been waiting. He wasn't a very tall man. In fact, Quarrah had him by at least an inch. His thinning hair was starting to turn gray at the temples, and he sported a thick mustache. His jowls were disproportionately flabby for such a thin man, hinting at a successful reformation from years of gluttony.

"Come in," he said. "Sit down."

It was an invitation Quarrah Khai rarely accepted, but she obliged today, seating herself in the soft chair beside his.

"Did everything go as planned?" Dulith asked.

The lingering presence of the servant at the door made her think that the lord wasn't keeping this job as tight-lipped as she'd originally suspected.

"It's here," she answered. That didn't mean it had gone as planned. Things seldom did.

"Male or female?" Dulith asked.

"It was a man," she replied. *Was.* Because that monster was hardly human anymore.

"How many were still in the compound?"

She shook her head. "I didn't go to Strind." Visiting the Moonsick compound would have been asking for certain death. It was a hole of misery created by King Pethredote in an effort to appear more humane. Instead of executing people with Moonsickness, he stuffed them all into a remote compound and let them waste away naturally, recovering their corpses to feed to the dragons for specialty Grit derived from human bones.

Quarrah had heard that the compound had been bursting to capacity during the war. Moonsickness had been spreading naturally, and it didn't help that the Realm was farming Bloodeyes for their own purposes.

"I thought you'd steal one from the compound," Lord Dulith pressed. "I was anxious to hear how many are still locked away, now that Moonsickness is on the decline—thank the Holy Torch."

Quarrah masked an exasperated sigh. How could anyone believe in the Holy Torch anymore? Up until a year ago the Wayfarist torch had been mysteriously failing. Now it was working better than ever? Couldn't everyone plainly see that the Torch's effectiveness directly coincided with the population of dragons on Pekal?

The little bull, whose egg Quarrah herself had stolen from Pekal, was doing his job more effectively than anyone could have guessed. Just over a year ago, new dragons had started hatching all over Pekal. Reports claimed that the population was now at a record high. And thus, Moonsickness was on the decline...

"The compound seemed too dangerous," she admitted. "I decided on a different method."

Dulith furrowed his brow. "*Is* there another method? Don't tell me luck ran out for those thrill-seekers tempting fate in New Vantage."

"The colony is fine," she replied. Although Quarrah thought anyone willing to live on Pekal during a Moon Passing seemed halfway crazy already.

"Then how did you acquire the specimen?" asked Dulith.

"New Vantage may be safe, but the Redeye line on Pekal is still a real threat," she replied. "If people travel far enough up from the shoreline, they'll still get Moonsick."

"I see," said Dulith. "And the fellow you found for me?"

"He was part of a group that didn't come down to the safety of New Vantage fast enough," said Quarrah. "Five of them got Moonsick. Harbor Regulation realized that they were in the early stages and tried to detain them, but the sick ones had friends who caused a skirmish so they could get off the island."

Dulith sat forward, his saggy cheeks jiggling. "Why would they do such a thing? They could endanger hundreds. A true friend would put a Roller ball through their heads."

*Not a very compassionate statement from an aspiring healer who claims to have a cure for Moonsickness*, Quarrah thought.

"Don't worry," Quarrah said. "The group was detained in Beripent. The Moonsick victims were chained and shipped off to the compound on Strind. I managed to steal one and brought him to you."

She made it sound a lot easier than it actually had been. She'd had to slip onto the transport ship before it left Beripent. Posing to be a friend of a friend, she freed one and led him out. By that point, he was approaching the second stage—already mute and losing his sight to a deep reddening of the eyes.

He'd been very cooperative until Quarrah had locked him in a box and slipped him onto a cargo ship headed for Talumon. The Prolonged Stasis Grit had kept him docile and slowed the decay a little, but by the time she met up with the coffin, he was well into the third stage and intent on murdering her when she'd opened the box. More Stasis Grit had put him down, subduing the insane creature long enough to haul him here.

Lord Dulith rose slowly. "Let us go inspect the monster. If I find everything to be satisfactory, I'll deliver the payment and you can be on your way."

If Lord Dulith was new to hiring criminals, he probably didn't know her reputation well enough to realize that her work didn't need inspection.

"Totshin, it's time," Dulith said to the servant. "Fetch my son." With a nod, the attendant ducked out of the doorway, moving so quickly that Quarrah couldn't see him by the time they'd reached the corridor.

"It's time?" Quarrah repeated.

"To put my cure to the test," Dulith answered.

"I'm intrigued," she said cautiously. "Healers have been searching for a cure for Moonsickness since the beginning of time. You really think you've found it?"

"I know others have dedicated their entire lives to the healer's art," Dulith said, "but I've only been studying it since my wife passed away nearly three years ago."

"Okay," said Quarrah, puzzled by how a mere trio of years would give him advantage over the professionals. Dulith cast her a hurtful glance, and she suddenly realized how insensitive her reply had been. "I'm sorry to hear about your wife," she added.

"I was holding her when she died," said Dulith. "Pasic was

there, too—just a lad of nine years, watching the life drain from his mother."

Dulith paused before a set of tall double doors, the engraved wood inlaid with gold leafing. A servant was waiting with a long coat and hood. He held out the garb to dress his master, but Dulith paid him no mind, seeming lost in thought.

"It's raining quite hard, sir," the servant insisted, but Dulith merely raised a hand in dismissal and continued speaking to Quarrah.

"I'd never felt more helpless in all my life," Dulith said. "I was filled with a hollowness after that. At times it gave way to rage. Eventually, I began to practice healing. Perhaps that way I would be more useful in the face of tragedy."

Lord Dulith grabbed the large brass handle and pulled open one of the tall doors. Over his shoulder, Quarrah had a clear glimpse into the manor's courtyard. It was paved with mossy bricks and abundantly adorned with greenery. Against the exterior wall of the west wing was a Heat Grit hearth surrounded by a handful of benches. On the right was a long stretch of sand, the stakes buried in place for a game of sailor's folly.

And in the center of the courtyard was the Moonsick man, his rain-soaked clothes already ripped to tatters from his inane fury. He was bound to a wooden light post with thick chains, wrapped like an insect in a spider's web so that only his head and his feet were showing. The lantern above him was glowing with Light Grit even though the dreary evening wasn't yet fully dark.

The four large workers framed the Bloodeye—two on either side. Quarrah noticed one of them nursing a fresh wound on his arm. It was a miracle they were all still alive! Even if they'd known what they were dealing with, those men would have been surprised when the coffin's lid came off, probably taking the motionless Bloodeye for dead until they moved his head outside the Grit cloud.

The common citizen of the Greater Chain didn't know about

Stasis Grit. That was a little something Quarrah had picked up from her time with the Realm. And she was lucky enough to have a supplier who knew how to re-create Portsend's liquid Grit solutions.

Lord Dulith stepped into the courtyard, stopping just arm's length from the Bloodeye. His wet face bore a steely expression that Quarrah couldn't interpret. It certainly didn't look like the face of a healer approaching a patient.

Something was obviously off, she'd sensed it from the moment she'd seen Dulith today. But she hadn't been detained, or even disarmed, so Quarrah had no reason to think she was in any real danger.

"Father?" came a voice from the doorway behind them. Quarrah saw a pale-skinned boy with shaggy hair and dark circles under his eyes standing beside Totshin, the servant.

Dulith turned to his son, arms out in a warm gesture. His expression gave way to unabashed excitement. "The day has finally come, Pasic!"

"What day?" the boy asked from the shelter of the doorway. Quarrah didn't think the lad had noticed the Moonsick man yet, despite the jangle of chains as he thrashed his head back and forth. "Father? Who are these people?"

"It's all right, my boy." Dulith beckoned. "Come. Come. Don't be frightened."

This statement seemed only to alert the boy that he *should* be frightened. With a gasp, Pasic finally noticed the Bloodeye and turned to run down the corridor. Totshin caught him by the shoulders, holding him fast.

Dulith hurried back to the doorway, and Quarrah tensed when she saw a Roller in the nobleman's hand. "Take it. Take it." He plunged the gun into his son's grasp, pointing it toward the monster chained to the light post. "Your mother was the most caring woman I have ever known. Honor her now, son. Honor her memory!"

In horror, Quarrah watched the boy's countenance darken. His youthful jaw clenched and his eyes narrowed as he stepped into the rain.

"*There* is the monster that took her from us!" coaxed Dulith, pointing wildly at the Bloodeye. "Hold nothing back! Make me proud, Pas!"

Quarrah's feet were suddenly propelling her forward, driven by a sick feeling of familiarity in her stomach. She didn't care if the Bloodeye died—sparks, he *needed* to die in this courtyard. But not by the hand of a grief-stricken twelve-year-old boy.

"What is this, Dulith?" she cried, stepping between the boy and the Bloodeye. "You said you had a cure."

"This *is* the cure!" he shouted, rain finding the lines in his droopy cheeks, coursing to stream off his chin. "My son will finally be healed. No more sleepless nights, filling the manor with his screams. We'll have vengeance. It will heal us both!"

She pointed at the Bloodeye. "He can't possibly be the man who killed her!"

"They're all the same," yelled Dulith. "This one, the ones in the compound, the one in the market that day…"

Quarrah felt her heart sink. A Bloodeye in a Talumonian marketplace, three years ago? That had to have been a creature farmed and released by the Realm. Designed to sow chaos and panic so the bulk of the Wayfarist population would grow fearful enough to sail away from the Greater Chain forever.

Lady Dulith was a wholly unnecessary casualty in the Realm's private war. But as much as the boy had to be hurting, this wasn't the answer.

"Listen to me." Quarrah turned to the lad. "Killing that Bloodeye won't make you miss your mother any less."

"Don't you *ever* speak about my mother!" shrieked the boy. He was crying, tears mingling with the rain. For a moment, she saw her own youthful face reflected there. Confused. Afraid. Manipulated into doing something terrible for a deranged parent. Not murder, but Jalisa Khailar had demanded other crimes of her young daughter that still stung if Quarrah wasn't quick to dismiss the memories.

The Bloodeye in the courtyard was already dead inside. And if Pasic Dulith pulled that trigger, he would be, too.

Quarrah lunged forward, seizing the boy's wrist and angling the gun downward. The hammer must have been cocked, because it went off with a deafening puff of smoke. She wrenched the Roller away, splashing through a puddle as she stumbled a few steps backward.

Lord Dulith screamed in fury, spittle flying with the rain. "You will not deny my son this chance to heal! That Bloodeye *must* die!"

Well, at least they agreed on something. Quarrah swiveled, pulling back the Slagstone hammer and sending a ball straight through the Bloodeye's face. She knew a single shot wouldn't kill him. People with Moonsickness had a terrifying ability to regenerate. She'd have to deal so much damage that death would claim him before he could heal himself.

She snapped off two more shots, one of them striking the chains across his chest, and the other biting into the man's neck. Then Lord Dulith tackled her and they both went sprawling on the wet brick courtyard.

Quarrah had spent much of her life learning to weasel out of an enemy's grasp, and she did so quickly, landing a kick between Dulith's legs and rolling into a crouch. Through the downpour, she saw one of the laborers drawing a Grit pot from his belt. She aimed and fired, putting the Roller ball into his leg.

With a grunt, the man went down beside the light post, his Grit pot shattering on the bricks. Quarrah had expected it to be a Barrier cloud meant to entrap her, but a Void cloud sprang up, flinging the fallen worker across the courtyard. He tumbled to a stop against the wall of the west wing and lay motionless.

Quarrah heard a crack of timber, and her attention returned to the Bloodeye. He was caught in the edge of the Void cloud, the outward rush of wind almost uprooting the light post and causing any slack in his chains to strain sideways. In the chaos, the Blood-eye had managed to free one of his arms. He was clawing franti-cally at his restraints, his body lurching against the push of the Void Grit.

The light post cracked again, this time separating from its base, the Void cloud hurtling it toward the east wing. No one moved for a moment, and then the Bloodeye slowly rose to his feet, tangled chains hanging from his shoulders while still attached to the post.

He opened his mouth in a scream, but no sound came out. Yel-lowish foam had clotted his gunshot wounds and the man's face looked broken and inhuman. He lunged at the nearest worker, but the chains pulled tight against the post, dropping him to the ground. In a fit of rage, he began to yank on his confines, shaking and tugging with a measure of strength enhanced by his horrible condition.

Quarrah scrambled back to where Lord Dulith was lying on the ground, propped on one elbow to witness the Bloodeye's escape. There was a cut on Dulith's forehead from his struggle with Quar-rah. The rain had washed the blood across his face, giving him a wild visage not unlike the Moonsick man.

"Get your son out of here!" Quarrah shouted at him. "Take him inside and barricade the door." Pasic was standing as still as a statue, his sunken eyes wide as the three remaining laborers kept their distance from the Bloodeye, stout swords brandished. Totshin was nowhere to be found.

Dulith shoved Quarrah back and rose to his knees. "Don't kill it!" he shouted at the workers. "That honor *must* go to my son!"

As he barked his demands, the Moonsick man finally broke away from the post. A length of chain whipped around in his raw hands, the end catching one of the laborers across the face, dropping him, writhing.

Quarrah fired the Roller again, the ball striking the Bloodeye's shoulder. She pulled the trigger once more, but the Slagstone hammer sent a sizzle of sparks into an empty chamber. Those six shots had gone much too quickly.

She tossed aside the Roller as the Bloodeye made a reckless charge across the courtyard. Wisely disregarding Dulith's instructions, one of the laborers took a swing at the passing man. His sword cleaved into the monster's left arm, severing it just above the elbow.

The heavy blow sent the Bloodeye reeling sideways, landing facedown on the bricks. Dulith hurled something and Quarrah heard the clay pot shatter. In response to the sparks, a dome of Barrier Grit sprang up behind the Moonsick man, enclosing only his legs and making it impossible for him to wriggle free.

"Pasic," his father cried, jolting his son from a horrified reverie. Dulith ran to him, somehow holding a fresh Roller. "Now!" He shoved the gun into the lad's hand. "Your mother would want this. Finish him."

The boy stepped closer to the Bloodeye. His thumb was too weak to pull back the Slagstone hammer, so he used the palm of his other hand to do it.

Quarrah moved to intercept, but Pasic saw her coming. He spun, leveling the gun at her. In the adrenaline of the moment, she had little doubt that he'd pull the trigger if she continued to provoke him. She stood still, raising her hands innocently.

"Father knows what's best," the boy said. Then he turned and fired the Roller at the Bloodeye's head. Quarrah winced at the spray of carnage, knowing that he'd found his mark.

"Again!" Lord Dulith bellowed, his hands clasped together as he watched.

Pasic fired once more, his aim as true as the first.

"Again! Again! Again!" Dulith was screaming, his face seized with the bitter throes of vengeance. His son unloaded the entire Roller into the Bloodeye's head until the skull was broken open and the corpse lay still. Rivulets of blood flowed with the rain, finding channels between bricks in a grid of gore.

"How did it feel, my boy?" Lord Dulith took a halting step forward, hands still clasped like a servant checking to make sure the food was satisfactory. "Do you remember her? Do you remember how much she loved you?"

Pasic looked up slowly through the haze of Blast smoke, his young face spattered with the Moonsick man's blood. His hollow eyes looked more sunken and hopeless than before, but there was a new spark of darkness in his gaze.

"I want another."

"Yes," the twisted man whispered. Then Dulith's eyes flicked to Quarrah. "Hold her!" he bellowed to the two remaining laborers.

Was Quarrah intended to be the boy's next victim? Or did Lord Dulith think she could get him more Bloodeyes? Either way, she didn't plan to stick around and find out.

She bolted for the doorway into the manor, but Totshin had finally reappeared with a gun in his hand. No problem. Quarrah had already surveyed the courtyard for every potential route of escape. At this point, her best option was to leap from one of those benches and Drift Jump to that second-story window.

Careening away from Totshin, Quarrah moved toward the benches, only to find her route blocked by one of the laborers who had taken up position in front of the sand pit.

Her hand flashed to her belt, plucking out a vial of purple liquid. She pitched it at the worker in a soft arc, watching him bring up his sword to deflect. The glass shattered against the broad blade and a cloud of Gather Grit sprung up, with him at the center. It wasn't Compounded enough to break his bones, but the inward pull—the reverse effect of Void Grit—would keep him contained.

The wet sand from the sailor's folly pit was drawn by the Gather Grit, glomming on to the worker until only his hands were visible, swiping desperately to clear the sand from his face. A few loose bricks from the courtyard also pelted into him, but he probably couldn't even feel them through his new coat of sand.

The distraction was exactly what Quarrah had hoped for. She skirted the perimeter of the Gather cloud, slipping a pot of Drift Grit from her belt. She hurled it ahead of her, sparking the Slagstone against the wall of the east wing. Leaping onto the bench, she sprinted two steps down its length before launching herself into the Drift cloud.

Weightlessness surrounded her, momentum carrying her upward until she hit the wall, her hands gripping the second-story window-sill with practiced precision.

She never felt as refined, performing stunts like these in her regular clothing. Her black thief's garb was much sleeker, and her Grit teabags were far less bulky than the wide leather Grit belt she currently wore.

Quarrah hoisted herself up, shoulder pushing the foggy glass open so she could roll into the room. This was clearly a bedroom, gratefully unoccupied. She crossed to the door, but her eye caught a silver hair comb on the stand beside the bed. A three-step detour, and she had the item in hand. Now that she was here, she realized that the painted vase would fetch a decent price, too. And that scarf was pure silk, with tiny gemstones embroidered along its length.

This was more than fair, considering it was unlikely that Lord Dulith was going to pay her now. With the comb in her belt pouch, the vase under one arm, and the scarf flung about her neck, Quarrah moved into the corridor. She was almost to the stairs when crescendoing shouts rose to meet her.

She doubled back, taking a moment to scan the great room she had previously blown past. She didn't see a suitable place to hide, but that old jeweled broadsword hanging above the mantel might be worth something...

Getting the sword down proved more difficult than expected. When it finally came free, the lump of steel turned out to be surprisingly heavy. The sword clanged to the floor, narrowly missing the vase she'd set down. A little adjusting and she'd probably be able to carry everything. But that gold sconce on the opposite wall looked mighty tempting.

She had just finished prying it loose with her sword when the voices reached her. Six armed staffers led by Totshin, who had donned a Grit belt to accompany his Roller. Quarrah was standing on the far side of the great room when they entered, laden with spoils that earned a loud curse from Totshin.

"Halt!" the attendant ordered. No one immediately opened fire, which reminded Quarrah that Lord Dulith still had plans for her.

If she'd had a free hand, a single detonation of Barrier Grit could have plugged the corridor between them. Instead, she'd have to settle for a footrace.

Quarrah turned and bolted back in the direction of the bedroom where she'd found the comb. According to her surveillance, she was headed in the direction of the servants' quarters. But there wouldn't be access to that area from the second floor.

Sparks! This was a dead end.

Wait. She'd seen a waste lagoon on the east side of the property. There were access chutes from this wing! If her spatial judgment was right—and it almost always was—the next door on the right would get her there. Now, if only she had a free hand to open it.

Taking a deep breath, Quarrah tossed the vase into the air, pushed open the door, and caught the fragile pottery against her chest as it came down. Ha! That was a fine trick. She kicked the door shut behind her and threw her back against it as she examined the room.

This was little more than a closet stocked with chamber pots and cleaning supplies. The foul odor of human waste filled the space and she quickly identified its source. Rising from floor to ceiling was the waste chute. It looked like a metal chimney with a hinged wooden door covering an opening on the side. Only about two feet square, but Quarrah had squeezed through many a tight space in her day.

She shuffled the vase into the crook of her arm so she could reach a pot of Barrier Grit on her belt. She'd need a little time to work her way down the chute, and if her enemies caught up to her before she reached the bottom, finishing her off would be as easy as shooting fish in a barrel. And conveniently for her attackers, Quarrah's body would be deposited in the refuse lagoon below.

Her hand had just found the pot she was looking for when the door bucked against her back. She lurched forward, the fragile vase slipping from her arm. She flinched as it shattered, the sound of lost Ashings clattering around her feet. But glancing down, she saw that it hadn't been empty. There was a folded piece of paper among the shards.

A grin touched her face as the door heaved against her back again. Noble folks were always stashing valuable documents inside other valuable items—gold-trimmed boxes, musical instruments, painted vases.

She kicked the broken pieces across the small room, the paper carried along with it. Then she leapt from the door, hurling the Barrier pot behind her. The door swung inward, stopping just a foot or two ajar as the Grit detonated, creating an impassible block. These people wouldn't know about Null Grit, so she had no reason to rush.

Stooping, she flicked aside pieces of the shattered vase and plucked up the folded paper. Unable to put off her curiosity, she unfolded it for a quick glance.

The sounds of the men struggling at the door faded as Quarrah's heartbeat seemed to fill the room. She forgot about the danger. She forgot about escape.

She reread the note.

*Quarrah Khai—Tofar's Salts. 8th of 3rd. Noon. Ask to see the Be'Igoth.*

She turned to the door and saw Totshin shoving helplessly against the transparent shell of the Barrier cloud.

Quarrah held up the note, her eyes narrowed in a suspicious glare. "Did you know..." But she trailed off on her own. Of course Totshin didn't know about the note in the vase. How could anyone have known she was going to flee through that particular bedroom, steal that particular item...

She tucked the note into a vacant pouch on her Grit belt,

returning to the matter of her escape. Taking the final steps, she lifted the cover to gain access to the chute. The rising stench choked her, and she turned away to cough. Holding her breath, Quarrah stuck her head inside to examine her last-ditch escape route.

The chute rose vertically to the third floor and dropped straight down about fifteen feet. At the bottom, she could see that the metal was bent at an angle, directing any dumped refuse outward to the waiting lagoon.

She had to admit, this wasn't the most desirable way to leave a manor. But she was committed to the plan now. Nothing to do but slide down the refuse chute.

*Flames*, Quarrah thought. *This sword better be worth a lot of Ashings.*

～

*We have all seen terrible things. But the memories that haunt me the most are of the mistakes I could have avoided.*

# CHAPTER

# 3

A rd hated studying. Sparks, he even hated *reading* most of the time. He'd gotten this far in life thanks to Raekon Dorrel, who'd been his tutor and primary exam-taker through Ard's last few years of schooling.

The fact that he was here now, tucked away in Cove 7, his desk littered with books and notes, was nothing shy of a genuine miracle.

And that he'd been studying earnestly like this for just over a year was unfathomable—even to himself.

As a Holy Isle, Ard had the right to block out certain periods of the day for private study, much to the chagrin of the long list of people hoping to meet with him each day for guidance. He enjoyed those visits, of course. Believing Wayfarists were prone to divulge all kinds of useful secrets in the privacy of the Cove. And Ardor Benn, doing what came naturally, would tell them whatever they wanted to hear to make sure they sang his praises across Beripent, solidifying his position at the Mooring.

Despite his distaste for the studying, that was what had brought him here. And his studies were what drove him forward in this strange new lifestyle.

Ard turned back to his notes, finger tracing under the scripture he'd just copied.

*All of life will move this way and that, rolling like a great sphere.*

All right, but what did that *mean*? Ard found the language in *Wayfarist Voyage* to be highly confusing. It was no wonder so many Homelandic religions had sprouted from this text.

What was he doing so far afield from his original topic of study? He'd joined the Islehood for one reason—to learn more about the Great Egress.

Over the last year, Ard had compiled an entire book of notes about the supposed mass exodus of the true believers. Naturally, all the writings he could find in the Mooring library supported the Wayfarist interpretation of that event—that the Great Egress was a metaphorical departure from a Settled lifestyle to a holier one of worshiping the Homeland.

The Realm had interpreted it as a physical departure, sending hundreds of ships sailing into the unknown sea with faith that would carry them to the Homeland. Of course, the Realm had been exploiting this idea, with hopes to purge the Greater Chain of Wayfarism and eliminate its influence on society.

Ard's personal findings on the topic remained very inconclusive, despite knowing so much about the truths of the world—the dragons' shield from Moonsickness, the time-traveling nature of Paladin Visitants, the forgotten kingdom at the bottom of the sea where all humankind had originated, the Trothians' devolution from a superior race, and Gloristar's transformation into it... None of that seemed to give him any definitive insight on what the scriptures called "the Great Egress."

When that topic had yielded nothing but frustration, Ard's attention had shifted to this.

The sphere.

Honestly, it was something Ard had entirely forgotten about until he'd stumbled across a certain verse about three cycles ago.

*Though we struggle in a line, the circle saves, and the sphere governs all.*

That simple line had reminded him of something Gloristar had said in the throne room on the fateful night of her transformation. Shad Agaul had been shot on the throne and Quarrah had asked Gloristar if there was anything she could do for the boy. Homeland knew they'd seen her perform other amazing feats that night.

Gloristar's answer had been cryptic. *"Not until the Sphere is complete. For now there is an order to life and a time for death."*

Ard turned a page of his book, studying his notes. Half the time, he couldn't even read his own handwriting. He really wasn't very good at this scholarly stuff. But in keeping with the meaning of his religious name, Ardor Benn felt compelled with a passionate drive to continue his work. Maybe he was close to finding something important. Then everything would make sense.

*The circle saves.*

Ard knew the circle was the symbol of the Homeland, so reverenced that it wasn't often displayed in a religious context. In Wayfarism, the sign of the anchor had largely replaced it, representative of the weight of life's troubles that threatened to cause believers to Settle.

*The sphere governs all.*

Ard had absently doodled all around that sentence, his jumbled notes a reflection of his mind on the matter. What *sphere*? Was it some kind of physical structure that needed to be built? If it had been completed, could Gloristar have stopped Shad Agaul from dying?

There was a knock at the Cove door. Ard perked up, glancing at the little mantel clock on the edge of his desk. All the Coves had them now—not Gregious Mas models, but that clockmaker wasn't the big fish he'd been two years ago. His competitors were making quality clocks at a fraction of the price. Mas's fame and notoriety had been short lived, a very telling aspect of today's society.

"Come in," Ard said, surprised that Raek was so early for their "guidance." He quickly closed his notebook and stacked a heavy book on top of it. It was fine to put on the *appearance* of studying, but Raek would know something was off if Ard looked too genuine in his work.

The door opened and Ard stiffened to see that it wasn't his old friend paying a visit. He rose from his desk, smoothing his sea-green robes and nodding his head respectfully.

"Prime Isle Trable," Ard greeted his visitor. "To what do I owe the pleasure?"

"Relax, Ardor," Trable said, closing the door behind him. "And have a seat."

Olstad Trable was young for a Prime Isle. A little digging and Ard had found out that the man was just a year his elder. He had black hair, tawny skin, and a trim beard to frame his square jaw. And according to public consent, he was by far the *handsomest* Prime Isle in the last century.

Trable sat down on the bench, crossing his legs under his purple robes. He exhaled slowly, rubbing his forehead with his fingertips.

"You're killing me, Ard," he finally said.

"I'm sorry?" he replied innocently. "Have I done something wrong?"

"Don't give me that slag," the Prime Isle replied. "You know why I'm here."

"Because . . . I did something wrong?" Ard guessed.

"We both know you've done plenty of that," Trable said. "I mean why I'm *here*, in Cove Seven."

"I hope you're delivering some of those lemon tarts that your wife's famous for."

Some thought that a married Isle would never be considered for Prime. Olstad Trable was proof that it didn't matter. In Gloristar's absence, a panel of experienced Holy Isles had deemed him the best person for the job. Ard could see why. An affable family man was a good image to display after Gloristar's unpopularity among the masses.

"Oh," Trable chuckled. "Isless Gaevala doesn't know I'm here. It's gotten to the point that I won't even mention your name in front of the girls. They're too young to see their mother's wrath." The Prime Isle sat forward, elbows on his knees. "Three summons of remediation to Cove One is grounds for suspension. I don't want to kick you out, Ard. I really don't. But you're not making it easy. You've got to help me out. I think it's important for the people to see that *anyone* can change." He paused. "Even someone like you."

Ardor Benn felt the prick of guilt stab at his insides. How much had he changed? Technically, his presence in the Mooring was another ruse. A long, patient ruse designed to get information—the location of the Islehood's store of dragon shell. Answers about the Great Egress that only the Mooring's library could provide.

But this ruse *felt* different than any job he'd done before. He usually felt a drive to finish, just so he could move on to the next. But this time, he wasn't sure if he wanted it to end at all. The thought made him feel dishonest, like he was cheating on the person he had always been. And in moments like these, when someone praised him for how much he'd changed, his past self would rise up within to convince him that he hadn't. To convince him that under these sea-green robes, Ardor Benn would never be anything more than an imposter.

"I assume you're referring to a little incident in the Char, day before yesterday?" Ard confessed. "For the record, I went with every intention of having a peaceful conversation. Anything you heard about was Dalfa Rhed's fault."

"I heard that one of my Isles was seen swinging from the Old Palace Steps in his holy robes."

"I was escaping," said Ard. "She sent her goons after me."

Prime Isle Trable raised his eyebrows. "You can't keep meeting with every old enemy that calls you out. I knew you'd be persecuted for your past, but you're part of the Islehood now. You've committed yourself to living a better life."

Ard nodded slowly. "I won't do it again," he promised. But even as he said it, he thought of the questionable meeting he'd scheduled for tomorrow. Assuming they could even find the place called Tofar's Salts, Ard didn't plan on wearing his Islehood robes. Not with so much mystery surrounding the note he'd found in the wall of the ruins.

"And what about the tattered Islehood robe the Regulators found in the bushes?" asked the Prime Isle. "It was recovered near one of the ruins that was vandalized by two men who locked themselves inside to avoid arrest."

Ard shook his head, biting the inside of his cheek. "I don't know anything about that."

Trable pursed his lips in thought. "I didn't think you would. I'm just saying that you need to be more careful. Your enemies would like to see you fail. Sparks, I'll admit that there are more than a few Holy Isles who'd like to see you thrown out." He leaned forward. "I'm not one of them."

"I understand," Ard said. "And I would hate for my misconduct to reflect poorly on the Prime Isle who let me in."

"You know I don't care about that." Trable waved his hand. "This is about you, Ardor Benn. You, and the condition of your soul."

"Every Prime Isle leaves a legacy," Ard said. "Frid Chauster started a war. Gloristar vanished into the night. Maybe you'll be known for getting a legendary criminal to the Homeland."

Trable squinted one eye, unamused. "I wouldn't say you're *legendary*. And for Gaevala's sake, let us hope I'm known for something else." He lifted his finger. "What about the Prime Isle who authorized the first female crusader monarch to reestablish peace across the Greater Chain?"

"Well, I mean…There's that, too," said Ard. "But it kind of sounds like you're taking credit for all the good work *she's* doing. How is Queen Abeth lately?"

"Impressive as always," he said. "I don't think anyone else could have reunited the islands so quickly."

Ard nodded. "Her bloodline and marriage made her uniquely suited." The former Sovereign States of Dronodan and Talumon accepted her lineage. The former Archkingdom acknowledged that she had been trained for years to rule Espar and Strind.

"And her training, and her experience, and her demeanor in court…The crusader queen really knows what she's doing. Unlike some of us." Trable sighed, standing up slowly. "Sometimes I think Gloristar is just going to show up one day and tell me all the things I'm doing wrong."

*Because you don't have the Anchored Tome*, Ard thought. But he certainly wouldn't say it out loud. Privately, Gloristar had confessed to Ard that King Termain had stolen the sacred book. And Trable had hinted enough times that Ard realized the book was never recovered. Without it, Trable was missing vital knowledge meant only for the eyes of the succeeding Prime.

Publicly, Prime Isle Trable had announced that he'd read the Anchored Tome. He lied to the Holy Isles and to the Wayfarist followers because telling them the truth would shatter their faith.

Perhaps that was why Olstad Trable had taken such a liking to Ard. They were both working to convince themselves that they were something they weren't.

"Ols?" Ard asked as the man moved for the door. "What do you think happened to Gloristar that night?"

The Prime Isle glanced back. "I issued my official statement."

"And I read it," said Ard. "But what do you think *really* happened?"

Queen Abeth had done a remarkable job covering up the truth. According to record, Ard and Quarrah had not been in the throne room that night. Termain had died at the hand of a mysterious woman who had forced entry through the balcony. There were rumors, of course. A handful of guards had been eyewitnesses, though speaking the truth of what they'd seen would contradict Her Majesty.

Trable ran a hand through his short beard. "I believe the Realm abducted the Prime Isless." Queen Abeth had spread word about the Realm far and wide, hoping that the attention would force down any remaining members of the organization.

"You think the Realm killed her?" Ard pressed. That's what he'd said in his official statement.

"I'm convinced of it more and more." Trable shrugged. "Otherwise, where could she be?"

His words mirrored Ard's thoughts exactly. For a time, he'd held out hope that Gloristar had survived her fall from the Old Post Lighthouse. But it had been *two years* now. And her glass skull had been badly fractured. Ard knew so little about her new condition. How long could she stay underwater? If she had truly become like the Trothian ancestors, they had survived in the deep for hundreds of years before coming to the surface to seek vengeance on the Landers.

There was still air down there, at the bottom of the InterIsland Waters. Ard had considered sinking himself in a bubble of

Containment Grit to search for her, but without a Trothian to detonate the Stasis Grit at regular intervals, he'd likely run out of air on
the way down. And the seabed was a large place. How would he
even know where to start?

"You have a visitor," Trable said from the doorway.

Ard glanced up from his thoughts to find Raek looming over the
Prime Isle. The two men exchanged a typical Mooring greeting,
shuffling awkwardly around each other on the dock. Then Raek
ducked inside and swung the door shut.

"You know that was the Prime Isle, right?" Ard said, double-
checking to make sure his study notes were out of sight.

"Olstad Trable. Yeah," said Raek.

"Most visitors in the Mooring would make a big deal about
bumping into the *Prime* Isle on the dock."

Raek shrugged his massive shoulders. "Did you want me to squeal?"
He plopped himself down on the same bench Trable had occupied, the
wooden boards groaning under his bulk. "I found Tofar's Salts."

"And?"

"It's an Agrodite soakhouse in the upper Western Quarter," he
said. "Plum full of soggy Trothians."

The saltwater soak was necessary for all Trothians to maintain
the health of their thick blue skin. Soakhouses had started springing up around Beripent during Pethredote's time, with seawater
being brought up from the harbors. But the baths had been shut
down when Pethredote had renounced the Inclusionary Act. Eventually, the need for the soak had driven all the Trothians to the
shore, where the Regulators had rounded them up and shipped
them back to their low sandy islets.

"And the *Be'Igoth*?" Ard wasn't even sure if he was pronouncing
that correctly.

Raek shook his head. "I just scouted the place so we wouldn't be
in for any surprises tomorrow. I didn't want to tip our hand by asking questions."

"What was it like?"

"Surprisingly big and more lavish than a lot of the soakhouses I've seen," he said. "Three Ashings a week for admittance. Whoever built that place is making a fortune off the Trothians."

Ard hoped it was another Trothian, not some cheap Lander looking to profit off their physical needs.

"You ever been to a soakhouse?" Ard asked his partner.

"I literally just told you I have," said Raek, massaging the spot on his chest where the pipe was buried.

"I mean before that," said Ard.

"In case you didn't notice, I'm a Lander," he replied, gesturing at the dark brown skin of his arm. "We're not really welcome there."

"You think that'll complicate tomorrow's meeting?" Ard asked.

"Based on that note, I'd say the *Be'Igoth* will be expecting you," he said. "Not sure if I should come, though. Your name was the only one on the note."

"You okay with that?"

"I'll hang around outside and warn you if I see any trouble."

"I'm expecting it." Ard drummed his fingers on the desk. "Who could have done it, Raek?"

"Done what?" he asked.

"Placed that note in the exact spot we would be—a spot *we* didn't even know we would be."

"I know that look," Raek said. "You've got a theory that's almost too crazy to say out loud."

Ard took a deep breath. "Time travel."

"Time travel?"

"We know it's possible," Ard explained. "Every successful Paladin Visitant has done it. Sparks! *I've* even done it. And we know the Islehood is gathering dragon shell. That could mean they're already making Visitant Grit."

"Leaving notes in stone walls... That's not how a Paladin Visitant works," said Raek. "Any interaction with the past—no matter how small—resets the timeline. If that had happened, we would cease to exist."

"I know, I know," Ard said. "But maybe it wasn't a Paladin Visitant."

Raek's face looked painfully skeptical. "Who else travels through time?"

"In the throne room that night," Ard began, "Gloristar said something."

"She said a lot of crazy stuff we didn't understand," he said.

"She said she was the Homeland," Ard recalled. "Said she was 'time and space perfected.' That sounds like someone who can travel through time."

"Gloristar's dead, Ard. Or if she's still alive, she clearly doesn't want us to know it."

"Maybe she planted the note *before* the lighthouse collapsed on her," Ard mused. "She could have had time between leaving you at the Moonsick farm and coming to the throne room to kill Termain. And how long would it take, traveling through time? She might have done it in the blink of an eye."

"Look, you're welcome to get your robes in a knot speculating over what the dead Prime Isless can and cannot do," said Raek, "but I'm not going to lose sleep over it until after the meeting tomorrow. I'm betting you'll get some answers from the mysterious *Be'Igoth*. And we can hope the job will pay well enough to warrant coming out of retirement."

"Job?" Ard faltered. "I...I can't take a job right now, Raek." He put a hand on his stack of books. "Prime Isle Trable was just here to reprimand me. Another infraction and he won't be able to sweep it under the rug. I'll be suspended from the Islehood. Or worse..."

"Worse?" Raek said, puzzled. "I assume you mean kicked out. Wasn't that in the plans all along?"

"Well, yes, but..." Ard's research felt hot under his hand. "I just need more time. If I get thrown out now, the whole last year will have been for nothing." He kept his voice low, always aware that someone could be listening from the dock outside the door.

"You need to step up your game in here," Raek said. "You said it yourself, it's a real possibility that they've already started processing Visitant Grit. We need to have our eyes on that shell, Ard. It'd only take one well-placed detonation to erase us all."

Ard swallowed. He was keenly aware of the risk. Keeping the location of the dragon shell from Raek was a risky move, but it was the only card in his hand. Raekon Dorrel wouldn't agree with Ard's true reasons for staying. Sure, Raek understood the value in good, hard research, but not the philosophical search for answers in old religious texts. He understood the patience involved in running a long ruse, but not the strange and comfortable satisfaction Ard was experiencing in this new life.

"It's time to start digging a little harder," Raek said. "I'm doing all I can from the outside, but the Islehood is taking advantage of this fresh start, covering their tracks to make sure no one gets their hands on Visitant Grit."

"I'll find it," Ard insisted. "But we have to be extra careful not to rock the boat until I do."

Raek nodded resolutely. "I'll keep her steady."

"I can put some pressure on Isless Banhue," Ard said. "She monitors a lot of the Islehood's resources."

"Do what you have to do." Raek stood up and stretched his tree-trunk arms in front of him. "And don't worry, pal. We'll get you out of here soon enough."

Ard ran his finger across the edge of his notebook. "Yeah," he said quietly. "The Mooring's no place for a guy like me."

~

*Every secret I hid felt like another life beginning.*

# CHAPTER

# 4

Tofar's Salts was noisier than Ard had expected, exuberant shouts and splashes reaching his ears as he approached the soakhouse along Tassel Street.

The hubbub implied good business, though. Ard knew surprisingly little about the ritual, despite having seen Trothians soaking in the harbors all his life. He understood that it had to be done with regularity to keep their blue skin smooth and healthy. Given the Trothian ancestry on the seabed, this connection to the water made sense.

Participating in the soak was considered an Agrodite religious practice. So by default, every Trothian was considered an Agrodite. As such, they were barred from becoming Wayfarists, which excluded them from certain societal benefits.

It was a broken situation, with fault falling on both sides. A stubbornness that kept a wedge between Wayfarists and Agrodites—and thus, Landers and Trothians. Would things change if they knew the truth about their joint ancestry?

Ard glanced over his shoulder one last time, but Raek was gone. His big friend would be lurking around the soakhouse perimeter, a Regulation-issue brass whistle on a chain around his neck. He'd blow it in a specific pattern—long, short, long—to let Ard know if it was time to get out of there.

The structure was simple but unique—a wide pavilion enclosed by a wooden fence rising almost halfway to the roof. Through the open gate, Ard caught a glimpse inside. It looked like a maze of wooden walls, the dividers partitioning off deep pools of salt water.

"Can I help you?" A voice turned Ard's attention to a Trothian woman standing just inside the gate. She was thin and willowy, with long braided hair falling down her back. Her ever-vibrating eyes studied Ard with a twinge of impatience, but not wholly without intrigue.

"Yes, um…" Ard flipped open the note in his hand to double-check the words. "Is this Tofar's Salts?"

"It is," she answered, speaking Landerian with no detectable accent.

"Sounds like business is good today," he said in an attempt to soften her expression.

"Our business is our own," she said. "This is an Agrodite place of ritual and healing. We do not allow *muckmus* inside."

Ard held up his hand. "I mean no disrespect in coming here. I'm supposed to meet someone. Could you please tell the *Be'Igoth* that Ardor Benn is here?"

Her thin face cracked into a smile and then a full snicker. She called to another Trothian woman who was passing by, exchanging a few brief words in their native language. Then both women had a good laugh that seemed very much at Ard's expense.

He shuffled his feet uncomfortably. "I probably didn't pronounce that right." He held out the note for her inspection, before suddenly remembering that Trothians couldn't see the written word. Their unique eyes perceived the energy of things, but text was washed out on flat surfaces.

"Your pronunciation was fine," she replied. "But *Be'Igoth* cannot see anyone."

"But I was told to come here and ask to see him," Ard said.

She laughed again. "And I was told to expect you. But it is past noon."

"Just a few minutes," Ard said dismissively. "But I'm sure *Be'Igoth* will understand." Arriving late was almost like Ard's signature of authenticity.

"*Be'Igoth* understands nothing." She was very amused by something. "Because *Be'Igoth* is not a person."

"Not a..." Ard trailed away. "Then what is it?"

"I will show you." But instead of leaving, she held out her hand expectantly. "Three Ashings for the week. Five Ashlits for a single day."

"Oh, I'm not going to soak," Ard said.

"No," she replied, still beckoning. "You are not."

Ard nodded, digging into his Grit belt for his money pouch. He hadn't brought his Rollers as a show of good faith, but he had a loaded Singler tucked into his vest.

He plucked out five metal Ashlits and dropped them into the waiting blue hand. The woman rubbed her fingers over the coins to feel for the marks and then plunged them into a pocket on her loose, flowing smock. Ard followed her closely into the soakhouse, wisely keeping his mouth shut so he wouldn't accidentally say something offensive.

A nice summer breeze kept the pavilion fresh, passing over the exterior fence and the interior maze-like dividers. The woman led Ard down a narrow wooden walkway in the middle of the floor alongside a deep central canal, where Ard saw several Trothians swimming.

From time to time, Ard caught a glimpse of one of the pools behind a partition. They were large enough to comfortably accommodate a dozen people. The baths were maybe four feet deep, recessed directly into the ground with canals running under the walkways to connect them.

Ard saw Trothian men, women, and children—many of them lying completely underwater. The noise wasn't yelling, Ard discovered. Rather, certain groups would burst out in chant-like singing. Cupping their hands, they would strike the water's surface in complex overlapping percussive patterns.

Walking the damp planks, Ard was suddenly struck by the depth of the Trothian culture. Their bright noise was a far cry from the silent reverence of the Mooring, but both were supposedly religious sites of worship. And despite the difference in behavior, Ard suddenly saw some startling similarities.

The soakhouse, with its interconnected pools, was not unlike the waterway of the Mooring. There, Landers took rafts across the waters, seeking dry Coves for spiritual healing and guidance. Here, the Trothians swam the central canal, ducking into shallower pools for their restoration.

*It's because we all came from the same place*, Ard thought. Isle Halavend had seen it, even if he hadn't understood. When Lyndel and the old Isle had embarked on their joint study, they had found a shocking number of correlations between their seemingly contrastive religions.

"The presence of your kind during *fajumar* makes many of my people uncomfortable," the woman explained.

"*Fajumar?*"

"It is our word for the saltwater soak," she said. Ard noticed a Trothian woman and child dive under the water's surface at the sight of him. "Your queen was right to open all borders to us again, but Lander offenses against Trothians in Beripent are not easily forgotten."

Ard nodded. "I just want to make it clear that I've always been on your side. What Pethredote did to your people was terrible. And Termain was no better. Queen Abeth is doing her best to set things right."

"That is what happens when you let a woman rule."

The narrow boardwalk reached its end near the back of the pavilion, where a genuine stone building rose to join the roof, unlike the wooden fence on the other three sides. In a way, it looked like this was a home, and the rest of the pavilion was some kind of extended covered patio.

"The *Be'Igoth*," the woman said, gesturing to the closed wooden door. The word sounded a lot smoother coming out of her mouth. "Or in your language, the *hot bath*."

Ah. He suddenly understood how foolish he must have sounded, insisting that he had an appointment with the hot bath.

The woman reached out her thin arm and knocked a quick rhythm on the door. It was answered almost immediately by a large Trothian man wearing nothing but a tight pair of shorts. The black hair on his chest was thick and curly, half concealing the pendant that dangled at the end of his gold necklace.

The man and the woman conversed briefly in Trothian before the big fellow stepped aside and gestured for Ard to enter.

"Thanks," Ard said to the woman.

"Geppel," she said by way of introduction. "I assume we'll be seeing more of each other in the near future." She winked one blurry eye in a distinctly Landerian gesture, then turned and walked away, leaving Ard to puzzle over her comment in the doorway.

"Come in, come in!" beckoned a gruff voice from inside the dark building. Ard casually checked to make sure his Singler was accessible, then stepped inside.

It felt like walking into a cave, the midday sun completely blotted out inside the windowless structure. Hot, heavy steam filled the expansive room, making Ard feel instantly sticky as he squinted.

The conditions wouldn't be a problem for the unique Trothian vision, but Ard felt half blind. At least someone had detonated a few orbs of Light Grit. They hovered in the steam like stars in a midnight fog.

The vapor in the room was rising from the pool at its center. It looked deeper than any of the ones he'd seen outside, but it took up only about half of the room. The rest of the floor was open, the high ceiling supported by stone pillars roughly hewn with square corners. A rack of Heat Grit pots lined the back wall and on both sides were individual stalls with privacy curtains for disrobing.

Ard startled at movement through the mist. The person had likely been there all along, visibility was so poor in here. Ard took a step closer, hand close to the Singler in his vest. There was something familiar about the hunkering mound of man crouched at the edge of the bath. The figure raised an ugly face, and Ard saw him clearly in the glimmer of the Light Grit.

"Hedge Marsool." Ard whispered the name. The King Poacher himself. He felt a chill, at odds with the sticky humidity.

"And here I thought you'd forgotten about me."

The man was an alarming sight, the left side of his face terribly disfigured with thick scars that looked like thin crisscrossing ropes of red and white. A leather patch concealed his eye on that side, and sparse brown hair grew only on the right half of his head, hanging almost to his shoulder.

His left arm was missing from the elbow down, and in its place he wore a metal spike, its length dewy from the steam, catching a shine in the soft light. Crouched at the edge of the pool, his good hand was plunged forward into the warm water and it looked like he was holding...

"Sparks." Ard shuddered. "Is that a *cat*?"

"Just a scrappy little Tom," Hedge Marsool said. He released his grip and the small animal's lifeless form bobbed to the surface, dark fur matted. "Mousing around the wrong soakhouse. You gotta hold them mewlers down a long time before the bubbles stop."

Ard took a step back, horrified by the barbarity. Yeah. This was the Hedge Marsool he remembered.

"Keeps me sharp, though," Hedge continued, rising from his crouch with a groan and an audible crack of his battered bones. "Good to feel the scales tip from life to death. Makes a man know what he's got. And what he could lose."

"Can't imagine the soaking Trothians appreciate that, though." Ard gestured at the drowned carcass.

"The *Be'Igoth* isn't a traditional Agrodite practice," Hedge said. His voice was somewhat strained, like his vocal cords might slip out of his throat at any moment. "You take a hearty dip in the InterIsland Waters during the winter cycles and you'll feel it cold enough to perk the titties of a dead man. But the cold don't bother the Trothians like it does us. That's why I find the *hot bath* so curious."

As he spoke, he moved toward Ard with his trademark jolting gait, a battered shell of a thin man draped in a damp cloak, a leather courier's bag over one shoulder. Nothing about his unfortunate appearance was too shocking to Ard. The man had looked this way the last time Ard had seen him—which was the *only* time. After that job, he and Raek had put the name *Hedge Marsool* on their personal blacklist, deeming him far too dangerous to be worth their while.

*This* was the man who had left the note in the wall of the ruins? The man who had predicted Ard's unpredictable escape? Deep inside, Ard had hoped it would be an old ally—or at least some enigmatic stranger. Hedge Marsool was neither.

"When the first inland soakhouses were set up during Peth-redote's reign, their construction required the oversight of a Lander landlord," Hedge continued. "*They* were the ones who demanded a building where the salt water could be kept hot. Made sense to them, and many of the Trothians found the experience more soothing on the blues. Good Agrodites would never debase themselves in the *Be'Igoth*, but the less religious Trothians are willing to pay extra for the novelty of soaking in hot water. I think that's why I like it. The room we're standing in is a rare hybrid of cultures. An illegitimate child, born of Trothian necessity and the overexertion of Lander control."

"Look, if this is about the gem cutter job..." Ard began. "I swear to you... that goat got a hold of the bag and shook those diamonds everywhere. We recovered what we could, but—"

Hedge held up his spike hand. "I didn't bring you here to shake you down for Ashings. I'm making plenty from Tofar's Salts."

"Wait. You're running this place?" Ard asked.

"One of my many enterprises," the crippled man said. "It's Ashlits to Ashings what I've done with this tub. The soak brings them in to Tofar's Salts, but I like to think they stay for the drinks."

"Drinks?" Ard said.

"Oh, yes. The Trothians can order food and drink from the comfort of their piss-water pools," said Hedge. "Like a genuine tavern."

"But with drowned cats." Ard glanced once more at the animal carcass.

"Oh, my people refresh the water every other day." Hedge's face cracked into a crooked smile. "Or at least, that's what I advertise."

Ard cast a glance at the large Trothian man beside him. Hedge's comment didn't seem to faze him, his blue face staring impassively into the mist.

"Don't worry about Eggat." Hedge pointed to the Trothian. "He doesn't speak a word of Landerian. But he and his brother are a fine piece of muscle."

Without so much as a hiccup, Hedge Marsool switched into Trothian, speaking to Eggat in long fluid sentences. That was the trouble with Hedge Marsool. He was terribly smart, but his brains were backed by a measure of ruthlessness that Ard found quite distasteful.

When Hedge had finished speaking, the Trothian nodded, sunlight flashing into the room like a beacon from a lighthouse as he opened and shut the door behind him.

"Eggat will stand guard outside," Hedge explained. "We wouldn't want anyone pressing an ear to our conversation."

"What conversation would that be?" Ard asked.

"The one where I hire you to steal me a dragon," Hedge Marsool declared.

"Sorry, what?"

"Draaaaagon." The man strung out the word patronizingly. "Mature sow. Alive and healthy. You'll bring her to me."

"*Here?*" Ard cried, not bothering to hide the incredulity in his voice. "Live dragon...Does the name *Grotenisk the Destroyer* ring any bells?"

Hedge chuckled slowly, as if the action pained him. "You're not going to bring her to Beripent, you wet goom," he said. "There's no place for her here. She'll be lodging in Helizon until I'm ready for her."

"Ready for her to do what, exactly?" he pressed. "You planning to raze the university? Destroy Talumon's prize city?" Ard scoffed. "Besides, why would the *King Poacher* need me?"

"Look at my body, Ardor." He held out his arms. "Pekal is a healthy man's game."

"From what I understand, you still have the contacts," Ard said. "Experienced poachers. Why do you need a ruse artist?"

"My poaching contacts do fine work," Hedge agreed. "On *Pekal.*"

"And your smuggling ring gets the goods into the Greater Chain without difficulty," Ard added, shrugging.

Hedge coughed something up and spit it onto the floor of the *Be'Igoth*. "I need you because I think it will be...amusing."

"Forget it." Ard turned to leave. This was some kind of vengeance hiring for the way Ard had cheated him out of those diamonds. "I'm not helping you with anything."

"Why haven't you asked me yet?" Hedge's question stopped Ard in his tracks. "Why haven't you asked me how I knew you'd be bashing your way out the back of that historic building in the Char last week?"

Ard swallowed. He'd come here with that sole question eating away at him. But his need to know had dried up the moment he saw it was Hedge Marsool. This man was as clever and conniving as they came.

"How many thugs did you have watching me?" Ard asked.

"None," he replied.

"Then how did you learn my escape plans?" Ard replied.

"Didn't," Hedge said. "We both know that ducking shelter in the Char ruins fell far outside your *plans*."

Ard narrowed his eyes. "I didn't come here to discuss what a clever note-dropper you are. I assumed there'd be a job, and now that I've heard it, I'm not interested."

"Oh, but you *are* interested." Hedge used his spike arm to make a reprimanding gesture. "That is, if you'd like to stay alive."

Ard breathed out in disbelief. "Are you *threatening* me, Hedge? You, of all people, should know I don't respond well to that."

"I'll admit my threats were insufficient last time," said the scarred man. "But things have changed."

"Nothing's changed," Ard said. "From your pungent stench to my superior intellect." He turned once more, this time determined to follow through with his exit.

"Be careful," Hedge said as Ard yanked open the door. "The steps are as slick as a toad's back from all that Trothian splashing."

Ard ignored the comment, pushing past Eggat, who seemed to be waiting for a command to pounce. The air outside felt fresh, a wake of steam following him down the stone stairs.

When Ard's boot hit the third step, he went down, slipping like a clumsy fool and taking a painful knee on the wooden boardwalk. But his heart seemed to fall farther, beating twice as fast when he heard the pained chortle of Hedge Marsool from within the *Be'Igoth*.

Ard righted himself, tugging self-consciously at his vest. *What the burning blazes?* Subtly, Ard inspected the slick step. It looked ordinary enough, with a touch of green algae adorning the ever-wet stone. Slippery, to be sure, but Ard had been watching his step.

Sucking in a deep breath, he skipped back into the room, avoiding the slickest step as he passed Eggat.

"How'd you do that?" Ard asked flatly, in no mood for games.

Hedge Marsool had moved to the far wall of the *Be'Igoth*, his back to Ard as he plucked a pot of Heat Grit from the rack. "*I* didn't do nothing," he replied. "You were the hobbledehoy who slipped. I knew you would, just like I knew you'd retreat into the Char ruins."

"What are you saying?" Ard whispered, not even sure if his voice was cutting through the steamy air.

Hedge Marsool tinkered with a long pole hanging on the wall beside the rack. A thin rope ran its length, tied to a small metal basket on one end. Hedge loaded the clay pot into the basket, and then removed the pole.

"I told you things have changed," he said, resting the pole against the shaft of his arm spike. Guiding it this way, he carefully lowered the end with the clay pot into the hot water. "I need a dragon, and you will get her for me."

Hedge tugged sharply on the rope and Ard saw the pot shatter underwater, the metal basket containing the shards as a fresh cloud of Heat Grit stoked the bath.

"And if I refuse?"

He shrugged, pulling the pole from the pool. "I know where you'll be. Ha. Even before you do. Haven't I proven that?"

"You've proven nothing," Ard said, agitated. His history with Hedge Marsool was enough to keep him on edge, but this latest turn of events was putting him over. "All you've done is left a note and told me to watch my step. In case you've forgotten, before I was a Holy Isle, I was a ruse artist—and a blazing good one. Rule number one: When you want to control someone, show them that you can predict their every move."

"I can do more than predict your move," Hedge said. "I can see your future, Ardor Benn."

"That would be something." But Ard didn't dismiss the comment as quickly as he would have liked. He knew firsthand that time travel was possible. But the lies and trickery of Hedge Marsool seemed even more so. "Why don't we put your claims to the test?"

Hedge leaned the pole against the rack. "What do you propose?"

"Something you couldn't possibly orchestrate," said Ard, digging in his pocket. "The flip of an Ashing." He produced a circular dragon scale—a three-mark.

Hedge tilted his scarred head. "What will this accomplish?" He casually reached his hand into his courier's bag. "You'll just whimper foul play when I predict each flip."

"The Ashing's mine." Ard hefted it in his open hand. "I'll be doing the flipping. I see no way you could cheat."

Hedge pulled his hand from the bag and Ard thought he saw something glint. He tensed, but the crippled man merely coughed. "Yep. Go on."

Flicking the Ashing with the edge of his thumb, Ard sent it spinning through the thick air. He caught it, glancing down at his palm to see the outcome.

"Marks up," Hedge declared.

Ard swallowed. It had indeed landed with the three indentations upward. Without a word, Ard flipped it again.

"Marks up," repeated Hedge. Again, he was right. Ard sent the scale spinning once more.

"Marks down," said Hedge. And the Ashing in Ard's palm had landed just as the man had said.

"Wrong," Ard lied, using a bit of sleight of hand to turn the Ashing over as he displayed it to Hedge. But Ard's own heartbeat told the truth he feared. Fifty-fifty chance to guess it right once. But three times in a row?

"What a rascal," Hedge said, squinting his good eye. "You know I was right. How else could I predict chance?"

"*Chance.*" Ard stuffed the three-mark Ashing into his pocket. "I would never take a job based on the fact that you *guessed* right three times in a row."

"I knew you'd be irked by it," Hedge said. "You demand more proof."

Ard nodded, an idea occurring to him. "A test of skill," he said. "Shooting."

"Explain."

"I'll set up six of those Grit pots—blanks, if you worry about wasting Heat Grit," said Ard. "I'll shoot at them and you can predict how many I'm going to hit."

"Oh," Hedge said, striding across the *Be'Igoth* toward the privacy stalls on the left. "Like this?" He pulled back the curtain to reveal six clay Grit pots propped side by side on a low shelf.

Ard's mouth went dry. What was happening? Maybe he should just leave. "I don't have a…"

He trailed off as Hedge reached into his vest and produced a Roller. He proffered it from his spike arm, the tip threaded through the trigger guard.

"All right." Ard accepted the gun. "Why don't you tell me how many I'm going to hit? And keep in mind that anything less than six is insulting." He pasted on a cocky smile, but he wasn't feeling it.

"I won't say," replied Hedge. "Influence your shooting, and whatnot. How about I write down the number on a scrap of parchment?" He held out a folded piece, pinched between his index and middle finger. "You can check it after the shots are made."

"Don't you need to write the number?" Ard asked.

Hedge's lips curled in a grin. "Did that before you came in."

Wordlessly, Ardor Benn took the scrap of paper and tucked it in his pocket. Hedge was playing a mind game with him, that was all. Ard's reputation would suggest that he'd hit all six. But Hedge would be aware of that, possibly assuming that Ard would intentionally miss one or two in an effort to throw his prediction.

But there was one number that Hedge Marsool couldn't possibly have guessed.

Ard leveled the Roller and snapped off six shots in rapid succession. Each found its mark, shattering a blank Grit pot. Ard's ears were ringing, his vision further obscured by the heavy smoke that filled the steamy bath house. But there was one more shot to be made.

Reaching into his vest, Ard withdrew the small piece of paper. But with it came his Singler, snapping off the last shot in Hedge's direction. The ball went over the man's shoulder, exploding into another pot of Heat Grit on the rack behind him.

While Hedge stood anchored, not even trembling from the close call, Ard unfolded the paper and glanced down at the single word.

*Seven.*

His eyes darted up to the thin man, whose chest was heaving with the exhilaration of victory.

"What the blazes?" Ard muttered. "How?"

"Same way I knew you'd be in that ruined building in the Char," he explained. "Same way I knew you'd flip three marks up. I can see the future. And that's how I know we're not alone in here."

Ard spun around, scouring the spacious *Be'Igoth* as if it might suddenly turn into an ambush. When he glanced back at Hedge, the man had crossed to the privacy stall next to the one Ard had shot at.

"I believe you already know the other rapscallion I invited to this meeting." Hedge Marsool pulled back the curtain and Ard found himself staring into the tense face of Quarrah Khai.

Quarrah didn't run. There was no sense in that. This stranger—Hedge Marsool—obviously didn't want her dead. Taking a deep breath of hot, misty air, she stepped out of the dressing stall, eyes locked with Ardor Benn.

"Quarrah?" he sputtered. "How did you...? What are you...?"

She gestured at the man with the spike for an arm. "Left me a note, same as you."

"Righty ho," said Hedge. "Though it's a blazing shame you had to break that vase to find it. Worth more in one piece."

Quarrah stiffened. Who was this creep? Claiming to see into the future? Sparks, she should have guessed Ard would somehow be involved. But judging by the conversation she'd just overheard, he didn't understand what he was up against, either. Unless he and Hedge were in it together, planning this entire thing to convince her to steal a dragon...

"This room only has one door," Ard said. "How long have you been in here?"

"Long enough," she replied. Patience was one of Quarrah's best qualities, but she didn't need to go bragging to Ard that she'd been inside the *Be'Igoth* since dawn.

"You look...good," Ard said hesitantly, as if he was aware that this wasn't the time or place for unnecessary compliments. Still, at least he was showing *some* restraint. Unlike the last time he'd seen her, shortly after he'd joined the Islehood—and what was with his sudden religious proclivities anyway?

Hedge Marsool reached into his courier's bag, withdrawing a folder of papers. "Documents and orders," he announced. "Captain Torgeston Dodset sits in command of my largest smuggling ship— the *Stern Wake*. The vessel can easily hold a mature sow, and with the right paperwork"—he waggled the folder tauntingly—"the captain can get you into and out of any harbor without a cargo inspection."

"Hold on," Quarrah said. "We haven't agreed to take the job."

"Sure you did," said Hedge. "What else are you going to do? When you leave Tofar's Salts, I know where you'll go. You try to hide, I find you. You try to run, I cut you off." He glanced at Ard. "You decide to double-cross me, I already know about it." Then he took a step closer to Quarrah. "You've got no idea what you're up against, dearie."

Quarrah drew back, his breath reeking of spicy fish. "I think I'll take my chances," she said. "You might scare Ard with your mystic abilities, but I'm not so easily hoodwinked—"

"Glassminds," Hedge said.

"What?" Quarrah and Ard replied in unison.

"That's what people are calling the creature that Prime Isless Gloristar transformed into."

"How do you know about—" Ard began.

"Rumors crawl the city," Hedge cut him off. "But I know better. I've got the cure."

"Cure to what?" Quarrah couldn't help but think of Lord Dulith's deranged claim. Hedge Marsool seemed no better.

"Moonsickness," said Hedge. "'Course, you have to catch the poor sap in a cloud of Metamorphosis Grit before the final stage."

Quarrah felt her heart skip, and Ard sucked in a sharp gasp. Only a handful of people knew about Portsend's final discovery. How did—

"Digested dragon teeth," the man went on, "extracted from a mound of Slagstone and processed to powder. Dissolved in a liquid solution with a balance level of negative flat five."

"Sparks," Ard whispered.

"I've got a few bruisers in mind for a quick transformation," said Hedge. "Just think how my smuggling business would soar if I had an army with powers like Gloristar had."

"How did you learn that formula?" Quarrah asked, her voice low.

"Oh, don't fuss." Hedge chuckled. "Secret's safe with me. So long as you get me what I've asked for."

"I, for one, think it sounds like a delightful challenge," Ard abruptly announced, swiping the folder from Hedge's hand. "Stealing a dragon, that is."

Hedge sniffed, turning his spike hand slowly like he might gore Ard where he stood. Then he reached out and took the folder back without any resistance from the ruse artist.

"Smarter than a stray tom, Ardor Benn." Hedge gave a twisted smile, tucking the folder back into his courier's bag. "I'll give you the documents you need to get aboard Captain Dodset's ship *after* you secure a place to store the dragon."

"My contacts in Helizon aren't—" Ard began.

"I'll give you the contact," Hedge cut him off. "There's a fat old baroness in Helizon by the name of Lavfa. A real ear-sore, but she's got the space to store the beast."

"And this baroness will agree to work with us?" asked Quarrah. "She's a friend of yours?"

"She doesn't know I exist," admitted Hedge. "But I understand she's willing to lease out her land to anyone if the price is right."

"A price you'll be fronting?" Ard ventured.

Hedge's scarred face contorted in a chuckle. "Don't play with me. They say the queen set you up for life when you signed her little pardon. I've heard figures over a million Ashings."

"Well, they're clearly exaggerating," said Ard. "It was only an even million."

Quarrah glanced at him, aware of the lie. According to Raek, the payment had been half that between both men. Queen Abeth had paid from her personal accounts, but most of her assets had been in the Guesthouse Adagio, which, regrettably, had been blown to bits in their battle against the Realm.

"The cost is yours," Hedge said. "Along with the negotiation. But I'm a fair man. Consider the *Be'Igoth* at Tofar's Salts exclusively yours until you get me that dragon." He strode between Ard and Quarrah, moving for the exit. "I won't even pop in to bother you."

"Thanks," Ard said, his tone bordering sarcasm. "In my negotiations, I'm sure the baroness will want to know how long we'll be renting the space. What are your plans for this dragon?"

Hedge laughed—little more than a rasping wheeze, but it must've been a laugh because his face was twisted into something like a grin. "You know what they say about you, Benn?"

"Best-smelling ruse artist in the Greater Chain?" Ard joked.

"You stick it in too deep." Hedge jabbed the air with his spike arm. "Don't know how to pull it out. Jobs need doing, not explaining."

Ard raised his hands defensively. "Just tell me how long to rent the blazing property, Hedge."

"I'll need the dragon for a full cycle," he finally said. "Don't worry your flimsy britches about what happens after that."

Hedge pulled open the door, and Quarrah saw the bare blue shoulder of the Trothian man standing guard.

"I'll send in Raekon Dorrel," Hedge called as an afterthought, carefully limping down the algae-slicked steps. "The Hegger's currently stuffing his face with a huckleberry turnover from the bakery across the street. That's what he calls keeping watch."

And then the door closed, plunging Quarrah and Ard into the steamy dimness of the waning Light Grit in the *Be'Igoth*.

"Care for a swim?" Ard finally asked, gesturing at the hot pool with the drowned cat. She could tell he was desperately trying to play it cool. Not to explode, like that day in the Char when he'd berated her for not letting him know she was alive after the Old Post Lighthouse had collapsed into the sea.

"Are we really doing this?" Quarrah asked.

"I mean, I was joking. But if you want to take a dip—"

Homeland, he could be annoying sometimes.

"I'm talking about the job, Ard." Quarrah sighed. She'd been extorted into a job before—when the queen dowager, Fabra Ment, had threatened to distribute a painting of her. At least there had been Ashings that time. In the years since, Quarrah had been living quite comfortably from the payout she'd collected before suspecting Fabra of being the masked leader of the Realm.

"Oh, we're doing it," Ard said. "We have to find out how he knows so much."

"Do you believe him?" Quarrah asked. "About predicting the future?"

Ard shook his head. "No . . . I don't know. Maybe. There's got to be a trick to it."

"Almost seems like the work of a ruse artist," she probed. But her suspicion went over Ard's head in a way that reassured her.

"Hedge Marsool is a lot of things," he replied, "but I wouldn't call him a ruse artist. He certainly has the skills to mastermind something as clever as a ruse, but he doesn't usually attach his face to it, because, well . . . you saw his face."

The disfigurement from the burn scars seemed to cause him a lot of pain. "Was he like that when you did the gem cutter job for him?" she asked.

"Yeah," Ard answered, a distant look on his face.

"How long ago was that?"

"Six or seven years," he replied. "Before I met you."

"He's been operating in Beripent all this time?" Quarrah wondered why his name had never reached her ears. He could have been part of the Realm.

"He covers a lot of the Greater Chain," said Ard. "But his real reputation is tied to Pekal. They called him the King Poacher. There wasn't a Harvester on Pekal that didn't fear him. Then old Hedge tangled with a dragon and his days of running the island came to a sudden end."

Quarrah felt the tingling of a dark thought in the back of her mind. Maybe it was born of her recent nightmare with Lord Dulith.

"Ard," she whispered. "What if this is a revenge job?"

"I thought of that. But it's been so many years since I double-crossed—"

"Not against you," she cut him off. "What if he wants a live dragon just so he can kill it?"

"He wasn't after a *specific* dragon," Ard said. "He said any mature sow would do."

And any Moonsick person would do for Lord Dulith. Revenge at that level wasn't logical. Quarrah had seen how twisted it could make someone. Working for a man like that would be beyond dangerous.

"Once he got back on his feet after the attack," Ard continued, "Marsool decided to work the other end of the poaching business. He became a notorious fence and know-all regarding dragon-related items. He's now as much a king of smuggling as he was poaching."

"What about those papers he had?" Quarrah asked. "You think they're really worth anything?"

"If we do this, we'll need a big ship and a willing captain able to convince harbor Regulation to look the other way. I'm not surprised that Hedge has these kinds of connections—especially when it comes to moving things out of Pekal."

But moving an entire dragon? Alive? Quarrah had single-handedly taken an unfertilized egg from Pekal, but this was going to be infinitesimally more perilous.

"Why would he pick the two of us?" Quarrah asked. "I'm known for stealing things, but usually only things I can pick up. And you... Well, I heard you were out of the rusing business."

Ard wiped some glistening dampness from his forehead. "Yeah," he said. "I'm part of the Islehood now. So you don't have to worry."

"Worry?" she said. What was he talking about?

"About me, you know..." He gestured awkwardly between them. "It's just... we can't be together. That's a choice I made when I became a Holy Isle."

She bit back a disbelieving chortle. Was he seriously working this angle with her? She didn't believe for a minute that Ardor Benn had actually joined the Islehood for a genuine purpose. He was clearly doing a long job. His new robes gave her no assurances that he wouldn't continue his hopeless attempts at winning her over.

"I'm just saying, if we *are* going to be working together again," said Ard, gesticulating more than normal with his hands, "then maybe we should talk about it."

"Talk about what?" She supposed it *was* fun to watch him squirm a little.

"Why you left that night," he said. "After Gloristar fell from the lighthouse. You could have been pardoned. You know Abeth would have done it. Sparks, I almost got her to do it while you weren't even there." His breath caught, like he didn't know which words to spend it on next. "Why didn't you come back?"

Quarrah wasn't sure how to respond. The answer to that question wasn't cut and dry. It was as complex and confusing as her feelings toward him.

"What good is the queen's pardon for people like us?" she finally settled on saying. *Us.* Her answer tied the two of them together in a way that visibly pleased Ard. But the look on his face quickly faded into an air of puzzlement.

"It was good for me," he said. "My entire life has changed."

"But for how long?" she interrupted. "Living outside the law is in my blood, Ard. And I know it's in yours, too. The queen's pardon would have only set me up for a bigger failure in the future."

*Better to keep on with the life I've always known*, she thought. *At least I know I'm good at that.*

The door burst open, causing both of them to whirl in surprise. Raek ducked inside, waving his hand through the air and making a sour face at the atmosphere in the *Be'Igoth*.

"Hedge Marsool!" he cried.

"Yeah," Ard said, clearly perturbed by the interruption. "We know."

"He knew right where I was," Raek continued.

"And let me guess," said Ard, "he caught you eating a huckleberry turnover."

Raek wiped self-consciously at the corners of his mouth, as if lingering crumbs had betrayed his appetite.

"Oh, hey, Quarrah," he finally greeted her.

"Raek."

It had been only two weeks since she'd seen him. Raekon Dorrel was a supplier unlike any other. Quarrah was completely capable of Mixing her own powdered Grit, but when it came to the new liquid solutions, Raek was her man. Their meetings were always brief, mostly out of fear that Ard would stumble across her like he'd done that day in the Char. Raek had done an excellent job pretending like he hadn't seen her in a year, but acting was harder for Quarrah.

"We're dealing with a fun case of extortion, Raek," said Ard. "Hedge has always been threatening, but he's upped his game. He knows the formula for Metamorphosis Grit. If we don't do what he wants, he'll transform his goons."

"What?" Raek cried. "He's bluffing."

Quarrah shook her head. "He told us the formula."

"But how did he—"

"Same way he knew everything else, I guess," said Ard. "He claims he can see the—" He interrupted himself with a snap of his fingers. "Memory Grit! That's how I would have done it."

"Done what?" Raek asked.

"Seen the future," Ard said. "The steam in the room would have made it impossible to notice the cloud. He must have tricked me into doing things so he'd know the outcome."

Quarrah tilted her head skeptically. Ard was obviously disturbed by Hedge's claims, but this was grasping at straws. "I was in the room the whole time," she reminded. "I would have noticed if you'd repeated yourself unknowingly."

"Not if you were in the Memory cloud, too," he tried, head bowed, eyes squinted shut as if trying to make sense of it.

"And Memory Grit wouldn't help him predict the outcome of an Ashing toss," said Quarrah. "Or the shots you fired."

"Maybe there was Illusion Grit in the mix," said Ard. "Maybe the coin in my hand wasn't what I was actually seeing."

"You know that's not how Illusion Grit works," Quarrah said. It was unlike Ard to ramble so inanely. She imagined it was always like that in his head, but he was usually more careful about screening the words that came out.

"Did either of you detonate liquid Grit in here?" Raek asked, crossing the room and taking a knee.

"No," Quarrah and Ard replied. She had needed nothing but a pot of Drift Grit to get over the soakhouse's outer fence and her lock-picking tools to get into the *Be'Igoth*.

"Then how do you explain *this*?" Raek pinched something tiny off the floor and held it up for their inspection. In the dwindling glow of the Prolonged Light Grit, Quarrah had no hope of seeing what he held. And she certainly wasn't going to don her wire spectacles in front of Ard.

"Slagstone chip," Raek answered his own question. He stood, brushing his boot across the floor with a grating sound. "Shards of glass and a little cork. All the evidence of a liquid Grit detonation."

Ard was nodding. "That's exactly where Hedge was standing when he predicted the Ashing toss and the shots." He took an anxious step forward. "What kind of Grit was it?"

"There's no way to tell," Raek said, peering down at the detonation site beside his boot.

"What color is the liquid?" Ard pressed, taking a knee to make his own inspection.

"The floor's damp, but probably just from the steam in here," said Raek. "Jonzan's Second Truth still applies to the liquid stuff—all ignited Grit is consumed upon detonation. No trace left behind."

"But what type would have been useful?" Ard asked.

In her mind, Quarrah ran through the list of new Grit types that Portsend Wal had discovered before his death. Ignition, Null, Containment, Stasis, Weight, Gather, and of course, Metamorphosis.

"Ignition makes the most sense," she answered. "It's becoming standard across the Greater Chain, and he could have used it to trigger other Grit types like Ard mentioned."

"Or..." Ard whispered. "Or this is something different."

"*New* new Grit?" Raek's voice was skeptical. "You're giving a lot of credit to a guy whose mother named him after a trimmed bush."

"Portsend developed seven types based on information that

Prime Isless Gloristar had given him from the Anchored Tome," Ard said. "But Gloristar told me herself that she'd lost the book. And she hadn't been able to read the entire thing before Termain took it."

"You're saying that there might have been other source materials that Portsend never knew about?" Raek said.

Ard shrugged. "I wouldn't have considered it before our time with the professor, but it seems possible. Likely, even."

Quarrah gave it some thought. "And you think that Hedge Marsool discovered the formula to a new type of liquid Grit that does . . . *what*? Shows him the future?"

"It's not a stretch to imagine it," said Ard. "Illusion Grit replays an image across time. Visitant Grit has the power to physically transport someone through time. What if Hedge has the next step?"

"Time Grit," Raek said.

"Future Grit," suggested Ard.

Raek shook his head. "I like Time Grit better."

"We don't know if it really shows him the future, or moves him through time," reminded Quarrah. "Sparks, we don't even know if some new type of Grit really exists."

"True," said Ard, standing. "But it's certainly given me good incentive to do Hedge's job."

"Out of fear that he'll use an unknown Grit on you?" she asked.

Ard shook his head. "Out of curiosity in finding it for myself."

Quarrah drew in a misty breath. Ardor Benn was notorious for digging too deep into his employers. But this time, she was actually onboard with him. They needed to prevent Hedge from turning his thugs into *Glassminds*, as he'd called them. And if there was a new Grit as powerful as Hedge was claiming, Quarrah needed to know more about it.

"All right," Quarrah said. "So we need to steal a dragon."

"And where do you plan to store a beast that size?" Raek asked.

"Hedge gave us a lead on that," answered Ard. "Someone named Lavfa, a Talumonian baroness. You ever heard of her?"

"Doesn't sound familiar," replied Raek. "I'll look into her and see what I can dig up."

"Once we find her, we'll need to win her trust before we can even ask about space to store a dragon," Ard said.

"Why?" Quarrah asked. "If we pay her enough, isn't it a fair deal?"

"Except our side of the deal is highly illegal," Ard reminded her.

"So I've met plenty of barons and nobles who were more than a little crooked," said Quarrah. "We can hope this Lavfa is one of them. I'll scout her properties and make certain she's not a straight arrow. Then Raek can set up a meet."

Ard held up his hands in a gesture that obviously dismissed what Quarrah had just said. Why was this man incapable of listening to anyone but himself? Even Raek's ideas had to pass through Ard's filter before they were acceptable.

"You're probably right," Ard said to her surprise. "I'm guessing the baroness is crooked. Which is even more reason to gain her trust. If she finds out who I am, then Lavfa might stand to gain more by turning me in. One little crime is all it'll take to get the queen's pardon revoked. Trable would have to throw me out of the Islehood and I'd lose everything I've been working for."

What *was* he working for? Quarrah thought he would probably answer her truthfully if she asked, but that would only show him that she was interested. If they continued working together, Ard's motives would certainly become apparent. And Quarrah had no trouble waiting.

"We have to approach this carefully so we don't spook her," Ard continued. "When we tell her that we have a very large, very dangerous, illegal item to store on her property, I want her to rub her hands together with excitement, not summon the local authorities."

Ard always did things the hard way. "And how do you plan to gain Lavfa's trust?" Quarrah asked.

"We need to get her away from the Regulation so she really has time to ponder our proposal before she reports us," Ard mused.

"Want me to abduct her?" Raek asked bluntly.

"*That'll* gain her trust," muttered Quarrah.

"Let's try something less aggressive," said Ard. "I'm talking about a little *ruse*."

Quarrah let out a slow breath. When was he not?

*It's impossible to know what comes next. I've survived this long by wearing out the toes of my boots.*

# CHAPTER

# 5

Holy Isle Ardor Benn sauntered out of the boathouse, the sea wind whipping his green robes as he studied the crowd on the broad deck of the catamaran. This vessel was like a genuine house floating on two long wooden pontoons. In addition to the covered deck, the house itself had three separate sleeping quarters, and a spacious social room with a kitchen at the back.

As large as the boathouse was, Ard found that there was nowhere he could go to escape Baroness Lavfa's voice. It was no wonder she'd never been invited to one of Lord Capsu's sightseeing excursions. Ard wished he could have captured the host's face in Illusion Grit when he realized that Lavfa had somehow received an invitation for today. Still, Capsu let her onboard without so much as a protest, proving to Ard that there was one universal trait shared by all noblemen—they hated admitting mistakes.

Far from an actual mistake, the forged invitation delivered to Baroness Lavfa had been carefully crafted. The plump woman had arrived in a fancy embroidered dress, haggling with the other guests before they'd left Grisn's southern harbor.

Even on the deck, with the fresh wind in his face and the pop of the big sail overhead, Ard could hear Baroness Lavfa inside the boathouse, trying to buy the earrings directly out of a noblewoman's lobes. She was an absolute shark of a businesswoman, but so far they'd not been able to find any evidence that she was crooked.

Lord Capsu silenced the quartet of musicians on the deck, earning everyone's attention as the string music paused. The man raised a stemmed glass in one hand as he addressed his wealthy guests.

"If you direct your attention off the starboard prow, you'll get your first glimpse of New Vantage." Capsu spoke of it with such pride, Ard would have thought he was the founder. His comment was met with great enthusiasm, the nobles swarming to the side of the deck, spyglasses in hand to ogle Pekal's first residential city.

Ard had already seen it from the *Double Take* a few months ago. He thought it was a fine accessory to the forested slopes of an otherwise virgin island.

To Ard, New Vantage represented everything that he loved to exploit about the upper class in the Greater Chain. It was a resort town—silver, gold, and glass sparkling above the eastern harbor. They weren't living on Pekal because they *should*. They were there to show that they *could*. It was an impractical site, populated by impractical people. Ripe for the rusing. If he weren't trying to stay out of trouble, Ard would have already run a dozen jobs on those haughty residents.

"I see the Mooring Station," exclaimed one of the women, her eye pressed to a spyglass. "There. You can see the waterfall pouring down the cliff to the sea."

Yes. Prime Isle Trable had been quick to establish a small remote Mooring. It had only one Cove and was easily staffed by a single Isle. The waterway had been constructed around an existing stream that flowed through the little Mooring, providing a place where the Holy Torch could be lit during the Passings to ward off Moonsickness.

Baroness Lavfa came bustling onto the deck, her pudgy cheeks rosy as she moved toward the group on the starboard side. "I've had my eye on several undeveloped acres on the east side of New Vantage," she said, her voice outperforming the wind. "It's a lease against the crown, you know. The crusader queen declared all of Pekal property of the throne."

Ard understood why Queen Abeth might allow some developments on the island. After all, her son had been held there for nearly two years, briefly shuffled off Pekal during every Moon Passing. A more permanent development would lead to regular residents. That would mean more eyes on the slopes to spot the kind of suspicious activity that had led to her son's detainment. In truth, Ard thought New Vantage was probably having the opposite effect, creating a more comfortable staging area for poachers and smugglers.

"Isle Ardor?" a servant asked. "Would you like something to drink?"

Ard turned to find Raek towering beside him. The servant's apron looked ridiculously small across his broad chest.

"I think I've had quite enough," Ard replied. "But I would enjoy another one of those sweet rolls if there are any left."

"Of course," Raek said, his voice unusually polite. "I will see to it myself."

Okay. That was the cue. Everything was in place. It was time to earn Baroness Lavfa's trust.

Ard moved to the starboard side of the deck, his steps natural and slow, like those of a person edging into a conversation that had started without him. He had already spoken individually with several of the guests, learning that his reputation preceded him, as it was wont to do.

"Of course, Her Majesty gifted the land to the Islehood for building the Mooring Station," Ard cut in at the back of the group, his gaze passing over their shoulders to the distant settlement. "As a crusader monarch, she works closely with Prime Isle Trable in all matters."

"Ah, the infamous Isle," said a woman Ard hadn't yet spoken with.

"I don't know about *infamous*," Ard replied with a coy smile, stopping beside Baroness Lavfa.

"What did Lord Capsu have to do to get you onboard?" asked a young man with vibrant red hair.

"Quite the contrary," said Ard. "I asked to come. It's a wonderful chance for me to speak with people of your standing."

*Second-rate Talumonian lords and nobles*, Ard thought honestly. Ones who couldn't actually afford to visit New Vantage but still wanted to feel like they were a part of it.

"And for us to speak with you," said Lord Capsu. "Your journey shines hope on anyone who has felt too Settled to go on."

"As does yours, good sir," said Ard, earning a few raised glasses for the comment.

It was common knowledge that Capsu had been a Hegger in his youth. The Compounded Health Grit had almost killed him one night, and his parents had locked him away for a year until his body no longer craved it. The man that had emerged was finally suited to inherit his parents' estate. He married well, had two children, and became a loud voice for better regulation of Health Grit in Talumon.

"You're both examples to us all," said Lady Capsu, squeezing her husband's arm affectionately.

"That's kind of you," Ard said humbly. "When Her Majesty

extended a pardon, the Homeland spoke to me. I've never doubted my decision to join the Islehood."

"Have you ever been to Pekal?" Lord Greyfeather asked.

"Once or twice," Ard admitted. "My old life had a way of getting me into places I didn't belong."

A few chuckles.

"Did you ever see one?" Greyfeather followed up.

"A dragon?" Ard clarified. "I glimpsed one in the wild once. The beast was standing so still, I thought at first that it was nothing more than a mossy cliffside. It was sleeping, thank the Homeland, but my companions were making such a racket, I thought for sure they'd awaken her."

"What did you do?" asked Lady Capsu.

"Well, my friend was walking past at that very moment and I grabbed his arm." As if to emphasize the story, Ard reached out and gripped Baroness Lavfa by the elbow. "I was too startled to speak, so I just pointed." He tugged his hand sharply away, pointing for dramatic effect. As he did so, he made sure to snag the silk strap of her petite handbag. It slipped from her ample arm, striking the deck and spilling its contents.

There was a moment of silence as everyone realized what they were seeing, scattered at their feet. Amid the expected handbag items—a small mirror and comb, a pouch of Ashings—were half a dozen rolled paper cartridges.

"Is that...?" someone muttered.

Lord Capsu abruptly handed his drink to his wife and stooped to snatch up a roll. Untwisting one of the ends, he poured a bit of gray powder into his palm, studying it under an intense eye.

"This is Health Grit," he said softly, his gaze falling on the baroness at Ard's side. "What are you doing with this?"

"I..." she stammered. "It isn't mine. I don't know..."

"This handbag is not yours?" Capsu's voice was already turning accusatory.

"The bag *is*—"

"Illegal possession of Compounded Health Grit is a crime," cried Capsu. "And you bring that filth aboard *my* vessel?"

"It was him!" came a loud cry from the deck behind. The whole crowd turned to find two servants standing beside the string quartet. Raek was awkwardly holding a basket of sweet rolls, looking as if he'd just been caught with his hand in the cookie jar. And Quarrah was beside him, dressed in a servant apron that actually fit her.

Ard would have waited a little longer before delivering the line, really letting Lavfa stew in confusion under Capsu's accusations. But he was pleased with the sincerity in Quarrah's voice as she stood pointing at Raek.

"I saw him drop the Health Grit into the lady's handbag," Quarrah continued when all eyes were on her. Ard could tell how much she hated this kind of acting and attention, but her part was nearly done.

Lord Capsu strode across the deck, hands balled into fists at his side. "You," he barked in Raek's face. "What's your name?"

"Wolden, sir." For a man his size, Ard thought Raek was doing a remarkable job of looking weak and frightened in the face of authority.

"Did you do this?" Capsu held out one hand, the paper roll smashed from his grip.

"No, sir." Raek stared straight ahead over the water.

"He has more," Quarrah said. "Search him." Then, having delivered her last line, she promptly excused herself, ducking out of the limelight into the boathouse. Too bad she'd miss the next bit. The fun part was yet to come.

Lord Capsu reached into Raek's apron pocket and withdrew another two rolls of Heg. The nobleman's face glowered a shade of red. "What are you doing on my boat?"

Raek remained impassive.

"Answer me!"

"Lord Capsu." Ard stepped forward and placed a hand on the angry man's shoulder. The host stepped away, violently hurling the fistful of Heg rolls over the railing of the ship.

"We'll detain him in one of the private rooms," said Capsu. "Turn him over to the harbor Regulation when we arrive back in Grisn."

"I'd like to speak with him, if you'll permit it," Ard said quietly. Lord Capsu flicked his wrist in a gesture of dismissive permission.

"Hello, Wolden," Ard said, stepping up to face Raek. What kind of a name was *Wolden*? Ard had suggested several winners, but Raek was clearly going off-script.

"I need you to tell me what you were doing with that Health Grit in your apron," Ard said.

"I don't know what you're talking about," said Raek.

"Come on. I saw it. We *all* saw it." He gestured to the group, making sure they stayed engaged in the exchange.

"I'm not a Hegger," Raek said stubbornly. It was a sentence that struck Ard to the core. His friend was supposed to be acting, but this conversation was steering awfully close to real life.

"Okay," Ard continued. "So you're not a Hegger. Are you a Wayfarist, by chance?"

"Yes, sir."

"Then you're probably expecting to be detained in a Wayfarist jailhouse once we reach Grisn?" Raek didn't say anything. "Did you know it is considered highly Settled to lie to a Holy Isle? Enough lies and people might begin to question whether you're Wayfarist at all."

Again, was this conversation mirroring reality a little too well? But this time, it was Ard's conflicted beliefs in Wayfarism reflecting in the glass.

"So let me ask you again," Ard said. "Why were you carrying Health Grit?"

In an impressive display of acting, Raek seemed to cave, his shoulders slumping forward as if Ard's words had dealt him a blow.

"I don't use it," he muttered. "I was working a job."

"What job?" Ard pressed.

"I was supposed to get close to Capsu," Raek said. "Catch him in a surprise detonation of Heg."

Lord Capsu looked like he would have rushed Raek if his wife hadn't been holding him back.

"Why?" Ard asked.

"Get him to relapse," said Raek. "Get hooked again."

"And did you plant that Health Grit in Baroness Lavfa's handbag?" Ard asked. When Raek didn't answer, he added, "You've got to be honest. At this point it's the only chance you've got of finding yourself in a decent cell."

Raek sucked in a breath. "I deposited the rolls while she wasn't looking. I've got quick hands, you know?"

Ard wanted to laugh. Raek had *steady* hands, but he was far from sneaky. Quarrah had actually been the one to deposit the incriminating evidence in Lavfa's handbag.

"Why'd you do it?"

"If Capsu relapsed, I knew everyone's possessions would be inspected," explained Raek. "I was trying to pin it on her." He pointed at the baroness. A gasp went through the crowd, and Ard saw a dangerous expression cross Lavfa's ruddy cheeks.

"Why her?"

"Isn't it obvious?" Raek spit. "Nobody likes her. She wasn't even *supposed* to be here."

"Like flames, I wasn't!" shouted Lavfa. "I was an invited guest just like everyone here."

"Your invitation was a forgery," Raek declared. "Capsu didn't want you tagging along, talking nothing but shop for three hours, striking your own Ashlit-pinching deals with his *actual* guests."

Lavfa spun toward Capsu. "Is this true?" The lord didn't answer immediately, which seemed to be all the proof she needed. The baroness stalked toward Raek, her excess fat quivering with rage.

At the last moment, Ard stepped between her and his partner, holding up his hands in a cry for peace. "The Homeland condemns violence."

"And what does it think of slandering one's good name?" she bellowed.

"He'll spend a night in a Wayfarist jail cell," Ard assured her.

"A single night?" cried the baroness.

Lord Capsu stepped forward, finally composed, now that Lavfa was enraged. "I'll escort him inside. We'll make sure he faces proper punishment."

"With respect," Ard said to Capsu, "I don't think you should risk escorting this man when his sole purpose aboard this ship was to inflict harm on you."

"Let me at him," cried Lavfa.

Ard held up his hands again. "I don't believe he would dare lay a finger on a Holy Isle." He grabbed Raek's arm. "Right this way, *Wolden*."

They moved across the deck, Baroness Lavfa following close behind. "We must interrogate him further," she said as they passed into the boathouse. Quarrah pulled open a door to one of the rooms as they drew near.

"If he's working for someone," said Lavfa, "we must find out who. I have enemies, you know."

"Enemies?" Ard asked, pushing Raek through the low doorway.

"A woman does not get where I am without stepping on a few toes," she said. "Ruffling a few feathers."

"Oh, I understand that as well as anyone," Ard said. Inside the room was a small feather bed with a hefty side table. A large window in the back wall showed the catamaran's impressive wake.

Ard led Raek across the narrow room, Quarrah shutting the door and standing watch outside once Baroness Lavfa was through.

"A single night in a Wayfarist jail…" Ard muttered, shaking his head. "It hardly seems a suitable punishment, considering how he humiliated you in front of the other guests." He stepped around Raek and opened the large window.

"A single night in a Wayfarist jail, and then he's back on the streets of Talumon, spreading his lies about you," Ard continued, walking around to stand between Raek and Lavfa again. "Or, we could decide on a better punishment for his crime."

Ard spun abruptly, throwing himself against Raek's chest. The big man cried out, staggering until the windowsill caught him in the back of the knees. Hopelessly grasping for Ard, he tumbled out the open window and fell some ten feet to the roiling water below.

Ard turned slowly, straightening his sea-green robes. Baroness Lavfa was staring, her small mouth slightly agape, a twitch of a smile at the corners.

"That was…unexpected." Her voice was soft for the first time since she'd come aboard.

"A terrible accident, wouldn't you say? That window really shouldn't have been left open," Ard declared. "And I was lucky I wasn't harmed when he tried to force his way past me."

Ard gestured for her to take a seat on the edge of the bed. The baroness obliged, daintily lifting the hem of her dress.

"Now that I have you alone," Ard continued, "I was hoping we could talk business."

"Oh?" She looked plenty intrigued.

"When you were speaking earlier, I heard you mention your land on Talumon," Ard said.

"I own a vast number of properties from Grisn to Lenthers," she said proudly. "I have over five hundred landlords and landladies in my employ, and more tenants than I could accurately count."

"The Homeland must look kindly on your enterprises," Ard said, sounding appropriately Isle-ish. "But I'm interested in your properties in *Helizon*."

Lavfa's demeanor changed ever so slightly, her round body stiffening at the mention. A common person might not have noticed, but Ard prided himself on reading people.

*Interesting*, he thought. *Why would that put her on edge?*

"I had a feeling you'd ask about that," she said.

"A feeling?"

"A holy man like yourself would probably call it an Urging from the Homeland." The baroness shuddered. "What do you need it for?"

"I'm working on something big," Ard said cautiously. "And I'm looking for a place to store a particularly *sensitive* item."

"How big, exactly?"

"Well, let's just say it wouldn't fit on this boat," said Ard.

Baroness Lavfa interlaced her thick fingers thoughtfully. "I might be able to provide a space. How long would you need it?"

See, Hedge? Of course she was going to ask that question. "Two cycles." Hedge needed it for only one, but Ard didn't think it would hurt to give themselves a little wiggle room. "But the property needs to be discreet. The item we'll be storing has the potential to attract a lot of attention. We need to make sure it doesn't."

"How well do you know Helizon's history?" Lavfa asked.

Ard shrugged cluelessly. "I'm from Beripent. Born and raised."

"Roughly three hundred years ago, a series of natural caverns were discovered under what is now Helizon," she explained. "One of them contained a massive underground freshwater lake. The early Talumonians attempted to distribute this water by carving tunnels to connect the various caves, making for more conveniently placed wells on the surface. The water is long gone, but the caverns remain." She pursed her painted lips. "I happen to own eighty percent of them."

Ard *had* heard about the caves under Helizon. Caverns of the sort were not uncommon all across the islands of the Greater Chain. Similar aqueducts to the ones Lavfa was describing were still used to run water into Beripent's Mooring. Lyndel had used an abandoned one to meet with Isle Halavend for cycles.

"What about access?" Ard asked. "Would we be able to move in something as large as, say, a dragon?"

"*Dragon?*" she whispered.

"I say that as a mere size comparison, of course," Ard said, watching her reaction. She wasn't as frightened by the prospect as she should have been. But then, she probably didn't take him seriously. Who would?

"I recently had the impression to expand one of my cargo hatches," she said.

"An impression?" Ard said. In his line of work, that usually meant *threat*. Maybe Hedge Marsool had primed the pump for him.

"Never mind that," she said. "The hatch is covered by an empty warehouse in a shabby neighborhood in the Picks. I have rope ladders for manual access. Large cargo can be lowered down with Drift Grit."

Sounded like the perfect place for a dragon.

"And you'll lend us the space?" Ard finally asked.

Baroness Lavfa tilted her head. "For the right price."

"I could do a hundred Ashings. Half up front." Ard knew he didn't have much hope of getting her to take this offer. She'd been running much harder bargains all morning.

"Pah!" She balked at Ard's offer. "The property's worth three times that."

"I could do two," said Ard. "But I can't go higher."

"I'm a very wealthy woman, Isle Ardor," she said. "Your best offer would be a mere drib in a bucket for me." She pursed her lips again. "But I could use a man with your expertise."

"There are many Holy Isles with much more experience than me," Ard began.

"I'm talking about your prior skill set. Yes, I heard you bragging about your exploits on the deck, too. You seemed unafraid to take risks in your former life."

That wasn't true. Ard had been plenty afraid, plenty of times. He just knew how to turn the fear into something useful. Something that would drive him forward at a relentless pace.

"Tell me what you have in mind," he finally said.

"I'd like you to acquire a few items for me," said Baroness Lavfa. "If you do so successfully, I will lend you my subterranean Helizon property and stay out of your business. Do we have a deal?"

"I suppose I should hear what the items are first," Ard said.

"Of course. How familiar are you with the Royal Concert Hall in Beripent?"

"Quite," Ard answered. He'd actually spent a great deal of time there as Dale Hizror, claiming to be the composer of the famous Unclaimed Symphony.

"Architecturally, the building is a throwback," said Lavfa.

"What do you mean?" Architecture was the last thing Ard had been thinking about when he'd been in that hall.

"Bricks," she answered. "Who uses bricks these days?"

Ard raised an eyebrow. "There are *thousands* upon *thousands* of homes in Beripent constructed from bricks."

Lavfa flicked her fingers at him dismissively. "Cheap homes in ragtag neighborhoods. But show me a manor or mansion built in the last two centuries that's made entirely of bricks. Drift Grit is the vehicle of impressive construction, and anyone with enough Ashings employs it. Slabs, blocks...Sparks, Lady Envire has a guesthouse made of just four pieces of stone—one for each wall."

"I don't see where you're going with this," Ard admitted.

"Excuse my tangent," Lavfa said. "A woman in my business finds that her heart beats for a well-built structure on a prime spot of land. Which leads me to the Royal Concert Hall, constructed ninety-eight years ago, when the use of Drift Grit for floating large masonry was in full swing. However, the architect of the hall thought it would be quaint to craft the entire structure from old-fashioned red brick and mortar. It was supposed to give the hall a friendly, neighborhood feel—which in my opinion was negated by the sheer size of that royal structure."

Ard scratched behind his ear. Baroness Lavfa could be exhausting. He understood why Lord Capsu had never invited her aboard his catamaran.

"But I digress again," Lavfa acknowledged. "For the purpose of our business deal, I need you to bring me four bricks from the wall of Beripent's Royal Concert Hall."

Ard wrinkled his forehead. It certainly wasn't the strangest job he'd taken. But why did she want common bricks? "That's all?"

"No, no. I'm just getting started," Lavfa said. "I'll also need ten panweights of Void Grit and the same amount of Barrier Grit. Those must be divided into sealed Grit kegs and placed in a black leather backpack with the bricks."

"Okaaay," Ard said, letting a little of his puzzlement shine through. Oddly specific. Maybe he should be writing this down.

"The last item I need will be the most difficult to obtain," said Lavfa. "Have you heard of Agrodite Moon Glass?"

At that comment, Ard nearly toppled out the open window himself. To his knowledge, he was one of the few Landers who had actually held a piece of the glass. Looking through the red lens had shown him something similar to Trothian vision. And Lyndel had said it did even more for her people.

Several years ago, the shard of Moon Glass had been given to Isle Halavend's assistant, a young Isless Malla. She had carried it to Pekal's summit to confirm what Lyndel and the old Isle had suspected—that the dragons absorbed the sickening rays from the passing Moon.

"I know they're very rare," Ard answered. Lyndel had said that there were only three pieces in existence among her people. Ard had seen a giant spire of similar red glass standing on the bed of the InterIsland Waters. That column had held the final testament of a race now forgotten.

"I need you to get me one," said the baroness.

Ard bit his lip in thought. That last part of Lavfa's order would be no simple task. He listed the items back on his fingers. "Four bricks, twenty panweights of Grit, and a piece of Agrodite Moon Glass?"

"Deliver those items to me in a black leather backpack and I will be happy to write you a lease to my subterranean property in Helizon," she said. "No questions asked."

That was more than Ardor Benn could say. His mind was swimming with questions.

*The key is never to be adrift. I've spent my whole life standing at the proverbial rudder.*

# CHAPTER

# 6

Quarrah stepped past Drot, moving up the slippery steps to the *Be'Igoth*. "Excuse me," she muttered, even though the Trothian man didn't understand a word of Landerian.

Initially, she and Ard had been suspicious that Drot and his brother, Eggat, might be merely feigning their inability to speak Landerian. It would certainly make them more effective spies for Hedge Marsool. More than four years had passed, but none of them were quick to forget how the Trothian baker, Mearet, had betrayed their hideout to the king.

Quarrah didn't worry about Drot and Eggat now. In classic Ardor Benn fashion, he had paid three other Trothians, unassociated with Tofar's Salts, to independently check the language barrier. And if that wasn't enough, he'd paid three more Landers to approach the brothers on the street with basic directional questions. In every case, the report came back clean.

It made sense to Quarrah. Hedge Marsool apparently spoke flawless Trothian. There weren't many Landers who risked learning it, since their language was considered Settled to traditional Wayfarist beliefs. Hedge's ability to retain two exclusively Trothian-speaking employees might give him a sense of security. After all, it was unlikely for another Lander to sway them with a better offer if they couldn't communicate.

"Quarrah!" Ard greeted her as she shut the door quietly behind her. He was dressed in his usual billowy-sleeved shirt and snug vest. Behind him, Raek was hanging a framed map of the Greater Chain on the stone wall. He looked quite recovered from last week's abrupt plunge out the back of Lord Capsu's catamaran. She hadn't liked the idea of relying on a common fisherman to swing by and reel him out of the water, but they'd paid the man well in advance to make sure he'd be in position.

"I made a few improvements to our hideout." Ard held his arms out, gesturing to the spacious *Be'Igoth*. "What do you think?"

A *few* improvements? This place barely looked like the same room where they'd met with Hedge. They'd stopped adding Heat Grit to the bath while they'd planned the catamaran ruse, greatly reducing the steam. But now Ard had taken the interior decorating to another level.

The first thing Quarrah noticed was the new flooring. Ard had laid wooden planks atop the stone floor. Well, Quarrah was sure Ard hadn't done it himself—he'd more likely hired it out or asked Raek, who was much less afraid of manual labor.

At any rate, the new flooring completely covered over the bath, effectively doubling the amount of usable floor space in the room. Ard had brought in an array of comfortable seating options— armchairs, couches, and a chaise against the far wall for lounging.

Quarrah noticed that a few sconces were mounted to some of the square pillars. They were the type with a Slagstone ignitor built into the bottom, making it easy to keep the Light Grit glowing brightly in the windowless room.

The rack of Grit pots was still against the back wall, but even the privacy dressing stalls had been given a makeover. The heavy curtains were gone, giving Quarrah nowhere to hide if the need should arise. Instead, the four empty booths were loaded with tables of Raek's Grit Mixing supplies.

"I'd say all you're missing is a personal cook," Quarrah remarked, remembering the lavish setup Ard had rused his way into at Queen Abeth's Guesthouse Adagio.

"Actually, we've got a whole kitchen staff," Ard said. "Hedge takes every chance he can to squeeze the purses of these good Agrodite soakers. Come to find out, Tofar's Salts is better known for its drinks and cuisine, served fresh to any Trothian taking a *fajumar.*"

Quarrah thought Ard was trying to sound abstruse, but he wasn't the only one who had picked up on the Trothian word for the saltwater soak.

"For obviously reasons, there isn't a written menu," Ard continued. "But Raek and I tried a sample platter last night while we were setting things up in here."

"Too salty," Raek said, finally turning away from the wall, satisfied that the map was hanging straight. "I think I drank the well dry when I got home last night."

"But rumor has it that one of the cooks knows some Lander dishes," Ard said hopefully. "And if that doesn't pan out, there's a great little bakery just across the street."

Quarrah walked forward slowly, passing between a pair of

armchairs as she tested the new section of flooring that covered the bath. She tried to peer down between the wooden floorboards, but they were nailed too tightly.

"How much do you trust these boards?" she asked, feeling them flex underfoot ever so slightly.

"A hundred percent," replied Ard. "We had a top-notch Trothian carpenter install it. And take a look at this special feature."

He strode over to a chair with a vibrant green cushion. Standing back, he grabbed the wooden arm and yanked upward. Instantly, a trapdoor swung downward on well-concealed hinges. The armchair went with it, but it must have been securely mounted to the hatch because it hung there, facing straight down.

"This is in case you still want to take a swim?" Quarrah asked. If someone had been seated in the chair, it would have dumped them face first into the bath.

"We drained the water," Ard explained, seating himself at the edge so his legs dangled into the dark opening. Then he reached down and grabbed the back of the mounted chair, using it as a brace to swing out of sight into the empty hole of a bath. "Come check it out," his voice floated up.

Quarrah glanced at Raek, who made an expression indicating that the space below wasn't anything to be overly excited about, but it would be best just to indulge the ruse artist.

She crouched down to grab the back of the armchair, and then nimbly lowered herself to join Ard.

"A hideout within a hideout," Ard said. "I know you're not fond of windowless buildings with only one door, but Hedge wouldn't allow me to install another exit. So I thought the next best thing would be to build us a good place to hide."

He reached out and grabbed a weighted rope. Giving it a long pull, the trapdoor with its mounted armchair rose back into place, plunging Quarrah and Ard into darkness, broken only by a few thin lines of light falling through some of the wider gaps in the boards overhead.

"This is where we're keeping our stores of liquid Grit," Ard said, rustling around in the darkness. "We've also got a cache of guns and ammunition and enough food and fresh water for the three of us to survive for a week."

Quarrah raised an eyebrow. "Do you really see that happening? I mean, the trapdoor is clever, but it's not entirely foolproof. Anyone familiar with Tofar's Salts would know about the existence of this bath."

"True," said Ard. "Still, I thought it wouldn't hurt to be prepared."

Sparks suddenly sizzled through the darkness, and Quarrah squinted at a little orb of Light Grit springing up in Ard's hand. A quick glance around the large space revealed all the supplies Ard had mentioned. He left his Light detonation hanging in midair and moved to the far end of the empty bath.

"Here's what makes this little hole really worthwhile." Ard dropped to a knee and pointed at a metal crank handle. It jutted out of the stone wall of the bath above a rectangular indentation.

With what looked like little effort, he turned the handle a few revolutions. The action was accompanied by a grating sound as the small rectangular section in the wall began to rise like a sluice gate.

"Behold, the complex plug to the bathtub," Ard said once the gate was fully raised. The opening at the bottom of the wall was about the same size as that waste chute she'd squeezed through while escaping Lord Dulith's manor.

"The Trothians pitch the seams when they fill the *Be'Igoth*," Ard said. "Between the seal and the weight of the water, they discovered that it was difficult to pull a plug on a pool this deep. So they installed this nifty mechanism to drain the *Be'Igoth* into the baths outside."

Quarrah dropped to her stomach and peered out the opening. She could see daylight through a grate on the other end. Based on the placement of the pool in relation to the layout of the room above, she guessed this tight passageway was about fifteen feet long. And now that she thought of it, she'd noticed the metal grate next to the steps outside.

"So if things go badly," Ard surmised, "we drop down here and shimmy our way outside. Hopefully before they find the trapdoor."

"How secure is that grate?" Quarrah asked. She'd have no leverage to kick it free once she was inside that drain shaft.

"That's a great question," Ard said, nodding. "I've got people looking into it."

"Oh?" She stood up as Ard ratcheted the sluice gate shut. "Who?"

"You?" He smiled awkwardly at her. "Will you look into that?"

"It's probably held in place by a handful of masonry nails," she said. "I can loosen them and install a latch that holds the grate in place from the inside. Something easy to undo in a hurry."

"Thanks," Ard said. "It's good to have your professional eye again."

The compliment hit Quarrah so unexpectedly that she couldn't decide whether to absorb it or shrug it off. Instead of doing either, she decided to point out another flaw in Ard's escape plan.

"Raek won't fit," she said, lowering her voice so the big man above wouldn't hear.

Ard scratched behind his ear thoughtfully, eyes lingering on the sluice gate and the small drain shaft. "Yeah. He knows." Ard crossed back over to the rope dangling from the trapdoor. "The trick is to stay ahead of Hedge Marsool so we never have to use this squirrel hole."

"How do we stay ahead of someone who claims to see the future?" Quarrah pointed out.

"Maybe we just keep the future unpredictable." Ard grabbed the rope and gave it a sharp tug.

Nothing happened.

He muttered something under his breath as he pulled again, but the trapdoor didn't budge.

"It doesn't open from the inside, does it?" Quarrah asked with a smirk.

Ard's face turned sheepish in the glow of the tiny Light cloud. "I guess we didn't specify that in the plans for the carpenter," he admitted, swatting the air hopelessly at the trapdoor eight feet above. "But hey. Look on the bright side. We've got more than a week's worth of food and water." He shrugged. "And the company's not half bad, either."

The trapdoor suddenly dropped open, causing Quarrah and Ard to flinch at the appearance of the falling armchair. Raek peered down at them, his bald head shining in the light from the upper room.

"Hope I'm not interrupting anything," he said, "but our appointment is knocking on the door, and it sort of ruins the whole *secret trapdoor* effect if you two come climbing up out of the floor."

He lent them both a hand, and with the support of the armchair, Quarrah found it quite easy to scramble out of the hole. In a flash, the floor was sealed, leaving no one to suspect that there was any way to access the empty pool with the new flooring in place.

Ard straightened his vest and ran a hand over his short styled hair. Then he strode to the front door of the *Be'Igoth* and pulled it open.

Drot was still standing guard, but now there were two Trothian women beside him. Quarrah recognized one of them as Geppel, the tall willowy greeter who collected payments at the entrance to Tofar's Salts. Geppel spoke perfect Landerian and Hedge paid her handsomely, which made Quarrah a little uneasy. But the woman had orders to let Quarrah, Ard, and Raek come and go from the *Be'Igoth* without charge. In many ways, Geppel had become their primary liaison with Hedge Marsool, passing messages and giving updates to the King Poacher.

"*Omligath*, Geppel," Ard greeted her. He waved the two women inside, closing the door behind them.

Geppel's companion was short, her black hair cropped tightly to her blue scalp. Her round face carried the plumpness of youth while somehow looking mature. If Quarrah had to guess—and it was difficult with Trothians—she'd say the woman was just out of her teens.

"Thank you for meeting us," Ard said to the short woman. "My name is Ardor Benn. These are my companions, Raek and Quarrah."

Geppel slipped into Trothian, translating Ard's words for her companion. "Vorish," the woman introduced herself.

"Come sit down." Ard led the way to the seating area over the empty pool. "Can I order you anything to eat or drink?"

After a brief exchange in Trothian, Geppel answered. "She says a glass of salt water would be fine." Then the translator gave a wily smile. "But if you're paying, I could go for a fish *hrav*."

Raek crossed back to the door to catch the attention of one of the many servers running the boardwalks outside. Ard carefully seated himself on the trapdoor chair with the green cushion, while Geppel and Vorish took the padded bench across from the coffee table. Quarrah remained standing. No sense in being caught off guard.

"Does she know why we asked to meet with her?" Ard asked Geppel.

"She knows it has to do with her home islet," she answered. "And the Agrodite Moon Glass. But she doesn't know you plan on stealing it. If you want her to talk, you'd be wise to keep it that way."

"Wait," Quarrah cut in. "But *you* know?" She stared pointedly at the Trothian translator.

"Relax," Ard said. "She works for Hedge. We're doing the job for him. Geppel is onboard." He turned to Vorish. "Tell us a little about the Trothian islets. Have you visited many of them?"

Geppel translated the request to Vorish and spoke her response.

"I have been to all of the islets in Ra Skal." Geppel drummed her fingers on the arm of the bench as if trying to think of the translation. "A *skal* is like a grouping," she settled on saying. "Or cluster."

"And Ra Skal?" Ard said. "Where is it located?"

"To the northwest," replied Geppel. "Between Strind and Dronodan."

Vorish continued speaking, and Geppel resumed the interpretation. "Our islets are much closer together than your great islands. There are no cliffs to divide us, just long beaches of soft sand caressed by the lapping waters."

"She's quite poetic, isn't she?" Ard remarked.

"That is the nature of our language," replied Geppel. "It's why so few of your people speak it well. On the other hand, my Landerian is so good because I mastered its secret."

"Oh?" said Ard.

"I just think of the least intelligent way to say something and it comes out sounding right," she replied bluntly. "Look, if I'd known your questions would be this basic, *I* could have answered them. Surely you've seen the islets as you sail past?"

The comment obviously bothered Ard. Quarrah knew he always had a masterplan to every conversation. "I'm *trying* to establish trust," he explained. "Show her that we're interested in something she loves." He leaned forward to better engage Vorish. "Tell us about your home."

"I hail from the Ennoth," Geppel translated. "It is the center for Agrodite worship on Ra Skal."

*Good*, Quarrah thought. At least they'd brought in the right person. It hadn't taken much digging to learn that Lyndel was last seen on Ra Skal. And since she was an Agrodite priestess, it followed that she'd be at the center of worship.

"What can you tell me about the features and layout of your islet?" Quarrah asked.

"It was low enough to be chosen as the Ennoth for our *skal*,"

Geppel translated. Then she added on her own, "In your tongue, *ennoth* would translate to something like 'sacred site.' Only two of the four *skals* have an island low enough to serve as an Ennoth."

"Low enough?" Ard questioned. "What does that mean?"

Geppel chose to translate that question and let Vorish answer. "Every cycle, our people excavate a network of canals through the sand. They run from beach to beach, filling with seawater that refreshes itself with the crash of the waves."

"And you do that to make it easier for the *fajumar*?" Ard said. Again, Quarrah thought he was just trying to impress Geppel with his simple knowledge of her language.

"Not only the soak," she translated, "but for drinking and cleaning as well. But that is not the primary purpose of the *pats*. The trenches also ensure that the Ennoth will drown properly during the Moon Passing."

"Hold on," Ard cut in. "What, now?"

"You have seen the water rise when the Red Moon passes?"

"It has little effect on our islands," Ard replied. Quarrah didn't agree. Throughout the Greater Chain, the nights of a Moon Passing were considered a time to stay indoors. The harbors basically shut down, halting travel between islands while the rising water swelled over the docks. People flocked to the Mooring to witness the lighting of the Holy Torch. Once a cycle, behaviors and routines were markedly different. Why was Ard downplaying that?

"During such a Passing, the water rises and every part of the Ennoth is covered with a blanket of seawater," Geppel translated.

"The whole island floods?" Ard exclaimed. "That's got to be hard on the crops and livestock. Can't you find a way to prevent it?"

Seeming amused, Geppel repeated the question and waited for Vorish's answer. "We look forward to the drowning of the Ennoth each cycle. Ranching and agriculture are Lander skills unnecessary for the survival of our race. Life on our islets is fully sustained by the sea that surrounds us."

Ard tilted his head skeptically. "The best bakery I've ever visited was run by a Trothian woman. You're telling me she just opened shop so she could gain my trust, betray me to the crooked king, and jeopardize everything I'd worked for?" He held up his hand. "Maybe don't translate that last part."

"Sounds like you're still working through it," Geppel said.

"I really liked her pastries," muttered Ard.

Geppel spoke to Vorish and translated the reply. "There are many Trothians who have found success farming and raising live-stock on our higher islets. We have traded and sold product to Landers for centuries. But I am saying that none of that is *necessary* for Trothian survival. If every Lander were to vanish tomorrow, the sea and the blessed Moon would sustain us forevermore."

The door suddenly opened and Raek reappeared, a tall wooden cup in one hand and a steaming bowl in the other.

"One lukewarm cup of fresh salt water for the young lady," he said, passing it to Vorish, who accepted it with a word of gratitude.

"And one fish *hrav* for the intrepid gatekeeper of Tofar's Salts. Careful, it's hot." Raek passed the bowl to Geppel and dropped into the seat Quarrah had been leaning against.

Undeterred by Raek's warning, Geppel lifted the bowl to her lips and slurped the steaming liquid. "Did Sochar make this?" she asked, her voice accusatory.

"Sochar?" Raek raised his eyebrows to show that he didn't know who that was. "Is it, maybe ... too salty?"

"It's fine," Geppel remarked. "I just don't like the way he cuts the shark tentacles."

Quarrah shuddered. She'd eaten shark before—the meat from its side was almost like beef. But she couldn't imagine slurping down those slippery tentacles from the big fish's mouth. It was no wonder Trothian cuisine hadn't taken root among the Landers.

"So what did I miss?" Raek asked. "Did she tell us where Lyndel keeps the Moon Glass?"

"We're getting there," said Ard. "She just finished explaining that the island where Lyndel lives completely floods during the Moon Passings."

Raek shook his head. "That's gotta be hard on the crops and livestock."

"That's what *I* said," Ard remarked, nodding emphatically.

Sometimes it was eerie how similarly the two men thought. And yet, at other times, they seemed so wildly different. Quarrah thought Ard would be a lot more tolerable if some of Raek's easy-going demeanor rubbed off on him. But then, Raek had his own issues, starting with his unwillingness to do anything about his Heg addiction.

"What happens to your homes during the Passing?" Raek asked Vorish.

"Our dwellings are built to withstand the rising water," came her answer.

"So do you just swim all night?" asked Ard.

"It is a night of celebration," she said. "The old and the weak can rest on the rooftops of our homes while everyone else sings and the priestesses recite poems. Some play *gras oronet.*"

"Is that a musical instrument?" Ard asked.

Vorish chuckled when the translation went through. "It is a game," she said. Then Geppel added, "The literal translation would be *lucky fish.*"

"Then why didn't you just say that the first time?" Raek muttered under his breath. "You *are* the translator."

"During the drowning of the Ennoth," continued Vorish, "fish will swim across the flooded islet. It is considered good luck in the cycle to come if you can catch a fish with your bare hands. The bigger the fish, the greater the luck."

"Is that even challenging?" Ard asked. "I've heard Trothians are experts at fishing by hand."

Quarrah remembered the first time she'd watched a group of

Trothian fishermen outside Leigh's southern harbor on Dronodan. She'd been a little girl then, ignorant of so much of the world, and fascinated by the blue-skinned divers. Four of them would take a net, each holding a corner, and dive deep into the InterIsland Waters. Long minutes would pass, and just when Quarrah had been sure they'd drowned, the divers would resurface with a full load of wriggling fish.

"Our vision normally allows us to see deep into the sea," Geppel translated. "But on that night, the reflection of the Moon on the water's surface creates an impenetrable glare to our eyes. It is as if the Moon has laid a great red blanket over the sea. Those who play *gras oronet* must keep their heads above water and go by feel alone as the fish swim past their legs."

"What do they do with the fish if they catch it?" Raek asked.

"Once they have proven a catch and shown off its size, they release the fish in gratitude," explained Vorish.

"Makes sense," said Ard. "It would probably be exhausting to swim around all night while holding a slippery fish."

"In many places, the water is shallow enough that we can stand," Geppel said for Vorish. "Especially near the *Ucru* at the islet's center."

"What is the *Ucru*?" Quarrah asked, already exhausted by the effort of keeping all these foreign words straight.

"It is a building designated for Agrodite worship," explained Geppel.

"What's it like?" asked Quarrah.

"It is constructed in the shape of a large dome," she answered. "Its base is sealed well, so the sand inside stays forever dry, even during the drowning of the Ennoth. A priestess is chosen to remain within the *Ucru* during the Passing. Bemdep is soaked in Stoshk and the root smolders inside the dome. The priestess sits in the haze, staring through the Moon Glass until her mind is awakened with a vision from the gods."

"So the shards of Moon Glass are kept in one of these *Ucrus*?" Ard confirmed.

Geppel repeated the question. "There are only three pieces of Agrodite Moon Glass. One is held in the *Ucru* on Ra Ennoth. The other is kept in the *Ucru* on Mei Ennoth. The third piece moves between locations, safeguarded by the *Shoka* priestess."

"Does that have a translation?" Raek asked.

"Of the tides," answered Geppel.

"What does this tidal priestess do?" Quarrah asked.

Vorish explained as Geppel translated. "She splits her time equally between the Ennoth on Ra Skal, and the one on Mei Skal. She also visits the Trothians who are living on the Greater Chain to assure that the Agrodite teachings are remaining pure and unin-fluenced. During the war, she was charged with military command over Trothian troops in council with our Sovereign allies."

Ard stood up abruptly, as if the excitement about what he'd just heard had propelled him out of his seat.

"Does this *Shoka* priestess happen to be called Lyndel?" Ard asked.

Vorish nodded. "Her name gained some renown during the war," translated Geppel. "But Lyndel is among the most devout of our Agrodite priestesses."

Quarrah and Ard shared a glance. Obviously, Lyndel's people had never heard about her research with Isle Halavend. Quarrah doubted she'd be referred to as *devout* if the Agrodites knew she'd consorted with a Holy Isle.

"We knew her before the war," Ard admitted. "And you're tell-ing me that Lyndel carries a piece of the Moon Glass with her wherever she travels?"

"Not exactly," Geppel said for Vorish. "But she does determine which Ennoth will receive it during the Passing. In such a case, *two* priestesses are selected to remain in the *Ucru* overnight."

"This makes so much sense," Ard muttered. "If she was the tidal priestess, it explains why Lyndel was in Beripent when she met

Halavend. It explains how she could give Isless Malla a piece of Moon Glass without raising questions."

"And it explains why she was in such a position of power during the war," Quarrah said, remembering how Lyndel had led an unprecedented capture of the Archkingdom's harbors on Pekal.

"Where is Lyndel now?" Ard asked Vorish.

"When I left Ra Ennoth three days ago," translated Geppel, "she was there, planning to stay for the Moon Passing at the end of the cycle."

"Then that's where we need to go," Ard said with far too much enthusiasm.

"Wait a minute," Quarrah looked at him. "Don't we want to *avoid* her? If I remember right, things didn't exactly end on a high note between you and Lyndel."

Going back on his promises, Ard had not let Lyndel use young Shad Agaul as a bargaining chip to stop the naval conflict against the Trothians outside the Pekal harbor. Quarrah vividly remembered the flat look of cold anger on the priestess's face and the words she had spoken.

*"You have made an enemy of me this day, Ardor Benn."*

Ard waved his hand. "That was nothing. Time heals old conflicts. Aren't you and I living proof of that?"

Quarrah didn't know how to take that. There had certainly been plenty of conflicts between the two of them, but were they truly healed? He obviously thought so, and the idea made her resent him a little more.

"So you just plan on taking a friendly walk along the beach with your old pal Lyndel?" Raek asked Ard.

"Seems like the perfect distraction to get her away from the *Ucru* so Quarrah can slip in and grab one of the pieces of Moon Glass." Ard's voice was backed with full confidence in her ability.

"But if both of the *Ucrus* already have a piece," Quarrah said, "then why bother with Lyndel at all?"

"Her presence on the Ennoth assures us that there'll be two pieces of Moon Glass lying around," explained Ard. "Raek can check my math, but I'd say that doubles our chances of swiping one."

"And Lyndel really doesn't worry you?" Quarrah checked.

"On the contrary," said Ard. "I'm counting on Lyndel to allow us to come ashore. Have you ever sailed up to one of the Trothian islets unannounced?"

Most things Quarrah did were unannounced, but not this. She'd never stepped foot on the sandy shore of an islet. From what she'd heard, Landers weren't typically well received.

"Ard and I gave that a try once. Before the war," Raek jumped in. "We'd been caught in some cross fire leaving Dronodan, and the *Floret* was taking water like a sieve."

"Technically, I don't think you can call it *cross* fire if it was intended for us," Ard interrupted.

"Unimportant," Raek brushed him off. "The point is, we were bailing with buckets in our teeth, limping our little boat across the waves toward the closest land, which just happened to be a Trothian islet. The minute we're in range, they send a warning shot over the prow."

"Never mind that we'd even thought to run up a white flag," Ard added.

"Your undershirt was gray, at best," Raek said to his partner. "Anyway, we have no choice but to lean into the rudder and make for Pass Harbor on Strind, knowing there's no way we'll reach it in time."

The two men shared a glance full of nostalgia, and then Ard spoke. "That's why we'll be counting on Lyndel to let us in."

"Hold on." Geppel raised a hand. "What happened in your story? Did you make it to Pass Harbor?"

Deep inside, Quarrah was interested, too, but she'd spent enough time with these two to know not to egg them on. Geppel's curiosity played right into their egos.

"We had a basket of fresh-caught fish," Ard started. "We put it on the sinking prow and took off the lid. Within ten minutes, a genuine flock of seagulls had gathered."

"I threw a net over the birds and lashed the ends to the bowsprit," continued Raek. "Those blazing seagulls kept us afloat and towed our ship all the way to Strind."

There was a moment of sincere contemplation among the women in the room, and then Quarrah called the story what it obviously was. "Dragon slag. What really happened?"

"Our ship sank and we were left treading water until some Homeland-sent cargo vessel pulled us aboard," answered Ard.

Raek reached over and smacked him with the back of his broad hand. "I thought we had an image to maintain. You *have* changed." He sighed melodramatically. "Anyway, the point of the story wasn't to explain our escape. It was to prove that we can't just sail up to the Trothian islets uninvited."

"We have Lyndel!" Ard exclaimed as if he'd been repeating the same logical phrase all afternoon.

"Who considers you an enemy," Quarrah reminded.

"We don't know that for sure," said Ard. "And maybe that's as good a place to start as any." He turned to Geppel. "Can you get a message to Lyndel on Ra Ennoth?"

She and Vorish conversed for a few seconds before Geppel answered. "Vorish's family returns home from their vacation in two days. She has agreed to share a message with the *Shoka*."

"Good," Ard said. "Tell Lyndel that Ardor Benn will be coming to see her."

"Would you like to tell her the reason?" asked Geppel.

Raek screwed up his face. "That we'd like to steal the Moon Glass?"

Geppel shot him a flat stare, then turned back to Ard. "Something that might convince her to allow you ashore?"

Ard took a deep breath and Quarrah saw a number of ideas flicker across his face. "Tell her that I wish to apologize."

Quarrah leaned in as if she'd misunderstood him. Did Ardor Benn say *apologize*? Without an official letter? Quarrah had been on the rare receiving end of profuse apologies from Ard—sorry for excluding her, sorry for not hearing her, sorry for a dozen other things. But the words always sounded brittle falling from his mouth.

Ard turned to Geppel and Vorish. "If you don't have any questions about my message, then that'll be all."

The two women stood, taking their cup and bowl with them as they exited the *Be'Igoth*.

"Are you sure it's a good idea to go over there wishing to apologize?" Quarrah asked when Ard turned around. "Won't Lyndel get suspicious when you don't?"

"Who says I won't?" Ard replied. "I'm not sorry for getting Shad Agaul home, but I do feel bad for the way things ended between Lyndel and me. I'll apologize for what I can and let her decide how much she wants to forgive me. Meanwhile, you'll be creeping your way into the *Ucru* to swipe a piece of Moon Glass. Would you prefer darkness or daylight?"

"Daylight," Quarrah said. "We're talking about sneaking past a village full of Trothians." Darkness would provide her no advantage against their superior vision.

"While you two do your thing, I'll keep the sails rigged and ready on the *Double Take*," Raek said. "I'm hoping we don't need a speedy getaway, but it doesn't hurt to be ready."

"Speaking of being ready," said Ard, "where are we with Lavfa's other requests?"

"I've got the Void and Barrier Grit divided into secure kegs," reported Raek. "And the black leather backpack was an easy purchase in the Char."

"And the bricks?" Ard asked Quarrah.

She pulled back her head. "Why are you looking at me?"

"We need four bricks from the Royal Concert Hall," Ard said, like it was self-explanatory. "I just assumed. Raek gets the Grit and the backpack, you get the bricks, and I get the Moon Glass."

She tilted her head. "Now, *who* gets the Moon Glass?"

"Well, technically, you do," said Ard. "I just meant that I was running point on that part since it was the most complex."

"And you don't think I can do complex?"

Ard held up his hands. "I'm sorry." See, there it was. How much weight did that word carry for him? "I'll get the bricks."

"Because you think I can't?" she retorted. "I know the Royal Concert Hall better than either of you. The southeast corner is the most worn. A cloud of Silence Grit, a pinch of Void, and I should be able to separate four of the bricks without any trouble. I'll get them tonight."

A subtle grin tugged at the corner of Ard's mouth, and Quarrah wondered if she'd just played right into his hands. Before she could grow any more upset about it, Raek changed the course of the conversation.

"I don't feel like we really explored any alternatives to Baroness Lavfa's demands," he said.

"She didn't leave a lot of wiggle room," said Ard. "And Hedge made it clear that he wouldn't give us the documents we need until Lavfa's property is secured."

"I know," said Raek. "But what about a forgery? Are we breaking our necks trying to fill her backpack, when it would be just as easy to present her with a regular shard of red stained glass?"

"How would we forge something like that?" Quarrah thought back to that day in Lyndel's Beripent apartment, surrounded by papers and writings from the recently murdered Isle Halavend. "Looking through the Moon Glass was unlike anything I'd ever seen before."

"*We* know that," continued Raek. "The three of us have seen a real piece, but it's unlikely that Lavfa has."

"I agree that the baroness might not recognize a forgery," said

Ard, "but getting the glass to Lavfa is only the first step in our job for Hedge. It wouldn't be hard for her to check the authenticity of the glass with a Trothian who actually knows. Then we show up on her doorstep with a dragon and she doesn't let us in?" He shook his head. "It's too risky. Better to do the job right."

"But what's the purpose behind this?" Quarrah asked, catching a smile from Ard. That was usually his line. "I mean, I've worked for plenty of people who accept goods instead of Ashings." She justified her curiosity. "But Lavfa's request is...unusual."

"Seems to me like she's planning on framing someone," Raek said. "I mean, it would look really incriminating if the Regulators were to apprehend someone wearing that backpack."

There was a pregnant pause in the room, and then Ard seemed to realize that Quarrah and Raek were staring at him. "*Me?*" he cried with incredulity. "You think she wants to frame me? Why?"

"Maybe she's among the many who don't agree with your *reformed* character," Raek said. "After all, she didn't name her price until *after* you pushed me out the window."

"That was supposed to gain her trust," Ard said. "To show her that I couldn't tolerate anyone plotting to abuse her good name."

"But what if it had the opposite effect?" Quarrah said. "Maybe Lavfa lost trust when she saw you—a supposed Holy Isle—reverting back to your criminal ways."

"First of all," Ard rebutted, "I'm not a *supposed* Holy Isle. I'm the genuine article. And I don't think Lavfa has anything so devious in mind. You both heard her on the catamaran. She's an absolute shark when it comes to business deals. And she couldn't stop bragging about her vast assortment of rare trinkets and baubles. I think she's just using us to expand her collection."

That had been Quarrah's first thought, too. Moon Glass made sense. Even the bricks from the Royal Concert Hall. But the twenty panweights of easily accessible Grit? And why specify the type of backpack to carry it in? Something definitely felt off about this whole thing—starting with Hedge Marsool's mysterious summons to the *Be'Igoth*

"Now I guess we just sit back and wait to hear if Lyndel returns our message." Raek kicked out his feet in a relaxed stance.

"We only have a week until the Moon Passing," Ard said. "If we wait until next cycle, Lyndel could move and we won't know where she'll be. I say we ready the *Double Take* to sail to Ra Skal in three days. That'll put us just a day behind Vorish's message."

"And what if Lyndel's answer is, 'Don't bother coming. Apology not accepted. I hate you'?" said Raek.

"Then we claim that the message must have been garbled in translation," said Ard.

Raek nodded in approval, but Quarrah stared at the cavalier pair. "Is no one else worried that the success of this job rests on Ard's ability to apologize?"

~

*More than anything, I'm writing this to clear my conscience. To acknowledge my vast shortcomings and misbehaviors.*

# CHAPTER

# 7

Ard peered through his spyglass at the line of Trothians waiting on the sandy islet beach. By now, their unique eyes certainly would have seen their flag, the fabric shredded into more than a dozen long strips that whipped in the wind. At the stern, Quarrah leaned on the rudder, keeping the *Double Take*'s nose aimed at their destination.

Raek swung down from the yardarm, the sail securely battened. But instead of dropping onto the rowing bench to take them the rest of the way, he began preparing the anchor.

"What are you doing?" Ard asked.

"This is how we have to make the approach," Raek said. "Macer's book says that every Lander vessel, regardless of size or crew compliment, must drop anchor no less than a half mile from shore. It's a safety precaution for the ships as much as anything, since the sand tapering away from the islets tends to shift and change with the movement of the waves."

Ard thought of the strange bed of the InterIsland Waters. The five big islands of the Greater Chain stood like stone columns, the depth of the sea plunging several miles straight down at their shores. Only the harbors had measurable depth, pocked into the rocky cliff sides.

Apparently the Trothian islets didn't share the same kind of abrupt drop-off beneath the water. Their clustered *skals* had foundations like great sandbars that would, if the InterIsland Waters were somehow drained away, act as sandy land bridges between the large Lander islands.

Ever since their discovery of an ancient civilization on the seabed, Ard had tried to picture the world as it had once been— without so much water. When the gods had used their powers to heap up towers for humankind's escape, it must have been a mighty ring of earth, with the forested peaks of Pekal freestanding at its center. Far below, the ancient Trothians would have been ringed in on all sides, seething for vengeance for hundreds of years before managing to rise to the surface.

Ard leaned overboard to watch as the anchor pulled down its rope. "I suppose Macer expects us to swim the rest of the way?"

"He says the Trothians will send a raft if they agree on a meeting," said Raek.

"Well, I think we could get a little closer," Ard remarked. "The *Double Take*'s not going to run aground."

"Don't question Macer," said Raek. "He literally wrote the book on approaching the Trothian islets. Every good sailor has a well-worn copy."

"Where was yours when we sank the *Floret* after the Denfar ruse?" Ard asked.

"It was on my 'to read' list," answered Raek, tying off the slack on the anchor rope. "I finally got around to it. Yesterday. I'll admit, it had some great tips. Did you know running up a dirty white undershirt on the mast is considered an act of war?"

"That was not in Macer's book," Ard argued.

Raek grinned. "How would you know? You haven't read it."

"There's that raft you were talking about," Quarrah said, squinting through a spyglass as she left her post at the rudder. She was wearing her black thief's garb, snuggly fit, with slim belts crossing her chest. The wind pulled a few long strands of hair from her ponytail and sent them tickling across her face. Ard smiled as she sputtered at a hair across her lips before tucking it behind her ear.

"I was planning on hiding in the boat while Ard drew the attention away," Quarrah said. "I didn't anticipate a swim."

Raek shrugged. "Guess you should have read the book, too."

"It's all right," Ard soothed her. "You're good on the fly. You can come ashore with me and slip away when the opportunity presents itself. After all, I'm sure Lyndel would like to see you."

Quarrah shook her head. "I think my presence will put her on edge. She knows what I'm capable of."

"You keep talking about Lyndel like she's our enemy," Ard said. "Just relax. We'll talk to her for a moment and then I'll think of a reason for you to go back to the *Double Take*. You can slip into the trees, raid the *Ucru*, and I'll meet you back at the beach."

Quarrah checked through her spyglass again. "Except I don't think there are trees on the Ennoth. Or any kind of vegetation for that matter."

"What kind of island doesn't have plants?" Ard balked.

"The kind that floods with salt water every cycle," Raek reminded him.

"I'm seeing lots of structures, though," Quarrah said, still inspecting the distant island. "They must have brought in building materials from other islets."

Ard looked for himself. Sure enough, the only variation on the sandy atoll was a row of houses that looked like they'd been built on stilts. His magnified gaze dropped to the raft, which was drawing steadily closer over the breaking waves. It wasn't like the flat rafts of the Mooring that sat high on the water. This one looked like a half-sunken catamaran with just a few wooden rails connecting the low-riding pontoons. A pair of strong Trothians were rowing, their bottom halves submerged, while two more swam behind to propel the vessel.

"Last chance to wear your robes," Raek said, offering Ard the sea-green Islehood outfit.

"By the looks of it, I'd get waterlogged and sink with that on," Ard said. "Lyndel will have to take my word about being a Holy Isle. Hopefully, she's already caught rumors of it. Besides, I don't think wearing that robe will be any more convincing. She knows we're capable of stealing so much more than a costume. And I don't want her to think I'm approaching her as an Isle. I'm just an old friend."

He'd expected the scoff from Raek, as he tossed the robe onto the rowing bench, but Quarrah's actually stung. Of course she thought meeting with Lyndel was an unnecessary risk. Quarrah Khai would definitely choose to raid the other *Ucru*, far away from anyone who might recognize her. But what would that leave for Ard to do? His plan had the dual benefit of utilizing his charismatic skills, and potentially repairing a relationship with a powerful Trothian ally.

"Hoy!" called one of the Trothians seated on the raft. They were holding their position, floating some twenty yards out.

"Why do you come to Ra Ennoth?" His voice carried a heavy accent, but he projected well enough that Ard had no trouble hearing him. In moments like these, Ard envied the superior lungs and diaphragm of the Trothians.

"My name is Ardor Benn," he shouted back. "We are here to meet with your *Shoka* priestess, Lyndel. She should have received a message to expect us."

The two Trothians conversed briefly in hushed tones that didn't reach the *Double Take*. "We will take you ashore!" the man called back. "Jump into the water and we will retrieve you."

Ard glanced at Quarrah as he unclasped his Grit belt. The clay pots were mostly waterproof, and wet Grit could still detonate under enough sparks. But the Blast cartridges he used for his guns were rolled in thin paper. Sitting half submerged on that raft would leave them too soggy to load, assuming they didn't dissolve completely.

Oh, well. It would probably prove his point better to go unarmed anyway. And he wasn't totally defenseless. Ard had one little Grit pot tucked away for emergencies. He slipped out of his boots and passed them ceremoniously to Raek. If that whole island was covered in sand, then he'd be more comfortable without them.

"What's this?" Raek asked, awkwardly accepting the boots.

"I want you to have these if I don't come back," Ard said in mock seriousness.

"They're not my size."

"Then you can wear them on your hands." Ard eased himself over the edge of the *Double Take*, dropping the short distance to the water, the cold splash stealing his breath for a moment. He'd been able to keep his head from going under, but Quarrah wasn't so lucky, plunging in beside him.

In a moment, they were seated on the Trothian raft as the swimmers turned it back toward the Ennoth's beach. It wasn't a comfortable vessel, requiring all of Ard's balance just to keep from falling between the rails and getting left in its wake.

They rode in silence, watching the beach draw steadily closer. The waiting Trothians stood shoulder to shoulder, forming a semicircle, those on the ends standing waste deep in the lapping water.

*Quite the welcoming party*, Ard thought. He knew Lander visitors were highly uncommon on the islets. The novelty must have drawn close to a hundred from their homes.

It wasn't long before the little raft touched sand. Ard stepped off the raft, amazed at the way the compact sand squished between his toes. It was strange and dizzying to see the water skimming in and out around his feet. To feel it pull at the sand beneath his soles. There was something rhythmic and soothing—even cathartic—about the steady undulation of the waves on a beach. How many Landers lived and died without ever touching Trothian sand?

He shot a sidelong glance at Quarrah, but she seemed much less interested in the feel of the beach. Her wet dark clothes clung to her tense body and he realized that this crowd might make it more difficult to slip away than they'd anticipated.

"Ardor Benn!" A familiar voice shouted his name, drawing his attention away from the soft sand. He saw Lyndel standing on the beach, the curved line of Trothians like a wall behind her.

The priestess seemed never to change, no matter the passing years. Her black hair was tinged with gray, falling thick and straight. She wore a simple gray tunic, with a necklace and belt of clay beads. Her shoulders were bare, but her arms were wrapped in red cloth from her elbows to her wrists.

"*Omligath*, Lyndel!" Ard called, beginning his charms with a warm smile. She was not smiling back as she trudged toward him, bare feet churning through the loose sand.

"Thank you for welcoming us," he continued when she was close enough that Ard didn't have to shout. "I assume you received my message—"

"Ardor Benn," she cut him off. "You will answer for your crimes against the Trothian people. You will surrender yourself willingly."

Ard took a faltering step backward, a high-reaching wave kissing his heels. He wanted to laugh off Lyndel's comments as a joke, but her vibrating eyes showed no mirth.

"Now, wait a minute." Ard held out both hands. "I don't know if you've heard, but I received a pardon for my crimes."

"Your queen cannot pardon crimes against people she does not rule," answered Lyndel. She reached behind her back, hand reappearing with a long knife, its hilt of polished bone.

Sparks, Lyndel looked like she meant business! Had he really misread this situation so greatly? *There's still time*, Ard told himself. *Time to talk my way out of this.*

"I understand that we didn't part on the best of terms," Ard said. "But that's why I am here. Why don't you put down the knife and we can talk?"

"You will surrender yourself to the ruling tribunal," she said. "You will come without a struggle to face the consequences of your actions."

"Lyndel," Ard said, his hand straying to his vest as she took an aggressive step closer. "It's me. Whatever problem you have, we can resolve it together. I've come to apologize. Tell her, Quarrah."

He glanced at his companion, but Quarrah had slowly backed away from him, standing knee deep in the waves, hands balled into ready fists.

"You will come with me now, Ardor," pressed Lyndel. "Or I will gut you where you stand." She raised the blade.

Okay. This was quite enough. Ard slipped his hand into his vest, yanking out the single pot of Barrier Grit he'd brought with him. Leaping backward, he hurled it at Lyndel's feet. It struck the soft sand, landing with a dull *thud* that wasn't enough to crack the clay pot.

"Quarrah!" he shouted, scrambling backward toward the raft. She stood frozen for half a second before springing to his side, catching one of the cross rails, and shoving the simple vessel back out to sea.

The nearest Trothian—one of the swimmers who had pushed the raft—moved to intercept Ard. The man swung a hefty fist, but Ard ducked it nimbly, following with an uppercut of his own. The blow landed, Ard grimacing at the jarring crack of the man's jaw against his knuckles.

He reached the raft, pushing alongside Quarrah while becoming painfully aware that the half circle of spectating Trothians was folding in on them.

"I told you this was a bad idea," Quarrah shouted.

Oh, really? Did she have to rub it in right now?

They were waist deep in their futile escape when something struck Ard in the back of the head. His hands slipped from the raft rail and he fell face first into the water.

Someone had a hold of him by the back of the shirt, jerking him upward until his head cleared the wave and he sputtered for breath, his vision threatening to go black from the blow.

"You have made a grave error coming here," Lyndel's voice sounded in his ear. The cold steel of her blade touched his neck as she held him securely, his face mere inches above the water like a sacrifice to the sea.

"Quarrah," Ard rasped. It was partly a cry for help, but mostly it was a question for her well-being. He had brought her here against her suggestions. If anything were to happen—

"My conflict is with you alone." Lyndel yanked him upright. Ard could now see Quarrah clearly, the water lapping at her chest, one hand still idly clinging to the raft. "Quarrah Khai is free to go."

"What will you do with him?" Quarrah called.

"We will deal with him in our way," Lyndel answered. "He will answer for the deaths that rest upon his head."

Ah, flames. This wasn't going to end well. Ard locked eyes with a startled Quarrah. "Tell Trable," he called, talking fast. "Tell him that I'm being detained. Spread the word to everyone in Beripent. Cinza and Elbrig. Get them to stir up the people. Tell them—"

Lyndel struck him in the back of the head again, causing the midday sunlight to flicker. His body drooped, but she held him above the water, dragging him up the beach.

At last, Quarrah hoisted herself onto the back of the raft, retrieving one of the long oars and paddling frantically. Lyndel shouted something in Trothian—an order that sent two Trothians swimming out to propel Quarrah toward the *Double Take*.

*At least this isn't falling on her*, Ard thought as a dozen Trothians pressed around him. He tried to put up a fight, but his head was throbbing and his arms felt weak.

Scratchy, fibrous ropes tightened around his wrists. In his dazed state, he considered this a good sign. If they were tying him up, it meant they wanted something. It meant he'd stay alive a little longer.

One of the Trothian women grabbed his face, forcing his mouth open as she shoved something in. Ard couldn't tell if it was a wad of fabric or a bunch of plants. Whatever it was, it had a distinct salty taste and effectively stopped him from saying another word. He chose to bite down instead of trying to spit it, grateful that he hadn't lost any teeth when she'd rammed it in.

Pushed from behind, Ard staggered, following Lyndel as she moved toward the houses. They passed into the neighborhood, Ard glimpsing between his Trothian escorts to catch a closer look at the structures.

He had always imagined Trothian dwellings to be run-down and primitive. It was the stereotype most Landers held, perpetuated by the less-than-ideal conditions in which many Trothians found themselves after immigrating to the Greater Chain. But what Ard was seeing wasn't primitive at all. It was different. Foreign. But there was a marked level of finesse to their construction and a simple elegance to their architecture.

The homes were made primarily of wood, with decorative accents of seashells. Not a roof stood over ten feet high, loosely thatched with what looked like dried aquatic vegetation. Ard supposed that a race whose island flooded once a cycle wasn't overly concerned with keeping out the rain.

The stilt-like framework of their buildings rose out of the sand, supported by stone at their foundations. But none of the walls actually touched the ground, giving the whole village the subtle appearance of floating in midair.

In the gap between the sand and the bottom of the walls, Ard could see blue feet shuffling—most of them hurrying to a doorless archway to get a glimpse of the passing commotion outside.

In Beripent, Ard had always considered Trothians to be rather reclusive—even secretive. But that was certainly not the case here. There was a perplexing level of openness and a shocking lack of privacy.

*There can be no secrets among us, for our eyes can see them.*

Unexpectedly, the line from the glass testament spire on the seabed came to his mind. He and Raek had done their best to write down what they could remember from it, and that particular line had definitely stood out to Ardor Benn, who valued his secrets above anything else.

In the context of his surroundings, it seemed completely believable that the Trothians had descended from a race like that. By comparison, Landers seemed stuffy and distrusting.

Ahead, Ard notice a trench full of water that dissected their path. Lyndel led the way and the group trudged into it without slowing. Glancing to the side, Ard saw that the trench ran all the way across the islet, giving him a clear view to the open sea.

This must have been one of the *pats* that Vorish had mentioned. A series of crisscrossing hand-dug canals that delivered salt water all across the Ennoth. They were deeper and wider than he'd expected.

Instead of passing through the *pat*, Lyndel turned their course, leading Ard and the others along the canal as though it were a convenient road. In fact, it seemed convenient for everyone except Ardor Benn, who stumbled time after time, the Trothians at his side keeping him from going under.

After a moment, the *pat* intersected another canal running perpendicular to the first. A pool had formed at the confluence, deep enough that Lyndel began to swim. Ard grunted a cry of help through his gag as his feet left the sandy bottom of the *pat*, but two of the Trothians quickly linked arms with him, dragging his floundering, wrist-bound figure through the pool until they reached the intersecting waterway.

They continued forward, Trothians lining up along the edge of the *pat* to witness the processional, as though Ard were some notorious criminal—which he *was*. But Ard hadn't expected his fame to have reached the Trothian islets.

He was surprised by the sheer number of people on Ra Ennoth. He'd heard that the islets were cramped and overcrowded—a significant motivator for some Trothians to relocate to the Greater Chain when King Pethredote had finally introduced the Trothian Inclusion Act. The close proximity of their many dwellings was perhaps the only similarity this place had with Beripent, and still it felt so different. Yet somehow, despite the overpopulation, it felt spacious. Like the sky itself was bigger down here.

All at once, the dwellings cleared and Ard saw what must have been the *Ucru*. It was by far the tallest structure he'd seen on the islet. Maybe twenty feet high and as many across. It formed a perfect dome, like an architectural representation of a Barrier Grit detonation against the sand.

The walls of the *Ucru* looked to be made of thick leather, draped over a framework hidden underneath. From this distance, Ard couldn't see a single door or window, but the very top of the dome was flat, indicating a hole.

Water had flooded all around the *Ucru* like a moat, and Ard realized that it was the confluence of all the *pats* coming together at the islet's center. He imagined seeing the Ennoth from a bird's-eye view, the network of canals laid out like the spokes of a wagon wheel, with the sacred building at its hub.

They were still a good fifty yards from the *Ucru* when Lyndel abruptly departed from the trench they'd been following, leading the group onto a narrow triangle of dry sand between the spokes of the wheel.

She stopped, finally facing Ard again. Slowly, deliberately, Lyndel wiggled her bare feet until they were completely buried in the loose sand.

She shouted a long sentence in her language, which caused all the Trothians that had escorted him to back away, retreating into the waist-deep water of the *pat*. Others were also filing into the canals, standing shoulder to shoulder on both sides of Ard's stretch of dry land.

Lyndel shouted again, only ten paces in front of Ard, but behaving like she was a world away. At her second command, a handful of Trothian women came forward. Ard instantly noticed that their apparel—specifically the red wraps around their forearms—matched Lyndel's.

*Priestesses*, Ard thought. *Maybe I can appeal to their religious side.*

The five women took their places next to Lyndel, digging their feet into the sand in the same ceremonious way. They each said something, and then Lyndel spoke to Ard.

"Do you desire a translator?" she asked flatly. Ard grunted against the gag in his mouth. He wasn't really trying to say anything, but he wanted to remind her that he couldn't.

"You may remove it," Lyndel said impatiently. Ard reached up and pulled the salty wad from his mouth, dropping it to the sand and coughing dramatically.

"Do you desire a translator?" Lyndel asked again.

"I'd say that would be mighty helpful," said Ard, "since I have no idea what we're doing."

Lyndel said something, which resulted in a Trothian man climbing out of the *pat* and coming to stand at Ard's side.

"Gorosad will speak for you," Lyndel said.

"Not you?" Ard asked in surprise.

"I will not defile my Agrodite station by speaking to my people on your behalf," she spit.

"Look, Lyndel," Ard said. "I realize you're upset. That's why I'm here. I'd like to—"

Lyndel cut him off with a raw, guttural scream. Ard took an involuntary step backward, the rest of his sentence stuck in his throat on a sudden lump of fear.

Lyndel's scream was answered by the five women next to her. In the *pats* on both sides, the gathered Trothians began to splash and wail.

"They mourn the victims of your crime," explained Gorosad.

Ard leaned over, lowering his voice to start building trust with his new translator. "Can you tell me what's going on? Lyndel's an old friend. I don't know why she's treating me this way."

"You are Ardor Benn," stated Gorosad as if it were news to Ard. "We have waited years for Denyk to bring you to our land."

"Denyk?" Ard repeated. "Am I supposed to know him? Was he one of the guys that pushed our raft?"

"He is the god of payment," said Gorosad.

"Sparks," Ard cursed. "Do I owe Lyndel money?"

"You would call it *justice*," Gorosad said, "but we have no such word in our language. The priestesses have taken a stand and cannot be moved until payment is made."

Lyndel held up her hands and the splashing and mourning came to an abrupt end. She began to speak, Gorosad translating over her words.

"Two years have passed since our brothers and sisters, fathers and mothers, bravely followed me into the final conflict that ended the war," he said with notably less enthusiasm than Lyndel's delivery. "All who sailed with me in the flying ships knew the risks of our actions."

She *was* talking about the capture and defense of the Archkingdom's Pekal harbors. Weaponizing the Trans-Island Carriages had been highly unorthodox, and Lyndel had acted without permission from her Sovereign States allies.

"When the Moon Passing came, our warriors were forced to sail to the safety of the Redeye line, where a fleet of Archkingdom ships awaited them," he translated.

Not only the Archkingdom, Ard recalled. The Sovs had been waiting with just as many vessels, intending to apprehend Lyndel and hold her accountable for her radical behavior.

"Many of our people were killed throughout the night," continued Gorosad, "and the fighting did not relent at break of day. But we were stalwart. We retook the harbors for the new cycle, and the subsequent pressure of being cut off from their precious supply of Grit forced the Archkingdom to yield."

"That's not exactly true." Ard decided to speak up. Gorosad called out his response in Trothian. "The Archkingdom and the Sovereign States reunited when the new Prime Isle selected Queen Abeth to rule as a crusader monarch. She called off the war that very cycle and both armies stood down so their rulers could set terms for lasting peace."

"This man"—Lyndel thrust her arm in Ard's direction as Gorosad translated—"would have you believe that our sacrifice was for nothing. That the political squabbling of their Isles and nobles was of greater importance than the deaths of our loved ones."

"That's not what I'm saying." Ard tried to defend himself. But by the time the translation had come through, Lyndel had already moved on.

"I was with Ardor Benn on the night of that Moon Passing. He had come to our harbor on Pekal, seeking my permission and assistance to make a last-minute expedition into the mountains. I was made to be convinced when he told me that the item he intended to extract from Pekal was no other than a missing Lander prince. The boy, he said, was presumed dead, and his sudden appearance would carry enough influence to end the fighting."

"And it *did*!" cried Ard, but the only person who seemed to be listening to him was his translator.

"Once we had retrieved the prince, we were forced to spend the night on a small raft, struggling against the waves to reach the battle ahead."

*Well, that part surely isn't true,* Ard thought. Obviously, Lyndel had not told her people about their trip to the bottom of the InterIsland Waters. But why? She had uncovered mind-boggling truths about her race's origins. Didn't she want to share that?

"By morning, our raft was spent," Gorosad continued with the translation. "We detonated Barrier Grit and were able to house ourselves in its bubble until one of our Trothian crews retrieved us."

Again, not quite true. But Ard understood why Lyndel wouldn't tell her people about movable Containment Grit. She had no idea how to manufacture liquid Grit, and the last thing she needed was to terrify the Trothian nation with the thought that Landers had new capabilities. It was already difficult enough for Trothians to get access to the Grit they knew about and understood.

"I agreed to let Ardor Benn search for his prince because he assured me that I could present the boy to the Sovereign fleet and regain their support," Lyndel went on. "This would have helped us vanquish the Archkingdom ships and the magnitude of the accomplishment could have exonerated me from the Lander laws of treason against our allies." She held up a finger. "But Ardor Benn did not follow through with his promise. Even delivering the prince to the Archkingdom fleet could have spared lives. With such precious cargo, they would have likely called an immediate retreat. But Ardor Benn did not do that, either."

Okay. Ard finally knew exactly where Lyndel was going with this. And put the way she was saying it, things didn't look good for him.

"Instead, this liar kept the single piece of salvation we had to himself and returned to Beripent, leaving our people to struggle against not one—but *two* Lander navies. This man alone is responsible for the deaths of thousands of our people."

She turned to look directly at him. He remembered that night when she'd touched the testament spire and her eyes had vibrated so quickly that they had begun to glow with a red hue—so akin to the perfected eyes of a transformed Gloristar. Lyndel's eyes were dark now. Full of nothing but hatred.

"Speak the truth, Ardor," she said in Landerian. "Confess your guilt to these crimes."

Ard took a deep breath. There had to be a way out of this. He just needed to convince the onlooking crowd that Lyndel was wrong. That he wasn't as guilty as she'd made him sound.

But he was.

Delivering Shad Agaul to his mother in the throne room had undoubtedly been the right decision. Deep down, he knew that he had never intended to fulfill his promise to Lyndel. He had never *actually* considered any other options.

Ard blamed his name for this stubborn determination. Once his mind had homed in on what he deeply wanted, there was little anyone could do to convince him otherwise. Sparks, there was very little he could do to convince himself.

Wasn't this the root of why Quarrah couldn't stand to be with him?

"It's true," Ard said, speaking slowly enough for Gorosad to translate comfortably. "I did what I thought was best at the time. I suppose I didn't pause to think what impact it would have on the Trothian fleet. That is why I have come here today. To apologize for my actions and beg your forgiveness."

"We have planted our feet," Gorosad translated Lyndel's words again. "There is no forgiveness for your crimes. Only payment. Because of you, our people have suffered grief. Because of you, I am unwelcome in the Greater Chain, unable to fulfill my *Shoka* duties."

"Let me talk to Queen Abeth," Ard said. "She can clear your name like she did for me. The Sovereign States have dissolved anyway. Sure, some of the Dronodanian and Talumonian nobles are probably still upset about the way you ignored their orders. But that was years ago. Water under the bridge. Just let me go back to Beripent and talk to the queen."

"Our feet are planted. We will not be moved until payment is made."

"You keep saying that," Ard shouted, "but I don't know what you want from me."

"There is only one payment sufficient for your crimes." Then Lyndel said a single word, and Ard guessed what it meant before the translation came through.

"Death."

The pronouncement struck him with a chilling force. Surprising, since it wasn't the first time someone had sentenced him with such conviction. Sparks, it wasn't even the first time an old acquaintance of his had threatened him with death. But hearing Lyndel say it was different somehow, and Ard felt a pang of genuine fear.

In unanimous agreement, the other priestesses repeated the word one at a time. Gorosad's emotionless echo only deepened Ard's feeling of dread. Lyndel might actually get her way.

She began speaking again, this time addressing the throngs of Trothians watching from the *pats*.

"Come, all who are grieved at this Lander's actions," translated Gorosad. "Make for him the bed in which *Nah* will drown him to sleep."

"Hold on. What?" Ard cried, taking a step backward. "Who the blazes is *Nah*?"

"The Bringer of Punishment. The Collector of Debts," said Gorosad. He pointed skyward. "The Red Moon."

"It's still six days before the Moon Passing, pal." Ard glanced up just to make sure Lyndel's pronouncement hadn't somehow altered the Moon's regular course. Sure enough, the clear blue sky was vacant, save for a distant flock of birds winging westward. "And what are you going to do—get me Moonsick?" They'd have to take him more than halfway up Pekal for that.

Before Gorosad could answer, Ard's attention turned to the *pats*, where dozens of Trothians were climbing out of the canals, advancing across the dry sand toward him. They stopped between Ard and the line of priestesses, dropping to their knees and digging up fistfuls of sand.

Singing—or at least chanting—rose from the Trothians waiting in the ditches. They splashed and cupped their hands against the surface of the water in that same rhythmic style Ard had glimpsed at Tofar's Salts. Only this time it seemed much less innocuous, the tone and tempo bordering on malice.

"What are they doing?" Ard asked his translator. He could no longer see Lyndel or the other priestesses through the digging throng.

"They dig a pit for you," Gorosad said.

"That's awfully nice," Ard replied. "But I really don't need a pit right now."

"All those who dig suffered grief at your hand," he said. "They are the kin of those whose deaths might have been avoided, had you fulfilled your promise to our *Shoka* priestess."

Ard looked over the crowd. Women, men, little children. They heaped up sand behind them, the pit growing rapidly deeper. And when one of them tired, there was no shortage of others waiting their turn in the *pats*.

*Homeland*, Ard thought. *What did I do?*

"Will they bury me alive?" Ard asked quietly. That would be one of the worst ways to go. Where was the heroism in lying unseen, choking for breath?

"When the pit is sufficient," said Gorosad, "you will be lowered down with great stones around your ankles. Then you will wait for *Nah*."

Ard suddenly realized exactly how this was going to go. When the Moon Passing raised the water levels to cover the Ennoth, his pit would be flooded. The Moon would be his executioner, but not through its horrifying sickness. It would kill him naturally. Ceremoniously.

"I'd like a final word with Lyndel," Ard said. If she'd just listen to him, maybe he could convince her to lighten the punishment to a few lashings, or something.

"I cannot take you to her," Gorosad replied. "And her feet are planted."

"Still?" Ard said. "For how long?"

"The priestesses do not take this punishment lightly," he said. "They will remain until payment is made and the same flood that drowns you washes the sand from their feet, releasing them from their responsibility over you."

"Lyndel's going to stand there for six days?" Ard cried, his voice spiking incredulously.

"Stand, sit, or lie upon the sand," he answered. "But the feet of the priestesses will remain buried."

"Aren't they going to get hungry?" Ard had no idea how long a Trothian could go without food and water, but he wasn't likely to make it a week.

"They will receive sufficient sustenance," said Gorosad. "As will you."

"That's very considerate," Ard said. "I'd hate to drown on an empty stomach."

He turned back to see the pit taking shape. It looked about ten feet in diameter, already several feet deep. The grieving Trothians showed no signs of slowing down, and fresh diggers continued to emerge from the *pats*.

He watched a little girl digging furiously with both hands. Her blue face was streaked with tears and her body shook with a mixture of sobs and apparent fury. Had she lost a mother? A father? A sibling?

Ard felt a knot in his throat and a subtle salty taste in his mouth that he recognized as the harbinger of tears. He swallowed hard, pushing it aside.

This was not his fault. Ard hadn't killed a single Trothian in Pekal's harbor. Lyndel claimed that he could have *prevented* deaths by turning over Shad Agaul, but that was purely conjecture. The tragedy of lost lives was the horrible result of war. A war that Ard had actually *stopped*. Instead of blaming him for lives he *might* have saved, Lyndel's people should have been praising him for preventing more deaths.

Based on where they were digging, Lyndel would probably be able to hear Ard's voice from the pit. That would give him six days to wear her down. Change her mind.

And if that failed... Well, Raek and Quarrah would know what to do.

～

*How did I manage to surround myself with such loyalty?*
*Loyalty of which I am sorely undeserving.*

# CHAPTER

# 8

Quarrah peeled back the curtain on the carriage window just enough to peer out. She had heard the crowd gathered on the palace grounds, but seeing them sent a shiver down her spine.

"I don't like this," she said to Raek. He sat across from her with his knees wide and his long arms hanging limply at his sides in a posture of utter relaxation. Was he burning Heg right now? She hadn't seen him load any into the pipe in his chest. But maybe he was always carrying a loose pinch in there, ready to detonate if the need overcame him.

"Why are there so many people?" Quarrah followed up, letting the curtain fall as she tried to decipher the words of their organized chants.

"That, my friend, is the work of the crazies," Raek replied, his eyes half closed.

On Ard's desperate request, Quarrah knew Raek had reached out to Elbrig Taut and Cinza Ortemion. But that had been just last night! The disguise managers had already worked up such a frenzy?

"Say what you will about them," continued Raek, "but Cinza and Elbrig get results."

"Then maybe *they* should be the ones going to this meeting," Quarrah returned. "Honestly, what could I say to possibly convince a room full of important people that they should rescue Ard?"

"Leave the convincing to the Prime Isle and the queen," Raek said. "Trable really seemed to care. And we know Abeth has a soft spot for Ard."

"Then why are we even going?" Quarrah cried.

Raek shrugged. "The Prime Isle asked for both of us to be there. Said it could help Ard's case."

"Seems like a trap," she muttered. *And once again I was foolish enough to take the bait.* She absently ran her finger over the head of a nail in the bench that wasn't quite flush.

"You have the queen's word, given to me by Trable himself just yesterday," Raek said.

"That's what you said, but—"

"For the purposes of today's meeting," Raek continued, "you'll be treated as if you had taken the same pardon Ard and I did."

"And I'm supposed to trust that word blindly?"

"Quarrah." Raek sat forward. "It's Abeth."

That was really why Quarrah had agreed to come this morning. They knew the queen well—or at least, they had two years ago. And the debt Abeth owed them for finding her son gave her word more weight than most.

The carriage rolled to a stop and the door whisked open. Quarrah couldn't help but tense at the sight of the red uniformed Regulator, despite knowing that he wasn't going to arrest her.

"Quarrah Khai?" Prime Isle Trable stepped into view, peering into the carriage. Quarrah had known he was a handsome man from a distance, but his looks actually held up under closer inspection.

"I told you I could get her to come," Raek said, leaning forward.

"You're late." The Prime Isle motioned hastily for the two of them to follow him up the palace steps.

Quarrah donned the oversized hood of the cloak she was wearing. There was no sense in letting people from the onlooking crowd recognize her. There may be a future client among them who would lose trust in her honor as a criminal if she were seen welcomed into the royal palace in broad daylight. Raek seemed less concerned, lumbering out of the carriage as they made their way to the grand entry.

"I can say with confidence that Isle Ardor would approve of our mild tardiness," Raek said. "And to be fair, how were we supposed to know that the palace grounds would be as crowded as a festival in the Char? Seems to me like we could use the delay to support our case."

"Let's hope the council sees it that way," said Trable. They were halfway down the hallway when the Prime Isle turned to Quarrah. "I hope I'm not overstepping here, but you might want to lose the hood."

"Unless you're trying to look like a Realm assassin," Raek added.

It was common knowledge across the Greater Chain that Queen Abeth hated anything clandestine or overly secretive. The moment the war had ended, she'd waged her own personal fight to purge any remnants of the Realm from the islands. Her ensuing queenship had been honest and remarkably transparent.

Pardoning Ard, and by association, Raek, had been a bold, but public stroke. So Quarrah could understand that Abeth would have some lingering doubts about her. Namely, why hadn't she come back to the palace after that night? Why hadn't she also taken advantage of the queen's generous pardon?

And the cowl probably wasn't helping.

Hesitantly, Quarrah pulled it down, feeling highly self-conscious without so much as a costume to hide behind. After a moment, they arrived at a guarded door. Following her mental map of the palace, Quarrah knew this would be one of the council chambers.

The guarding Regulators stepped aside, nodding respectfully to the Prime Isle as they pulled open the door.

In all her years, Quarrah couldn't remember entering such a stuffy, bloated room. The air was actually quite fresh, a scented bouquet of herbs hanging in a window that opened to a small courtyard. But the people seated around the large rectangular table were putting off their own air—and Quarrah found their self-importance downright stifling.

Everyone stood when they entered the room, even Queen Abeth, at the table's head. Did kings and queens always rise for the Prime Isle? Or was that just a show of respect since Abeth was a crusader monarch? After all, her right to rule was intrinsically tied to the Islehood's approval.

Quarrah heard Raek snicker beside her. She could already hear the way he would retell the story to Ard, claiming that the entire noble council had risen for Raek alone.

"Thank you all for convening on such short notice." Trable held up his hand in a silent approval for everyone to be seated.

As they carefully lowered their pampered backsides into their padded chairs, Quarrah took the opportunity to scan the faces of all the nobles in the room. In addition to the Prime Isle and the queen, there were three women and four men. Quarrah recalled stealing from only two of them, and the thefts had gone off well enough that they'd have no reason to suspect her.

"The matter at hand is as much political as it is religious," said Trable, seating himself at the opposite end of the table. Quarrah and Raek took up the empty seats on either side of him. "By now, I'm sure you've all heard—it seems that everyone in Beripent has—that one of my Holy Isles is being detained on the Trothian islets. I brought the matter to Her Majesty's attention and she recommended we meet to discuss what can be done."

"I was not aware that the preaching of the Holy Isles was permitted on the islets," said a pale young noblewoman with large green gems set in her earrings.

"He was not there to preach," answered the Prime Isle.

"Then what business took him to the islets?" asked a bald man.

"He was there to apologize." It was the queen who answered.

At once, all eyes turned to Abeth. It had been only two years, but she looked so different than when they'd sheltered her in the Guesthouse Adagio after faking her death. She exuded an unmistakable air of confidence, complemented by an enhanced measure of the determination she had always shown. Quarrah liked her. Sparks, it seemed everyone did. And the fact that she was willing to assemble the royal council for Ard's sake only made Quarrah respect her more.

"The Isle in question is none other than Ardor Benn," Abeth continued. "I believe you're all familiar with his unique path to the Islehood?"

"Does this arrest void his pardon, then?" asked a plump noblewoman, a little too anxiously.

"I hardly consider it a crime to sail to Ra Ennoth for an apology," answered the queen. "During the war, Ardor made an enemy of a particularly powerful Trothian priestess. The reports we're receiving say she plans to execute him during the upcoming Moon Passing."

"I fail to see why this news warranted a meeting," said a harsh-looking nobleman with a beak nose.

"The issue before us today is whether or not to mount a rescue on the Isle's behalf," said the Prime Isle.

The bald nobleman threw his hands in the air. "The Kinter family does not see any good in meddling in Trothian affairs. We are open to their presence and contributions in the Greater Chain, but what happens on their islets should remain their business."

"Was it legal for this priestess to detain him?" asked a dark-skinned noblewoman with an elegant hat.

"Technically, yes," answered the queen. "She waited until he stepped foot on Trothian sand."

"Then the Werner line must agree with the Kinters," continued the noblewoman. "This is purely a Trothian affair."

Prime Isle Trable leaned forward, clearly growing agitated by the lack of concern. "I would side with you if this were an ordinary citizen. But we are talking about a well-known Holy Isle. Over the last year, Ardor has become much loved by the citizens of Beripent."

"The people love Isle Ardor the way they love a three-legged street dog," said the sharp-nosed nobleman. "He is an oddity. A curiosity. And when he does a trick for a treat, the people gawk and applaud."

Quarrah watched the Prime Isle's jaw tighten under his trim dark beard. "Regardless of your personal feelings, I expect a level of respect when discussing my Isles. Ardor provides perspective that many find helpful. He listens without judgment and guides with insight drawn from diverse life experiences."

Was this *Ard* he was talking about? Quarrah wanted to laugh, but that wouldn't help Ard's case. Seemed like he really had Trable wrapped around his little finger. That was what Ardor Benn was best at—convincing powerful people to give him what he wanted. But there was something about the conviction in the Prime Isle's voice that gave her pause. It made her believe for a moment that maybe—just *maybe*—Ard really had changed.

"Like him or not," continued Trable, "word of his capture has already spread through the streets. The people are watching to see what we'll do about it."

"That's actually why we were late," Raek cut in, raising his hand. "Have you seen the crowd out front? Tough to get a carriage through while everyone's chanting about freeing their favorite Holy Isle."

"And who exactly are you?" asked the large noblewoman, turning a lazy eye on Raek and Quarrah.

"I'll be happy to make the introduction," Queen Abeth said. "This is Raekon Dorrel and Quarrah Khai, known associates of Ardor Benn."

"Criminal associates?" asked a muscular, broad-shouldered man.

"In the past, yes," said Abeth. "But I have extended my pardon to them for their assistance in finding my son and dismantling the Realm."

She shot a pointed look at Quarrah, who was aware of the way she had phrased the sentence to protect her. Abeth had *extended* her pardon. Didn't mean Quarrah had taken it.

"Prime Isle Trable and I thought it best to invite these two to our council today," continued Abeth. "They were with Ardor at the time of his arrest and they know him as well as anyone."

"So now we're inviting friends to the royal council meetings?" questioned Lady Werner. Frightfully disrespectful tone when addressing the queen. But then, these seven were here because their family bloodlines were being considered for the monarchy. While the common citizen adored and respected Abeth, these families saw her only as a placeholder queen. Someone to rule until a new bloodline was instated to replace the Agauls.

"The crusader *queen* can invite whomever she chooses to the royal council meetings," Abeth replied sharply. The insulted look on Lady Werner's face brought a quiet smile to Quarrah's.

"They are here to provide an eyewitness account to what happened on the Trothian islet," said Trable. "They are happy to answer any questions you might have."

*Happy* was pushing it. Quarrah found the wooden chair beneath her growing more uncomfortable as the focus of the meeting bore into her.

Raek cleared his throat and she let out a relieved sigh, grateful that he would be taking point.

"Better ask Quarrah," he said, causing her to turn. "She was actually with Ard when the Trothians nabbed him. I was waiting on the ship a half mile out."

Quarrah felt her fingertips begin to tingle with nerves. Why did it feel like Raek had just betrayed her? And what was she supposed to tell them anyway? The truth? She hadn't heard Lyndel say the exact reason for the arrest, but it hadn't been hard to deduce.

She drew in a deep breath. "I believe the Trothians are blaming Ard for the naval skirmish to retake the Pekal harbor two years ago," she finally said.

"Why would they blame him?" asked Lord Kinter.

Quarrah glanced at Raek, but he didn't come to her aid the way Ard would have. Instead, he simply gave her an encouraging nod.

"We were there," she said, the words tripping over themselves in her mouth. "We had just rescued Shad Agaul from Pekal and were attempting to transport him back to Beripent. The Trothians thought we should have leveraged the boy to stop the fighting."

"Were there not Archkingdom ships in the fight?" asked the man with the sharp nose.

"There were," replied Quarrah.

"Then the Trothian plan seems a good one," he followed up. "Why would you not relinquish the prince to the Archkingdom navy?"

"Lord Blindle raises a good point," said the plump woman. "The Archkingdom vessels could have assured him safe transport back to Beripent."

"We couldn't trust them," said Quarrah. "We didn't know how far the Realm's reach had extended. Ard thought it best to see the boy back to Beripent in our care."

"And what did *you* think?" asked the woman with the earrings.

Quarrah hesitated. Could they have saved lives that morning? Ard hadn't put the question up for debate. Like so many things, he'd taken control and Quarrah had had little choice but to hang on for the ride. It was what she found so frustrating about him. And yet, that same irritating quality was what had restored the dragon population, causing Moonsickness to recede.

"I think he made the right choice," Quarrah finally said.

"Wouldn't it have been best to present the prince at the battlefront to spark a ceasefire?" said Lord Kinter.

"Or turn him over to the Sovereign States," said Blindle. "They didn't want him dead. They could have used the lad to initiate peace talks. Termain would have had to listen."

Queen Abeth rose from her seat slowly, but with an intensity that silenced everyone in the room. She stood at the head of the table, her hands visibly trembling and her voice low.

"We are talking about my son. He was not a commodity. He was not a bargaining chip. Anyone who chooses to see him that way is no better than the Realm. And there is no question about how I dealt with them."

She let the silence hang in the chamber, daring anyone to meet her eye. When the group was sufficiently cowed, she smoothed the bodice of her dress and sat down again.

Prime Isle Trable finally recovered the meeting. He leaned forward, his voice soft but intense. "Let us consider that to be the testimony of our crusader queen regarding the character of the man who rescued her son. And I will vouch for the reformed man, Isle Ardor." Then he turned to Quarrah and Raek. "Now, perhaps a few words from his longtime associates might convince you that he is worth saving. What can you tell us about the ruse artist, Ardor Benn?"

Quarrah's mind immediately went blank. When thoughts returned a moment later, all of them were highly incriminating. Luckily, Raek started talking this time, buying her an extra few moments to compose a testimony.

"My parents died when I was sixteen," he said, his voice a low rumble. "I was old enough—smart enough—to survive on the streets, but I didn't have to because Ardor Benn invited me home as a brother."

"Was that here, in Beripent?" Lady Werner asked.

"Yes, ma'am."

"And are his parents still alive?" came the follow-up from Lord Kinter.

Quarrah managed to catch Raek's eye, but she couldn't tell

what he was thinking. How honest should they be, walking a line between saving Ard and betraying his secrets?

"I don't know," Raek replied. "But if they are, I can tell you they are no longer in Beripent."

"How can you be sure?" asked the muscular lord.

"Because I moved them out of the city myself," he answered. "Look, we weren't always criminals. We tried for years to make an honest living. We were delivery boys, message carriers, students at the university, miners, Harvesters on Pekal. But when Ard's old man got into a debt he couldn't repay, we turned outside the law. Our first ruse put enough Ashings in our pockets to set us up for life. But do you know what Ardor Benn chose to do with that money? He paid off his father's debts and asked me to move them far away from Beripent so they could live out their old age in peace and quiet."

"And you went along with that?" asked the young noblewoman.

"Absolutely," he said. "For two reasons. Ard's parents were good to me. They were like a second family and I had a chance to thank them for it."

"And the other reason?" asked the plump noblewoman.

"Because going along with Ardor Benn's plans is always the best bet." He interlaced his large fingers on the table.

"Thank you," said the Prime Isle. He turned toward Quarrah expectantly.

Oh, where to start?

"Ard doesn't know when to stop," she said. "I've seen him throw caution to the wind to accomplish his goal. I've seen him put his own life on the line to rescue a friend in need." She glanced at Raek, who just happened to be pressing one hand against the hole in his chest. "I've seen him think of solutions when there didn't seem to be any left. I've even seen him throw away something good"—she swallowed hard—"because he couldn't stop."

"So the man is driven," said Kinter. "We all have our ambitions."

"Think of the thing that you are most passionate about in this world," said Quarrah. "Then imagine that's how Ard feels when trying to decide which pastry to eat for breakfast."

Across the table, Raek burst out in an uncontrolled snicker, his bald head nodding in agreement.

"Ard went to Ra Ennoth because he doesn't know when to stop," Quarrah continued. She didn't feel like that was lying at all. She had proposed an alternative, but Ard had been determined to use Lyndel to get the Moon Glass. Well, look where that had landed him.

"I can speak to that," seconded the Prime Isle. Quarrah leaned back, grateful to be out of the hot seat.

"Since his entry into the Islehood, Isle Ardor has been determined to make things right with former unsavory associates who seek to take advantage of his reformation," explained Trable. "I have counseled him more than once to avoid these encounters, but he feels an obligation to meet with anyone who has a qualm with him, in an effort to put it to rest. Hence, his excursion to the Trothian islets is not entirely unexpected."

Lord Kinter leaned forward, gently placing a hand flat on the table. "I suppose I'm still unclear on what exactly you're proposing we do."

Queen Abeth took over. "We would like the council's blessing to send an emissary to Ra Ennoth to negotiate the release of Isle Ardor. I have already taken the liberty to have the *Leeward Pride* prepped to sail. She stands ready in the western harbor."

"When you say *negotiate* the release of the Isle, what assets are you offering on his behalf?" asked the lazy eye.

The queen held out her hands. "That is up for discussion."

"I am told that the Trothians care little for Ashings on their islets," said Lord Kinter.

"Then perhaps we can trade something," said Trable. "A ship? A generous supply of Grit? Homeland knows they have a difficult time obtaining it."

"Oh, yes!" cried Lord Blindle. "Let's be sure to arm our enemies."

"Need I remind you that the Trothians are not our enemies!" snapped the queen.

"Offer them a thousand Ashings," said Lady Werner dismissively. "If they refuse, we can reconvene to discuss further options."

"We are a mere three days from the Moon Passing," said the queen. "And the islet where he's being held is not down the street. Our first offer must be our best. And it must be convincing."

"Still, I agree with Blindle," said the lazy eye. "Even a thousand Ashings is too high a price for the life of one man. And if we pay this ransom, what's to stop the Trothians from abducting another Holy Isle to milk us for more?"

The Prime Isle held up his hand. "To be clear, this is not a ransom. And Isle Ardor was not abducted."

"Then why are we working so hard to save him?" cried Lord Blindle. "Sounds to me like the Trothians have every reason to execute him."

"That's not—ugh..." Prime Isle Trable let out an exasperated sigh. "I suppose we should put it to a vote, then." He wiped at his forehead, shiny with nervous sweat. "Those in favor of sending an emissary to Ra Ennoth for negotiations?"

"Not just yet," said the woman with the earrings. "Why does Her Majesty even need the council's blessing to authorize an emissary? It is well within your rights as queen to act alone on this. As the crusader monarch, you need only the approval of the Prime Isle, which you clearly have."

"We are dealing with a very public incident," said Abeth. "I don't know how word spread so quickly, but Raekon is right. The citizens are incited."

Quarrah imagined Cinza and Elbrig working the streets, donning and doffing disguises as quick as a sneeze. They'd done it just as efficiently the night Pethredote had been eaten by the dragon.

"I'm concerned about the political consequence of sending an emissary," continued the queen. "My connection to Ardor Benn could make it seem like I am extending a personal favor by coming to his aid. I think it would look better to the Trothian nation if we acted as a council."

"And what exactly *is* your connection to Ardor Benn these days?" asked the woman with the lazy eye.

Queen Abeth remained straight-faced. "I invite you to see my official statement regarding the rescue of my son."

Such a document existed? Quarrah suddenly found herself hoping that her name hadn't made it in there.

"That is," added the queen, "assuming you have someone to read it to you, Lady Heel."

Quarrah couldn't tell if that was an insult, or if Lady Heel really didn't know how to read with that wandering eye. Either way, it didn't faze the plump noblewoman.

"Oh, I've read it," Lady Heel said. "And I would just like to point out that you couldn't possibly have written it without the help of the very man in question. Which leaves me to wonder just how factual the account really is? For example, there was no mention of what we just learned—Ardor Benn's choice not to leverage the prince for the benefit of the Trothians."

Sparks, these nobles were a school of circling sharks.

"I've read it, too," Raek cut in. "And speaking as a person who was actually there, I can tell you the whole thing is blazing true."

"Excellent," said Lord Blindle. "We have the word of the criminal's best friend."

Prime Isle Trable suddenly stood up. "We are not here to question the authenticity of the Shad Agaul Papers. Can we *please* return to the matter at hand?"

"Ah. The matter of why Her Majesty is unwilling to authorize an emissary without the council's support," said Lord Kinter.

"She already explained her motives," Trable said, reluctantly seating himself again.

"Allow me to propose another theory," Kinter went on. "Perhaps Her Majesty wants the blessing of the council so she will not have to shoulder full responsibility when this entire fiasco detonates in our faces like a keg of Blast Grit."

"Here, here!" cried an old man who hadn't yet spoken a word. He thumped the tabletop with his wrinkly fist and winced at the pain from the impact.

"I believe we can now move to a vote with confidence," said Lady Werner, to nods from the other nobles.

Quarrah felt this entire thing slipping away from them. The queen and the Prime Isle were feeling it, too. Raek's head was downcast, his fingers massaging his chest as if trying to work the pipe free.

Well, in Quarrah's opinion, this whole approach had been ill-advised. Trable and Abeth had done their best, but it simply wasn't enough for the deep water Ard was in.

She sighed, clearly seeing the way out of this, but loath to risk so much for Ard's sake. Why couldn't she just let him die?

"On the matter of sending an emissary to Ra Ennoth to negotiate the release of Holy Isle Ardor Benn," said Trable. "How does the royal council vote?"

"Nay," each of the nobles said in turn.

"I recognize that the Islehood has no vote in this matter," said Prime Isle Trable, "but it is the will of the Homeland to protect and preserve the Holy Isles. Her Majesty has my support should she choose to pursue this endeavor single-handedly. However, let it be noted that she is under no obligation to do so, and my words here reflect only advice, not mandate, for the crusader monarch." He let out a slow breath. "How would Her Majesty like to proceed?"

Once again, all eyes went to Queen Abeth at the head of the table. "I withdraw my request for an emissary," she said quietly, defeated. "The fate of Ardor Benn now lies in the hands of the Trothian nation to do with him as they see fit." She looked down the table at Quarrah, Raek, and Prime Isle Trable. "I am indeed sorry for your friend."

~

*Advice. Counsel. Recommendations ... What does any of that matter when I'm just going to do whatever the sparks I want in the end?*

# CHAPTER
# 9

Ard used both hands to dig another hole in the sand at the bottom of his pit. Oh, flames. He was running out of places to bury his vomit. He rocked back on his knees, groaning. Maybe he could hold this one in.

The last time he remembered being this sick was more than a decade ago—Ard had collected nearly twenty Ashings from the bet, but apparently, his constitution was no more equipped for whatever the Trothians were feeding him than it was for licking poisonous toads hiding under benches at the University in Helizon.

Ard looked skyward, wondering when the flooding seawater would surge over the edge of his pit and put him out of his misery. This would be the night, though there was still a glimmer of daylight above.

But something new was happening on the Ennoth, Ard could tell. It had started about an hour ago, with Trothians running past his pit to exchange words with the priestesses before racing off. Probably making preparations for the big night.

After four days, Ard had given up talking to Lyndel. He couldn't see the priestesses from down here, but he could hear them taking up a song or a chant from time to time. Sparks, they had to be almost as miserable as he was, with their feet stuck in the sand.

He'd also given up trying to climb out. Ard had a shackle around each ankle with a short length of chain connected to two large blocks of stone. Even on his first day down here, he could barely drag them across the bottom of his pit. And that was when he'd been healthy and strong.

Ard had managed to drop one of the stones on top of the other, breaking off a small corner of the block. That fragment had then become the sole object of his time, using it to scrape, hoping to loosen the pitons that held his chains in place.

But even that had come to a discouraging end when his makeshift tool had broken, slicing the palm of his right hand and shaving off the skin on his knuckles.

Ard's thoughts oscillated between hope that his friends would mount a rescue and resigning himself to die. The latter would consume him whenever he closed his eyes, the image of that weeping Trothian girl flooding his mind. Her body shaking with sobs, her small hands dusted with pale sand as she had literally dug his grave.

A voice called out from somewhere above. In his weakened state, it took Ard a moment to realize that the person was speaking Landerian.

"Priestess Lyndel. I thank you for allowing me to approach you here." It was a man's voice, with a distinct Dronodanian accent. "Communicating from the beach was growing tedious. Your messengers were fast, but I'd say we've got less than an hour until that Moon rises."

"What is your name?" Lyndel's voice called.

"Stamon Grau," he replied. "Chief emissary to Queen Abeth Ostel Agaul, crusader monarch of the unified Greater Chain. I have been sent to negotiate the release of the prisoner."

The words caused a sudden numbness to wash over Ard's aches and weakness. He rose slowly to his feet, head cocked slightly to one side so he wouldn't miss another word of the conversation.

"That will not be possible," replied Lyndel. "This matter is not open to negotiation."

"Then why did you even allow me ashore?" Stamon asked. "A few more hours and it would have been too late. You would have gone through with the execution and the issue would have resolved itself."

"We brought you ashore because of the second addendum to the Trothian Inclusionary Act. As long as my people are allowed the freedom of coming and going from the Greater Chain, we must receive any royal flagship that hails our islets."

"Yes," said Stamon Grau. "I wasn't sure if you—"

"We may not be able to read," Lyndel cut him off, "but your *stakdash* King Pethredote made sure we knew the wording of the Act."

"And again, I thank you for honoring it in allowing me ashore," Stamon said.

"The alternative was to risk tension between our nations," said Lyndel. "And I don't think either of us want that."

"No, indeed," said the emissary. "Which is why I have come. Are you aware that the man you are holding is a Holy Isle of Wayfarism?"

She was definitely aware. Ard had been shouting it for several days. Lyndel had probably thought he was lying, but the queen's emissary was proving it now.

"I do not care what titles or status this man has on your islands," she replied. "Once he set foot on Ra Ennoth, he became our prisoner."

"He is very popular back home," said Stamon. "All of Beripent is abuzz about his capture. That puts us in a bit of a delicate position, see? The Landers want him back—the citizens, the Prime Isle. The queen. I would hate for his execution to cause *tension* between our nations."

Ard grinned. This man was a fine negotiator, using Lyndel's words against her. And if what he said was true, then it sounded like Raek had reached Cinza and Elbrig in time for the two of them to spread word of his detainment through Beripent.

"Are you threatening us?" Lyndel asked.

"I am only trying to help you understand the delicacy of your situation," the emissary said. "Following through with this execution will be considered an act of aggression against Wayfarism. And Her Majesty currently rules as a crusader monarch under the direction of the Islehood. I think you can see where this is going."

"Executing him might be an insult to your religion," said Lyndel, "but freeing him would be an insult to ours."

"With all due respect, there is a difference between insulting one's religion and starting a war," said Stamon.

Ard gawked in silence at the bottom of his pit. Queen Abeth had really gone all out to save him if she was willing to threaten the Trothians with war.

Above, Lyndel began speaking with the priestesses in their language. The conversation stretched on, the sky growing dimmer by the minute. After some time, Ard couldn't help but wonder if the priestesses were merely stalling. Perhaps their plan was to drown Stamon Grau along with Ard and claim that the whole thing was the result of bad timing.

Then silence fell. Ard could see a reddish tinge to the darkened sky. Lyndel spoke in Landerian once again.

"We have required the life of Ardor Benn as payment for the deaths of our people," she began. "But if doing so will bring about more Trothian deaths in a war against Landers, then we must consider what is best for our people." She paused for a long time. "You may take him."

Ard felt a rush of relief that quickly gave way to nausea. Instead of celebrating his freedom, he dropped to his knees, gripping his stomach and trying not to lose its contents.

"And the name *Stamon Grau* will be remembered as the one who robbed *Nah* of due payment," continued Lyndel. "Should you ever step foot upon Trothian sand again, you will find yourself in a pit much like this one. In the meantime, take this message to your queen." Lyndel cleared her throat. "Your actions have offended the Trothian nation. Should the time ever come that you need our assistance, we will stand by and watch you suffer."

As she spoke, Ard saw movement at the edge of his pit. A couple of Trothian men lowered a simple rope ladder. Then one of them sprang down, his bare feet leaving imprints in the sand beside Ard. He wrinkled his nose at the reek of the pit and then wordlessly unlocked the shackles around Ard's ankles. He muttered something in Trothian and gestured to the way up.

Ard staggered across the pit, gripping the looped rope rungs, wincing at the effort it took to hoist himself. The Trothian above heaved on the ladder, hauling him up like a limp fish in a net. Ard remained on hands and knees for a moment, feeling ill. Then he stood up slowly, realizing he was just feet from Lyndel.

She studied him with her dark vibrating eyes, her face an unreadable stone. "You have powerful friends, Ardor Benn," she said.

"I've always counted you among them," he replied.

She leaned forward, her feet still buried in the sand. "The next time I see you"—her voice was a whisper—"I will kill you where you stand."

Ard swallowed against the rising bile in his throat and turned away from her. Was it really going to end like this between them? Full of animosity and distrust? Isle Halavend would have sorrowed at the discord between the two individuals who had once saved life and time itself. The sorrow nipped at Ard, too, but Lyndel seemed wholly calloused by her desire for vengeance.

There was a Lander man standing on the other side of the pit who must have been Stamon Grau. He wasn't very tall, mostly bald, with prominent ears and two front teeth that Ard could see even in the darkness.

Behind the emissary, the Red Moon was rising on the horizon. Sighting down the nearest *pat*, Ard thought the glowing crimson curve looked like a crown of fire on the sea.

"Thank you," Ard said, staggering toward the emissary.

"Thank the queen," he remarked coldly. "I'm now an enemy of the Trothian nation."

"We've got to get out of here," Ard said. "I assume you have a ship waiting?"

"The queen's own *Leeward Pride*," answered Stamon. Then he turned once more to Lyndel. "We will stay anchored through the night and depart at dawn."

"What?" Ard cried. To give the Trothians a chance to recapture them? "Why?"

"The InterIsland Waters are swollen during the Moon Passing and the harbors are closed," replied Stamon. "And the crew of the *Leeward Pride* would prefer to spend the red night belowdecks."

"You will maintain the distance of a half mile," said Lyndel.

"Understood," answered Stamon.

Ard risked one last glance at Lyndel, but her head was downcast. She had reached out, gripping the hands of the priestesses on either side of her.

The Trothian men that had freed Ard from the pit led the way, dropping into one of the *pats* and moving seaward, setting a pace much too swift for Ard's weakened condition.

Ard noticed that the canals were noticeably deeper than before, forcing him to swim more than once. The water actually felt fresh and cleansing after so many days sitting in his own filth.

Every minute they traveled, the water seemed to grow deeper. In some places, Ard saw that the banks of the *pats* had overflowed, seawater flooding under the raised walls of the Trothian homes.

By the time they reached the beach, the open sand where he'd been arrested was completely underwater. Ard stood chest deep in the sea, the *Leeward Pride* silhouetted against a solid red backdrop of the rising Moon.

One of those half-submerged rafts was waiting for them, a pair of Trothian swimmers ready to push. Ard and Stamon hoisted themselves onto the rails and the simple vessel streamed through the water, effortlessly propelled.

Stamon Grau said nothing, but clung to the raft like he might be bucked off at any moment. Ard felt exhilarated, the fresh wind against his wet face, moving *away* from what he had thought would be his certain death.

When they reached the *Leeward Pride*, a salty-looking sailor woman was waiting with a rope ladder over the hull. Stamon went first and Ard followed, nearly slipping twice. When he finally reached the deck, the Trothian raft was out of sight in the darkness.

"You look like slag."

Ard pulled himself up at the sound of the voice. "Raek?" What was his partner doing with the queen's crew? "You cut it kind of close."

"It's a long ways to Beripent and back," Raek replied.

Ard nodded. "I knew Trable would pull through for us. But this..." He gestured at the ship. "He went above and beyond getting the queen involved." Ard scanned the deck. "Skeleton crew, eh?" Only three sailors besides Raek and the woman. "I would have thought Her Majesty would send some Reggies for backup."

"She probably would have," Stamon Grau said. "But *we* didn't have that kind of pull."

"Huh?" Ard turned just in time to see him reach up and wipe off one of his sagging earlobes.

"On the bright side," the man said, "Stamon Grau now has a significant and memorable encounter. I'd say the value of his character just went up by at least a hundred Ashings."

Ard leaned forward, peering at him through the red-hued darkness. "Elbrig?"

"Not so loud, Ardy," he replied. "I'm still Stamon Grau to the crew."

"I assume Cinza's here, too?" Ard said.

Elbrig pointed at the woman who had thrown him the ladder. She cast him a sidelong wink.

"But..." Ard stammered. "The *Leeward Pride*..." If this wasn't the real ship, then it was a stunning replica.

"Queen Abeth made the mistake of telling us where it was docked," Raek said. "Quarrah swiped the necessary departure papers and we sailed out of the western harbor without any opposition." Raek held up a finger. "I have a sneaking suspicion that Queen Abeth could have stopped us, but chose to turn a blind eye. She was in your corner, Ard. She and Trable. But the council of royal morons wouldn't authorize an emissary."

"Where do we go from here?" Ard asked. "I can't imagine they'll welcome us back into the harbor."

Raek shook his head. "In the morning we'll sail the *Leeward Pride* as far north as we dare and then abandon her. I made arrangements with Frent Bailor to pick us up in the *Double Take*."

"I haven't seen Frent in ages," Ard said. "I thought he retired after that barrel of dead rats pinned him against the back of the greenhouse."

"He was willing to do a simple pickup run for you," Raek said. "And he'll keep it under his cap so it shouldn't jeopardize the queen's pardon or your standing in the Islehood."

Ard tapped his chin in thought. "We'll need an airtight story for Trable."

"Too many witnesses for anything to be completely airtight," Raek said. "You could always claim that you escaped."

Ard shook his head. "That would be a crime—not against the Greater Chain, so maybe I'd keep the pardon. But Trable could never justify keeping me in the Islehood after that."

"That might not be a bad thing," said Raek. "If you haven't

found what we're looking for yet, what difference do you think a few more cycles will make?"

Ard held up his hand. "We can spread the word that the Trothians released me after I talked Lyndel's ear off."

"Paint it blue and here's proof." Elbrig held out the wadded prosthetic ear.

"That story won't hold up forever," Raek pointed out.

"It doesn't need to." Ard thought of his studies in the Mooring. Maybe he was close to uncovering the true meaning behind the Great Egress. "I just need a little longer."

"Cinza and I will start working out the details of the story," Elbrig said. "We can brief you in the morning." He strode away, keeping one hand over his missing ear so the crew wouldn't notice anything amiss.

"Raek?" Ard scanned the deck one more time just to be sure. "Where's Quarrah?" He was afraid to hear the answer. Afraid that this little hang-up with Lyndel had put her over the edge. Driven her away yet again.

"She's not on the ship," Raek answered his searching eyes.

Ard felt his spirits fall, stomach turning with something more than just his food poisoning. "Do you think we'll see her again?"

"Oh, we better," said Raek, looking starboard toward the dark Ennoth. "But she's only got until dawn to steal the Moon Glass."

Quarrah lay on one of the flat-roofed Trothian homes, giving her arms and legs a break from the endless swimming. Of all the nights to try to steal a Moon Glass . . . The Ennoth was completely flooded, both of the Moon Glass shards would be in use inside the *Ucru*, and the *Leeward Pride* would set sail at dawn whether she was onboard or not.

By now, Elbrig would have gotten Ard safely back to the ship. The disguise managers thought it a little overambitious to couple the rescue with the theft, but what choice did they have? After tonight, they'd never get a Lander ship within a half mile of the islets. Lyndel would spread the word of Ard's release, and the Trothians would be more guarded and vigilant than ever.

Quarrah stared at the massive red orb in the darkness above her. It was always a majestic sight, the Moon seeming to fill the entire sky. It was no wonder the Trothians worshiped it. Lying on the roof of the house, Quarrah felt like she was on the top of the world. Without the thick smoke and looming buildings of Beripent, the sky looked incredibly vast. Out here, she could almost *hear* the Moon, grinding so slowly past the net of stars above.

Although she couldn't see them with her naked eye, Quarrah imagined the red rays of the Moon streaming toward the distant summit of Pekal, the growing population of dragons absorbing them into their huge scaly bodies to shield the world from the sickness. She thought of the poor Bloodeye man she had stolen for Lord Dulith's sick purposes. What had taken him and his friends so high into the mountains? What had been his final thoughts before the madness had broken his mind and twisted his body?

There was a cure. The Metamorphosis Grit didn't work once the Bloodeye had reached the final stage, but Quarrah had intercepted that man earlier. If she had been carrying Meta Grit, she could have saved his life.

Saved his life, or simply altered it beyond recognition? Would the man have transformed like Gloristar—his body enlarged, skull turned to thick red glass, and his eyes ablaze with an inhuman light? Would he have become a Glassmind?

A family of Trothians swam past, laughing and splashing. If she'd sat up, she would have seen them clearly enough, their naked blue bodies illuminated in the red glow of the Moon. But Quarrah stayed on her back, regulating her breathing, hoping to go unnoticed. With their enhanced ability to see the energy of all things, Quarrah wondered if they could even see her breath pluming up from the rooftop.

The family passed harmlessly and Quarrah waited until their splashing had faded into the distance before refitting her cork nose plugs, pulling the breathing reed over her mouth, and sliding off the roof into the chill water.

She had dressed for the occasion, wearing a tight sleeveless shirt and pants that were cut off so her bare legs would move easily through the water. She had her belts, loaded with her usual compliment of Grit. Knowing she'd be in the water, Quarrah had opted for wax-coated Grit pots instead of her stealthier teabags.

She was glad she had followed Raek's suggestion to swipe the nose plugs and breathing reed from a Grit processing factory. The items, designed for submersion in the liquid Scouring Pits, allowed her to stay very low in the water, just her eyes and forehead above the surface.

She swam slowly and cautiously, no longer pushing herself now that she'd reached the cover of the half-submerged houses. Someone with a less astute sense of direction might have been disoriented in the flood, but Quarrah maintained a course that she knew would take her to the Ennoth's center.

The Trothians had formed into large social groups, occupying any significant stretch of open space, which left the densely constructed neighborhoods a navigable maze of cover. And it certainly helped that most of the people were distracted with their chants or trying to catch a fish in a game of *gras oronet*.

It was just past midnight when she finally saw the *Ucru*. The domed building rose more than ten feet out of the water, smoke wafting skyward from an opening in the top. There was no door or windows, but she saw something that looked like a covered ladder leading to the high opening.

Between the *Ucru* and the house where Quarrah now hid was a wide stretch of water occupied by hundreds of Trothians. They filled the space around their religious building, the water shallow enough that many of them stood chest deep. How was she supposed to—

A cheer went up from a group of Trothians nearby. Quarrah squinted, cursing the dim lighting and her poor vision. But she could see that one of the women was holding a fish the length of her forearm. It wriggled and bucked as she held it aloft. When the applause of her peers died down, the woman lowered the fish through the red glare on the water's surface and released it.

The glare!

Vorish had said that the Trothian vision was hindered by the reflection of the Moon. If Quarrah could stay underwater the whole way, they wouldn't be able to see her. The distance was much too far to hold her breath, but she might be able to angle the breathing reed to draw air. Hopefully, the reed itself would blend with the flotsam of twigs and leaves—even some unsecured belongings— that she'd seen adrift all night.

Working quickly, she used two replacement reeds and some extra forming wax to triple the length of her breathing tube, making sure there was a watertight seal over the seams. She made a couple of experimental dives, adjusting the angle of the long reed so the opening was behind her head. She sucked water once, but managed to blow it out through the end of the reed without surfacing.

Okay. This was going to work. Quarrah took a moment to get her bearings, sighting toward the *Ucru*, gauging the distance. Then she ducked underwater with barely a ripple.

Lit with penetrating red Moonlight, it was like another world under the surface, with so many Trothian legs between her and her destination. For the most part, they swam in place, legs kicking lazily to tread water. But as she swam closer to the *Ucru*, the water grew shallower with the incline of the sand.

The Trothians were mostly standing now—except for some of the little children who couldn't reach. Navigating between them was getting tighter, too.

One of them sidestepped directly into her path and she threw out her arms, frantically paddling backward. At the disturbance in the water, his hand plunged down, grasping blindly mere inches in front of her face.

*Sparks! They think I'm a lucky fish!* And this was suddenly a life-and-death game of *gras oronet*.

Quarrah touched her bare feet down on the sand, remaining bent in half to keep her torso below water and her breathing reed up. The desperate fisherman gave up, and Quarrah heard boisterous laughter from his friends as he withdrew his empty hand.

She resumed her route to the *Ucru*, skirting the group and trying to keep her bearings. She didn't need to swim now that she had her feet in the sand. It was definitely slower to move bent over like this, but it gave her better control among the crowd.

She was almost there, just squeezing between two muscular men. Suddenly, one of them grabbed the unnaturally bobbing reed, yanking her breathing tube out of the water. It came apart at one of the wax seams, Quarrah's mouth instantly flooding with seawater. She lunged forward, swimming with both arms outstretched until she touched the side of the *Ucru*. Holding tightly to the wall, she raised her face above the surface, spitting the water and gasping fresh air.

It seemed she *was* the lucky fish tonight, because nobody noticed her against the *Ucru*'s wall. And the covered ladder was only a few feet away. She ducked under the water once more, palming along the wall until she felt the first rung. Peering up, she saw that the ladder was little more than simple wooden slats nailed to the arched frame of the *Ucru* dome. But the whole ladder was enclosed in a vertical tunnel made of bent twigs and a covering of tanned hides.

Quarrah hoisted herself into the tunnel, the wooden slats of the ladder feeling warm to her bare feet and hands. Concealed like this, she didn't have to worry about being spotted as she ascended the side of the *Ucru*.

She got her first whiff of the smoke about halfway up. It was acrid and caustic, not at all like the typical smoke of a hearth fire. Sparks. Were they burning garbage inside this structure?

By the time she'd reached the top of the dome, Quarrah's head was spinning. The ladder led to a circular opening no more than five feet across. The Moonlight that spilled down was quickly choked out by the haze of gray smoke, making it impossible to see anything below. But Quarrah noticed a rope descending into the dome.

*These priestesses must be pretty agile if this is the only way in and out,* she thought. As much as she hated the idea of lowering herself into the unknown, Quarrah knew she couldn't stay here all night, leaning over the opening and breathing the heady smoke. If Vorish had been right, there would only be two priestesses below—one looking through the resident piece of Moon Glass, and the other using Lyndel's shard.

It was awkward to maneuver from the covered ladder onto the rope. The smoke brought a sudden bout of coughs and Quarrah felt like she might as well have announced her arrival with a shout. The rope was knotted at regular intervals, her bare feet finding good purchase as she slithered downward.

In here, the air was hot and astringent from the gray haze. It stung her nose and made her throat feel raw. She dangled fifteen feet above the dry sandy floor as the dome's interior came into focus through the smoke.

Directly beneath her rope was a smoldering fire, its coals providing enough glow to light the interior of the *Ucru.*

Lyndel was down there. She was lying on her back beside the fire, unmoving, a piece of red Moon Glass gripped in one hand, which rested limply at her side. Another Trothian woman, identically dressed, lay across the fire from her, a second Moon Glass clutched loosely over her chest. Both women appeared to be staring up at Quarrah, but strangely, they showed no signs of noticing her.

*Maybe they're asleep,* Quarrah thought. It was the middle of the night, after all. If she moved quietly enough, she might be able to pry one of the glass pieces away and get out without disturbing anyone.

Blowing out a breath against the pervasive smoke, Quarrah lowered herself another few knots until she felt the heat of the fire directly beneath her. She reached out an arm, pumping it back and forth to give her some momentum on the rope. Once it was swinging like a clock pendulum, Quarrah let go, dropping to the soft sand at Lyndel's feet.

Now that she was closer, Quarrah saw that their eyes were open, staring flatly upward. Not asleep.

Dead.

There was blood everywhere. How had she missed it from above? It pooled in the sand, making a crimson paste beneath their heads. With a wave of nausea, Quarrah saw the lines across their throats. Clouds of black flies buzzed on the gaping, gory wounds, and the smell of rotting flesh suddenly assaulted her.

"I've been waiting for you, Quarrah," a voice said from behind. It was a voice she had known her entire life. And one she had tried hard to forget.

She whirled around and saw the woman crouching against the wall of the *Ucru*, a dripping blade dangling casually from one hand.

Quarrah opened her mouth, trying to eke out the woman's name. But it wouldn't come. Another word fell from her mouth— one she didn't like to say.

"Mother."

Jalisa Khailar rose slowly to her feet, tossing the knife from one hand to the other. Her knuckles were red, and the front of her tan tunic was splattered with the blood of the priestesses. But she looked so much the same. Wild, unkempt hair, crooked teeth, foggy look in her bloodshot eyes.

"You didn't come home," her mother said, voice small. "When I got back from the market... you were gone."

Quarrah shook her head, fighting tears that flooded to her eyes. "You..." she whispered. "How did you find me?"

"I looked for weeks," she said. "I waited. But you didn't come home."

"No," said Quarrah. "It was *you* who didn't come home that day. Or the next. Or the week after that."

"You abandoned me." Jalisa took a step forward. "I was delayed at the market, that's all."

Quarrah choked on a sudden sob. "I didn't think...you were coming back."

"But I did," her mother said. "And you were gone. I needed you, Pockets."

*Pockets.*

It was a name only her mother had called her. A name that showed how this woman saw her daughter—nothing more than an extra pair of pockets to hold her stolen goods.

"I didn't..." Quarrah gasped. "I didn't need you."

It was why ten-year-old Quarrah had waited only a week for her mother to return. Jalisa Khailar had been gone for stretches longer than that, but Quarrah had wanted an excuse. Any excuse to be free.

Her mother's face began to contort in anger. Quarrah was transported to a helpless time almost forgotten. She felt every fiber of her body tighten to weather the coming blows.

"You wretched little twit," Jalisa spit.

But Quarrah didn't have to take it this time. She was grown. She was strong. She was ten times the woman her mother could ever be.

Jalisa lunged with the dagger and Quarrah sidestepped, pushing her weapon aside. Her mother's arm felt so frail beneath the tunic sleeve, and her elbow buckled with surprising ease. She fell on her face, and Quarrah heard the soft squelch of the knife as it plunged into her mother's stomach.

"Sparks," Quarrah muttered, staggering backward, blinking against the tears and smoke in her eyes. "Oh, blazing sparks." She dropped to Jalisa's side as the woman sputtered on her own blood.

Carefully, Quarrah rolled her mother onto her side, drawing back at the grisly sight of the wound in her torso.

Jalisa Khailar's hand slipped from the hilt of the knife. She reached up, fingertips drawing lines of red across Quarrah's cheek as she caressed her daughter.

"My…little girl," she rasped. "Point into the Homeland." Her hand dropped heavily to the sand. Her eyes glazed.

Wait. Not just glazed. Her eyes were changing, turning red, filling with blood. Moonsickness? How? What was happening? They were glowing now. Like Gloristar's.

Quarrah scrambled backward as the knife pushed itself free of her mother's abdomen, hovering in midair. But this weapon was unlike any Quarrah had ever seen. The blade was thick red glass, like a shard broken from a piece of Agrodite Moon Glass. The handle was little more than a tapered tang wrapped in thick rawhide, stained with her mother's blood.

Transfixed by its appearance, Quarrah reached toward the floating blade. But before she could touch it, the weapon dissolved into red smoke, quickly mingling with the haziness of the *Ucru*.

Jalisa Khailar's body suddenly convulsed and Quarrah saw dozens of spindly black legs reaching out from the wound in her stomach. Then at once, thousands of spiders erupted from her mother's dead body, flowing onto the sand like a black wave.

Quarrah screamed, falling backward, landing dangerously close to the fire. The embers crackled, the rush of wind from Quarrah's fall breathing new life into them. Flames leapt up, orange and yellow with hints of blue. But there was something else in the fire. Faces. Yawning faces caught in the mad, silent screams of a Bloodeye.

Quarrah stumbled to her feet, dancing away from the spiders and kicking sand across the coals. The priestesses were burning more than wood. Quarrah could see a blackened lump that looked like a withered potato balanced carefully atop the coals.

Something Vorish had mentioned suddenly came racing back to her mind. The priestesses who spent the night in the *Ucru* breathed a special smoke that supposedly awakened their minds to visions from the gods.

This wasn't real. Her mother's body, the glass knife, the spiders...It was some kind of hallucination—a far cry from a godly vision.

Quarrah coughed against the smoke. Lyndel and the other priestess were still alive. A second look proved that there was no blood on their bodies. Their eyes were indeed open, but they seemed to be in some kind of meditative trance.

She took a step backward and a giant snake dropped from above, coiling itself around her arm. She struck at it, crying out in fear and confusion. Part of her knew that the snake was nothing more than the rope she had used to climb down, but her mind was unable to separate the delusion from reality.

She drew a small knife from her belt and slashed at the reptile. Quarrah felt the blade bite into her own arm as it severed the snake, which fell writhing into the fire.

The very air of the *Ucru* was poisoning her. She needed to grab one of the Moon Glasses and get out. But Lyndel was now one of *four* priestesses lying on the sand, and Quarrah's head was reeling.

She lunged toward the nearest, tripping as her hand touched the leather-wrapped edge of the red glass. The piece pulled free of Lyndel's grasp, skittering across the sand.

When she moved to find it, the entire interior of the *Ucru* changed. The walls became reflective red glass, casting her image in both directions ad infinitum. She reached for the piece of Moon Glass on the floor, but it turned to sand in her grasp, a mere apparition.

She had to get out of here. This wasn't a vision. It was a nightmare. Maybe the Trothian constitution meant their reaction to the smoke was more meaningful—or at the very least, less severe. Or maybe Quarrah would soon slip into a catatonic trance like Lyndel and the other priestess.

Quarrah pounced at another piece of Moon Glass on the ground, only to feel it slip through her fingers. Confusion clawed at her mind like a wild animal desperate to escape its cage.

She screamed again, maybe for no other reason than to prove she still had a voice. To prove that she wasn't turning Moonsick.

"Vethrey," Lyndel's voice said from behind her.

"Vethrey," repeated the other priestess. Quarrah saw her lips form the word, though she had no idea what it meant.

"Vethrey. Vethrey. Vethrey." The chant started slowly, building into a swift and chilling accelerando. The two women repeated the word over and over until Quarrah's brain ached from the sound.

She reached out, at last gripping the tangible piece of glass, warm and smooth beneath her fingertips. It was larger than she remembered, thick and irregularly shaped, with two leather loops fastened to the sides like handles. No sooner did she hold it than the entire *Ucru* turned upside down.

Quarrah pushed her wrist through one of the loops on the glass, digging her hands into the sand to hold on. If she let go, she'd fall into the sky, careening upward until she splatted against the great red sphere of the Moon.

No way out.

"Vethrey. Vethrey."

Quarrah groped at her belts, yanking one of the wax-coated Grit pots free. Was it Drift Grit? Probably. Quarrah couldn't be sure of anything right now.

With a grunt, she hurled the pot as hard as she could against the red mirror wall of the *Ucru*. It struck, the clay shattering and the Slagstone chip sparking in the darkness. The Grit exploded with a deafening crack and a gush of flames.

Not Drift Grit.

Blast Grit.

Quarrah was thrown backward as the wall of the *Ucru* blew wide open. There were screams outside and cool seawater suddenly rushed across the dry sand.

The fire went out in an angry hiss, the cold wave splashing Quarrah's face. The *Ucru* turned right side up again, and she staggered to her feet, the large Moon Glass dangling from her wrist, droplets of water streaming off its red pane. But what was this?

Broken.

A shard of the glass must have cracked off in the explosion, leaving a new shape along the bottom. And there! The broken fragment was glimmering against the sand by her feet, churning beneath the surface of the rising water.

Sparks...It was the same shape as the blade that had stabbed her mother.

A lingering hallucination. It had to be.

There was still so much smoke in the air, stinging Quarrah's eyes and cloying at her throat with every breath. She looked away from the shard of glass, focusing on the hole in the side of the *Ucru*. Broken timbers of the framework jutted upward from the sand, the leather covering of the dome hanging like torn skin. Water poured through the waist-high opening, and Quarrah pushed against the flow, not thinking clearly enough to glance back and see if Lyndel was drowning in her trance.

*Vethrey. Vethrey.*

Their chant still rattled in Quarrah's skull as she pulled herself through the opening. Her foot caught the ripped leather, sending her sprawling underwater. She resurfaced outside the *Ucru*, gulping in the fresh air and clinging tightly to Lyndel's thick piece of red glass.

The Trothians outside had scattered in fear of the explosion. Chaos reigned on Ra Ennoth, and Quarrah took full advantage of it, dropping low in the water and making her way toward the distant *Leeward Pride*.

It was going to be a long swim, but her mind cleared a little more with every stroke that took her away from the *Ucru* and its foul smoke.

She paused only once to feel the edge of the Moon Glass. It was weathered smooth except for the bottom edge. The razor-sharp profile confirmed that a piece really had broken off. And its shape . . .

Quarrah heard her mother's voice. *"Point into the Homeland."*

She swam on through glowing red waters.

～

*There were moments when my mind felt stretched too far and a certain kind of madness hedged its way in. But I always found a light to shine my way back to sanity.*

# PART II

The Settled, with their drowned prayers and their false gods, can in no way reach the Homeland.

—Wayfarist Voyage, *vol. 1*

Beat the water and cry out. *Nah* will see to justice in the end, as he did in the start.

—*Ancient Agrodite song*

# CHAPTER

# 10

Nemery Baggish stared down at the unsightly blemish of New Vantage. Why did people have to encroach on her space like this? If the Landers continued developing Pekal at this pace, would she live to see a day when there was no unspoiled place?

"You know," Nemery said, turning to Mohdek, "I'm only doing this because I love you."

The Trothian simply grinned, his dark, vibrating eyes studying the harbor below. He knew it. Nemery didn't have a doubt about that.

"Just don't take too long," she continued. "I'm not sure how long I can stand New Vantage today. Remember last cycle? That nobleman had over a dozen people in the street, staring up at the sky with their hands covering the sun, talking in highly educated tones." She altered her voice in a horrible impersonation of a nobleman. "Yessir, that is a *dragon*. You can tell it's a sow by the curve of the tail and the ample breast—"

"He did not say that," Mohdek replied, laughing. She noticed his awkward posture. Standing with his legs slightly apart, arms hanging so they wouldn't touch his sides. He'd even stopped itching his cracked skin because it caused more pain than relief. Flames. They really should be getting to the water more often for his sake.

Nemery broke character. "It was a seagull, Moh. A dozen nobles gawking at the silhouette of a blazing seagull." She shook her head. "At least you can pretend not to speak their language. Ugh. Sometimes they try to ask me for directions... Like I know my way around that Homeland-forsaken town."

"I thought you liked talking," he said.

She snorted. "To you."

"I caught you having a sit-down chat with Burdal two cycles back," Mohdek said.

"Okay. Sometimes Burdal. And maybe Sheren. And Gohk. But that's it." Nemery adjusted the bow that was strung across her back, making sure the single arrow stayed tied in place. She needed to move on before Mohdek accused her of any more casual conversation.

The two of them merged onto a well-trodden path, the low spots still a little muddy from last night's rain. Visitors to New Vantage would consider this trail a rugged descent, but it felt like a regular highway to Nemery and Mohdek.

A careful analysis over the last year had taught them that the first week after the Moon Passing was the best time to visit the pretentious mountainside town—if a visit became strictly necessary. The best time for Nemery meant the fewest tourists.

The trail widened and they entered an area of new construction. The borders of New Vantage were growing faster than mold on damp bread. There must have been nearly a hundred workers on this site alone. They didn't pay any attention to Nemery and Mohdek, keeping their focus on their tools and the large blocks of stone they were maneuvering through clouds of Drift Grit.

"Give me three hours," Mohdek said in Trothian.

"Take all the time you need," she replied in his language. After almost three years with him, there was very little she couldn't say. And nothing she couldn't understand.

"I'll meet you at Burdal's to help you carry the salt," he said.

Nemery shook her head. "Just meet me here."

"How much are you buying?"

"Depends on how much I get for the bow," she said. "I'm hoping for fifty panweights. Sixty, if Burdal's in a good mood."

"That's half your weight, Nem. I'll meet you in town. We can share the load."

"Moh," she called as he turned to a narrow street leading toward the harbor. "Be careful." She said this in Landerian so she'd get the tone just right. Nemery wasn't expecting any trouble, but she always hated separating. They'd spent very little time apart since he and his brother had captured her.

Mohdek smiled. "You, too, Salafan." Then he moved out of sight.

Nemery headed toward the town center, spotting the Mooring Station perched on the edge of the cliff shoreline. She hadn't been inside that building, but the mere sight of it churned a mix of feelings inside her. Feelings of who she had been, versus who she was now.

Part of her still longed for the simple belief in Wayfarism that had sustained her through childhood. Another part of her felt guilty, even shameful, for not believing it the way she used to. She still loved Wayfarism. And she believed the parts of it that made sense to her. But her heart was at odds with her faith. And Mohdek would always win that battle.

The town center was busy, as usual. Finely dressed people milled about aimlessly, their fancy shoes clicking on the bricks underfoot. At the center of the circular courtyard stood a large stone statue of a dragon. The arrangement of its tail spikes was not quite right, and the sculptor had depicted the dragon perching upright in the most preposterous manner. Hah! Dragons didn't sit like that. Well, maybe Polnaj. But he was still a hatchling of three cycles. Just a silly little bull.

Nemery moved past the inaccurate statue, heading for Burdal's Provisions on the far side of the courtyard. No one spoke to her, but she noticed the way their eyes stuck to her as she moved. What must she look like to them? A wild Lander who seemed at least half Trothian.

Nemery Baggish was nearly eighteen now, though her small frame probably made her look younger. Her dark skin was calloused and tough from so much exposure to the elements. She kept her black hair cut short, the side braided across her scalp in the Trothian tradition.

She wore clothes of her own making. Not a perfect fit, though each pair she sewed was better. Her pants were knitted wool taken from wild mountain sheep, and her tunic was a blend of weathered animal hides—mostly rabbit and goat, for this one, with a snakeskin belt.

And she walked with a limp—so subtle, she could often make it look like a strut. Pekal had given her that scar. Under the rage of a confused dragon, Nemery's thigh had been pierced with a broken tree branch. She didn't resent it. In fact, she had told Mohdek that she considered the injury a touch of fate. Pekal's way of sticking its hooks in her. Giving her a taste of the island's wild danger to ensure that she'd come back someday.

Now that she was here, she hoped she'd never have to leave.

Nemery was almost to the shop when she heard someone shout her name.

"Salafan! Salafan!"

The few people in New Vantage that knew her called her only by her Trothian name. That was just fine with Nemery Baggish. No sense telling people who she really was. She'd hate for word to reach her parents that she was still alive.

Nemery turned to find Ednes Holcatch running across the courtyard toward her. Sparks, not Ednes. This woman was the hub of gossip in New Vantage, the very type Nemery tried to avoid.

"Praise the Homeland," Ednes said, catching up to her. "Just the person I needed to see."

For a moment, Nemery thought about nocking her single arrow

and staking the hem of Ednes's dress to the ground. She resisted the urge. "Hullo, Ednes."

The woman was shaped like a ripe pear, with extra-wide hips and a torso that tapered to a head that looked one size too small. Perhaps in an effort to compensate, she wore an obvious wig of thick, curled brown hair that spilled past her shoulders.

"Have you been to see Raston this cycle?" Ednes asked. She was out of breath from her run, but Nemery thought the huffing might be a bit melodramatic.

"Why would I go see Raston?" Nemery asked flatly.

"Well, I thought you reported there when you came down from—"

"I don't work for him, if that's what you're getting at."

"Then why do you spend so much time up there?"

Nemery glanced up at the towering mountain that formed New Vantage's backdrop. "I like the view."

Ednes waved her hand. "Never mind that. You need to see Raston. He has a client—"

"I don't work for Raston," Nemery repeated with more emphasis.

"Then that's more reason for you to see him," said Ednes. "No one will take this client up—"

"And I don't take clients," said Nemery. "I'm not a blazing tour guide, Ednes."

The woman scoffed at Nemery's bluntness. "He's offering good money," she pressed. "And you're the only one who could take him."

"Why is that?" Nemery asked.

"He wants to summit."

Nemery's breath caught in her throat. Her gaze went out of focus on the slopes of greenery over Ednes's shoulder.

She and Mohdek had summited Pekal only twice. The journey was not for the faint of heart. The air was thinner up there, and the glacier could freeze an unprepared hiker in their tracks.

"Who's the client?" Nemery asked.

"He said his name is Legien Dyer." Ednes leaned forward, lowering her voice to a hoarse whisper. "He's singing to the tune of five thousand Ashings for whoever will take him."

*Five thousand Ashings?* Nemery nearly hiccuped. Sparks, it was more money than she'd ever seen in her life. Ardor Benn had once promised to pay her a hundred and fifty for joining his motley expedition, but she had come to consider mere survival her payment for that job.

"Where is this Legien Dyer?" Nemery finally asked.

"He's staying at the Elegant Perch," said Ednes. "Been in New Vantage three days already. But you'll probably find him hanging around Raston's during shop hours. The man is desperate."

"I'll swing by," Nemery said, glancing at Burdal's Provisions, "but I've got something to take care of first." Mohdek would definitely need salt if they were going to summit.

"As long as you can get there today." Ednes smiled. "And if you don't mind, tell Mister Dyer I sent you. I've been trying to get his attention since I saw him disembark."

Oh, flames. There was always an angle with Ednes Holcatch.

"Don't suppose you want to buy an authentic Trothian bow, do you?" Nemery asked, slipping the weapon from her shoulder.

Ednes drew back as if Nemery had struck her. "Homeland! What would I want with a heathen weapon like that?"

*Heathen . . .* Nemery used a bow almost every day. Not this one— her personal hunting bow had a much heavier draw.

Ednes scurried away like a rabbit. Nemery hadn't expected the woman to take her up on the offer, but at least it had put an end to their conversation. She scanned the sunlit courtyard, eyes darting around until she found a likelier buyer. A father and son, both sporting oversized hats of bright green.

*There's a man out to impress his kid,* Nemerey thought. The boy looked no older than eight. Easy target.

Nemery swallowed down any jealousy she felt for the boy.

Her first visit to Pekal had been with Ardor Benn and his crew of criminals. Nemery's parents had been so angry when she'd returned home...they'd barely seemed happy that she'd survived the ordeal.

"Sir?" Nemery said, causing the man in the hat to turn. She held out the bow. "Can I interest your boy in his first weapon?"

The man smiled arrogantly. "Tervol has had his own Singler since he was six."

"Of course," said Nemery, "but has that Singler drawn blood from a dragon?"

The boy looked up at his dad, and then back to the bow. Nemery dropped to a crouch in front of the kid, offering him the single arrow.

"See this?" she asked, pointing to a dark mark on the shaft just above the stone arrowhead. "Dragon blood. It's so hot when it come out of the beast that it chars the wood."

The boy rubbed his fingers along the arrow in obvious admiration. In reality, the arrow was a reject, a hidden knot in the shaft making it too weak to shoot from her heavier bow. The charred mark came when Mohdek had used the blank shaft to stoke the campfire. Then the next morning, Nemery had decided to throw on some fletchings and an arrowhead so she could sell it at New Vantage.

"And where did you come by this?" asked the father.

Nemery stood to face him, taking the arrow from the boy's hand. "Shot it myself. I'm part of a Harvesting crew," she lied. "We spooked one of the hatchlings last cycle and I got a shot off before it killed two of my companions and fled."

"Aren't you a bit young for Harvesting?" he questioned.

"Aren't you a bit old for fathering?" she followed up. "It takes all kinds."

Nemery grimaced. Her quick tongue had probably just spoiled the deal. She needed to work on that. Ardor Benn had once told her that words were a tool, to be used carefully, and only for their intended purpose.

"Can we get it, Father?" the boy asked.

"A gentleman's weapon is a gun," he replied. "Your attention should be on mastering that. Not shooting some antiquated tool."

He was one to talk about antiquated. Guns and Blast Grit fit the racket of the cities. Pekal demanded something more reverent. Something with greater finesse.

"Please, Father? You told me I could have a souvenir from New Vantage."

The man sighed wearily. "And you choose this? Very well." He looked at Nemery. "I'll give you seven Ashings for the bow."

She couldn't hold back a smile. That was far more than it was worth. "Done," she replied. The man dug into a velvet pouch and produced a seven-mark Ashing. She handed the bow to the boy and turned to leave.

"Hold on," the man called. "You forgot to give him the arrow."

"Oh," she remarked in mock surprise. "You said seven for the bow. It'll be three more for the arrow." Ardor would have been proud of that technicality.

The man huffed a bit, but he was committed now. He handed her a three-mark and Nemery gave the arrow to the boy.

Nodding in gratitude, she skipped across the courtyard and onto the porch of Burdal's Provisions, reaching up to swat a bell as she passed through the open door.

Well, *that* wasn't here last cycle. A Caller instrument had been set up in the corner of the shop, a sign propped in front of the wide brass bell.

FOR DISPLAY ONLY—NOT FOR SALE

Nemery examined the silken pull cords, little decorative wooden balls fastened to the ends. The vibration box looked like it was made of tempered steel, and there wasn't a dent or a scratch in the brass.

Well, she didn't need a fancy, top-of-the-line Caller instrument anyway. The cobbled, mismatched piece that she and Mohdek used worked just fine in the few situations where they actually needed to call a dragon.

"Look what the dragon dragged in!" cried a voice from behind the counter, pulling her attention away from the instrument. The man had a pleasant expression, his gray mustache drooping clear to the second fold of his chin.

"Morning, Burdal," Nemery greeted. "You're looking well. How was the Passing?"

"A real boost for business," he said with a wink. "You know how it is here. They brought in the largest orchestra yet."

"Always sounds like a party," Nemery admitted, though not one she wanted to be invited to. "On a clear, calm night, I can hear those trumpets halfway up the mountain."

He folded his eyebrows. "You shouldn't be up that far. Too close to the Redeye line."

She waved away his concern with a flick of her wrist. "The line's pushed clear up to the summit these days. Moh and I weathered the last Passing a mile up from Rock Creek."

Burdal shook his head like he didn't understand her fascination with the slopes. "What can I do for you, little Salafan?"

"I'm after salt today." She wasn't going to wait three miserable hours in New Vantage just so Mohdek could help her carry it. She'd make her way back to the outskirts, leaving a trail of clues in the streets that he couldn't miss.

"Salt again?" replied Burdal. "You just about cleaned me out, cycle before last. What kind of meat are you curing up there?"

"Mohdek," she replied with a half smile.

"Where is the strapping rascal?"

"He went down to the harbor for the *fajumar*," she answered. "My salt paste only goes so far."

"Ah," said Burdal, finally seeming to understand why she was buying in such large quantities. "Didn't know that worked for his kind."

"There's a lot you don't know about them," she said, perusing the nearest shelf. There was a jar of apricot preserves that was calling her name if she had an extra Ashing. Everything was so expensive here. "For example, did you know that Trothians snore through their eyes?"

Burdal leaned his stout form across the counter, thick brows knitting together. "No…"

Nemery laughed. "I'm yanking your chain, Burdal. They're not all that different than us. I think Trothians and Landers have more similarities than differences. People just decide to notice the latter." She slapped the seven-mark Ashing down on the counter. "How much can I get for this?"

"Salt?" Burdal clarified. "I'll give you twenty-five panweights."

"I need double that."

"Then it'll cost you twice that much."

Nemery forked over the three-mark—all she had. "There. Two coins. Twice as much."

"You know, that's not how numbers work…" Burdal said good-naturedly.

Movement at the door drew Nemery's attention. Two older men had entered the shop, stopping to admire the Caller instrument in the corner. One had a deep frown weathered onto his face, and the other wore a lacy neckerchief.

"I'd like sixty panweights of your coarsest salt," Nemery said, turning back to business with Burdal.

The shopkeeper chuckled. "Sixty, eh? I could have sworn I'd said fourteen Ashings would buy you fifty."

"Well, let's be honest, Burdal. Your memory probably isn't what it used to be," Nemery whispered out the corner of her mouth.

He shrugged. "You drive a hard bargain, Salafan." Then he disappeared into the storage room in the back of the shop.

THE LAST LIES OF ARDOR BENN

Nemery leaned casually against the counter, eyeing the two men in the corner. The one with the neckerchief was trying to explain to Frowny how the complex instrument worked. The instructions were only half correct, proving to Nemery that he understood less than he was claiming to know.

Burdal reappeared, lugging two large burlap sacks around the end of the counter. "*Fifty-five* panweights of salt for you, m'lady."

Nemery nodded in gratitude. Sixty had been pushing it, and Burdal was kind to throw in the extra five.

"Hey, Burdal," she said. "You heard of a guy named Legien Dyer?"

He stroked his long mustache. "Doesn't sound familiar."

"Word is, he's hanging around Raston's looking for a guide to help him summit," Nemery said.

"I didn't think you took clients," he replied.

"Who said I was thinking about it?" she asked.

"That look in your eyes."

"Excuse me!" called Neckerchief. "Would you mind terribly if I gave this a go?" He pointed at the Call.

Burdal reached out and gave Nemery's arm a squeeze. "If you and Mohdek decide to summit, make sure you're prepared."

*He has no idea I've done it before*, she thought.

"Supplies and equipment aren't cheap," Burdal continued, "but if it comes to your safety and survival, I want you to know I'd accept credit to make sure you have what you need."

Nemery acknowledged his generous kindness with a nod as the shopkeeper turned his attention to the two men in the corner.

"What exactly can I help you with?" he asked.

"My friend doesn't believe that I know how to work one of these," said Neckerchief.

"And if you do," said Burdal, "then we'll soon have a dragon flying down on New Vantage."

Neckerchief laughed awkwardly. "A valid point."

Burdal waved a joking hand at him. "Ten Ashings and I'll give you a pot of Silence Grit. That'll buy you ten minutes to play with the Call at no risk of being overheard."

"Sounds fair," he said, reaching into his pocket.

Fair? Ten Ashings was a gouge, and Burdal knew it. Money was flowing on New Vantage like cheap ale in the lower Eastern Quarter.

The shopkeeper reached behind the counter and withdrew a clay pot. Nemery took her time picking up her salt, curious to see how this would play out.

Burdal dashed the clay pot into the bottom of a pail that he'd set in front of the Call. The air in the corner of the shop turned hazy and the men's voices were instantly silenced, despite the fact that Nemery could still see their mouths moving.

Slowly, she hefted the two bags of salt. The drawstring ropes were thick enough to use as carrying straps, and she slung one over each shoulder.

By this time, Neckerchief was on one knee in front of the mouth-piece, his fingers pulling the silken cords to prime the rattlers in the vibration box. But his posture was all wrong. Crouching like that, he'd never get the breath support he'd need to achieve any sort of sustained Call.

Nemery sauntered toward the door, passing into the Silence cloud just in time to hear the man deliver a pathetic blast through the instrument. She winced, but told herself to keep moving. Neckerchief tried again, this time producing a louder sound that was even more upsetting.

Nemery was almost to the door when Burdal and Frowny clapped for the man's performance. She stopped. That sound was *not* clap-worthy. Before she realized what she was doing, she had lowered her bags of salt to the floor and turned to the men.

"That's not how it's supposed to sound," she stated. All three of them looked at her in silence. "The rhythm of the vibrations was off. And you didn't even touch the reed valves."

"Well…" said Neckerchief indignantly. "My apologies, little miss. I don't suppose *you'd* like to show us how it's done?"

"Actually, I would," said Nemery, gesturing for the man to get out of her way.

"Salafan…" Burdal muttered.

Nemery felt her heart race as she took a knee behind the instrument, her fingers pulling the cords at a steady tempo, priming the vibration box.

The Silence Grit would really allow her to let loose. She was about to see if she remembered the Calls her master had taught her more than four years ago. Calls she couldn't risk sounding on the mountainside of Pekal—*Fertilized Egg, Nesting Sow, Injured Hatchling.*

She decided on *Sparring Bull*, remembering it to be the most impressive. Her lips touched the brass mouthpiece, the metal still warm from Neckerchief's pitiful attempt.

Drawing in as much air as her lungs would take, she breathed life into the instrument. Her fingers danced across the valves, bending the long double reeds to change the pitch of the grating whine that screeched above the rumbling bass tones of the horn.

She held it a long time. Unnaturally long, her master would have said. But she liked the feel on her lips and the buzz on her fingertips. She held it because she could. And because she didn't know when she'd get the chance to sound that Call again.

When Nemery was finished, Burdal's Provisions fell eerily quiet, the three men staring in speechless wonder. Nemery stood up, walked around the large instrument, and hoisted her bags of salt over her shoulders. Reveling in the awed silence, she moved through the open door.

Maybe New Vantage had its perks. Mohdek would have accused her of showing off. But Nemery was glad to know that she could still handle herself in a social setting with strangers. That she hadn't lost her touch, living among the critters of the woods.

She stepped off the porch carefully, the ropes from the salt bags digging into her shoulders. As she moved across the courtyard, every heavy step seemed to remind her that she was walking away from five thousand Ashings and a *reason* to summit again.

She could buy a lot of salt with that kind of money. And she had three hours to kill before Mohdek was ready to leave. At the very least, it was worth swinging past Raston's to meet the client and decide if he seemed trustworthy.

Nemery turned, heading east across the courtyard. Fewer people looked at her with the salt on her back. She probably looked like a common servant girl.

She reached Mountainside Expeditions in little time, the architecture of the building intentionally rustic and adventurous. A smoky fire burned in a barrel out front, three muscular guides with sticks taking absentminded prods at the coals while swapping stories of the mountain.

"Bottle," Nemery called, recognizing one of the men. "I'm looking for Raston."

Raston Strick had been guiding hikes on Pekal since well before New Vantage—even before the war. His people guided single-day excursions mostly. If the price was right, and the weather cooperative, Nemery had heard of Raston's guides extending as far as week-long trips. But never to the summit.

"You got an appointment?" asked the woman by the fire barrel.

"She don't need an appointment," Bottle said to his companion. "Ain't you never met the infamous Salafan?"

"Salafan?" said the other man. "Isn't that a Trothian word?"

"Yeah," Nemery said. "It means *one who doesn't need an appointment*." All three of them chuckled.

"Boss is out today anyway," said Bottle. "Think he's trying to put some distance between him and the squeaky wheel."

"Legien Dyer?" Nemery asked.

"You know him?" asked the woman.

"Not yet," replied Nemery. "Where is he?"

Bottle gestured to the building with his smoldering stick. "Sitting inside. Moping."

"Why do you think we're out here?" said the other man. "We don't got the time or the fittings for what he's asking."

Nemery strode past the three guides, moving up the half-log steps and pushing open the door with her shoulder.

There was only one person inside the spacious room—a man seated on a bench against the wall. He had been slumped forward, his face in his hands in anxious boredom, but he sprang to his feet as Nemery moved through the doorway.

"I hear you're interested in summiting," she said, getting straight to business. Sunlight angled through one of the glassless windows, catching the man's hair in a way that accentuated the white on his temples.

"Yes," he said. His face, which seemed to have worried itself into a few extra wrinkles, lit from within. "Yes! Do you know someone who can take me?"

Nemery cleared her throat, setting down the salt bags. "I know a guide."

"I need to speak with him at once."

"You are," Nemery said. "And she's not impressed with what she sees. It takes an experienced hiker ten days to reach the summit. No offense, but you're old. And you don't look experienced." She was basing that assumption on the way Dyer's stomach hung slightly over his belt.

"You don't understand," he said. "I *have* to go up. If not to the summit, then as far as you can take me."

*Well, he didn't have any trouble swallowing that*, Nemery thought. No demands to hear her qualifications, or talk to someone who could vouch for her reputation. Maybe Dyer wasn't as chauvinistic as his initial comment had let on. Or maybe he was really as desperate as people were saying.

"I heard you were offering six thousand Ashings," Nemery said.

"Yes, of course," he replied quickly, earnestly.

Sparks. She should have said seven.

"And you'll still pay, even if we don't reach the summit?" she checked.

"As long as you do your best to get me up there," he replied. "I give you my word as a Wayfarist."

Nemery studied him for a moment. Despite her shift in faith, that word still carried weight to her. A person with strong convictions—which she could tell he was—did not swear it away lightly.

Besides, there was something pitiful and sad about Legien Dyer. She could see it in his stooping posture and the way he wrung his hands as if they were dishrags.

"All right," Nemery said. It might take some work to convince Mohdek. But the pay was unbeatable, and lately she'd been feeling the draw to summit again. This was just a good excuse.

"You'll want to get your pack together," she said. "Water skins and rations, you'll need a good blade, and a—"

"Everything is ready," he said. "Raston sold me a pack yesterday. Filled it with everything I'd need."

*Probably just trying to get rid of you, poor old man.* "Perfect. We'll leave the morning after the next Passing. Three weeks from now."

"What?" he cried, lurching forward a step. "We can't wait until next cycle. Please. We have to leave *now*."

Nemery drew back in puzzlement. "What's your problem?" she asked bluntly. "I'd heard you were pushy, but this just doesn't make sense. At the pace you'll be setting, we have the best chance of reaching the top if we give ourselves a full cycle."

He came forward another step. "I'm begging you," he whispered. "Just take me up the mountain. As far as you can. But we have to go before the Passing. Please. I have half the payment in my room at the Elegant Perch. I can get it to you before we leave."

"Ha. So I can carry three thousand Ashings up the mountainside?" Nemery scoffed. "This salt is heavy enough."

"No need to take the money with us," he said. "You can keep the payment at your home."

Oh. That made more sense. Except that her home was the mountain.

Nemery took a deep breath and picked up the salt bags. "I'll collect the money when we get back."

"Then you agree to take me?" he asked hopefully.

"Only if you calm down," she said, hoping she didn't regret this decision.

"Oh, Homeland bless and keep you," he muttered. "When do we leave?"

Nemery turned to the door. "As soon as my boyfriend gets his skin put back together."

~

*Time spent on Pekal is not without its consequences. For some, it is a spark of wildness in the heart. For others, a desperation to return to the Greater Chain. For me, it is a reminder that there are forces out there greater than anything I could ever hope to be.*

# CHAPTER

# 11

Ardor Benn glanced over his shoulder one more time, despite feeling confident that no one could have followed his erratic route from the Mooring. Cupping a hand around his mouth, he cooed twice like a pigeon. Then he waited, leaning against a punky wooden beam holding up the wall of a run-down healer's shop.

Ard had no interest in the healing store. It was the cheap kind that sold mostly herbs, tonics, and bandages, too lazy to acquire the necessary licensure for selling Health Grit. Instead, Ard's eyes lingered on the low, flat-roofed building across the street.

Most of the businesses were already closed for the evening, leaving the street quiet and peaceful. Pinkish-golden hues of sunset spilled over Ard's shoulder, lighting a little cloud of gnats that hung like a cloud in front of the building's sign.

TALL SON'S MILLINERY

Ard didn't know if the shop was named after a son in the Tall family, or if the son was actually tall. The only thing he knew was that hats weren't the only things the millinery was keeping in stock.

"Didn't think you was coming," a small voice sounded behind him.

The street urchin couldn't have been ten years old. His bare feet were filthy and scabbed, his brown hair long and unkempt. But his pale skin looked a little less peaky each time Ard saw him. Maybe he was making a difference.

"Hello, Tobey," Ard said, smiling. "I was expecting Marah. I thought she was taking the evening shift."

"Is," Tobey replied. Ard noticed that he was holding what looked like a round ball of twigs about the size of his head. "But she weren't feeling good today, and we knew you was coming, so…" He shrugged and pointed at himself.

"Is she going to be all right?" Ard asked.

"Just the sniffles," Tobey said. "She's holed up out back of Genni's place, sleeping it off."

Ard held up a paper bag with spots of grease bleeding through the sides and bottom. "I brought you something."

The little boy set down his ball of twigs and crossed to Ard without hesitation, snatching the sack before moving to a bench in front of the healer's shop. Ard joined him, the wooden boards bending and creaking under his weight. No sooner had they settled in than Ard noticed the twig ball rolling across the street, seemingly of its own accord.

"Um…" Ard said as the boy reached a grubby hand into the bag, withdrawing a buttery croissant with an ooze of chocolate coming out the ends. "Your twigs are on the move."

"That's just Bunson," the boy said before taking his first bite.

"It has a name?" Ard raised an eyebrow.

"'Course," he replied, setting the bag aside and jumping down from the bench. "He's my pet." Tobey picked up the ball and held it out for Ard's inspection. Peering through the tightly woven twigs, Ard could see a brown-and-white rat inside.

"Is he stuck in there?" Ard asked.

Tobey laughed as if the notion were ridiculous. Then he cradled the ball in the crook of one arm while working a straight twig out of the weave. This allowed him to open a little door in the side of the ball, through which he dropped a flaky piece of croissant.

The rat squeaked its gratitude and Tobey closed the door, pushing the stick in place to hold it shut.

"Did you make that thing?" Ard asked, impressed with the creative engineering.

"Yup," Tobey replied, setting the twig ball down on the street. "I keeps him in there so he don't get lost." He walked over and took his seat on the bench again.

Ard didn't point out that maybe Bunson *wanted* to get lost. That rats could fend for themselves in this city better than orphans. But Tobey clearly liked having something to take care of. And Ard wasn't going to ruin that.

"Anything to report?" he asked as the boy picked up the pastry bag again.

"I got inside a few days back," the kid said proudly.

"Tobey, no!" Ard scolded, his voice a little harsher than

intended. Sparks, maybe it was a terrible idea to employ homeless children. He took a deep breath and tried again. "I appreciate your enthusiasm, but I hired you and the girls to watch the *front* of the shop. I'm not paying you extra to get inside."

"It's just hats, Mister Ash," Tobey said through a mouthful.

Ard hadn't told the orphans what to call him, so Kelse had made up her own nickname a few cycles back. Mister Ashing. It stuck with the others, eventually earning a subtler abbreviation. Ard went along with it now. After all, he'd certainly been called a lot worse in his time.

"They gots all kinds," Tobey said, swallowing. "Rain caps, sun hats…lots of those three-point kind the rich folk like."

"That's a good report," Ard said. "You'd almost think it was a hat shop."

"Is," Tobey said, missing the sarcasm as he dove for another pastry. "And I don't think there's nothing more to it."

"Leave that for me to decide," Ard said. "You see anything else this week?"

"Delivery, day before yesterday," Tobey said.

"What was it?" Ard asked. "Did it come in a box?"

"Not this time," Tobey answered. "Just some cloth. Bundle of straw—what's that about?"

"Probably for weaving sun hats," Ard said. Nothing unusual.

"Guess that figures," the boy said. "Marah said she saw a delivery, too. Same night. Just after dark. Couple of big heavy boxes. Like the ones I saw two cycles ago."

Ard nodded silently. There was the news he'd been hoping for. Why hadn't the boy led with that? He didn't need details—the amount being delivered didn't actually matter. Ard just needed to make sure that Tall Son's Millinery was still serving as the storage place.

"Think they're hiding something, Mister Ash?" Tobey interrupted his thoughts, a flaky piece of croissant clinging to the corner of his mouth.

"Nah," Ard said dismissively. He didn't think it. He *knew* what they were hiding.

Dragon shell.

After the debacle of Prime Isle Chauster and King Pethredote destroying centuries' worth of shell, Olstad Trable had been wise not to make the storage site publicly known. It was even a secret in the Mooring, except among a handful of the most trusted Holy Isles. It had actually taken Ard longer than he'd like to admit to figure out its location, though no one suspected him of knowing it—not even Raek.

"Anything shipping out of the shop?" Ard asked. His biggest concern about the millinery in the Western Quarter was that it would only be a temporary place to store the shell. That, more than anything, was why he'd hired the orphans to keep watch.

"Between Kelse, Marah, and me," said Tobey, "counted only two hats sold this week."

That was a good sign. Ard had told them to keep an eye out for large boxed shipments going out. "Business is slow for the tall son."

"Don't know why it's called that," said Tobey. "Isn't even a son what runs the place."

"What makes you say that?" Ard checked.

"Only gots two folks working there," said Tobey. "Fat old woman and a man."

"Is he tall?" Ard asked. "Maybe he's the son."

Tobey shook his shaggy head. "Can't be. He's too old."

Ard chuckled. "That doesn't mean he's not a son. Everyone had a father sometime."

"Not I," said Tobey, like it was something to be proud of.

"Yes. Even you," Ard said. "I guarantee it."

The boy suddenly turned to him, pausing mid-chew with his eyes open wide. "Ashes and soot," he muttered. "Are you my pops, Mister Ash?"

Ard cuffed him playfully on the shoulder, downplaying the boy's utter sincerity.

"Flames, no, you little street lizard." Ard dug a pouch of Ashings from his belt. "Now get out of here before I gut you and take back those pastries."

Tobey jumped off the bench, rolling the paper bag shut over whatever was left of the croissants.

"Hup!" Ard cried, flicking an Ashing into the air. The polished dragon scale went just high enough to glint in the setting sunlight. Then Tobey caught it with a grin.

"Here are some for the girls," Ard said, passing him two more Ashings. "Make sure those get to them." He gave the boy a stern look. "And next week, I'm going to start getting suspicious if I don't see Marah or Kelse."

"Don't worry, Mister Ash," Tobey said. "Wouldn't try nothing. Not strong enough to hide the bodies."

"Sparks," Ard muttered as the little boy scooped up his rat ball and ran off. "You're too young to make jokes like that!" he called as Tobey disappeared around the corner. Ard chuckled to himself and turned one more glance toward Tall Son's Millinery.

He needed to tell Raek about this place. Ard knew his partner wanted to steal the dragon shell—all of it—to make sure the Isle-hood could never make more Visitant Grit. To make sure that no one would be capable of traveling through time and erasing this existence.

Ard wasn't convinced that taking the shell was the right move. After all, that was essentially the same thing Pethredote and Chauster had done nearly a decade back. Look at the trouble that had drummed up.

Maybe it was better to let the Islehood store it. Let them keep tinkering with it. Prime Isle Trable wouldn't likely succeed in summoning a Paladin Visitant without the knowledge he needed from the Anchored Tome.

And what was the point in stealing all the shell anyway? The dragons were flourishing now, with more being born every cycle.

Steal the shell now, and the Islehood would just get more. Raek was sure they could stay ahead of it, but Ard wasn't convinced that he wanted to live out his days as a habitual shell thief.

And then there was the matter of Ard's studies. If he told Raek about Tall Son's Millinery, his partner would insist that it was time to leave the Islehood. Ard's research would come to an abrupt end, and he'd never discover the true meaning behind the Great Egress.

Not that he was making big strides in that area anyway. After a year of studies, did he understand it any better? The only thing he really knew was that all the signs had come to pass. Signs that predicted a huge departure to the Homeland.

But which Homeland? A long-lost distant continent? The remnants of an ancient civilization on the bed of the InterIsland Waters? Or the transformation to a more powerful and perfected being like Gloristar?

A scream cut through Ard's thoughts. It was close. Familiar. It sounded again, this time punctuated with a cry for help.

Tobey.

In a flash, Ard was moving down the quiet street, slipping a loaded Roller from its holster. His other hand clutched a small pot of Barrier Grit as he clenched his jaw and sprang around the corner.

Hedge Marsool stood in the middle of the narrow lane, his half-bald scalp covered with a black tricorn hat. Tobey's small figure was grappled tightly against the man's body, held in place with Hedge's one good arm. Bunson had fallen to the street, the ball of twigs rolling away as Hedge's spike hand pressed against Tobey's back.

"Let him go," Ard said, keeping his voice calm. He couldn't help but picture the man holding that cat underwater in the *Be'Igoth*. Skewering a helpless street orphan seemed like the next step.

"But I caught him stealing," Hedge said pragmatically.

"What did he take?" Ard asked.

Hedge reached out a toe and kicked the greasy paper bag that Tobey had dropped to the stones. "Your dessert."

Ard lowered his gun, risking a step forward. But he didn't fool himself into thinking that the situation was actually diffused. "He's not a thief. I gave the boy some food."

"And the Ashings?" Hedge asked, spreading the three coins between his fingers like a performer in the Char.

"What can I say," Ard remarked. "I was feeling charitable tonight."

"Pandering to the beggars…" Hedge said. "What does that teach them? Like feeding a stray. Don't know about you, but I'd like to keep the Western Quarter a nice place." He flexed and Tobey let out a scream.

"Stop!" Ard shouted, raising his Roller again. "The kid is just passing through. Let him go."

Hedge tilted his head, ugly face darkly shadowed beneath the brim of his hat. "And here I thought the boy watched these streets for you."

Ard felt the grip of hopelessness reaching out for him, remembering the kind of adversary Hedge Marsool had become. Unbeatable.

"Fine," Ard spit. "I've been paying the boy."

"Why?" Hedge asked. "What's around here that strikes your fancy?"

Ard shrugged, keeping his gun up. "I'm sure you already know."

"That's not how it works," he said. "But I could find out easily enough."

*Not how it works?* This only supported Ard's hypothesis that Hedge's ability to see into the future was not omniscient. It was reliant on something. He remembered the broken glass vial in the *Be'Igoth*. If it was Grit, Ard needed to make sure his enemy didn't detonate any right now.

"He's watching the hat shop!" Tobey blabbed, his face turned sideways against Hedge's chest.

The crippled man glanced back down the street toward Tall Son's Millinery. "Got your eye on a new cap?"

"I've never really been a hat guy," Ard said, trying to stall. Anything to keep that pike from killing the boy. "I mean, I'd love a big tricorn like yours, but I don't think I could pull it off. As a fashion statement, you understand?"

"Slinking around behind my back," muttered Hedge. "Keep that up and you won't have a thinker to put your new hat on."

"That's why you followed me?" Ard said. "More threats?"

"Followed?" cried Hedge. "You forget. I always know where you'll be."

"Then you're just here to prove a point?" Ard said. "I'll consider this a reminder."

"I'm here to kill two birds with one stone," said Hedge.

*Homeland*, Ard prayed. *Don't let one of those birds be Tobey.*

"I wanted to have a little chat about the job," Hedge said. "At the same time, you tell me your obsession with the millinery."

"And the boy?" Ard said. "What part does he play in your big plans?"

"He stops you from trying to shoot me," said Hedge.

Fair enough. At this distance, hitting Tobey was too great a risk.

"If the boy is only here for your protection," said Ard, slowly clicking down his Roller's hammer as he lowered the gun, "then I'll put down my weapons and you let him go. You and I can talk to each other like civilized men."

"Civilized!" Hedge chuckled. "That would require a good amount of pretending from both of us."

"Sure." Ard slowly holstered his Roller and unbuckled his Grit belt. With overly exaggerated movements, he set them in the street and took a step backward, fully realizing how vulnerable he'd just made himself. But his own safety wasn't really in question here. Hedge wouldn't kill his own employee. At least not until the job was done.

"Now, release the kid," Ard said.

Hedge beckoned with his pike arm. "Come closer."

Ard stepped over his weapons and approached the man, stopping at arm's length. Beneath Hedge's long brown coat, Ard could see a well-stocked Grit belt—a Roller holstered on the right, an array of clay Grit pots nestled in hardened leather pouches, and something else. Something Hedge Marsool should not have had…

Hedge's scarred face slowly twisted into a smile. He grunted, thrusting his pike arm through the back of Tobey's shirt.

Ard cried out, lunging for him. He barreled into the awful man, pawing desperately as he tried to grab Hedge's arm.

But Hedge Marsool merely laughed. He let go of Tobey, who, to Ard's surprise, did not slump to the ground. Instead, the boy jumped away with a yelp. In relief, Ard saw that Hedge's spike had merely torn through the urchin's ragged shirt, leaving not so much as a scratch on his skin.

Tobey scampered around the corner, tripping once as he scooped up his pet rat, the twig ball having gotten stuck in a pothole of a missing cobblestone. Then the poor kid dashed away, never looking back, his bare feet slapping the street.

"Walk with me," Hedge said, shrugging away from Ard.

Ard cast a glance at his own belt and guns lying in the street. The poacher must have noticed, because he added. "Fine gear, but nobody's going to take it. The street is ours for now."

Well, that explained the lack of foot traffic for such a lovely evening. Hedge's goons must have blockaded both ends of the street.

"The millinery," Hedge said. "Why is it important to you?"

Ard cleared his throat. "It's personal," he began. "I'd rather not—"

"I like what you did with the *Be'Igoth*," Hedge cut him off unexpectedly.

"Um…thanks?" Ard said. He wasn't surprised to learn that Hedge had stopped by the soakhouse while Ard wasn't there. After all, the King Poacher had the run of Tofar's Salts. As far as secret hideouts went, Ard realized it was their least secure, since their evil employer actually had a key.

"I assume you drained the bath before you floored it over?" Hedge asked.

Ard took the question as a good sign. It meant that Hedge hadn't noticed the trapdoor, either on his own, or using his ability to predict the future.

"We had it drained, yes," answered Ard. "Though I don't know how they removed all that water." This comment would lead Hedge to believe that he didn't know about the sluice gate drain, Ard's secret escape route.

"You realize what a leech you are to my business?" Hedge said. "Every day you're in the *Be'Igoth* means Trothians aren't. That's Ashings down the drain."

"You said we could use it—"

"Forever? No. I expected you to be making better progress in getting my dragon."

"We've actually been making great headway," Ard countered.

"Ho, really?" Hedge's mouth twisted in a grin. "Last I heard, you were being held in a hole on Ra Ennoth waiting for the seawater to fill your lungs."

"All part of the plan," Ard said. "They let me go eventually. I knew they would."

"There are no dragons on the Trothian *skals*." Hedge stopped walking. His tone was unamused.

"We were just doing things in the order you specified," Ard replied. "You made it clear that we needed to secure a space for the dragon before we moved it off Pekal. Baroness Lavfa's demands sent us to Ra Skal. We got what we needed."

"Then why haven't I seen the agreement for Lavfa's property in Helizon?" Hedge demanded.

"Well, we didn't get it *yet*," Ard said. "We have her payment. We're just waiting to deliver it."

"Waiting?" Hedge snapped. "I did not hire you to wait."

"Technically, 'hiring' us would imply that there'll be some kind of payment," Ard dared.

"Not all payments are in Ashings, son," said Hedge. "I'll uphold my part."

*Not to transform your men into Glassminds*, Ard thought. *How kind of you*. He would have said it aloud to almost anyone else, but Hedge Marsool was not to be trifled with.

"I find myself in a delicate position," Ard explained. "I was the one who met with Baroness Lavfa, so I need to be the one to deliver the goods she asked for. Unfortunately, I can't exactly go galavanting over to Talumon right now."

"Oh?"

"I'm in a bit of hot water with the Prime Isle right now," Ard said. "Well, maybe just uncomfortably *warm* water. You see, Trable didn't exactly sign off on having me go to the Trothian islets. In fact, the whole thing sort of reflected poorly on him. When I got back, he should have pulled me into remediation, but I've already had too many warnings and that would have gotten me suspended from the Islehood. Trable's a good guy and he didn't want that to happen—especially since so many people were paying attention after the Trothians released me. Instead, we reached another agreement."

"What's that?" Hedge seemed only mildly interested in the story.

"No time off," replied Ard. "For two weeks straight, he wants me putting in time at the Mooring—sunup to sundown. The sunup part isn't going great for me, and I had to skip out a little early today. But otherwise, I've been doing what he asked."

"And this is why you haven't delivered the payment to Baroness Lavfa?" Hedge clarified. "Because you made a promise to the Prime Isle?"

"Yeah," Ard said. It was the truth. The black backpack was loaded and ready. But Raek couldn't make the delivery—he'd insulted the baroness and been shoved out the window of the catamaran. Quarrah's face would be unfamiliar to Lavfa, which might spook her. Ard had worked hard to earn the baroness's trust, and he felt it important to be the one to make the delivery. Even if it meant waiting a couple of weeks.

"Only four more days," Ard said, "then I'll be setting sail for Talumon so I can—"

Hedge spun on him, raising his spike arm and stopping the point under Ard's chin with frightening precision. "I don't know what game you're playing with the Islehood, but let me be clear about something. Your first job is to get me a dragon. I'm waiting—patient as a man can be. And I know you'll do what I ask, because I've seen the future. But the amount of *prodding* to make it happen"—he jabbed his pike tip until it pressed into Ard's skin—"is up to you."

"I'll get it done," Ard croaked. "Sparks."

"While I have you here…" Hedge's single eye bore into Ard. "What's your interest in the millinery?"

"I said, it's personal."

"I like personal," replied Hedge unyieldingly.

"My folks," Ard whispered. "My mother and father own the business. They thought I was killed in a Harvesting accident on Pekal over ten years ago. I didn't want them to know that I'd taken up rusing, so I stayed dead to them."

The lie had been inspired by his little conversation with Tobey about the hat shopkeepers, but there was actually quite a bit of truth to it. Those made for the best kinds of lies.

"I hired a few street urchins to keep an eye on the shop," Ard continued, aiming to extinguish the last bit of distrust in Hedge's eye. "The kids tell me how my folks are faring. Sometimes I swing by to peek through the window myself."

Hedge Marsool stepped away abruptly, dropping his spike. Taking up a fistful of his long coat with his other hand, he polished the sharp point as if it were a habit to wipe it clean of his enemy's blood.

"You lied to me," he stated flatly.

"I swear I didn't—"

"Arelia and Sidon Castenac are living in a comfortable little cottage on a hillside above the farmland village of Sunden Springs—southern leeward Espar."

Ard stood in speechless horror. Raek was the only other person in the world who knew where his parents were living. Raek had moved them suddenly—secretly—using the Ashings they had coined from their first ruse.

If Hedge Marsool knew this, then nothing was safe.

"They do indeed believe you're dead," continued Hedge, "but you never so much as peeked through a window at them."

"How…" Ard finally stammered. "How are you doing this?"

"If you won't tell me the truth about the millinery," said Hedge, "then I'll do some digging on my own."

He let go of his long coat and shrugged his shoulders so it would hang straight. "Get me that dragon, Ardor Benn." He turned and limped away, calling over his shoulder. "I won't ask again!"

Ard stood still long after Hedge had turned down a side street, vanishing as night came on. Then he finally dared look at the item he'd been clutching in his closed fist for most of the conversation.

It was a small glass vial.

He'd taken it from Hedge's belt when Tobey had wriggled free. It was hard to see it clearly with the darkness setting on, but Ard could see a fragment of Slagstone submerged in a liquid solution. And what was stranger still, the liquid had no color.

Portsend Wal had dyed all of his liquid Grit solutions for ease of identification. But even before the color was added, the liquid was usually hazy, or even milky, depending on what had gone into the solution.

As Ard held his newly acquired glass vial up to the darkening sky, he saw that this liquid was glass-clear, like pure water.

*Raek will be thrilled to analyze this*, Ard thought, pocketing the vial and turning back to find his belt and guns.

Ard was thrilled, too. If the item he had just stolen was what he thought it was, then Hedge Marsool was about to lose his advantage.

And the future would belong to Ardor Benn.

～

*I only ever bit off what I knew I could chew. I only ever tackled the enemies I knew would go down.*

# CHAPTER

# 12

Nemery glanced up from the muddy tracks just in time to see Legien Dyer's foot slip from the log and plunge calf deep into the crystal-clear stream they were crossing. The man's boots were barely holding up after a week of hiking, and a wet foot inside them was only going to lead to more blisters. Still, he managed to stay upright, slogging with one foot in the water and the other on the log until he reached the far side.

Mohdek was there to greet him, helping him through the mud with an encouraging pat on the arm. Dyer was actually faring better than Nemery had expected. He never complained. In fact, he rarely said anything, his eyes constantly fixed on the trail ahead and the sweeping greenery of Pekal.

Nemery understood his awe. This island was so vastly different from any other—in its terrain, the way it teemed with life, the very energy that seemed to emanate from the soil itself. Even after an uninterrupted year exploring its ravines and ridges, Pekal never got old to Nemery Baggish.

Unlike so many others, she wasn't here to take or exploit. Nemery considered herself a daughter of Pekal, like Izmit, in the Trothian legend. The island was her master, and she and Mohdek felt fortunate to learn at her feet and experience her majesty each day.

Nemery pulled off her wide-brimmed woven grass hat and dunked it in the stream. She put it back on, cool rivulets of water tracing lines down her sweaty neck. Summer on Pekal brought beautiful crisp nights, but the days were quite hot. And the sun was closer the higher they hiked, quicker to burn unconditioned skin.

She scanned the messy array of tracks one last time before leaping nimbly to the log and crossing to the other side of the stream to hear Mohdek's report.

"I count a dozen," she said in Trothian. "Maybe a few more."

"Me, too," replied Mohdek, stepping away from Dyer, who had seated himself on a rock to remove his wet boot.

"That's a big party, Moh," she said. "And I'd say they're less than a day ahead of us."

They'd picked up the poachers' trail a few days ago, not far out of New Vantage. Going by the tracks, the group had had a week's head start, but they clearly weren't as experienced as Nemery and Mohdek. They knew enough to take the easiest route up, though. And now that she had finally gotten a better headcount, Nemery was beginning to rethink their usual strategy.

"Maybe we should cut over to Rangdon's Pass," she suggested to her partner. "See if we can get around them."

"Come on," Mohdek said playfully. "What have you done with my Salafan? Poachers, Nem. Isn't that why we're here?"

Nemery cast a glance at their battered, weary client. "How are you holding up?" she called to him in Landerian.

"What about the poachers?" Legien Dyer questioned. "How far ahead are they?"

He asked about them often, and Nemery regretted ever telling him that they were behind the group.

"We're not worried," she replied. "It's almost midday. What do you say we stop for lunch?"

"Oh, I can go a bit further yet," he replied, reaching for the large pack he had dropped next to his rock. He was a blazing hardy old man, and Nemery admired his resolution.

"But what will we do if we catch up to them?" he asked.

*We kill enough of them to make sure that those who survive never come back to Pekal*, Nemery thought.

Large snares and traps were Nemery's preferred method, set quietly around their camp in the dark of night. That way, she and Mohdek didn't even need to stick around to watch them struggle.

But sometimes, the terrain and supplies didn't allow for that. In such cases, Nemery would have to find a good perch and maim a few of them with arrows. So far inland, an injured poacher would have slim chances of making it out alive. And if he did, he'd certainly rethink making a return expedition.

There was another method to eliminate poachers, of course. By far the most effective. But Nemery had sworn never to do it again. The carnage had forever scarred her mind and the tactic had left her empty. Guilt-ridden.

And it had earned her yet another name among the poachers, this one cold and ruthless—misrepresentative of who Salafan should be.

"If we don't bother them, poachers'll generally leave us alone," she lied instead.

Dyer tugged on his boot and rose with a groan.

"With a group this size, we'll definitely have to hit them at night," Mohdek said in Trothian. Then he switched to Landerian. "I should go ahead and make sure we don't run into any surprises."

"Good idea," Nemery said. "Stay within whistle range."

Mohdek pulled down the front of his loose shirt. Flames, was he tempting her in front of Dyer? His hairy blue chest hadn't started chapping yet, but Nemery could still see a crust of the dried salt paste she'd rubbed on him last night.

Mohdek tapped the wooden whistle hanging from a twine around his neck, wrinkling his nose at her—a cultural sign of coy affection, the Trothian equivalent of a wink.

She watched him move quickly up the switchbacks leading away from the stream. His legs were so strong and they carried his brawny form with ease. Mohdek was only a few cycles older than Nemery, but he was muscular and broad shouldered, well settled into his physical maturity. To most people, Nemery probably still looked like a rangy youth—small, flat-chested, light on her feet. It seemed she had sprung straight to womanhood with little change to the shape of her body.

Legien Dyer cleared his throat conspicuously. He'd probably noticed the way she'd been staring after Mohdek. The man hadn't said anything about their relationship, but Nemery could tell it made him uncomfortable, especially when they snuggled into the same hammock at night.

Any good Wayfarist would view their relationship as base and Settled. Landers and Trothians were incompatible races, unable to produce children. But Nemery and Mohdek had found their love to be quite compatible. And they were well past caring what other people thought about it.

Dyer swung his pack onto his shoulders, grunting at the weight. Raston had done a decent job equipping him, but even Pekal's top guide packed too heavily for Nemery's liking. She and Mohdek carried much smaller backpacks, which would make them far nimbler in a pinch. They were loaded with only the bare essentials—Slagstone ignitor, rope, blanket, hammock, and a single water skin. Her heaviest item was a sack of salt to be rationed on Mohdek throughout the trek.

"Shall we?" Nemery led Dyer up the switchbacks, noticing that Mohdek had already vanished through the trees.

Halfway up, she pointed to a low bush on the side of the trail. "Those look a lot like the rockberries we ate last night, but these are actually mildly poisonous. You have to count the number of points on the leaves. What did you think of those rockberries? They're kind of an acquired taste, but they're packed with nutrients…"

She trailed off, noticing that Dyer didn't seem interested in the berries. Or if he was, the man had no breath to waste on a reply. He was doubled over, gasping. Sparks. Nemery wasn't even winded. They'd just started again.

"Anyway," Nemery said, "we'll get some game snares set around our campsite tonight. With any luck we could have some meat in the morning again."

That was supposed to be an encouraging thought, but it had no visible effect on the elderly man. This wasn't the first time Nemery had wondered if Legien Dyer would die on her. The thought had obviously crossed his mind, too. By the third night, he had given her the key to his room at the Elegant Perch, just in case. He had also told her the name of the treasury where she could withdraw the remaining amount, but Nemery didn't understand much of that. Besides, no amount of money could get her to sail off Pekal.

After two more short rests, they made it to the top of the switch-backs, the trail leveling. It was mostly up and down on Pekal, so Nemery had learned to appreciate the occasional stretch of flat trail. Although still nestled between two slopes, the view opened up a little more here. Across the canyon, Nemery could see a moss-covered cliff and—

"Look!" she cried, stopping abruptly. Legien Dyer must have mistaken her enthusiasm for a warning, and the poor man dropped into a defensive huddle.

"It's okay," she said, helping him up. "Over on that cliff. Do you see that mess of branches at the top?" She was pointing, and this time she wanted to make sure he acknowledged her.

"I…think so," he wheezed.

"Nest," she said reverently.

"What kind?" he asked.

She snickered before realizing he was sincere. "Dragon, of course. No other creature would build something that big. Every nest is made specifically for each egg."

"Has that one got an egg?" Dyer was at least pretending to be excited, though Nemery thought it was genuine.

"No way to tell from here," she said. "Dragons lay eggs year round—like people. Well, people don't lay eggs, but you get what I'm saying. There's not a season for it."

She squinted at the distant nest, wishing she had brought her spyglass despite the added weight.

"A sow dragon lays an unfertilized egg in a quiet, protected place. Then she leaves to build a nest," explained Nemery. "When a bull finds the gelatinous egg, he breathes fire to fertilize it and the shell becomes hard as stone. Once the deed is done, the mother's sense brings her back to retrieve the egg and she takes it to her nest to incubate. When it's time to hatch, the mother leaves and the baby dragon has to do it on her own."

"You've seen one hatch?" he asked.

"Not that lucky," she replied. "But Moh and I have found hatch sites and old nests."

"You've seen dragon shell?" said Dyer in unmasked amazement.

"Mostly little pieces," she said. "It's common for the hatchling to trample his shell to bits as his first show of strength. But we've found a couple of shell fragments big enough to process into Visitant Grit."

"What did you do with them?" he asked.

"We left them where they were," she answered honestly.

"You didn't take them to the Mooring Station on New Vantage?"

"For what?" she asked.

"The Islehood," he said. "For Visitant Grit. It's the law."

"Not my law," she said. "The dragons are not a resource. They're living creatures. Beautiful living creatures. They were almost wiped out once. Mohdek and I are here to make sure they're respected."

"How many of them have you seen?" he asked.

"*All* of them," she replied. "At least, Cochorin and all the mature sows."

"Cochorin?"

"Moh and I name them," she explained. "It means *saving breath* in Trothian. He's the miracle bull. And he's been doing his job. There are so many hatchlings it's been difficult to accurately record them. I think Fernleaf has mothered eight in the last year. They can lay up to three unfertilized eggs each cycle."

Legien Dyer stared at her, a new expression on his face. "How do you know so much about them?"

"I read a lot of books when I was a kid," she said. "Of course, all the books in the world can't beat practical experience." Another lesson she'd learned from Ardor Benn. "I've only been on Pekal for a year, but I've been able to disprove a number of—"

She stopped talking. Sparks. Why had she been talking so much? She could have missed it altogether . . .

Mohdek's whistle.

Nemery waited in silence, her hand raised to prevent Dyer from asking what was wrong. There it was again, a common listener sure to mistake it for the cry of a bird. Long. Long. Short.

That meant come quickly, with no particular need for stealth. Nemery broke into a run down the trail, slipping her bow from her shoulder and an arrow from her quiver.

"Hey!" Legien Dyer called. "Where are you—"

"Keep moving up the trail until you reach us," she called over her shoulder. "It's not far."

She sprinted through a patch of shade that held the telltale chill of never seeing daylight. Her short boots skipped over rocks and fallen trees, consistently finding the best footing on the rugged terrain.

In a moment, she caught up to Mohdek. He was standing in a clearing just off the trail, dappled light flecked across his square shoulders.

"Another one of the poachers' camps," she whispered in Trothian, coming alongside him to get a better look at the site. By this point they'd seen enough of them to know that this group took a terrible toll on the land. Healthy trees were carved up and cut down for no apparent reason, trash and debris carelessly littered.

"This one is the worst yet," Nemery remarked.

Camp had been set in a half circle clearing in the trees, all of the surrounding underbrush trampled or burned. It looked like they'd lost control of a fire, the scorch marks extending well beyond the campfire's ring of rocks.

Mohdek shook his head. "Something happened here. Something more than a rowdy night's rest."

She saw the signs of a hasty departure. One of the poachers had left a hammock strung between two trees. There was a half-cooked boar on a collapsed spit next to the fire. Its carcass had been mostly devoured, and Nemery saw the signs of wild animal scavengers.

"Did you find anything interesting?" she asked.

"I waited for you so I didn't disturb the tracks," he said.

"True love," Nemery whispered. But Mohdek seemed too distressed for her frivolousness. His vibrating eyes had homed in on something, she could tell.

He set across the clearing, careful where he put his feet. Nemery followed, only ten steps in when she saw the blood. It covered the grasses, laying them over to the south.

"Dry," Mohdek said, crouching to inspect the blood. "But not old. I'd say this happened last night."

Nemery took five more steps in the direction the grasses leaned. Her heart rammed to a stop against her ribs and she recoiled.

"Moh!" she cried, pointing.

There was a body in the underbrush. Or at least part of one. His head was intact enough for Nemery to realize it was a young man. But his middle had been ripped open, and it looked like every bone in his body had been broken.

"Dragon," Nemery whispered, holding her stomach together for another look. "It had to be." What else could shake a man with such bone-shattering force? And that would explain the scorched clearing.

"What is it?" gasped Legien Dyer, finally catching up to them, thundering haphazardly off the trail. "What do you see?"

Nemery held up her hand. "This isn't for the faint of heart," she warned. "Looks like one of the poachers got a taste of Pekal and we didn't even have to interfere."

Dyer's face paled and he desperately pushed past Nemery to get a look for himself. "Oh," he muttered, almost gagging. "Oh, praise the Homeland."

*Praise the Homeland?* That a poacher got gutted? Sparks, maybe there was a dark streak to this guy that Nemery hadn't seen.

"Well, maybe that'll spook the party back down," Nemery continued.

"Tracks," Mohdek said. He was walking away from her, heading into the trees at a crouch. "Oh, Nem," he whispered. "It was a baby."

She scrambled over to him, seeing the first clear track in the soft soil. The print was significantly larger than her open hand, but it was small for a dragon. So small. And there was blood here, too. But not human.

"No!" Mohdek shouted, breaking from his tracking posture and sprinting forward.

Nemery saw it then, the little hatchling lying on its side among the ferns.

"She's still breathing," Mohdek said, dropping to the hatchling's side.

"Can you see where she's hurt?" asked Nemery. They were both speaking in their native languages, too shocked and frantic to use any extra brainpower to translate.

The dragon was small. Maybe a runt to begin with, or just younger than any hatchling Nemery had seen before. Still, it was at least the size of a Dronodanian buffalo.

The hatchling's scales were such a pale green, they looked almost white, with darker stripes developing on her flanks. Nemery reached out, pausing with her hand above the creature's side. This was the moment. She had dreamed of it for as long as she could remember, though the circumstances were spoiling it a bit.

She touched the dragon.

Her dark skin was a stark contrast to the shimmering creature, its raspy breath gently pushing Nemery's hand up and down. The hatchling's scales hadn't hardened yet, still relatively soft and supple, like a tanned leather.

"She's losing a lot of blood from the underside," Mohdek said, his Trothian eyes perceiving something that Nemery couldn't. "We need to roll her over. On three. You ready?"

Nemery repositioned herself, sliding aside one of the hatchling's wings, which lay unfolded like a discarded blanket.

Mohdek counted, and the two of them strained against her hulking form. The sudden movement seemed to send a shock of panic through the animal and she let out a cry that Nemery immediately recognized.

*Hatchling in Distress.*

It wasn't very loud, but if the mother was anywhere nearby, this situation could turn deadly in a matter of moments. Still, their effort was enough, and the small dragon flopped onto her other side when she couldn't find the strength to stand.

"Holy sparks!" shouted Legien Dyer. "It's still alive!" Nemery hadn't even realized he had joined them. "You've got to kill that thing," he continued. "Kill it fast before it gets up."

Nemery ignored their ignorant onlooker, finally getting a clear look at the cause of the hatchling's pain. A spear had pierced the dragon's side, just behind its foreleg. Nemery didn't know how deep it had penetrated, but the broken shaft protruded a few inches from the hatchling's skin.

"We need to pull it out," said Mohdek.

"She's so young," Nemery said. "Maybe only a day or two old. That could have been her nest across the canyon."

"And she attacked this camp so soon?" cried Dyer.

"She probably smelled the cooking meat," Nemery answered, remembering the hog on the spit. "Poor thing came to investigate and the poachers attacked her."

"Unless she attacked first," Dyer said.

"They're not like that," Nemery insisted. "Especially the young ones. Dragons are more reclusive than you might think. If they had given her the hog, she probably would have left them alone."

"Something doesn't add up," said Mohdek. "If the poachers attacked her, why didn't they finish her off?"

"Maybe they thought she got away," said Dyer.

"She's too close to the camp," Nemery pointed out. "And her soft scales would be worth a fortune."

"Scales, teeth, talons..." Mohdek listed. "All of her."

"So why didn't they kill her and strip her for parts?" Nemery asked.

She'd tracked a lot of poachers in her time on the island. If there was one commonality among them all, it was greed. Specifically when it came to dragons. An infant hatchling like this should have been easy prey.

Mohdek knelt down and gripped the splintered end of the spear with both hands.

"You really think we can do this?" Nemery asked.

"We can't leave her like this," he pointed out. "The moment I pull out the spear, I'll need you to put pressure on the wound."

"Okay. Okay." She nodded, trembling hands at the ready.

In one quick motion, Mohdek pulled out the spear with a squelching sound. The hatchling tried to bellow, but her body went limp, great green eyes rolling back in her head.

Nemery pounced on the wound as dark blood spewed upward. It was hot and sticky, and the smell was strangely sweet. She thought of that tale she'd told the young boy in New Vantage, grateful that the dragon's blood wasn't hot enough to burn her hands.

"Is she dead?" Nemery noticed that the dragon wasn't moving at all.

Mohdek cast aside the broken weapon, its metal spearhead basic and barbless. Daringly, he placed a hand on her muzzle, marring her beautiful nose with her own dark blood.

"She's still breathing," he whispered. "Just overcome by the pain. We need to stitch her up."

"You're trying to *save* it?" Legien Dyer exclaimed.

"I have a needle and sinew in my pack." Nemery gestured with her head to the spot where she'd dropped her things at the edge of the trees.

Mohdek hurried over and started digging through her belongings. "You think it'll be strong enough?"

"Get the big needle," she said. "The one for leather. And use the thick sinew that I spin for bowstrings."

In a flash, Mohdek was at her side as Nemery did her best to pull the wound together. It was difficult to see through the steady flow of blood. Mohdek tried to push the stout bone needle through the thick skin, but it wouldn't puncture.

"Try starting the hole with your knifepoint," Nemery suggested.

Mohdek dug the tip of his knife into the dragon's flesh, sliding the leather-stitching needle along the flat of the blade until he successfully punched through.

Through it all, the dragon remained unconscious, which was good, since the job was hard enough. It wasn't a pretty stitch, but Mohdek managed to close the wound. Still, blood flowed from the injury. Less than before, but steady enough that Nemery wondered if they were already too late.

"She needs Health Grit, Moh. She's not going to make it."

"Peeker's Hollow," Mohdek exclaimed, standing abruptly. "We've got Grit, and supplies, and—"

"It's more than a day's hike from here," Nemery cut him off. "In the wrong direction."

"It's our closest cache," he replied.

She and Mohdek had established stashes of supplies all over Pekal. They'd tried to spread them equidistant from one another, providing the greatest chance that they'd be able to reach one in a moment of need.

"Keep pressure on the wound until the bleeding stops," Mohdek instructed, shedding his backpack. "You," he said to Legien Dyer. "Try to find something to use for a bandage."

Mohdek stepped over and placed a hand on Nemery's shoulder, his speech slipping back into Trothian. "Once the bleeding has slowed, she might wake up. Try to get her to drink some water. I'll be back in two days."

Nemery nodded. Two days? Was this really happening? As much as she didn't like it, the Peeker's Hollow cache was probably their best shot at keeping this little dragon alive.

"If she squawks enough to call her mother," Nemery said, "Dyer and I will retreat downhill to that stand of Pichar trees. Did you see it?"

"I'll look for you there first," he said.

"We'll need to give her a glorious name if she survives," Nemery said.

"And a noble one if she doesn't," replied Mohdek. He stooped and kissed the top of Nemery's head. Then he pushed past Legien Dyer and disappeared through the trees.

Nemery kept her hands on the wound, feeling the hot blood between her fingers, praying for it to stop.

"Are you just going to stand there?" she finally snapped at Dyer.

"They're not poachers," he said quietly.

"What?" Nemery looked over at him.

"I know who we're following, and they're not poachers. That's why they weren't interested in this dragon."

"What are you talking about?"

"They're members of a religious cult known as the Glassminds."

Sparks. What was this nonsense? And if Dyer really knew something, why hadn't he mentioned it before?

"Bandages," she snapped. "Leaves. Vines. Anything you can find to keep some pressure on this wound."

"My son is with them," continued Dyer. "He's caught up in the ideals and beliefs of this cult. Their leader is a persuasive man. He's drawn my son in too deep, with promises of power and change. Feltman isn't much older than you." Legien Dyer let out a sudden sob. "They're going to kill him."

"Kill him?" Nemery cried. "Like…a sacrifice?" She didn't know much about cults, but she'd heard enough to know they could be dangerous.

"Yes," he said. "There is a group of them willing to die."

"They *know*? And they're going along with it?"

There were very few things Nemery Baggish considered worth dying for. Mohdek was one. Protecting Pekal and its dragons was another. And she supposed if she ever saw Ardor Benn or Tanalin Phor again, she owed them her life.

"They don't think they'll die," explained Dyer. "True believers within the cult think they can overcome death. That's why they're going to the summit." He paused, struggling against his emotions. "To get Moonsick."

As intrigued as she was, Nemery didn't have time for this conversation. The *hatchling* didn't have time for this conversation.

Realizing that Legien Dyer was useless, Nemery slowly released pressure on the dragon's side and stood up. It was still seeping, but the bleeding wasn't as intense as before.

Acting quickly, she plucked a dozen large green leaves and draped them over the wound. She hated to part with the coil of rope on her pack, but this was a worthy cause. With some difficulty, Nemery managed to bind the leaves in place.

She stepped back from the unconscious dragon, wiping a bead of sweat from her forehead. The sweat was replaced with a smear of dragon blood, and Nemery shook her hands at her sides.

"Poachers or not," she said to Dyer, "your son and his friends did this."

"I'm sure they were frightened," the man replied. "Feltman's never been to Pekal before. I don't think the cult is particularly violent, but—"

"But they just take their friends to the top of Pekal to get them Moonsick," Nemery cut him off.

"They don't think it will hurt them," said Dyer. "The cult's leader claims that the true believers will be transformed by the Moonsickness. Into something magnificent."

"And he got people to believe that slag?" she cried, not caring how insensitive it might seem toward Dyer's son.

"Feltman tried to convince me of it when I discovered that he'd aligned himself with the group," continued Dyer. "Their leader is a man named Garifus Floc. Feltman said he was a palace Regulator who survived the events in the throne room that night."

"That night?" Nemery questioned.

He looked at her curiously. "The night King Termain was killed."

"Oh," she replied. "I think I missed all that gossip." She and Mohdek had been living in the woods of Dronodan at that time. They hadn't found out about Termain's death until a cycle after the war had ended. By then, the details were so stale that Nemery had heard a hundred different versions, choosing to ignore them all.

"Garifus Floc is among those who claim that Prime Isless Gloristar assassinated King Termain," said Dyer.

"Wouldn't she have been executed for that?" Nemery said.

"At the very least, she would've been questioned…but no one can find her."

"The Prime Isless is missing?" Nemery cried. She'd heard that a man named Olstad Trable was now serving as Prime, but she'd assumed Gloristar had been simply replaced when Queen Abeth Agaul was made crusader monarch.

"Oh, yes," he said. "The logical public admits that Gloristar was also killed that night, her body never recovered. But Garifus Floc claims to have seen her transform."

"Transform?" Nemery said. "What does that even mean?"

"My son explained that her body had transformed into a perfected state—like one who had reached the Homeland. They call it a *Glassmind*."

"And your boy saw this?"

Dyer shook his head. "No. But this palace Regulator, Garifus, did. And he has been spreading the word. Quietly, of course. They don't want the Islehood coming after them for heresy. Still, they're gaining followers. Feltman told me that this Glassmind cult is more than five hundred strong."

That was actually not very big, considering the vast population of the Greater Chain. Beripent alone had a million citizens. This Regulator's cult was a drop in a bucket.

"Why do they call it Glassmind?" Nemery asked.

Dyer scratched his chin. "Feltman told me it had to do with the Prime Isless's new form. Her skull was made of pure red glass."

"I wouldn't call that perfected," said Nemery. "Sounds kind of fragile to me. And they're saying Moonsickness did this to her? How?"

Dyer shrugged helplessly. "It's the teachings of a madman leading my son to a horrible, Settled death. This is why I hired you.

Every Ashing I have…It'll be worth it if I can reach my son before the summit. Before the Moon Passing. I'll talk to him. Help him see the foolishness of his actions."

Nemery drew a deep breath. That sounded an awful lot like the conversation her parents had attempted when she'd returned from Pekal with an injured leg. Their words had not helped her see the "foolishness." They had pushed her away. She'd been back on a boat to Pekal as soon as her leg had been strong enough to run away from home.

"Children have their own ideas," Nemery said. "What you see as foolishness, he might see as the very reason for living."

"Or a reason for dying," the man muttered. "I don't care what Feltman thinks or believes. As his father, I have to do everything I can to stop him from throwing away his life." He shifted his awkward backpack. "You said the group is less than a day ahead of us. Let's go."

"We're not going anywhere." Nemery pointed at the hatchling. "Not until Mohdek gets back and we make sure she's going to survive."

"That could take days!" cried Dyer.

"Or weeks," said Nemery. "We're below the Redeye line here, so we can stay for cycles if we need to."

"That's not what I paid you for," he bellowed. "I need to find my son! Isn't his life more important than this little dragon?"

"Little dragons like this are what keep us *all* from getting Moonsick," she retorted.

Dyer moaned. "Of course, you're one of those Settled lunatics who doesn't believe in the Holy Torch."

That had been the first breaking point in her faith. When Nemery had heard the theory of the dragon shield, it had resonated with her. She had seen the majesty of the beasts, and she had no doubt that they were capable of protecting all humankind with their very presence.

"You're welcome to go ahead," Nemery said. "But I'm staying with her."

Surprisingly, Legien Dyer slipped out of his backpack and dropped to his knees in the ferns.

"Homeland," he prayed aloud. "End this dragon's life quickly, that a greater good might be served."

Then he rocked back, sitting on his heels, a steely glare cutting into Nemery. "When she dies, promise me that you will show as much care for my doomed son as you have for this hatchling."

Nemery felt her heart breaking for the desperate man. The strained look on his face . . . the tears moistening his eyes. Maybe he did deserve one last chance to speak with his son. "All right," she said.

"Swear it," he whispered. "Swear by whatever you love most in this world."

"I can't promise that we'll catch up to them," she said. "But I swear I'll get you as high as I can."

"And you're a woman of your word?"

"I swear it on my love for this place."

Tears began streaming down Legien Dyer's face. "Thank you," he said, voice so soft it was barely perceptible. Then he lunged forward, a dagger clutched in one hand. He fell upon the hatchling's still form, stabbing. *Stabbing.* Nemery let out a cry of horror, latching on to his back, trying to wrench him away.

But the older man was too determined. He had plunged the knife half a dozen times before finally giving up, leaving it buried hilt-deep in the dragon's neck.

Nemery wrestled him back, Legien Dyer slumping weakly into the blood-spattered ferns, sobbing. She crawled back to the hatchling, her own tears wetting her face. It was clearly too late.

The infant dragon was dead.

Nemery slowly reached out a hand, touching the creature's lifeless face, feeling the little ridge of raised scales on her muzzle.

"*Oropsi*," Nemery whispered, giving the dragon a Trothian name.

A name that meant *heartbreak*.

~

*Some have died for me. Some have died because of me. I never took any of it lightly.*

# CHAPTER

# 13

The *Double Take* listed on a wave and Quarrah watched the black backpack roll over. Ignoring whatever Ard was rambling about, she moved to midship to check the load.

Loosening the cinch on the top of the leather pack, she peered inside to make sure that the bricks from the Royal Concert Hall hadn't smashed the Agrodite Moon Glass to shards. It was an unnecessary worry. The red glass was much more durable than anything the Landers could make. It had taken a direct explosion from Quarrah's pot of Blast Grit to even break off that thin knife-shaped shard.

The events of that night still bothered her like a festering blister. Itching, making itself constantly remembered throughout the day. Making ordinary, routine things sting with pain. She smelled her hallucinations in the woodsmoke of Beripent. She saw them in a common spider on the wall, or a ratty-haired woman in the market...

And her mother's final words still rattled in her mind.

*"Point into the Homeland."*

She hadn't told Ard or Raek what had happened to her in the *Ucru*. The three of them had met at Tofar's Salts a handful of nights since, but she was grateful for Ard's commitment to be in the Mooring these past two weeks. It had given her plenty of time alone to process what had happened.

She had killed her mother. Never mind that it wasn't real. It had *felt* real, all the way down to the hot blood on her hands. Quarrah didn't know what kind of vision that smoke was supposed to induce, but she'd drawn her own conclusions.

She had killed her mother.

For so many years, Quarrah had wondered what had become of Jalisa Khailar. She couldn't imagine that the broken woman was still alive. And now Quarrah knew she wasn't.

Whether Jalisa still wandered Dronodanian streets or not, she was dead to Quarrah. And the smoke had forced her to face the question that had nagged her for most of her life. Had Quarrah been abandoned? Or had she run away?

The truth had been spit in her face during that horrific vision, and Quarrah was not at peace with it. Was she a runner? Had she ever stayed when the going got really rough?

She glanced at Ard. There was the opposite of running. The man who overstayed and overshared. Quarrah had left him because he didn't know when to run. He'd promised to change for her. But maybe Ard wasn't the only one who needed to change.

"Let's change course," Raek's deep voice shouted to Ard, cutting through her thoughts. "Three clicks to starboard."

"Why?" Ard called back from the tiller, making the adjustment anyway.

From his perch at the prow, Raek pointed off the port bow. "Bigger ship on the same course to Helizon."

"Shouldn't matter," said Ard. "We're far enough out."

He was right. They were in the middle of the InterIsland Waters between Espar and Talumon. Neither island could be seen on the horizon, and the naval traffic was far from congested.

Quarrah squinted in the direction Raek had pointed, but she could only see a blurry speck on the water. One of these days she'd wear her spectacles unabashedly in front of Ard. But today she wasn't in the mood to try to decipher how genuine his compliments would be.

"I'll bet they haven't even noticed us," Ard said. "I call it the big ship complex. Always expecting the little guys to change course, even if we were here first."

Quarrah cinched the backpack shut. It was about time they got this package delivered. The Moon Glass had been burning a proverbial hole in her apartment for half a cycle. They hadn't dared leave it in the *Be'Igoth* for fear that Hedge Marsool would come across it. So Quarrah had stored it in her Southern Quarter apartment.

"Quarrah," Ard called. "I've been thinking more about what you said."

Regarding...? And when had Ard had time to think? He was always talking.

"I'd like you to come with me to meet the baroness," he continued.

She definitely hadn't said anything about that. The fewer meetings she could attend in her life, the better.

"I'd rather not." She ducked under the yardarm and walked toward him. If this turned into a debate, she didn't want to be shouting her rebuttal.

"You said you wanted to come," pressed Ard.

"I said I'd do a sweep of her property to make sure you weren't walking into a trap." Quarrah drew even with him, noticing how he fidgeted with a particular glass vial in his right hand.

"You brought *that*?" Quarrah cried.

See, this was why Ard shouldn't be trusted with their only sample of Future Grit. And that was precisely why Quarrah had swapped his vial for a fake.

He quickly slipped it into his pocket as though she might steal it from him. Ha. Too late for that…

"Raek told me to bring it," said Ard. They had inspected the real vial in the *Be'Igoth*, but it was unlike any of the other solutions Portsend Wal had discovered. Raek had even dared taste it, declaring the clear liquid to be as sweet as nectar. But short of detonating it, there was nothing more they could learn.

"And if you lose it?" she asked. "Or drop it?" Or worse, *use* it? Quarrah knew Ard was itching to try it out—another good reason for her to keep the real vial hidden in her Northern Quarter apartment.

"It'll be fine," Ard said. "Raek has an old acquaintance at the University in Helizon. He's going to swing by and show it to her while we deal with Lavfa."

"No!" she snapped. An expert would only confirm the truth— that Ard's vial contained nothing more than sugar water. "I just…" Quarrah stammered. "I think we should be careful who we show it to." Then, as an afterthought. "What if she tries to claim it as her own discovery?"

She thought the reasoning was sound. The scientific world had turned upside down in the last two years. Ignition and Weight Grit were being mass-produced now, their cost steeper than powdered Specialty Grit. But more than that, the introduction of liquid Grit had proven that there were more types out there. The race to discover more was on, although no one had been successful yet.

The Realm had known about all the liquid Grit types except Metamorphosis. So even if Hedge Marsool had employed one of the few survivors of the Realm, it still wouldn't explain how he knew about creating Glassminds. Or how he'd developed yet another solution to show him the future.

"Raek's not going to give her the whole vial," Ard assured. "He'll separate some of the liquid and see if she can help him identify what went into the solution. If they can figure it out, we'll be on the fast track to making our own *Future Grit*. We'll see how Hedge Marsool likes it when we level the playing field."

"Hey, you two!" Raek swung under the yardarm, a spyglass in one hand. Quarrah found herself grateful for the distraction, her face turning red at the string of lies she was coming up with. She didn't regret taking the real vial. Ard's recklessness with the fake only confirmed her decision. She would take more cautious steps to uncovering the truth behind Hedge Marsool's mysterious Grit solution.

"We might have a situation." Raek pointed to the large ship that was sharing their heading. The vessel was close enough now that Quarrah could see the dual masts with her bare eye.

"Looks like they've set a new course," Raek said. "To intercept."

"Sparks!" Ard beckoned for the spyglass. "Who are they?"

"There's the clincher." Raek tossed him the item. "It's the *Shiverswift*."

"The *Shiverswift*?" Quarrah repeated.

"Pirates," Ard said, sighting down the spyglass. "You've been aboard that ship, remember? Captain Sormian Dethers and his crew picked us up after we encased the Slagstone in ice. They towed us away from Pekal."

Quarrah exhaled hopefully. "Friends, then."

"Not exactly," Raek muttered.

"Let me guess," said Quarrah. "You didn't pay them."

"Half," Raek said. "We paid them half upfront. The rest was... well..."

"I don't understand," muttered Ard. "It's been four years. This has never been a problem before."

"It only needs to be a problem once," Quarrah pointed out. "Didn't you write them an apology?"

Ard let out a mocking laugh. "My official letters of apology were limited to the rich and noble who might whine about my admittance into the Islehood. I hardly thought to include pirates." He tossed the spyglass back to Raek and gripped the tiller with both hands. "We'll have to outrun them."

"We're sharing the same wind," Raek said. "And as much as it pains me to admit, the *Shiverswift* is faster than the *Double Take*."

"Then what's our plan?" Quarrah asked.

"How much money do you have on you?" Ard asked drolly.

"Ha!" Raek laughed bitterly. "Unless she's packing the royal treasury in her shirtsleeves, there's no way we're paying him off today. See, Captain Dethers has his own special way of calculating interest."

"Do I want to know?" Quarrah asked.

"Well, he multiplies the outstanding cost by the number of weeks overdue," Raek began. "Then—"

Quarrah held up her hand. "Oh, it's an actual calculation? I thought you meant..." She pantomimed a knife slitting her throat.

"Flames, no," said Raek. "Sormian Dethers is a civilized pirate."

Quarrah remembered that much. When they'd first met, the man had been dressed for a night at the orchestra, a stemmed wineglass in one hand while he proffered her a silk handkerchief and a butter mint.

"Then we have nothing to worry about," Quarrah said. "Right?"

"As a pirate," Ard said, "how successful do you think Captain Dethers would be if nobody feared him?"

"Then, what's his method?" she asked.

"He won't kill us," said Raek. "He'll just take everything we have, sink our ship, and watch how well we swim."

"How civilized," she muttered.

"He usually only has to do that once or twice before his debtors do whatever it takes to gather the money," Raek continued. "People always go crawling back to Sormian Dethers."

"Listen, Quarrah," Ard said. "I'm sorry to drag you into this. I just want to say that you're welcome to leave at any time. No hard feelings."

She looked around at the vast expanse of open water. Was that some sort of joke? It was probably his harmless sense of humor, but she couldn't help but wonder if he was making a subtle stab at her penchant for running.

"Battle stations, then?" Raek asked.

"We're kindling if it comes to that," said Ard. "What about enclosing the *Double Take* in a cloud of Containment Grit?"

"I only have three vials," said Raek. "And even if we could pull it off and keep the Containment dome moving with the ship, they'd just follow us until we got to Helizon. This strikes me as a problem that's not going away."

"But why now?" Ard whispered. "Why bother hunting us down four years after we stiffed them? And how did they know our heading before we even recognized their ship?"

"Are you saying they knew where we'd be?" Raek said.

"So it seems." Ard tapped his chin in thought.

"Hedge Marsool, then?" Quarrah guessed. Anticipating their movements was definitely in his wheelhouse. "Maybe he wants to stop us from making the delivery."

"That makes no sense," said Ard. "When I saw him, he was upset that we hadn't secured the baroness's property yet."

"Then you think this is just a coincidence?" said Quarrah.

"Not sure I believe much in those anymore," Ard answered. "But I don't think Hedge would be behind this. More likely Captain Dethers caught our names on an outgoing harbor manifest and decided to make his move today."

"Battle stations, then?" Raek repeated in the exact same tone as before.

"At the very least, we need to hide the backpack." Quarrah crossed past Raek to midship.

"Where?" Ard asked. "If they decide to board us, they'll rip this ship apart plank by plank."

"Then we don't hide it on the *Double Take*," continued Quarrah. "We trap it in a bubble of Containment Grit and throw it overboard. It'll float. We can collect it once they leave."

"You mean we can swim around looking for it in the flotsam of our ship?" Ard said.

"The Containment bubble would only last ten minutes anyway," Raek said. "Then that pack would sink like, well... like it was full of bricks."

Quarrah looked out at the fast-approaching ship. Sparks, had it already covered *that* much water? She could see the sails clearly now. It wasn't flying a flag of any kind.

"All right," continued Quarrah, unwilling to give up yet. "We've got well over a hundred feet of rope on this ship. Let's tie one end to the backpack and drop it like an anchor. We can tie the other end to something buoyant. Something that doesn't look valuable—that barrel."

She could tell the small barrel was full of pitch, the sticky black substance oozing down the side. But they could empty it easily enough.

Raek nodded his bald head. "I think that'll work. As long as we can find the barrel in the aftermath and reel it in without any trouble."

Ard suddenly snapped his fingers. "I've got it!" His face spread into a wide smile. "We hide the backpack in the one place we know they won't shoot."

Quarrah stared at him in confusion. Had he not heard her plan at all? He seemed like he was in his own world over there.

"And where would that be?" Raek asked, ever the enabler.

"On the *Shiverswift*," Ard declared proudly. "Sormian Dethers is always good for a chat. He'll hear me out, even if his ultimate goal is to take everything we own and blow up the *Double Take*. I'll engage him and his crew in stimulating conversation"—he looked at Quarrah—"and you sneak the backpack onto his ship."

She couldn't help but guffaw at the plan. "We might as well surrender it."

"Not if you stay with it," Ard went on. "Once Dethers runs out his cannons and dusts the *Double Take*, you can spring out of hiding and jump overboard with the goods."

"And then we swim to shore?" Quarrah asked sarcastically.

"Raek's got a couple of emergency Grit flares," said Ard. "We can stay afloat on the ship scraps until we see another vessel. Then Raek will light 'em up and we hope somebody comes to rescue us."

"You realize that would be twice in two cycles that you've left me treading water, hoping for a pickup," Raek said to his partner.

"Well, if it makes you feel any better," replied Ard, "we'll be together this time."

Quarrah bit the inside of her cheek, trying to decide if she should say anything more about her idea. Ard's plan was decent, if she could figure out how to get aboard the *Shiverswift*. She had a basic memory of the vessel—its size and general layout. But she'd have no way of knowing the crew compliment or where the best hiding spots would be.

She drew in a deep, steadying breath. The approaching *Shiverswift* sailed steadily forward like a burning fuse. There really wasn't time to argue about plans, but—

"Hold on," she cut in. "What about my idea? The floating barrel plan?"

Ard looked at her, his expression softening as he seemed to realize how blunt he'd been.

"It's good," he said. "Solid backup plan. I just think we ought to get the backpack onto the *Shiverswift* because that's the safest bet."

Quarrah picked up the backpack. "Well, I think we ought to tie it to the barrel." She stepped forward as Raek picked up a coil of rope and held it out to her. Okay. Maybe she didn't mind him being such an enabler.

She was nearly to Raek when she heard a splash behind her. Whirling, Quarrah saw Ard dusting off his hands, a bit of black pitch on his palm. The barrel was bobbing out of reach, carried on the swell of the waters.

Quarrah felt something bubble up within her. It made her woozy with incredulity and astonishment.

"I'm sorry," he said. "But there just wasn't time to debate." He wouldn't look her in the eye, quickly moving back to his position at the tiller.

Silently, Quarrah pulled the backpack onto her shoulders and turned to watch the big ship.

"Your plan better work," she finally said. But deep inside, there was definitely a part of her that hoped it wouldn't.


"Captain!" Ard greeted with a respectful bow of his head. "Good to see you again. It's been too long."

He was choosing not to acknowledge the rough way the *Shiverswift* had sidled up to them. The *Double Take* was now snug against the hull of the pirate ship, held in place by a handful of grappling hooks.

A bit of fast talking on Ard's part had earned him a chance to go aboard the *Shiverswift* and speak with the captain. But it hadn't staved off the boarding party. Raek was still on the *Double Take*, watching the pirates tear apart his ship in search of valuables.

How Quarrah had managed to vanish during all this was beyond Ard's comprehension. He thought he'd seen her slip over the port side rail before the pirates reached them. With any luck, Sormian Dethers and his crew would think there were only two men aboard.

The captain's face was shaved smooth, his tanned wrinkles

deep and worn. Dethers ran a hand over his silky silver hair, and Ard noticed that his fingernails were painted green in the fashion of the northern Strindian nobles. Ard was pretty sure the man didn't have a drop of noble blood, but he understood the value in pretending.

"I'd say it's better for me to see you than the other way 'round," said the captain. "I believe you owe us some money."

"There must be some misunderstanding," Ard said. "We left the amount agreed upon in your treasury account at the Symphonette guesthouse on Strind, as per your instructions. That must have been, what... two years ago?"

"Four," said the captain. "And unfortunately for you, the payments never arrived."

Ard pulled a face. "I don't understand. My partner and I delivered the remaining portion of the payment within the cycle." He sucked in a breath as though something had just occurred to him. "This sounds like a bookkeeping error. Or worse. You know what I heard? Fifteen percent of deposits made into treasury accounts are incorrectly reported." He shook his head. "If there's a discrepancy with my payment, I'd check the bookkeeper first. Meredy... no Molli... I don't remember her name, it's been so long."

"His name is Fedor," said Captain Dethers. "He's been the chief of my estate for nearly two decades. I trust him with my money, and thus my life."

"Ah," Ard muttered. "I don't think he was working that day..."

This wasn't really about getting out of trouble. Even Ard realized he was far beyond that. He was having this conversation to buy Quarrah enough time to get aboard with the backpack. But in the meantime, there was one thing he was dying to know.

"Why today?" Ard asked bluntly.

"Excuse me?" replied the captain.

"You obviously tracked us down to question me about the payment," Ard said, "but why today?"

"I can answer that," came a new voice. It was tinny, carrying a bit of a whine that Ard remembered at once.

Moroy Peng descended the steps from the stern deck. Ard had last seen the thin runner aboard this same ship four years ago. Moroy had been one of the few lucky ones in Ard's illegal Harvesting crew who had survived Pekal after feeding the Royal Regalia to a dragon.

"I've been looking forward to this moment," the man said, strutting across the deck with an arrogant gait.

"You're running with this guy now?" Ard said to Captain Dethers. "He's a weasel. Can't you smell him?"

"I'm not part of the crew," Moroy said. "Just along for today's voyage."

"He came to me a couple of days ago," explained Dethers. "Said he had a lead on your whereabouts."

"That's hardly a mystery," said Ard. "You can find me in the Mooring in Beripent. Seven days a week."

"You make it sound so easy," Moroy said. "But you're actually a hard man to follow."

"Thank you."

"After we Harvested that Slagstone, you disappeared," said Moroy. "Then the war was on and it was impossible to find anyone across island borders. By the time I heard your name again, you were serving as a Holy Isle. Gone legitimate, they were saying." He clucked his tongue. "Untouchable that way, but I've been watching you. The moment Raekon rigged up the *Double Take*, I got word."

Ah. So it *was* a coincidence. No whiff of the King Poacher's involvement, here.

"But you couldn't get your own ship," Ard hypothesized, "so you had to convince Dethers to sail you out here."

Solid plan, actually. Basically the same strategy Ard had used to separate Baroness Lavfa from the mainland. There were no Reggies out here in the middle of the InterIsland Waters. No law.

"We had a mutual interest," Captain Dethers said.

"I didn't pay Moroy because he didn't do what I hired him to do," Ard said. "First sign of a dragon and he turned tail and ran. I don't pay cowards."

"I'm not interested in Ashings anymore," said Moroy.

Ard looked at Sormian Dethers. "But I thought—"

"*We* are interested in Ashings," he specified. "But Moroy has something else in mind."

Instinctively Ard leapt back as Moroy Peng drew a long knife, the slightly curved blade winking in the midday sunlight.

"Whoa," Ard said. "Easy there, fella. Don't want you to cut yourself—"

Moroy lunged, Ard barely sidestepping the attack.

"Come on, Captain," Ard protested, his eyes never leaving Moroy, who tossed his knife playfully from hand to hand, circling for another strike. "This isn't your style. It's going to stain the deck."

The pirates were gathering into a wide circle on the deck, making an arena of sorts. Like he and Moroy were Karvan lizards fighting in the ring. The pirates' brightly colored clothing was a visual distraction as he tried to keep his eye on Moroy's knife.

"And if you let him kill me," Ard continued to the captain, "who will bring you the money?"

"I believe there are two of you." Captain Dethers pointed a thumb at Raek aboard the *Double Take*.

*"Two of you." Good. They hadn't seen Quarrah.* At least that part of his plan was going right. Now he just needed to stay alive.

"At least give me a knife," Ard coaxed. "I'd hate for my partner to spread the word that I died unarmed in a knife fight. Doesn't reflect well on the killer."

"You can't ruin my name any more than you already have." Moroy sprang again, Ard twisting to the side.

"You give me too much credit," Ard said. "I actually never

mention you. In fact, I intentionally leave you out of the story when I'm talking about Pekal. Makes me look bad, hiring a coward."

"Word got around that I was on your crew," Moroy said. "Wasn't so bad during the war. But after you got the queen's pardon, nobody would hire me. Known associate of a do-gooder Holy Isle."

"Really?" Ard said. He genuinely hadn't seen that as a possible side effect when joining the Islehood, but it made sense. If Ardor Benn had gone legitimate, then he might be willing to flip on old associates and tell the Reggies how to make a few more arrests.

Moroy stabbed again, but this time Ard was ready for him. He leaned back, catching the man's arm with both hands. Moroy's other hand came around, dealing a shocking blow to the side of Ard's head. He let go, falling to one knee on the deck.

This was a fight Ard wasn't going to win without a weapon. Maybe the pirate standing closest to him wouldn't mind if he borrowed her dagger.

Ard sprang past his wiry opponent, grasping at the pirate's dagger. It slid free of its sheath, but one of the crossbars snagged in the lace of her vest, bringing his whole plan to a grinding halt.

The woman shoved Ard aside and he used the momentum to press through the ring of onlookers, breaking into a dead sprint across the deck. There was no way to escape, but the *Shiverswift* had to be littered with guns and blades. Ard circled around the mizzenmast, the pirates shouting and pointing his route to Moroy.

Why was this the tidiest ship he'd ever been on?

An ammunition closet sat beneath the stairs that led to the quarter deck. The large cabinet door squeaked as Ard yanked it open. A terrible hiding place, but it would probably be full of sixes for the light cannons. He could set a trap, closing himself inside the closet, ready to smash one of the cannon balls over Moroy's head.

Ard threw himself into the cramped dark space, slamming the door shut behind him.

What the blazes? There was something more than six-panweight cannon balls tucked away in here. Something wet...Ah! Something moving!

"What are you doing?" a familiar voice snapped through the darkness.

"Sparks! Quarrah?" He was basically sitting on top of her. "What are *you* doing?"

"This is my hiding spot," she retorted. "You told me to get onboard."

"You thought this was a good place?" Ard cried. "What happens when they start grabbing sixes to open fire on us?"

"This is a starboard closet," Quarrah whispered. "The *Double Take* is port side. They'll take the cannon balls from over there."

"Huh. Sounds like you really thought this through," Ard said. "You got a weapon?"

"No," she said. "Why?"

"Moroy Peng is trying to kill me."

"The Tracer?"

"No," said Ard. "*I* was the Tracer on that expedition, remember?" Suspicious of a traitor in their midst, Ard had shuffled assignments once they'd reached Pekal. That had been the beginning of the animosity between Moroy and himself.

"You realize this is bad, right?" Quarrah said. "Based on the way things sounded out there, I'd say they saw where you're hiding."

"Yep."

"And that's going to lead them straight to me. To the backpack."

"Yep."

"And we're unarmed."

"Not completely." Ard pulled something from his pocket. A thin sliver of sunlight angling through the doorframe glinted on the glass vial Ard had stolen from Hedge Marsool.

"No, no, no," Quarrah whispered. "I really don't think that's a good idea. It's not going to work, Ard."

"I think it will," he replied. "We can—"

"It's not going to work!" she snapped.

"It's our best shot," Ard insisted. "They're already fishing through the *Double Take*. If they see you with that backpack, they're going to know it's something valuable. If this Grit can really show us the future, we could get out of here with our lives, the backpack... maybe even the *Double Take*."

"Ugh," Quarrah grunted. "Listen, Ard. It's not going to work. There's something I—"

The cabinet door jerked open and Moroy appeared in a flood of daylight. From Ard's awkward position sitting on Quarrah's lap, he kicked. His boot caught Moroy in the stomach, knocking him back a few feet.

"Here goes," Ard announced to Quarrah. Holding his breath, he hurled the Grit vial against the deck in front of him. The glass shattered, and the Slagstone fragment sparked against the liquid that spilled out.

Nothing happened.

"You feeling anything?" Ard asked desperately.

"Aw, sparks," muttered Quarrah.

"No, I saw the sparks," Ard insisted. He reached out with his foot and stomped the little Slagstone chip, hearing another sizzle beneath the heavy sole of his boot.

Still nothing.

"Come on," Ard muttered. Their only shot was a dud? Or maybe he had sorely misunderstood Hedge's vial. Perhaps it was like Illusion or Visitant Grit, requiring a second detonation to truly activate the first...

Moroy bellowed a battle cry and threw himself forward. In Ard's stupor over the failed Grit vial, Moroy might have stuck him if Quarrah hadn't hurled a six from behind him.

The iron ball dropped Moroy face first on the deck, but he was still breathing. Ard scrambled out of the ammunition closet, turning back to help Quarrah. She'd been clutching the black backpack against her chest, but a few of the cannon balls had cascaded, pinning her leg.

"Here!" She threw him the backpack. Between four bricks and twenty panweights of Grit, the bag nearly bowled him over.

Moroy was rising, so Ard swung the backpack around, feeling a satisfying *thunk* as it clubbed him upside the head. He threw one strap over his shoulder and grabbed Quarrah's hand as she finished digging herself out of the cannon balls.

"What now?" she asked as they raced across the deck, weaving through pirates who whooped and taunted, but otherwise remained uninvolved.

"We need to get you and the pack aboard the *Double Take*," Ard said. "You and Raek cut loose and sail as fast—"

Quarrah went down, hitting the deck hard. Ard turned to see Sormian Dethers hauling her back up, a Roller in one hand.

"A stowaway," the captain said. "This day is full of surprises." He pressed the barrel of the gun to Quarrah's neck, holding her arm with his other hand. "How long have you been onboard, lass?"

Quarrah blew at a wet strand of hair that was plastered against her forehead. "No handkerchief this time?"

Captain Dethers chuckled, glancing at Ard. "I like her spirit."

But Ard didn't have time to respond. Moroy Peng came barreling through the crew, face bleeding and one arm hanging limply at his side.

Ard caught his other arm, which brandished that same curved knife, but Moroy's charge forced them both stumbling across the deck.

The port rail rammed into Ard's back, knocking the wind out of him. The backpack swung over the side of the ship, dangling from the single strap over his shoulder.

Moroy's face was strained with anger, his teeth bared and a bit of spittle flecking across Ard's face as he grunted to overpower him with the knife. The point was mere inches from Ard's chest, drawing nearer through Moroy's sheer desire for vengeance.

The *Double Take* was behind Ard, but the raiding party had concluded, leaving Raek alone on the boat. The grappling hooks were still in place, but the vessel was floating at least twenty feet away from the *Shiverswift*'s hull. Too far to jump, even if he could manage to throw off Moroy.

"Ard!" Raek shouted.

Ard turned his head, risking a glance at the *Double Take* just in time to see his partner lob a knife in a gentle arc toward him.

Ard let go of Moroy's arm with his right hand, reaching out and catching the hilt in midair. He brought it around, plunging the blade into Moroy's unprotected stomach.

The man went limp, his breath catching in his throat. He coughed, his teeth smearing with red as the blood came gurgling up. His eyes were confused, as if his brain had not yet registered the pain, but his body wouldn't respond like he wanted.

"The pack?" he mumbled, his strained words sounding unsure.

"What?" Ard said, sure that he'd misunderstood the man.

"Cut the pack." With his final drib of energy, Moroy Peng reached out and sliced through the strap of the backpack.

Ard felt it slip from his shoulder, falling in what seemed like slow motion as he rolled away from Moroy. He saw the pack splash into the water between the *Shiverswift* and the *Double Take*, the already-soaked leather instantly sinking out of sight. Ard and Raek made stunned eye contact across the distance, then Raek dove into the water.

Ard gripped the rail, barely aware of anything else as he waited for his friend to surface. After painstaking seconds, Ard saw Raek's bald head break the water's surface. He looked up and shook his head, a look of glum defeat on his broad face.

Gone? Had they really just lost the backpack? The bricks and the Grit were replaceable. But the Agrodite Moon Glass…Stealing another was out of the question.

How would Ard explain this to Hedge Marsool? He felt the whole job falling apart, sinking like the pack. And how long would it be before Hedge's smugglers surfaced, transformed by Metamorphosis Grit into something terribly powerful?

"Dust her!" Sormian Dethers gave the command to the pirates at the cannons on the port side.

"Raek!" Ard shouted. "Look out!"

His friend dove, swimming toward the *Shiverswift* as sparks fell into the first cannon. Ard felt the deck shake under his feet as the resounding *boom* set his ears ringing.

At such close range, it was almost impossible to miss. The cannon ball tore into the hull of the *Double Take*, timbers cracking as the little boat bucked.

A second *boom*. Through the cloud of smoke that wafted past, Ard watched his ship take water at an alarming rate.

One more cannon sounded and the *Double Take* capsized entirely, the short mast snapping, broken planks skipping across the water's surface.

His ship! Ard could hear Raek screaming obscenities from the water below. Well, at least he hadn't gone down in the wreckage.

"I think our business is concluded here," said Captain Dethers, lowering his gun and shoving Quarrah forward.

Ard cast a regretful glance at the corpse of Moroy Peng slumped at the base of the port rail. He hadn't meant to kill the man, even in self-defense. If word got back to Beripent about this, it could jeopardize his pardon and his position in the Islehood.

They'd lost everything in this unexpected fiasco—the backpack, the *Double Take*, even their single vial of mysterious liquid Grit.

"I'll expect your outstanding payment delivered by the end of the cycle at four times the original amount." The debonaire pirate captain dusted his hands together. "Now, do you prefer to jump or be pushed?"

~

*So much has settled to the depths of my soul over the years.
And once it's gone, I know there's no recovering it.*

# CHAPTER

# 14

They weren't going to make it to the summit. It had been obvious to Nemery and Mohdek for several days, and it was time to break the news to Legien Dyer.

"This is it," Nemery announced. It was midafternoon, and they had just passed Goldred's Scramble, an area of jagged boulders and loose scree that spilled out in front of the glacier. The last trees were behind them, and they were onto the ice now, snow crunching underfoot.

"But the summit..." said Dyer. "We haven't reached it."

"And we're not going to," Nemery replied.

This was the most she and Mohdek had said to him since he'd murdered little Oropsi seven days ago. After burying the hatchling, Dyer had insisted that he and Nemery set out immediately. Leaving obvious clues and a trail for Mohdek, Nemery had intentionally dragged her feet up the mountain. The slow pace had given Mohdek a chance to catch up, but it had also granted the Glassmind cultists a significant head start.

"I can see the summit right there," Dyer said, breathing extra hard in the cold, thin air. "If we push, I think we can reach it before nightfall."

"We could get there," Nemery admitted. "But Goldred's Scramble marks the Redeye line. Unless we retreat back through those rocks, we *all* get Moonsick tonight."

"What about my son?"

Nemery gestured vaguely up the icy slope, like a broad river of white, frozen between great spires of stone. "I imagine he's somewhere up there. But it's time for us to turn back."

"Not yet," Dyer begged. "We still have time. The sun won't set for hours."

"And by then it will be too late," Mohdek said. "You are welcome to continue on your own. It doesn't take a tracker to follow this trail." He pointed to the stampede of footprints in the snow. "But Salafan and I are going back."

Nemery turned to Mohdek, switching to Trothian so Dyer wouldn't understand. "Do we tell him that there are only eight sets of tracks in the snow?" That left a handful of the party unaccounted for.

"It would be bitter irony if his son has backed out," Mohdek said. "Especially if the old man goes up and gets Moonsick."

It was wonderful, speaking fluent Trothian. Legien Dyer squinted into the distance with no idea that they were discussing his fate.

"We could tell him that prints matching his son's height and build are not here," Nemery said. "It wouldn't be hard to convince him to turn back with us—"

"Why should we save his life?" Mohdek cut her off, taking a deep breath to steady himself. "There is a Trothian saying: *The man who weaves his own net catches his own fish.* His net was woven when he decided to hike this high. If he catches Moonsickness, he should not be surprised."

Honestly, Nemery felt bad for Legien Dyer, a man so desperate that he was willing to murder a helpless infant dragon. She'd been furious at first, but she had enough self-control not to let her passionate, emotional side take over. Because, Homeland, if it did, Nemery was likely to leave this man to the wilds of Pekal. But she'd given her word to see him this far and the man deserved to make his decision with all the facts.

"Dyer!" Nemery called. "There's something you should know." Behind her, Mohdek moaned. "Your kid might not be up there."

The man whirled so quickly, his pack almost knocked him over. "Why would you say that?"

"The party split," she explained. "Only eight of them are going to the summit."

"Is Feltman with them?" he cried.

"How should we know?" said Mohdek.

"What happened to the others?" asked Dyer.

Nemery shrugged. "We lost their trail in the rocks. I'm guessing some of the cultists got some sense knocked into them when they realized that the Scramble marked the Redeye. Can't say I blame them for chickening out and turning back."

"What are you going to do?" Mohdek asked him.

The older man was frozen in pure indecision, the magnitude of his choice as heavy as those boulders they'd scrambled across.

"It's not what *I* would do," he finally said, his voice almost lost in the wind. "I wish I could say Feltman would back out, but he's never been one to do what I wished."

"Then you're going up?" asked Mohdek.

He closed his eyes, jaw trembling. "Homeland forgive me if I'm wrong." He shrugged out of his backpack, the overstuffed load landing with a thud in the snow. "I'll move faster without it," he said, opening his eyes. "I'll find Feltman and we'll get below the Scramble before the Moon rises. I can do this. When he sees me, he'll understand..."

Legien Dyer's words faded away as he moved up the mountain, trudging after the trail of footprints.

Mohdek instantly headed back the way they'd come, but Nemery bent down and scooped up a handful of snow. It was a curious thing, snow. The vast majority of people in the Greater Chain had never seen it, let alone packed a ball of it and thrown it at their lover.

The snowball hit Mohdek right at the top of his pack, breaking apart and showering icy crystals down the back of his neck.

He turned with a playful grin. Before he could retaliate, a shadow passed overhead, turning their eyes upward. A large sow dragon was winging her way toward the summit, her soaring green body at least a hundred feet above them.

"Jothdet?" Mohdek asked, squinting against the sun.

"Shadespring, I think," replied Nemery. "See the way the tip of her right wing turns in?"

So far, that was six adult sows, and nineteen hatchlings this afternoon. Still no sign of Cochorin, but the miracle bull dragon was often among the last to roost before the Passing.

"I'm a little envious of him," Nemery remarked as they resumed their downhill trudge.

"Dyer?" said Mohdek. "I knew you secretly always wanted to be a Bloodeye."

She snickered at him. When Mohdek joked, it was always worth obliging. "I mean, to see them all up there... Every dragon roosting in one place. Soaking up the Moon rays. It's got to be an incredible sight."

"One of the last you'll see," said Mohdek. "And you'd never be able to tell anyone about it."

"I don't know," she said. "I might be fast enough to get down to New Vantage before I lost my voice."

"You know that's impossible." Mohdek shook his head. "Though I'm sure you could make it before the madness struck."

Nemery shivered against the cold wind. "I'd say the air's thin enough up here to make anyone go a little mad."

They made their way back down the glacier and into the field of loose rock. Nemery enjoyed hiking the Scramble, but it was tiring. The going was strenuous, either climbing over boulders, or trying not to get swept away in a slide of loose scree. She'd sleep well tonight, despite the fact that they were closer to the Redeye line than she liked.

She slid a few feet, gravel clattering around her boots until she stopped herself against a smaller boulder. This was strange. The rock was painted pink. At first, she thought it was a trick of the waning sunlight, but when she stooped to inspect it, she realized it was still quite fresh.

"Moh!" She beckoned him over for a closer look. "What do you make of this?"

"What?" he asked, vibrating eyes examining the rock. It was such a thin application, maybe he couldn't make it out with his unique vision.

She scraped a bit with her fingernail. "Tracer's Dye." She stood, squinting across the slope.

"You see another?" he asked.

"Yeah," she replied. "How did I miss this on the way up?"

"We weren't expecting it," he said, giving her every benefit.

"The paint is on the uphill sides of the rocks, so someone is marking a route down," Nemery said. "It has to be the other cultists. The ones who turned back." She moved in the direction of the next marker.

"Yes," said Mohdek, following.

"That was a long way to haul the dye powder," Nemery said. "Someone in their group actually knows what they're doing, even if Legien Dyer said his son has no experience on Pekal."

"And it seems like the ones who turned back did so amicably," said Mohdek, "if they want the hikers to find them again."

She loved seeing what they could learn from the marks on the land. Speculating and unraveling mysteries with Mohdek, just like Namsum had taught them.

Nemery nodded. "Maybe they didn't chicken out. Maybe they only ever planned for part of the group to get Moonsick."

"It's possible that the ones leaving this trail are not part of the cult," added Mohdek. "Perhaps these are the wilderness guides."

"Guides that agreed to meet up with a bunch of Moonsick people after tonight?" Nemery shook her head. "I can't imagine. I'd say it's more likely that they're the sacrificers. They stayed behind to put a knife in their friends in case the faithful don't actually end up undergoing this mystical *transformation*."

Mohdek said nothing, but she knew he was considering her morbid words.

They followed the splattered dye markers across the Scramble, the afternoon advancing quickly. They counted a few more dragons in flight before Mohdek stopped and pointed upward.

"There he is."

Nemery looked to the sky, its clouds tinged orange and yellow from the setting sun. Against this picturesque backdrop, she saw Cochorin winging his way to the summit.

Nemery estimated him to be almost four years old—mature enough to fertilize, but still a juvenile. Still growing.

Six little hatchlings flew behind him in a flock. Even from this distance, Nemery could see that at least four of them were male. Nemery smiled. Cochorin had broken an ancient tradition. He had disregarded a law among dragons that dated back to the beginning of time.

He had ended the Bull Dragon Patriarchy.

Since humans first observed the dragons, there had never been more than three males in existence. A son, a father, and a grandfather. When the eldest died, the youngest would be allowed to fertilize a male egg, keeping the trio intact.

It had never made sense to Nemery. Renowned dragon scholars like Eilmer and Toom had written theories—a limited number of bulls assured that the dragons wouldn't overpopulate their singular habitat. Or that the bulls were capable of fertilizing only one male egg in their lifetime.

Whatever the reason had been, Cochorin didn't seem to care. By Nemery's count, he had sired more than forty new dragons, over half of them male.

It'd be a couple of years before the other bulls would be mature enough to fertilize eggs of their own. For now, Cochorin was the father of all dragons. And the Trothian name she and Mohdek had given him reflected that.

Cochorin dipped left and then streaked right, twirling in a barrel roll with his broad wings tucked back. The hatchlings shrieked behind him. Ha! He was always such a showoff. Especially in front of his offspring.

Nemery watched until he was out of sight. She liked to imagine him finding an unoccupied spot to roost at the rocky, ice-crusted peak. His plentiful progeny would tug at his wings and pull his tail while he tried to enjoy soaking up the Red Moon rays.

She turned her attention back to the rugged terrain, scanning for the next splotch of pink dye. They were almost out of Goldred's Scramble, and she felt some apprehension about who they'd find waiting at the end of this trail.

Darkness crept over the mountain, but it didn't last more than a few minutes before a reddish hue heralded the rising Moon.

The terrain below the Scramble was mellow and easygoing. Glacial streams trickled through the rocks, happily bubbling down a gentle grassy slope. They wound around scattered, wind-stunted trees before disappearing into a dense forest a few hundred yards below.

In the failing light, the dye marks were harder to spot now. Nemery was grateful for Mohdek's vision as he quickly picked up the footprints of the party they'd been tracking.

The Moon was halfway over the horizon, the slopes of Pekal glowing red, when Mohdek reached out and grabbed Nemery's arm. A campfire winked at the edge of the forest ahead, the blaze unnecessarily large to ward off the high mountain chill and the uneasy feelings that came with a Moon Passing.

A couple of large boulders had rolled down from the Scramble, their journey stopped by the tree line. The travelers had made their camp there—protected on the uphill side by the huge stones, and concealed by the thick forest below.

"What's our plan?" Nemery kept her voice low, even though there was little risk of being heard at this distance. "Can you see how many of them there are?"

Mohdek held up a finger for patience.

"I think we should go in for a closer look," she continued.

"I see five people," he whispered.

"That's not bad," replied Nemery. "With the element of surprise, maybe we could—"

"One of them is Trothian," he cut her off. "And she's keeping watch."

"Well, that complicates things." It probably wasn't smart to get much closer than this. "Maybe we should move into the forest."

"They'll be watching the trees," said Mohdek. "We should wait here with a clear line of sight. I can keep an eye on them through the night. If that Trothian lowers her guard, we can move in."

"Or," Nemery said, sweetening her tone since she knew Mohdek wouldn't like her proposal. "I could creep through the field, putting those boulders between me and the campers. Then I advance slowly. Trothians can't see through rock, right?"

"And what do you plan to do when you get there?"

"I'm going to climb up the back side of that boulder, perch on top like a roosting dragon, and see what I can learn about them."

"Here's what we already know," said Mohdek. "They're part of an extreme religious cult that is willing to sacrifice their companions to Moonsickness." He paused. "And don't forget about what they did to Oropsi."

"You can keep watch from out here," she said. "If it looks like I've been detected, give me a signal on your whistle and I'll get the blazes out of there."

Mohdek bunched his eyebrows together in disapproval. "What are you hoping to see over there?"

"Feltman Dyer," she whispered. "We have to know if he's there."

"What good will that do?" asked Mohdek. "His father is already gone."

"I know, but aren't you curious?" said Nemery. "And who knows, maybe they've got cake. You know how long it's been since I've had cake?"

"I can learn to make it," Mohdek pleaded. "Does that change your mind?"

"Nah," said Nemery. "Besides, I have a feeling your recipe would be too salty. Speaking of salty…"

Nemery leaned over and pecked him on the cheek. It felt a little dry and chapped, and they had enough salt for only one more application of the paste.

"I won't stay up there all night," she promised. "And once I get back, we can decide where to place the traps."

"You want to treat them like poachers, then?"

"I haven't forgotten about Oropsi." Before he could protest, she slipped through the grass in silent determination.

Nemery swung wide, moving silently until one of the boulders blocked her view of the campfire. Then she cut toward it as quickly as she could.

She hadn't always been so sneaky. With some embarrassment, Nemery remembered how clumsily she'd tried to follow Ardor Benn on her first trip to Pekal. But as a musician, she knew the value of focused practice. And the last three years with Mohdek had granted her many opportunities to hone her skills in the wild.

She reached the back side of the rock and began to climb, her tired arms and legs trembling by the time she finally pulled herself onto the top. Lying on her stomach, she inched across the rough stone, passing under pine boughs that stretched across the boulder from the trees that had grown up around it.

She could see only two Lander men from this angle, sharing a seat on a large downed tree. Both of them seemed too old to fit the description of Feltman Dyer. Their provisions and gear were scattered in a way that was consistent with all the other campsites Nemery and Mohdek had come across. With the messes they'd left behind, she'd always imagined them to be a lively, merrymaking band. Tonight, however, the ones below were a quiet, somber bunch. With good reason. Their companions had taken a doomed journey. The same large Moon that was watching over these campers would be making their friends irreparably sick.

Nemery lay there for a long time, keeping an ear out for any signal from Mohdek. Little happened in the camp below. She could see just the tips of the flames from the crackling fire, the flickering yellow light dancing across the trunks of the forest trees.

At one point, another Lander man with dark skin stepped into view, passing something edible to his seated companions before moving back to where he'd been.

That left two unaccounted for. Mohdek had identified one of them as a Trothian woman, but what if the last one was Dyer's son?

"Where are you going?" came a man's voice from below.

Finally. Something. Nemery tilted her head to catch every word.

"I have to pee," came the reply. It was a woman's voice.

"Trenchy," said the same man. "Go with her."

One of the Landers on the log spit on the dirt. "She's a big girl. She can wet the grass on her own."

"Garifus wouldn't like her wandering off like this," came the reply. "Not when we're so close."

*Garifus Floc.* That was the name of the Glassmind leader. The palace Regulator who claimed to have seen Prime Isless Gloristar get Moonsick and transform into a perfected being.

"I'm not wandering off, Carpen," said the woman. "Besides, can't Shopaj see me in the dark?"

"Only for a ways," Carpen replied. "What if you decide to run?"

The woman let out an incredulous laugh. Youthful, but full of animosity. "Where would I run? I'm just looking for a bit of privacy."

"Afraid that's a luxury you can't afford," replied Carpen. "It's for your own safety. I promised Garifus that I'd keep you safe until morning. Can't have you getting mauled by another little dragon while you're doing your business."

"I'll be fine," she continued to protest. "The dragons are all up there."

"Trenchy!" snapped Carpen. "I told you to go with her."

The man called Trenchy finally stood, muttering something incoherent. He picked up a short sword and stepped out of sight. A moment later, he reappeared, accompanied by the Lander woman.

In the red light of the Moon, Nemery thought the stranger didn't look much older than her. The woman was as thin as a broomstick, with pale skin that looked painfully sunburned. Her fair complexion was enhanced by hair as yellow as straw. It was straggly and unkempt, pulled back into a messy braid.

Whoever she was, it seemed obvious to Nemery that she didn't want to be with the cultists anymore. The overwhelmed, regretful look connected on a deep level with Nemery's first trip to Pekal. She had loved the island, but the company had been frightfully Settled, which was what had led her to confide in Ardor Benn—a man with a religious name she could trust.

But this woman didn't seem to trust any of the campers. And they seemed just as wary of her running away.

*A prisoner?* Nemery wondered. Had they brought her from the start, or picked her up along the way? Whoever she was, she seemed important to Garifus Floc. A wife? A daughter?

"That was unnecessary," said the other man in view. "She's not stupid enough to run."

"Not worth the risk," answered Carpen. "Without that girl, Garifus and the others get Moonsick tonight."

*What?* What did that even mean?

At least Nemery understood that Garifus Floc was here. And by the sound of it, he had gone with the rest of the party to the summit. That was the sign of a committed leader.

"*Real* Moonsickness," Carpen continued. "Is that what you want?"

The other man drooped his head in shame. "Right. Sorry. Garifus wouldn't want us fighting like this. I guess we'll see what the girl can do in the morning."

"You have doubts?"

"I left my doubts in the harbor," he replied. "Just like the rest of you." The man looked up and pressed the tip of his middle finger against his forehead in a ceremonious manner. "Tomorrow we change the world."

Nemery slowly inched backward. The conversation had given her more questions than answers. She'd wait until Trenchy and the young woman returned. If they didn't have anything else to say, she'd retreat and report to Mohdek.

But their tactic in dealing with these people had to change. No traps. No lethal force. At least not until they could see what part this young woman was supposed to play. Then Nemery would do whatever it took to free her from the cultists. Find out what she knew.

*We'll see what that girl can do in the morning.* The cultist's words echoed in Nemery's mind. *Tomorrow we change the world.*

～

*Ideas can drive people to the brink of insanity. And when the detonation clears, what do they have to show for it?*

# CHAPTER

# 15

A rd slipped through the outer gate of Tofar's Salts, pressing through the crowd of Trothians inside the soakhouse. Busier than normal tonight, under the red glow of the Moon Passing. Most Landers would be indoors, but this was a night of celebration for the Trothians—their Agrodite religion worshiped the terrifying Moon.

The baths were so full that the salt water flowed over the plank walkway, wetting Ard's boots. He wasn't excited for tonight's meeting in the *Be'Igoth*. The last two had been wholly unproductive, and it was only a matter of time before Hedge Marsool decided to drop in and check on them.

Eggat and Drot were both on duty outside the hot bath house tonight. "Gentlemen." Ard tipped an imaginary hat at them, moving up the stone steps and slipping into the remodeled structure.

"Sorry I'm late," Ard said to Raek and Quarrah.

"No surprise there," Raek muttered. He was stooped over a table, studying a map. Above his head was a large orb of Light Grit. Ard's thoughts took hold of him for a moment, his eyes lingering on the brightly glowing ball.

Another sphere.

In his studies, Ard had started listing all the naturally occurring spherical shapes in the real world.

It was the shape of a detonation cloud.

The Red Moon.

The bleeding eyes of a Moonsick person.

"Did you get lost on your way here?" Raek followed up.

"Had to shake a tail," Ard lied. He certainly couldn't tell them the actual reason for his tardiness. He *had* been lost. In his studies.

The split focus between the Islehood and Hedge's job was draining. It shouldn't have been—Ard had run plenty of simultaneous ruses in the past. But maybe that was just it. Maybe he didn't view his position in the Islehood as a ruse anymore.

Sure, he was using the Mooring to get what he wanted—the location of the dragon shell, and clarity about the Great Egress. But he'd found more than he'd expected there.

"Hedge, or Captain Dethers?" asked Quarrah, standing up from one of the padded armchairs.

"Huh? Oh, I didn't get a good look at them. Suppose it could be any number of spiteful enemies," Ard said, artfully evading an honest answer. "Where are we with getting another Moon Glass?"

"Um…" Raek glanced up from his map. "Nowhere. That ship has sailed, my friend. Or rather, *sunk*."

"But Baroness Lavfa—"

"The job is shot, Ard," seconded Quarrah. "Time to move on."

Moving on was not one of Ard's strong suits. She, of all people, should have known that. Looking at her pierced him with a pang of regret, still fresh even after days of profuse apologies.

Sparks, why hadn't he listened to her plan on the *Double Take*? If he had, they might still have the glass. Ardor Benn actually knew the reason. It was the same reason he had insisted on meeting with Lyndel—it kept him relevant. Useful.

Quarrah's way of doing things was always simpler, but it didn't give him a chance to impress her. Of course, the logical side of him acknowledged that she'd probably be far more impressed if he actually listened to her ideas.

Ard had always prided himself in his ability to read people and manipulate them. But when it came to Quarrah Khai, he was helpless. He knew what it would take, but he could never quite commit to the lie—pretending to be something he wasn't just to win her over.

His feelings for Quarrah exacted nothing short of perfect honesty from him. But this time around, all the honesty did was make Ard realize how much he hated himself.

"Baroness Lavfa's unnecessary anyway," said Raek. "Hedge told us to contact her because he needed a place to store his dragon. There are other places besides the cavern under Helizon."

"You weren't here when he hired us," Ard pointed out. "Hedge was pretty adamant that we secure the baroness's Helizon property. Tell him, Quarrah."

She shrugged. "Hedge talked like that was the only option. But I don't see why we couldn't persuade him otherwise."

"Hedge Marsool isn't really a flexible, understanding fellow," Ard said. "If we don't play by his rules, I'm afraid he could—"

"Right here." Raek tapped the map with his finger. "There's a sizable cave just a few miles south of Beripent. In the Pale Tors. Actually not far from that abandoned granary where we hosted the Karvan lizard fight."

"I've heard of that cavern," Ard said. "Doesn't Jaig Jasperson have the run of the Pale Tors?" He turned to Quarrah. "Jaig was a smuggler during the war. Moved cannons and ammunition out of the Archkingdom and sold them to the Sovs for Ashlits." Then to Raek. "You think that cave's big enough to house a dragon?"

"The entrance is too small right now," he admitted, "but I think a couple of well-placed kegs of Blast Grit could open it up without collapsing."

Ard snorted. "As if Jaig would agree to that."

"I actually swung by this morning and had a word with him," said Raek. "Showed him my plans for blasting."

"You did *what*?" Ard cried. "If Hedge finds out—"

"Relax," Raek cut him off. "I told Jaig we were looking to hide a sailing ship."

"What did he say?" asked Quarrah.

"He wasn't *completely* opposed to the idea of widening the entrance," Raek said. "I think I could bring him around."

"Threats, or money?" Ard asked.

"Maybe a little of both."

Ard shook his head. He didn't like changing plans on Hedge like this, even if all their efforts were still aimed toward finding a place for his dragon.

"If you'd rather stick to the original plan," Quarrah said, "I've got a solid lead on a glassblower who I think could make a convincing replica of a Moon Glass."

"We went over this," Ard said. "There's no such thing as a convincing—"

"Quiet," Raek hissed, holding up his hand for silence.

The cheerful sounds of the bathing Trothians outside had come to an abrupt silence. Then Ard heard a man grunt just outside the door to the *Be'Igoth*. The wall shuddered as something slammed against it.

"I thought you shook your tail..." Raek reached for a Roller lying on the table beside the map.

Oh, sparks. Had someone *actually* been following him? Ard reached for his own gun belt, but it wasn't there. He needed to figure out a way to secretly arm himself when leaving the Mooring.

The door flew open. A single figure filled every inch of the doorway, cowled head ducked low just to squeeze inside the room. Draped in an ill-fitting black cloak, the stranger was terrifyingly large and imposing. With the backdrop of the reddish night behind, Ard saw a waterfall of sparks tumble from the figure's hand.

Quarrah had wisely retreated to take shelter behind a table stocked with Raek's Grit Mixing equipment. Ard was doing the same when Raek pulled the trigger. His Roller spit flame and lead, striking the stranger squarely in the chest.

Instead of stumbling or flinching, the figure reached up and cast off the large hood.

Impossible...

It was Prime Isless Gloristar.

Ard stood rooted in speechless shock. Could it really be her? Alive and looking no different than when they'd seen her plummet from the top of the Old Post Lighthouse. Her enhanced body rippled with muscles, enlarged beyond any natural frame. Pale blue skin shimmered with veins of pure gold, and her hairless scalp was made of thick red glass. Her eyes blazed like coals of crimson.

"Shoot first, ask questions later?" she declared, her voice resonating unnaturally. "Honestly, where is your discipline, Raekon Dorrel?"

Raek lowered the gun slowly, as if it had suddenly grown too heavy to keep raised. Gloristar made a dismissive gesture behind her, the door suddenly swinging shut, seemingly of its own accord.

"Flames, Gloristar," Ard finally managed. "We thought... Everyone thought you were dead!"

"That's understandable, I suppose," she stated. "But death does not come so quickly to me now. I was merely... out of sight."

"Where were you?" he followed up.

"I was stranded for a while," she said, "in the depths of the Inter-Island Waters."

"And how did you..." Ard found himself stumbling on his words, an uncharacteristic testament to his shock. "How did you get here?"

"Now, that is something altogether miraculous." Gloristar strode into the room, swinging an object from her shoulder and dropping it heavily on the table.

It was a black leather backpack. And it was still wet.

In the corner of the room, Quarrah Khai stood up from her hiding place. She stepped around the Mixing table, moving quietly toward Gloristar, who seemed unsurprised by the thief's sudden appearance. Maybe the woman had already spotted Quarrah with those glowing red eyes. Maybe there was nowhere safe to hide from the perfected creature Gloristar had become.

A Glassmind.

"Well, I'll be sparked," Raek muttered, drawing closer to inspect the backpack. There was no mistaking it. Ard could see where the shoulder strap had been severed by Moroy's knife in his final desperate moments.

Slowly, as if expecting Gloristar to stop her, Quarrah reached out and loosened the pack's drawstring opening. The transformed woman watched in silence as Ard, Quarrah, and Raek peered inside.

The soft glow from the Light Grit glinted magnificently on the thick red Agrodite Moon Glass. Beneath it, Ard saw two Grit kegs and four bricks resting in the bottom of the pack.

"And how…" Ard started. "How exactly did you come by this?"

"I didn't," Gloristar replied. "It came by me."

Raek gave a grunt of annoyance. "Look, I realize that you're fluent in cryptic. Makes sense, from all that scripture you must have read as Prime Isless. But we're simple folk here, and I think I speak for all of us when I say you need to explain things a bit more clearly."

"Things are unclear, even to me," said Gloristar. "How long was I gone?"

"Two years," Quarrah answered.

Gloristar lifted a hand, fingers sparking absently as she tapped them together. "Two years. Time was a blur to me without the rising and setting of the sun."

"The pack," Ard said. "We lost it in a struggle just four days ago."

She nodded her glass head. "It settled to the depths, where I was waiting."

"Whoa," Raek remarked. "That's one blazing lucky backpack."

"Not so," said Gloristar. "It was directed to me by a power beyond your comprehension."

"What do you mean?" Quarrah asked.

"In my current state, my body has developed a bond with *renna*—what you and the Trothians call Moon Glass." She placed one hand on the pack. "I sensed the presence of this piece the moment it entered the water. It is corrupted, having spent so many centuries in the hands of those who cannot access its true power, but my mind still perceived it. I drew that Moon Glass toward me, feeling it push and pull against the natural currents of the sea until at last it was in my possession. The *renna* was imprinted with the history of those who had touched it, and I knew exactly how to find you here."

Ard rubbed his chin. "Incredible," he whispered. "This is unbelievable."

"I am drawn to the *renna*," said Gloristar. "And it is drawn to me. That is how I survived these last two years. There are great spires of this glass scattered across the bed of the sea. Each is protected by a pocket of air—residual effect from ancient detonations that are sustained by the glass spires."

"We know," Ard said. "We saw one."

Gloristar tilted her head and Ard saw that her glass skull was still broken—a spiderweb of thin cracks across her scalp.

"How is that possible?" Gloristar asked.

"We enclosed ourselves in a bubble of Containment Grit and sank down during a Moon Passing," said Raek. "Just happened to land in one of those handy air pockets."

"Lyndel," Quarrah whispered. "She believed that some spiritual power had guided us to that spire of Moon Glass."

Ard remembered perfectly. The priestess had been determined to snuff out their protective Containment bubble so they could go out and investigate. She had called it a test of faith. And she hadn't been wrong.

"Lyndel," Gloristar repeated. "She is an Agrodite priestess. Her history is deeply imprinted into that piece of corrupt Glass. Her Trothian form is a mere shadow of its glorious ancestors, but the power of the spire would have been sufficient to detect her heritage and draw your sinking bubble toward it."

"The testament spire attracts Trothians?" Raek said.

"Only if they are alive at such a depth in the sea," answered Gloristar. "And Lyndel's connection to this piece of Moon Glass would have made the draw even stronger."

"So the only reason we survived that night was because Lyndel was with us," Quarrah said.

Ard already knew that. Without Lyndel's unique ability to limit her breathing, they would have had no one to stay awake and ignite fresh Containment Grit to keep their bubble safely intact. It made the sting of their falling out even more intense. But Ard didn't want to acknowledge their reliance on Lyndel now.

He shrugged. "Maybe we would've gotten lucky and landed in one of the air pockets."

"No," said Gloristar. "The spires of *renna* repel common debris. It keeps them safe and protected."

"Are you calling us debris?" Ard muttered.

"That explains why the seabed was so clean," Raek said. "Not a scuttled ship or skeleton in sight."

"Once you found the pack," said Quarrah, "how did you get back to the surface?"

"In this state, I am able to absorb detonations and reignite the Grit clouds in any shape or manner I choose," said Gloristar. "But my reserves were spent from stopping the Cataclysm flood. I was pushed deep with the sinking rubble of the lighthouse. By the time I had recovered from the fall, I was miles down. Too far to swim unassisted to the surface. I needed more Grit."

Ard glanced at the backpack, realizing that the two kegs were empty. "And suddenly, you found it." That was a blazing happy coincidence.

Gloristar nodded. "Your Barrier Grit shielded me from the water, and your Void Grit propelled me upward."

"When did you surface?" Raek asked.

"Not more than an hour ago," she said. "I pulled myself out of the water and found this cloak in the harbor. I came directly here."

"We were your first stop?" Ard checked. "That's quite the honor, but why didn't you go to the queen? There's a lot of speculation about what happened to you that night. You could set the record straight."

"After killing Termain, I had no idea what political state the islands would be in," said Gloristar. "The Moon Glass let me know that the three of you were safe. You have not seen him, so I felt I could trust you."

"Excuse me. *Him?*" Ard leaned forward, as if he hadn't heard her correctly. "Who is *him?*"

Gloristar closed her glowing eyes for a long moment. "There is much to explain." The three of them waited for her to go on, but she wouldn't even open her eyes.

"Would you like to sit down?" Ard asked. "We can get you something to eat. Drink?"

"My perfected frame no longer requires sustenance," she replied. "Nor do I tire of standing or wakefulness."

"Oh, well…" Ard said. "I hope you don't mind if my *im*perfect frame has a seat while we talk. My dogs are barking."

Gloristar opened her red eyes slowly. "Forgive my rudeness. I will sit." She moved toward the large armchair with the green cushion.

"But maybe not there." Raek gestured her away from the trigger for the trapdoor. The woman took a seat on the short couch, making the furniture look comically small beneath her enlarged figure.

"The Homeland, as I once understood it, does not exist," Gloristar began. "There is no distant shore where the righteous go. There is no existence beyond this one."

"Okay," Ard said, seating himself heavily on the edge of the table. "Let's just get the discouraging bit out first, then."

"I am the true Homeland," Gloristar said, "and any who become like me can find this perfection. I am what was once called Othian."

"We've been calling you a Glassmind," said Raek.

"Is *Othian* a Trothian word?" Quarrah asked.

"It is from a language that precedes Trothian," she answered. "It is the pure language that revealed itself to my mind at the time of transformation. In your tongue, *Othian* would be translated to mean *one who is like the gods.*"

"The gods…" Ard leaned forward. "What do you know about them?"

"Only what I learned from the *renna* spire on the seabed," she replied. "The gods attempted to keep humankind contained. A portion of the people strayed beyond the borders and were inflicted with Moonsickness. Using dragon teeth, they transformed themselves into Othians. A great battle ensued, and the gods took those who had not transformed and created these high islands, filling in the rest of the world to drown the rebellious Othians."

Ard clenched his fists in frustration. None of that was new. Gloristar's surprise arrival should have brought all the answers he craved.

"But what happened to the gods?" Ard pressed. "Why is there no mention of them in Wayfarism?"

Gloristar shook her head. "That knowledge, among much else, was kept from me at the time of my transformation."

"Kept from you?" Quarrah asked.

"By one who calls himself Centrum," said Gloristar. "He was the first Othian in existence."

"I don't understand," said Ard. "All the original Othians swam up from the depths. *Ships unseen,*" he quoted the historical reference. "Their race devolved and they turned into Trothians."

"Yet I am here," she said.

"Yeah, but you came later," said Raek.

"And Centrum was before me." Gloristar looked at each of them with her burning eyes. "He began the next wave of Othians, of which I am second."

"So somebody figured out Metamorphosis Grit before Portsend?" Raek asked.

"It would seem so," answered Gloristar. "All I know is that Centrum had already transformed before Portsend Wal came to my rescue at the Realm's Moonsickness farm. Centrum was waiting for me."

"You met him?" Quarrah asked.

"Not in the traditional sense." Gloristar reached up and tapped a finger on her temple, sparks sizzling from her fingertips. "He was waiting for me here."

"What did he say?" asked Ard.

"He told me we needed to join forces," she replied. "To end civilization as we know it."

"And I'm hoping you said, 'No thanks'?" Ard checked.

"He told me that our minds must be aligned for this to happen." She closed her terrible eyes again. "I resisted. He tried to kill me."

"When?" Quarrah asked.

"After the transformation," she said. "The night of the Cataclysm."

"I don't understand," said Ard. "We were with you."

"So was Centrum," Gloristar said, opening her eyes. "He was with me in the throne room. And in the Old Post Lighthouse. He was in my mind, trying to extinguish my existence like the flickering flame of a candle."

"You didn't say anything," said Ard. Not a word about her mental battle. What had she been going through?

"I didn't understand it," she replied. "I knew Centrum had information that I needed, but he would not yield it unless I submitted to him."

"Well, it sounds like you did the right thing," said Raek. "This Centrum fellow sounds like a real piece of slag."

"You beat him?" said Ard. "Or is he still in there?"

"When that beam fell in the lighthouse, it cracked my skull." Gloristar lowered her head to show the fractures. "After that, I could no longer hear him."

"You think that crack broke the link between your minds?" Ard asked.

"Yes," she answered, "though I am fortunate the damage was not more extensive. As an Othian, I am close to immortality. Age and disease have no hold on me, and my skin is too thick to be pierced by ball or blade. Shattering my skull is the only way I can taste death. If that beam had injured me any more than it did, I would not have recovered."

"Hah!" Ard exclaimed. "That's what I call a lucky break."

"Ugh." Quarrah shook her head at the pun.

"Too soon, Ard," said Raek disapprovingly.

"What do you mean, too soon?" he retorted. "She's been alive for two years. It's not like her skull is suddenly going to cave in."

"Do you think Centrum is still out there?" Quarrah asked, getting them back on track.

Gloristar nodded. "I have little doubt of it. But the fact that you have heard nothing from him gives me hope. It means he hasn't completed the Sphere."

Ard felt a chill pass through him, his mind begin to tingle. "You said something about it that night," he said, voice soft. "When Shad Agaul died on the throne, Quarrah asked if there was anything you could do to help him. You said—"

"Not until the Sphere is complete." Gloristar nodded. "Centrum was tempting me. He told me if we united, we could complete the Sphere. Then life, death, and time itself would be ours to shape."

"The Sphere." Ard squinted in puzzlement. "What is it?"

Gloristar drew a deep breath. "It is time and space perfected through an Othian."

"I'm afraid I don't follow," said Raek.

"Imagine time as a line," Gloristar began, drawing her finger through the air. "Events unfold, days unfold, in a linear fashion—one thing after the next."

"Yep," Raek said. "I'm with you so far."

"But sometimes, time is circular." Gloristar looped her finger backward.

"You're talking about a Paladin Visitant," said Ard.

"You know their true nature?" she asked, surprised.

Ard glanced at his companions. "We have it on good authority."

Gloristar raised her hairless eyebrows. "This will simplify my explanation, then. Time becomes circular when a Paladin Visitant successfully appears at a point in the past. But that resets the timeline, starting a new line going forward."

"Right," Ard said. "Linear. Circular."

"But what happens to the other lines?" Gloristar asked. "The timelines that *were*? Or the ones that *might have been*?"

Ard shook his head. "They don't exist. There can be only one timeline. This one."

"Yes," said Gloristar. "But once the Sphere is complete, time can roll forward. And backward. *And to either side.*"

Ard slowly reached up and grabbed the sides of his head. What was Gloristar even describing? This was pure madness. A scripture from *Wayfarist Voyage* suddenly made sense to him.

*Though we struggle in a line, the circle saves, and the sphere governs all.*

"So you're saying," Raek said slowly, "that if Centrum builds his little Sphere, he could roll us all over to a different timeline? A timeline where he likes things better?"

"Not exactly," answered Gloristar. "Life can only exist in one timeline. This one. Centrum referred to this as the Material Time. When time circles backward with the appearance of a Paladin Visitant, the Material Time begins anew from that point. The previous line is erased, becoming one of an infinite number of shadow timelines where things are *Immaterial*."

"Sparks, that hurts my brain," Ard admitted. He'd had four years to iron out the idea of circular time. It was what had scared King Pethredote into killing the dragons. He'd tried to eliminate any possibility of another Paladin Visitant resetting the Material Time and turning this one into an immaterial shadow.

"I can't wrap my head around this Spherical idea," Ard continued. "If things only exist here, what benefit would Centrum gain by having time roll sideways into an immaterial shadow?"

"I do not fully understand it myself," Gloristar replied. "As I said, he blocked much from my mind. But he promised me that Spherical Time would usher in a new era of limitless power."

"You believe him?" Ard asked. "You think something like that is possible?"

"I do," Glorisar answered solemnly. "Wayfarism teaches something very similar. A time when anything would be possible. When wealth would be found in overabundance, and death would have no power."

"The Homeland, right?" Quarrah asked.

But Ard shook his head. "She's talking about the Final Era of Utmost Perfection."

"That is the time when all living souls will dwell in peace upon the Homeland," explained Gloristar.

"Well, I don't like it," Raek declared. "Sounds like utmost horror to me—time rolling this way and that…"

"How does Centrum plan to complete the Sphere?" Quarrah asked.

"He withheld that information from me," Gloristar answered.

"Surprise," muttered Raek.

"But I know he can't do it alone," she continued. "Wherever he is, Centrum will try to create more Othians. And when he does, that will be the beginning of the end of human civilization."

"Hedge Marsool," Ard whispered.

Quarrah's eyes grew wide. "He told us he knows how to make

more Othians. Flames. What if he created Centrum in the first place?"

Ard nodded. "It's possible. Even likely. And it makes the job that much more important. We get him a dragon and he doesn't create more Glassminds."

"Spark the job!" Raek cried. "I don't trust anything Hedge Marsool says. Here's another idea—kill Hedge and deal with Centrum when, or *if*, he ever shows himself."

"If we kill Hedge, we lose the chance to find out what else he knows," said Ard. "Or *who* else knows what he knows. And right now, he has us at an advantage with that Future Grit."

"Future Grit?" questioned Gloristar.

"That's what we're calling it," he said.

"We're not committed to the name," Raek cut in.

"Anyway," continued Ard, "we think it's a new liquid Grit type that allows our unwanted employer to see what we're going to do before we do it. Have you heard of anything like this?"

"No," replied Gloristar.

"We're not even sure it's a thing," said Quarrah. Why was she fidgeting so much?

"It's definitely a thing," Ard rebutted. "I snagged a vial of it off his belt."

"You snagged a vial of *something*," Raek corrected. "And now we'll never know what it was because you smashed it on the deck of the *Shiverswift*."

Quarrah let out a self-satisfied laugh over that.

"What effect did it have?" Gloristar asked.

"As far as I could tell," said Quarrah, "the only thing that Grit did was create a look of pure stupefaction on Ardor Benn's face."

This time Raek burst out laughing, and Ard stood up, trying to regain control of the conversation.

"I think we digress," he said. "The point is, we can't abandon Hedge's demands now. Come on, Raek. We've never been ones to turn our backs like that. We continue with the job. Especially now." He reached out and shook the backpack on the table. "All our hard work came right back to us. If that isn't a sign that we should continue, I don't know what is."

~

*I always had a strong grasp of my role in things. It only started slipping when I finally admitted that others had more to offer.*

# CHAPTER

# 16

Nemery woke with a start, even though Mohdek's touch had been gentle. She was surprised to see that the sun was up, though it hadn't been bright enough to awaken her between the shade of the trees and the thick storm clouds overhead. Either that, or she'd just been *really* tired.

"I told you not to let me fall asleep, Moh," she scolded.

Silently, Mohdek pointed across the grassy slope to a line of figures descending from Goldred's Scramble. But Nemery quickly counted nine of them, instead of the eight sets of footprints they'd seen going up.

"Legien Dyer is with them." Mohdek answered her unasked question. She squinted at the hikers, but couldn't see faces at this distance. Yet one thing was true, even if she couldn't see it.

"They're Moonsick," she whispered, as if the truth of it were hitting her for the first time. "All of them."

Nemery had seen her share of Moonsick people during her time on Pekal. Blind and mute, their wanton violence falling on anything that moved. And even sometimes things that didn't.

She'd had to put down a handful of them. They were terrible, frightening creatures, with bruised skin thick enough to stop her arrowheads. Their blood-red eyes were the most effective targets, as brutal as it sounded. Perhaps it was callous of her, but she always felt like she was doing them a favor by snuffing out their miserable existence.

But Nemery Baggish had never seen anyone so fresh into Moonsickness. These nine hikers walked like civilized people, their eyes and minds not yet tainted. Only a few hours in, they would still have their voices. But Nemery didn't fool herself. They were dying. An awful, torturous death.

"This was a mistake," Mohdek said. "We should have rescued that young woman last night when their numbers were fewer."

Nemery shook her head. "We talked about it, Moh. We have to see how this plays out. If she really has something that could save people from Moonsickness, isn't it worth sticking around to watch?"

"I fear you place too much faith in this Glassmind cult."

"*Faith* is too strong a word," replied Nemery. "I'm just curious to see what happens. Besides, we've got time. We can follow them for days, so long as we rescue her before those Bloodeyes get ripe and start tearing the group apart."

She gathered her quiver and began tying it around her waist. "We need to get close enough to hear what they're saying. I'm going back to the boulder."

"In broad daylight?" Mohdek cried. "You'll be noticed for sure."

"Then we cut through these trees and sneak up on them from the downhill side," she proposed.

Mohdek nodded. "All right. But we need to act fast."

Nemery pulled on her pack and bow. "I'm just waiting for you."

They moved deeper into the trees, the scent of dust and pine filling her senses. The forest quickly grew dense, the crisp air untouched by today's sunlight, still clinging to night's chill.

In the dim lighting, Nemery let Mohdek take the lead, picking their path carefully through the thick underbrush. They moved straight downhill at a slow and steady pace before hooking back around, following a ravine until the camp came into view through a tangle of branches.

She and Mohdek shed their packs in the ravine's bottom. Here, the canopy of trees was thin enough that a crusty bank of snow had fallen through, lying untouched by the summer sun. They crawled up the slope on their bellies, finally cresting the side of the ravine just in time to see the hikers reach the campsite.

"My friends!" called the man leading them. He was tall and well built—the figure of a man who took exceptional care of his body. His skin was browned from the sun, and his sandy-colored hair was cropped short. He looked to be roughly the age of Nemery's father, though her papa hadn't been nearly as robust when she'd last seen him. Despite this man's militant stature, his face was friendly, and his expression warm.

"Herald Garifus!" Carpen greeted the man with a firm embrace. "How do you feel?"

The two men pulled apart and Nemery could see that Garifus Floc was smiling. "We have slept among the dragons," he announced to the campers. "And we have discovered that they snore." This was met with boisterous laughter from both hikers and campers.

*He's trying to keep everyone at ease*, Nemery realized. The man was charismatic, she'd give him that. A man like that could certainly gain hundreds of followers. But Nemery didn't think he was charming enough to hike all the way to Pekal's summit to get Moonsick...

"Hold on. Who is *this*?" Trenchy pointed a finger at the rear of the group. From her spot, Nemery could barely make out the worn face of Legien Dyer.

"The father of our very own Feltman Dyer," introduced Garifus. "He came all this way to join us on the summit."

Legien didn't protest. Had he already lost his voice? Or maybe he had simply said everything he could, with no more words to spend. Maybe he'd finally come to terms with the fact that he couldn't save his son. Too late now. Legien Dyer looked like a broken man—physically and emotionally.

"I thought Feltman said his father died," replied one of the other campers.

"He will." A young man stepped forward. The physical likeness to Legien Dyer was immediately obvious to Nemery. "Soon enough."

"Peace, Feltman," said Garifus, reaching out and placing a hand on the lad's shoulder. "The Moon has taken him the same as us. He will undergo the transformation at our side."

"But he's not one of us," said a woman standing next to Legien Dyer.

"Would the Prime Isless forbid any worthy person to reach the Homeland?" Garifus rebutted. "Would she deem him Settled because of his love for his son? Legien Dyer may not be one of us, but he has sacrificed everything to come this high. One day soon, every commoner will join us. Why not begin today?"

"But how will we know if he's worthy?" asked another woman.

"The Homeland will judge him," replied Garifus. "But come! Let us speak of more hopeful things. The hour is finally at hand, my friends. Take a moment to remember the faithful who have tried before us." He bowed his head in reverential silence. "But the Homeland has smiled upon us, and this morning's outcome will be more favorable. I feel it in my bones."

Garifus gestured through the group. As the people parted, Nemery saw the young woman step forward. The prisoner looked even more tired and afraid than the night before.

"Is everything prepared?" Garifus asked her. She nodded, a

gesture so small it was almost imperceptible through the foliage. Then she held out her hand to show him something. Glinting in the morning sunlight, Nemery saw a glass vial. What was that about? A tonic or elixir?

Garifus Floc held out his hands. "Let the chosen ones gather with us." The young woman stayed by his side, but the three Lander men and the Trothian woman who had spent the night in safety backed away.

The hikers came forward, gathering into a circle. One of the women pulled along a hesitant Legien Dyer, but Feltman wouldn't even look at his father. Once in position, Garifus joined them, leaving the young woman alone in the ring of nine Moonsick people.

"The world may not understand what we are doing here today," preached Garifus Floc. "But tomorrow they will. The Homeland beckons us, and we must be transformed to receive its glory."

He reached up and pressed the tip of his middle finger against his forehead, spurring all the others to copy the effect. All except the sunburned woman. She had closed her hand around the vial, clenched fist raised slightly above her head. Her face was knotted with so much worry, she looked like she might be sick.

The group began to speak, their voices sounding in unison as they recited a memorized phrase.

"All things form a great Sphere. And we have now come to the top. We are the Homeland. We are time and space perfected."

Their recitation ended as abruptly as it had begun, the chorus of voices seeming to hang among the branches of the forest like a morning fog.

Then Garifus Floc nodded to the young woman. She brought her fist down, hurling the glass vial at the stony ground. Nemery didn't hear it break. She couldn't see if something sparked. But at once, the campsite was enveloped in a perfectly formed vaporous mist.

Like a Grit detonation.

The dome easily encompassed the ten participants in the circle. Part of the detonation was contained against the boulders on the far side, but the perimeter of the cloud rippled into the trees, stopping just yards in front of Nemery and Mohdek.

Her attention snapped back to the campsite as the ring of hikers began to scream and howl. Something was happening to their bodies. They were growing rigid. Paralyzed. Attempting to break their formation, but somehow unable.

Then they went silent, their faces frozen in various expressions of shock and fear. Legien Dyer was stiff as a board, desperately reaching out for his son.

Homeland! What kind of Grit was this? Nemery thought she knew all the types, but she'd never heard of one that could do something like this.

In the middle of the circle, the fair-headed young woman turned this way and that, tears wetting her eyes as she gasped. Nemery couldn't tell if she was horrified or relieved.

Then Garifus Floc's face split straight down the middle. His scalp ripped like a thick piece of parchment, skin falling away to reveal a new skull.

A skull of red glass.

His figure rose out of his former flesh, the new Garifus significantly larger than the one before, like watching a great winged butterfly emerge from the cramped confines of its cocoon.

The other nine began the same process, wriggling through their skins to reveal figures unlike anything Nemery Baggish had ever seen.

Their skin was pale blue like the morning sky, laced with veins of gold that rippled with an otherworldly iridescence. They stood so tall that their hairless glass skulls nearly touched the boughs overhead. Shed strips of human skin littered the ground at their feet, but torn scraps of their clothing still clung to their enlarged forms.

And their eyes... They burned with an unholy red glow. It

seemed as if the Moon itself had pocked their faces with bits of its power.

Garifus Floc rose to his new height. He looked so different. Had she not just seen him transform, she might not have even recognized him.

"We are the Homeland." Even though he spoke softly, his voice was oddly resonant. "For now, we may be few, but together we can usher all of civilization into the Final Era of Utmost Perfection."

"Perfection!" echoed the others.

Then Garifus stepped forward, finally breaking the ring. "I sense that there is one among us who does not share our ideals." He crossed to stand before Legien Dyer.

Like the others, Dyer had been entirely remade by the power of that unknown Grit. His new look seemed ageless, no longer overweight, standing every inch the height of Garifus Floc.

"You are hesitant to share our perfection with the world," said Garifus. "But I do not understand why. Haven't your aches subsided? Hasn't your mind cleared?"

Legien Dyer said nothing that Nemery could hear, but Garifus paused and then resumed as if the man had spoken.

"*I* have saved your son," said the cult leader. "Look at him. Sense him. His mind is open to you, and it is clear he has no guile. Why do you wish to withhold this state from others?"

Again, he paused before resuming his monologue. "It cannot be like that. We must all be united in deed and purpose. Our individual strengths and knowledge become part of the whole. Soon to be part of the Sphere. But we cannot fit a square peg into a round hole. If you cannot see the merit in what we must do, then you have no place in the Homeland."

"Please!" Legien Dyer shouted, his voice booming through the woods. "You said there was room for every commoner to join you."

"There is," said Garifus. "Every commoner who shares our ideals."

"I...I do!" It was strange to see such a powerful-looking figure beg. "I'll go along with your plans."

"There is dishonesty in your heart," said Garifus. "It is laid plainly before our minds. The Homeland does not need you, when there are thousands of others who will come without a fuss."

Suddenly, the red glass of Garifus Floc's skull began to glow. It pulsed at first, but quickly became steady as others in the group responded in kind. One by one, their glass scalps began to radiate an eerie light.

"Wait!" pleaded Legien. "I can change. Feltman!" He turned to his son. "Feltman, please!"

Feltman Dyer's skull was the last to illuminate. Then it ignited like an orb of red Light Grit.

The moment the glow was unanimous, Legien Dyer's skull shattered. Nemery flinched as shards of thick red glass sprayed outward from his cranium. He fell—first to his knees, and then to his face, a wisp of red smoke rising from the blasted crater of his brain.

The woman beside Feltman reached out, gently squeezing his arm in condolence. Then the lights in their minds were extinguished, heads darkening to smooth red glass.

"We have sensed another matter," said Garifus. Nemery tensed, preparing to run, but the huge man turned to the young woman who had backed against the boulder.

"I believe congratulations are in order," Garifus said to her. "You were right about everything."

He held up his hand and took a deep breath. Suddenly, the vaporous Grit cloud cleared, snuffed out before its usual ten minutes. No. Not snuffed.

*Absorbed.*

Nemery could see the final wisps of the cloud flowing into Garifus Floc's raised hand.

"Your secrecy had bought you relevance," Garifus said to her. "But we now understand your... *Transformation Grit* on a new level."

"I...I..." The poor girl was so shaken, she couldn't get more than a word out.

"Your once-impressive mind is nothing to our perfected collective consciousness," Garifus continued. "And now you have overstayed your welcome."

He stooped and lifted a long dagger from the litter of his former body. *Sparks*, Nemery thought. *He's going to kill her the traditional way.*

The woman grunted, springing past Garifus with surprising agility, making for one of the backpacks on the ground beside the fire pit. The Lander man, Carpen, reached it first, snatching the pack away and leaving the woman to fall on her knees in a hopeless pounce.

Nemery had an arrow on her bowstring before she even realized it. She wasn't going to stand by and watch this woman—this *prisoner*—get murdered for doing everything the cultists had asked of her.

"Salafan!" Mohdek hissed as she rose to her knees, drawing the bowstring and releasing in one fluid motion.

At this range, she hadn't even needed to aim. The arrow took Carpen just below the collarbone. He dropped the pack in front of the woman, staggering backward with a gurgle.

The nine Glassminds turned in unison, their glowing red eyes shining through the dense trees, locating her immediately.

"Oh, flames..." Nemery cursed, scrambling to her feet. No sense in hiding. Two of the transformed beings were already moving in her direction.

An explosion ripped through the camp, throwing everyone outward in a blast of fire and smoke. Broken chips of rock sprayed from the boulders and one of the dead trees caught flame.

It would seem the young woman had found the Blast Grit in that backpack.

Before the dust had settled, Nemery was on her feet, running. Not away from the campsite, but directly toward it. She burst through the black smoke, stumbling over the body of the dark-skinned Lander man she had seen last night. He was unconscious from the explosion, maybe dead.

Nemery was at the young woman's side in no time, yanking her to her feet without a word of introduction.

"Leave the pack," Nemery said.

"But it's full of Grit," said the young woman.

Nemery nocked another arrow, one of the Glassminds sprinting toward them. She loosed, but she might as well have shot the boulder. The stone arrowhead didn't break skin, and the shaft splintered against the man's pale blue chest.

The blond woman plunged her hand into the backpack and withdrew a clay Grit pot marked with a yellow dot.

Nemery caught her arm before she could throw it. "More Blast Grit?" she cried. "You're lucky you didn't blow yourself up the first time."

The woman pulled out of Nemery's grasp. "Eight and a half granules," she said. "Mixed it myself. We'll be fine at this distance."

She hurled the pot at the incoming Glassmind. It shattered against his shoulder, sparks dancing as the Slagstone fragment struck. This explosion was much smaller, flinging the Glassmind sideways into the boulder. That Blast would have blown a normal man to paste, but the Glassmind promptly rose, glowing eyes narrowing to slits.

"Come on!" Nemery cried, sprinting back into the trees.

"We can't outrun them," the woman replied, following nevertheless. "Garifus said their new forms would be capable of great speeds."

*Can't outrun them. Can't outfight them. Can't outthink them . . .* Nemery suddenly regretted her decision to reveal herself.

"Nem!" Mohdek was waving a hand through the trees. He wasn't where she had left him, having retrieved their packs and repositioned himself on the other side of the ravine. Smart. The trees were thinner over there. Easier for a hasty getaway.

In Mohdek's enthusiasm, he didn't see the Glassmind racing toward him. Nemery screamed a warning, neither in his language, nor in hers. Simply a guttural cry, punctuated by frantic gesturing.

Mohdek realized what was happening as the Glassmind leapt the ravine in a single bound. The Trothian stepped back, swinging the short sword he already held at the ready. But the Glassmind caught the steel blade in one hand, halting his blow. Then the enhanced woman reached up with her other hand, seizing the tip of the sword and snapping the blade with the sheer strength of her grip.

Mohdek let go of the broken weapon, staggering backward and slipping down to the snowy bottom of the ravine as Nemery loosed another arrow. It was as useless as the last, splintering against the Glassmind's side.

Sparks! And she thought *Bloodeyes* were hard to kill... That was it! She needed to treat this foe like a thick-skinned Bloodeye.

"Hey!" She nocked another arrow, turning the woman's attention away from Mohdek. In a single bound, the Glassmind leapt over the ravine, landing nimbly in the loose soil. Now Nemery was only a few yards away, and those glowing red eyes were like targets begging to be shot.

She let the arrow fly, the shaft flexing under the force of her bowstring. Her aim was true, she could tell the moment her fingers released.

The Glassmind's hand came up with superhuman speed, catching the shaft of the arrow. It slid a few inches through her grip, the pointy arrowhead stopping just a leaf's width from her glowing eye.

Nemery felt her legs threaten to give out. She could see Garifus Floc leading the rest of the Glassminds toward them, shouting commands.

"Get behind me!" The prisoner woman shoved Nemery down into the ravine toward Mohdek. She remained at the edge, gripping two more Grit pots, a small linen pouch dangling from her mouth by its drawstrings.

She threw the first pot only a few feet in front of her, a distinctive Barrier cloud forming instantly. The detonation had a small radius, no more than three feet, but it encompassed the trunks of several trees, standing as an impenetrable dome between her and the charging Glassminds.

Acting quickly, she tucked the remaining Grit pot into the small linen pouch, leaving the drawstrings open. Then she lobbed the parcel over the top of her Barrier cloud, not even waiting to see where it landed.

Nemery saw it, though, peering up over the edge of the ravine. It was Void Grit, obviously Mixed with Compounding Grit beyond any level Nemery had ever seen.

The outward rush of energy instantly broke or uprooted every tree within its radius, sending whole trunks flying like massive spears in a hailstorm of rocks. Down in the ravine, the three of them were protected, any limbs or stones bumping over the small Barrier dome and clearing their heads.

"Blazing brilliant," Nemery exclaimed. "Why didn't you lead with that?"

"Didn't think of it until I saw the ravine," she replied. "That pouch had all the loose Compounding Grit we brought."

"Come on," Mohdek said, leading the way along the snowy bottom of the draw. He was right to keep moving. As destructive as that technique had appeared, there was no telling how much damage it would do to the Glassminds. Or even how long it would delay them.

"I'm Salafan," Nemery introduced, sprinting alongside the stranger. "You got a name?"

The young woman flinched as a low-hanging branch whipped at her face, threatening to snag her ratty blond hair.

"Lomaya," she replied. "Lomaya Vans."

They ran in silence, too winded to ask questions or give answers. Mohdek moved in front, choosing their path without a second's hesitation.

Nearly an hour had passed when Lomaya finally collapsed to the forest floor, heaving from the prolonged exertion.

"We have to..." Nemery gasped in Trothian, "to rest."

Mohdek nodded, breaking his pace to begin a quick search of the area. There were no signs that the Glassminds had followed, but that didn't mean they were safe.

"You care to explain how you just turned a bunch of Moonsick folks into blazing superhumans?" Nemery uncorked her water skin, offering it first to Lomaya.

"You care to explain how you just came out of nowhere?" she retorted. Nemery dropped wearily to sit at her side, back against a tree, as sweat streamed down her neck. Nemery briefly explained about Legien Dyer's desperation to reach his son while Lomaya alternated between long gulps and gasps for breath.

"Your turn," Nemery said when she was finished, taking back the water skin and finishing the last two swallows.

"I call it Transformation Grit," Lomaya said, her breathing finally regular. "My friend and I developed it a few cycles back."

"You developed a new type of Grit, and you thought it would be a good idea to turn that information over to the local cult?" Nemery cried.

"We weren't the first to create it," she said. "Our professor must have been successful two years ago, based on the reports we heard about Prime Isless Gloristar."

"So you're a believer in this Glassmind cult?"

"Sparks, no," Lomaya said. "But San and I had to test our theories somewhere. We caught wind of the Glassmind cult. They seemed to have more information about what happened to Gloristar than anyone. Garifus Floc was an eyewitness to the Prime Isless's transformed state. From him, we learned that Gloristar had been Moonsick before she'd turned into a Glassmind. When San and I told Garifus that we had a strong hypothesis about creating more Glassminds, the cult held us captive."

"And your friend, San..." Nemery started. "Where is he now?"

"He's in Beripent," Lomaya replied, "waiting for our return with the rest of the cultists."

"How did Garifus convince you to hike up here with him?" asked Nemery.

"San was supposed to be the one, but he got sick the night we left Beripent. Garifus said he'd only slow them down, so I had to come in his place," she answered. "San and I spent cycles trying to keep the formula for Transformation Grit out of Garifus's hands. We had convinced him that one of us needed to be present in order to successfully create the detonation."

"Ah," said Nemery. "That explains why he wasn't very happy with you after he absorbed the detonation cloud. Did you know he could do that?"

Lomaya shook her head. "Honestly, San and I had no idea what the Glassminds could do. We thought Garifus's description of Gloristar's abilities was exaggeration...Now I'm realizing that he didn't even know the whole of it."

"You knew he would transform when you broke that vial?" Nemery asked.

Lomaya nodded. "The cultists have been coming to Pekal to get Moonsick for nearly two years now," she explained. "To them, it's like the Wayfarist Voyage. The most devout cultists make the sacrifice, believing that the worthy would transform into a Glassmind... Like what happened to Gloristar. Of course, they were missing the Grit until San and I came along."

"Then why'd you do it?" Nemery asked. "If you really believed it would work, then why did you go through with it?"

"Have you heard of the Realm?" Lomaya asked.

"No," Nemery said. "Where is it?"

"Not *where*," she replied. "The Realm was a secret organization. Criminals. They controlled my professor, assassinated Prince Shad Agaul, murdered someone I was close to..." She drew in a steadying breath. "Queen Abeth has done her best to stomp them out, but Garifus Floc was one of them."

"Legien Dyer told us he was a palace Regulator," said Nemery.

"He was," answered Lomaya. "But he was also a second-tier member of the Realm, known as the Faceless. He puts on a charismatic air, but the man is driven by a wicked desire for power. He told me that if I didn't come with him to the summit, he would kill San."

"Still, couldn't you have thrown a different type of Grit?" Nemery suggested. "Claimed it didn't work?"

"Then he would have killed me," she said quietly.

"Not to be insensitive," said Nemery, "but he kind of tried to do that anyway."

"I was hoping for a different scenario this morning," Lomaya said softly. "I knew a lot could happen between the harbor and here, but Shopaj was an excellent guide, and we lost only one person along the way."

Nemery thought of that mangled corpse near the dragon hatchling. She didn't feel anything for that stranger, but her heart still ached for little Oropsi. This was not the justice she had planned for the poor hatchling. Instead, the dragon's murders had become powerful beyond reckoning.

"I underestimated the power of the Transformation Grit," Lomaya admitted. "I thought, even if it works, what harm would come from eight Glassminds on Pekal's summit?"

"That depends," said Nemery. "What does Garifus have planned next?"

"He'll go back to Beripent and rally the rest of the cult. There are nearly a thousand anxious to see if he returns. When they see what he's become, they'll follow him to the summit without hesitation. And if Garifus really knows how to make more Transformation Grit, he'll have hundreds of Glassminds after the next Passing."

Eight of them were unstoppable enough. Nemery couldn't imagine *hundreds*.

At the sound of a snapping twig, Nemery leapt to her feet with a startled boost of energy she didn't know she had in her.

Mohdek appeared, still breathing heavily. "They've moved past us," he said quietly. "Looks like they're making for Dornik's Pass."

Nemery helped Lomaya to her feet. "Then we'll take Skyline Loop," she said. "It'll take us an extra day or two to get down, but we won't have to worry about running into them again."

"What?" said Lomaya. "No. We have to get back to Beripent before them."

Nemery snorted. "We're not going to Beripent."

"They'll kill San," she whispered. "I need to help him escape before Garifus and the others get back."

Mohdek shook his head. "At the rate they were moving, they'll be to the harbor by tomorrow morning."

"If they're that far ahead, then we don't need to worry about running into them again," Lomaya said. "We could take that Pass—the faster way down..."

Nemery turned to Mohdek, switching to Trothian. "What do you think?"

"She won't know if we take Skyline Loop," he replied. "We could tell her it's the Pass, just to be safe."

"The Glassmind cult is holding her friend," said Nemery. "We should get her down as quickly as we dare. If you think it's safe."

Mohdek nodded.

"Look," Nemery said to Lomaya. "We'll take Dornik's Pass and see you safely back to New Vantage. We can be there in as few as four days. After that, I'm afraid you're on your own."

Lomaya Vans stiffened. "Thank you," she managed to say through the disappointment on her face. "Where will you go?"

"Us?" Nemery glanced at Mohdek. "We'll be here. Pekal is our home."

"Then you'd better get yourselves ready," said Lomaya. "By the end of next cycle, your home is going to be crawling with Glassminds."

~

*Something needed to change. I've known it for years now. Something major.*

# PART III

Is there any greater than the Homeland? Any who could rise above perfection? Nay. For if it were so, the blessed Homeland would be vanquished.

—Wayfarist Voyage, *vol. 2*

All that we have, and all that we are, is given by the Moon. If it gives again, we will stand with our faces upturned and our minds aglow.

—*Ancient Agrodite poem*

# CHAPTER

# 17

The Elegant Perch was a top-notch establishment, in Ardor Benn's humble opinion. New Vantage's premier inn was aptly named, the structure built right on the edge of Pekal's shoreline cliff. For an extra ten Ashings, he could have scored a balcony that hung right over the InterIsland Waters. But he'd seen that view plenty. He was interested in the other side of the inn, and the green slopes of Pekal, rising out of sight on a foggy morning like this.

Things had gone quite smoothly since Gloristar's return. With the Agrodite Moon Glass and the backpack, they were able to complete their transaction with Baroness Lavfa. She had given them a signed agreement for the subterranean property below Helizon, which Ard had left with Geppel at Tofar's Salts. The next evening, the Trothian gatekeeper had turned over the documents and paperwork that Hedge Marsool had promised.

That information had connected them with Captain Torgeston Dodset, a woman with insane connections that would allow her to get a ship in and out of any harbor without a cargo inspection. And the *Stern Wake* was certainly large enough to hide a fully grown sow.

Captain Dodset had provided plenty of strong arms to carry equipment and fend off attacks on Pekal. She even had a pair of Tracers that claimed to know their way around the island.

But they were still looking for a Caller in New Vantage.

Hedge Marsool's papers had given them a name. Well, it wasn't a name so much as an overwrought moniker.

The Terror of Wilder Far.

Cryptic, and quite off-putting. Raek had left early this morning to chase down a lead. Yawning, Ard moved down the stairs leading to the Elegant Perch's common room. It was spacious and well lit from large, east-facing windows. There was no bar or counter, but diners were free to seat themselves at any number of tables with padded chairs, waiting for servants to ask what they'd like to eat.

Ard wouldn't have breakfast here. Not delicious enough for the price—he'd learned that yesterday morning. But he swept the room to make sure that Raek wasn't waiting to give him a report.

He didn't expect to find Quarrah here, though she had rented a room next to Ard and Raek. She would be...Well, Ard didn't even have a guess as to how Quarrah was spending her time in New Vantage. There was certainly no shortage of rich people to pickpocket.

Ard wondered how Gloristar was holding up, staying onboard the *Stern Wake*, cooped up belowdecks for two days now. Her appearance was just too startling for a room at the Elegant Perch. It had been difficult enough to get her onto the ship in Beripent's harbor.

At first, Ard had questioned Gloristar's decision not to go to the queen, but her reasons to stay in hiding were valid. Cut off from Centrum's mental connection, the evil Glassmind had no reason to suspect that Gloristar was alive. If she made a public reappearance, word would spread like wildfire, which might provoke Centrum into attacking. And they couldn't risk that.

Ard finished his sweep of the common room, noticing only well-dressed breakfasters. From the snippets of conversation he'd picked up, it sounded like most of them had been in New Vantage for the Moon Passing, and were preparing to head back to the Greater Chain in the next few days.

Ard was almost to the inn's exit when the door burst open. He reached for his Rollers until he saw that the intruder was absolutely harmless.

It was Ednes Holcatch, just the type of person Ard wanted as a contact in a place like New Vantage. He'd found her in the town center yesterday, practically bubbling over with gossip and information.

"Oh, Mister Ardor! Praise the Homeland!" The plump woman was breathing heavily in the most dramatic fashion.

"What's wrong, Ednes?" he asked.

"Wrong?" she cried, giggling. "Why, quite the opposite. Salafan has returned ahead of schedule. She rarely visits New Vantage this early in the cycle."

"Salafan?" Ard asked.

"I told you about her yesterday," Ednes said with some degree of annoyance. That really didn't narrow it down. Ednes Holcatch had told him about a *lot* of people yesterday.

"That girl," she continued. "I've known she was a wild thing for some time, but according to Amma, who heard from Poless, who heard from Burdal, she has some skill as a Caller. Ha! Who knew that rat's nest of a hairdo had such finesse?"

Ard held up his hand with hopes that she'd stop talking.

"You *were* looking for a Caller, were you not?" she said.

"Yes, yes," replied Ard. "But not just any kid that can blow a horn. I hardly think that this *Salafan* could be the one they call"—he lowered his voice—"the Terror of Wilder Far."

"Well, I don't know anything about that," she said. "Why, a name like that sounds absolutely chilling." The woman shuddered. "But if you've tried Raston's Expeditions—"

"We have," Ard interrupted.

"Then you might as well talk to Salafan," continued Ednes. "She might know more about this *Terror* you're looking for. Rumor has it, the wild girl is unregistered, unaffiliated. And Homeland knows she's discreet."

Ard sighed. It was worth a shot. "Where is she?"

"Well, her Trothian boyfriend's down at the harbor for a soak." She paused. "*Trothian* boyfriend," she said again, as if it should have gotten a bigger response from Ard. But why would he care whom other people were loving? He had enough trouble with his own love life.

"And where is this Salafan?" he asked again.

"Oh, she stopped at Burdal's Provisions, not fifteen minutes ago," said Ednes. "She's with a young woman I didn't recognize."

"Burdal's Provisions?"

"A shop in the town center," she answered.

"Ednes, you're a gem," he said. "I don't know how I could possibly repay you."

She giggled again. "Dinner?" she suggested. "Somewhere quiet?"

Ard stopped himself from recoiling. The woman was more than a decade older than him and, quite frankly, too chatty to be his type. He wouldn't get a word in edgewise at dinner with Ednes Holcatch.

"Dinner…" Ard nodded slowly. "Yes. Definitely. Probably not tonight, though." He moved past her, slipping outside into the cool summer morning. "I'll contact you!" He broke into a jog down the street. Phew. Hopefully, he wouldn't have to follow up on that.

He found his way to the courtyard in the town center easily enough, keeping his eye out for Raek and Quarrah as he went. No sign of his companions, but he did see a Holy Isle preaching on one street corner. It was unlikely that the man would recognize him, but Ard kept his head low anyway. He'd told Prime Isle Trable that he needed some personal time to visit his aged and estranged grandmother in Strind before she died. Trable had given him two weeks. Ard figured that would be plenty of time to steal a dragon.

He entered the courtyard, moving around the impressive statue of the dragon at its center. There was a string quartet performing under a covered awning. Unlike street musicians in the Char, no one was throwing them money, though a decent crowd had gathered to watch. Maybe this was an actual concert.

Ard stepped onto the front porch of Burdal's Provisions. The door struck a little bell hanging from the top of the doorjamb, announcing his arrival.

A portly man with a droopy mustache stood behind the counter, conversing with two young women. The first was a sunburned blonde, who turned nervously the moment Ard entered. The second was smaller, dark skinned, and dressed in clothes more rural than a field worker. There was a well-worn pack at her feet and a longbow strung across her shoulder. She didn't pay any attention to the door chime, obviously working some kind of deal with the man Ard presumed to be Burdal. This had to be the girl Ednes had told him about.

Ard left the door ajar, stopping next to a fine-looking Caller instrument on display. He cleared his throat, but he only got a response from Burdal.

"I'll be with you in a moment."

"I'm looking for Salafan," Ard announced.

The dark-haired girl turned and Ard's heart leapt. If he looked past her rough appearance and wild hair, if he changed the expression on her face from pure confidence to frightened insecurity, if he pictured her younger... naive and innocent... By the Homeland.

It was Nemery Baggish!

He opened his mouth to say something, but she beat him to it.

"Ardor?" She took an unsure step forward. "Ardor Benn? What are you doing here? How did you find me?" Then she tilted her head skeptically. "Did my parents send you? Be honest."

Ard let out a laugh. Same talkative spirit, even if nothing else about her seemed familiar. "Your parents? Nemery, I've never even met them. I promise."

She visibly relaxed. "Then why were you looking for me?"

"I didn't know it was you," he admitted. "Ednes told me that you—"

"Ednes Holcatch?" Nemery cut him off. "You can't believe half of what that woman says."

"Well, she was right this time." Ard took a step toward her. "She told me Salafan was a Caller. And I happen to be looking for one."

Nemery broke eye contact, seeming suddenly interested in the stocked shelves. "Yeah, well...I can't help you this time."

"Oh, no. It's...I'm actually looking for someone they call the Terror of Wilder Far."

Her dark eyes snapped up, making intense contact with his. "Maybe we should talk outside."

"You know him?" Ard asked.

Nemery strode past, stepping through the open door, the morning sunlight glinting off some metal beads she had woven into her black hair. Ard followed her, but the girl was talking before he had even swung the door shut.

"It's me, okay?" she whispered. "*I'm* the one they call the Terror of Wilder Far."

Ard started to chuckle, but the serious look on her face quashed it. "You?" he said. "What does that name even mean?"

"Never mind that," she snapped. "Who sent you to find me?"

"I got the name from Hedge Marsool."

"Who?"

"The King Poacher?" Ard said. "Grizzled fellow with one eye and a spike on his arm?"

"I have no idea who you're talking about."

Ard scratched his chin. "He named you specifically in a document—"

"Me?" she cried. Then she lowered her voice to a whisper. "Nemery Baggish?"

"Not your real name," Ard said. "Not even Salafan. Is that what you're going by now? How long have you been here?"

"Listen, Ardor," she said. "I'm sorry I can't help you, but I'm not taking clients into the mountains anymore. There are a handful of decent Callers in New Vantage. You should try the Harvester's Exchange on the south side—"

"I'm not interested in a *decent* Caller," Ard cut her off. "Not when I'm talking to an extraordinary one." He didn't miss the tug of a smile at the corner of her lips. "Besides, Raek has already shaken down most of the legitimate Callers on New Vantage. They want to see our Harvesting papers and..." He shrugged. "Well, I'm sure you remember how I work."

Nemery looked up at him. "I'd like to, Ardor. I really would. But I—"

"You don't have an instrument?" he guessed. "I'll buy you that one." He gestured back toward the one in the shop.

"You can't buy it," she said.

"Oh? I'm not bothered by a little NOT FOR SALE sign."

"You can't buy it," Nemery repeated, "because I just did."

Ard raised his eyebrows. Where did little Nemery Baggish come up with enough Ashings for an instrument that fine?

"I recently came by some Ashings," she explained. "From a job...Burdal's an old friend, so he cut me a deal."

"If you have an instrument," said Ard, "then what's the holdup? Is it payment? I can offer you—"

"I owe you my life, Ardor Benn," she cut him off. "I'm not letting you pay me."

Well, that was a new phrase. This girl was dealing one surprise after another.

Nemery strummed absently at the bowstring across her chest. "I'm sorry, but I just don't have time. Something's happened. On Pekal. And until I figure out what to do about it, I can't spend my time as a Caller on a simple Harvesting expedition."

Ard studied her youthful face, trying to figure out what she meant. Something had obviously spooked her. Only more reason for

Ard to convince her to join them. If Nemery was frightened about Pekal now, wait till she saw what would happen if Hedge didn't get his dragon... There would be Glassminds all over these slopes.

"What if I told you it wasn't a Harvesting expedition?" Ard ventured.

Nemery chewed on that for a moment. "What do you have in mind?"

"There's a lot at stake, Nemery Baggish," said Ard. "I'm here for a job. And if we don't get it done, my employer has plans to make a lot of people Moonsick."

Her entire expression darkened. "Are you talking about Moonsickness," she whispered, "or Glassminds?"

Ard's breath caught in his throat. "How do you know about—"

"I think we need to talk somewhere else."

Nemery stood between Lomaya and Mohdek on the dock, staring up the ramp to the *Stern Wake*. It was a massive ship—larger than any she had ever set foot on, with three great masts topped with Esparian flags.

"How sure are you that this isn't a trap?" Mohdek asked in Trothian.

"Come on, Moh," she replied in his language. "It was Ardor Benn."

"Yes," he said, tone markedly unenthusiastic. "The famous Ardor Benn. Known criminal and ruse artist."

"Apparently, he's reformed," she replied. "He said he's a Holy Isle now."

"And I'm a Lander nobleman," he remarked, less a joke than a cutting statement made to prove a point. "We should have met on more neutral ground. He's had hours to get ready for us."

"He had to round up his friends," she explained. "And I had to round up *you*." Mohdek's *fajumar* had been cut a little short, but his blue skin was still glistening smooth.

"Are we going aboard, or not?" Lomaya asked, tired of being excluded from their many conversations in Trothian.

"See," Nemery said to Mohdek, switching to Landerian. "I'm not the only one who trusts him."

"I don't know about *trusting* him," said Lomaya. "But he knew too much about my professor and his secret work. If he isn't an ally, then he's a lingering part of that group I was telling you about."

"The Realm," said Nemery.

"Which means he might know Garifus Floc," Mohdek pointed out.

"Fine," Nemery said. "You two are welcome to stay on the docks, but I'm going to talk to him. The Ardor Benn I knew might have been a criminal, but he was a good person."

"And how much have *you* changed in the last four years?" asked Mohdek. She didn't answer. "Is it not reasonable to think that he might have, as well?"

"Of course," she said. "And it sounds like it's been for the better." Without waiting for her companions to deliberate any further, Nemery headed up the ramp.

"Nemery Baggish?" She was greeted by a woman with a shaved head and a handful of glittering jewels in both of her ears. Tattoos of curling flames spread up her arms and neck.

"I go by Salafan," Nemery said.

"And I go by Your Highness, but nobody calls me that," said the woman. "Captain Torgeston Dodset." She reached out for an introductory shake, her hand in a fingerless leather glove.

"I'm here to see Ardor Benn," Nemery explained, aware that Mohdek and Lomaya had come up behind her.

"He's expecting you." The captain pointed to a door beneath the quarterdeck. "I'm loaning you my cabin for this meeting. Make sure Ard doesn't move my favorite chair."

"You're not joining us?" Nemery asked.

Captain Dodset shook her head. "I've got a very specific set of skills. Traipsing across Pekal is not one of them." She ran her hand along the ship's rail. "I'll keep the *Stern Wake* ready to run in case you all come back."

*In case?*

With a nod, Nemery moved past the woman, leading the way across the deck. She didn't like the harbor, let alone boarding a ship. It felt too much like leaving Pekal.

At the door to the cabin, Nemery glanced at Mohdek one last time, giving him a chance for a final rebuttal. He must have known that she'd shut him down regardless of what he said, because he kept his mouth closed, merely acknowledging her with a resigned shrug.

Nemery knocked.

There was a quiet stretch, when the only thing she heard was the beat of her own heart. It really hadn't slowed since she'd seen Ardor Benn in Burdal's Provisions. After all these years, imagining what it would be like to reunite, but realizing its absolute improbability, she felt enlivened and a little bit frightened.

So many old memories had awakened at the sight of his face. Memories of the girl she'd been on that first terrifying trip to Pekal. The validation she'd felt from her obsessive study of dragon books, and her hard work studying with a Master Caller. Ardor Benn had been the first person to see her true potential, and now she felt tremendous pressure not to let him down.

The door opened, and there he was, waving the three of them inside. She saw Raekon Dorrel first, sitting on a chair with his huge arms resting on the edge of a square table. Raek had been the one who'd actually hired her for that ill-fated job all those years ago. Nemery hadn't trusted him the same way she had Ardor. He'd seemed rougher, more Settled. Strangely, she didn't feel the same judgment toward him now. After hunting poachers for so many cycles, she knew what a real villain looked like. And it wasn't Raek.

Quarrah Khai was seated beside him, and Nemery smiled at the sight of her. She remembered Ardor kissing Quarrah outside the Caller hut four years ago. He had been unsure about their future then, but the fact that she was here now must have meant things had worked out between them.

As Ardor swung the cabin door closed, Nemery turned, spotting a new figure standing against the wall. She let out an involuntary yelp, drawing an arrow from her quiver and clumsily pulling the bow off her shoulder.

It was a Glassmind.

The woman stood so tall that she was hunched to avoid bumping her cowled glass head on the cabin ceiling. Even with the dark cloak, she was easy to recognize with that pale blue-and-gold skin and those red eyes shining through the dim room.

"It's all right." Ardor reached out, placing a hand on her bow. "She's with us." Nemery tried to relax, but she noticed that Mohdek didn't lower his sword.

"Prime Isless Gloristar," Ard introduced, "meet my friend Nemery Baggish."

"Prime Isless..." Nemery started. But her awestruck rambling was nipped in the bud as the tall Glassmind woman moved across the room in three long strides.

"Homeland afar," Gloristar whispered, fiery eyes piercing over Nemery's shoulder. "Lomaya Vans?"

Nemery glanced back at her companion, who looked paler than ever, staring up at the Glassmind. Finally, she bowed her head in respect.

Gloristar reached out, fingers gently touching the young woman's chin and lifting her gaze. "Portsend Wal would raise a prayer to the Homeland to see you safe and well. He worried about you until his final breath. You, and San—"

"Oh," Ardor cut in. "So you two already know each other?"

Behind the table, Raek rose abruptly, chair sliding out behind him. "I know her, too," he said.

"I met you once," Raek continued to Lomaya. "Not sure if you remember."

"I remember." Lomaya seemed much less enthused to see Raekon Dorrel. In fact, if the touch of a Glassmind hadn't sent Lomaya running, Raek's attention nearly did.

"Well, this is turning out to be quite the reunion, isn't it?" Ardor clapped his hands together contentedly.

Raek was massaging his sternum in a peculiar way and Nemery could see something bulging beneath his sleeveless shirt. Perhaps a pendant on a necklace, or something?

"The Prime Isless is right," Raek continued to Lomaya. "There was a time when old Portsend thought he'd lost you. Keeping you safe was what drove him on. He spoke of you and San often." Raek tilted his head curiously. "Where have you been?"

"Perhaps a great place to start," Ardor said, gesturing for Nemery and her companions to take a seat at the table next to Quarrah. Nemery remembered the thief to be a quiet one, rarely speaking unless it was necessary.

*A good balance for Ardor Benn*, she thought. *Like Moh and me.*

"When Professor Wal sent us away," began Lomaya, seating herself across from Raek, "San and I fled to northern Talumon. We knew the formulas for six types of liquid Grit, and we knew the source material for the seventh. When the war ended, we got ahold of some digested, powdered dragon tooth and began our own experiments."

"You didn't go back to the college?" Raek asked.

Lomaya shook her head. "We'd heard that Professor Wal had been killed. And we didn't know who to trust in Beripent. The Realm..." She trailed off, and Nemery could see the fear on her face. For a group Nemery had never heard of, this Realm had really shaken up a lot of people.

"About a half a year ago," Lomaya continued, "San and I had a breakthrough. We'd been successful in creating a detonation cloud with the dragon tooth solution, but we didn't know what it did. After literally hundreds of tests on mammals, we decided to vary the experimentation, using birds, reptiles, and amphibians. The cloud had no measurable effect on a mature frog, but when we tested it on a tadpole—"

"It immediately turned into a frog," Raek finished. "The professor's tests reached a similar conclusion."

"But we knew there had to be a better application for this Transformation Grit," she said.

"Transformation Grit?" Ardor cut in. "Portsend called it Metamorphosis Grit."

"Don't think it matters which name you call it," Quarrah said.

"I just want us all to be on the same page," replied Ardor defensively. "We should decide which one to call it."

"She can call it what she wants," Quarrah pressed. "We're all smart enough to track this conversation."

Yep. Nemery grinned. Only a couple in love could argue like that.

"How did you figure out the Moonsickness connection to the Grit?" Raek asked Lomaya.

"I'm afraid we can't take credit for that," Lomaya said softly. "A few cycles back, San and I were trying to put together more details about Professor Wal's death. We'd heard it somehow involved the Prime Isless." She glanced at Gloristar, still standing beside the table. "But reports about what had happened to you were as numerous as the stars. Eventually, our search led us to a religious cult—a group of zealots that had splintered from Wayfarism over one particular point." Her gaze was fixed on Gloristar. "You."

"Me?" whispered the Glassmind. The complexity and resonance of her voice sent a chill down Nemery's spine.

"They called themselves the Glassmind cult," continued Lomaya. "Their leader is a man named Garifus Floc, Faceless in the Realm, and a former palace Regulator who claims he saw you after your transformation."

"That's probable," Ardor said. "There were half a dozen Reggies in the throne room that night."

"Well, the Prime Isless made an impact on this one," said Lomaya. "He promptly left the Regulation and dedicated himself to finding out exactly what had happened to you. By the time San and I crossed his path, Garifus knew that you had been Moonsick, and that someone had transformed you using unknown Grit. The cultists were crazy. Garifus was sending the most devout up to Pekal, telling them that if they believed, they could change like Gloristar."

Quarrah suddenly sat forward. "How long had these groups been going up?"

"Several cycles," Lomaya answered.

"I stole one of them."

"What?" Ardor and Raek cried in unison.

"That's what I was doing the night I found the note in the broken vase," Quarrah explained. "Lord Dulith had hired me to steal a Moonsick person. He'd claimed to have a cure, which had interested me enough to do the job. But it was just a cover."

"Then why did he want a Bloodeye?" Ardor asked.

"Revenge," answered Quarrah.

Nemery shuddered. She didn't understand exactly what Quarrah was saying, but it reminded her how demented "civilized" people could be. They put on airs in their fancy manors, or common neighborhoods, but people in the city were every bit as savage as the animals on Pekal.

"And you told Garifus about the Transformation Grit?" Gloristar asked.

"Not directly," said Lomaya. "Some of his followers had just come back from Pekal. They were chained up, their minds lost to Moonsickness. When we saw them, San and I asked if we could try to save them. That got Garifus's attention."

"Did it work?" Nemery asked.

Lomaya shook her head. "They were too far gone—into the final stage. But by that point, Garifus was intrigued by us. He held us hostage, demanding that we improve our Grit formula and try again. We explained that we couldn't alter the Grit, but perhaps if we had a fresher specimen..."

Lomaya didn't seem excited to finish the story, so Nemery took over.

"We rescued Lomaya at the summit, but nine of them had already transformed. One of them didn't want to play by Garifus's rules, so they killed him without lifting a finger."

"What?" said Ardor. "How?"

"I don't know," she replied. "It was like they could read each other's thoughts. When they didn't like what this guy was thinking, they just shattered his head. Tell them what you saw, Moh."

Clearly uncomfortable by the sudden attention, Mohdek shifted his feet where he'd been standing behind Nemery's chair.

"My eyes saw what Nemery describes," he began, his nerves making his accent more pronounced than ever. "Their skulls began to glow, and a network of energy connected their minds. I don't know how to describe it. It was like..."

"Like seeing thoughts," finished Gloristar. "My mind was once connected to another. I felt him try to break me as you have described." She turned to Lomaya. "In your time with Garifus Floc, did he ever mention the name *Centrum*?"

Lomaya wrinkled her forehead in thought. "No. I don't think so."

"We believe Centrum is the first Glassmind of this new generation," explained Ardor. "He's planning to change civilization as we know it."

"Then Garifus will get along great with him," Lomaya said. "He's a dangerous man. And now that he's transformed..."

"We don't know where the Glassminds are now," Nemery said. "They were moving down the mountain faster than anyone I've seen, and we were happy to let some distance come between us. We lost their tracks when we came out the bottom of Stormflood Gap. But we don't think they passed through New Vantage."

"Right," said Ardor. "We've been here for two days and I'm sure we would've heard from Ednes Holcatch if eight giant people with red glass heads came within ten miles of this town."

"Then, where did they go?" Quarrah asked.

"Garifus will go back to Beripent," said Lomaya. "The cult makes their headquarters on the eastern outskirts of the city. Are you familiar with Winter Barracks?"

"It was a reserve during the war," said Raek. "Termain bunked injured Archkingdom soldiers there until they recovered enough to go back to their deaths. Doesn't that property belong to the queen?"

"Garifus Floc purchased it from the crown about a year ago," explained Lomaya.

"The guy must be rich," said Ardor.

She shook her head. "His followers pooled the money. Garifus promised it would be a safe place for the gathering of the Glassminds."

"In other words," said Ardor, "when his followers came back in the violent throes of Moonsickness, there would be a secure site to lock them up."

"But everything's going to change when they see Garifus and the others transformed," continued Lomaya. "He'll rally as many as will follow him back to Pekal's summit to undergo the change themselves. That's why I have to get to Beripent. Quick as I can."

"To face Garifus?" Raek cried. "Gloristar took a lighthouse to the head and sank to the bottom of the InterIsland Waters for two years, and she's here to tell us about it. I don't think these Glassminds are people you want to mess with."

"Trust me, we know," Nemery said.

"He has San," Lomaya whispered. "And Garifus claims that his new form has given him understanding of the formula for Transformation Grit."

"That's true," said Gloristar. "As an Othian, we can absorb detonation clouds and gain a perfect knowledge of their composition."

"That's why I have to go now," said Lomaya. "If Garifus tried to kill me after he learned the formula, I can only imagine he'll do the same to San."

"Then we better get going," said Raek, rising to his feet again.

"You're...coming with me?" Lomaya whispered.

Raek nodded his bald head. "It's what the professor would have wanted."

At Nemery's side, Lomaya let out a sudden sob of gratitude, muttering her thanks in tones of disbelief.

"Hold on. Hold on!" Ardor looked at his partner, injury on his face. "What about the job, Raek?"

Raek pointed at Prime Isless Gloristar. "She's got a perfect knowledge of Grit...And she's got muscles. As long as you have her, I'd say I'm redundant."

"That doesn't mean I don't need you," Ardor cried.

"Oh, I know you need me," said Raek. "You can barely find your way from Tofar's Salts to the apartment without me. But I think you've got things covered here. We can rescue San and keep an eye on these crazy cultists until you get back. Besides, I was planning to head back early anyway..."

"But not until after we get the dragon," said Ardor.

"Dragon?" Nemery asked. "What dragon?"

"Wait," Quarrah jumped in. "Why was Raek going to leave early?"

"I have to take care of some business in Beripent," he answered.

"What business?" Quarrah asked.

Ardor and Raek shared a glance. "He's talking about the clocks," said Ardor.

"Clocks?" she repeated suspiciously.

"I thought we'd take a page out of the Realm's book," he explained. "To free the dragon."

"Free *what* dragon?" Nemery asked, her frustration mounting.

Ardor held up a finger, as though indicating that he'd heard her question and wasn't ignoring her.

"It's the best way to make sure she goes free before the next Moon Passing so she doesn't get sick," Ardor continued to Quarrah. "Raek's going to rig up enough of those chainspring mantel clocks to detonate at a certain hour. It'll blow the shackles off our beast and she'll be free to fly home."

"And that's not the only reason I was going home early," Raek said.

"It's not?" Quarrah asked.

"It's not?" Ardor repeated.

"Well, somebody's got to contact Hedge and tell him to go check out the goods in Helizon," explained Raek.

"Oh, of course," said Ardor. "That goes without saying."

"You'll be fine, Ard," Raek continued. "Now that we know there are more Glassminds in play, the plan has to change. Lomaya and I can get passage on the first ship back to Beripent."

Quarrah narrowed her eyes in thought. Then she stood up. "I'm going with him."

"Come on, Quarrah," moaned Ardor. "We're stealing a dragon! I need a thief."

"Wait, what?" Nemery cried. "We're stealing *which* dragon?" Why wasn't anybody answering her?

"I think you'll be fine," Quarrah said, ignoring Nemery. "It's not like I was going to pick up the dragon and sneak her down to the harbor anyway."

"I believe that is *my* job," said Gloristar.

"Exactly," said Quarrah. "But Raek's right. We need to find out what the Glassminds are up to. And if it comes down to sneaking into their cult to rescue Lomaya's friend, that's more in my wheelhouse."

Ardor let out a heavy sigh. "Wow. After all the work to get here, you two are leaving me alone."

"You're not alone," Raek said. "You've got Gloristar, Captain Dodset and the crew, Nemery, and...him." He pointed at Mohdek.

"Mohdek," he introduced himself.

"Wait. Who says Moh and I are going anywhere?" Nemery cut in.

"We need a Caller," said Ardor, as if that explained it.

"But now you're talking about *stealing* a dragon?" said Nemery. "Why?"

"I guess I'm getting ahead of myself." Ardor held up his hands. "A real dirtbag retired poacher named Hedge Marsool figured out how to see the future and he's manipulating us into stealing a dragon for him."

Nemery's eyebrows rose and she heard Mohdek mutter a disbelieving curse in Trothian.

"Why?" she finally asked.

"We're not clear on that," Ardor admitted. "But unfortunately, Hedge also knows the formula for Metamorphosis Grit, and he's threatening to transform more people into Glassminds if we don't get him a dragon."

"You believe him?" asked Nemery.

"Absolutely," said Ardor.

"Where are you going to take this dragon?" she followed up.

"We've got a spot ready in a cave beneath Helizon," he explained. "Of course, we're only going to hold her until Hedge sees that we've made the delivery. After that, the dragon is going to 'break free.'" He made little quotes in the air with his fingers.

"The clocks," said Nemery, finally making sense of that earlier bit. "Which dragon does he want?"

"All he said is that it has to be a mature sow," said Ardor.

She threw her hands in the air. "So just one of the largest living creatures in the world. Do you have a plan for this?"

Ardor Benn simply pointed at Prime Isless Gloristar.

"After we get her onboard," said Ardor, "we should be able to keep her subdued with Stasis Grit."

"What's that?" Nemery asked.

"Think deep sleep," said Raek. "Except your heart stops and you don't even breathe."

"Sounds terrifying," admitted Nemery.

"It's a little disorienting," said Ardor. "But it's harmless."

Nemery turned in her chair so she could see Mohdek. "What do you think about this?" she asked in his language.

"I think your hero is turning out to be much crazier than you ever described him," he replied.

"You shouldn't be surprised. I told you how he crash-landed a Trans-Island Carriage into the side of Pekal."

"I spent all these years believing that was a tall tale," said Mohdek.

"Nemery!" Ardor interrupted. "When did you learn to speak Trothian?"

It wasn't his first attempt to get her to tell him her life story. He'd asked a million questions at Burdal's Provisions, but she'd evaded them all. Nemery's journey since their last encounter hadn't all been pleasant. She certainly wasn't the same little girl that he'd hiked with. What if Ardor Benn disapproved of the choices that had brought her here?

"I don't like the idea of moving a dragon," Mohdek continued in Trothian without acknowledging Ardor's question. "We've spent so long protecting them. Doesn't this feel like a betrayal?"

"But we have to consider the consequences," she said. "Is it worth giving up one dragon to prevent more of those Glassminds? And it doesn't sound like anyone would be hurting her. He said they plan to free her as quickly as possible."

"You can't possibly be considering this, Nem!" Mohdek cried. "We're talking about moving a dragon to the Greater Chain. Don't you remember what happened last time? Dragons and cities don't mix. If we go through with this, innocent people could die."

Ardor cleared his throat. "Going by his tone, I'm guessing Mohdek is all for it."

Nemery looked at her boyfriend, dark vibrating eyes fixed on her, boring into her soul. Mohdek knew her too well to be fooled by her alleged logic. Did she think it was a terrible idea to relocate a dragon to the Greater Chain? Yes. And if anyone else in the world had come to her with this request, she would have laughed them off in an instant.

But this was Ardor Benn.

"Moh," she said, feeling awkward in front of everyone, even though they couldn't understand the conversation. "We have to help them. *I* have to help. If I'm honest, I don't agree with it, but I owe him—"

"Your life," Mohdek finished for her. "I know."

She turned away from his glum face. "We'll do it," she said to Ardor. "But only if your crew promises to respect Pekal. And no one hurts the dragon."

"In my experience," said Ard, "those that don't respect Pekal, die there."

"I'm talking about the land," said Nemery, "the plants. The animals. We go up and back without a trace. Small fires, controlled campsites, and no senseless target practice."

Ardor nodded. "Captain Dodset is staying here to hold down the ship, but she made it clear to her crew that I'm in command as soon as we head up the mountain. I'll make sure everyone understands."

"We'd better get going," Raek said to Quarrah and Lomaya. "Hopefully, we can catch a midmorning ship and we can be to Winter Barracks by midnight."

"I'll send word to you the minute we set sail for Helizon with the dragon," Ardor said. "That'll give you and Quarrah time to notify Hedge and then meet me at the cavern with the clock explosives."

"How many days are you thinking it'll be?" Raek asked.

"That's a better question for Nemery," said Ardor.

She turned to Mohdek, but his face was downcast in obvious disapproval of this entire arrangement.

"Best-case scenario, five days," she answered. "But it depends on if she returned to Red Banks after roosting for the Passing."

"You know where the dragons will be?" Ardor asked with unmasked amazement.

"We know most of their haunts," Nemery admitted.

"And this Red Banks area..." said Ardor. "It's the closest?"

"Not necessarily," answered Nemery. "But trust me, if she's there, she's the dragon we want."

"Why is that?" Ardor asked.

Nemery stood up. "Because I believe she already knows your scent."

～

*My responsibility, like it or not, has always been to act on the information I uncover. It's something I owe to myself, lest I dither into uselessness.*

# CHAPTER

# 18

Outside the wall of Winter Barracks, Quarrah moved through the darkness until she reached a cluster of tall elm trees. Neither Raek nor Lomaya was well concealed, and she spotted them instantly. Were they even *trying* to hide?

"What did you see in there?" Lomaya asked impatiently.

"Glassminds," Quarrah replied. "And a lot of fanatical people." A surprising number, if she was honest.

The three of them weren't ready for this. Sure, they'd grabbed some supplies from Tofar's Salts after disembarking in the Western Harbor, but this was going to be a complicated rescue.

"What about the seventh barracks?" asked Lomaya.

"Empty," answered Quarrah. "But they're holding someone in the officers' quarters on the far side of the compound. I heard him try to shout for help, but he was silenced."

"You didn't see if it was San?" Lomaya followed up.

Quarrah shook her head. "Do you think they're holding more than one prisoner?"

Lomaya shrugged. "Garifus and the other cult leaders were living in the officers' quarters. San and I were being kept in barracks number seven."

"Well, it's empty now," Quarrah repeated. "And the officers' quarters was the only building guarded by Glassminds."

"Sounds like San got an upgrade to his living accommodations," said Raek.

"The rest of the soldier barracks appear to have large groups of people living in them."

"Yes," said Lomaya. "It was about half full when we left for Pekal."

"Well, it's got to be getting close to capacity now," she said. "I estimate over four hundred people in there. Men, women, children…"

"And more coming by the minute," Raek added. "There's been a steady stream arriving through the front gate. What are they doing in there?"

"They're gathering everyone in the training yard," Quarrah said. "Garifus and three of the Glassminds are mingling among them."

"They'll be preaching," said Lomaya.

"That's what it looked like," said Quarrah, "though I didn't get close enough to hear what they were saying."

"Can you give me a rundown of the layout in there?" Raek asked.

"Ten-foot stone wall surrounds the entire compound, with a single guard tower by the main entrance," began Quarrah.

"I spotted a Glassmind up there," Raek said.

"Me, too," she replied. "Once you pass through the front gate, there's a large open training yard. Might have been grass once, but it's so trampled, it's mostly dirt now. To the right of that are the stables. They're not big. Probably just enough to hold horses for the officers during the war. There aren't any animals, but people are living in there. In the center of the compound are the kitchens and mess hall—more of a social pavilion, really. Lots of tables and chairs. Beyond that, you come to the barracks. Rows and rows of low-roofed buildings with little windows. Every now and again, a storage shed pops up between them. They would have held Grit and weapons during the war, but I don't know what's in them now."

"And the officers' quarters?" Raek asked.

"It's a big square building in the middle of the barracks, taller than the rest," she said. "A Glassmind at the front door, and another at the back. Decent windows all around, but it would take a Drift Jump to reach them."

"So Garifus and three Glassminds in the yard," listed Raek, "two Glassminds guarding the officers' quarters. And the one on the guard tower."

"That leaves one unaccounted for," said Lomaya.

"Maybe that's a good thing," Raek said. "Maybe he's gone, making a doughnut run."

"Or he's inside the officers' quarters," said Quarrah, "guarding the person we're trying to rescue."

"Love that positive attitude, Quarrah," said Raek. "Keep it up." She watched him unbutton his shirt. Time for another hit of Compounded Health Grit.

"Plan for the worst," she said, "and at least you have the possibility of being pleasantly surprised."

"The worst is that the kid is already dead," Raek pointed out. "If that's the case, then we're going in there for nothing."

"He can't be," whispered Lomaya. "What's our plan to get in?"

"Through the front gate," replied Raek, untwisting a paper roll of Heg.

"Are you insane?" Lomaya cried.

Raek shrugged. "Quarrah said there are hundreds of people inside. We wait until a new group is heading through and we fall in behind them."

"We'll be recognized," Lomaya said.

"You can wear my hat." He pulled his black knit cap from his bald head and tossed it to her. Then he placed a pinch of Heg into the pipe in his chest and replaced the cork, igniting it with a sharp rap. Raek sighed, closing his eyes. "Garifus and his cronies have never seen Quarrah or me, so that shouldn't be a problem."

He pulled a Roller from the holster on his belt and offered it to Lomaya, who accepted it without hesitation. "Go for the head," he instructed. "Gloristar said that shattering their glass skulls was the only way to kill them."

"I hardly think this is going to do the trick." Lomaya eyed the weapon. "I hit them with pure Blast Grit and it barely knocked them over."

"I'm with Lomaya on this," Quarrah said. "I'd rather rescue San without being seen at all. If we open fire on Garifus, it's not just the Glassminds we'll have to contend with. I don't think four hundred devout followers will stand by and watch their leader get assassinated."

"You have a better idea?" Raek asked.

"Maybe..." She shook her head. "No. Never mind."

"Oh, come on," pressed Raek. "Out with it."

"I don't have it with me anyway..." she stammered. "We'd have to swing by one of my apartments, and we don't even know what it does."

"What are you rambling about?"

She groaned, angry with herself for bringing it up and knowing that she had to come clean with Raek now. "Future Grit."

"But we don't have—"

"Ard's vial was a fake," Quarrah said. "I took the real one after you were done inspecting it in the *Be'Igoth*."

Raek's scarred face glowed with a huge smile. "Why, you little—"

"I didn't trust Ard with it," she explained. "He's not careful with things like that and…well, just look at what he did on the *Shiverswift*."

"Oh, I'm not questioning why you did it," Raek said. "In fact, I've never been prouder of you."

"Thanks?" Quarrah said, grateful that Raek wasn't asking why she hadn't told *him*. It wasn't that she didn't trust Raek to keep a secret from Ard—he'd been doing that while supplying her with liquid Grit for the past year. It was just Quarrah's default to keep things to herself.

"It's a bad idea," Quarrah went on. "If we use the Future Grit without understanding it, that makes us no better than Ard—"

"Future Grit?" Lomaya cut in.

"I wanted to call it Time Grit," said Raek.

"It's a new liquid solution…" Quarrah trailed off as Lomaya shook her head.

"You're saying there's another source material?" the young woman asked. "One we didn't know about?"

"We weren't able to identify it," Raek said.

"Did you use a light filtration scope?" she asked.

"Ha. Because I have one of *those* lying around," Raek answered sarcastically.

"There's one at the college," Lomaya said. "Professor Wal taught us how to use it."

"That's not exactly open to the public," said Raek.

"I've still got connections there. I could run the vial through the scope myself."

"That's not going to help your friend tonight," Quarrah said, bringing the two scientific minds back to earth. She should never have suggested the Future Grit. All it did was expose her secret. "We've got to get San out of the officers' quarters." She thought about their options. "What if we smoke him out? Literally. We light the officers' building on fire and wait for him to emerge." It was a bit flashy for her taste, but it would be right up Raek's alley.

"That would send the whole compound into chaos," said Lomaya.

"Exactly," continued Quarrah. "We use the chaos to get close enough to grab your friend and escape."

"I'm in love with this plan." Raek swung his pack around and untied his crossbow. "In *love*, do you hear me?"

"How do we start this fire?" Lomaya asked.

"Blast Grit's our surest bet," said Raek. "I can rig up a bolt and we can shoot it through one of the windows... *Boom!*"

"What if San is up there?" Lomaya asked, a trace of panic in her voice.

"All the rooms will be on the first floor," said Quarrah. "I assume that's where he'll be. We can shoot through the third-story windows and blow up the top level. It should be just a map room."

"*Should* be," Lomaya repeated. "How do you know this?"

"Winter Barracks is an Archkingdom compound," Quarrah explained. "Its layout and design are virtually identical to Forward Barracks in the Northern Quarter, and Midway Barracks to the south."

"And you've been there?"

"Both of those barracks were used as redistribution centers when the war ended. Lots of valuables in the officers' quarters."

Lomaya looked aghast, but Raek chuckled, a pleased expression on his rugged face as he worked on filling a blank Grit bolt.

"I don't know," Lomaya said. "If they're planning to kill San anyway, what makes us think they'll bother pulling him out of a burning building?"

"If Garifus was going to kill him, don't you think he'd already be dead?" Raek asked. "Sounds like the Glassminds have been back for two days. Why bother keeping him prisoner?"

"Raek's right," said Quarrah. "Garifus must have something else in mind for your friend."

"Still," said Lomaya, "even if they do exit the quarters, we have no way of knowing where they'll take him."

"We'll have to be ready for anything." Raek carefully dropped a chip of Slagstone through the opening on the end of the bolt. "I'll stick with going through the front gate. If they bring him my way, I'll be there."

"And I'll come over the back wall," Quarrah said.

"I think you should take the shot since you're likely to get closer to the officers' quarters." Raek passed her the crossbow. "And be careful," he said, melodramatically handing over the Grit bolt. "This baby is stuffed fuller than a nobleman's wallet. It's not going to fly too well, but it'll pack a serious punch."

Quarrah nodded in understanding. She'd handled plenty of crossbows. And she'd have ample time to line up a good shot from atop the low barracks roofs.

"What about me?" Lomaya asked.

"You should go with Quarrah," Raek said.

"Why me?" Quarrah asked, before realizing that it made Lomaya sound like unwanted goods.

"You'll need someone to help you identify San Green," Raek explained.

"And you won't?" Quarrah asked.

"I've seen him twice," answered Raek. "I spoke with him in

Portsend's lab, and then I saw a very convincing wax replica of his severed head."

"What?" Lomaya cried in horror.

"Don't be jealous," Raek said. "There was one of you, too. Anyway, I'm thinking I'll recognize him when I see him again."

"All right." Quarrah glanced at Lomaya Vans. The girl didn't look overly stealthy, but Quarrah had a bit of Silence Grit if they needed it.

Raek slung his pack onto his shoulders again. "Give me at least twenty minutes to get into position. Then light it up. If we get separated, don't wait. I'll meet you back at Tofar's Salts."

Lomaya followed Quarrah closely as they set off in the opposite direction. They took their time, but not just for Raek's sake. Over the years, Quarrah had learned that rushing a stealth mission was the quickest way to get caught.

They rounded the corner, moving along the back side of the compound wall until Quarrah brought up a hand to stop them. She reached to her belt, pulling out a little mesh bag of Grit.

"I've never Drift Jumped before," Lomaya suddenly whispered in her ear.

*Oh, great. How many ways could this go wrong?*

"You'll feel a sensation of weightlessness," Quarrah whispered back. "Makes some people sick the first few times."

"Oh, I've been in a Drift cloud," Lomaya replied. "I've just never had to jump through one. I understand the basic concept. I'm just wondering how you compensate for wind resistance and aerodynamics."

Sparks. Lomaya was really overthinking this.

"I just sort of line it up and...jump," Quarrah replied. That answer was clearly too basic for Lomaya's scientific mind. "Listen," she continued, "we only need to make it to the top of the wall. You should be able to see enough from there while I move onto the rooftops to make the shot."

Quarrah crouched down, Lomaya following suit.

"Hold on to something," Quarrah whispered. Innocently, Lomaya reached out and grabbed her arm.

That would do.

Quarrah gripped a fistful of grass and pitched her little bag of Drift Grit against the face of the stone wall. It detonated successfully, enveloping her and Lomaya in a cloud of weightlessness.

"We can jump together," Quarrah said, throwing an arm around the other woman's shoulder. Lomaya nodded vigorously, visibly anxious. Quarrah counted down from three and they sprang upward.

The Drift cloud was large enough to see them all the way to the top of the wall. Quarrah reached out and gripped the capstone, steadying the two of them until Lomaya could successfully swing her leg over the wall, straddling it like a horse.

Quarrah pointed across the flat roofs of the soldiers' barracks and waited for Lomaya to acknowledge that she recognized the officers' quarters. The only movement came from a few tired cultists adjourning to their rooms after a late-night gawking at their Glassmind leaders.

Multiple orbs of Light Grit illuminated the area, easily allowing Quarrah to spot the Glassmind stationed at the back door to the officers' quarters. She gestured for Lomaya to stay low on the wall. Then she gauged the distance to the nearest roof. There was enough overspill from the Drift cloud that she had no trouble making it.

She landed nimbly on the roof, but one of the clay shingles broke, clattering down the eave and tumbling over the edge. She cursed silently. Weren't these barracks only three years old? Why were they already in such disrepair?

Quarrah held still until she was sure the sound hadn't attracted any attention. Then she pulled the crossbow off her back and ratcheted the string into place. Carefully, she took Raek's bolt of Blast Grit from her side pocket and laid it into the weapon.

This was a long shot for a crossbow with a bolt this heavy. Luckily, she didn't have to be accurate. Still, she'd have to aim high to compensate for the fall over such a distance.

Kneeling for stability, Quarrah tucked the crossbow's stock against her shoulder. Sighting down the bolt, she squeezed the trigger, not even seeing where it hit before her eyes squinted shut against a deafening blast of flames and smoke. She dropped to her stomach, dust and fine debris raining over her back.

Screams tore through the night, spreading across the compound like a landslide of terror. Quarrah lifted her face to examine her handiwork. A good portion of the roof had been blown off, and the top floor was all aflame.

The Glassmind guard crouched at the base of the building, both hands over her head. The falling debris sloughed to either side of her, blocked by some sort of unseen shield. Probably Barrier Grit, manipulated in a moment's notice to create a uniquely shaped shield.

"That's him!" Lomaya screamed from atop the wall, her voice blending with the chaos. It took Quarrah a moment to see who she was talking about. A young man, accompanied by another Glassmind, had just emerged from the back door, his captor pushing him forward frantically. Before Quarrah could even rise, they had disappeared around the corner of the building.

*All right, Raek,* she thought. *They're coming your way.*

But Quarrah wasn't going to leave him to face the enemy alone. She dropped the crossbow. No point in lugging that thing around without any bolts. Turning over her shoulder, she shouted instructions to Lomaya.

"Jump down! Circle around the outside of the compound and meet us by the front gate!"

Without waiting to see how she'd respond, Quarrah leapt to her feet and sprinted across the barracks roof. Reaching the edge, she twisted, dropping down and catching the eave to break her fall. She braced her feet against the wall and dropped to the packed dirt.

It wasn't going to be hard to slip past that backdoor Glassmind—Quarrah would just blend in with the people running in every direction. Maybe there was more merit to this bombastic tactic than she'd ever given credit. It was certainly a far cry from her usual leave-no-trace approach.

As Quarrah sped past, she saw the Glassmind woman reaching her arms toward the burning building, manipulating some kind of Grit cloud in an effort to quell the fire. What type could do that? It looked like Gather Grit, Compounded to such an intensity that it was drawing the flames together to a central point, pulling them away from fresh combustibles and choking them out.

If Quarrah was right—if the Glassminds had Gather Grit, then they probably knew about the other types of liquid Grit, too. Sparks, she and Raek would have no advantage over these beings.

Ahead, she saw San Green and his Glassmind escort entering the open dining pavilion. Beyond, the training yard was a jumble of chaos as hundreds of cultists tried to pour out the front gate with no semblance of order.

Quarrah doubled her speed. San wasn't shackled or tied. If she could pull him away from the Glassmind, they might be able to slip into the throng and escape without a fight.

She caught up to them on the far side of the pavilion. The Glassmind man had paused, one hand gripping the back of San's neck as if he were a small child in need of discipline. Quarrah couldn't tell what the man was doing, holding perfectly still, overlooking the confusion in the yard.

She was close enough now that she regretted not having a gun. Her knife seemed sorely insufficient against the muscled figure ahead. She needed something big and blunt. Some way to shatter her foe's skull before he knew what had hit him.

Quarrah yanked out another bag of Drift Grit and hurled it ahead of her, the detonation filling the aisle between two long tables. She'd judged the distance perfectly, the perimeter of the cloud stopping just behind San and the Glassmind, not tipping them off to her presence.

With a grunt, Quarrah hoisted one of the wooden benches onto her shoulder. She ran forward, trying to gain as much momentum as she could before reaching the cloud.

She hurled the long bench into the Drift detonation, watching it sail forward. Her own momentum sent her tumbling into the cloud behind it, but she managed to grab the edge of a grounded table, steadying herself in time to see the bench find its mark.

It struck the Glassmind in the back of the neck, missing his red skull by mere inches. But the unexpected force was enough to send him toppling forward, losing his grip on his prisoner.

"San!" Quarrah shouted, pulling herself along the edge of the table. "Run!"

The young man looked back at her, confused. Frightened. Then he bolted for the yard. Quarrah exited the Drift cloud and hit the ground running just feet behind him.

Just when she thought they might make it, something grabbed her from behind. She swatted at it, but an invisible force had yanked her off her feet, dragging her back toward the pavilion.

Partway there, she collided with San, a tangle of arms and legs as they squirmed against the power drawing them in. Quarrah saw the Glassmind on his knees, just outside the Drift detonation, hands outstretched to manipulate a cloud of his own.

This was Gather Grit without a doubt. And with seemingly little effort, their enemy was gathering them both back to him.

"I have found the intruder," she heard the Glassmind say. His strange enhanced voice was calm and controlled, not possibly loud enough for anyone but her and San to hear. "I'll hold them in the dining area."

He rose to his full height as Quarrah and San rolled to a halt at his feet. Dizzy and disoriented, she pushed herself up onto her elbows just in time to see a figure sprinting through the pavilion toward them.

It was Raekon Dorrel. He was unarmed, but wearing thick leather gloves, gripping a short iron rod in each hand. His fists seemed to be enclosed in a shimmering orb of Grit.

With one fluid motion, he leapt onto the table, boards bowing under his weight. He sprang forward, entering the Drift cloud with an acrobatic twist. Quarrah kicked the Glassmind in the knee as hard as she could, sending him staggering a step back, falling into the detonation just as Raek passed over his unprotected head.

Raek's Grit-clad fist came down in a thundering blow, shattering the Glassmind's skull into a hundred shards. The transformed being lurched awkwardly in the weightless cloud, his glowing red eyes going dark. He floated forward, regaining his weight as he left the perimeter, thudding onto his face between Quarrah and San.

Raek's momentum carried him out the other side of the Drift cloud and he came down hard, cracking one of the tables in half.

"Sparks," San Green hissed. "Who are you?"

Firelight from the burning building glinted on the shards of red glass that spun lazily in the Drift cloud. Raek pulled himself up with a grunt and stepped over to them, nudging the dead Glassmind with his foot.

"Come on," Quarrah said, turning toward the panicked crowd. But she couldn't run. She couldn't say anything, staring in speechless shock at what was coming over the front gate.

It was another Glassmind.

And he was *flying.*

His arms were at his sides, columns of Grit detonations flowing from his downturned palms, reaching all the way to the ground. The people below were scattering, the crowd parting down the middle to make a path for the airborne Glassmind. And those who didn't move quickly enough were thrown aside.

Of course. He was manipulating the push of Compounded Void Grit to lift himself from the ground. And he was flying right toward them.

"This way!" Raek cried, moving around one of the dining tables and heading east. The three of them exited the pavilion with a clear line of sight to the outer wall.

"Tell me you didn't toss my crossbow," Raek said.

"It was useless," Quarrah replied.

"Not to me," he said. "That crossbow was my friend. Now we'll have to do this the old-fashioned way." He ground to a halt, twenty yards away from the stone wall.

"I need you to get a little keg of Blast Grit out of my pack," he said.

"Why don't you get it?" She didn't see the sense in digging around if he knew right where it was.

Raek held up his gloved, Grit-covered hands. "I might as well have hooves at the moment."

He turned his back and Quarrah reached into his pack, yanking out the keg he'd used to fill the Grit bolt earlier.

"Throw it at the wall," Raek instructed her.

"But that's a storage keg," San cut in. "It won't detonate without a Slagstone pin." His sparsely stubbled face was sweaty, and he looked a bit peaky.

"Ignition Grit, kid," said Raek. "You know the stuff. There's a vial of it on my belt."

Quarrah hurled the keg. It landed a few feet short of the wall, cracking open and spilling its contents as it rolled against the thick stone. She turned back just in time to see San pitch the little vial of liquid Ignition Grit. It struck, creating a flash cloud that ignited the spilled Blast Grit.

The wall exploded, throwing the three of them back with a gush of hot air and a blinding belch of flames. The size of this explosion made the officers' quarters look like a smoldering cooking fire.

Between the darkness and the smoke, Quarrah couldn't see how effective it had been. Didn't really matter anyway. Through the wreckage, the Glassmind was slowly descending.

Quarrah scrambled to Raek's side, pulling San up along the

way. There was blood on the young man's forehead but he didn't seem to notice.

"Garifus," San whispered as the Glassmind's feet touched down on the blasted soil.

"San, San, San," the huge man said. He stood in a curtain of dust and smoke, blocking their path to the hole they had surely blasted in the wall. Garifus's glowing eyes turned to Quarrah, and he tilted his head as though she were a curiosity.

"And your name is Quarrah." His voice was a hum and a whisper rolled into one. She shivered at the attention.

"You were trapped under a Barrier cloud with a man named Ardor on the night Gloristar killed the king." Garifus smiled. "Don't flatter yourself by thinking you made an impression on me. I remember all things. My memory, like the rest of me, is operating at complete perfection."

"Well, you don't know *me*," Raek grumbled, racing forward and banging his Grit-covered fists together as if priming them for a mighty blow.

Garifus Floc merely stretched out one hand, his fingertips sparking in the darkness. A wall of Barrier Grit streamed from his palm, colliding with Raek so hard, he was thrown backward. The Barrier wall folded downward, becoming a dome that enclosed Quarrah, Raek, and San.

"Oh, you're going to toy with us?" Raek called, mustering the strength to sit up and spit. The bridge of his nose was cut, and going by the amount of blood streaming down his upper lip, the bone was probably broken. "Let me take you in a fair fight. We'll see who gets a perfect kill."

"I'm not going to kill you," Garifus said. "I don't *want* to kill anyone. All must have a chance to reach the Homeland. Only then will you be judged."

"Slag," Raek moaned. "You're a blazing lunatic. And I'm getting a whiff of coward coming off your shiny little head."

Through the thick dust of the broken wall, Quarrah glimpsed movement behind Garifus. She squinted, trying not to make it obvious, since Raek was clearly fighting to keep the Glassmind's attention.

A significant portion of the wall had crumbled, a U-shaped opening clogged with chunks of stone. Standing on the rubble was Lomaya Vans, Raek's Roller in her outstretched hand.

She was sighting down the barrel, her elevated position providing the perfect angle for a shot at the back of Garifus's glass skull.

"Come on!" Raek goaded the man. Or maybe he was shouting to Lomaya. He reached out and punched his orbed fists against their impenetrable prison dome. "Come on!"

Lomaya's Roller cracked. In the darkness, Quarrah saw a tongue of flames lick the end of the barrel. The moment the gun sounded, Garifus Floc's hand shot out behind him, fingertips sparking.

A cone-shaped detonation met the Roller ball and Quarrah actually saw the projectile come to a halt in the air not three feet from Garifus's head. The lead ball spun, suspended in midair as the Glassmind turned toward his shooter. Then he pushed his hand outward.

The ball returned along the same path it had come, speeding so fast that Quarrah didn't have a chance of seeing it. But she saw where it hit.

Lomaya's head snapped backward as the metal took her in the forehead, her body crumpling on the rubble of the blasted wall.

Beside her, San Green let out a scream. Raw. Almost tangible with its grief.

Garifus Floc turned to face them once again, his pale blue-gold face wearing an obvious expression of discontentment. "I am the Homeland," he said. "And the Homeland's strength lies in perfection. I hope you believe me when I say that I am as disappointed in her loss as you are."

San Green was sobbing at Quarrah's side, big gasping breaths that seemed insufficient to deliver air. He shouted something, but it was too inarticulate to decipher through his grief and anger.

Garifus looked past the trapped trio, his red eyes seeming to lose focus for a moment. His stance was oddly detached, similar to the Glassmind that had been holding San at the edge of the pavilion.

"I must go," he said, eyes regaining focus. "You have made my followers feel unsafe. Some of them are saying that I was killed in the explosion. I cannot allow this rumor to spread among my scattered believers."

He lowered his arms, palms earthward as his fingertips sparked again. His feet left the ground as columns of Void Grit propelled him upward.

"We shall speak again soon," Garifus called. "And perhaps I will convince you of the Homeland's perfection." Then he angled his body and sped toward the front gate.

In the silence that followed, Quarrah reached out and placed a hand on San's back. He shrugged it off with a moan of despair.

"You really think he'd leave us unattended like this?" Raek asked. The clouds of Containment Grit around his fists had gone out and he was sliding his hands out of the leather gauntlets.

"I'm guessing another Glassmind is on the way," she replied quietly. "And we've got at least five more minutes before this thing burns out." Quarrah reached up and knocked on the Barrier dome.

"That's what I'm counting on," said Raek. "For all his talk about having a perfect mind, there's one thing Garifus Floc doesn't know about us."

"What's that?" Quarrah asked, in no mood for Raek to be clever.

"We were friends with the guy who invented Null Grit." He held up his hand and Quarrah saw a little vial pinched between his fingers. He dashed it against the Barrier cloud, which was immediately snuffed out.

"Come on…" Quarrah pulled a numb San Green to his feet.

"This is our best chance of getting out of here, but I need you to run."

He wiped his face with the sleeve of his shirt—blood, tears, snot. Then he nodded resolutely and the three of them sprinted for the crumbled wall.

Quarrah climbed over the chunks of rubble, coughing at the smoke and dust that lingered from the explosion. She paused only once, reaching down to close the eyes of Lomaya Vans. Quarrah's stomach turned, and her heart ached in unison with San's grief-stricken wail.

Then she was running again. Running through the night.

*It's strange to think that everything hinges on trading one life for another. Stranger still that I feel no remorse about it.*

# CHAPTER
# 19

We make camp here," Nemery called. With less than an hour of daylight remaining, they weren't likely to find a better spot. The steep cut to the east would block wind. There was a fresh-water stream not thirty yards south, and plenty of well-spaced trees for hanging their hammocks. The soil here was a deep red that stained their boots and the hems of their pants.

"Good work today, everyone," Nemery added as heavy backpacks and tiresome Drift crates were lowered to the ground. Captain Dodset had provided ten people for this expedition, which felt like an army to her and Mohdek.

"We found tracks today," she continued her morale-boosting speech. "That means we might actually see her tomorrow." *And I might finally get to do some Calling on my new instrument.*

"Ha!" cried Senso. "Tracks don't mean trail."

Nemery took a deep breath. Senso had been bothering her since the minute they'd left the harbor. For the first five days it was, "She don't know where she's going. Where are the tracks?" And now that they'd finally found some, he was griping about that.

"Can't have a trail without tracks," Nemery said to him. She knew she shouldn't engage. It never ended well. But he was just so stupid.

"Look around, girly," Senso said. "These trees gotta be no more than ten feet apart. The dragons I've seen are at least double that in girth. You expect us to believe that one passed through here?"

"She didn't pass through here," Nemery said. "She passed through over there." She pointed down toward the stream where the trees were slightly denser. "And your logic doesn't hold water. Rats can squeeze through spaces less than half their size. Same with foxes."

"Yeah, but we're talking about dragons," said Senso, in case she'd forgotten.

"We're tracking a creature whose *dung* has magical properties," Nemery snapped. "You don't think it's possible for them to fit between two trees without knocking them over?"

She and Mohdek had seen it plenty of times. The dragons could manipulate their great bulk in a surprising way, stretching, elongating, even flattening themselves to fit. It was almost as if their bones could collapse. She'd read a book on that in her younger years, though there was no hard evidence to support it.

"We're on her trail," Nemery promised. She glanced across the developing campsite. Dargen and Phel were pulling together some kindling for a cooking fire. Most everyone else was stringing hammocks or readying rations.

Several yards away, Ardor Benn and Prime Isless Gloristar were conversing in quiet tones. Nemery was finally getting used to the large woman's appearance. At least now she didn't think it was Garifus and his Glassminds every time she glanced behind her on the trail.

"You don't need to prove anything to them," Mohdek said in Trothian. He swung his pack off his shoulders and began untying the hammock he had wadded at the top.

"Well, not all of us can pretend like we don't speak their language," she replied, looping a rope around a suitable tree.

Mohdek looked up, his vibrating gaze serious. "This is probably our last chance to lead them astray. If we keep following her tracks, we'll be close enough that even a half-witted *muckmus* like Senso will be able to find her."

"I know." Nemery tugged on the knot. "But we have to remember, as much as we may dislike this crew, we're not giving up the dragon for *them*."

"Right." Mohdek shook out the hammock. "We're giving her up for a madman ex-poacher who is threatening to create more Glassminds."

Nemery swallowed. "I was thinking Ardor Benn. But yeah. I guess you're right. From what we've heard, this Hedge Marsool guy sounds a lot worse than Senso."

"Which is why we head south in the morning," said Mohdek. "Move out of Red Banks. They'll never know. We can lead them along until they tire of the chase and beg us to take them back to the harbor."

Nemery stepped past him and began fixing the second rope. "I can't do that, Moh. Ardor is... He's counting on me. And I can't let him down."

He took a slow breath, fraught with annoyance. "Then, are we sure this is the right dragon? Why not give up one of the yearlings? Smaller, less dangerous, easier to transport…"

"But not what Ardor is looking for," she said. "It has to be a mature sow. You know she's the best fit."

"But…" he stammered. "It's Motherwatch."

*Motherwatch.*

Nemery and Mohdek had decided on that name. The Trothian translation sounded even more elegant, as he spoke it in reverence.

As far as Nemery was aware, the people of the Greater Chain had never named the sow that had killed King Pethredote. Perhaps in time, someone else would give her a name—maybe even celebrate her as they did Grotenisk. But for now, she was Motherwatch to them.

Of all the dragons on Pekal, Nemery Baggish was most fascinated by her. Cochorin's mother. The sow that had flown so many miles to Beripent to retrieve her egg, remaining ever vigilant for fertilization, despite the fact that there were no more bull dragons to do the job.

"She's getting old, Nem," pressed Mohdek.

"Exactly," said Nemery. "She hasn't produced an egg in nearly a year. All the other sows have dependents, but Motherwatch isn't as vital to the reproduction of her race anymore. Not to downplay her role, since she hatched Cochorin…"

"What if she's not strong enough for the flight back to Pekal?"

"She is," said Nemery. "That's another reason why it should be her. She's the only dragon that has left Pekal. We know she can find her way home. And she's smelled people before."

*She's smelled Ardor Benn.*

All these years, Nemery had believed it was him on the palace steps, facing off with Motherwatch. And in the last few days she had finally confirmed the story with Ardor, though he'd been dodgy when it came to telling her exactly *how* Cochorin's egg had been fertilized.

"Motherwatch will be frightened," Mohdek continued. "She still bears scars from her first visit to the Greater Chain."

"I know," said Nemery, "and I have my fears about this, too. But Ardor is confident in Gloristar's abilities. She'll keep Motherwatch in Stasis until it's time for her to break out and come home."

"It is hard for me to see you swept up like this, Salafan," Mohdek said, moving past her to tie one end of the hammock to the rope.

"Swept up?" she asked. "What are you talking about?"

"Him," Mohdek said. "He has great influence over you, whether you realize it or not."

Was he *jealous*? "It's not like that, Moh." She reached out and squeezed his arm. "Namsum used to say he'd do anything for us, remember? You know why?"

"Because he was my brother," said Mohdek.

"Because we saved his life," she added. "I feel the same way about Ardor Benn. That's all there is to it."

He nodded his head. "I suppose it was easier for me to be grateful to him when he was just a name in a story."

"I love you, Moh," she said in Landerian. "And nothing's going to change that." Nemery stepped away from him as he moved to tie up the other side of the hammock.

"We're losing daylight fast," she said. "I'm going to run down to the stream. I'll fill our waters." She snatched the skin off his pack as she passed, moving through the camp and into the trees.

The sound of the tumbling water drowned out the voices behind her as she dropped to her knees, making two little depressions in the soft red earth. She plunged her hands into the cold water, feeling it wash away the grime of the day. Stooping forward, she splashed her face.

Behind her, a twig snapped and she heard a conspicuous cough announcing his approach.

"I'm tired of these people, Moh," she said in his language. "Can't wait until it's just us again."

"Sorry," came the reply in Landerian. "But I've got no idea what you're saying."

Nemery turned in surprise. It was Ardor Benn.

"I thought you were Mohdek," she admitted.

Ardor chuckled. "Not nearly so muscular. Or wise." He took a seat on a moss-covered rock just downstream from her, dipping his fingertips into the passing water. The stream looked black in the waning light.

"You're doing a great job," he said. "I know I'm technically the leader of this group, but we're not fooling anyone. Without you, this expedition would be doomed. Half of us would've probably been eaten by a dragon already."

She smiled at his compliments, even though he was demonizing dragons again.

"Sometimes it seems like just yesterday that the two of us were out here," he said wistfully, "chasing that confounded sow with the Royal Regalia in her belly, trying to stay ahead of our group. You didn't like that crew. At least that much has stayed the same." He dried his fingers on the leg of his pants. "Is Mohdek okay with this?"

"With us talking?" she replied quickly.

"I meant stealing Motherwatch," said Ardor.

"Oh, of course." She turned her head, hoping he didn't see her blush in the fading light. "He's warming up to it."

"I know that's all thanks to you," Ardor said. "So... thank you."

Nemery shrugged. "He can be stubborn. But he's got a good heart."

"The two of you make a good pair," Ardor said. "An ambitious pair, living out here in the wilds like this."

"It's home," she said.

"But it wasn't," said Ardor. "The home I asked Tanalin to deliver you to was in Beripent." He leaned forward, forearms resting across his knees. "What happened to Nemery Baggish?"

She looked up at the treetops above. Two-dimensional black leaves were silhouetted against a dusky sky that already winked with a handful of stars.

Was she ready to tell her story? She'd been avoiding it since the first time he'd asked in New Vantage. She was Salafan now, and part of her feared that explaining how she got there would make her miss bits of her former life.

"Everything changed when you took me to Pekal the first time," she began. "You know that? Take a little girl with a dream, and make that dream come true…"

"Sure," Ardor said. "Because seeing your companions get eaten alive and getting sent home with a hole in your leg is every little girl's dream."

She shrugged. "Things weren't good with my parents, even before I joined your crew."

"I remember," he said. "Your mum wanted you to stick with the orchestra, but your pops got you lined up to learn from a Master Caller."

She smiled. After all these years, he remembered those details about her unimportant little life?

"That changed when I got home," Nemery said. "My father never wanted me to come back to Pekal, and my mother was against it from the beginning. But their anger only made me want it more. Soon as my leg healed up, I struck out. The war was on, so it wasn't hard to get hired as a Harvester for the Archkingdom."

"You were a Harvester?" Ardor exclaimed. "Hard to imagine you lugging a Drift crate."

"I pulled my weight," she said defensively. "I was on track to become a Tracer, too."

"Not a Caller?"

"Nobody knew I could Call," she said. "And I never had a

chance to show them. On my second expedition, we ran into trouble over by Leafy Reach." Nemery glanced at the dark water. "My crew was attacked by a group of Sovereign Harvesters. Our captain was killed, and the rest of us were taken captive."

"Homeland, Nemery," Ardor whispered. "You were a prisoner of war?"

"At the ripe age of fourteen," she said.

"Did they... Did they treat you okay?"

She looked up at him. "It was Mohdek. He and his older brother were part of the Sovereign crew. They marched us down to their harbor and loaded us onto a ship. The plan was to take us over to Dronodan and keep us in Leigh with all the other prisoners. The Sovs thought they might get King Termain to care if they amassed a large enough group."

"Clearly, they didn't know him," Ardor said.

Nemery picked up a short stick on the bank beside her and jabbed the tip into the red soil, thinking about what had happened next.

"We didn't make it to Leigh," she said quietly. "Naval blockades pushed our ship farther and farther south until an Archie fleet finally opened fire on us. Didn't matter that some of their own were aboard. They shot us to scraps. Everyone was drowning... people shot to bits..."

The stick broke in her hand and she tossed the piece she was holding into the little stream.

"I was trying to swim for Dronodan when I heard someone screaming for help," she continued. "It was Mohdek. His brother was unconscious and he'd managed to pull him onto some of the floating wreckage. We worked together. Got Namsum to Dronodan, but we still had a cliff to deal with."

Despite the fear that came with remembering, she smiled at the thought of those first experiences with Mohdek. It should have been obvious to them then, what an effective pair they'd make. But neither had considered it for a moment.

"Believe it or not, we made it to the top." She felt smug about it, even so long after.

"And Namsum?" Ardor asked.

"He was tied to Mohdek's back," she said. "And when he didn't think he could go any farther ... he was tied to mine."

That came across as a slight exaggeration, but she let it stand. Namsum had been far too heavy for her to carry. But she had lashed him on, waiting on a narrow cliff shelf until Mohdek could recover his strength to go on.

"It took a couple of days, but Namsum recovered," Nemery continued. "The three of us found ourselves in the southernmost reaches of Dronodan. You ever been down that way?"

"Never been south of Marow," Ardor replied.

"Mostly all wilderness," she explained, "and much drier than here. Luckily, Namsum knew everything it took to survive. He taught us to read the land, track animals. He taught us how to identify poisonous plants—although, I must say, some of the leafy greens that Namsum called *delicious* sat like sand in my gut."

"I know a thing or two about the superiority of the Trothian constitution," Ard said.

Nemery laughed. It was fun to tell someone about Namsum. Painful, yes. But there was a joy to it that she hadn't expected. She knew Mohdek didn't feel ready to remember his brother that way, but maybe it would be helpful.

"After a couple of cycles, Namsum felt strong enough to undertake a longer journey. He and Mohdek decided it was time to head north so they could check in with the Trothian warriors and report that they'd survived the attack on their ship. The first town we came to was a backward little place called Sprigton. Namsum decided to stop in to check on the state of the war."

She stopped talking, thinking through her next sentences so she could say them as painlessly as possible.

"Folks in Sprigton were confused, I guess," she whispered.

"Apparently, the Trothian forces had gone against Sovereign orders and attacked the Archkingdom harbors on Pekal. The way word trickled down to southern Dronodan, the Trothians were now the enemy."

She swallowed a lump that threatened to end the story.

"They killed Namsum. Thought he was a spy, or an enemy...I don't know."

"I'm so sorry," Ardor said, his voice soft.

"Mohdek and I got away. We went back into the Dronodanian wilderness and only came out of the trees when it was time for Moh's *fajumar*. We must have lived a year like that before we crossed paths with a Trothian hunting guide, who told us that the war had been over for cycles. And since the queen had reinstated the Trothian Inclusionary Act, we were free to go wherever we wanted."

She picked up her waterskin and pulled out the cork. Now that she was through the hardest part of the story, she suddenly remembered the original reason for coming to the stream.

"Here." Nemery dipped the skin into the cold water. "We came here. Of course, we couldn't stay, because the Redeye line had stretched too far with the dragon population on the decline. But we spent every available hour on this island, sailing to one of the Trothian Ras during the Moon Passing. After about a year of that, Cochorin became of age and the Redeye line started retracting. Seemed to happen really quick, pulling farther up the mountainside each time a new dragon hatched. By the time they started building New Vantage, Moh and I were already living here full time."

She corked her waterskin and began to fill Mohdek's.

"Guess that gets me up to speed," said Ardor. "All except one thing...Why did Hedge Marsool tell me to find the Terror of Wilder Far?"

Nemery shrugged innocently. "I don't know the man, honest to Homeland."

"He's obviously heard of you," Ardor said. "And it sounds like he's not the only one who calls you that. Why does—"

She held up a hand. "Please. Can we talk about something else?" Her heart was tender enough right now without going into that. And she didn't want to admit to Ardor that she had borrowed Tanalin Phor's most brutal tactic.

"That's fine," he said, rocking back and sliding his heels together through the red mud. "We've all got secrets, Nemery. Doesn't make us bad people."

She scoffed. "We've done other things for that."

"Hey, now. Go easy on yourself. You've been through more than most people see in a lifetime." He plucked a leaf off a low-hanging branch. "What about your parents?"

"What about them?" she retorted.

"Do they know you're here?"

"I'm guessing the last thing they heard was that I died as a prisoner of war when that Sovereign ship was sunk."

"And you're okay with that?"

She corked Mohdek's waterskin. "Look at me, Ardor. Do I look like someone my parents would be proud of?"

"I'm proud of you," he said. "To hear what you've been through...You were a brilliant kid when I knew you. But you lacked experience. Now you have more of it than anyone I know. The way you handle yourself on these slopes...I think that would make anyone proud to say they knew you when."

She smiled. "Thanks."

"I died once, you know," Ardor said unexpectedly. "My parents are still alive out there, but they think I've been gone over ten years now. Still hurts to think about them. So I try not to. I try to tell myself that I'm a completely different person. That they wouldn't like this version of me."

"Would they?" she asked.

He took a deep, uncertain breath. "I don't think there's any version of me that my mother and father wouldn't love. But I have to keep telling myself lies. Have to keep rusing."

He looked at her, his face a dark shadow in the night that had fallen around them. Perhaps they were more alike than Nemery had ever supposed. In a way, it was comforting to see that even someone as strong and confident as Ardor Benn harbored quiet doubts and insecurities about who he had become.

"And I guess I should come clean with you about something," he said. "You asked me about Quarrah yesterday. We...we aren't together. Not sure we ever really were, actually."

"Sorry to hear that."

"No, it's fine. Really." He exhaled very deliberately. "I understand her hesitation. I mean, I know I'm not an easygoing person. I keep telling myself that I'll change, or I *have* changed, or even that I *could* change. But I know I'm still the same. And I know...I always will be."

Nemery suddenly felt an intense gratitude for Mohdek. He didn't want her to change. And if she did, fine...he'd probably love her still. He was constant and unwavering. She didn't know who she'd be without him. Certainly not Salafan.

Ardor stood abruptly. "Well, tomorrow's the day, you think?"

"To see her, at least," answered Nemery. "These dragons are important to me, Ardor. You think we're doing the right thing, taking her to Talumon?"

Ardor pursed his lips in thought. "Honestly, I'm not so sure. And that isn't something I like to say very often. The whole point of this job was to stop Hedge Marsool from creating Glassminds. But Garifus Floc already beat him to it. I can't help but think that they're connected somehow. I know Hedge is keeping a lot of secrets. And until I can get some answers, following his rules is the best play."

Nemery nodded. "I trust you."

She stood still, holding the plump waterskins as he strode away into the darkened trees. The sound of the gurgling brook filled her ears and her mind swam with thoughts of who she'd been and who she was now.

And of who she wanted to be tomorrow.

~

*The moment we stop regretting our past mistakes, we lose a portion of our humanity and find one more thing in common with the beasts of Pekal.*

# CHAPTER

# 20

It was windy on the campus green of Beripent's Southern College. Quarrah sat on a wooden bench, silently observing the flow of students as the bell tolled the midday hour.

The academic setting was strange to her. As a little girl, Quarrah remembered climbing a stout tree in the Porter District of Leigh. Perched on one of the lower limbs, she'd had a perfect view through a classroom window. Her "school tree" had taught her the letters of the alphabet, but the streets had taught her to read.

Ah, there was San Green moving toward her, clutching a book satchel as though he were a regular student. The young man didn't move like the others, though. There was a furtiveness to his gait and an uneasiness in the way he turned his head. The look of a person who felt like death was always closing in.

San reached her, but didn't sit down. "Where's Raekon?" he asked.

"He only saw me as far as the college gate," Quarrah answered. "Said he had some personal business south of the city."

"What do you think he's doing?"

Quarrah shrugged. "He's got some demons, San." Raek was probably meeting a contact to purchase some Heg. Ard would have tried to stop him, but Quarrah wasn't one to meddle. She had talked to Raek about it once. With his condition, she honestly didn't know if he could survive without the Compounded Health Grit in his chest.

"Did you do it?" she asked.

San seated himself on the bench beside Quarrah, flipping open his satchel. "It took longer than I thought because Professor Baruss kept hanging around. You're not going to like what I discovered anyway." San pulled the thin glass vial from his satchel. "Sugar water." He held it out for her examination.

"What?" She rolled it between her fingers, utterly confused.

"Raekon was right," San said. "There's no source material at all. It's not even technically a Grit solution. Just plain sugar water."

"He must have switched them back," Quarrah muttered.

"Hedge Marsool?"

"No, Ard," said Quarrah. "He stole a vial from Hedge and we were examining it in the *Be'Igoth*. I was too afraid Ard was going to try to use it without understanding it, so I stole the vial and replaced it with one filled with plain sugar water."

"You think he realized it?" San asked. "When would he have switched them back?"

"He couldn't have," Quarrah said, mind racing over the last few weeks. "I've had this vial locked in a safe box in an apartment that Ard doesn't even know about."

"Huh..." San scratched his head. "Maybe you made a mistake and never actually switched them. That's a possibility if they looked identical, right?"

"A small possibility," said Quarrah. "Very small." But if the vials had been switched back, then that meant Ard really had shattered their only sample on the deck of the *Shiverswift*. Quarrah had seen the sparks, but there had been no detonation.

"I don't understand what this means," she admitted.

"Let's consider the options," said San. There were definite perks to keeping a scientist brain around. "First. You didn't switch the vials. The one you're holding is the sugar water you made. Second. Ardor caught on and switched the vials back. The one you're holding is your own sugar water again. Third. The switch was successful."

"But the third option would mean that Hedge Marsool had sugar water in his vial all along," finished Quarrah. Highly improbable. Unless the King Poacher truly was predicting the future somehow. Unless he knew Ard was going to steal a vial. Unless he knew she was going to swap it with sugar water.

Sparks, this was all so confusing! She knew she hadn't made a mistake. Sleight of hand was her area of expertise, which ruled out option number one. And the only way she could rule out the second option was by confronting Ard about what she'd done. That wasn't going to go over well...

Quarrah tucked the glass vial into her pocket. Sugar water. Bah. At this point, she might as well use its contents to sweeten her tea.

"You think he's really going to do it?" San asked. He lowered his voice even though nobody was around. "Get a dragon?"

Quarrah sighed. "It'll be that or the dragon getting him. Ardor Benn doesn't stop once he's put his mind to something."

"You heard any updates?"

"Any day now," she replied.

"What are you going to tell him about that vial?"

"Don't know yet," she said. "For now, let's keep this between us and Raek."

He nodded, gaze distant as he stared across the campus green. "I don't like being back here..." He didn't need to finish the sentence.

Quarrah knew he meant *without her*. The lad was actually handling himself quite well. Still, she didn't know what to say to someone hurting like this.

"We used to study over there." He pointed to a pair of trees to the west. "On summer evenings the cicadas would buzz so loud we could barely hear each other..." San leaned forward, elbows on knees, face in his hands.

*Do I clap him on the back? Say something comforting?* She was lost enough in her own frustrations over this sugar water puzzle.

Quarrah decided on standing up. "Let's get you back to Tofar's Salts." So much for comforting. The young man wiped at his tears and rose with a weary sigh.

"Thanks," Quarrah added. "Lomaya was right. You had the equipment and the contacts to use it."

"Wish it gave us answers," San replied.

"Maybe it will yet."

In all his life, Ardor Benn had never expected to see this dragon again. Motherwatch was curled up at the top of a long draw, wings folded over her back, head tucked down. Her position was relaxed, making no real effort to conceal herself. Ard supposed that was one of the benefits of having no known predators.

His memory of the dragon was burned deep into his mind, but every time he thought of her, she was on the palace steps, the building ablaze behind her and the blood of King Pethredote on her chin. She looked different in her natural habitat. More peaceful, and yet somehow wilder still.

Ard and the crew were on a rise above the draw, their camp established in a tangle of dead trees. Strips of limp bark drooped and swung in the breeze like miniature corpses from a gallows, catching Ard's eye and making him start.

"Why isn't she moving?" he whispered to Nemery.

"I don't know," the girl replied.

She was kneeling behind her new Caller instrument, the wide brass bell covered with a leafy fern so it wouldn't glint in the mid-morning sunlight.

Ard didn't know much about the dragon Calling devices, but this one looked nicer than the one Nemery had used on their first journey to Pekal. The girl was proud of her purchase, he could tell. And happier still to have the crew lug it up the mountainside for her.

Ard wasn't sure how often she'd been able to practice the Calls, living wild on this island for so long. But based on the rich sound she'd just made through the instrument, he still considered her an expert.

"Let's give it a minute," Nemery whispered. "She's clearly on edge, which means she recognized the Call."

"I thought she looked relaxed," he said.

Nemery chuckled. "They don't flex their tails like that when they're relaxed."

"If she recognized that Call," Ard said, "won't she realize that the only one who could make it is Cochorin? Maybe Motherwatch just isn't afraid of her son."

Nemery shook her head. "*Territorial Bull* should work anyway. The Call simulates a bull dragon looking to . . . well, let's just say he wants the place alone so he can search the area for any unfertilized eggs."

Over their shoulder, Senso chuckled. "Well, that explains it. Takes a man to make that Call."

Ard glared in disgust at the annoying man.

"Maybe you ought to head down and provide some backup for Gloristar," Nemery retorted.

That got him to back off. Nobody wanted to join Gloristar, stationed like an army of one at the bottom of the draw. There, the sides of the canyon steepened into a narrow chute. If all went according to plan, Gloristar would soon be facing off with this dragon one on one.

In the clearing below, Motherwatch bobbed her head up and down like a bird searching for predators.

"This whole thing is a bad idea," said Shenya. Ard was growing tired of the crew's dissolving attitude. "We should have approached her in the night," the smuggler continued. "Dragons sleep with their eyes closed, don't they?"

"Not tonight, she wouldn't," said Nemery. "Motherwatch smelled us this morning, well before we saw her for the first time. If she doesn't consider the area safe by sundown, she'll take flight and it'll be days before we can locate her again."

"Funneling her down to Gloristar is our best option," Ard said. "And since our transformed Prime Isless has no detectable scent, she should be able to take Motherwatch by surprise."

"And what makes you think she'll go the direction we want her to?" Shenya asked. "If I had wings like that, I'd definitely fly."

"Motherwatch wouldn't dare," Nemery explained. "Taking flight would provoke the male into giving chase. When a bull makes this Call, he wants the sows in the area to quietly slink away."

"Sounds like a man." Shenya slugged Senso in the arm.

"Let me try the Call again," Nemery said. "I think we can risk once more. Then we'll need to hold off until dark."

"And then we lose her," Ard said, discouraged.

Nemery gave him a helpless little shrug and turned back to her instrument. She made a few adjustments, primed it, and then pressed her lips to the brass mouthpiece.

*Whomp! Whomp! Whomp!*

Ard felt the vibrations of the Call rattling his rib cage. He peered through the white, dead limbs of the trees to see Motherwatch spread her huge green wings in response. For a moment, Ard thought she might take flight. But she stayed low to the grass, puffing up her torso, drawing deep breaths until Ard could see glowing lines appear between her scales.

*Whomp! Whomp! Whomp!*

Nemery's Call faded, the reverberations echoing down the wide draw. Ard tensed, holding on to hope until Motherwatch folded in her wings and burrowed down again.

"Sparks," Ard whispered. "We may have to switch to our backup plan."

"No," Mohdek snapped. He'd been seated silently on the ground beside Nemery all this time. Sometimes it was hard to even know if he was listening. "We can't risk frightening her. A scared dragon can injure herself when trying to flee."

"Flames, Mohdek," said Ard. "You talk about her like she's some delicate mountain deer. For a minute, I thought you were worried about what might happen to the *people* involved in the backup plan."

Nemery's boyfriend was certainly hardheaded. He'd made it clear that he didn't care much for Ard or the purpose of this expedition, despite Ard's plentiful attempts to butter him up over the last week.

But Ard was past that now. He'd resigned himself to a moderately cordial, if not slightly discordant, relationship with the Trothian. On the other hand, Ard was grateful, realizing that Mohdek's no-nonsense, bullheaded characteristics were likely part of what had kept Nemery Baggish alive over the last few years. He was a good man, just not one Ard would want to grab a coffee with.

"It's our only option," Ard said about the backup plan. He turned and waved to Cadlon and Popin. They were the crew members to talk to if you wanted to get something done. Not nosy layabouts like Senso and Shenya.

"We're going to flush her out," Ard explained as the crew began to gather around. "We'll have five of you drop in from the top of the draw. I want you firing guns, making noise . . . But don't get closer than fifty yards or she could hit you before you have a chance to scream. I want everyone else in pairs, positioned on both sides. If she comes your way, you make a racket. We don't want her taking flight. She has to get down to Gloristar."

Nemery suddenly gripped Ard's arm with such intensity that he fell instantly silent. His attention turned back to the area below, and he leaned forward, not believing his eyes.

Another dragon was emerging from the trees on the far side of the slope. A small dragon. A hatchling.

The creature was a similar deep green shade to Motherwatch, though it had stripes of black running down both sides. It measured only a quarter of the length of the mature sow, with wings that looked too small for its body. Its muzzle was rounded, lacking the intimidating hook-jaw distinctive to the adults of its species.

The little dragon was carrying a dead boar in its mouth with little difficulty, like a cat with a prize mouse. It dropped the carcass in front of Motherwatch and pranced a few steps, thwacking its tail against the ground, its underdeveloped, nub-like spikes laying down the grasses and tilling up red soil.

Nemery and Mohdek were speaking in hushed tones, their conversation exclusive in his language. But Ard heard them say Motherwatch's Trothian name. He'd picked up on that much over the last few days.

"What's that hatchling doing here?" Ard finally whispered, watching Motherwatch nudge the dead boar back toward the little dragon. "Is Motherwatch going to fight her?"

"The little one's a male," corrected Nemery. "And I'd say that his *mother* has been teaching him to hunt."

"You've got to be kidding me," Ard muttered.

Nemery watched the little bull tear a leg off the boar and swallow it whole. He sneezed, or belched, an unthreatening spurt of flame escaping his muzzle.

*Proud of yourself, aren't you, little guy*, she thought. Perhaps Proudflame would be a suitable name for him.

"I thought you said Motherwatch wasn't laying anymore," Ardor said.

"She must have had one more in her," said Nemery. "Based on the wing development, I'd say this one is barely two cycles old. That's why Motherwatch wouldn't leave even when she heard the *Territorial Bull* Call. She didn't want to risk getting separated from her little one. And I guess it explains why she's been hanging around Red Banks. It's common for a mother to train her hatchlings in the area near where they hatched."

"Well, does this change your mind?" Mohdek said, switching the conversation to Trothian.

Nemery breathed out slowly. "This changes everything."

Ardor cleared his throat. "I really hope the two of you are scheming on how to separate that little dragon from Motherwatch."

"What?" Nemery turned on him, hoping he was telling some kind of morbid joke.

"I'm just saying," Ardor continued, "we don't have the space or the resources to take them both."

"We're not taking *either* of them," snapped Nemery.

Ardor's expression rapidly shifted as he processed her words. From focused, to confused, to disappointed.

"Nemery," he said. "We have to—"

"No," she cut him off. "The first three cycles of a dragon's life are critical. The bond with their mother teaches them survival, social interaction, and maybe a lot more that we don't understand…"

"Well, he seems plenty big to me," said Ardor, pointing down at the draw. "And he obviously knows how to hunt…so I'd say he'll be fine."

"How can you say that?" Nemery cried. "He's a hatchling with—"

"Will he survive?" Ardor asked.

"There are so many skills they—"

"Will he *survive*?" he asked again, forcefully this time.

"Well, I mean…probably," she stammered. "Maybe. But it's not a risk we're going to take."

"It's a risk we *have* to take," he said. "Gloristar's in position. Everything is ready. We have to do this. Or would you like to come back to Beripent and explain to Hedge Marsool why we don't have a dragon?"

"Sparks, Ardor," she muttered. "This was never my fight." Why was he coming at her like this? She had only agreed to this expedition as a favor. Because she owed him her life.

Ardor turned to the crew. "Nothing changes about the plan. Let's go." He clapped his hands together, jolting them into action.

"You can't do this, Ardor," said Nemery. "You and your crew promised to play by my rules."

"Happy to follow the rules," Ardor said, "but you can't change the game. Phel!" He called one of the Tracers over. "I want you to get down to Gloristar as quickly as you can. I'm guessing she's seen the hatchling by now, but make sure she's prepared."

With every word he spoke, Nemery felt the situation slipping away from her. It had been so many years since she'd felt betrayal like this. Ardor Benn had seemed so vulnerable at the stream last night. So honest and trustworthy. But with a single step, he had crossed a line. And if he thought she would simply stand by and watch this happen, then he clearly didn't know how much she'd changed.

"We only take Motherwatch," Ardor concluded his instructions to the Tracer. "Am I clear?"

"Aye," Phel said. But before he could turn, Nemery had drawn an arrow on him.

"You're not going anywhere," she whispered, heart hammering as loudly as a dragon Call in her ears.

The Tracer stood stiffly, unsure of how to respond. Nemery was shaking. It had been a mistake to make a full draw on her bowstring. This bow was too stiff to hold for more than a couple of seconds. But that wasn't the only reason she trembled.

Slowly, with an air of absolute confidence, Ardor Benn stepped between her and Phel. Her hand-carved arrowhead was wobbling just inches from his chest, and she feared she might loose whether she meant to or not.

"Nemery," Mohdek said from behind her. She couldn't tell if his tone was encouraging, or forewarning. All she could think about was the feel of the bowstring as it bit into her three fingers, the straightness of the arrow shaft, the screaming of her own voice inside her head.

"Before you make this decision," Ardor said calmly, "remember whose side Gloristar is on. She's taking Motherwatch to Beripent with or without me."

Behind him, Phel was gone, already out of sight to deliver his message to the Glassmind Prime Isless. The other crew members were moving into position. He was right. This ball was already rolling too fast for her to stop it. Shooting Ardor Benn wouldn't change the outcome. But it would change her.

Unable to hold on to the string any longer, Nemery jerked her bow to the side, the movement finally loosing the arrow. It missed Ardor's arm by mere inches, burying into the pale trunk of a dead tree behind him.

"We're even, Ardor Benn," she said, fighting a sudden surge of tears that threatened to fill her eyes.

"I'm sorry it has to be like this." Ardor stepped away from her.

So was she. For four years, she had put him upon a pedestal. And suddenly, in the course of just a few sentences, he had come tumbling down headfirst.

Ardor cast her one last regretful look before turning to sprint through the trees. Just when she thought she might collapse, Nemery felt Mohdek's steady hand slide around her waist. She dropped her head onto his firm shoulder and let a few tears spill. One for Motherwatch. One for Proudflame. And one for the shattered foundation upon which she had started her new life.

"Come," Mohdek said softly. "We should gather our things and go."

She was surprised that he didn't suggest fighting the crew. But he knew just as well as she did what a Glassmind was capable of. The fight would be over before it began.

"No," she replied, standing up tall. "We have to stay and see what happens. In case the hatchling needs us after they take Motherwatch."

Mohdek smiled sadly. "It will not be easy to watch. You know which side I'll be rooting for."

From the top of the draw, gunshots sang out through the mountain stillness, sending birds into the air.

It had begun.

Ard stopped running as the gunshots echoed down the draw. A tiny part of him was surprised that Nemery hadn't shot him in the back. He cursed at himself for the way things had just unfolded. Little Nemery Baggish...Did Ard have to destroy *every* relationship in his life?

The walls of the draw were steeper as he got closer to where Gloristar was hiding. Best not to go much farther, for fear of spooking Motherwatch into taking a different path.

Peering down the slope, he could see that the dragon wasn't moving yet. The spines on her back were raised, wings elevated in an aggressive stance as the little hatchling huddled under her breast.

More shots sounded and Ard saw a blur of movement in the trees at the top of the draw.

*Don't get any closer*, Ard silently urged the crew. *She could lash out.* Maybe Mohdek had been right. This plan wasn't turning out to be as effective as Ard had hoped. And the risk...

One of the crew members shouted something that sounded like a warning. Then Ard saw a Grit pot come hurtling through the trees. It struck the open grass, detonating with a ball of flame and smoke.

Ard doubted a fiery explosion would do any damage to a dragon's hide, but it certainly scared her more than the gunshots. The Blast Grit caused Motherwatch to rear up on her hind legs. At the same time, the hatchling screeched, darting down the draw.

Motherwatch dropped, moving after him. For a moment, Ard thought their plan might be successful. About halfway to Gloristar's position, the hatchling decided to scamper up the slope on the opposite side of the draw. There must have been crewmen in place, because two pairs of Rollers sounded in answer to the charge. Ard saw the hatchling flinch, lead balls pinging off his tough scales. He growled, swiping his short tail back and forth in rage.

With a pounce, Motherwatch reached her baby on the hillside. Scooping one of her stout forearms around the smaller dragon, she flung him back down to the grassy draw.

Motherwatch hissed, her huge mouth opening with a snarl. Blindly, she blew a mighty breath into the trees. Not a breath of destructive fire, but a rush of vaporous air so hot that Ard saw shimmering waves. Every leaf and twig of green vegetation instantly wilted as screams rose and unseen flesh scalded.

Motherwatch dropped to where the hatchling was scratching and nuzzling at a spot on his shoulder. Ard couldn't see any blood, but maybe one of those Roller balls had pierced the little guy.

Sparks, they weren't supposed to hurt it! He'd told them to fire into the air. If the hatchling was hurt, what chance it had of surviving without his mother would be drastically reduced.

Motherwatch nudged the small dragon with her nose, pushing him ahead as they continued toward the narrow passage where Gloristar waited.

Ard held his breath, shrinking behind a bush as the two creatures barreled past. Motherwatch hadn't likely smelled him on the downwind side of the draw. And at this point, the dragon seemed more interested in getting her little one safely away.

The hatchling moved through the passage, out of Ard's sight. But Motherwatch suddenly ground to a halt, her hooked talons gouging grooves in the red dirt. She drew her head back, producing a frantic chirping sound that was surely a warning for the baby.

Prime Isless Gloristar sprang into view. Ard had no idea where she'd been hiding; it was as though she had just flown into sight from behind that boulder.

Mid-chirp, Motherwatch's sound changed to a hiss. Her long neck sprang forward like a striking snake, but Gloristar reached up, sparks dancing across her fingertips.

Motherwatch collapsed. Her huge form slumped to the ground, head narrowly missing a jagged rock protruding from the steep slope.

"We got her!" Ard shouted as he scrambled down toward the dragon. The slope was so steep that he couldn't find a proper footing and ended up sliding downward, hands grasping for any twigs or roots to break his fall. Knuckles scratched and knees bruised, Ard picked himself up, finding that his reckless descent had landed him just feet from Motherwatch's tail.

He moved slowly alongside her elongated figure, in awe of her size and the complexity of her features. Her green scales were knobby and weathered, the knuckles above her talons gnarled. She was as still as a statue, Gloristar's Stasis Grit having suspended even her breathing.

Ardor Benn had seen several dragons in his life. First, as a Harvester. Then standing face to face with this one on the palace steps. Quarrah had even brought down a sow with Stasis Grit during their expedition to rescue Shad Agaul.

But for the first time in his life, Ard felt like he was *really* seeing a dragon. Seeing her without the usual fear of being eaten. He reached out and placed a hand at the base of her neck. Her scales were surprisingly smooth, and her body was quite hot to the touch. Majestic in every sense of the word.

Gloristar stepped around the dragon's nose. One arm hung casually at her side, but the other was extended, a thin trail of detonated Grit connecting to the hazy cloud surrounding Motherwatch's head.

Ard pulled his hand away, ending his reverential connection with the beast. "How long will she be out?"

"I have enveloped her entire head in Stasis Grit," Gloristar explained. "I can keep fueling it with Prolonging Grit, but she will regain a degree of consciousness as the Stasis effect wanes."

"How much consciousness?" The last thing Ard wanted was for Motherwatch to awaken in a stupor like a delirious drunk.

"Her heartbeat will resume first," Gloristar answered. "And then her breathing. As long as we don't let her get beyond that point, we should be fine."

"And then you can dose her again?" Ard checked. "With more Stasis Grit?"

She nodded. "Until my internal supply is spent. I should have plenty to get us back to the harbor."

"And we've got more Stasis Grit on the *Stern Wake*," Ard said. "Raek already sent another batch ahead to Helizon so we should have plenty to keep her as long as we need."

"Blazing sparks!" Dargen muttered, coming into view behind the dragon's folded wing. Shenya and Phel were behind him, sharing his astonishment. The three crew members circled slowly, desperate to get a clear view of her face.

"Do you realize how much she'd be worth?" Dargen continued. "The scales alone..."

"Don't even think about it." Ard recognized the greedy looks on their faces.

"How are you going to move her?" Phel asked.

"Like this." Gloristar stretched out her free hand, fingers sparking. Ard saw a cone of detonated Grit stream from her palm. It flowed over Motherwatch's entire body, from the heat-crusted nostrils to the tip of her tail.

There wasn't much overspill. Not like there would have been had the cloud been spherical. Gloristar was manipulating its shape to fit around the dragon's body like a loose glove. When she was finished, tendrils of wispy cloud connected her hands to the motionless dragon like an immaterial leash.

Ard knew Gloristar could manipulate only two clouds at a

time—one with each hand. As soon as she released her hold on them, they would either dissipate, or assume their natural spherical shape.

Prime Isless Gloristar lifted her hands, the clouds of Drift and Stasis moving upward with no apparent difficulty. Motherwatch's still form rose from the ground, clods of red dirt falling from her, floating lazily through her shroud of Drift Grit until they exited the perimeter and plopped back to the earth.

Ard stared up at the floating dragon. She stayed perfectly centered in the oblong cloud, oddly stiff and motionless.

"Phel," Ard said, snapping the Tracer out of his awestruck wonder. "Round up the rest of the crew and get back to the campsite. Gather our things and meet us at the stream crossing on the other side of that rise. We need to get out of here before that hatchling comes back looking for his mother."

*Or before Nemery and Mohdek change their minds about letting us take her.*

Ardor Benn pushed past the twist of guilt he felt in his stomach. Homeland forgive him, but he was doing what needed to be done.

～

*I would take a beast on the mountain over one in my head.*

# CHAPTER

# 21

Ard quickly reread the note he'd just scribed onto the tiniest piece of thin paper. He noticed one little misspelling. Raek would chide him for that, but it was difficult to focus in here with all the cooing and flapping of wings.

*Job is done. We sail from New Vantage at sunset on the 8th. Notify Hedge to meet us at Helizon property at dark on the 9th. Come with Q imediately. Bring doughnuts.*

*Doughnuts* was just code for the explosive mantel clocks that Raek was rigging up, but Ard hoped his partner would bring both.

He turned to the blank side of the note and wrote: *Deliver to: The Short Fuse—Tofar's Salts, Upper Western Quarter.*

"That'll be ten Ashings," said the young man behind the counter, carefully rolling Ard's note like a Heg wrapper.

"Ten Ashings!" Ard cried. New Vantage was bleeding him dry. "I should hope at least half of that goes to the pigeon."

"Of course," said the lad. "The pigeons are well fed, and their travel accommodations back to Pekal are—"

"And you knit them little caps for the winter cycles, I hope," Ard said. "Give them soup if they're not feeling well?"

This befuddled the worker quite wonderfully. "But, sir. They're … birds."

Apparently, Ard was the first client in New Vantage with a sense of humor. He dug out three Ashings and a seven-mark, slapping them down on the counter.

"That goes to Beripent, see," Ard confirmed, reading the labels over the pigeonholes behind the young man. Ha! They even had a pigeon for the little Strindian township of Duway. New Vantage was still a fledgling town, but its services were already competing with any major city on the main islands.

Ard watched the young man select a pigeon from one of the Beripent holes, sliding the scrolled note into a little tube fastened to the bird's leg. Ard waited to leave the shop until he saw the bird go out the window, flying into the flat gray sky of a stormy midafternoon.

Flightsome Messages was an absolute ripoff, but it was definitely the quickest way to get in contact with Raek. Pigeons were fairly reliable throughout the Greater Chain, and Ard didn't see why they'd be any less so, coming from Pekal.

He moved up the street, passing a vendor roasting sausages over an open fire. They smelled delicious, reminding Ard that he hadn't eaten lunch yet. But there was no time for that. He was already running late for his meeting with the harbormaster.

"Mister Ardor!" called a familiar voice. Speaking of having no time...

"Hello, Ednes," he said, not slowing his pace. How had she found him so quickly? They'd returned to New Vantage only a few hours ago, and they'd be leaving just as soon as they could get Mother-watch onto the *Stern Wake*. Hopefully before dark if everything went according to plan.

"How was your little hike?" she asked. "Did you see any wild animals?"

"Just you," Ard said, pasting on a smile.

"I'd be happy to show you my wild side." She lowered the pitch of her voice in an attempt to sound sultry. "But there's not a room available at the Elegant Perch."

"I noticed New Vantage is busier than when we left." Ard pretended not to catch her implication.

"I know! Busiest it's ever been!" Ednes was happy enough to talk through any direction the conversation might lead. "They're saying *all* the inns are at capacity. I don't know what they're going to do when the rest of them get here. We can't have tents on the streets!"

Ard looked at her for the first time. "When the rest of *who* gets here?"

"You didn't hear?" She was noticeably excited about the nugget of gossip that was about to spill across her tongue. "They say it's a *cult*."

Ard stopped in the middle of the street. The Glassmind cult? Had Garifus Floc already returned to Pekal with his followers?

Ard's eyes darted to the myriad pedestrians traveling this way and that. Suddenly, he could trust no one.

Ednes chuckled softly. "A ship with over a hundred visitors arrived earlier today. Word is that they're the first in a big group. Over the next week, we should expect to receive four times that number."

*Sparks!* Over four hundred cultists heading to Pekal?

"Who's their leader?" Ard kept his voice quiet as he resumed his path down the street.

"How should I know about cults, and such?" Ednes asked. "I'm a good little Wayfarist. Honest to Homeland."

Ard was relieved by her comment. If there was a transformed Glassmind in New Vantage, Ednes Holcatch would surely be talking about it.

Perhaps Garifus and the other Glassminds were keeping a low profile on their ship in the harbor. Maybe even hiding outside the town. But Ard thought it more likely that the leader of a cult would remain in Beripent to oversee everyone's departure. Make sure none of the human cultists got cold feet.

"Listen, Ednes," said Ard. "I've got to run up ahead. But do me a favor?"

"Anything."

"If you happen to see Salafan, warn her about the cultists," he said. Nemery would surely realize who they were on her own, but it didn't hurt to put Ednes on it. "And tell her I'm sorry. Truly sorry."

The plump woman seemed excited by his parting words. Ard took advantage of her giddiness to slip into a mossy alley, making for the harbor.

He knew why the cultists were here. There was only one good explanation for it. They were coming to get Moonsick. Having seen Garifus Floc, they were ready to make the leap of faith—or the hike to the summit, as it were. And if they were successful, it would mean more Glassminds by the start of the next cycle. *Hundreds* more.

Ard slipped out of the alley, pausing for a moment to decide which direction to go. He was easily turned around in New Vantage—especially since the once-familiar harbor had been completely redesigned since New Vantage's establishment. Steep, rickety ramps that had once been used only by rugged Harvesters now had handrails and carved grooves dusted with sand for traction.

Ard went left, passing a cart full of wooden toys where a family of four was examining the trinkets. Were they cultists, too? Would they be dragging *children* to Pekal's summit to expose them to Moonsickness?

Ard reached the checkpoint, noticing a queue of departing tourists lined up to show their bags. Queen Abeth had made sure that security wouldn't grow lax with the increased tourism. The place was crawling with harbor Regulators determined to search every outgoing person, regardless of the visitor's rank or social standing.

Moving past, Ard saw the harbormaster's office, a quaint little log structure that was already pocked with spots of black mold. It was situated well above the harbor, far enough from the entrance checkpoint so the harbormaster wouldn't be bothered by the sounds of tourists coming and going.

Ard spotted Captain Dodset loitering near a tool shed, an oversized hat with a floppy brim pulled over her shaved head. A smoking reed was clutched between her lips and she gave him a lazy salute to show that she was ready and waiting for his cue.

Ardor Benn usually liked to be the closer on a job, but he didn't mind playing the part of the opener today. This was why they had gone through so much effort to secure Dodset's allegiance, along with that folder of papers.

Ard cracked open the office door without knocking, stepping quietly inside. It was a simple room with one hearth for Heat Grit, and another for burning wood. Neither were in use on a pleasant late summer afternoon like this. Instead, windows on opposing walls were wide open, providing a gentle cross breeze that rustled stacks of papers on a desk in the center of the room.

Behind the desk was an elderly man with wrinkled features and a prominent rosy nose. He was so thin that the shoulder pads on his uniform had slumped down with nothing to hold them up.

Ard would have expected a man of his age to be lavishly retired at New Vantage, not overseeing the entire harbor. But he supposed it was a good thing to be dealing with a veteran harbormaster. A bright-eyed, bushy-tailed new leader might not have been as susceptible to the coming threats.

"Harbormaster Pike?" Ard said. "I hope I didn't catch you at a bad time."

"Not at all." The man gestured for Ard to have a seat on one of the chairs in front of the desk. "What can I do for you, Mister...?"

"Crosser," Ard introduced. "Elt Crosser." He didn't have any paperwork for the name he'd just made up, but he certainly couldn't use his real one. Holy Isle Ardor Benn was supposed to be visiting his estranged grandmother on her deathbed in Strind.

"I'd like you to authorize a Drift repair on my ship," Ard said.

"Well, we don't typically do those here," said Pike. "Not unless the damage is bad enough that you won't make it back to the Greater Chain. How much water are you taking?"

"Who said we were taking any water?" said Ard.

"You just requested a lift."

"Exactly," continued Ard. "I want your Reggies to Drift my vessel to Repair Field Number Two on the south side of New Vantage."

"Now, wait a minute—"

"Don't worry," Ard cut him off. "We'll take care of the repairs ourselves. Won't need more than a half hour. Then your Reggies can Drift our ship back down to the water, where we'll set sail without a cargo inspection."

"Who do you think you are to tell—"

"I'm the man with the gun." Ard quickly drew his Roller,

keeping it at hip height, conspicuously pointed in Pike's direction. "Now, I'm sure you've got one, too. In a drawer, maybe in a holster at your side. That's why I'm going to need you to place your hands on top of the desk where I can see them."

"You listen to me, Mister Crosser," Pike said, nevertheless doing as Ard had instructed. "Fire that Roller and you'll have two dozen harbor Regulators on your back before you reach the first checkpoint. You'll never get out of the harbor. Not you, nor your crew, nor your ship. Let alone whatever illegal material you're attempting to smuggle out of here."

"What do you say we test your theory?" Ard pulled the trigger. The shot went past Pike's head, lodging into the mortar between two of the logs in the wall behind him.

Harbormaster Pike nearly jumped out of his skin. His hands left the desk, but Ard cocked the Slagstone hammer, readying another shot while clucking his tongue disapprovingly.

The cabin door flew open, but Ard didn't need to turn to know that it was Captain Torgeston Dodset. He recognized the way she cleared her throat, and the draft of tobacco smoke that accompanied her wherever she went.

"It's been a while, ole Pikey boy!" She slammed the door behind her, strutting across the room. A silver-handled knife with a wide blade rested loosely in one hand.

"Dodset," the man muttered. "I should have known."

"I believe my compadre already told you what we need." Casually, she used the edge of her knife to trim one of her fingernails.

"I cannot allow it," Pike said firmly.

Outside the cabin door, Ard heard shouts in a chain of command. The Reggies were responding as quickly as Pike had promised, and the harbormaster seemed to be holding out for their rescue.

Captain Dodset slapped a paper envelope on the desk between his splayed hands. "Hedge Marsool sends his regards."

The door burst open again, two eager-looking young men in uniform trying to squeeze through the doorway at the same time. Ard shifted his stance to conceal the drawn gun at his side, all the while keeping it homed in on the harbormaster.

"It's all right, lads," Pike said weakly. "Just a faulty hammer on my Roller. Nearly put a hole in my foot." He paused, but the Reggies looked too suspicious to dismiss themselves. "Give us the room," he said in a tone that demanded compliance.

The Regulators pulled the door closed behind them.

Captain Dodset used the tip of her knife to flick the envelope closer to Pike. "Go ahead and give it a read," she said. "There's some good stuff in there. I especially like the last line."

With trembling hands, Pike tore open the envelope. The letter inside was written on a single page, which the harbormaster read with tears of fear in his eyes.

It killed Ard not to know what Hedge Marsool had written, but this was one of the few benefits of working for the King Poacher. After all, that letter was only in play because Ard had done his part—negotiating with Baroness Lavfa, stealing the Moon Glass, surviving an attack from the *Shiverswift*.

Harbormaster Pike slowly lowered the page, face blanched. "I will instruct my people to do as you said. Your ship will be Drift-lifted to repair field two, where you'll have thirty minutes—*thirty minutes*," he stressed. "After that, your vessel will be returned to the harbor and you'll be free to go."

"Pleasure doing business." Dodset sheathed her knife.

"Please let Marsool know that I was cooperative." Pike's voice was trembling.

"I'll be seeing him tomorrow evening," Ard said. "Happy to sing your praises." He'd be happy to say *anything* to keep Hedge's attention during their upcoming conversation—to keep him from noticing what they were really planning to do with the dragon.

A lot was riding on that meeting. But first they had to get

Motherwatch into the baroness's storage cavern. Captain Dodset had promised that she'd be just as persuasive in the Helizon harbor, so hopefully they wouldn't run into any trouble unloading the dragon.

"You don't know who you're dealing with," Harbormaster Pike dared. "Hedge Marsool isn't your ally. He works only for himself."

Ard put on a smile. "So do I."

Quarrah maneuvered the handcart into the spacious warehouse. A small hunchbacked man in a tattered cloak was waiting just inside, quickly pushing the sliding door shut behind her. It was dim in here without a single window to let in the final hour of daylight. A handful of small Light Grit orbs illuminated Ard as he jogged toward her, his boots echoing on what sounded like a metal floor.

"Perfect timing, Quarrah," Ard said. He looked like he wanted to greet her with a hug, but he didn't go for it. "We were almost out of Stasis Grit, and Hedge Marsool won't be here for at least another hour." He glanced toward the door. "Where's Raek?"

"He decided to stay in Beripent," Quarrah said. "But he sent me with everything we need." She pulled the canvas covering off the handcart. Two wooden boxes filled with vials of Stasis Grit, and six chainspring mantel clocks, rigged to explode twelve hours after being wound.

"Everything okay back home?" Ard asked. "Did you find Lomaya's friend?"

Quarrah tilted her head, trying to decide how to break the news to Ard. "That's partly why Raek stayed. We rescued San Green, but Lomaya..." Even a week later, Quarrah could clearly see the still form of the young woman lying upon the rubble of the wall.

"Sparks," Ard whispered mournfully.

"Garifus Floc was more powerful than we expected," Quarrah justified.

"You saw him?" Ard asked anxiously.

She nodded. "The Glassmind cult might be a bigger problem than anticipated, Ard. There are hundreds of them."

"I know," he replied. "The first shipload had arrived in New Vantage by the time we left."

"And our reports tell us that Garifus and the other Glassminds are gathering more people every day. But he doesn't have Portsend's students anymore, so hopefully it'll take them a while to figure out the formula for more Metamorphosis Grit."

Ard winced. "Gloristar said they probably already know it from absorbing the cloud that transformed them." He scratched his chin in thought. "After all this, I still can't figure out what part Hedge is playing."

"The part of our boss, I'd say," Quarrah pointed out.

"I mean, he knows the formula for Metamorphosis Grit, but he's not the one making Glassminds," Ard continued.

"As far as we know," said Quarrah.

"He seems unrelated to Garifus and his followers," continued Ard. "But if the Glassminds are going to be such a problem, shouldn't Hedge have foreseen that with his Future Grit?"

"About that…" Quarrah took a steadying breath. She wasn't ready to tell him what she'd done, or even what she'd found out. But she needed to know if he had switched the vials back after her sleight-of-hand trickery.

"What did you do with that single shot of Future Grit you stole from Hedge?" she asked. Far too direct. He was going to know that something was off.

"Umm…" Ard raised an eyebrow. "I smashed it on the *Shiverswift*. Are you really trying to rub this in right now?"

"Have you ever been to my apartment in the Northern Quarter?"

"Is that an invitation?"

"Sparks, Ard! I'm trying to figure something out." Why did he have to fluster her with that coy smile. Still, he seemed sincere enough that Quarrah found herself ruling out the option that Ard had switched the vials back. That left only one possibility of the three she and San had listed.

Hedge was carrying sugar water.

"Whatever you're so worked up about is going to have to wait until later," Ard said. "Right now, we've got to deal with Motherwatch." He gestured over his shoulder.

"You *named* the dragon?" Quarrah said. Like it was some kind of pet...

"Actually, Nemery can take credit for that," Ard said. "I'll have time to fill you in on everything later." He stepped over to the handcart and popped open one of the boxes that held a clock.

"But she's down there?" Quarrah pointed to the huge metal hatch that Ard had walked over. It took up the entire floor, save a ten-foot border around the edge.

"Oh, yeah." Ard lifted one of the clocks from its sawdust packaging to inspect it. "Sleeping like a baby. Well, in Stasis, so technically not sleeping. But she's been quite comfortable down there since this morning."

"How the blazes did you move a dragon through Helizon in broad daylight?" Quarrah asked.

"This is the Shipping District," Ard said. "Close to the harbor and not exactly the nicest part of town."

"Still..." Quarrah said. There had to be more to it. Ardor Benn would never risk parading his hard-earned dragon through any neighborhood unless he *wanted* people to see it. "Did you show her off?" Quarrah accused. "Does everyone in Helizon know she's here?"

Ard drew back. "Don't be absurd. You realize how fast the Regulators would be on us? And the queen would surely get involved for something as big as a live dragon. That would be a glaring blemish on my inscrutable new name." He carefully set the clock back into its box.

"How'd you do it, Ard?" She hated when he did this, stringing her along so that his final reveal would seem more impressive.

"Well, Hedge's papers and Captain Dodset's threats to the Helizon harbormaster got the *Stern Wake* Drift-lifted to a repair yard above the harbor," Ard began. "Then Gloristar manipulated a detonation of Shadow Grit, spreading it across the sky to look like a thunderhead. She kept Motherwatch in Stasis and used Drift Grit to push the dragon straight up. Half a mile in the sky, at least, hiding her in the cloud. Then we just walked down the street until we got here."

Quarrah glanced back at the sliding door to the warehouse. It was large, but she'd seen a mature sow dragon. "And she fit?"

"Roof lifts off," Ard said, pointing up. "Part of Baroness Lavfa's recent renovations. We opened it up and Gloristar quickly lowered the dragon out of the cloud, through the roof, and into the cavern below."

"So basically Gloristar did everything," Quarrah pointed out.

"Well, it was mostly *my* idea," Ard said defensively.

These days it seemed like *ideas* were all Ardor Benn could manage. His ability to execute them was waning like an overly Prolonged cloud of Light Grit.

"Where is Gloristar now?" asked Quarrah.

"She left with the *Stern Wake* once the dragon was in place," replied Ard.

"Where did they go?"

"Back to Beripent," he answered. "You would have passed them in the InterIsland Waters. Gloristar still has no interest in being discovered, and Captain Dodset has the unique ability to move our Glassmind friend through harbors without questions. Gloristar was going to wait for us at Tofar's Salts. I'm guessing she'll meet up with Raek and San before we get—"

Ard was interrupted as the heavy sliding door rolled open, spilling flat evening light into the warehouse.

"Pincher!" Ard barked at the strange little man attending the door. But he stepped back, raising his dirty hands to show that he wasn't moving it.

Instinctively, Quarrah reached out, flicking the edge of the canvas over the handcart as a familiar misshapen silhouette appeared in the threshold.

Hedge Marsool. Woefully ahead of schedule.

The King Poacher limped forward, his spike arm tucked against his side and his other one swinging extra-wide to compensate. This evening, he was accompanied by two massively muscled Trothian men wearing Grit belts and more knives than Quarrah could count at a glance.

"Hedge!" Ard cried, his voice carrying an edge of forced merriment. "I take it my message reached you. We weren't expecting you for another hour—"

"Now, that gives me the puzzles," the man replied. "You weren't expecting me, but you're already here...Didn't I say to give me a holler the *moment* the dragon was in place?"

"You did," Ard said. "We were just giving ourselves a bit of flexibility in case something unexpected happened during transport—"

"Unexpected? Bah!" Hedge cut him off. "Nothing is unexpected to me."

"Then why were you surprised that I was already here?" Ard dared.

"Boys," Hedge said to his Trothian companions. "Kill him."

Quarrah's hand strayed to her pockets, making a quick decision about which type of Grit to throw in Ard's defense.

"Whoa! Wait!" Ard held up his hands as the Trothians advanced. "I'll show you the dragon!"

Hedge grunted, holding up his spike to call off his men.

"Sparks, Hedge," Ard gasped. "You're not supposed to go straight from banter to *kill him*. What happened to foreplay?"

"You waste your reeking breath in words," said Hedge. "Show me the beast."

Ard nodded, glancing anxiously at Quarrah before turning around and clapping his hands. "Pincher! Otella! Let's open it up!"

The hunchbacked man left his post at the door, making his way across the warehouse toward another figure who had just appeared from the shadows. The woman was as dirty as Pincher, with ratty gray hair and a mouth that puckered in a telltale sign of toothlessness.

The two vagrants moved to a large crank mounted next to the warehouse wall. A chain led to the rafters far overhead, passing through a block and tackle and hooking into the metal floor. Quarrah noticed that the hatch was split down the middle of the warehouse, an identical crank and pulley system on the opposite side, ready to open the floor like a pair of double doors.

Pincher and Otella were teaming up on one crank, the chains tightening with audible vibrations as they pulled. The hinges groaned and squeaked as half the floor began to rise.

Hedge stepped forward and Quarrah could see his twisted, scarred face ripe with excitement, peering into the dark crack. For a moment, she thought about giving him a solid shove, sending him tumbling to the dragon below. Would he see it coming if it were unplanned—truly impulsive? Well, she'd thought about it for too long now...

"Too dark," Hedge muttered, using the tip of his spike to pull aside his long leather cloak. Quarrah eyed his Grit belt—a single Roller with Blast cartridges wrapping around the back, four hardened leather pouches for Grit pots, and half a dozen loops holding thin glass vials with clear liquid.

More sugar water?

Ard stepped forward, a pot of Light Grit in his hand. "Allow me," he said, pitching it through the widening hatch. Quarrah heard it shatter. She turned her attention back to the cavern, a draft of hot air wafting upward from the beast below.

A flare of Light Grit filled the space, and Quarrah couldn't help but gasp at the sight. The cavern was larger than she'd expected, certainly much bigger than the warehouse that concealed its entrance. The walls below were rough stone of black and gray, unshaped by human tools except for one smooth stretch where a ladder descended into the depths. It was a surprisingly sturdy-looking thing, metal rungs anchored directly into the stone. Ard's Light Grit had detonated against a protrusion in the wall on the way down. And at the bottom...

*Motherwatch*, as Ard had called her, was a hulking terror of scales and spines, unconscious beneath one of the Greater Chain's most prestigious cities. It was hard for Quarrah to admire her beauty and unrivaled power when it seemed like she might spring upward at any moment.

Sure, she was shackled—one on each leg, one around her neck, one at her tail—and the heavy chains were staked directly into the cave's stone floor. But would those restraints really hold her if she slipped out of Stasis?

That was the very thing they'd be counting on Hedge to believe. The clock explosives would knock out all six of her chains, but the King Poacher needed to think Motherwatch had burst her bonds with her own unimaginable strength. Which she very well might.

"Why isn't she moving?" Hedge grumbled.

"Stasis Grit," Ard explained, stepping over to the handcart and pulling the canvas partway back. "We've got plenty more here. Should keep her as still as the grave well into next cycle. Just like we agreed."

Quarrah raised her eyebrows at the answer. The next cycle was nearly twenty days away. They barely had enough Stasis Grit to keep her more than a day. Luckily, the dragon would be gone by midmorning tomorrow.

Hedge Marsool began moving along the side of the hatch opening, his single eye never leaving the dragon below.

"I assure you, she's just as big from every angle," Ard said as Hedge stopped at the spot where the ladder dropped into the cave.

He raised his spike arm, pointing it directly at one of his Trothian associates, speaking something in his language. Quarrah readied herself for the worst, but the big thug merely moved around to join his boss.

"What's going on?" Ard asked. Was that a hint of nervousness in his voice?

"Frush is strong as a Dronodanian buffalo," answered Hedge. "He's taking me down." The Trothian positioned himself with one foot on the top rung.

"You won't make it," Ard said flatly.

Hedge was about to swing onto Frush's back when he paused. "Oh? And why in the name of your mother's corset won't I?"

"Because you'll get about three quarters of the way down and your head will enter the cloud of Stasis Grit surrounding the dragon," said Ard. "You'll fall twenty feet, at least."

Hedge barked something in Trothian and Frush climbed up.

"I'm surprised you didn't realize that," Ard continued. "After all, *you're* the one with the Future Grit. But then, I'm sure you've noticed by now that I nicked one of your vials."

Quarrah sucked in a breath and held it. What was Ard saying? Why would he tip their hand like this?

"I had my people examine the liquid solution," Ard said.

"Ard..." Quarrah warned. He was going to make himself look stupid.

"We're calling it Future Grit," he continued, "based on the way it shows you a glimpse into the future."

Across the square opening in the floor, Hedge Marsool stood perfectly still for an unnerving moment. Quarrah swallowed. If the stolen vial was as useless as Quarrah assumed, Hedge would call Ard's bluff.

"That so?" Hedge finally rasped. The man didn't sound

particularly angry or bothered. In fact, his tone revealed an expression Quarrah hadn't previously seen from him—surprise.

"We're mass-producing it now," Ard carried on, nodding. "So I suppose there was a good payout for this job after all. You got your dragon. We got Future Grit."

"Don't know what you think you got," Hedge said. "But it's not my secret to success."

*It's not the Grit*, Quarrah realized, the King Poacher's words rattling in her head. *There is no Future Grit. The vials are just a decoy.*

Hedge slowly began limping around the opening in the floor. "Close the hatch," he ordered Pincher and Otella as he strode past them. "I'm finished here."

The hinges screeched as the chains rattled through the massive pulleys, lowering the metal door. Quarrah wanted to say something about the vials, but it didn't seem right to call his bluff. Let Hedge think they were still blind to his tactics.

"Frush and Calo will stay here," Hedge said. "And there'll be a dozen more of my blue boys standing guard at the warehouse by sunup."

"There's no need for that," Ard said. "I've already got a security detail here." He pointed at the scrawny forms of Pincher and Otella struggling not to lose control of the crank.

"Them?" Hedge scoffed.

"They'll be happy to stay on as long as you need them." Ard leaned forward, lowering his voice to a whisper. "Locals from the Labor District, so they know how to handle themselves if anyone gives them trouble. Plus, they're so cheap, they're practically free."

"My boys stay," said Hedge. "Posted outside. And if you're smart, you won't leave your jacket behind. Once you walk out of here, your ugly mugs are no longer welcome back."

"Well, I didn't even bring a jacket, so…" Ard trailed off as Hedge stopped dangerously close to him.

"A real joy, doing business with you," he hissed through his deformed lips. Frush pulled open the warehouse door.

"Wish I could say the same," Ard replied. "Now that you have your dragon, I trust we won't be seeing you again?"

Hedge Marsool smirked. "If you'd really figured out the secret behind that Future Grit, wouldn't you know the answer to that?"

Hedge limped away down the darkening street, his thugs taking up their new posts outside the warehouse door. With a huff of annoyance, Ard stepped over and rolled it shut.

"He's planning to keep her over the Moon Passing," Quarrah whispered, glancing at the closed hatch in the floor. "Do you think he knows? That dragons can get Moonsick?"

"That's what I'm afraid of," Ard answered. "If history has taught us anything, it's that a raging Moonsick dragon can wreak a lot more destruction than a healthy one."

"Because the healthy ones just want to fly home," said Quarrah.

Across the room, one of Ard's hired hands let out a loud yawn. The two looked to be bedding down next to the crank, probably grateful for any roof over their heads tonight.

"You really thought you could convince Hedge Marsool that those two vagrants were enough to guard her?" Quarrah asked.

"Worth a shot," Ard replied. "The real reason I hired them was to give ourselves an easy scapegoat. Now that Hedge has seen the looks of those two, he shouldn't have a hard time believing that they'll forget to replenish the Stasis Grit. And that's how the dragon gets away."

Clever. Hedge's own guards would be much better equipped. Maybe even stand a chance at stopping the beast, or at least slowing her, before she got away.

"So what now?" Quarrah asked.

"I think it's time to accelerate our plans," Ard said, moving to the handcart. "The clocks are set to detonate in twelve hours. If we move their hands before we wind them, we can make that six."

Quarrah nodded. "Letting the dragon break free before the rest of Hedge's guards arrive."

"But still giving us plenty of time to get away from Talumon," said Ard. "What ship did you bring?"

"Rented a little sloop," she replied.

"You should head down to the harbor and get her ready," Ard suggested, lifting the mantel clock from its box again. "I'll change the clocks and set them in position."

"How will you get down there with the Stasis Grit?" Quarrah asked.

Ard scoffed. "The Stasis Grit is only a small cloud around the dragon's head. I just didn't want Hedge going down there to see how rusty the chains are. Of course, he probably already knows if he's detonated Future Grit—"

"It's not real," Quarrah blurted out. Well, she was committed to telling him now. "Hedge seems to be predicting the future, but it's not with those vials of liquid Grit."

Ard set down the clock he was winding. His brown eyes were intense as they turned on her. "What makes you say that?"

She spilled it all in a matter of seconds, from her swap with Ard, to San's analysis of the liquid solution. When she was finished, the ruse artist stood in stunned silence as the clock in front of him *ticktocked* auspiciously.

"Sugar water?" Ard finally said. Quarrah nodded. "Hedge just happened to be carrying the same mixture you stirred up in the counterfeit vial?"

"I know it seems unlikely—"

"That's beyond unlikely, Quarrah. The way I see it, Hedge knew which vial I was going to steal off his belt that day. He knew you were going to swap it for sugar water, so he made a sugary mixture himself to prove that he saw it coming."

"I considered that," Quarrah said. "But didn't you hear what he just said? The vials are not his secret to success."

"Oh, great. So he has *another* way of seeing the future?"

She nodded with conviction, despite how crazy it seemed.

"Why bother with vials at all?" Ard said.

"A ruse for the ruse artist," she answered. "Something to keep you guessing in the wrong direction."

"Then what is the *right* direction?" Ard was losing his patience, perhaps annoyed because there was merit in her discovery but he hadn't been the one to learn it.

"I don't know," Quarrah admitted. "But next time we see Hedge Marsool, I intend to find out." She turned, running her fingers along the edge of the handcart. "I'll go ready the sloop."

Nemery Baggish wedged her final pouch of Blast Grit into a cleft in the rock. The stuff was barely fine enough to be considered powder. Blast Grit so coarse would never be sold in New Vantage or the Greater Chain. But Nemery had made this batch herself, grinding down a chunk of Slagstone in an anti-ignition liquid of her own making.

Satisfied with the arrangement of things, Nemery let go of the rock, dropping a few feet to land beside her partner.

"There's no undoing this, Salafan," Mohdek said hesitantly.

"I know," she replied, picking up her pack and her bow. "And I'm not happy about it. But I don't see what else we can do. There are two of us, and hundreds of them."

"We could go back to New Vantage," Mohdek said. "Hit their supplies again."

"Too many have already set out for the summit," she shot back.

"Then we set traps... Treat them like poachers."

"Too many children with them, Moh. You saw. That's innocent blood I won't risk."

"But the men and women," he said. "They're followers of Garifus. You heard the way they were talking back in New Vantage. It's a dangerous mindset."

Nemery had overheard a number of startling conversations. The Glassmind cultists considered themselves superior to anyone else. They found strength in numbers, which only fed their majority-rules mentality.

"I know," Nemery said. "That's why we're doing this."

Mohdek glanced up at the towering rock face, now dotted with pouches of Blast Grit. "Collapsing Gateway Rock isn't going to stop them," he said softly.

"But it'll slow them down," she said. "Passing through Gateway is the fastest way to the summit from New Vantage. The first group has already turned at Twin Springs Canyon, so we know they're coming this way. A caravan that size moves slowly. By the time they get clear up here and realize that the trail through Gateway Rock is impassable, they'll have to turn around and take Willowswitch Bypass. It'll add *days* to their journey and they only have seventeen left to reach the summit. If we can keep delaying them—"

"At what cost?" Mohdek cried. "Destroying the face of Pekal? *Our* island? And what if we *do* slow them down enough to prevent them from reaching the summit this cycle? The Moon will pass again in thirty days and they'll already be that much closer. We need a more permanent solution."

"We've discussed them all," Nemery said.

"There is one..." Mohdek paused in thought. "We're far enough ahead of them. We could get to Red Banks and—"

"And what?" she snapped.

"Your new instrument is still there," he encouraged. "If you had it, we could..." But he trailed off at the dark look on her face.

"You know better than to suggest that. Never again, Moh," she whispered, striding away. "Taking down Gateway Rock is the only way."

"You're more like him than you want to admit," Mohdek called after her.

Nemery stopped in the middle of the trail. "What did you say?" she hissed.

"You spent so many years talking about him." Mohdek switched to Trothian, probably to make sure he expressed himself correctly. "Thinking you'd make him proud if he only knew what you were up to. Then he came, and it wasn't what you...what you thought it would be."

"I'm nothing like Ardor Benn." She breathed deeply to calm herself. "What he did to Motherwatch and Proudflame—"

"Is the same thing you are doing now," Mohdek cut her off. "Destroying something natural. Something beautiful. Just so you can accomplish what you think is best."

Nemery clenched both fists at her sides. "You helped me pack the Grit pouches. You held the rope so I could place them higher up. You carved the Slagstone arrowhead...I thought we were in this together."

"I'm in this," he said, "because I love you." Nemery knew that, though it was rare to hear him say it aloud. "And I owe it to you— and this place—to ask you one more time." He swallowed hard. "Do you really think this is the right thing?"

"Making sure our place is not overrun with Glassminds," Nemery said. "That's the right thing."

She struck off toward the spot she had chosen to take the shot. Her thoughts churned with every step. Was she like Ardor Benn? A week ago, she would have taken that as the highest of compliments. Now it was an insult. The Trothians had a saying that went something like: *A tree only admires the work of a carpenter until it meets his axe.* The Landers said it more simply: *Never meet your heroes.*

Nemery wished she had stopped Ardor from taking Motherwatch. At the very least, she wished she had forced him to stick around and see the distress of little Proudflame. After the crew had departed, the hatchling had returned to the draw where he'd been hunting for his mother, cooing sadly as he waited all through the night.

He'd been injured in the fight, a Roller ball having pierced his developing scales. Nemery and Mohdek had followed him long enough to make sure he'd recover. Then they'd gone back to New Vantage only to find the place overrun with cultists. And shiploads more were arriving every day.

She and Mohdek had put a desperate plan of sabotage into action—stealing, burning, or otherwise destroying as many of the cultist supplies as they could get their hands on. The plot was short lived, however. The cultists quickly began posting more guards over their supply camps just outside New Vantage. And now that the first of them had set out on their expedition to the summit, it had come to this...

Nemery scampered up a muddy slope and took a seat on a flat rock. Sliding an arrow from her quiver, she took a last look at Gateway Rock. It was a magnificent structure—a stone tower carved by centuries of wind and rain. It seemed to be hanging desperately on to the steep mountain slope beside it. In fact, the amount of Blast Grit she had stuffed into the rock was probably far more than was needed to bring it down. The structure would tumble quite easily, the loose rock choking the narrow trail that led between two impassible slopes.

She glanced down at the special arrowhead, grooves carefully chiseled into the Slagstone so it could be tied onto the shaft. The impact would make a huge spark, definitely enough to ignite the pouch of Blast Grit she had marked with a cairn of stones.

Making sure Mohdek had moved out of the way, Nemery nocked the arrow on her bowstring, heart pounding. She drew, sighting down the shaft toward her mark.

She heard Mohdek's words in her mind. *"There's no undoing this, Salafan."*

Salafan. Salafan. Salafan.

She had heard it so many times, it was easy to forget its meaning. Then she thought of the first time Mohdek had spoken it, standing over the grave of his brother, Namsum.

*"He used to call you little Salafan behind your back,"* he had said.

*"What does it mean?"* she'd asked.

*"It is the name of a bird that digs in the sand of the Trothian islets,"* he had explained. *"To hear one sing is a good omen. It means that your enemy can look you in the eye and you'll feel no remorse about the way you treated them."*

Nemery screamed in frustration, loosing the arrow straight into the sky. How could she do something like this and ever hope to look Mohdek in the eye again? How could she betray the very land that had given her purpose and strength? How could she stoop to the level of Ardor Benn, so wrapped up in her own ideas that she was blind to the way they affected those around her?

There was always another way.

Nemery Baggish set down her bow. She scooted off the rock, slipping down the steep slope as Mohdek moved toward her.

"Thank you," he said.

She lowered her head in shame, but he reached out, stroking her cheek.

"We will do what we can to stop them," he continued. "And we will do it without sacrificing what we love."

Nemery nodded, brushing away tears with the back of her hand. "We need to go back to New Vantage," she said. "Find new ways to sabotage them."

Mohdek grinned. "Let the cultists fear the mountain."

"We need to target their Grit supply," Nemery went on. "Without Drift Grit, they won't be able to carry the crates."

"And without the crates, they'll have no gear. No rations."

"We need to pay extra attention to any vials of liquid Grit they might be carrying," said Nemery. "Take away their Transformation Grit, and the worst we'll be dealing with will be a horde of Moonsick Bloodeyes."

"If we run them ragged enough," said Mohdek, "I'm betting more than half of them will turn back before they reach Three-Quarter Circle."

"No," said Nemery. "We can't follow them that high." Mohdek gave her a puzzled glance, so she explained herself. "Garifus Floc. If he and the other Glassminds return to Pekal, we have to be ready for them."

Mohdek nodded in understanding. "We'll stay within a day's hike of New Vantage. That will give us more than enough room to make those cultists miserable as their groups set out."

"Thank you." Now it was Nemery's turn to say it. "Thank you, Moh."

She felt a freedom and a power in having done what was right. And she was proud to have earned the name *Salafan*.

~

*There always comes a breaking point. I try to bend around it,
but I'm splintering inside.*

# CHAPTER

# 22

Ard couldn't help but feel like Isle Halavend—albeit a younger, handsomer Isle Halavend—as he sat in Cove 23, waiting for an unsanctioned visitor to climb through the trapdoor at his feet. Although, today it was more of a gaping hole than a trapdoor.

Ard had done his part, prying off the wooden planks that the Islehood had nailed over the forbidden entrance. It was a poor attempt to seal it up, but nature had done a better job, collapsing portions of the tunnel years ago. Still, Ard wasn't worried. A half mile of fallen rock and timbers would be no obstacle for Prime Isless Gloristar.

Ard double-checked his piles of notes. Organization had never been one of his strong suits, but he was proud of what he'd done. One stack of papers regarding the Sphere. One for the Great Egress. And one for his questions on the topic of Wayfarist gods. He had another stack of scribblings, but those were more of a personal matter.

Ard wiped his forehead with the back of his hand and stood up. It was hot in this small room, and his heavy Islehood robe wasn't helping. He could risk cracking the door for some fresh air as long as he stayed close so he could pull it shut the moment his transformed visitor arrived.

Ah. That felt better, a little cool draft coming off the Mooring waterway...

"Sorry I am later than expected."

Ard jumped so high, he nearly whacked his head on the Cove ceiling. He slammed the door shut with a bang that must have echoed through the whole Mooring. Whirling, he saw Gloristar standing with elegant poise beside the hole in the floor.

"Sparks, Gloristar." He took deep breaths to calm his racing heart. "I didn't hear you come in."

"Silence Grit," she said, a spark bouncing across her fingertips and fizzling out. "I thought it best to approach in stealth."

"Yeah, well... good job." He'd only had his back to the secret entrance for mere seconds. "Thanks for meeting me here."

Ard had seen her at Tofar's Salts that morning, but sailing through the night had left him too tired for a conversation of this depth. Besides, he couldn't talk about his scriptural studies in front of Raek and Quarrah. A good long nap, a late lunch, and a couple of hours alone in the Cove to collect his thoughts... Now Ardor Benn felt impatient to get started.

"It is surreal to be back," she said, glancing around. "Everything seems... smaller."

Indeed, at her enhanced height, she had only inches of clearance above her cracked glass scalp.

"What is it you wanted to discuss?" She reached out, splaying a stack of papers as if she could read multiple pages at once.

"Nothing there." He quickly collected the papers out of her hands. Why did she have to look at *that* stack? It was almost embarrassing.

"With fervent ardor go thy way, walking paths of increasing progress." Gloristar quoted one of the verses he had copied on those pages.

"That's just a random note," Ard tried.

"A study into your name as it appears in scripture," said Gloristar.

Sparks, she was good.

"It's not really important." He rolled up the pages.

"To whom?" she asked. "You are the one who gets to decide what is important to you. Are you aware that the word *ardor* appears fifty-nine times throughout all volumes of *Wayfarist Voyage*?"

Fifty-nine! Ard had been jotting them down as he'd encountered them, but so far he'd found only fourteen. "Well, I guess there's a reason why it's one of the most popular Wayfarist names."

"*Your* name," she said.

"Not that it means anything to me." Ard's words brought back a conversation he'd once had on the dock outside this very Cove. Isle Halavend had asked him why he'd kept the name *Ardor*, despite changing his last name and living the lifestyle of a Settled criminal. He'd dismissed it then, but the fact that he was now holding a full sheaf of papers on the topic told him that he still might be searching for the answer to Halavend's question.

"Do not be so quick to discredit the appearance of your name in holy text," continued Gloristar. "I speak from a place of solemn experience."

Ard cleared his throat, setting the notes on the corner of the desk and gesturing to a different stack. "I wondered if we could talk for a moment about the mention of gods in Wayfarism."

"You mean in Agroditism?" she clarified. "The Homeland is the only deity worshiped by the Wayfarists."

"I know," said Ard. "But there has to be more to it than that. The testament spire on the seabed..."

"The gods grew angry at our progress and they smote us with a plague of mind and body," Gloristar began to quote. "But we were many in number, and we rose up against our encroaching madness, taking salvation out of the open mouths of the dragons. From their teeth we rose to higher heights, granted new sight and power beyond our imaginings."

Ard remembered that passage, although maybe not word-perfect. It was what had led Portsend to understand Metamorphosis Grit and transform Gloristar.

"Did you memorize the entire testament?" Ard asked.

"With my perfected recall, it took only a single reading," she replied. "Though I certainly had enough time down there to memorize any length of text—my mind perfected or not."

"Then you know the way they talked about the gods," said Ard.

She nodded. "But that testament was left by the Trothian ancestral race. It is no surprise that a notion of gods lingers in Agroditism. And the worshiping of the Moon."

"Yes, but if the testament is to be believed, then there really *were* gods," Ard pressed. "And they lived with ancestral Landers, too."

"The unchanged stood with the gods," Gloristar continued her helpful recitation.

"And it said something about how the gods brought us up to live on these islands," Ard continued.

"In the still of night, the gods made preparations, building towers of stone and soil reaching almost to the Red Moon itself. Then, taking the last remaining unchanged, they whisked them high up out of our reach."

"Good," said Ard. "But what happened after that? Where did they go?"

"The testament continues," said Gloristar. "The gods were spent from such expenditure of their power. Already, we saw them begin to decay. They had sacrificed themselves for the unchanged, and given us nothing but scorn. They loved what they could control, and they despised us when we ascended to be like them. With their final measure of power, the gods filled our kingdom with the depths of the sea."

"So as far as I understand it, the gods are more powerful than the Glassminds," Ard analyzed. "And the Glassminds—*you*—claim to be the Homeland, correct?"

"Not a mere claim," she said. "It is the truth."

"Then what is more powerful than the Homeland?"

"Is there any greater than the Homeland?" Gloristar began quoting a verse from *Wayfarist Voyage*. It was one Ard had written down in his stack of notes, but by the time he'd riffled through them, she'd finished the scripture. "Any who could rise above perfection? Nay. For if it were so, the blessed Homeland would be vanquished."

"Exactly!" Ard felt validation that she'd cited a verse he'd studied. "Whoever the gods were, they must have had the power to vanquish the Glassminds."

"That is a lofty claim," said Gloristar. "I think you underestimate the power of the Othians. If these gods *could* defeat them, why did they flee all those centuries ago?"

"I don't know," Ard shrugged. It was a discouraging thought. One that admitted to the Glassminds having no equal.

"And as powerful as I may seem to you now," continued Gloristar, "Centrum claimed that the strength of the Othians would only increase if the Sphere is completed."

"Okay. The Sphere..." Ard moved to the next pile of papers. "Though we struggle in a line," he read, "the circle saves, and the sphere governs all." He looked up at her. "That's because Time will be able to move sideways into alternate realities that might have been?"

Sparks, maybe that's how Hedge Marsool was doing it. Maybe his Grit created Spherical Time and he could see countless possible outcomes to any given scenario. Ard tapped his chin in thought. "We're sure this isn't happening right now?"

"It cannot come to pass until Centrum completes the Sphere," said Gloristar. "And that's not something he can do on his own."

Ard felt a chill pass through his body, head to toe, but lingering in his heart. "He's not on his own anymore. Garifus Floc and the other Glassminds. If Centrum contacts them—"

"He surely already has," answered Gloristar. "He spoke directly into my mind mere moments after my transformation."

Ard brought a hand to his forehead. "I've been a fool," he muttered. "I should have gone to Winter Barracks the minute I disembarked this morning."

"What would you have done?" she asked.

Ard grunted in frustration. "Watched them. Followed Garifus. See what he's up to. Blazing Raek…Why didn't he keep any eye on them?"

"I believe Raekon was sufficiently busy carrying out your other, more discreet, orders," said Gloristar.

"Quarrah, then!" Ard shouted. "What's she been doing all last week?" He immediately regretted blaming her for inactivity. Ard knew the answer to his accusation. Before she'd met him in Helizon, Quarrah had been seeing to the security of poor San Green.

"I'm sorry." Ard quietly bowed his head. "I should have done something to stop it sooner. Centrum will obviously try to use Garifus and his followers." He started piling up his papers. "I should go to Winter Barracks right now."

"That may not be necessary." Gloristar canted her head just slightly in a pose of active listening.

"Why not?"

"Because I believe Garifus Floc is here."

Ard dropped his notes, the papers scattering across the Cove floor. "Here?" he whispered. "As in *here*?"

"The voices of the Othians resonate at a different frequency than those of Landers or Trothians," Gloristar said quietly. "I hear the voice of one who has transformed entering the Mooring at this very moment."

"What's he saying?" Ard asked. "Sparks, we've got to get you out of here."

"I can't understand his words at this distance," she said. "But he has surely heard me as well."

"Then *stop talking*!" Ard hissed. A man's scream echoed through the Mooring. Ard didn't need enhanced ears to hear that. It wasn't a scream of fear at seeing a figure so starkly different than any other human. It was an unequivocal scream of pain.

Ard moved to the other side of the desk, yanking open the bottom drawer and pulling out a pair of Rollers. He'd started packing them in and out lately, but he tried to have the decency not to wear them inside the Coves.

"Have you still got some Grit in you?" he asked.

"My reserves are—"

"Quiet!" Ard screeched. "I asked you a yes-or-no question on purpose. I'm assuming Garifus can't hear you nod."

She nodded.

"He *can*?" Ard cried.

"Of course not," she whispered. "That was in answer to your question about Grit."

Right. Ard crossed the room, pausing beside the closed door. "I've got a raft tethered at my dock," he whispered, hiking up his robes and tucking both guns in the waist of his pants. "I'm going to go out there and draw them down this way. If you stay quiet, maybe they'll think you've fled. Once they're in position, I'll shout your name. You burst out of here and start smashing glass heads."

Another scream sounded outside the Cove door. This time closer. A woman. It was promptly answered by the jarring crack of gunshots.

"If you don't approve of this plan," Ard said, "then spin around three times, touch your toes, and pat your head."

"I'm not doing that," Gloristar rebutted.

"Then you approve," said Ard.

Gloristar reached out and grabbed Ard by the back of his neck, stopping him from opening the door.

"Perhaps there is a better way." She dragged him several feet back and released him. "One that will not come to violence."

Ard looked at her skeptically. "You heard Quarrah's report. These guys killed Lomaya."

"But they did not kill San," Gloristar pointed out. "And Quarrah said Garifus was planning to spare their lives as well."

"What are you getting at?"

"Perhaps they can be reasoned with."

"Are you nuts?" Ard said. "These people are insane cultists dedicated to..." He trailed off, realizing the good fortune of their situation. "Oh, oh, oh!"

"What?" Gloristar asked.

"Dedicated to *you*," Ard finished. "The entire Glassmind cult was founded on your transformation. According to Nemery, they basically worship you!" He smiled. "I think it's time for Garifus Floc to meet his idol."

Without waiting for her thoughts on the matter, Ard swung open the Cove door and moved onto the dock.

The first thing he noticed was the temperature—much too cold for a late summer afternoon like this. Then he saw why.

The Mooring waterway was frozen solid.

Walking down the icy path were three Glassminds. They looked quite similar to one another, all of them standing at exactly the same height, with the same coloration on their glistening bluish skin and red scalp. They wore sleeveless, hoodless cloaks of black that had clearly been tailored to their enhanced figures. All three moved with grace, their bare feet finding sure purchase even on the slippery surface.

On the distant stairs that led from the waterway to the foyer, Ard spotted two broken bodies in Regulation uniforms. More Reggies had gathered, but they were pounding against a Barrier wall in a futile attempt to break through. Ard wasn't the only Holy Isle who had emerged onto the docks in curiosity, but he was one of the few not ducking back inside the moment they saw what was coming.

The trio of Glassminds continued on an undeviating route down the waterway toward the Holy Torch, exuding a power and authority that went unquestioned.

Gloristar emerged from the Cove, stepping past Ard with one giant stride. The opposing Glassminds stopped the moment they saw her striding across the frozen waterway. They didn't speak a word, but somehow, Ard thought they seemed to be communicating. Gloristar slowed her pace, the wrought iron brazier of the Holy Torch rising from the ice between them.

"Can it be?" said the Glassmind who stood slightly ahead of the other man and woman. His voice echoed through the Mooring with more than natural resonance. "Can it truly be?"

He raised a sparking hand, and a line of detonated Grit shot from his palm, rending the metal Torch down the middle. With a gesture from his other hand, the scraps of the brazier bent to either side, thick iron bowing like wilting flowers.

The three Glassminds strode into the wreckage, coming to a halt in the middle of the demolished Holy Torch.

"Isles and Islesses of Wayfarism," the leader called, his voice booming and authoritative beyond any natural frame. "Consider yourselves among the first to lay eyes upon the Homeland." He dropped his glass head in a reverential bow. "Prime Isless Gloristar."

"Who are you?" she asked.

The Glassmind looked up sharply, his red eyes narrowing. "Why is your mind dark to us? We cannot see your true intent."

"Who are you?" she repeated. "And what are you doing here?"

"I am Garifus Floc," the man said. "We have come to usher in a new era of civilization. The Final Era of Utmost Perfection." He took a step forward. "We are here to complete the Sphere."

"You have spoken with Centrum," Gloristar said. "Surely, you could see *his* true intent. A man of greed and thirst for greater power."

Garifus tilted his head. "You speak in riddles, Prime Isless. Do you share in our goals of perfection or not?" His glowing eyes darted to her cracked skull. "Ah. I see now. You have been separated from our collective thoughts. Step forward and I can mend the *renna*." He stretched out a hand, but Gloristar didn't move.

"I will not rejoin my mind to Centrum," she said. "I will have no part in creating Spherical Time for a mind as ill intentioned as his."

"I do not know of any *Centrum*," Garifus said. "But our desire to create Spherical Time is not for one mind alone, but for the minds of the many. The majority will always rule among the Othians."

"Then I suppose you should not count me among them," Gloristar said. Ard saw her fingertips begin to sizzle with sparks.

"Your words grieve me, Prime Isless," said Garifus. "You were the catalyst for all of this. You should be leading this charge. But what do the scriptures say? 'Go forth, every one. And cease not in your labors until the Homeland is reached. Let none stand in your way, neither the weak, nor the mighty. The Settled, nor the—'"

Gloristar's hand shot out, a wave of Void Grit emanating from her pale blue palm. It caught all three Glassminds, flinging them upward and away. Midflight, Garifus somehow regained control, using a detonation to pull himself straight down, landing with such force that the ice beneath his bare feet cracked all the way across the channel.

His companions recovered a moment later, breaking their fall with detonations from their own hands.

"I have great mercy for those unchanged," said Garifus, striding toward her. "But you should know better, Gloristar."

He held both hands in front of him, launching small orbs of Barrier Grit from his palms like balls from a Roller. Gloristar met the attack with a flat Barrier shield suspended in front of her, deflecting the orbs, which seemed to fizzle out the moment they ricocheted.

Gloristar pressed forward until she stood at the heart of the broken Torch brazier. Her other hand came up, glowing eyes narrowing in concentration. Then she dropped her Barrier shield and sent out another detonation. Her cloud reached Garifus, but not before his final projectile struck her in the shoulder.

It ripped through her heavy cloak, peeling back her bluish skin with a spattering of gold blood. She let out a cry of pain, but maintained manipulation of her own cloud.

The hazy streamer from her hand wrapped around Garifus, instantly dropping him to the ice.

Dead? No, his eyes were still wide open and glowing. It had to be Stasis Grit. Just enough to encompass Garifus's head. Maybe that was all she had left.

Gloristar released her hold on the Stasis cloud, allowing it to form a natural sphere around her enemy. But already, the other two Glassminds were racing to his aid.

With a cry, Gloristar threw a ribbon detonation of what must have been Gather Grit. It caught the other Glassmind man by the side, yanking him away from Garifus's still form, sliding him across the ice to Gloristar's feet.

She caught him by the neck before he could recover, heaving him upward and slamming him down against the warped iron bands of the brazier. Ard heard the distinctive sound of cracking glass, but Gloristar didn't stop.

She hefted him and struck again. And again. Her fingers were sparking, a brief detonation forming around her fist each time she brought him down. Weight Grit, making her blows heavier. Deadlier.

The man's glass skull shattered, thick red shards raining down on the white ice. His eyes instantly darkened and his enhanced figure went limp, draped across the warped Holy Torch.

But across the waterway, the Glassmind woman had dragged her leader out of the Stasis cloud. Garifus was rising, shaking his head against the disorientation of regaining consciousness.

"Gloristar!" Ard shouted, yanking up his robe unceremoniously and pulling one of the guns from his waist. He cocked the hammer and squeezed off one shot—two shots. But the lead balls pinged harmlessly off the impenetrable skin of the Glassminds.

Gloristar released her grip on the dead Glassmind just as Garifus Floc pulled back his arm and let something fly in a flurry of sparks.

A spear of Barrier Grit entered Gloristar's mouth at an upward angle, bursting out the back of her skull with a spray of red glass. The spear vanished as quickly as it had come, and she collapsed in a heap at the heart of the Holy Torch. Her eyes dimmed as a wisp of red smoke vented from the blasted hole of her skull.

Gloristar! A woman powerful enough to carry a dragon by raising one finger. A woman who had fulfilled scripture and found her way to the true Homeland.

Ard slunk back into the doorway of Cove 23, a mortal fear summoning the cowardice that lurked in the depths of every man's heart. He might be able to escape out the secret tunnel. He could bear the terrible news to Quarrah and Raek.

"Heretic!" cried a daring voice from across the waterway. Ard paused in his escape to see Isle Swick standing defiantly on the dock entrance to Cove 18. Of course, the older man was opinionated, judgmental, and often cantankerous. If anyone would shout "Heretic!" at a mysterious stranger who had just killed the Prime Isless with little more than a wave of his hand, it would be Swick.

Garifus turned toward his challenger, and Ard finally had a clear view of the back of his head. The thick red glass was flawless and shiny. Practically begging for a Roller ball.

But he couldn't summon the courage to lift the gun.

Garifus's hand stretched out in Swick's direction. An unseen force grabbed the Isle by the front of his robes and sucked him toward the Glassminds. He went down on the ice, skidding to a halt just arm's reach from Garifus's feet.

"Perhaps you can be of more help than the former Prime Isless," said the Glassmind leader. "We have come here because we are in need of vast quantities of Visitant Grit."

*Visitant Grit?* Why?

Isle Swick rose to his knees on the ice. Even from here, Ard could see that his lip was bleeding. "Who are you people?"

"Visitant Grit," insisted Garifus.

Swick shook his head. "You won't find any. The Prime Isle doesn't authorize a single granule to be processed unless there is a need for it."

"There is a need greater than you could possibly comprehend," said Garifus. "As for processing it to powder, I can see to that myself. I know the Islehood keeps a supply of dragon shell, some of it already digested. Where is it?"

"I am a faithful servant of the Homeland," Swick declared. "If you think I will—"

Garifus brought up his hand, the ice instantly thawing in a perfect circle under Isle Swick. He plunged into the hole of water, disappearing below the surface just as it refroze around him. One of the man's hands rose out of the ice like a tree of flesh, the ice pinching around his forearm. His hand opened and closed frantically, the futile grips of a dying man.

"Who would like to be more cooperative?" Garifus boomed, turning to look down the waterway again.

Ard's hand trembled around the gun's wooden stock, the

opportunity for a shot squandered in the shock of Isle Swick's sudden demise.

The Glassmind woman next to Garifus threw one hand to the side, a Grit cloud blasting the door to Cove 16 right off its hinges. Across the waterway, Ard could see young Isless Nett drop to cower beneath her desk.

Garifus extracted her, his beam of Gather Grit plucking her out of her Cove and dragging her, screaming, toward him. Unlike Swick, her approach was slow and she remained upright, the toes of her shoes dragging across the ice. Her sea-green robes and her auburn hair stood straight out, caught in a wind that was sucking her toward the huge man.

Garifus Floc seized her by the neck, extinguishing the Gather cloud and holding the young woman aloft with the raw strength of his arm.

"What about you?" he asked. "Do you know where the dragon shell is stored?"

"I don't know anything. Please! Only a few people have that information," whimpered Isless Nett. "Some of the senior-most members of the Islehood. I've only been in the Mooring two years. Please!"

Garifus dropped her, his other hand melting the ice. She plunged into the water, the ice instantly re-forming with another spark from his fingertips. Young Isless Nett, enclosed in a frigid coffin.

"Stop!" came a shout from the far end of the Mooring. "In the name of the Homeland! Stop!"

Ard turned to see Prime Isle Olstad Trable standing on the dock outside Cove 1. His hands were outstretched in a commanding gesture, but he looked weak in comparison to the immutable Glassminds. His purple robes, once so authoritative and grand, now looked like the costume of a child playing dress-up.

"Prime Isle Trable," said Garifus. "To be honest, I didn't expect you at the Mooring so late in the afternoon."

"Whoever you are," Trable replied, "I'm sure we can reach an agreement that doesn't involve killing my Isles."

"Certainly," said Garifus. "My needs are simple. All of the dragon shell in the Islehood's possession, as well as any processed Visitant Grit you may have."

"What you ask is impossible," called Trable. "Visitant Grit is the sacred responsibility of the Islehood."

"You speak to *me* of sacred things?" replied Garifus. "You don't understand the half of it. The time has come to create a detonation that will complete the Sphere and change everything you know about the world. There is no responsibility more sacred than this."

Ha! So Garifus needed Visitant Grit to create Spherical Time…

"Whatever you're planning…" Trable said. "Let us talk about it."

"Your feeble mind would not comprehend its complexity." He tensed his hands at his sides. "Where is the Visitant Grit?"

*Don't be a hero, Trable*, Ard thought. Surely, he saw that the Glass-minds wouldn't hesitate to kill him and move on to someone more cooperative.

"I am not afraid of your threats," said the Prime Isle in what Ard considered to be a monumental lie. "The Homeland is with us."

"Yes," Garifus said. "I am." He raised both hands and Trable's feet lifted from the dock. The Prime Isle appeared to be caught in some kind of oblong Drift cloud, the fabric of his robe looking stiff and unnatural. Garifus's hands sparked again and Trable suddenly dropped a couple of feet. But instead of reaching the ground, his arms flung out to his sides, caught in hazy detonations like shackles, leaving him hanging in midair.

"I don't believe you are familiar with Gather Grit," said Garifus, his own arms outstretched to maintain the clouds. "Right now, I hold your arms in two separate clouds of it, the centers of the detonations just beyond your fingertips. I have Compounded the Grit enough to hold your weight, pulling your arms in opposite directions. Allow me to add a little more Compounding Grit."

Ard couldn't see a change in the clouds, but Prime Isle Trable grimaced.

"I can continue adding Compounding Grit until the strength of the Gather is enough to pluck both of your arms out of their sockets," said Garifus. "Or you can tell me where to find the dragon shell."

"You should know I can be quite stubborn," Trable said. "Just ask my wife. I think you'd be better off to go ahead and kill me."

Garifus must have increased the pull, because Trable couldn't hold back a cry of pain.

"I actually hope you survive," said Garifus. "Perhaps it would even give you incentive to join us."

"Why is that?" grunted Trable. "You need a certain number of armless followers?"

*Sparks, Trable. Don't be sassy!* Ard usually appreciated that about the man, but not at a time like this!

"If you join us," continued Garifus, "any physical ailments or imperfections will be made right in the transformation."

"You mean, I'd grow new arms?" said Trable. "What if I like the ones I've already got?"

"Where is the shell?" pressed Garifus.

"Even if you should find it," said Trable, "you will never be worthy enough to summon a Paladin Visitant."

"We have no use for such a hero," answered Garifus. "We are only interested in completing the Sphere."

"I don't know what you're carrying on about," Trable said.

"We will detonate the Grit on the site of the oldest failed Paladin Visitant," said Garifus.

Ard tensed. He *would* be worthy. That was the very trick to *becoming* a Paladin Visitant! But wouldn't doing so reset the timeline, effectively erasing the Glassminds from existence?

"Once it is done, all of time and space will be rolled into one great Sphere."

No. Garifus was describing something different. A Paladin Visitant appeared if a mortal person stepped into a Visitant cloud, but what would happen if a Glassmind did it?

"Now," said Garifus. "I will not ask again. Where is the dragon shell?"

"I don't remember..." Trable trailed off into a scream.

Ard shut his eyes, hoping Isless Gaevala couldn't hear it. Hoping she was home with the kids so she didn't witness her husband's death. Ard couldn't help but think of the girls, their little faces drooped with sadness and confusion about why their daddy wasn't coming home. Trable probably thought this would make them proud, but his death would only break their hearts.

"In fact," the Prime Isle said, "I don't think anyone remembers—"

"I do," Ard shouted, stepping off the dock. The ice was ridiculously slippery and he went down hard on his backside. So much for a heroic entrance...

Garifus and the Glassmind woman both turned on him. Trable kept hanging with what appeared to be no reprieve from the Compounded effect of the Gather Grit.

"Ardor Benn." Garifus's unusual voice echoed across the frozen Mooring.

"Hold on. You know me?" Ard picked himself up off the ice with as much decorum as he could muster. "I mean, I'm flattered, but—"

"You were in the throne room the night of Termain's death," said Garifus. "You and Quarrah left the palace with the Prime Isless. Tell me, has Gloristar been with you all these years?"

Ard glanced past them at the still corpse of Gloristar lying in the Holy Torch.

"I know where the shell is being kept," Ard said, ignoring Garifus's other question.

"Ard!" Trable shouted from his precarious position. "I know what you're trying to do."

Ard held up a hand. "It's all right." Then to Garifus. "I can lead you there, but only if you release the Prime Isle."

"No," Trable gasped. "You don't have to do this, Ardor. Think it through. It's only going to cause more problems."

"What is he talking about?" asked the Glassmind woman.

"I don't have a clue," said Ard.

Prime Isle Trable groaned in frustration. "This man is trying to deceive you. He's new to the Islehood, still a fledgling," he blabbed. "He doesn't know the shell's location."

"Actually," Ard said. "I do." To prove it without giving too much away, he reached up and pretended to don a hat—a subtle gesture that said Tall Son's Millinery.

"What?" the Prime Isle muttered, crestfallen.

"I've known for cycles, Trable." He shrugged. "You really thought you could keep that information from me? It's why I joined the Islehood in the first place." He drew in a deep breath. "It's who I am."

He couldn't bring himself to look at the Prime Isle's face—a man who had given him chance after chance, believing when no one else would. A man Ard actually considered a friend.

Garifus Floc lowered his hands. All at once, the twin clouds of Compounded Gather Grit winked out and Trable fell, landing in a purple heap on the ice.

The Glassmind leader turned to Ard. "If you are deceiving us," he said, "you will be killed."

"Yeah," said Ard. "I sort of figured that."

"And then we will return to the Mooring and resume this unpleasant business until we find the shell."

"Take it easy," Ard said. "I'm not lying."

"Where is it?"

"Not so fast," Ard continued. "Who's to say you won't kill me the moment I tell you?" He tried to read their expressions, but the Glassminds looked stoic. Hopefully this next line would go over all right. "I'll take you to the dragon shell."

Okay. *Now* he was lying. There was no way under the sun or Moon that he was going to lead Garifus Floc to the Visitant Grit so he could create Spherical Time.

His only play here was a wild-goose chase. Traipse these two Glassminds around every corner of Beripent until he thought of a way for the search to end without him dying. And along the way, hopefully he could figure out exactly what the Glassminds intended to do with the Visitant Grit.

Sparks, he'd really stepped in it this time...

"Trable," Ard called. "Send my regards to the hot bath at Tofar's Salts." Hopefully, Raek and Quarrah would be there. Hopefully, they'd know what to do.

Then Ard turned and proffered his arm to the Glassmind woman. "Shall we?"

~

*If you could open a spyglass into my heart, you would see that everything stems from a misguided sense of integrity.*

# CHAPTER

# 23

Quarrah pushed the needle through the black cloth, pulling the thread tight. The hole in the knee of her pants was nearly fixed, and it was a good thing. She didn't know how much longer she could sit in the *Be'Igoth*, listening to Raek and San talk about Mixing Grit.

"That joiners fuse is a waste of money," Raek carried on. "All you have to do is twist the fuse back onto itself, pull the next one through the loop and cinch it all down with regular twine. Just as effective, and saves you an Ashing."

The two men were stooped over the Mixing table on the side of the room, whipping up another batch of... Quarrah didn't even know what. Something liquid.

"That was the last of the processed shale," San said, passing the bigger man an empty container.

"Not so, my friend." Raek reached down to produce another vessel from a box below the table.

San let out a jovial laugh of pure excitement. It was good to hear happy sounds from him. He was a tough young man, and he'd come to their hideout almost every day since escaping Winter Barracks. Perhaps Mixing with Raek made him feel something besides the overwhelming grief at the death of Lomaya.

While Raek was brilliant without a doubt, there was no question that San was more expert when it came to liquid Grit. Quarrah had given him the vial she'd stolen from Hedge Marsool, asking for a quiet analysis. He'd quickly come back to her with conclusive results, and Quarrah was still trying to decide how best to share that information with Ard.

San took the canister from Raek, shaking his head in disbelief. "Potter's Independent Harvesting... I approached them over a year ago. They said they didn't take Specialty Grit orders, let alone asking them to isolate something as unique as digested shale. Plus, they cost a fortune."

Raek smiled. "Clearly, you didn't say the right things to the right people."

"Ah. I can venture a guess at how that played out," said San.

"I'll let you use your imagination," Raek replied. "Potter's people have been very good to work with. I've accumulated a lot of uncommon source material for the liquid Grit over the last two years." Raek bent down, measuring a tiny pinch of powdered shale on the scales. "Who did you end up using to get your source materials?"

San scoffed. "We didn't. Imagine being some of the only people in the Greater Chain who actually understood all the new Grit types and not being able to get your hands on the source material to make it."

"Now that Ignition and Weight Grit are common knowledge, more and more Harvesters are including gold and horse vertebrae in their dragon bait," said Raek. "And they're isolating them from the Slagstone during processing."

"Sure, but it costs a fortune," said San. "Lomaya and I saved up and got some, but we wanted more than just Ignition and Weight Grit."

Quarrah looked up from her stitching, deciding to join the conversation, now that it had turned away from the hard mechanics of Mixing.

"Garifus Floc seemed to know about all of them," she said. "Or at least Gather Grit."

"Where did they get the source materials for that?" Raek followed up.

San lifted a finger like they weren't going to believe what he was about to say. "They've been sifting. *By hand.*"

"What do you mean?" Quarrah asked.

"The Glassminds. They would upend a canister of Prolonging Grit—normally a blend of common rocks that the dragon might have digested," explained San. "And they'd pick through the pile of powder, meticulously separating the grains of marble for Gather Grit, and shale for Null Grit. Or they'd sift through Light Grit, picking out the birchwood to isolate for Stasis Grit."

"How is that possible?" Raek asked. "It's virtually indistinguishable in a blend like that."

"It was something about their eyes," San said with a shudder. "They can see better than us—better than Trothians. And their hands were so steady. They had patience like I've never seen, but they made quick work of it."

"But what about the Metamorphosis Grit?" Raek asked. "You and Lomaya had obviously made some of it *before* Garifus and the others transformed. How did you get the digested dragon teeth?"

He looked down, his face shadowing with pain. "That's different."

"How so?" asked Raek. "Lomaya told us that you'd been experimenting with processed dragon teeth for cycles before you had a breakthrough. Where'd you get it?"

"We had a contact in Talumon," he said. "A smuggler with poaching connections. She called herself the Widow."

Quarrah didn't recognize the name, but it obviously rang a bell for Raek. "Widow Bloodrust?"

San nodded shamefully. "You know her?"

"Not personally," said Raek. "But her name came up when I was looking into Hedge Marsool. The Widow's part of his ring."

"That's the connection," Quarrah said. "That must be how Hedge learned about Metamorphosis Grit."

"We never told the Widow what we were doing," San said defensively. "She didn't even ask any questions. She got us the first shipment of digested dragon teeth at a bargain price. But there were additional fees that she didn't tell us about."

"She roped you in," said Raek.

"And when the debt got too large, Lomaya and I fled back to Beripent, trying to get away," he explained. "It was a mistake. We never should have done business with her. Sparks, we never should have..." He slammed down the canister. "Now Lomaya's gone and there are blazing monster humans outside Beripent!" He got control of his emotions, planting both hands on the table's edge and leaning forward. "We should have abandoned the experiments. We should have let it all die with Professor Wal."

Raek clapped a big hand on the young man's shoulder. "This isn't your fault, San."

Actually, it kind of was. But Quarrah silently returned to her stitching.

"You and Lomaya developed Transformation Grit on your own," Raek went on. "But that's the thing about creating something. Once you've finished, it's out there in the world. What people decide to do with it isn't up to you."

San looked up, his eyes wet. "What do *we* do about it?" he said quietly. "The Glassminds are..."

"We're working on it," Raek said.

Were they? Seemed like business as usual to Quarrah. She was mending her pants and Ard was putting in useless hours at his "day job" in the Mooring. What *were* they going to do about the terrifying Glassminds?

"We have Prime Isless Gloristar on our side," Raek said. "And Ardor Benn is probably out there right now, working up some brilliant plan."

The door to the *Be'Igoth* flew open. Quarrah sprang to her feet, going for the Roller on the side table. But the stranger at the door was not a figure to shoot at.

"Trable?" Raek muttered.

"The Prime Isle's coming in!" Geppel's voice shouted lazily from outside. "Couldn't stop him."

The room seemed to spin around Quarrah in confusion. The Prime Isle of Wayfarism at an Agrodite soakhouse? At their hideout? Sparks, whatever was coming wasn't going to be good.

"Are you friends of Isle Ardor Benn?" Trable was winded.

"That really depends on the day," Raek replied, which was nicer than Quarrah would've put it.

"He's gone," Trable announced.

"Gone," said Raek. "What do you mean?"

"There were people...monsters," he stammered. "They came into the Mooring."

"Slow down." Raek stepped around the table.

"He called himself Garifus Floc."

Yep. Not good. Quarrah reached down and yanked the needle off the end of her string. Now the whole thing would unravel. Only a stitch short of finishing, too. *Rather symbolic*, she thought.

Raek put a hand on his bald head. "Where are they taking him?"

Trable shook his head. "*He's* taking *them*," he corrected. "To the location where the Islehood stores the dragon shell."

"What?" Raek cried. "Ard doesn't know where that is. He's been trying to find out for cycles."

"He knows," insisted the Prime Isle. Quarrah saw a dark look of betrayal pass over Raek's face. He reached to his chest, absently pressing a hand against his old wound.

"But I think he's trying to lead them away," continued Trable. "I just received a report that he's in the Char, heading toward the Northern Quarter."

"And the shell storage isn't in the Northern Quarter?" Raek pressed.

"No," answered Quarrah. "It's in the Western Quarter. Hidden in a hat shop called Tall Son's Millinery."

All eyes in the *Be'Igoth* went to her.

"Excuse me," said the Prime Isle, "but who the blazes are you?"

"You knew?" Raek bellowed. "How long have *you* known?"

"Just over a year," she answered.

"Why didn't you tell us?" Raek cried.

Quarrah shrugged. "Nobody ever asked me."

"Unbelievable," the Prime Isle muttered, studying his feet. Then he swallowed his pride and went on. "I've sent word to dispatch every available Regulator to the millinery. If we're lucky, they'll reach—"

"Call them off," Raek said. "Call them off immediately."

"You don't call the shots here." Trable folded his arms stubbornly.

"He's right," said Quarrah. "Ard is obviously leading them astray, but if you start amassing Reggies in the Western Quarter, the Glassminds will realize what is happening. They'll kill Ard, and your attempt to protect the shell will lead them right to it."

"There will be over a hundred Regulators between them and—"

"You don't know what they're capable of," Quarrah cut him off. "If you want to protect that shell, you need to call off the Reggies. If you want to save Ardor's life . . ."

That last part was wishful thinking. Did Ard even have a plan, stringing the world's most powerful beings on a sightseeing tour through Beripent? And why did he think it was worth his life to keep them from reaching the shell?

"We need to find Gloristar," Raek said.

Trable shook his head. "She's dead."

"Actually," said Raek, "she's back. She transformed into—"

"I know," Trable interrupted. "And she's dead. Garifus shattered her skull in the Mooring."

Quarrah wanted to collapse onto the couch. Their one powerful piece, their only shot at a level playing field . . . Dead?

"Flames, this is all my fault," Trable whispered. "The Homeland is punishing me."

"Hey, now," said Raek. "Don't give yourself so much credit."

"I haven't followed the Urgings like I should," he confessed. "There's something I should have done. I feel it, but . . . I don't understand why."

"Sounds like you've got some issues to work through," said Raek. "Maybe we could talk about it *after* you call off the Regulators."

"I can't stand by and do nothing. I'm the Prime Isle, for Homeland's sake!"

"Tell you what," said Quarrah. "Order the Reggies to stand down and I promise the Glassminds won't steal the shell from the millinery."

"How can you promise such a thing?" he asked.

"Because we're going to steal it first," she said. It was really the only option. Taking possession of the shell gave them the most control over the situation. They could work out a deal. Maybe hand it over to the Glassminds in exchange for Ard's life.

"No...Flames, no..." Trable was muttering incoherently, nervously scratching his beard.

"You might as well go along with this plan," said Quarrah, strapping on the first of her thin belts. "It's happening with or without you."

"Fine," said Trable. "I'll call them off. I'll notify the queen and start redirecting the Regulators to the grounds. The moment you have the shell, I want you to take it to the palace. It's the most defensible location."

That definitely wasn't going to happen, but Quarrah nodded anyway. The sooner Trable got out of their hair, the better.

The Prime Isle nodded as if in an effort to convince himself that he was doing the right thing. Then he turned and walked out the open door.

"It was an honor to meet you!" San Green called after him. The young man had been so quiet that Quarrah had almost forgotten he was there.

Raek shut the door behind him. "How are we doing this?" he asked Quarrah.

"Simple." She fastened her final belt. "I've had my eye on Tall Son's Millinery for cycles. I know exactly how to rob the place. They're keeping the dragon shell in a storage cellar. There's a hidden entrance in the back room of the shop. I'd rather do this in the dark after they'd closed for the night, but I don't think we've got that kind of time."

"Still, you've got one big advantage that I'm guessing you hadn't counted on," said Raek.

"What's that?"

He shouldered a pack that he kept ready for such a hasty departure. "Me."

Quarrah was already thinking of a way to use him as a distraction. But sneaking all the shell outside was going to pose a challenge.

"What about me?" San asked as the two of them headed for the door.

"You should stay here," said Raek. "Hold down the fort in case Hedge Marsool shows up, wondering how his dragon got away."

"And *I'm* supposed to answer him?" San squeaked.

If the intent was to make the lad feel comfortable in the *Be'Igoth*, Raek had really botched that.

"What we're about to do is highly illegal," said Quarrah. "And the Prime Isle knows we're doing it. If you come with us, that's the end of your clean record. It makes the most sense for you to lie low here. We might need somebody on the outside if things go wrong."

San nodded curtly. Raek pulled open the door and they set off across the boardwalks of Tofar's Salts.

"You got any Shadow Grit?" Quarrah asked as they jogged down the street.

"A little," he answered. "What do you have in mind?"

"Tall Son's Millinery is surprisingly secure for a shop in the Western Quarter," Quarrah explained. "Single story. Flat roof. One door and two big windows into the shopfront. There's an interior door leading into the rear room, which is always locked. There was a window back there, but they boarded it up when the Islehood started using the shop as a secret cache."

"And the way into the cellar?"

"I don't know yet," she said. "Never made it that deep inside. It'll be disguised, but I'm sure I can sniff out the entrance. It's getting me into the back room that's the hard part."

"You want me to throw Shadow Grit around the door?" he asked, following her onto the street.

"That's what I was thinking," she said. "But that only gets us in. How do we get out with hundreds of panweights of dragon shell in tow?"

Raek chuckled. "Leave that to me."

"You're going to blow a hole in the wall, aren't you," she said.

"No," he replied defensively. "I'm going to blow a hole in the roof. We can use a cloud of Drift Grit, inside a bubble of Containment, to haul the shell up and out."

They moved at a steady jog for quite some time, Raek's breathing raspy and shallow until he paused to take a detonation of Heg in his chest.

The streets were getting narrower, but the buildings were very well cared for. The Islehood certainly wasn't going to hide their assets in a slum.

Nearly there.

They passed a couple of Regulators who looked confused, running to and fro. Trable must have called them off, even if it was taking some time for the message to trickle down to the first responders.

The hat shop finally came into view. The street was no busier than would be expected on a late afternoon. Pedestrians coming and going, a painter touching up the door to a nearby flower shop, a vendor selling bread from a basket...

Quarrah squinted through the front windows of Tall Son's Millinery, but it was too dark to see inside.

Raek produced a small round Grit pot. "I'll leave the front door open and give you a signal once the Shadow Grit is in place."

"What's the signal?" she asked.

"I'll break the window. Don't worry. It'll happen naturally."

Before Quarrah could ask any follow-up questions, Raek strode across the narrow street and pushed open the door to the millinery, a bell chiming on his way in. He moved out of sight, leaving the door open as promised.

Waiting at an inconspicuous side street, Quarrah pulled on her black thieving gloves, making sure that the Slagstone fragment was squarely situated on the tip of her middle finger, ready to spark with a snap.

*The Glassminds might have sparking fingertips,* Quarrah thought, *but I came up with it first.*

She checked the thin pockets on her palm, filled with convenient, quick-access Light Grit. From within the hat shop, she could hear voices raised in argument. They escalated quickly, and she was able to make out Raek's words.

"I didn't ask you if my *head* looked funny! I was talking about the hat!"

Suddenly, the front window shattered as a man came flying through the glass, landing in a painful heap on the street. Passersby screamed, and several pedestrians raced to his aid. In the confusion, it was easy for Quarrah to slip into the shop through the front door. She quickly ducked behind a tall hat display to analyze the situation.

Raek was standing in the middle of the room, a ridiculously undersized child's riding cap perched atop his bald head. He was holding an elderly man under one arm in a headlock.

"Not so fast," Raek said. "Can't have you running to the Regulators until we get this sorted out. This hat is half the size of my head. Therefore, it should be half the price!"

Suddenly, a fat old woman popped up from behind the counter. She had wispy gray hair and a long-barreled Fielder tucked against her shoulder. Behind her, Quarrah saw an area enveloped in a cloud of impenetrable shadow. Perfect.

"Let him go!" the woman shouted.

Raek released the man, who quickly scrambled back behind the counter, cowering under the woman with the gun.

"Now, now," Raek said. "I'm just trying to understand your questionable business policies. My apologies for the window. I didn't like the way that customer looked at me."

"Never mind that," the old woman answered. "He was no customer of ours. Now, turn and get. Take the hat. I don't care."

With the woman's focus on Raek, Quarrah advanced unseen through the racks of hats until she reached the end of the counter.

"Oh, I wouldn't dare leave without paying," said Raek. "It's a fine cap, worth the asking price for someone with a smaller head."

"Then pay what you want and go!" shouted the woman impatiently.

Quarrah shrank against the back wall, moving with absolute stealth behind the elderly couple. She knew Raek could see her clearly, and he seemed to double down on his distraction tactics. He ripped off the tiny riding cap and threw it to the floor.

"On second thought, it *is* a bit small," he said. "Giving me a blazing headache. What about this one?" He reached out and grabbed one of the popular tricorn hats with a gaudy yellow plume stitched into the band.

Quarrah slipped into the pocket of shadow to see that Raek had done a fine job using it to conceal the door. As expected, the knob was locked, so she withdrew her picking tools and set to work.

Only a few feet behind her, Quarrah heard the old man's voice in a panicked whisper. "We've got none left, Suze. I already pulled them all."

With both hands tied up in the lock, Quarrah risked a glance over her shoulder. The nature of the Shadow cloud allowed her to see out, although she would be completely hidden.

The old man was fidgeting with a series of strings, each ending in a metal pull ring. Quarrah had seen enough of these to recognize it as a security alarm system. The strings would be rigged to a number of Light Grit pots at distant locations. Pulling them would break the pots and the Regulators could quickly respond to the millinery when they saw the bright detonations.

But the strings were already slack.

"Shut up, Carl," snapped the woman with the Fielder. Suze, he had called her. "They didn't even work the first time."

Quarrah sprang the lock, her hands finishing the job by feel even while her attention was elsewhere. *Didn't work the first time?* Quarrah thought. Had the millinery had a break-in before?

"Tell you what," Suze shouted to Raek. "You keep perusing those hats all you want. Just let Carl outside. He's got an important delivery to make."

"Not until we get this sorted!" Raek shouted. "What about this hat? I like what it does to my ears…"

Quarrah swung the door inward on silent hinges. Raek seemed to have things under control, although she thought he was risking a lot in front of a loaded Fielder. Still, the millinery owners would be good Wayfarists employed by the Islehood. They weren't likely to pull the trigger on a man who just wanted to find the right hat for his oversized head.

Quarrah moved into the back room, closing the door behind her so nothing would look amiss when the Shadow cloud burned out. She raised her left hand and snapped her fingers, igniting a small orb of Light Grit, which revealed her surroundings.

This was clearly a storage area, with hat-making materials stacked high along every wall. Bolts of fabric, stacks of leather, bundles of straw. She even saw a few finished hats with delivery tags hanging from their brims.

There was clearly not enough space here to house all the dragon shell—an observation Quarrah had made cycles ago while viewing the property from the outside. And since there was no upper story, a cellar was the only possible explanation.

She'd had a knack for finding secret spaces and hidden rooms since she was a young girl. The key was in looking for little details that were out of place—a wear pattern on a rug, accumulated dirt from repeated fingerprints on a wall. Or in this case, a floorboard with a nail hole, but no nail.

Quarrah worked her fingers under the loose board and pulled. It was part of a larger panel that lifted free to reveal a short ladder dropping into darkness.

People just didn't know how to hide things from Quarrah Khai.

She moved down, using only a few rungs of the ladder before dropping nimbly to the dirt cellar floor. It was musty and cool down here. She could sense that the space was large, even though she couldn't see anything, the faint glow from her Light Grit above doing little more than illuminating the spot where she stood.

Quarrah moved a few steps forward, feeling blindly with her feet. Then she raised her right hand and snapped her fingers. In a little burst of sparks, her second detonation of Light Grit ignited, illuminating the oversized basement cellar.

It was empty.

Rough timbers framed the low ceiling, with dusty wooden support posts standing between packed dirt walls. There were no boxes or crates, bags or barrels.

There was no shell.

"If you're not early, you're late," said a familiar voice.

Hedge Marsool stepped out from behind one of the thick wooden posts. Quarrah's hand flew to her belts, whipping out one of her mesh bags of Barrier Grit, holding it at the ready.

"What did you do with the shell, Hedge?" Quarrah asked.

"My people finished moving it out of here less than an hour ago," he replied. "But I thought I'd stick around to say hello to you." Sparks. He knew she was coming and he'd anticipated her move. How?

"How did you get down here?"

"Front door, lass," replied the King Poacher. "We gave those pathetic shopkeepers little choice but to show us the way down."

Of course. That was why Carl had already pulled the strings.

"You cut the signal strings," Quarrah assumed.

Hedge nodded. "I left Drebsky upstairs to make sure those shop-keepers didn't try to run for help before you got here. He said he'd warn me when you arrived, even though I assured him that was unnecessary."

The man Raek had thrown through the window. *"He was no customer of ours."* He'd been holding the old couple hostage! And now Raek was up there doing the same thing, playing right into Hedge's hand.

"What did you do with the dragon shell?" Quarrah asked again.

"I hear your friend, Ardor Benn, is in a bit of a sour pickle again," he replied. "Would you like to know what happens to him?"

"How would you possibly know?"

In response, he held up his gloved hand and Quarrah saw a thin glass vial delicately pinched between his fingers. "How quickly you forget."

"It's fake," she said. No more time for tricks and lies. "Your *Future Grit* is nothing more than sugar water."

She saw him swallow, his sharp apple sliding along his thin, scarred neck. It was the truth, and Hedge hadn't expected her to call him on it so bluntly.

"And yet, Ardor claims to have uncovered all its secrets, mass-producing this *Future Grit*," said Hedge. "You should really get your stories straight. Which is it?"

"Ard was rusing you," said Quarrah. "He stole a vial off your belt, and I gave it to an expert, who confirmed the truth." She nar-rowed her eyes. "It's not real Grit. And you said it yourself... That's not the secret to your success."

Hedge Marsool began to laugh, a painful-sounding crackle that originated somewhere in his scarred chest. He lowered the vial and raised his spike playfully, as if he wanted to spar.

"You wanna know what happens to Ardor Benn or not?" he asked.

Quarrah stared at him. Future Grit or no, the man had proven to know things in the past. "Humor me."

"He is currently having a wee stroll with two Glassminds in the Northern Quarter," said Hedge, "racking his tender brain for a way out of this. In a few moments, the Glassminds will grow impatient and he'll be forced to lead them somewhere. He'll settle on the storage room behind a soot-smudge tavern called the Puckering Lizard. Ardor knows the owner and he'll hope to slip away as the Glassminds move in to investigate."

"And will he be successful?" Quarrah taunted. "What do you say?"

"Oh, what do I know?" Hedge said melodramatically. He dropped the glass vial to the hard cellar floor and crushed it with the toe of his boot. In the dim lighting, she saw the flash of sparks under his sole, but just as she'd predicted, there was no detonation cloud.

Hedge smiled with only half his face. "I'm just an old fool with sugar water in my Grit vials." He lifted his spike and dragged the tip down the length of the wooden post beside him. "Personally, I have no use for dragon shell. I just wanted to move it to a new location."

"Why?" Quarrah asked.

"Payback." Hedge spit. "For not properly securing my dragon."

Quarrah looked up at him, trying to keep her expression impassive. "I don't know what you're talking about."

"The dragon's gone," he said. "By the time my men arrived at dawn, Frush and Calo were dead and the warehouse in Helizon was a smoldering ruin."

"She must have . . . broken free." Quarrah didn't think her words sounded very convincing.

"Broken free or *set* free." He growled. "Ardor's fault, either way. But I'd say we're even now. And should he try to cross me again . . ." Hedge tapped the tip of his spike against his forehead. "I'll know it."

"How?" she said. "How do you know it all?"

Hedge sighed wistfully. "Just a feeling in my gut. I'd even call it an Urging if I were a religious man."

"An Urging?" Quarrah shook her head. "You?" His ability to see the future was based on a gut feeling?

"I've been having them stronger and stronger for almost a year now," said Hedge. "A tickle in the tummy. A whisper in the brain."

"You think the Homeland has been telling you the future?"

"Homeland? Sparks, no." Hedge chuckled. "It's my own voice, dearie. Clear as a bell. Making me promises that I'd be a fool to refuse."

"What are you talking about?"

"Nothing mystical or secretive about it," he said. "I'm just a man with a premonition."

"No," said Quarrah. "What you're doing is more than a premonition. More than an Urging." It was too specific. Too precise. And if Hedge's predictions about Ard's current situation were true, then he was in terrible danger.

"Would you like to know where I put the dragon shell?" Hedge asked casually. "If you hurry, you might find it. I moved it to the storage room in the back of the Puckering Lizard tavern."

Quarrah's mind reeled. She needed to get up to the shop and tell Raek. She needed to find Ard—

Quarrah bolted for the ladder.

~

*Nothing useful ever came from a feeling unless it was chased to its resolution.*

# CHAPTER

# 24

Ardor Benn was getting used to the dramatic response that two Glassminds received while walking down the streets of Beripent's Northern Quarter. Most of the citizens scattered. A few lingered awkwardly, staring unabashed. Certainly, no one spoke to them or dared approach.

"On your right, we've got Beetle's Acquisitions." Ard gestured to the first floor of a tall building. "It's a decent place if you're looking to sell back household items, or buy things used at a discounted rate—"

"Is this the location of the dragon shell?" Garifus asked.

"Well, no," said Ard, "but I thought you might be interested—"

Garifus's hand shot out and the whole shopfront of Beetle's Acquisitions imploded. Glass broke, timbers cracked, and bricks crumpled.

Ard flinched, throwing up his hands against the debris. "Sparks! What was that for?"

"The next building you point us to will have the dragon shell inside," said Garifus. "Am I clear?"

"Of course," Ard replied. "But it might take a while to get—"

"We are seventeen blocks from the northern border of the city," said Garifus. "Even at the dawdling rate we have been walking, it will take us no more than thirty minutes to reach the edge."

"You really know your way around town," Ard said, grateful that he hadn't tried to kill more time by doubling back on his route to nowhere. "Did you spend a lot of time in the Northern Quarter?"

"I have never been on this street before," Garifus admitted. "But I benefit from a perfected sense of recall."

"I'm pretty sure you can only recall things you've experienced before," Ard pointed out.

"*Collective* recall," Garifus clarified. "The minds of the many have become one."

Ah, flames, it was going to get progressively harder to lie to these Glassnoggins. Ard remembered a scripture about the Homeland. Something about how one could not whisper without all hearing, and none could act without the knowledge of all. He thought about what Nemery had said about Legien Dyer after his transformation. Garifus and the others had sensed his opposition to their ideals and their heads had illuminated to kill him with a thought.

"Alumay worries that you intentionally mislead us," Garifus said.

Ard glanced at the Glassmind woman. She certainly hadn't said anything aloud about it. "That's hurtful," Ard said. "I might get a little directionally turned around from time to time, but I know where we're going."

Oh, Homeland, where *were* they going? The plan had been to wander until Raek and Quarrah hatched a brilliant rescue plan. But what if no one had been at Tofar's Salts to hear the news from the Prime Isle? Or worse, what if Trable had decided not to take the message at all? He *had* looked pretty devastated by Ard's admission about knowing the shell's location. Maybe he viewed this as a simple way to rid the Islehood of Holy Isle Ardor Benn.

Regardless, Ard couldn't wait much longer. He had to decide on somewhere to take Garifus. He didn't know the Northern Quarter as well as other sections of Beripent, but he had a few contacts there who might be able to provide him some desperate help.

What about that fellow in the cleaning business? The one with three toes. Oh, Raek would remember his name... Or there was Betnis Fawn. She ran a laundry service with a back room full of guns and Grit. No, wait. Betnis had threatened to cut off his knee-caps if she ever saw him again.

Pirel Gulwar! His tavern wasn't far from here, and the man had given Ard many a free drink in exchange for a good story. Pirel had an enormous storage room behind the kitchen, where he always kept a stash of unlicensed Grit to sell to the right customers. If Ard remembered the room correctly, it had enough doors that he might be able to lead Garifus through one and slip right out another. Especially if he could convince Pirel to pull off a distraction.

Now that he'd decided, Ard found his heart beating at a rate that doubled his footsteps. He led Garifus and Alumay around a cor-ner and three more blocks before he saw the building. The tavern's name was burned into a wooden sign that hung above the front door.

THE PUCKERING LIZARD

"This is it." Ard stopped long enough to point at the tall build-ing. Pirel's tavern only occupied the first floor, while the upper two were mostly rental rooms. "I've tracked shipments of dragon egg-shell to this tavern, but I'll have to speak with the owner to find out exactly where they're storing it."

"We will make sure he is compliant," said Alumay.

"That shouldn't be necessary," Ard said. "I know him. And he'll recognize me as an Isle so he'll think I have authorization. But it might be best if you two stay out here—"

"You will not leave our sight," said Garifus.

Well, it was worth a shot. Ard led his abnormally large compan-ions onto the porch and pushed open the door to the Puckering Lizard.

It was a well-lit tavern designed for sociality, with three incred-ibly long tables that stretched nearly wall to wall. Ard counted ten people on the benches, sharing drinks or catching an early dinner.

But all conversation stopped when they saw the new arrivals. Ard was framed in the doorway, flanked by towering Glassminds that must have looked like monsters.

"Well, I'll be sparked…Ardor?" one voice called through the silence. Pirel Gulwar was wiping down the bar with a damp rag. He was a man who looked thin on all counts except his belly. His hair was long, but it was quite thin on top. From Pirel's angle, Ard was sure he couldn't see Garifus and Alumya.

"*Isle* Ardor!" Pirel let out a laugh. "I heard you was wearing the green these days, but I didn't actually believe it."

"I'm afraid the Lizard is closing early tonight," Ard announced, stepping inside. The customers promptly rose, making for the back door when they saw the Glassminds following him in.

"What in the name of the Homeland?" Pirel screeched, holding out his rag like a shield and dropping to a crouch behind the bar.

"It's all right, Pirel." Ard walked over to him. "They're with me. We've come for the goods. Where are you storing it these days?"

Pirel rose slowly from behind the bar, speaking to Ard, but unable to take his eyes off the Glassminds. "Usual storage room behind the kitchen. I can take you back."

Ard held up a hand. "I think we can find the way."

He led Garifus and Alumay into the kitchen, passing a watery-eyed cook who paused from cutting an onion to gawk at the Glassminds.

"Time to go home." Ard clapped his hands to expedite the command. "Closing early. Get out of here."

Wordlessly, she set down the knife and moved out the door where they had just entered. Good. That was one less person to get in the way of this slapdash escape. He led them around a deep wash basin, stopping in front of the closed door to the storage room.

"Open it," Alumay ordered.

"Me?" Ard's head was spinning, trying desperately to plot a way out as he grabbed the doorknob. Maybe he could swing it shut the moment the Glassminds were across the threshold. Bracing himself, Ard pulled open the door. But his fear suddenly turned to dread, his anxiety to astonishment, as Garifus Floc looked at him with a smile.

"Well done, Ardor Benn," said the Glassmind.

On feet that were quickly growing numb, Ard pushed past Garifus and peered into the Puckering Lizard's storage room.

Impossible.

The space was filled with dragon eggshell. Ard saw the black boxes that Tobey and Marah had described, the ones the orphans had said were delivered to Tall Son's Millinery. Many of the boxes were lidless, and Ard could see the sparkle of eggshell in cream and amber as late afternoon sunlight angled through the back window.

*Impossible!*

Yet it was all here—or at least an impressive collection of it. Ard was the first to walk into the room, dazed and completely speechless as he moved between two aisles of shell fragments.

How had it gotten here? Nobody knew Ard was heading to the Puckering Lizard. Not even Ard himself, until a few minutes ago. How had the shell magically transported from—

Hedge Marsool.

It had to be him. The King Poacher and whatever he was using to see the future...Now the Glassminds would have Visitant Grit. Garifus Floc would complete the Sphere, and Centrum would have his way. This was the end.

"You have earned the right to live on," Garifus said to Ard. "You will have the opportunity to reach the Homeland. To transform like us."

Ard shook his head. "That's not going to happen. I'm not joining your blazing cult on a hike up Pekal."

"That won't be necessary," he said. "A day cometh when all must speedily go unto the Homeland."

"That verse..." Ard whispered. "It's about the Great Egress."

He had first heard it from the Realm, but he'd read it a hundred times since in his own studies in the Mooring.

"Yes," said Garifus. "It is a time when every man, woman, and child will have the opportunity to transform—to become part of the Homeland."

"How?" Ard said. "People won't go along with you just because *you* transformed."

"They don't have to go anywhere," said Garifus. "We will bring the transformation to them."

"Moonsickness?" Ard muttered.

Garifus nodded. "Once the Sphere is complete, the dragons will pose no threat to our strength. We will wipe them from the slopes of Pekal, and the next Passing will bring Moonsickness to every living soul in the Greater Chain. We will then provide Transformation Grit to those who share our ideals. Civilization will become perfected."

Ard felt weak. He needed to sit down. *This* was the true meaning of the Great Egress. Why hadn't he seen it sooner?

Alumay passed him, carrying six huge boxes toward the back door of the room. Manipulated clouds of Drift Grit enclosed her load, allowing her to move with ease.

"Why?" Ard asked. "Why are you doing this?"

"The world is evil, Ardor Benn," said Garifus. "Don't you see it? In a civilization where we all share consciousness, there will be no more crime. No more lies. People will do the right thing because they will see the value in it."

"Or because they'll be afraid," said Ard. "Afraid that doing anything against the majority could cause their minds to be snuffed out like a candle."

"You do not understand perfection as I do." He sent two more boxes of shell floating over to Alumay with a wave of his hand.

"What you're describing isn't perfection," Ard said. "It's... dominion."

Garifus shrugged. "We will see if your mind is changed when the great day of egress is upon us all." He crossed the room, pushing both hands in front of him. In a tremendous rush of Void Grit, the entire far wall blew outward in a spray of dust and debris. Somehow, the roof remained intact, likely held by an unseen Barrier detonation.

Alumay lifted all the boxes of dragon shell at once, reminding Ard how Gloristar had once transported Motherwatch. Without a backward glance, she moved into the street.

"We will meet again, Ardor Benn," said Garifus Floc. "And when we do, you will beg for the transformation from your Moonsick state."

Ard couldn't say anything, barely standing on trembling legs as the two Glassminds disappeared with the Islehood's entire storage that shouldn't have been there.

"I'm sorry, Ardor," came a voice from behind. Pirel Gulwar was standing in the kitchen, face downcast in shame, empty hands clutched in front of him.

"They told me you'd be coming," said the barkeep. "Swore me to secrecy until after them Glassminds left with the shell."

Ard turned, his anger boiling up in Pirel's direction. "Who did this?" He moved after the man, who retreated through the kitchen until Ard cornered him against the bar. Nowhere to go.

"Who did you sell me out to?" he bellowed in the barkeeper's face.

"Don't know," Pirel squeaked. "They just showed up an hour or two ago, started loading that stuff into the storage room like they owned the place. I was going to put up a fuss, but they offered me a thousand Ashings to keep my mouth shut."

"That's how much I'm worth to you?" Ard grabbed the man by the front of his stained apron. "After all these years?" Honestly, it was a fair price. Ard had sold people out for much less. People he knew better than Pirel Gulwar.

The front door to the Puckering Lizard flew open. Ard released Pirel, who dropped behind the counter in fear. But the figures at the door were not enemies.

"Ard!" Raek shouted. "You're not dead!"

"Hedge moved the dragon shell here," said Quarrah.

"Yeah." Ard moved around to greet them between two of the long tables. "He knew I was coming before I did."

"Where's Garifus?" Raek peered into the kitchen through the open door.

"Gone," replied Ard. "And he took all the dragon shell with him."

"Let him have it," Raek said. "At least he left you alive."

"No," said Ard. "He needs Visitant Grit to complete the Sphere. And once he does that, he's going to eliminate the dragons in order to cause mass Moonsickness. It's the Great Egress."

Raek dropped heavily onto one of the benches, nearly breaking it under his weight. Ard heard him let out a world-weary sigh, running one hand over the top of his sweaty bald head. His hands were shaking. Looked like he was due for another Health Grit detonation.

"How do we stop him?" Raek asked.

"By beating him to the punch." Ard looked from Raek to Quarrah. "We detonate Visitant Grit and I become a Paladin Visitant again."

"Are you insane?" Raek croaked. "That'll destroy everything."

"Not destroy," Ard corrected. "This will *reset* everything."

"Yeah, and we'll puff out of existence with it," Raek reminded him.

"It's been done before," Ard said, "to save civilization. Every successful Paladin Visitant has reset the timeline. The Prime Isles of the future made that call. They erased their own existence in order to give humanity another chance to do things better." He gripped the edge of the table. "I don't see that we have any other choice."

"I see one big problem," Quarrah said.

"Just one?" Raek muttered.

"We don't have any Visitant Grit," she pointed out.

"But we know who does," said Ard, pointing over his shoulder toward the kitchen.

"The Glassminds?" Quarrah said. "We won't survive another theft from Winter Barracks."

"That's not what I have in mind," Ard replied. "To complete the Sphere, Garifus said they were going to ignite Visitant Grit on the site of the oldest failed detonation. We know where that is."

"We do?" asked Quarrah.

"It's here, in the oldest city in the Greater Chain," he said. "The site is well known by everyone in the Islehood. The fame of its failure is second only to Oriar's botched detonation against Grotenisk."

"Why don't you just tell us where," said Raek, "for those of us who haven't spent the last year reading books in the Mooring."

"Beripent's Western Harbor," Ard said. "Detonated by Isless Onsto centuries ago. Well before Grotenisk. Even before the Strondath Era. We're talking at least seven hundred years back. It was the first recorded detonation of Visitant Grit intended to summon a Paladin who would defend the harbor against a fleet of attacking Trothians."

"How do you know so much about this?" Raek asked.

"I actually did read when I was in the Mooring," he said.

"Huh," Raek said. "You finally learned how."

"So that's where Garifus will detonate the Visitant Grit?" Quarrah checked.

"Yep," said Ard. "And he made the mistake of telling Prime Isle Trable, which means the harbor will be swarming with Reggies."

"Do we have any idea when this might happen?" she asked.

"I don't think Garifus will waste time," said Ard. "The Glassminds have the dragon shell, but it's not Visitant Grit yet."

"They're taking it to Pekal?"

Ard shook his head. "There are already a few shell fragments that have been through a dragon."

"So all they need to do is grind it to powder," said Raek. "They might be able to do that with their bare hands."

"True," said Ard. "Which is why we should get in position as quickly as possible."

"Position where?" Quarrah asked.

"Above the docks," said Ard. "We can lie low in one of the ship repair fields. The moment the Glassminds show up and engage with the Regulators, we strike."

"And by 'strike,' you mean steal the Visitant Grit, take it down to the harbor, and detonate it on the failed site," Quarrah said.

"Exactly!" Ard cried. "The moment we enter that cloud, we'll appear to people seven hundred years in the past. As soon as they see us, the timeline will reset, and the Glassminds will never come into existence."

"Neither will we," Raek said.

"So all of this will have been for nothing?" Quarrah said. "Our entire lives…"

"I don't like it, either," said Ard. "But we owe it to humanity."

"How altruistic of you," Raek said bitterly. "I'd almost think you were a Holy Isle."

"Hey," Ard said. "You know I couldn't keep that up forever."

"Really?" Raek replied. "Because it seemed like you wanted to." He shook his head in disbelief. "How long had you known? About the dragon shell at the millinery?"

"It's not what you think, Raek," Ard began. He'd really hoped this would come out on his terms, not forced upon his partner in a way that made it seem like Ard didn't care. "I was going to tell you. I just had some other things I needed to take care of."

"Like what?" spit Raek.

"The Great Egress. Didn't you hear what I said?" cried Ard. "Moonsickness is going to destroy everyone. Destroy them or turn them into Glassminds."

"But you didn't learn that studying in the Mooring," Raek pointed out. "Garifus just told you."

"I was...I just..." Ard trailed away, truly at a loss for words. Raek was right. He had stayed too long in the Mooring.

"I guess I just need to know who I'm dealing with," Raek pressed. "Are you a Holy Isle, or a ruse artist?"

Ardor Benn took a deep breath. He was honestly sad to see his associations at the Mooring come to an end, but there was no way he'd be allowed to stay in the Islehood after breaching Prime Isle Trable's trust like he'd done.

His time in the Islehood was clearly over, but he hadn't done anything illegal... The queen's pardon was still intact.

"I suppose it doesn't matter," Ard said, noticing Raek's shoulders droop. "Being a Holy Isle, having the queen's pardon...I'm sorry, Raek. But once we enter that Visitant cloud, none of this will have ever happened." He took a deep breath. "Everything starts over."

Raekon Dorrel stared at the floor. "It doesn't change what you are today."

~

*Sometimes everything seems so straightforward. So blatant that I can't see why I didn't understand it all a long time ago.*

# PART IV

---

Through Settled smoke they will chant a name, and the one who restored life will send all hope to the Homeland in the red of night. Behold, this is zeal and ardor beyond Perfection.

—*Wayfarist Voyage, vol. 1*

Be as the eyes in the *Ucru*, alight with visions. Be as the ears, hearing wisdom. And be as the voice, calling answers into the flood.

—*Poem of the Agrodite Priestesses*

# CHAPTER

# 25

Ard peered down at the Western Harbor, squinting against the setting sun.

"Did it ever occur to you that maybe Garifus Floc is yanking our chain?" Raek asked.

"What do you mean?" Ard asked.

"What if he only *said* he was going to detonate Visitant Grit on the oldest failed site, knowing that you and the Prime Isle would focus all your attention here?"

"It certainly worked," Quarrah pointed out. "How many do you think are down there?" She was gesturing to the Reggies, packed so tightly on the ramps and docks below that Ard could hardly see space between them. The harbor entrance was blockaded for a hundred yards in either direction, cannons at the ready.

Ard and his companions were positioned at the edge of the ship repair field, a wide grassy stretch where damaged vessels could be Drift-lifted. The harsh cliff shoreline was less intense here—more like a steep slope of dirt and crumbling rocks with a series of switch-backing ramps to access the docks at the water below.

"Got to be at least a thousand of them," Raek wagered.

"That's what I call a fast response," said Ard. It hadn't been five hours since they'd left the Puckering Lizard.

"Trable had already put out a city-wide alert to the Reggies,"

Quarrah explained. "He just had to redirect them from Tall Son's Millinery to the harbor."

"Possibly a perfect game of misdirection," Raek pressed.

"I don't think so," said Ard. "In the Mooring, Garifus said that he can only speak the truth. Apparently, that's part of being a transformed Glassmind."

"Oh, okay," said Raek. "We should probably believe everyone who says they can't tell a lie."

Ard grimaced. The whole thing *could* be a big ruse, but there was an arrogant honesty to the way Garifus handled himself. At the very least, he seemed to think lying and deception were beneath him in his mighty transformed state. And Ard was inclined to believe that.

"Looks like he was telling the truth after all." Quarrah pointed across the repair field, Ard's breath quickening as six Glassminds emerged from the neighborhood that marked the edge of Beripent's developments. Garifus was leading them, and they were moving at a steady pace without a trace of haste to it.

At the sight of them, a shrill whistle sounded and the first rows of Regulators fell into attention. Ard lifted a spyglass to his eye and examined the approaching enemies.

"Garifus isn't carrying any Visitant Grit," he said, the first indicator that their plan was about to fall apart. "Or at least, nothing I can see. Flames, they're all empty-handed."

"Of course," Raek said. "They've absorbed it. They absorb detonations and cast them out their fingers."

"Well, how in the blazes am I supposed to steal that?" Quarrah cried.

A cannon sounded and Ard saw a billow of smoke from one of the big guns mounted next to the ramp entrance. Instantly, a shimmer of Grit shone in the evening light and the large ball was deflected with a wave of the nearest Glassmind's hand. It came hurtling across the repair field, digging a gouge through the grass.

Next came a barked command, and the discharge of at least fifty long-range Fielders. The Glassminds didn't even bother to deflect these, taking the shots directly with barely a flinch.

"Reggies'll learn quick enough," muttered Raek, "that's not going to do any good."

The two Glassminds behind Garifus suddenly moved in perfect unison. They waved their hands in opposite directions as clouds of Grit emerged from their fingers. At once, the army of Reggies at the ramp entrance parted down the middle, bodies flying out of control, swept aside as if they were grasshoppers.

*The unchanged stood with the gods, but they were like insects beneath our feet. We slaughtered them without resistance.*

With a chill, Ard remembered the words from the testament spire on the seabed.

Fifty yards out, the six large figures broke into a run, their inhuman speed perfectly synchronized. It was a free-for-all now, the remaining Regulators emptying their guns, two more cannons shaking the earth.

Then Garifus Floc leapt into the air, both arms stiff at his sides. Twin columns of Void Grit struck the ground, propelling him higher and higher until he cleared the archway entrance to the ramp in a single bound.

"Great sparks," Ard muttered as the other five took to the sky in the same manner, figures silhouetted against an orange sunset. Their flight cleared a trail directly below them, throwing Reggies aside as the six Glassminds soared down to the docks.

"I told you they could fly," Quarrah stated.

There seemed to be no spoken command between the Glassminds, and yet they acted with perfect unity. Their bare feet touched down on the planks of the docks, hands redirecting the Void Grit that had propelled them. They sent the wind outward, shoving back the nearest Reggies and clearing a space as two of the Glassminds manipulated a ring of Barrier Grit that surrounded their party on all sides.

The Regulators still standing on the docks continued to fire at the impenetrable wall, sending lead balls ricocheting in every direction. They probably didn't understand the nature of the shield in front of them, having never seen Barrier Grit take such a unique shape. Or maybe they just couldn't help but pull their triggers in fear.

"I think this sets the record," Raek declared.

"For what?" asked Ard, not tearing his eyes from Garifus below.

"Fastest job ever to go to slag." Raek leaned back and began loading more Heg into his chest pipe.

"What are they doing down there?" Quarrah asked.

Ard peered through his spyglass. Garifus and Alumay were pacing something off as if measuring the docks.

"Looks like they're trying to figure out exactly where the original detonation occurred," said Raek.

"Makes sense," replied Ard. "Isless Onsto failed that Visitant Grit detonation seven hundred years ago. The docks would have been very different back then."

Raek replaced the cork in his pipe. "Are there any records or drawings of what they might have looked like during her time?"

"I don't know," said Ard. "Why?"

"They might be trying to overlay the original layout of the harbor." He rapped on the pipe and took a deep, soothing breath. "It would give them a better idea of where the first detonation happened all those years ago."

"If there are maps, we better hope none of those Glassminds have ever laid eyes on them," said Quarrah.

She made a good point, with their perfect, collective recall. "At least it's slowing them down," Ard said. "Buying us some time."

"Time for what?" cried Quarrah. "There's no way we can reach them. And don't try to tell me that the great Ardor Benn can smooth talk his way past *that* many Regulators. Not even the queen's pardon will get you through them."

Ard took a deep breath. This was not his day. Why did it feel like the last *years* of work were all falling apart in a matter of hours?

"Maybe it's finally time to lose that pardon." Ard glanced at Raek. "What do you say, partner? You think Ardor Benn and the Short Fuse have one more ride in them?"

"Don't call me that..." Raek sighed wearily.

"I say we leave this timeline in a blaze of glory." Ard clapped his hands enthusiastically, but his energy wasn't as contagious as he'd hoped.

"Do you even have a plan?" Quarrah asked.

"Always." Ard turned to Raek. "How much Containment Grit do you have?"

"I've got a vial or two of everything in here." He jabbed a thumb at his backpack.

Ard smiled. "I know a little kid in the Western Quarter who keeps his pet rat in a ball of twigs. Rolls around all on its own."

"Neat," Quarrah said flatly, but he knew Raek could already see where he was heading.

"Ho, no." He shook his bald head.

"It would work, wouldn't it?" Ard said. "We close ourselves in a ball of Containment Grit and roll all the way down the ramps."

"What?" Quarrah shrieked.

"I hate your ideas," Raek said, though he was already digging in his pack for the vials.

"We're not seriously going to—"

"This spot looks good," Ard interrupted, staring down a sheer fifteen-foot drop. The stretch of ramp directly below was scattered with a dozen Regulators. He couldn't really tell them to move without tipping their hand.

"Ready?" Raek said, holding out his hand. Two vials of red liquid shimmered in the fading daylight.

"Wait," said Quarrah. "What do we do when we get down to the docks?"

Raek held up another vial with yellow liquid. "The minute our Containment ball hits their Barrier wall, I'll dash this Null Grit."

"Then we run like sparks," Ard said. "We may not be able to steal their Visitant Grit, but we can try to beat them into the cloud."

"And what's our exit strategy?" Quarrah asked.

"Exit strategy?" Ard said. "I don't think we need one this time. If everything works like we're hoping, our future won't even be here to welcome us back."

Ard stepped over to the edge of the cliff, holding out a hand, hoping Quarrah would accept it. She did. And even though it was probably just to make the jump smoother, he liked to think there might have been something more behind it.

"This is going to be a direct assault on a whole lot of Reggies," Raek said, taking Quarrah's other hand. "Might even squash a few. You're okay with this, Ard?"

He shrugged. "I think I should go out of this world the same way I came into it."

"Crying?" Quarrah asked.

"A criminal."

"Ready?" Raek checked. "We jump on three. One."

"I just want to say," Ard began, turning to Quarrah, "since time is about to stop for us anyway…"

"Two," Raek continued.

"I still love you," Ard said. "I've never stopped."

"Aw, thanks," Raek said.

"Sparks, I was talking to Quarrah!" Ard cried.

"Three!"

Hand in hand, they sprinted the final steps and jumped from the repair field. Midflight, Raek gave a mighty cry and Ard heard him shatter the red vials of Containment Grit. Airborne as they were, the Containment bubble formed a perfect sphere, barely enclosing the trio as they plummeted to the ramp below.

Warning shouts sounded as the Reggies tried to throw themselves out of harm's way. A few even managed to get off a couple shots before the ball came crashing down on them.

Inside the sphere, the landing impact knocked the air out of Ard's lungs as his legs buckled. Quarrah and Raek slammed into him with jarring force as their ball bounced and skidded, cracking through the ramp's railing but managing not to go over the edge.

The rat ball centered itself on the wooden ramp, the steep grade immediately sending it rolling. The Reggies were screaming, barking commands, some diving out of the way while others stood their ground with Rollers spitting lead.

But there was no stopping the three criminals in the impenetrable ball. In moments, they were rolling fast enough that Ard was plastered against the inside of the sphere, Quarrah and Raek smashed against him. He watched the world spin—the sky, the ramp, punctuated by the occasional mug of a Reggie pressed to the Containment cloud like a child making faces on a glass window.

He felt sick. Dizzy beyond belief. He was only vaguely aware that the Containment cloud had banked on the hillside, successfully making the switchback turn and picking up more speed on the final stretch to the docks.

Then, *wham!* The Containment ball struck its equal, jolting to a halt with force that threw Ard and his partners to the other side of their vehicle. Through eyes that could barely focus, Ard realized they had hit the Glassminds' Barrier wall.

"Ha!" Raek shouted, and Ard heard the crunch of the Null Grit vial.

The smooth glassiness of the Containment sphere disappeared and Ard found himself on his hands and knees on the damp dock, trying to get his head on straight. Fewer than thirty yards away, he saw Garifus Floc, flanked by Alumay and another Glassmind. The cult leader's hand was outstretched, fingertips sparking as a detonation streamed from his hand.

No! Ard had to be the first one into that Visitant cloud! He pulled himself up, staggering sideways. His body ached from their tumble, his nose bleeding. Quarrah moved beside him, having just as much difficulty walking on a dock that appeared to be pitched at an impossible slant. Behind, Ard heard Raek give a war cry as he ran straight off the edge of the dock, hitting the water with a splash.

Garifus cast a sidelong glance at them and Ard knew he had lost. The confidence on the Glassmind's face held an undeniable victory. An expression that Ard himself had worn, so many times.

With a grin, Garifus Floc stepped forward, vanishing into the cloud of Visitant Grit.

Ard fought against the feeling of dizziness and failure. Maybe it wasn't too late...Maybe Ard could still fling himself into the cloud and become a Paladin Visitant. The timeline would reset and humanity would have another chance to stop Garifus from transforming.

Ard lurched toward the cloud, his head finally righting enough for him to run in a straight line. He was almost there when something erupted out of the water beside the dock. A figure blasted upward and landed on the planks with a shower of droplets. It was a Glassmind. No, wait...

It was Garifus Floc!

He stepped past a stupefied Ardor Benn and stretched out one hand, absorbing the Visitant Grit cloud into his pale blue palm. Where the blazes had he come from? And why did he wear that unsettling smile, face raised to the sky?

"I am here!" the man bellowed. "I am seen again!"

The Glassminds around him all gave the cultist symbol, touching their middle fingers to their foreheads.

"We literally saw you ten seconds ago!" Raek yelled, hoisting himself out of the water.

Garifus looked at the trio of dizzy humans. "Ten seconds for you..." His voice was soft. "Seven hundred and two years for me." He closed his eyes as though relishing the moment. "At last, the Sphere is complete. I have lived a great loop in time, from the first detonation of Visitant Grit until this very moment. From the shadows, I have watched history unfold. I have seen kingdoms rise and fall. Seven centuries of war and peace. Seven centuries alone. Unseen. But along the way, I have come to understand exactly who I am." He opened his eyes, glowing red. "I am Centrum."

"That can't be," Quarrah whispered. "Gloristar told us that Centrum was the first to transform. But she did it two years before you."

"Not the first to transform," he said. "The first in existence. When I traveled back in time, I predated Gloristar by seven centuries."

"She heard your voice," continued Quarrah. "You called yourself Centrum. She said you tried to kill her."

"Yes," he said hesitantly. "Gloristar's views were not aligned with mine."

"Meaning...?" Ard probed.

"She did not agree with the Great Egress," he answered. "She was not ready for a mass transformation."

"But you couldn't snuff her out," said Ard.

"As there were only two of us, I did not have the strength of mind that comes with the majority. She and I found ourselves in a mental duel. I would have defeated her if our telepathic link had stayed active."

"But Gloristar's skull cracked," said Raek. "And the two of you were disconnected."

"No matter," he said. "I dealt with her in the Mooring. Time always runs out for those unwilling to join with the majority."

"So you're a dictator?" Ard said. "You don't allow anyone to think differently."

"I am a god," said Garifus. "I have ascended to become something unrivaled. Those who understand that will *choose* to think as I do. I'm not controlling anyone. Each of us maintains our individuality. But all is shared freely, so there can be no guile. Everyone must become of one mind. I have seen the petty differences of the minority tear civilization apart century after century."

"Hold on," Ard said. "If you were there all along, why aren't you in the history books?"

"If I were seen, all of time would have folded in upon itself," explained Garifus. "I cloaked myself in Shadow Grit and remained silent so history considered Isless Onsto a failure."

Ard scoffed. "That's *my* thing. I came up with that first..."

"*You* were a Paladin Visitant," Garifus went on. "But it was different for a Glassmind. When Isless Onsto's Visitant cloud closed, I remained in the past, forced to hide until the present day."

"So you've just been slinking around dark alleyways for the last seven hundred years?" Few things sounded more boring and tedious to Ardor Benn.

"I spent most of the years in the sea beyond the Greater Chain," said Garifus.

"Swimming?" Ard cried.

"Or adrift on wreckage from unfortunate ships," he said. "My body needs no food or water. No sleep."

"Still..." said Quarrah.

"I did it for you," Garifus replied. "For all of you!" He shouted to the Regulators looking on from the hillside. "Now that time has become Spherical, I can make you feel the truth of it!"

His fingertips sparked, a small detonation forming. Garifus reached into it, his hand disappearing up to the elbow. As he withdrew his hand, Ard suddenly felt an overwhelming sensation of peace wash over him. He knew he should have been frightened of Garifus. At the very least, he should have been angry. But he felt calm. The only thing he could compare it to was...

"You feel the Urgings from the Homeland," said Garifus. "Calming your nerves. Soothing your concerns."

Across the hillside, Ard saw the Regulators relaxing, lowering guns that had been raised all this time.

"How are you doing this?" Ard whispered, fighting to feel something other than the peace Garifus was blanketing them with.

"A world of infinite emotions is at our fingertips," Garifus said. "Timelines upon timelines. Things that once were. Or things that might have been. All of it has been rolled into one great Sphere. My people can easily access it with Visitant Grit."

"That's why you're making us feel like this?" Quarrah said. "I don't understand."

"The Visitant Grit now acts as a kind of portal for the Othians. I merely had to sift through millions of alternate timelines until I found one where you all felt peace in this location."

"Merely millions…" Ard repeated.

"I was able to reach into that nonexistent timeline and retrieve that emotion, applying it to you in reality."

Garifus said it so matter-of-factly, but Ard's head was reeling. He should have been shaking, but he still felt calm.

"Get out of my head," Raek muttered.

Garifus raised an eyebrow. "I don't think you understand. I am not controlling your mind. I cannot make you think or feel something you haven't already experienced naturally."

"I've been in your presence twice now," Raek said. "*Calm* wasn't the natural takeaway."

"Perhaps not in this Material Time," he said. "But in an alternate timeline, you have felt peace in my presence. I am able to turn that emotion into something material and apply it to you now. Those who have lived Wayfarist lives should not find this hard to accept. It is the very nature of the Homeland's Urgings."

"But I've felt those Urgings in the past," Ard said. "Years before you were…" He trailed off, realizing that Garifus—Centrum— had always been out there.

"Past. Present. Future," said Garifus. "Time means little now that the Sphere is complete. Every Urging that has ever been felt was intended to direct time to the Homeland. To us. My Glassminds will soon reach back through time, applying direction and emotion to key individuals to assure that everything will unfold as it has."

"But the Urgings..." Ard stammered on. "They've been more specific than that. I've read about Isles and Islesses who saw visions...heard voices directing them."

"Yes," Garifus said. "Much in the same way we apply emotions from alternate timelines, we can also apply visions and whispers. In a Sphere of infinite possibilities, there is nothing a person has not seen or heard. We merely take those immaterial memories—those shadows—and impose them upon your mortal minds."

"If you can manipulate people with such ease," said Ard, "why not reach back in time and have your enemies destroyed before they become a problem?"

Raek smacked him on the shoulder. "Sparks! Don't give him ideas!"

"The Glassminds can only influence the past with great care," explained Garifus. "Now that time is locked, nothing can jeopardize the creation of the Othians. If something in the past prevented our transformation, time and space would collapse entirely. There would be no existence whatsoever."

Ard breathed a sigh of relief. He, Raek, and Quarrah, were all instrumental in bringing the Glassminds into existence. Did that mean they were safe? But that same instrumentality meant that he'd received Urgings to bring to pass this very end. Sparks! Had he been a pawn in Centrum's plans all along?

"As Othians," said Garifus, "we can move freely through the Sphere, traveling backward through time to leave the Urgings that will assure we *do* come into existence."

"And the future?" Quarrah asked. "You can travel there as well?"

"In a sense," he answered. "Through the Visitant Grit, we can see an infinite number of possible futures. It is impossible to know which will unfold as the Material Time."

That was a relief. Centrum and his redheads could tweak the past, but not the future. But wait, going back in time *was* foreseeing the future for those in the past.

Ahh! Hedge Marsool! That had to be the answer! The King Poacher had told Quarrah that he'd been guided by his feelings and a whisper in his mind. Wasn't that exactly what Garifus was describing? Centrum had manipulated Hedge to steal the dragon. But why?

"We can still stop you," said Ard. "We can find our own Visitant Grit and become a Paladin Visitant—"

"Did you hear nothing I said?" Garifus cut him off. "Now that the Sphere is complete, there can be no more Paladin Visitants. No more resetting of the timeline. The linear progression of time was only ever a means to an end." He gestured to his fellow Glassminds. "*We* are the end. Humankind was *meant* to evolve. The trouble was, we kept destroying ourselves before we had the chance. Paladin Visitants allowed for the resetting of time, putting us back on a linear track to total evolution. The moment that end was reached—the moment a Glassmind transformed—time was finally fulfilled. There can be no more circling back to undo us, because we are the very fulfillment of time. Time is now locked and it can only be influenced to this selfsame end."

"That's a lie," Ard said. "You're just saying that so we won't try it."

In response to his words, Garifus stretched out a hand and ignited a detonation from his palm. The cloud hung in front of Ard, shimmering softly in the fading daylight.

"Visitant Grit," explained Garifus. "By all means, human, step inside. Become that Paladin Visitant you so boldly speak of."

Ard's eyes flicked from Garifus's face to the cloud and back. A bluff?

Would Centrum jeopardize everything he had just accomplished for a simple bluff? Ard couldn't get a tell from those glowing red eyes.

"What will happen if I step inside?" Ard asked, pushing the bluff.

"You will be lost in a state of endless limbo, caught in the center of the Sphere, held perfectly still while all of time rolls around you in every direction. Your existence will be scrubbed from the Material Time, and in so doing, there will be no trace of you in any alternate timeline. It will be as though you had never existed."

"Sounds like my afternoon naps," said Ard. "How do I wake up?"

"There is no way back." But for the first time, Ard thought he saw a flicker of hesitancy cross Centrum's face. Just a drib, but enough to tell Ard that Garifus wasn't a hundred percent confident in this bluff. The Glassmind's outstretched hand flexed and he began to absorb the Visitant cloud as if to say that the conversation was over.

"Wait!" Ard shouted, not ready to fold yet.

Garifus's face suddenly twisted in impatience. "You doubt my words?" His other hand shot out, a cloud of Grit jetting from his fingertips. The ribbon-like cloud streamed past Ard, sliced through the Barrier wall, and seized one of the Regulators. The man was sucked toward Garifus in an obvious Gather, his boots dragging across the dock, arms flailing. He was mid-scream when Garifus brought his hands together, hurling the Reggie into the Visitant cloud.

The Regulator disappeared in a wisp of vapor.

Ard swallowed. Maybe Garifus wasn't bluffing.

"Satisfied?" the Glassmind asked, drawing the Visitant cloud into his hand.

Ard was. At least for now. Garifus clearly wouldn't have done that if the Reggie had a chance at becoming a Paladin Visitant. But where had the man gone? Into the Sphere? Erased from time, like Garifus had threatened?

"What now?" Ard asked. "Where will you go now that all of time and space is your oyster?"

"We go to Pekal," answered Garifus. "Many of my followers are already venturing to the summit. We will assure that they arrive before the night of the Passing. After their transformation, our mind will be hundreds strong."

"Your cultists have quite a head start," said Ard. "What'll they do if you don't catch up to them in time?" It was an empty threat. If a thousand Regulators couldn't stop Garifus, what hope did Ard and his companions have?

"We now travel through the Sphere," explained Garifus. "By stepping into a cloud of Visitant Grit, my kind can travel freely through alternate timelines, returning to the Material Time in a different location without a second spent."

Oh, flames. What *couldn't* these people do? Ard would never be at peace again, knowing that Glassminds could pop out of thin air directly in front of him.

"But your human followers..." said Quarrah. "They'll have to hike to the summit on their own?" Centrum couldn't move them through the Sphere or they'd end up just like that poor Reggie.

"They are full of faith and a desire to transform into the Homeland," said Garifus. "They will undergo the change first. And then our numbers will be sufficient to destroy the dragons. And once they are gone, *all* humankind will have the opportunity to transform."

"You mean, get Moonsick," spit Raek.

"That is a natural step in the evolution of our species," he replied. "The dragons will fall, Moonsickness will spread to every corner of the Greater Chain, and we will begin a systematic process of mass transformation."

"Sounds like you've got it all planned out," Ard said. "Where does that leave *us* in your master scheme?"

"Standing on the docks," said Garifus, "waiting for your fate." He turned, detonating a cloud of Visitant Grit at his fingertips. He stretched it wide, bringing a portion of the detonation to the other five Glassminds. Then, moving in perfect unison, they all stepped into the Sphere, instantly vanishing.

The peaceful feeling—that Urging from the Homeland—vanished as the Barrier wall was suddenly snuffed out. Ard flinched as the thousand spectating Reggies on the ramps opened reckless fire. Quarrah's reaction saved their lives, throwing down a mesh bag of her own Barrier Grit to form a small dome over the three criminals abandoned on the dock.

In moments, Ard's view of the docks was blocked as Regulators pressed around their protective Barrier dome, guns drawn and shackles hanging ready for an arrest that some had said was inevitable.

Ardor Benn and the Short Fuse. With the elusive thief, Quarrah Khai, at their side.

Ard turned to his companions, realizing there was no fighting their way out of this one. He swallowed hard. "I think we should have had an exit plan."

~

*I have dueled the clock and lost more times than I care to admit. It has a hand far more deft than mine.*

# CHAPTER

# 26

Quarrah leaned back against the cold stone wall of the jail cell, annoyed to be here, and even more annoyed to be sharing the small room with Ard and Raek. Couldn't the Reggies at least have given her a cell of her own?

She was well acquainted with the palace dungeon. Two years ago, she and Ard had rounded up the surviving members of the Directorate—the Realm's highest-ranking position—and locked them away down here.

It wasn't the kind of place one broke out of. The stone walls between cells were at least two feet thick, and the door was a heavy slab of wood with a narrow viewing slat at eye level. Tonight, it had been left open, allowing a rectangle of dim Light Grit to shine into the cell. The door would be barred from the outside, with a padlock hanging in a spot she couldn't even see, let alone reach.

Not that she'd be able to pick it anyway. The Regulators had basically stripped them, taking every granule of Grit along with anything else that seemed suspicious or useful. They'd even taken the belt to Ard's pants, which had obviously been serving a purpose, since he could barely keep them up as he paced in the darkness.

"What time do you think it is?" Ard asked. "Got to be past midnight by now."

"Time . . ." said Raek, who was lying on the cell's single cot, one muscular arm drooping off the side. "What is time? Is it a ball? Is it a line? Is it a doughnut?"

The big man wasn't doing well. His bald head was shiny with sweat, his hands trembling. And when he wasn't jabbering, he was moaning and groaning. Obviously going through a Health Grit withdrawal, but Quarrah thought the discomfort was even more than that. Raek had been a prisoner here, four years ago. Maybe in this very cell. King Pethredote's healers had planted that awful pipe in his chest, intending to keep him alive only long enough to beat more information out of him.

This had to be hardest for Raekon Dorrel, back in the place where he'd thought he would die. Where Ard had rescued him, only to find that his life would forever be plagued by a cursed Heg addiction.

"Do you think Garifus went straight to Pekal's summit to wait?"

Ard continued. "Or would he have appeared to the cultists to help them hike?"

"Doesn't matter," moaned Raek. "We're down here. They're out there. And even if we did get out... What would we do about it?"

Quarrah was still in favor of escaping, but Raek had a point. They had lost. The Glassminds had been too powerful. And now that they had access to Spherical Time, they could be anywhere, manipulating people's emotions, and whispering Urges... Maybe this really would be the end of human civilization.

Ard hiked up his pants and dropped to sit beside Quarrah on the sawdust-littered dirt floor. "We've got to get that guy some Heg," Ard whispered, jabbing a thumb at Raek. "His downer attitude is really making me depressed."

"He has a point, though," she said quietly. "What would you do if you got out?"

"I'd start by not getting executed."

"Yeah," she said. "That would be nice."

"You might be spared since you didn't sign the queen's pardon," Ard said. "It explained in no uncertain terms that committing any additional crimes would void the pardon, holding Raek and myself accountable for every questionable deed we've ever done."

"That definitely warrants execution."

"Thanks," he said. "As long as you don't confess, you'll probably just be locked up in a Reggie Stockade for the rest of your life. But I bet you'll grow one of your fingernails really long and use it to pick a lock and escape."

"This just reminds me that you don't know anything about picking locks," Quarrah said, but she smiled at the idea nevertheless.

Ard sighed. "Remember how a few hours ago, we thought we were going to become Paladin Visitants and reset time and puff out of existence? Yeah... Well, I might have said a few things..."

Quarrah reached out in the darkness, taking his hand in a gesture so sudden it even surprised herself.

"You didn't have to say it, Ard," she whispered.

"I'm sorry."

"That's not what I mean." She shook her head. "I knew...I always knew how you felt."

Sparks. Was she really having this conversation? It was the right thing—the *considerate* thing—to give closure to a doomed man. That was all she was doing here. Nothing more to it.

"I guess I'm not as good at hiding my feelings as I'd like to think." He squeezed her hand.

What was he talking about? The man was like a walking emotion. Quarrah closed her eyes, feeling the warmth of his hand in hers, remembering a time when her heart had found such comfort and trust in that warmth.

"If things had been different..." Ard spoke in the darkness. "Could this have worked between us?"

*If you had been different*, she wanted to say. She knew that was what he was really asking.

"There was a time when I thought so," she whispered.

"When did it fall apart?"

The memory of that night came back to her, followed by half a dozen other times when Ardor Benn's ceaseless motivation had driven a wedge deeper between them. When his own goals came at the cost of everyone and everything around him.

She pulled her hand away from his. "I think you know."

It suddenly felt like fate to have this conversation in the palace dungeon. In a sense, this was the place that had delivered the first blow to that wedge—when Ard had been determined to get down here and rescue Raek. She had suggested they make a more calculated plan, with a careful extraction. Instead, Ard had jeopardized the newly fertilized dragon egg—the only real hope for humanity at the time—alerting the Reggies to its location with three gunshots into the night sky. Three shots that had sent Quarrah running. And despite whatever force kept bringing them back together, she couldn't seem to move past those gunshots. They had shown him for who he really was. And she'd seen it too many times since.

Quarrah could tell there was so much more Ard wanted to say, but he was waiting for her to go on. Fortunately, she didn't have to.

Outside the jail cell, the sound of an opening door turned all three heads. It was followed by clicking footsteps descending the stairs as the door shut.

"Hey, Hal." Ard stood up, moving toward the door. He had been calling their guard Hal for the last several hours, like they were old friends. The guard hadn't said a single word in all this time, so Quarrah didn't think that could possibly be his real name.

"Is that you, buddy?" Ard went on. "Sounds like you got some new shoes." He was almost to the view slot when the cell door swung open.

Queen Abeth Ostel Agaul stood in the threshold, her hair and makeup looking pristine despite the late hour. She wore a simple gown of green and pale blue, the blending of the colors indicative of the Islehood robes. A subtle reminder of her Islehood-sanctioned position as a placeholder ruler and crusader monarch.

Quarrah sprang to her feet. Even Raek managed to sit up on the squeaking, dirty cot.

"Your Majesty." Ard bowed his head. "I've been asking Hal for a word with you since they locked us up. Let me tell you what really happened."

"Quiet, Ardor," she snapped, holding up her hand, jeweled rings twinkling on her fingers.

Their relationship with Queen Abeth was admittedly strange. They had pretended to assassinate her, then lived with her at the Guesthouse Adagio before saving her son, blowing up said guesthouse, and failing to keep Shad alive for more than a few moments on the throne. Quarrah knew that Abeth didn't blame them for that last part, but her mercy toward Ard could extend only so far.

"Would someone please tell me what the blazes is going on?" Abeth cried. Ard glanced over her shoulder, but she shook her head. "We're quite alone down here."

The queen of the Greater Chain, alone in an open jail cell with three criminals...Strange relationship, indeed. But it showed her implicit trust that they wouldn't bowl her over, take her hostage, or otherwise use her to escape.

"So there are these Glassminds..." Ard began. Quarrah watched in silence as he explained everything to the queen, using far more words than necessary and really playing up his own heroics. Every time Abeth took a step or shifted her weight, Quarrah eyed the doorway, resisting the urge to bolt. It was instinctual for her, and standing still took all her willpower.

"I'd heard the reports from the Regulators," Queen Abeth said when he was finished. "Your explanation fills a lot of holes. What I want to know is why you didn't try to stop this Garifus from escaping into the Visitant cloud?"

"There was no stopping him!" Ard cried. "Besides, he was making us all feel peaceable. And for the record, we never hurt any of your Regulators. I'd say this whole thing is just a big misunderstanding."

"Fifty-nine of them have broken bones from your little rat ball stunt," Queen Abeth fumed. "And I didn't bother to find out how many more have cuts and bruises. I realize that you were trying to stop Garifus. But there are over a thousand witnesses, and most people thought it looked like you were *helping* the Glassminds."

Raek snorted. "I couldn't even walk in a straight line."

"Either way..." said Abeth. "You broke the law. You assaulted Regulators on duty, trespassed onto an area that was closed to civilians, resisted arrest."

"We went willingly!" cried Ard.

"My reports state that you enclosed yourself in a detonation of Barrier Grit," said Abeth.

"That was to stop your guys from filling us full of lead," Ard argued.

"Don't forget reckless detonation of Grit in a public space," Raek added. "And using Grit detonations contrary to their intended purpose."

"Raek!" scolded Ard.

"What?" said the big man defensively. "We lost the pardon. I just want to make sure people know we went down doing something more heroic than trespassing."

Queen Abeth pointed a finger in Ard's face. "Above all, you betrayed my trust. I took a risk in extending you that pardon. The entire council was against it, but I thought you could behave yourself. You're a disappointment to me, and to Prime Isle Trable."

Quarrah thought she saw a shadow of regret pass over Ard's face. But it was short lived. He held up his hands innocently. "I think we need to stay focused on who the real villains are here."

"I've already dispatched a fleet to Pekal," said the queen. "They'll apprehend this Garifus Floc and anyone who swears allegiance to him."

Raek chuckled, flopping back on the cot. "Good luck with that."

"There is little more I can do," she said. "And now I have to turn my focus to preventing the widespread panic that follows wherever you go."

"People have reason to panic this time," said Ard. "If Garifus kills the dragons—"

"Then we all get Moonsick. I know!" shouted the queen. She cleared her throat and went on, composed. "The noble councils are calling for your execution."

Ard turned to Quarrah. "See?" he said with an I-told-you-so tone.

"But I'm afraid it's more complicated than that," said Abeth.

"More complicated than killing us?" Raek asked through chattering teeth.

"The Trothians have already caught word of your arrest," the queen went on. "I have an Agrodite priestess upstairs who is demanding that I turn you over to her."

"Oh, flames," Ard muttered. "Does her name happen to be Lyndel?"

"Yes," said Abeth. "She has been in Beripent, looking for you. She claims that you were never released from Ra Ennoth like the reports claim. She says you hired someone to impersonate an official emissary who levied threats against the Trothian nation on behalf of the queen. Is that true?"

"No!" Ard cried. "That might have happened, but I didn't hire anybody."

"Then who was this mysterious emissary?"

"Must have been one of my fans, bailing me out of a sticky situation." He shrugged. "And to think, all this time, I thought *you* had rescued me. I figured, after all I'd done for you, you wouldn't stand to see me drown on some Homeland-forsaken islet."

Trust Ardor Benn to flip the situation and make Queen Abeth feel like the moral degenerate in this story. The queen took a deep breath, pressing her fingertips to the side of her head as if trying to stave off a headache.

"I have a difficult decision to make by morning," she said. "Do I have you executed in Beripent, or turn you over to the Trothian nation?"

"Either way, he's a dead man," Raek called from the cot.

"You're one to speak!" Ard snapped.

"Your fate is more straightforward, Raekon," said Abeth. "You and Quarrah will face the firing squad at dawn."

"What?" Quarrah shouted.

"Hold on," Ard interceded. "Quarrah didn't do anything—"

"We're well past that," said the queen, turning to Quarrah. "The noble council has had their teeth set on you since you showed your face to petition on Ard's behalf."

"Quarrah?" Ard said. "You did that for me?"

A mistake, apparently. Quarrah stepped toward Abeth. "I had your word that I wouldn't be held accountable for anything I said at that meeting."

"And you weren't," she replied. "But now that you've been officially arrested, the other council members are seeming to remember things you may or may not have said about your past associations with Ardor Benn."

Quarrah shot a glowering gaze at Ard. It wasn't enough to be executed for her own merits over decades of thieving? In the end, she'd meet the firing squad just because she'd spent time with Ard...

"You don't want to execute us," said Ard. "Any of us."

"And why not?"

"We're valuable. We know things." Ard cleared his throat. "We have good ideas."

That was the best Ard could do right now? Quarrah shook her head.

"The noble council isn't going to be appeased with *good ideas*," said the queen. "But if you could give me something concrete... Perhaps the name of the man who impersonated my emissary?"

"And what happens if I remember it?" Ard asked.

Quarrah gasped. He wasn't really thinking about betraying Elbrig?

"Then the noble council might be satisfied long enough for the three of you to escape."

"I like the sound of that," muttered Raek.

"How?" Quarrah asked.

"There could easily be a miscommunication among the Regulators after the queen visited the dungeon." Abeth straightened the bodice of her gown. "Your cell was left unguarded. And I hear one of you is an expert at picking locks."

"You're serious?" Ard said.

"The name and location of the man," demanded the queen.

Quarrah leaned back against the wall. So much for their one chance of escaping. Ard would never betray the disguise managers . . .

"Elbrig Taut," said Ard. "He goes by a lot of names, but I know him as Elbrig Taut. His partner is a woman named Cinza Ortemion. They are masters of disguise and they spend years developing well-connected personas to sell to criminal contacts. They're difficult to reach, and you can never be sure what they'll look like on any given day. But this is my method of reaching them. Have your people go to Drune's Haberdashery on Leaf Street in the Eastern Quarter. Have them tell the attendant at the front desk that they'd like to see something more exotic. The attendant will ask if the fabric is for them. They should reply by saying, 'It will be, if the season is right.'"

Quarrah stared at him, mouth agape. Was he seriously doing this? Turning Cinza and Elbrig over to the queen? Of course not. This was a lie. Just something to convince Abeth to let them go. By the time her people tracked down Ard's lead, the three of them would be long gone.

"How can I trust you?" the queen asked, obviously coming to the same conclusion.

"It's the truth," Ard said. "I swear to you."

"You'll understand if I have a hard time believing your word."

"Raek will confirm it."

Abeth scoffed. "Oh, that's much better."

"Why would I lie?" Ard asked. "If I give you a fake lead, it'll only put you back on our trail faster. If you get Elbrig and Cinza, we'll have a little breathing room after we escape."

Sparks! Maybe he *was* telling the truth. When he put it that way, it seemed quite convincing.

The queen pursed her lips in thought. Then she took a step closer to Quarrah and conspicuously dropped something on the dirt floor. Quarrah recognized her thief's tools immediately.

"In one hour, the Regulators on the first floor will change," said Queen Abeth, turning to leave. "The hallway that leads to the palace's east exit will be vacant. I hope you can make my decision easier before sunrise."

"Abeth," Ard said, forgoing the formality of her position. "Thank you."

She glanced over her shoulder at him. "We're even, Ardor Benn. Do not expect mercy the next time we meet."

Then she closed the heavy cell door and Quarrah heard her footsteps *click clack* up the stairs.

"Please tell me that was some Heg she dropped." Raek sat up on the cot again.

"Better," said Ard. "Quarrah's lock-picking tools."

"Though it doesn't matter much." Quarrah picked them up and put a hand to the door. "I still can't reach…" She trailed off as the door swung open on its own. "She didn't even lock it."

"This is how legends are born," Ard said. "Palace Reggies for decades to come will talk about how Quarrah Khai picked a lock through a solid door."

Raek staggered forward, bumping into her. "Let's get out of here."

"Not yet, big guy." Ard grabbed his friend's arm to stabilize him. "Got to wait another hour for the guards to change."

He helped Raek back to the cot while Quarrah pulled the cell door shut. Safer to maintain appearances in case a guard peered in over the next hour.

"See," Ard said. "I knew we could get out of this."

"Cinza and Elbrig…" Quarrah turned to look at him. "Was that an honest lead to find them?"

He shrugged. "Didn't seem like we had another choice."

"But you…" she stammered. "You *betrayed* them."

"I don't really see us needing a disguise in the near future," Ard said. "Those Glassminds would see right through anything we put on."

"So you turned them in?" Quarrah cried. "Because their services no longer suit you?"

"No skin off my teeth," Raek replied. "Never liked the crazies anyway."

"It's not like that, Quarrah," Ard tried. "I had to get us out of here. Abeth would've seen through a lie."

"Elbrig put his neck out for you with the Trothians," said Quarrah.

Ard nodded. "And now that neck is going to meet the chopping block. It was either his or mine. Elbrig would've done the same in my position. He'll understand."

At the back of the cell, Raek groaned and Quarrah thought he might throw up.

"I promise we'll get you some Heg the minute we get out of here." Ard went to his friend's side. "Once you're fixed up, we'll swing by and check on old Vethrey."

Quarrah felt goose bumps racing down both her arms. "What did you say?"

"Oh, it's nothing," said Ard. "Just a little something Raek and I have been working on."

"Say it again." Her heart was hammering.

Ard cleared his throat. "Um...Vethrey?"

"What does it mean?" Quarrah's voice spiked. "You have to tell me what that means!"

"Sparks! Relax, Quarrah," Ard said. "It's nothing to worry about."

"They were saying that word," she muttered. "When I was in the *Ucru*...the night I stole the piece of Moon Glass. They were chanting it."

"Who was?"

"Lyndel and the other priestess," said Quarrah. "They were burning that turroc root. The whole place was full of smoke. And they were chanting that word. *Vethrey*. What does it mean?"

Ardor Benn covered his mouth, a look of pure astonishment on his face. "It's a Trothian word I learned from Nemery," he whispered. "It means *Motherwatch*."

Ard's thoughts were racing so fast, he could barely focus long enough to verbalize one. Quarrah's words had brought sudden clarity to everything—Hedge Marsool, Motherwatch, Gloristar's reappearance, the scriptures. And above all, they had given Ard the first glimmer of hope that they just might take down these impossible Glassminds.

"Through Settled smoke they will chant a name," Ard began to recite. It was a verse he had memorized because it referenced his name. "And the one who restored life will send all hope to the Homeland in the red of night. Behold, this is zeal and ardor beyond perfection."

"What the blazes are you carrying on about?" Raek asked.

Ard looked at Quarrah. "You said they were chanting the name *Vethrey*. *Motherwatch*. She's going to save us."

"The dragon?" Quarrah asked. "How?"

"By becoming something even more powerful than she is right now," said Ard. "Think about it. Humans and dragons are the only two species known to get Moonsick. If *we* can evolve into Glassminds...what will a dragon become?"

Raek shuddered, sucking in a deep breath. "A god."

"You can't know that for sure," said Quarrah.

"It says it right there in the verse," Ard replied. "The one who restored life will send her away to get Moonsick. And she will become something beyond perfection. *Beyond* a Glassmind."

"The one who restored life?" Quarrah questioned. Ard nodded, but she obviously didn't understand. With a humble bow, he gestured at himself.

"You?" she cried. "You think that scripture is talking about *you*? How did Ardor Benn restore life?"

"The dragon egg," said Ard. "I saw to the fertilization of that bull dragon egg. I restored a dying species. Trust me. I spent the last year studying these things. It even mentions my name explicitly. I'm supposed to get Motherwatch sick and help her transform— send her to the Homeland in the red of night."

"Even if you're right," said Quarrah. "Even if that verse does talk about turning a dragon into a god, I see one big problem." She stared at him as if expecting him to see it, too. "We don't actually have Motherwatch anymore."

Ard scratched behind his ear. Time to come clean with Quarrah. "Yeah. About that…Raek and I sorta decided to stash Motherwatch somewhere else."

There was a speechless pause, and then Quarrah attempted a response. "How could you…When did…" She trailed off into something that sounded like a growl of frustration. *"What?!"*

"We couldn't risk letting Hedge get his hands on her," explained Ard.

*"Hand,"* Raek corrected.

"But we thought she might be good to keep around for a bit," he said. "After all the work to steal her…"

"I saw her!" said Quarrah. "In the cavern below Helizon."

"You saw the Illusion Grit likeness of Motherwatch," explained Ard. "With a detonation of Heat Grit to make it feel convincing."

"Where was the real dragon?"

"She had quite the trip," Ard said. "We had to bring her to Helizon first so we could create the Illusion Grit image to fool Hedge. But she was only in Baroness Lavfa's cave for about a half hour. Then I stayed behind and Gloristar returned Motherwatch to the *Stern Wake.* We needed Captain Dodset's influence to get the dragon through Beripent's harbors unseen, so I paid her a hefty fee. Most of my life savings, actually. Raek was waiting at the other cave. The one we told you about. South of Beripent, in the Pale Tors."

"You knew about this?" Quarrah spun on Raek.

"It was why I had to leave Pekal early," Raek affirmed. "Needed to square things away with Jaig Jasperson and make sure he had enlarged the cave's opening so we could get her inside."

"But the escape..." said Quarrah. "Hedge said the warehouse exploded when the dragon broke free. Killed two of his men."

"That was the work of Cinza and Elbrig," Ard said. "Or as you might remember, the hunchback, Pincher, and the hag, Otella."

Ard knew this truth would sting, but he was surprised by the depth of the betrayal on Quarrah's face. "Why didn't you tell me?"

"I knew you wouldn't like it," he said.

"How about next time, you let *me* decide what I don't like."

"Well, do you?" he asked. "Like it?"

She clenched her jaw. "No."

"See?"

"I think it's one of the stupidest things you've ever done," said Quarrah. "Keeping a live dragon in the largest city in the Greater Chain..."

"Technically, she's outside Beripent's city limits," said Raek.

"Who's been watching her all this time?" Quarrah asked. "Doesn't she need regular detonations of Grit to remain in Stasis?"

"Jasperson's on it," Raek explained. "And I told San if we didn't return from the harbor by morning, he should instruct Jasperson to release the dragon."

"*San* knows about her?" Quarrah cried.

Raek shrugged, a childish grin on his face. "No secrets among lab partners."

"I should have told you, Quarrah," Ard said. "But I didn't. I'm sorry. What's important is that we still have her! We'll keep her locked up through the coming Moon Passing. Away from the other dragons, she won't get the rays she needs. Once she's Moonsick, we'll expose her to the Metamorphosis Grit and see what happens."

"*See what happens?*" Quarrah threw her hands in the air. "This is a huge gamble, Ard! If Garifus succeeds in destroying the other dragons, Motherwatch will be the only hope we have to shield anyone from Moonsickness."

"I know," replied Ard. "It's right there in the verse. We will 'send all hope to the Homeland in the red of night.'"

"I think you're grasping at straws," said Quarrah. "We need to release her. Let her fly back to Pekal and get the Moon rays that she needs to stay healthy."

"And be right where Garifus wants her so he can slaughter Motherwatch along with all the others," said Ard. "The number of Glassminds is going to soar after the Passing. Do you doubt that they can track down and kill every single dragon on that island?"

She shook her head.

"But think about what could happen if this works," pleaded Ard. "We'll have a *god* on our side."

"Probably a goddess," Raek interjected, "but I guess we'll see."

"A more powerful ally than Gloristar was," said Ard.

"We don't know that," Quarrah emphasized. "And if it doesn't work, then our only hope will be as raging violent as Grotenisk was."

"Then maybe she'll put up a better fight against the Glassminds," said Ard.

"And maybe Dale Hizror will write an aria about her," added Raek. "I heard you like to sing about killer dragons."

She scowled at him.

"For all we know," said Ard, "a Moonsick dragon can still absorb Moon rays. We have nothing to lose in trying this."

"Nothing to lose?"

"In fact," Ard pressed, "keeping Motherwatch in Beripent gives us two things we want. We get a Moonsick dragon to experiment on."

"Can't say we *want* that," muttered Quarrah.

"And we keep her away from Garifus a little longer. I think we can safely assume that no one knows we have her."

"What about this Jasperson fellow?" said Quarrah.

"Okay, well, *obviously* he knows," Raek said.

"And we did everything we could to keep this from Hedge," Raek said. "We're pretty sure we've stayed ahead of him. Even though he was the one to hire us for this job in the first place."

"No," said Ard, holding up a finger. "He didn't." He took a deep breath, assuring himself that this had to be the truth. "*I* did."

Oh, boy. If it had been hard to sell them on the concept of a transformed dragon goddess, then this next bit was going to be a wild ride of naysaying.

"Wait...what?" Raek and Quarrah shared a look of confusion.

"All right. Bear with me for a moment," Ard began. "I'm going to say something that's not going to be easy to digest."

"Well, that's new..." muttered Quarrah.

"When Garifus completed the Sphere, he said that any Glassmind can go back in time to leave Urgings—feelings and whispers—so long as they didn't jeopardize the creation of his kind."

"Based on what Hedge said to me, he's been manipulated by a Glassmind all this time," Quarrah added.

"Yes," Ard agreed. "But not just any Glassmind...*me*."

"But you're not a—"

"Not yet," Ard cut her off. "But there's still time to reach the summit before the Passing. I've got nine days."

"And Nemery said an experienced hiker could make it to the summit in ten," Raek said.

Ard nodded. "It'll be quite the hike, but it's doable."

"Why in the blazes would you even consider this?" Quarrah cried. "The moment you transform, Centrum will be in your head. He'll know what you're planning and he'll kill you on the spot."

"Not if I disconnect myself quickly enough," Ard explained.

Raek nodded. "Just like what happened to Gloristar."

"We have no idea what kind of a crack that takes," argued Quarrah. "Too much, and you'll shatter your own skull."

Ard held up a hand. "It'll be all right. I have a way to do it safely." That was mostly a lie, but he had studied Gloristar's glass scalp quite closely. A solid blow to the skull would—

"Let's say it works," Raek interrupted his thoughts. "You become a Glassmind and you reach back in time to hire us to steal a dragon. Why would you pick *Hedge Marsool* as your mouthpiece? We hate that guy!"

"Exactly," said Ard. "I have to hire someone intimidating enough to scare us into doing his bidding. You know that's not a long list, but Hedge is at the top of it."

"If it *was* Hedge," said Quarrah, "then how did he know which vase to put the note in at Lord Dulith's manor?"

"Because you told me," Ard said. "And I'll tell him. A whisper in his mind. Isn't that what Hedge said? It's the very way Garifus described the Urgings!"

"But which happened first?" she questioned. "I told you about the note because I'd already found it. But you haven't passed that information along to Hedge yet. How can something happen if it hasn't happened yet?"

"Look, this is going to get messy." Ard tried to remain calm. "I don't claim to fully understand this time travel slag, but hear me out."

Quarrah nodded. Raek shivered. Ard went on.

"Once I become a Glassmind, I'll reach into the past, imposing feelings and whispers on Hedge Marsool to convince him to hire us to steal a dragon."

"There's not a more straightforward way to get one?" Raek asked.

"Sure, there is. But not with the limited time we have left," said Ard. "All of this was to plan ahead, knowing that we wouldn't have time to go to Pekal and hunt down a dragon when we finally realized we needed one. Hedge's job was to make sure we had everything we needed, *already* in place."

"Like what else?" asked Quarrah.

"Think about what Hedge required of us before he surrendered the paperwork for Captain Dodset and the *Stern Wake*," said Ard. "He specifically told us to seek out Baroness Lavfa."

"Because of her underground property," said Quarrah.

"Or because Glassmind-Ard told him to," said Raek. "Why?"

"Because Hedge Marsool isn't the only person I'm going to manipulate in the past," said Ard. "Remember how Baroness Lavfa mentioned the Urgings?"

"You think that was you?" Quarrah asked.

He nodded. "I'll reach back to the baroness and put the whispers in her head. Tell her exactly what to demand when someone comes asking about her subterranean property beneath Helizon."

"A black backpack with ten panweights of Void Grit, ten panweights of Barrier Grit, four bricks from the Royal Concert Hall, and a piece of Agrodite Moon Glass," Raek reviewed.

"Everything Gloristar would need to resurface," said Ard.

"Why the bricks?" Quarrah asked.

Raek chuckled. "Those are just to make sure it sinks."

"Exactly. And when I'm done hiring Lavfa, I'll pay a mental visit to our old friend Moroy Peng. He said he had good intel on exactly where to find us."

"Because you told him," said Quarrah.

"Well, I haven't yet," said Ard, "but I will soon. Moroy's dying words were 'Cut the pack.' At the time, I didn't understand what that was all about. But I'm going to chalk it up as another oddly specific Urging. He'll sink the black backpack so it'll be sure to reach Gloristar in the depths. After that, we'll get Motherwatch and I'll stop sending the Urgings to Hedge so he won't know that we're keeping her in Beripent."

"But you *will* tell him to move the dragon shell from the millinery to the Puckering Lizard?" Quarrah shook her head. "Why?"

"Because that's where he told you about the Urgings," said Ard.

"It's what led us here. I'll convince Hedge to make vials of sugar water and pretend to have Future Grit. That's what kept us guessing about him. Once you confront him about it, I'll let him know it's okay to tell you the truth about the Urgings."

"I don't know, Ard," muttered Raek. "It sounds to me like you're just saying you're going to do a bunch of stuff that already happened...because it already happened."

"I get the feeling that's how time travel works," replied Ard. "With Visitant Grit, I'll be able to make all these visits in a matter of minutes, maybe seconds. After that, things should run smoothly to the present moment."

"I wouldn't say smoothly," said Quarrah. "Gloristar and Lomaya died. Why didn't you do something about that?"

"And we got arrested," said Raek. "Why don't you tip us off that the rat ball is a bad idea?"

Ard held up his hands. "I don't think I can take requests," he said. "I don't understand how this works, but I know that what's happened has happened. It's too risky to change anything else."

"If this is the truth, I'm going to need a sign," said Raek. "Something to prove that you really will turn into a time-traveling Glassmind."

"Fine. You want a sign?" Ard said. "I'll add it to the list." He pretended like he was writing on a piece of paper. "Give Raek a sign so he'll believe me."

The cell fell into absolute silence.

"Come on, future me," Ard muttered after a pregnant moment.

Quarrah sighed. "Do you think it's been an hour?"

"Beats me," Ard said. "It's not like we have a clock in here—"

From under Raek's cot, Ard heard the soft chiming of a mantel clock. He looked at Quarrah, then at Raek, making sure they were hearing it, too. Ard dropped to one knee, squinting to see it half buried in rank sawdust. As the chime concluded, he saw a flash of sparks. Ard fell back as a detonation cloud erupted from the clock, encompassing Raek, who sat directly above it.

The big man instantly stopped shivering, his breathing calm. There was a blissful look on his scarred face as he passed his hand through the hazy air around him.

"That's some fine-quality Heg," said Raek. "I'm officially convinced."

~

*Some things I took for the Ashings. Some things for the fame and recognition. But the things I took for myself are what really mattered.*

# CHAPTER

# 27

Ardor Benn led the way through Tofar's Salts, moving clumsily across the boardwalk in the darkness. A regular glow of Light Grit was an unnecessary expense in a soakhouse where all the patrons could see in the dark.

The carriage driver had agreed to wait on the street, but Ard knew he had to hurry if he hoped to catch a ship to Pekal before sunrise. He pushed open the door to the *Be'Igoth*, snatching a pot of Light Grit from the rack and smashing it against the wall. The room came into focus as the clay shards tumbled into a waste pail by his feet.

Someone sprang from the couch, causing Ard to reel backward, crashing into Quarrah.

"Sparks, San!" Ard cried. "What were you doing in the dark?"

The young man bounced anxiously on his toes, eyes bleary as he rubbed them with the palms of his hands. "I heard you were arrested. I waited here in case it wasn't true. Must have fallen asleep."

Raek quietly shut the door behind them.

"So *was* it true?" San asked.

"You don't have to rub it in, kid," said Raek.

"How'd you get out?"

"Probably better if you don't know," Ard replied.

The escape had gone perfectly, the hallway empty of Regulators just as Queen Abeth had promised. Being the middle of the night, it had taken a little longer than Ard had wanted to flag down a public carriage, but the privacy of a coach was worth it.

Ard moved to one of the cabinets where they kept some limited provisions. "Nine-day trek to Pekal's summit…I'm gonna need more than crackers and cheese."

"Wait," said San. "You're going up there? Like Lomaya? Are you going to stop Garifus?"

"I don't think that's possible right now," Ard replied. "But I'm going to level the playing field, at least."

Quarrah cleared her throat. "We should come with you."

Ard was surprised to hear her say it, knowing how much she disliked that island. "I wouldn't ask that of you. Only one of us needs to become a Glassmind for this to work."

"That's not what I'm talking about," said Quarrah. "I just think you're going to need help on the hike. Let's face it, you'll never make it to the top on your own."

"How hard can it be?" Ard asked. "If I'm going up, I'm going in the right direction."

"Yep. He's definitely going to die up there," Raek muttered.

"So maybe I don't know the way," Ard said. "But I know some-one who does."

"I thought you burned that bridge," said Raek.

"With Nemery?" Quarrah asked. "Did I miss something?"

Ard had been forthright with Raek about the undesirable conditions under which he'd taken Motherwatch, but he had purposefully withheld that information from Quarrah. That story was just the kind of thing she had been talking about in the jail cell—Ard's insistence on doing what he thought was right at the cost of his interpersonal relationships.

Quarrah was angry at him for keeping Motherwatch. Nemery, for separating her from the hatchling. Raek was still mad about Tall Son's Millinery, and Queen Abeth about breaking the pardon. Prime Isle Trable was upset that he'd learned Islehood secrets, and Lyndel wanted him dead for crimes against the Trothian people. And the minute Elbrig and Cinza realized he'd turned on them, they'd want him dead, too.

Sparks, his life was really falling apart. But he couldn't stop now. Not when he was so close.

He was going to bring back the gods.

"Nemery and I aren't really on speaking terms anymore," Ard admitted to Quarrah. "But I can win her over. It'll be fine."

"What happens if you *do* make it to the summit?" San asked.

"I get Moonsick and then detonate some of that fancy Metamorphosis Grit around myself," Ard explained. "I turn into a beautiful butterfly."

"You can't become a Glassmind!" San shrieked. "Garifus will control you."

"Garifus said that his transformed followers still retain their individuality," corrected Ard. "Their thoughts are linked and their bodies become perfected. We can—"

"It should be me." Raek was looking down at the *Be'Igoth* floor, a distant expression on his face. "I should become the Glassmind, not you."

"I appreciate the offer," said Ard, "but I've got this."

"This isn't like anything we've done before," Raek said. "We're not talking about putting on one of Cinza and Elbrig's costumes." He looked up. "This is a permanent change."

"I understand the risks," said Ard. "But it has to be me."

"Why?" Raek asked.

"To give the Urgings to Hedge Marsool and the others," said Ard. Why did his friend suddenly seem so intense about this?

"I know what happened, too," Raek said. "I could plant the Urgings just as easily as you."

"Raek…" Ard held up a hand. "It's okay. I can—"

"I *want* to do this," his partner suddenly barked.

"Of course you do," Ard returned. "A chance to be a superior being… To manipulate Grit at your fingertips."

"You're not hearing me, Ard," said Raek. "This is something I *need* to do."

"Why?" Ard rebutted. He wasn't going to let anyone take this brilliant plan from him. Not even Raekon Dorrel. This was about the millinery. Because he didn't tell him where the shell was being stored. "I get it, Raek. You're tired of being the *partner*. The Short Fuse. Hanging out in the corners while I get all the attention."

Was that *jealousy* in Raek's eyes? Oh, this made sense now. Raek had always been the muscle. If Ard went through with the transformation, he would loom over his partner. He'd take away the one thing that—

Raek let out a roar like an angry bear, rending his sleeveless shirt down the front. He took a lurching, challenging step toward Ard, the metal pipe protruding conspicuously from his muscled chest.

"Look at this!" Raek yelled. Ard dropped his eyes to the floor. "Look! Does this seem *perfect* to you? Does this look like a body that feels no pain?" He let go of his torn shirt, seeming suddenly embarrassed. Striding across the room, he leaned against the back of the green chair, his head downcast.

"Humans are blazing fragile," Raek muttered. "But some more than others."

Another kind of embarrassment hit Ard. Embarrassment for his own selfishness. For not having seen it sooner. For not having understood. To be honest, Ard rarely thought about the pipe in Raek's chest anymore. The Chimney, as Ard liked to call it, seemed almost like a natural part of his friend now. Raek never complained about it, and Ard must have mistaken that silence for acceptance. What kind of friend did that make Ard, pretending like the pain had gone away?

"I'm sorry, Raek." He took a quiet step closer to him. "I didn't realize."

Raek sighed. "Sometimes I think I could be living another life altogether...and you wouldn't realize."

Ard clenched his jaw. Was his friend *trying* to twist the knife of guilt? So much of their life intersected. Ard knew those parts as well as himself, it seemed. But they weren't *always* together. And while Ard was usually quick to give a full accounting of his day, Raek had never felt the need to share as much. Over the years, Ard had asked fewer and fewer questions. Had they been drifting apart right under his nose?

"I'm ready to be free of this." Raek tapped his chest. "And for the first time...I see a way."

Ard walked over to him, trying to decide how to handle this situation sensitively. "If we can pull this off..." he said softly. "If we can actually succeed in separating a Glassmind from Centrum's collective mind...I promise you'll be the very next one to transform."

Raek squinted his eyes. "You're not going to let me do this?"

Ard rubbed a hand across his face in exasperation. Couldn't Raek see how delicate this whole situation was?

"We're talking about becoming a *Glassmind*, Raek. This isn't like taking a trip to the healer's shop."

"I understand that," Raek retorted. "And by the sound of it, the trip is about your ego."

Ard huffed. "I'll say it again. I am the best person suited for this, having been present every time Hedge Marsool pretended to know the future."

"Experiences you told me about in great detail," said Raek. "And you weren't there when Quarrah met him under the millinery."

"This isn't up for negotiation!" Ard cried. "I am going to Pekal on my own."

"I guess we'll have to see who gets there first." Raek stepped around the chair, his hand shooting out, catching Ard in the chest and throwing him backward. Ard landed in the chair, gasping for breath.

"I won't screw this up," Raek promised. "But I have a feeling— maybe even an Urging—that you might."

Raek's eyes dropped to the chair arm. Sparks, not *this* chair! Ard tried to leap up, but his partner was faster. Raek pulled the wooden arm, and Ard felt the seat drop out from under him. He reached out desperately, managing to grab a fistful of Raek's torn shirt, but it wasn't enough to hold his weight. The fabric ripped and Ard fell, landing in a heap on the floor of the empty bath.

"Raekon!" he yelled.

"I'll be back in a couple of weeks." Raek threw something down and Ard saw it shatter on the floor beside him—a little vial of liquid Grit, sparks sizzling as a detonation engulfed him.

He fell limply to the floor and everything went black.

Quarrah stared at Raek, completely speechless over the conflict she had just witnessed. He pulled the trapdoor back into position, the arm of the green chair clicking into place.

"Does anyone else have a problem with me becoming a Glass-mind?" He dusted his hands together, turning to face her and San. The poor man…he was desperate to shake the pains that had plagued him. And looking at his weathered face, Quarrah knew it was the right choice.

"You've earned this, Raek." She nodded at him. "I'll stay here and make sure Ard doesn't follow you."

"That might not be as easy as it sounds," Raek said. "He's going to be livid when that Stasis cloud burns out."

"How much more of that stuff do we have?" she asked.

"There's a box of vials right here." San moved over to the Grit Mixing table. "Most of them are Prolonged, so that should give you..." He pulled off the box's lid and silently counted. "Well, it should keep him out cold until morning, at least."

"Then that's what I'll do," Quarrah replied. "And since there's no way to open that trapdoor from the inside, I could potentially keep him down there for days."

"That's right," said Raek. "You'll want to plug the drain so he can't weasel his way to the baths outside."

"Of course," she said. "But I have to ask... Whose idea was it to put a trapdoor under that chair?"

Raek scratched his head as if trying to remember. "Mine, I think. Why?"

She nodded. "Now I'm sure we're doing the right thing." If Ard were truly destined to become a Glassmind, wouldn't he have Urged the past to change the remodel of the *Be'Igoth* in order to avoid this little mutiny?

"While I'm gone," said Raek, "San's your man if you need more Grit."

The young man stood with his hands clasped in front of him, a notably nervous posture. "Actually, I'd like to go with you."

Raek smiled. "That's nice of you to offer, kid. But there's no sense in putting more lives in danger."

"Flames, Raek," Quarrah cried. "Don't be like Ard. If he wants to go, let him."

He looked at her, his contempt over the comment quickly giving way to acknowledgment of his error.

"Why?" he asked San.

"When Lomaya and I were being held at the Barracks," San started, "we told Garifus that detonating the Transformation Grit was more complicated than it really was—that one of us would have to be there in order to make it work correctly. It was a simple lie designed to stall him. Perhaps convince him to bring the Blood-eyes to us. We didn't think he would actually take one of us with him on the trek."

San swallowed hard, and Quarrah could see the pain of remembering his friend.

"The night they set out from Winter Barracks," he continued softly, "I was supposed to be the one to go with Garifus. But I got sick. I tried to tell Garifus that I could still hike, that I'd be feeling better by the time we reached Pekal." He shook his head. "Garifus took Lomaya instead."

"Going with me to the summit won't bring her back," said Raek.

"I know. That's not what this is about," San said. "After Lomaya had left with Garifus, I was working in our laboratory at the barracks when I found a little vial of Thornleaf oil…"

"You think she *poisoned* you?" Quarrah asked. She was familiar with Thornleaf's undesirable properties. She had used it plenty of times to make sure that certain rooms of a manor would be unoccupied—and others *occupied*—in order to simplify a burglary.

"My symptoms were consistent with the effects of Thornleaf," said San. "Vomiting, diarrhea, a rash on my chest and back…"

"All right, bud." Raek held up a hand, face disgusted. "Save it for a healer." He shuddered. "What kind of person poisons her friend so she can take his place on a death march?"

San looked him squarely in the face. "What kind of person traps his friend in an empty bath?"

"Watch it, kid," Raek whispered.

But San didn't back down. "Lomaya talked and talked about how weary she was of this world. How she saw her boyfriend dying every time she closed her eyes, and she was tired of living with the pain. She had begged me to let her go with Garifus, but I convinced her that I was better suited for the hike. That it had to be me. I thought she wanted to go because she figured Pekal would be the end of her. A quick way out of her suffering."

"But she survived the island," said Quarrah.

San nodded, eyes glistening in the faint glow of their single Light detonation. "And that's when I realized...She'd given me a lot of selfish reasons for going, but when it came right down to it, she didn't do it because she wanted to die. She did it because she wanted to keep me safe. So you asked what kind of person would do that to their friend..."

Raek stared at the young man for a long, hard minute. "You got a pack?"

San shook his head. "I've got one change of clothes to my name."

"Then you should probably bring it," said Raek. "There's an outfitter in New Vantage. We'll set you up with everything you need when we get there. But we'll want to take as much Grit from here as we can reasonably carry."

"We only have six vials of Transformation Grit." San wiped tears from his face, springing into action.

"We'll take two," said Raek.

"Only two?" Quarrah questioned.

"I should only need one detonation to undergo the change," he pointed out. "But I'm not the only one who needs to transform after the Passing."

"You're talking about Motherwatch?" Quarrah checked.

"Wait...the *dragon*?" San cried.

"Long story," Raek said. "She might be a goddess. I'll fill you in on the way." He turned back to Quarrah. "We don't know if the transformation will work the same for her. She might need more than one dose, so you should keep the four remaining vials."

"Can't you make more when you get back?" Quarrah asked. "You have the source material you need here?"

"Dragon tooth," Raek affirmed. "We've got a little left." He crossed to the open cabinet and withdrew an empty backpack. "I'll leave you the formula just in case the dragon doesn't respond to the first four doses."

"I'm no Mixer, Raek." She had packed plenty of powdered Grit in her day, but she'd never attempted anything as complicated as the liquid solutions. "And we both know Ard won't be any help there."

"Well, hopefully, Motherwatch transforms on the first detonation and you don't have to worry about it."

*Or hopefully, you and San will be back by then.* Quarrah didn't say it out loud. Raek was obviously leaving her the formula for a worst-case scenario.

"So you're trying to get that dragon Moonsick?" San said, still hung up on it. "How are you storing her?"

"In Stasis Grit," answered Quarrah.

"Isn't that going to be a problem?" San checked.

"Seems like a bigger problem if she's *not* in Stasis," Raek pointed out.

"But how do you expect her to react during the Moon Passing?" San probed. "I feel like I'm pointing out the obvious, but a creature in Stasis isn't supposed to change in any way."

"Actually, I kept a Moonsick man in Stasis a few cycles ago," said Quarrah. "He still progressed through the phases."

"You *what*?" San turned to her with a horrified expression.

Quarrah shrugged. "It was for a client." As if that would be a reasonable explanation.

"It's something we already discussed with Ard," Raek said. "Quarrah's experience shows us that Moonsickness cuts through the Stasis. We're counting on that to work for Motherwatch."

"How do you plan on getting to the summit?" Quarrah asked.

Raek dropped an entire keg of Health Grit into his pack. "I know a guide."

"Nemery? I thought you said Ard burned that bridge."

"He did," said Raek. "But luckily, I wasn't on it."

～

*This will save so many lives, but I'm doing it just as much for myself. In time, I'm sure my arrogance will be remembered as selflessness. But those who really knew me will see through it.*

# CHAPTER

# 28

Nemery peered through the trees, overlooking the wreckage—two broken Drift crates, a handful of collapsed tents, a smattering of backpacks strewn through the tall grasses of Bo's Glen. She was especially proud of the deep talon gouges she'd raked into the soil and the goat entrails she'd splattered against the side of the crate.

The destruction looked good, but Nemery was starting to worry that the cultists weren't even going to notice the scene.

"Their guide should have stopped them by now," Nemery whispered to Mohdek.

"You use the term *guide* too loosely," was his reply. "This one seems even less capable than the last."

They had quickly noticed that none of the large summiting parties had hired true professionals. But that didn't surprise Nemery. Who would be willing to lead entire families to the top of Pekal on a one-way trip to Moonsickness?

The guides were obviously fellow cultists with some Pekal experience. Probably ex-Harvesters. Maybe even poachers. Still, the guiding got easier with every passing group, trampling a veritable highway up the slopes.

By Nemery's estimation, there were eighty cultists in this party, with at least fifteen of them younger than her—some of them little enough to be carried in packs or on top of Drift crates. Bo's Glen was a common camping site for the first night out of New Vantage, but this party was moving so slow that it had taken them two days to reach it.

"Here we go," muttered Mohdek. Halfway across the meadow, Nemery saw the guide hold up his hand, bringing the procession to a grinding halt. Packs were slipping from shoulders and people were collapsing into the grass, grateful that their leader had called a break. But Nemery could see the concern on the faces of those in the front of the group as they drew closer to the first crumpled tent.

"You better get into position," said Nemery. "Signal me when you're ready." Mohdek nodded with a grin, moving off through the trees.

The guide and a handful of others were now spreading upward through Bo's Glen, examining the wreckage that Nemery and Mohdek had put out. The cultists' anxiety was palpable, especially once they recognized the brand on the gear, matching the same supplier as the equipment they carried. The tension began to ripple through the large crowd, even managing to bring some of the laziest-looking people back to their feet.

She heard Mohdek's whistle through the trees, easily mistakable for the chirping of a small bird. He was in position. Now it was her turn to signal back.

Nemery crawled forward, pulling aside a broadleaf branch to reveal the shiny mouthpiece of her Caller instrument. It was disguised well, even though she hadn't built a full hut. That had seemed like overkill. Staying hidden from the eyes of eighty fright-ened cultists would be much easier than going unnoticed by one determined dragon.

Nemery reached up and began to prime the little box. She loved the subtle rattle as she pulled the cords in a steady, rhythmic fash-ion. She had decided on *Territorial Bull*, the same Call she had used when trying to frighten Motherwatch. It was really her only choice, since any other Call would risk bringing a curious dragon down on them. And Homeland knew she wasn't going Wilder Far on these people.

Nemery drew a deep breath and placed her lips on the mouth-piece. The brass buzzed, her whole face vibrating as she unleashed the impressive sound.

Twenty yards to her side, there was a tremendous rustle in the trees. Like a gale force, it bent trunks and broke limbs, sending them careening toward the cultists in a maelstrom of leaves and twigs. This was accompanied by a blast of heat that even Nemery could feel from her position in the trees. She squinted one eye against it, pealing on with every bit of breath she had.

The cultists were screaming and running back the way they'd come. The guide and a few others had drawn guns, taking blind potshots into the woods ahead. Nemery heard one of the Roller balls crack into the stump in front of her, chipping up splinters.

*See, Moh*, she thought. *I told you it was a good idea to barricade.*

Her breath ran out, but she sucked in another, putting it through the instrument and feeling the rumble of the great horn all the way down to her toes.

There were a lot of things that didn't add up about their little trick, but Nemery was counting on fear and ignorance to overlook them. For example, a bull dragon would rarely, if ever, cry twice in a row like that. And as for Mohdek's part, that was pure theat-rics. She supposed the combination of Void and Heat Grit—both of which they had stolen from a previous group of cultists—was meant to represent the hot breath of a dragon. But if that were so, how could the dragon bellow a cry at the same time it was breathing heat? And Nemery was banking on no one sticking around long enough to realize that the dragon's breath seemed never to waver for a full ten minutes.

Sure enough, the relentlessness of their deception was working. The guide and front guards stood their ground only until the bulk of the cultists had made their retreat. Then they, too, began backing away in haste.

Nemery sounded the instrument one last time, blowing until the last person had moved out of Bo's Glen and disappeared from sight. She knelt back, sitting on her heels, flapping her lips to shake out the tingling sensation leftover from the instrument.

"Just the person I was looking for," said a deep voice from behind her.

Nemery lunged to the side, drawing her dagger from a thigh sheath. She whirled to face the intruder, but she didn't even need to bring up her blade.

"Raekon?" She relaxed at the sight of him, but only a little. The big man was wearing an overstuffed pack with a crossbow dangling from it. There was a short sword on his hip, the type commonly used to clear underbrush when hiking off the trail. His bald head was bare, and his sleeveless shirt showed his massive biceps.

"How did you...?" Nemery sputtered. "Why are you...?"

"I enjoyed your little performance," he said. "Sent those Bloodeye-worshipers running with their tails between their legs. But I know a ruse when I see one."

"You were with them?" she asked.

"Only for a little while," he said. "We caught up to them an hour or two ago, and we were just hanging around long enough to ask if any of them knew where I could find someone called Salafan."

Nemery stiffened at his use of the word *we*. "He's with you?" she asked.

"If by 'he,' you mean Ardor Benn," said Raek, "then no. I'm with a Mixer named San Green. An old friend of Lomaya's."

"I know the name. Did Lomaya come, too?" Nemery checked.

"It's just San and me." Raek slipped his pack off his shoulders and shrugged to stretch, lines of sweat marking his gray shirt where the straps of the pack had been. "Lomaya...she didn't make it."

What? She had been so brave! So strong! It was hard to imagine that the young woman had bested Pekal only to fall in Beripent. "What happened?"

"Garifus Floc," Raek answered.

"I'm sorry to hear it." She tried to shrug off the heavy feeling. "Where's your companion?"

"Soon as I decided that was a fake dragon Call, we slipped away from the group and made our way around the sides of the glen. I sent San along the north edge so we'd be sure not to miss you. He should be here any second."

"What tipped you off?" Nemery gestured to the glen.

"Well, those weren't *human* guts spattered on the side of that Drift crate," he answered. "So unless there's a dragon with an exclusive taste for goat, I'm guessing nobody actually died here. That, and the apparent lack of carcasses."

"The cultists didn't seem to notice," said Nemery. "Of course, regular folk tend to think that an attacking dragon eats every scrap of every person in sight."

Raek glanced through the trees in the direction that the group had fled. "Not sure what you were hoping to accomplish, though. They'll just find another way up."

She shook her head. "Any guide worth their salt knows that there's an alternate route just half a mile back. We only need them to get to the fork in the trail."

"Then what?" asked Raek.

"Regulator Chief Lampar has a regiment waiting there," said Nemery. "Once the cultists come into sight, she'll have them."

Raek grinned. "A trap. How'd you arrange that?"

"A fleet of Reggies sailed into New Vantage just two days ago," she said. "Moh and I were there when they started rounding up the cultists and packing them onto their ships by the hundreds. Taking them in shackles if they didn't go peacefully. This group struck out as quick as they could, and Chief Lampar was pretty chapped that she couldn't get permission from the higher-ups to go on a chase across the mountainside. Moh and I offered our services to herd them back into reach. We're hoping this should be the last of them."

"Should be," Raek agreed. "The queen herself dispatched that Reggie fleet. Completely closed down Pekal until Garifus Floc could be dealt with and—"

"Garifus is *here*?" Nemery cut him off.

Raek gave a gesture that was part nod and part shrug. "At least he made a public announcement that he was on his way."

"Well, he didn't come through New Vantage," she said. "Ednes Holcatch would have told me if she'd laid eyes on a bunch of oversized people with glass heads. They must have sailed around to one of the other harbors."

"They don't need harbors," Raek said gravely. "The Glassminds are stronger than before."

"Stronger?" she croaked. Was there no end to their powers? "What do you mean?"

"It's complicated," said Raek. "In a nutshell, they have changed the way they perceive time."

"Huh?"

He rubbed his chin. "They can use Visitant Grit to create... portals. Once they step through, they can move through parallel timelines and pop out anywhere they want in the world."

Nemery blinked hard. "I don't..." What was he talking about? "They can... appear out of thin air?"

"Basically," he replied. "Although I thought the Glassminds

would have appeared here." He jabbed a thumb at the Glen. "To be with the cultists."

"They're probably with the first caravan," she whispered.

"You mean there are more of them?"

Nemery nodded, discouragement clouding her face. "There are three groups on the mountainside already. Mohdek and I have been waiting outside New Vantage for days, hitting the caravans as soon as they set out. We turned four of them back to regroup. I assume the Reggies have gathered them up by now."

Raek didn't bother to hide how impressed he was. "Same tactic every time?" He glanced at the Caller instrument.

"Actually, this was new," she replied. "Our usual method is to wear them down. Steal and destroy their provisions until the going looks so bleak that they turn back to recuperate. We poisoned the third group, but that made a mess of the mountain."

"Sparks!" he exclaimed. "There were children in those caravans."

She held up a hand. "It was just a drib of Nightsure extract. Nothing serious. And they were less than a day out. Made them miserable enough to head back to New Vantage in a hurry. Anyway, between the three groups that got past us, Mohdek and I estimate that there are close to two hundred people already on their way up."

"Let's make that two hundred and two," Raek said. "San and I are heading to the summit. And I was hoping, just *hoping*, that you and Mohdek might be willing to—"

"Flames, no!" She turned away from him, her face growing hot. "I'm never going up there again. Certainly not for you!"

Raek scratched his chin. "I'm sorry, did *I* do something wrong?"

"Motherwatch," she whispered.

"The dragon?"

"Ardor took her," Nemery said. "She had a hatchling."

Raek sighed loudly. "Ard makes a lot of stupid decisions. Especially when I'm not around to keep him in check."

"What's he doing now?" She didn't want to know, but she had to.

"Oh, I imagine he's probably pacing the floor, scheming up all they ways he could get back at me once I get home."

"What?" Nemery risked a glance at him. "He didn't send you?"

"Definitely not," said Raek. "In fact, I had to push him down and knock him out just to get away."

"You?" Nemery said in disbelief. Everything she'd ever heard about Ardor Benn and the Short Fuse spoke of unbreakable friendship. "Are you lying to me?"

He raised his hands. "No. Not I. 'Tis the honest truth."

She felt like he was being forthright, but there was obviously more to this story.

"In fact," Raek continued, "nothing would spite Ard more than if you were to guide me to the summit."

She felt her heart beat a little faster at the thought of vengeance against Ardor Benn. Still, she couldn't shake a lingering feeling that Raek might be manipulating her to Ardor's benefit.

Gratefully, her reply was postponed by the sound of a twig snapping in the trees. Nemery and Raek both turned, the big man putting a hand on the hilt of his short sword.

"Back away from her," Mohdek called to Raek. Sparks! He had a young man in a vise grip, a long knife pressed to his throat.

"Oh, good," Raek said, letting go of his sword. "You met San Green."

"It's all right, Moh," Nemery said in Trothian. "You remember Ardor Benn's companion, Raekon Dorrel?"

Mohdek lowered his knife, but he didn't release his hold on San. The young man looked terrified. He was probably just a couple of years older than Nemery, but there was a softness to his features that Pekal had taken from her a long time ago.

"What are they doing here?" Mohdek asked her.

"They want us to guide them to the summit," she replied, their conversation still in Trothian.

Mohdek scoffed. "What kind of saps does Ardor Benn think we—"

"Raek said they came on their own," Nemery interrupted him. "Against Ardor's wishes."

"And you believe him?" Mohdek asked.

Nemery nodded. "I do."

Mohdek finally let go of San, pushing him forward. The man stumbled under the weight of his backpack, but didn't go down.

"You're the one who rescued my friend," San said, staring straight at Nemery. She couldn't tell if it was a question or a statement.

"Lomaya Vans," Nemery affirmed. "She had a lot of good things to say about you." She paused. "Raek told me what happened. I'm sorry."

"Garifus has to be stopped," San hissed.

"That's why you're here?" Mohdek asked him. "For revenge?"

"I don't know what I could do against someone like Garifus." San blinked away tears, steeling himself as he gestured at Raek. "I'm here with him. I figure what he's doing is pretty important if he was willing to turn on his partner for it."

Ah. So San Green corroborated Raek's story. Either that made it true, or the two of them had discussed it before entering Bo's Glen. But she was inclined to believe him even more than Raekon. San didn't have the look of a liar about him.

"How do you intend to defeat Garifus once you catch up to him?" Mohdek asked.

"I'm with San on that one," said Raek. "I'm not sure we can hold a candle to him. Garifus has plans after his followers transform. He blabbed all about them on the docks in Beripent. And he's more powerful than ever, now that he's tinkered with time itself."

"What are you talking about?" Nemery shook her head.

"It's a lot to wrap your head around," he said. "Luckily, we have several days of hiking ahead of us. I should be able to catch you up on everything by the time we reach the summit."

"We're not going to the summit," Nemery insisted.

"Garifus is planning to kill the dragons," Raek said bluntly. "That's his big plan. Destroy the dragons and everyone in the Greater Chain gets Moonsick."

"Which will allow him to transform *everyone* with massive controlled detonations of Transformation Grit," added San.

A sudden wave of terror gripped Nemery's insides. It was the kind of fear that quickly turned to panic if left unchecked. The kind she had felt first on this island, when that branch had punctured her leg during the dragon fight years ago. She'd felt it again when her Harvesting party had been taken by Sovereign soldiers, and again when their ship had been scuttled off the Dronodanian coast.

She glanced at Mohdek, finding the comfort and strength she needed to control that terror before it transformed. But even he looked shaken, his blue face blanched, dark vibrating eyes staring out through the trees.

The idea of the entire world overcome with Moonsickness was upsetting enough, but Nemery was stuck on what would have to happen first.

"Nobody's going to touch my dragons," she whispered.

"Then I assume you'll be heading up?" Raek asked.

"Fine," she said after a moment of final deliberation. "We hit the cultist camps along the way. The fewer that make it to the top, the fewer the Glassminds. The better chance the dragons will have at defending against them." She stepped between Raek and San, picking up her bow and quiver from the spot where she'd leaned them against a tree trunk. "I expect the two of you to keep up."

"I can go hours when I'm full of Heg," Raek said.

Nemery shared a concerned glance with Mohdek. They were becoming regular summit guides at this point. First a desperate father, and now a Health Grit addict?

Raek picked up his pack. "Lead the way, Salafan."

~

*I have been a mighty dragon, commanding respect from everyone in the room. But inside I often feel like little more than a Karvan lizard with claws of thin foil.*

# CHAPTER

# 29

Quarrah sprang awake with a gasp.

No, this wasn't waking up. It was something less natural. Coming to.

Stasis Grit.

She was still sitting on the couch in the *Be'Igoth*, but...what the blazes had happened here? The place was completely ransacked! Cabinets were open, some of the doors broken off their hinges, contents scattered across the floor. One of Raek's Grit Mixing tables was completely overturned, expensive equipment bent and ruined.

The wooden floor in front of her had been hacked apart, boards splintered to make a jagged hole to the hidden bath below. Across from her, the green armchair remained upright with the trapdoor latched. Ard was still seated there, his legs crossed, hands resting loosely on the arms.

Had he done this? At least he hadn't run. Quarrah wouldn't have blamed him after being cooped up in the soakhouse for a full week.

But Ard probably realized there was nowhere to go. Every Regulator in the city was looking for them, and there wasn't enough time to reach Pekal's summit with only two days until the Moon Passing.

"What happened?" she asked softly into the quiet room. Based on the waning of the Light Grit, she guessed she'd been out for at least half an hour. Ard didn't respond. Sparks, he didn't even move!

"Ard!" she said a little more forcefully. She leaned forward, squinting through the dimness just in time to see a Grit cloud wink out around Ard's head. He gasped, lurching up from the armchair and nearly tumbling headfirst into the hole in the floor.

"Hedge!" he barked. "I saw him! He was here!" Ard spun around, scanning the wrecked room for their enemy.

"I think he's long gone," Quarrah said. The question was, why hadn't the King Poacher killed them? He'd obviously been successful at taking them by surprise.

Ard yanked up on the armchair, releasing the trapdoor. Quarrah followed him down, feet crunching on broken glass as she landed in the empty bath. A couple of very dim Prolonged Light Grit detonations still illuminated the area, showing the full amount of damage Hedge Marsool had done.

Packaged sawdust from their Grit storage boxes was littered across the floor, pieces of broken clay in the mix. Shards of shattered glass twinkled in the low light. Some of the boxes had been reduced to kindling. Others lay upended or tilted on their sides.

It had been bold of Hedge to trash their Grit supply like this, considering that a single spark could have sent the whole *Be'Igoth* up in a ball of flames. That was the very reason Raek had always insisted on storing the Slagstone fragments far away from the prepared, packed Grit.

As she surveilled the damage, Quarrah's heart stopped when she realized what all this meant. She crossed to the few boxes that were still intact, scanning them, pushing them aside, hoping that the worst had not happened. But Ard's attention was elsewhere.

"Thank the Homeland!" he cried from across the empty bath. "He didn't find the books."

Why would Hedge care about those stupid books? They'd been a way for Ard to pass the time, locked away in the empty bath, but did he really think they were that important? The past had already happened. Why did it matter if Ard wrote down every little detail of how it was *supposed* to happen?

Quarrah finally saw what she'd been looking for. And it made her heart plummet.

"The Transformation Grit," she whispered. The empty storage box was in her hands, one side broken from being hurled across the bath. The four vials Raek had left behind for Motherwatch were gone— either shattered to bits or stolen by the King Poacher.

"Why?" Ard muttered, moving to her side. "Why would Raek tell Hedge to do this?"

"Raek?" Quarrah cried. "You're seriously blaming Raek for this?"

"He's going to be the Glassmind that sends the Urgings," Ard explained. "He must have gone off the books, because I'm definitely not going to write about this."

"Just because you're Urging him doesn't make Hedge Marsool your puppet," Quarrah said. "He can still act on his own." Why did there have to be time travel? The world was complicated enough when time moved in only one direction.

"It'll work out, though, right?" Ard was trying to calm himself now. "We know it has to work out because...it already happened."

"What about Motherwatch?" Quarrah dropped the empty box of Transformation Grit. "We don't know how that turns out."

Ard clenched his jaw. "Tell me again why the only two people who know how to make that stuff literally took a hike?"

"They're not the only ones." Quarrah sucked in a hopeful breath at the thought. "Raek left the formula." She rose suddenly, jumping to catch the dangling armchair and hoisting herself out of the large bath.

*Please be there*, she thought frantically, realizing anew the awful state of disarray in the upper portion of the *Be'Igoth*. Gratefully, the cabinet where she had put the written formula was still standing. Quarrah nearly ripped the small door off its hinges, reaching blindly to the uppermost shelf. Her fingers brushed the envelope and she pulled it down, hands trembling as she withdrew the single piece of paper.

Praise the Homeland—or the gods...Or whatever deserved praising. The formula for Transformation Grit, scribed in Raek's careful hand, had gone untouched by Hedge and his goons.

Glancing over the instructions, Quarrah realized that this was a task far out of her comfort zone. Using scales to measure the powdered Grit was simple, but steeping this list of herbs and bark just long enough for the liquid to reach a balance level of negative flat five...Where was she even supposed to find these ingredients?

She turned her attention back to the Mixing table lying on its side, some of the jars and canisters having rolled clear across the room.

Powdered dragon teeth.

That was the source material for Transformation Grit, and Raek had said they had only a little left. Her heart lurching in her chest, she picked up the nearest canister, checking the label chalked onto the side.

COMMON STONE: PROLONGING GRIT

She dropped that canister, a mere dusting of powder still inside, and moved to the next one on the floor.

COPPER: HEAT GRIT

QUARTZITE: COMPOUNDING GRIT

MARBLE: GATHER GRIT

Her eye caught the canister across the room, the label only half visible. But the letters she could see were enough.

DRAGON TOOTH: TRANSFORMATION GRIT

She dropped to one knee, anxiously reaching out to pick up the lidless container, tipping it upright to peer inside.

Empty.

She tapped the bottom of the dented metal canister against the floor, hoping to gather what little might remain. But there was only enough to make her fingertips dusty as she swiped them desperately along the inside.

A sudden hopelessness reached out of the empty canister, seizing her by the throat and making it hard to swallow. There would be no more Metamorphosis Grit. In two nights, Motherwatch would get Moonsick and they would have no way to complete the transformation. She would become a mad beast, filled with a violent rage like Grotenisk of old.

"Quarrah," Ard whispered.

In her haste to find the formula, she hadn't even seen him crawl up through the trapdoor. Now he was standing beside the *Be'Igoth* exit, his face drained of color. A single piece of paper was staked to the inside of the door.

She stood slowly, the empty dragon tooth canister hanging limply at her side. There was writing on the page, but without her spectacles, she had no hope of reading it from this distance. She moved closer to Ard, who seemed to be reading it again and again as if expecting the message to change.

Finally, he read the words aloud. "I know where you're keeping her."

Ard reached up and pulled the small knife from the door, the page fluttering to the floor. He turned to Quarrah, face lined with distress.

"Hedge is going after Motherwatch."

The thundering hooves of their stolen horses mimicked the relentless pounding of thoughts in Ard's head. They left Beripent on the southern road, making all haste for the Pale Tors.

How had Hedge Marsool discovered Motherwatch's hiding place? Ard hadn't even made it that far in the instruction books he was writing. If it was an Urging from the future, it wouldn't have come from Raek. Was another Glassmind trying to manipulate Hedge to work *against* him?

Urgings aside, Jaig Jasperson could have spilled the beans to the King Poacher. Ard had never trusted that double-dealing middleman. There would be a steep price to pay if anything happened to that dragon.

Well outside of town, they passed the abandoned granary where Ard had once posed as a ringmaster for a Karvan lizard fight. His days of such straightforward, entertaining ruses seemed long behind him, replaced with little more than an ongoing struggle to stay ahead and stay alive.

Ardor Benn felt his life unraveling, relationships too badly frayed to salvage with a simple stitch. He was tired, but too stubborn to sleep. Hoarse, but opposed to whispering. He didn't like what he was doing—or even what he had become. Part of him screamed in frustration, *Why won't you change?* But he was incapable of that. Incapable, or unwilling.

He needed a transformation.

If he were honest with himself, this, above all other reasons, was why he had been so desperate to go to the summit. Maybe Garifus's claims of perfection had gotten into his head, because Ard felt limited by his current state. As if his mind had already reached capacity, but he didn't know if its contents were good enough.

It was why, deep down, he was no longer mad at Raek for taking his place. His friend's discontentment in life was as visible as the scarred metal protruding from his chest. Even as obvious as that should have been, Ard had missed it, caught up in his own deeper dissatisfactions.

He was no longer mad at Quarrah for locking him in the *Be'Igoth*, either. He had fumed for the first three days, trapped under the floor, surviving on stale rations. But his perspective had shifted by the time Quarrah had let him up. He understood why his companions had done what they'd done.

Ard led his horse off the road, slowing to a walk as they took a dusty single-file trail leading into the Pale Tors. The area ahead was an undeveloped section of rolling hills punctuated by crags of white rocks. Not true mountains—those only existed on Pekal, but the Pale Tors area was some of the highest terrain in the Greater Chain.

Trails were well worn through the Tors, but they weren't typically traveled by the lawful types. It was an area known among the criminal networks as a good place to stash things or take shelter when the heat was on from the Regulation.

"Keep an eye out," Ard cautioned. "Jasperson's king of the Tors now."

"Just because he has a dragon?" Quarrah asked. "I should hope he's been keeping that discreet."

"It's not the dragon that's put him on top," said Ard. "It's what I paid him to store her here. Raek said Jasperson hired enough thugs to drive out the competition. By now, he'll have claimed their stashes and sold the goods to generate even more wealth. See?"

Ard pointed ahead as a squat, surly-looking Lander slipped out from behind the nearest rock, a pair of Rollers held at the ready. On either side of the trail, Ard saw the glint of metal as more guns nosed through cracks between rocks. Evidence of Jasperson's new empire.

"This here area be closed to common traffic," the man on the trail said.

"Glad to hear that," Ard replied. "Because my companion and I are anything but common. We're here to see Vethrey."

The man's demeanor changed at hearing the dragon's name. "Leave the horses."

"Vethrey?" Quarrah whispered as she dismounted.

"That's the password we've been using with Jasperson," Ard explained.

"Should you really be so straightforward with something so important?"

"Straightforward?" Ard cried. "It's the Trothian translation of a dragon's name that a girl and her boyfriend made up in the wilds of Pekal."

"It's the fulfillment of prophesy," hissed Quarrah.

"Well, I didn't know that at the time I used it as a password," said Ard. "But it's not like people are going to recognize it."

Quarrah huffed, lashing her reins around a protruding nub of rock.

They followed their guide through the craggy landscape for at least twenty minutes. After their third turn, Ard was hopelessly lost and stopped paying any attention to their route. Especially since Quarrah was beside him. He was sure she was marking the path in her mind, noting how to retrace their steps and get out.

"Jas!" shouted their guide. "Ya gots company what knows the password!"

A hut came into view, a series of canvas tarps strung between rocks, supported by a framework of timbers. A man was exiting the structure through a tent flap. Though it had been years since Ard had seen him, he recognized Jaig Jasperson immediately.

He was shirtless, and Ard noticed that the dark skin of his chest was marred with a fresh tattoo, still too scabby to recognize the design. The man had prominent ears, and both lobes were pierced, golden studs peeking out through a mess of curly black hair. His feet were bare, but there was a pair of simple shoes in his hand as if he'd been in the act of putting them on when his name was called.

Jaig's face lit up when he saw Ard, and he broke into a good-natured chuckle. "Well, if it isn't the grand founder of my little kingdom in the rocks," he said. "Ardor Benn!"

"Good to see you again, Jaig, old boy," Ard greeted him. He resisted the urge to draw a gun and demand to know if Hedge Marsool had been around. But that would only tip his hand. Better to play this off as a routine check-in. At least it would give Ard a chance to read the situation.

"How's my dragon?" he asked.

"Oh, she's an absolute sweetheart." Jaig gingerly stepped over the rough ground toward them. "Sleeping so sound, half my guys are convinced she's dead."

Well, that was a good sign.

"I've positioned somebody at the cave around the clock," Jaig continued, "smashing those vials just like the Short Fuse showed us."

Ard studied Jasperson's eyes. There was no trace of a lie, but that didn't mean all was well. Sounded like there were plenty of others in Jaig's employ who could have sold out to Hedge.

"I want to see her," Ard said.

Jasperson nodded. "Of course." He reached down and slipped into the shoes he'd been holding. "Watch the hut, Basgid," he said to their stout guide. Then he set off down a worn footpath, waving for Ard and Quarrah to follow.

"Has anyone else come to see her?" Ard asked when the three of them were alone.

"Short Fuse was here to check in over a week ago," he answered. "Been quiet since then. Hey…What's that I heard about you getting nabbed by the Regulation a spell back?"

Ard shrugged, putting on a puzzled expression. "I'm here, aren't I?"

Jaig chortled. "Blune said there were a thousand Reggies piling on the docks to take you down. And some of them glass-headed folk…Like the old Prime Isless."

"Only a thousand Reggies?" Ard said. "And you believed it?" He was quick to turn the conversation away from the Glassminds. Jaig already knew too much, having seen Gloristar when she'd moved Motherwatch into his cave.

"Now, I didn't say I believed it," Jasperson defended.

"What would you do if I had been arrested?" Ard asked. "If Short Fuse and I both got nabbed, what would you do with the dragon?"

Jaig ran a hand through his messy hair, breathing out slowly like he might exhale the right answer. "Suppose I'd wait for word from you," he said. "Even in a Reggie Stockade, I figure you'd have a way to get a message out."

"That's not what I'm asking," pressed Ard. "Kill her? Or set her free?"

"Are those my only two options?" he asked.

"Can you think of another?" Quarrah chimed.

"Could sell her," said Jaig. "Parts from that beauty would be worth a blazing fortune."

The mere fact that he was suggesting it made Ard think he wasn't in talks with the King Poacher. It took a daringly confident person to talk openly about things they were trying to hide. Ardor Benn did it all the time, but he didn't peg Jaig Jasperson for that caliber of liar.

"Let her go, I guess," the man finally answered, glancing back at Ard. He knew the answer was less a reflection of how Jaig actually felt, and more indicative of what he thought Ard wanted to hear.

Jasperson led them across a marshy low spot where a freshwater stream cut its way through the Pale Tors. Halfway up the steep hill ahead, Ard saw the opening to the cave.

He'd been here before, many years ago. But even if he had remembered it better, the cave's entrance had been drastically altered to accommodate contraband as large as Motherwatch.

Once, the natural opening had barely been large enough to fit a standard-size Drift crate, but now it appeared as a massive hole in the hillside, some thirty feet wide by fifteen feet high. Broken rock from the Blast Grit had been piled up around the entrance to form something of a rugged patio, a few scrubby trees hanging above the hole.

"Tajis!" called Jaig. "We're coming up!"

A lone Trothian guard scrambled into action at the sound of his name, hastily strapping on a gun and Grit belt. Not the best reaction from the person who was supposed to be guarding the sole hope of humankind.

They moved quickly up the grassy incline, Jaig leading them onto the pile of rocks. Now that they were up here, Ard saw that the guard's post was adorned with a chair, a couple of cushions, several blankets and animal pelts, and even a little canvas awning to give shelter from rain and sun.

"All quiet up here," Tajis reported to Jaig. The Trothian's vibrating eyes looked a little bloodshot, and Ard didn't miss the half-empty jug of liquor beside the chair.

"She better be in there," Quarrah said to Ard. "I mean, really in there, this time." She moved past Tajis, who glanced nervously at Jasperson. The man assured the guard with a nod and the wave of his hand.

Ard stepped across the rocky landing to join her, holding his breath as he peered inside. His anticipation didn't have much time to build, because Motherwatch was there. *Right* there. He was shocked by how close she lay inside the natural cavern.

"You're lucky she fit," Quarrah pointed out.

It was a fair observation. Jaig Jasperson's cave had been bigger in Ard's memory. It was a mere fraction of Baroness Lavfa's cavern beneath Helizon.

Motherwatch's folded wings rose almost all the way to the cave's jagged opening. Her tail and long neck were both curled to fit, leaving her head facing the exit. It would be an easy escape if she came out of the Stasis cloud that surrounded around her head. Luckily, the same oversized shackles and chains that had been used for the Illusion in the baroness's cave were clamped onto all four of the dragon's legs, her neck, and tail.

"Tajis," Jaig scolded. Ard turned to see what was the matter. Jasperson was pointing at a large hourglass standing on a rock under the awning. The top chamber was nearly empty, and Ard knew exactly what that meant—Time for more Stasis Grit. It was a good sign that Jasperson was coming down so strict on his man. They had no way of knowing that Raek had set the hourglass nearly ten minutes shorter than the potency of the Prolonged Stasis Grit. This allowed for a slight margin of error, because Homeland help them all if that Stasis cloud completely burned out.

Tajis retreated to the covered area, pulling back a sheepskin to reveal a small wooden box. Raek had cut circles in the top to hold the vials of Stasis Grit upright. Tajis selected one and pushed his way between Ard and Quarrah.

"We do it just like this," he muttered, leaning into the cave's spacious opening. Ard glimpsed a rope ladder descending into the dimness, but Tajis didn't need it to reach the dragon. Taking careful aim, he hurled the vial, striking the mammoth beast somewhere on the nose. Ard heard the glass shatter and saw the sparks as a fresh Stasis cloud surrounded Motherwatch's horned head.

How long could they keep her like this? The Moon Passing was fast approaching, but what did it matter? Without Metamorphosis Grit, there would be no cure to her Moonsickness. Motherwatch's only hope relied on the safe return of Raek and San. Quarrah had said they'd taken two vials.

Tajis turned away from the cave. But his grin instantly faded as he looked over Ard's shoulder. Without hesitation, Ard spun, drawing a knife and whirling on Jaig Jasperson. He ducked past the bare-chested man, coming up behind him with the blade pressed to his throat.

Jasperson made no move to escape, arms limp to both sides without so much as a weapon drawn. "Ashes and soot," he cursed. "Did I do something wrong?"

"Ard..." Quarrah pointed toward the two opposing hillsides on the other side of the stream they had crossed. He saw the problem at once—six Trothians scattered across the slopes, sheltered behind crags of pale rocks. Each had a Fielder trained on the cave's opening, ready to fill Ard and Quarrah with lead.

"I don't know what you're trying to do here," Ard said in Jaig's ear, "but I need you to call off your men."

Jasperson was breathing heavily, his bare shoulder sweaty in Ard's grip. "Problem, Mister Ardor. Those aren't my men."

"*Eyoo-hoo!*" called a voice from below.

Keeping Jaig in tow, Ard stepped forward, peering down the slope. Hedge Marsool stood calf-deep in the creek, the hem of his long cape pulled downstream with the current.

"What's he doing here, Jaig?" Ard hissed.

"I don't even know who that is!" he replied. At Ard's side, Quarrah was clutching one of her Grit bags.

Hedge limped forward, stepping out of the water and starting up the trail toward them.

"Hedge Marsool, the King Poacher," Ard whispered. "Does that ring a bell?"

"Him?" Jasperson cried. "Flames...I haven't seen him since the accident. You got to let me go, Ardor." Now that Jaig knew who was coming toward them, he dared to wriggle in Ard's grasp just a little.

"Not until I know you have no part in this," Ard replied. And even if Jaig was being honest, Ard wasn't sure he wanted to give up his human shield with all those Fielders pointed in their direction.

"Jaig Jasperson!" Hedge called, taking his time coming up the hill. "Quite the royal setup you've got here in the Tors. You've come a long ways from sitting on guns and Grit. I hear you're storing a beastie now."

That didn't sound like a greeting between two men working together...

"Just trying to make a living," squeaked Jaig. "Opportunity came along, and I took it. Didn't know you were involved."

"*Involved?*" cried Hedge. "That sweet sow is rightfully mine. I used these double-crossing whelps to pinch her from Pekal for me. You know what she's worth, Jasperson."

"How'd you know we were here?" Ard asked. "And don't tell me it was a *feeling*."

"No, not this time." Hedge finally arrived onto the uneven rock landing. "Somebody came squeaking to me a few days back. Told me that the dragon's escape from the cave in Helizon had been as fake as a stone-cut Ashing."

"Who?" Ard asked. Who even had access to that information?

Hedge suddenly stooped over, his already deformed body imitating a hunchback. "I think you called him Pincher." He chuckled. "You shouldn't trust the street scum."

Elbrig Taut.

Ard let go of Jaig Jasperson as a wave of nausea passed over him. He looked to Quarrah for support, but she was staring across the Pale Tors at the Trothian marksmen.

Not Elbrig and Cinza…But then, Ard shouldn't have been surprised. Betrayal begot betrayal. And by the sound of it, the disguise managers had slipped through the Regulators' grasp. Ard should never have given their names to the queen. He should've listened to Quarrah and tried to negotiate another way out of the palace dungeon.

"That sorry beggar didn't know where you had taken the dragon," Hedge continued. "But it wasn't hard to follow you here."

"The note on the *Be'Igoth* door . . ." Ard muttered. "It was a lie?"

"A little ruse for the ruse artist." Hedge winked his single eye. "My boys and I were hiding outside Tofar's Salts. You stormed out in a hurry."

"How did you get past my security at the edge of the Tors?" Jasperson asked.

"You mean those pubescent rats hiding in the rocks?" said Hedge. "Everybody's got a price for the King Poacher, son." He wiped his spike hand against the leg of his pants. "Pincher sold me information for a wee dozen Ashings. Pirel Gulwar let me use the Puckering Lizard for a keg of Visitant Grit. And the folks at the millinery—"

"Hold on," Ard cut him off. "You *paid* Pirel Gulwar?" That little weasel had said Hedge had threatened him. "In *Visitant Grit*?"

Hedge shrugged. "We had no shortage of it when we found the Islehood's shell. Half a dozen kegs already processed and packed. Ready for a worthy detonation."

"Half a dozen kegs..." Ard muttered. "You left it all for the Glassminds?" Maybe that's what they had absorbed... The detonation Garifus had manipulated on the docks.

"Sparks, boy. You take me for a charity?"

"You took it," Ard accused.

Hedge grinned. "One for the barkeep. Two for me. The rest for the Glassminds. Pleasure doing business."

"Where are the kegs you took?" Ard asked. Hedge wouldn't have been fool enough to attempt a detonation already.

"Don't you fret over that," said the King Poacher. "I've got them squirreled away for a rainy day."

Hedge looked past Ard and Quarrah, calling out to Tajis in Trothian. The guard nodded vigorously, terrified. Hedge said something else and Tajis replied. Then Hedge waved his hand and the Trothian man took off running down the hillside.

"Tajis!" barked Jasperson.

"He works for me now." Hedge limped over to Jaig. "And so will everyone else in the Pale Tors by the time our conversation is over."

Jasperson held up his hands. "Listen, I can sell you the dragon for—"

Hedge brought up his spike arm, skewering Jaig Jasperson through the stomach. The shirtless man opened his mouth, producing a squelching sound not unlike a boot in the mud.

Ard thrust for Hedge's exposed back, but the King Poacher turned sharply. He brought his spike around in a defensive swipe, spraying Ard with a line of Jasperson's blood as he turned aside the incoming knife. In the same fluid movement, he brought up his good hand, a Roller aiming at Ard's forehead.

"Not a twitch from you, dearie," Hedge snapped at Quarrah. She had retreated right up against the cave's mouth, arm raised, clutching her Grit bag. "Why would I settle on a price with Jasperson when the dragon is rightfully mine?"

"It's two against one, Hedge," Ard pointed out.

"I have half a dozen marksmen with a clear line of sight on you from any angle," the King Poacher countered.

"And their shots are useless the minute Quarrah throws that Barrier Grit around us," reasoned Ard. He actually had no idea if that was what her little bag contained, but he needed to keep Hedge talking.

"Two of my men have crossbows," said Hedge, "bolts tipped with Null Grit for just such an occurrence."

Sparks. Did Hedge know about *every* type of liquid Grit? But the poacher's comment turned a gear in Ard's head. It caught the cogs of another idea, and soon a genuine plan was taking shape. It would be exceedingly dangerous...reckless beyond belief. But those were exactly the kinds of ideas that made him Ardor Benn.

"You're probably wondering how I did it," Ard said. "How I made it look like there was a dragon in the baroness's cave when there never was."

"Illusion Grit," spit Hedge. "Pincher spelled out your tricks."

"And you think I'd tell all my secrets to a vagrant I hired off the streets?" said Ard, mind racing. "How could I use Illusion Grit if the dragon was *never there*?"

This got a reaction; Ard could see it in Hedge's lone eye.

"See, it's not about having a dragon," Ard continued. "It never was. It's about making people *think* you have a dragon."

"What the blazes are you talking about?" muttered Hedge. With his gun still trained on Ard, he took a few shuffling steps toward the cave opening. "I can see her down there."

From where he was standing, Ard could see her, too, frozen in Stasis, her giant nostrils stuck mid-flare, as if she'd been drawing a mighty breath when the cloud had overwhelmed her.

"Just like you saw her in Helizon?" Ard pressed.

"Just another trick, then?" Hedge grunted.

"The world has been changing with the discovery of those eight types of liquid Grit," said Ard. "And I think you—"

"*Eight* types?" Hedge cut him off. Ard held back a smile. He knew the King Poacher would be sharp enough to catch that. Playing right into Ard's hands.

"Of course," lied Ard. "Did you not catch wind of the latest type?"

"What's it called?" Hedge questioned.

"Portal Grit," explained Ard. "Discovered by San Green and Lomaya Vans, pupils of the late Portsend Wal." He was borrowing a tactic straight from Hedge himself. If the King Poacher had been able to string them along with pretend Future Grit for weeks, Ard could return the favor, if only for a few moments.

"Yes," Hedge said reluctantly. "I'm familiar with Portal Grit."

Slowly, his body language asking silent permission, Ard reached into his pocket and withdrew a glass vial. "Then you'll know that that dragon is actually in a cave on Pekal at the moment," continued Ard, "with two corresponding clouds of Portal Grit connecting both locations."

"Portal Grit..." Hedge muttered again.

"Of course, sufficiently Compounded like this one"—he held aloft the vial in his hand—"the Portal can actually stabilize the connection to make a permanent bridge between locations. Imagine the smuggling possibilities with a doorway onto Pekal's mountainside."

Hedge scoffed. "My Mixers have Compounded it at numerous levels. They have told me of all the benefits."

"Did they seal the cork with wax?" Ard asked. It was something he had heard Raek and San blathering on about. "Like this..." Gently, he tossed the vial in an underhand arc toward Hedge Marsool. Easy to catch, even for a person with only one hand.

Hedge took the bait. It was that, or let an unidentified vial of Grit shatter at his feet. He flipped the Roller under his arm and snatched the glass projectile just as Ard barreled into him, avoiding the spike of his missing hand by mere inches.

They grappled, but Ard knew his opponent's weak side, and he pushed against Hedge's bad leg. The King Poacher lost his footing, his ankle turning on a loose rock as he toppled through the cave's mouth to the dragon below. Ard wrenched himself away, teetering. In the darkness, he saw a little sizzle of sparks as Hedge's body struck the stone in front of Motherwatch's resting face.

That would be the Null Grit he'd just tossed to the King Poacher.

A flash cloud erupted from the broken vial, instantly snuffing out the Stasis surrounding the dragon's head. Hedge's prone body lurched in fear as Motherwatch's huge eyes flicked open. She completed the breath she had started on Pekal more than half a cycle ago. Then she exhaled in a terrifying snort and Ard felt a blast of hot wind ride up the side of the cave to tousle his hair.

As promised, shots sounded from Hedge's marksmen across the way. But Quarrah had been faster, sealing them under Barrier Grit the moment Ard had made his move. Sparks, they *were* a good team, even if she never wanted to admit it. Still, if the shooters had crossbows with Null Grit, Ard and Quarrah would be safe under this shield for only a moment.

Below, Motherwatch slowly lifted her majestic head off the cave floor, chains jangling around her long neck. Somehow, Hedge Marsool was on his feet after the fall. He discharged his Roller in a gush of flame, the lead bouncing off the thick scales along the underside of her jaw.

The dragon let out a screech that rang in Ard's ears louder than a hundred trumpets. Then Motherwatch opened her mouth and she struck at Hedge. The King Poacher made one more valiant effort to stave her off, thrusting his spike at the roof of the dragon's mouth.

If anything, Hedge's final blow only made his death more painful. Motherwatch jolted at the prick, but one of her long bottom teeth had already punctured the man. He fell backward out of her mouth, the single tooth ripping him open like a sack of flour.

Ard flinched, staring down through squinted eyes as the dragon cleaned up the mess, jostling the broken man in her maw until he went straight down, spike and all.

Ard was aware of the chorus of ongoing gunshots, but the lead wasn't pinging off the Barrier Grit that still shimmered around them.

"Tajis came back," Quarrah whispered, drawing his gaze across the hillside.

By the looks of it, the Trothian had brought a bunch of Jasperson's people with him. And they were firing against Hedge's marksmen enough to keep the attention away from the cave opening. "Must not have wanted to work for Hedge after all," Ard said. "Hopefully, Tajis—"

Ard was cut off as a massive green foreleg reached up with the terrifying sound of snapping chains. Black talons bit into the rock at the cave's wide opening, causing Ard to fall backward, scrambling across the rough stones as the second foreleg gained purchase, thick broken chains dangling from useless iron shackles.

Then the dragon's great head appeared, rising slowly like a snake from a bush. Ard stared into her giant emerald eyes and a calm sensation of familiarity overwhelmed him. It held at odds with the sheer terror he felt, her hot breath washing over him and nearly making him lose control of his bodily functions.

Motherwatch's head thrust forward, the spines of her neck scraping along the top of the cave, raining loose bits of rock. Her face emerged into the daylight, sparkling green.

Ard gave up his backward shuffle, raising a hand as though she'd want to sniff him like a common hound. He had only one hope at survival, and that was to appeal to Motherwatch's mercy the same way he had on the palace steps after she'd eaten King Pethredote.

"Easy, girl…" Ard tried to keep his voice calm and smooth. "Easy." Her cavernous nostrils flared as she seemed to sniff the air. Ard couldn't smell anything but the irony tang of fresh blood and the stench of the wild beast.

"That's it," Ard coaxed. "Lie back down. You can—"

Motherwatch came for him. Not with the speed of a striking snake, but with the steadiness of assured victory. She hoisted her body halfway out of the cave, mouth opening, long yellowed teeth streaked with red.

Something sailed over Ard's head, smashing against one of the dragon's horns with a sizzle of sparks. Motherwatch instantly went limp, green eyes rolling back as she collapsed across the cave's threshold. The shimmering detonation cloud encompassed Motherwatch's head, spilling partway down her neck. Ard's feet were mere inches from the cloud's perimeter, and he could still feel the heat of the dragon's breath through the soles of his boots.

He tried to stand up, legs giving out twice before he found Quarrah's arm for support. In the hills beyond, all shooting had ceased at the sight of the beast.

"Was that your plan?" she asked.

"She got rid of one of our problems." His voice was unusually shaky.

"By the looks of it, she nearly got rid of you," Quarrah said.

"She wasn't going to eat me," Ard said, more to assure himself.

"Oh, really? That's not what I saw."

"She didn't before"—he stared at the still dragon—"on the palace steps."

"Maybe Motherwatch just wasn't hungry that night."

But Ard didn't want to believe it was something so ordinary. He'd felt a connection with her then. Something he couldn't explain. Something beyond her animal instincts. Even that verse in

*Wayfarist Voyage* alluded to their bond—that he, Ardor, would be the one to send her to the Homeland and see her transformed.

Would she have eaten him just now? If Quarrah hadn't thrown that Stasis Grit, would Motherwatch have looked Ard in the eyes with that same measure of mercy she had shown him on the palace steps? Or would the dragon have felt, like Queen Abeth did, that any debt she might have owed him was now paid off? That ripping her away from her hatchling on Pekal made them even for the egg he'd delivered. And like Lyndel, would Motherwatch be willing to kill a man she had once considered an ally?

"Looks like the threat of a dragon was above their pay grade," Quarrah said, gesturing across the hills. Hedge's surviving shooters were making a hasty retreat through the Pale Tors.

Ard cast a glance at Jaig Jasperson's dead body, lying in a pool of blood near the canvas shade awning.

"Let's hope Tajis and the others are open to having a new leader," Ard said. "We can't chance moving Motherwatch again. I don't know where we'd put her. We'll ask this crew to stay on. Tell them we'll hire them at whatever rates they had agreed on with Jasperson."

"Can you afford that?" Quarrah asked.

"Does it matter?" said Ard. "We just need to keep her contained here for a little while longer."

"She's not very contained now." Quarrah pointed toward the dragon's huge body spilling out of the cave. "And what are we supposed to do when she's Moonsick and we have no Metamorphosis Grit to transform her? Sparks. We don't even know if that'll do what we hope it will do."

Ard didn't appreciate Quarrah's skepticism, but he wasn't going to call her on it moments after she'd saved his life.

"Raek and San will have an extra vial of Grit when they get back," assured Ard. "I'll just hang tight until then."

"Here?" Quarrah cried.

He shrugged. "Someone has to make sure Motherwatch gets her regular doses of Stasis Grit. Especially now that she's not chained down." Not that those shackles had done much.

To Ard's surprise, Quarrah shook her head. "It should be me."

"What?"

"Raek and San will go straight to the *Be'Igoth*. You need to be there for Raek. Tell him exactly what information he needs to communicate into the past."

"It's all in my books."

"I didn't think you'd finished them."

"I'm close," said Ard. "And you know the information that's missing."

Quarrah shook her head. "Too much pressure for me. If we screw up one little detail, all of time and space could collapse in on itself. That sounds like something only Ardor Benn would dare tinker with."

Ard wasn't sure how to take that, but he was grateful for Quarrah's offer. "You'll be all right?" He felt bad leaving her alone in the Pale Tors, especially with Motherwatch dangling out in the open. "Raek and I might not make it back here until a few days into next cycle."

"I can handle myself," she assured him.

Ard had no doubt about that. He glanced back at the motionless dragon. He felt a strange debt to the creature already. After all, she had now disposed of two of Ard's biggest enemies.

*Now I just need you to turn into a god and take care of all our other problems.* Ard took a deep breath. Was that too much to ask?

~

*So many ways to die. I've spent more time than I'd like to admit wondering which way will claim me.*

# CHAPTER

# 30

The rain was bitterly cold at this altitude. Nemery had watched it fall all night, rose tinted in the light of the Red Moon. It was a mere drizzle now in the momentary darkness between the setting of the Moon and the rising of the sun that would mark the first day of the Sixth Cycle—the start of autumn. Behind her, the eastern horizon was starting to lighten, the blackness over the sea turning to pale blue.

Pale blue—the color of the Glassminds' skin. It was as if dawn itself was heralding the coming mass transformation.

"Here they come," Mohdek said, peering up the slope toward Goldred's Scramble. He said it in Landerian, probably for the benefit of San Green, who was lying under a conifer with dense, low branches. The young man was wrapped in a blanket and his eyes were closed, but Nemery didn't think he was asleep. How could any of them sleep on a night like this?

"Is he with them?" she asked.

"I can't make it out from this distance," Mohdek replied. They had parted ways with Raekon Dorrel just before sunset last night, the three of them remaining at the tree line while Raek had gone ahead on his own, crossing the open slope, making his way up the scramble of rocks, and moving onto the glacier. Past the Redeye line toward an inevitable fate.

It had been a grueling week of hiking to make it to the summit in time. San was hardier than he looked, though he basically collapsed whenever they stopped to rest.

Nemery had quickly learned that Raek's endurance was completely reliant on regular detonations of Compounded Health Grit inside his chest. He had told her the story of Pethredote's sword and the experimental and unethical surgery to keep Raek alive so they could beat information out of him.

His stories had reshaped the way she viewed him. Raekon Dorrel was more than Ardor Benn's right-hand man. He was a complex individual constantly torn between his loyalty to a childhood friend and his desire for a life of his own. Nemery now understood his need to transform, and she supported it fully, despite any concerns she had about their plan to crack his skull afterward.

"Garifus is leading the group," Mohdek whispered in Trothian. "I don't see the other Glassminds yet." He glanced over at her, his face lined with concern. "You still want to go through with the plan?"

Nemery gritted her teeth. "We have to." She tried not to think of the children among them. She tried not to think of Wilder Far.

Nemery and her companions had managed to turn one of the cultist caravans back to New Vantage, depriving their camps of food and destroying their tents. That group had given up several days ago, making empty promises to try again next Passing. Clearly, they didn't understand their leader's plan. If Garifus Floc was successful, then the Moonsickness would come to *them* next Passing.

Nemery had celebrated that small victory, but had it even made a difference? There were still a hundred and forty cultists that had crossed the Redeye line, now ready to undergo the transformation. A hundred and forty new Glassminds. And with their ability to move through Spherical Time, as Raek had explained it, they could spread across Pekal in the blink of an eye.

Would her dragons even stand a chance? She and Mohdek had counted them as they'd come to roost at the summit last night. The numbers looked good, even without Motherwatch. There were several new hatchlings, and some of the adolescent dragons had really hit a growth spurt last cycle. Would they be enough against a united force like the Glassminds?

Nemery heard a rustle in the dark woods behind them. Before she had a chance to wonder, Mohdek spoke. "Raekon comes."

His statement was finally enough for San to open his eyes. The young man slid out from under the tree, blanket draped across his shoulders. Coming alongside Nemery, he peered into the darkness, the three of them waiting as the rustling grew louder.

She had learned over the last week just how little stealth Raek possessed. Not surprising for a man of his stature, but Nemery hoped that he would never mention the way he'd crept up on her that day in Bo's Glen.

Raek appeared suddenly through the trees, and Nemery reared back in surprise. She couldn't see his eyes in the darkness, but his arms were outstretched blindly and his mouth kept opening and closing as if trying to speak.

Sparks! How had this happened? Only hours into his Moonsickness, and the man looked like he was bordering the third phase.

"Stop it, Raekon," snapped Mohdek. "There is no humor in that."

"Aw…" Raek dropped his arms. "How could you tell?"

Nemery's expression swung from frightened to annoyed, without a trace of amusement. It was hard to be too upset with him, though. By now, she knew Raek well enough to know that joking was the best way for him to deal with the unthinkable fear he must be feeling.

"Moonsick people put off a very different energy than what I'm seeing from you," explained Mohdek.

"But I *am* Moonsick," Raek said, his tone more somber than usual.

"I meant real Bloodeyes," Mohdek said. "The ripe ones."

"Well, let's hope I never get that far." Raek glanced up the grassy slope in the direction of the Scramble.

San stumbled over to him, a glass vial clutched in one hand while he rubbed his eyes with the other. "You ready?"

"Wait," said Nemery. "You're doing it here? Now?" She didn't like the idea of the transformation happening so close to Garifus's position.

"Sooner the better." Raek pressed a hand to his chest.

"How are you going to...you know..." She pantomimed hitting Raek over the head.

The big man stooped down and plucked a fist-sized rock from the soft ground. "I suppose this'll do the trick."

"There's no science to it?" she croaked. "What if it doesn't work?"

"Then I guess you'll have to hit me again." He held out the rock, but Nemery tucked her hands behind her back.

"I'm not doing it."

"Then I'll have to do it myself," he said. "You don't happen to have a mirror?"

Nemery reached out with trembling hands and took the rock.

"The Transformation detonation should only affect Raekon, since he's the only one Moonsick," San explained, holding out the vial.

"San," grunted Raek. "Just do it already. This isn't a college lecture."

San took a deep breath and hurled the small vial at the ground. Nemery saw the thin glass break, but there was no spark. No detonation.

"What happened?" Mohdek took a step closer.

"Oh, flames." San Green dropped to his knees, touching the damp soil that had absorbed the undetonated liquid. "I'm an idiot. A blazing idiot..."

Raek sighed wearily. "You forgot to add the Slagstone fragment."

San looked up, his tired face strained. "I wasn't thinking...I've been keeping them separate while we hiked so there wouldn't be an accidental detonation."

"Now what?" Nemery cried. "You'll have to go up there and use one of Garifus's detonations?"

"No." San sprang to his feet. "We brought another vial as a backup."

"Wait." Raek caught the young man by the elbow as he moved for his pack. "Something's not right."

"What do you mean?" asked San.

"I can't explain it." Raek shook his head, an ironic chuckle on his lips. "It's just a . . . feeling."

"You don't think—"

"We need to get out of here," Raek cut him off. "We need to get back to Beripent. Back to Ard."

"What about your transformation?" Nemery asked.

"If we move fast, we can get home before I slip into the final stage of Moonsickness."

"Why?" she said. "Why would you risk that? Just because you have a *feeling*?"

"I know how this must sound," said Raek. "And I'm not a religious man. But we've learned things about the Urgings . . ."

"You told me," she said. "But how do you know this Urging is coming from you? What if Garifus or one of the other Glassminds is trying to make you feel something? Trying to prevent you from transforming because it's the only chance we have to stop them."

"The plan was never to stop them," Raek admitted.

"But the dragons . . ." stammered Nemery.

"Yeah," Raek said. "They're probably all going to die."

She felt anger bubbling up inside her. "And you're okay with that?"

"I mean, I wish there was another way, but I have to get back to Beripent—"

"To check in with Ardor Benn?" Nemery cried. "I thought you were here to spite him, not to go running back to him."

"Listen to me." Raek's tone was stern. "It's not *your* skull on the line here. I know what I just felt. Detonating our last vial of Transformation Grit isn't supposed to happen. At least . . . not now."

Nemery dropped the rock she'd been holding. "I guess this is it then. This is where we part ways. I trust you can find the trail back down to New Vantage?"

Raek sniffed against the nip of the cold dawn. "You're not coming with us?"

"You may be done here." She glanced at Mohdek. "But this is our home."

"You're going to stay and fight them?" Raek shook his head again. "Look, Nemery. We did our best to stop them all from getting here. But now that they've made it, what do you really think you can do?"

Her breath caught in her throat and she swallowed hard. "If they're planning to kill the dragons, then I'm going to start the fight before they're ready."

"What?" San took a curious step forward.

"The last caravan was toting a Caller's instrument," explained Nemery. "Moh got his hands on it a few hours ago."

"You're going to Call the dragons down from the summit before the cultists transform?" Raek cracked his knuckles. "Bold plan. What are you waiting for?"

"The dragons are lethargic on the summit during the Passing," said Nemery. "I have to wait a little bit longer for them to come out of it."

"How many will come?"

She shrugged. "I'm hoping for one or two. And maybe the sound of a Call will send the other dragons scattering so the Glassminds have a harder time finding them."

"You know a Call that'll make them want to fight?" Raek checked.

Nemery blinked hard against the memory. "I've done it before . . . in Wilder Far."

Raek studied her as if seeing her for the first time. "The Terror of Wilder Far."

"Don't call me that." Nemery held up her hand.

"What happened?"

"I don't want to talk about it."

Mohdek stepped forward. "She has nothing to be ashamed of. She brought justice to our enemies. The justice of Pekal."

"Sounds poetic," said Raek.

"It's what Tanalin Phor called it," Nemery suddenly blurted out.

"Tanalin?" Raek repeated. "As in, Ard's old lover?"

Nemery nodded. "She Called those dragons to attack us while we were harvesting the Slagstone mound with the Royal Regalia."

"I remember."

"She'd been so matter-of-fact about it," Nemery went on. "Said our little group had got what it deserved. The justice of Pekal." She jabbed the toe of her boot into the soft earth. "It wasn't so easy for me to forget."

"Wilder Far," said Raek. "That's a plateau on the south side of Pekal."

Nemery reached up and plucked a leaf off a tree. She felt cornered into telling it now. And maybe speaking of it would be good. Maybe it would help her do what she needed to do to the cultists this morning.

"Moh and I had been following a big group of poachers," she began. "Trying to decide how to deal with them after they harvested an illegal Slagstone. After a couple of days, they rendezvoused at Wilder Far with a group of smugglers who were supposed to move the goods back to the Greater Chain."

She ripped the thin leaf in half, tearing it along the central vein.

"They were all there. Forty of the worst men and women the islands had to offer. I told Mohdek to move downhill. Start scouting potential spots so we could blockade the trail. But I had something else in mind."

She dropped the torn leaf. "I snuck into their camp, stole their Caller instrument, and retreated to the edge of the plateau. Then all I had to do was signal *Trespassing Sow* and wait for the dragon to come. She must've been nearby, because the sow was on them before they could get armed."

"How many did she kill?" San asked.

"Thirty-eight," answered Nemery. "I guess the two who escaped knew someone had used their instrument."

"And a legend was born," said Raek. "The Terror of Wilder Far—a person who could wield the most dangerous weapon in the world. A dragon."

But she didn't feel like a legend. The night had sickened Nemery, causing a deep ache in her scarred leg. Who was she to play like a god, turning nature against humans who didn't stand a chance?

Over the cycles, she had come to decide that the remorse was less about the lives lost than it was about the weapon used. She admired the dragons too much to manipulate them like that. To turn them into a weapon that perpetuated humankind's demonization of the most elegant creatures.

"That must have been hard to watch," Raek said. "But today is different. This is a fight the dragons will have to face sooner or later. They'll have a better chance of killing those cultists *before* they transform."

"Killing them..." Nemery didn't even realize she'd said it aloud. She'd killed plenty of poachers, impersonally, from a safe distance. She told herself that this would be no different.

Except that there were entire families on that slope.

Raek reached out and put a hand on her shoulder. "You'll be doing them a favor, Nemery. Every person on that mountainside is already doomed. There are only two ways this could end for them. They get Moonsick. Or they turn into Glassminds."

"And even those who transform aren't really saved," San chimed in. "If they so much as think differently than Garifus and his majority, they'll end up dead in a matter of seconds."

"At the risk of sounding overly dramatic," said Raek, "the more Glassminds, the quicker the world ends."

Nemery nodded, drawing in a slow breath. The reasoning from Raek and San made her feel slightly more justified in employing Tanalin Phor's brutal tactic once again. But there was only one person's opinion she truly cared about. Only one stamp of approval she needed.

"Moh?" Nemery turned to study him. His skin was dry and flaking. She could see painful cracks that had split open and scabbed over. In their haste to leave with Raek, they hadn't brought enough salt for the paste treatment. Mohdek was obviously uncomfortable, but he never said a word of complaint.

"Raekon is right." Mohdek looked off through the trees. "They're all doomed anyway."

"That's not what I was asking." She switched to Trothian. "What will you think of me if I put my lips to that horn?" It was a direct question, the kind Mohdek preferred. And she had to know the answer.

"I got the instrument for you, didn't I?"

"Because you'd help me do anything I asked," she cut him off. They were suddenly rehashing the same conversation they'd had at Gateway Rock. Only this time human lives were at stake.

"Their logic is sound." Mohdek gestured to Raek and San.

"But what do *you* think?" she pressed. Then quietly, "What would Namsum think?" It was another way to ask a question even deeper inside her. *Would he still call me Salafan if I go through with this?*

She saw Mohdek swallow. "My brother always trusted you. And so do I. You're not a killer, Nem. You're a savior."

"Then you *don't* think we should do it?" She was confused by his cryptic response.

"That's not what I said," he replied. "We did everything we could to save those poor souls. Now it is time to save the rest of the Greater Chain. And if that means destroying those who are already lost, then I proudly stand by your side."

Nemery drew a deep breath, filling with confidence.

"What will you do after you make the Call?" Raek asked.

She picked up her bow. "Moh and I will keep doing what we came here to do. We will defend the dragons against those who would take advantage of them."

"They're fire-breathing monsters," Raek said with a chortle. "You really think your protection means anything to them?"

"Maybe not," she said. "But I know their names. And they have spoken to me since the first time you brought me here. So I guess we both have our heroes to go running back to."

Raekon stiffened, crossing to pick up his pack. "This is goodbye, then, Nemery Baggish. The next time we meet, you can count on me looking a little different."

"I think you can count on there not being a next time," Nemery replied.

"Come on, San," said Raek. "Going downhill is a lot faster than going up."

"It better be," replied San. "We've only got five days until you're beyond the point of transformation."

Raek pulled a leather pouch from his belt and tossed it to Nemery. "A parting gift," he said. "You're going to need it a lot more than I will."

Then Raek headed deeper into the trees, turning his back on the open slope full of cultists. The slope where a hundred and forty people would transform into Glassminds, sworn to destroy the great shield against Moonsickness.

Nemery tugged open the drawstrings of the leather bag and peered inside. "Health Grit." She lifted out a paper roll.

The contents of the pouch were probably worth more Ashings than she'd ever held in her life. A generous gift, indeed. And she knew the stuff was Compounded enough that it might even heal an injured dragon.

San Green picked up his own pack, nodding respectfully to

Nemery and Mohdek. "Thank you for everything," he said, hurrying through the trees after Raekon Dorrel.

Nemery looked over at Mohdek. Somehow, it felt comforting for the two of them to be alone again. She shrugged off any lingering feelings of responsibility toward Raek and San. They were surrendering themselves back to Ardor Benn, to schemes that were a little too big, and stakes that were out of their control.

But Nemery Baggish had a bow in her hand, an arrow on her hip, and the only person she truly loved standing at her side.

"I'm ready."

The two of them crept forward, using every technique Namsum had taught them about stealth and caution. Mohdek led the way, silently pointing to the Caller instrument he had concealed with leaves and twigs. She took a knee, but here at the edge of the trees, Nemery could finally see what was happening on the grassy mountainside.

Dawn's faint glow illuminated Garifus and five Glassminds standing apart from the rest of the cultists. As she watched, the transformed beings ushered five of the cultists out of the crowd, positioning them in a circle around their leader. Two men, two women, and a lad who looked no more than ten years old.

"Only five of them?" she wondered aloud.

Mohdek didn't respond, watching closely as Garifus greeted the newcomers with the cult symbol—a finger raised to touch his glass forehead. They responded in kind, seeming nervous, but visibly excited about the promised transformation. Then Nemery saw the first ray of sunlight twinkle against a glass vial in his hand.

"Salafan." Mohdek gestured at the instrument, urging her to act. But she let her hand slip off the priming box. She couldn't do this. If a dragon responded, it would kill that boy in cold blood. He looked so innocent and eager.

Garifus smashed the vial between his fingers in a flurry of sparks. The detonation cloud instantly sprang around the group, sunlight dancing through the haze.

The five humans in the circle went deathly still for a moment. Then their skin began to tear open. It fell away in fleshy ribbons, their new glass heads appearing first, majestic figures rising out of their insignificant husks.

Even the boy transformed, his new body no smaller than the other Glassminds around him. Once changed, he didn't look youthful or underdeveloped in any way. The metamorphosis had propelled him instantly into a fully mature state. Nemery should have predicted it. The Glassminds touted perfection, which meant there was no room for growth.

She didn't know what had happened to the boy's personality, or his developing mind. Garifus claimed that his transformed followers retained their individuality, but one thing seemed apparent. The transformation would steal their childhood.

"Let our minds be one!" Garifus's enhanced voice carried easily to the edge of the trees where Nemery and Mohdek crouched. He turned his ember eyes to one of the women beside him. "What is this I sense? There is no place for dishonesty in the Homeland." Then he looked at the man next to her. "And there can be no self-serving ambitions when you are part of the whole."

Garifus's glass head began to glow and Nemery tensed. Not this again... One by one, the lights flickered on across the Glassminds' scalps. The boy, if he could even be called that anymore, was quick to light his, and with their united minds, the kid had to know what the result would be.

The man and the woman joined hands, turning to flee. But they made it only a handful of steps before their skulls shattered. Their transformed bodies crumpled to the grass, eyes dimmed and heads blown wide.

Garifus turned back to the onlooking cultists. "Eight," he called. "I need eight of you to come forward for the transformation to the Homeland!"

Mohdek glanced at Nemery. "Eight now?"

"Garifus needs the assurance of the majority," she explained as the truth dawned on her. "There are nine Glassminds who have already proven their thoughts and faithfulness to his ideals."

"And if all of these transform faithfully, then there'll be seventeen of them," said Mohdek. "They'll be able to turn sixteen in the next round."

"That number will grow exponentially until they've tested everyone," Nemery said.

"You need to make that Call."

She began priming the instrument as three of the Glassminds moved into the crowd, choosing the next cultists to come forward. Suddenly, there was a cry and someone bolted from the back of the group. The man's desperate sprint seemed to inspire a few others to do the same. In seconds, the reverent atmosphere over the party had devolved into near-chaos.

Some of the more faithful were attempting to restrain those who meant to flee, but none of the transformed Glassminds were making any move to stop them.

"Let them go!" cried Garifus. "Ye shall know that the great day of egress is upon you when the miserable shall forsake their habitat and walk among you, wild and uncontrolled."

Nemery recognized his quote as a verse from *Wayfarist Voyage*. Her faithful upbringing meant she was usually quite good at deciphering the archaic speech, though in the moment, the meaning of this particular verse was lost on her. It seemed to have the desired effect on the crowd, however. Those who wanted to flee—maybe fifteen or twenty—were released, and they ran down the mountainside toward the woods, gratefully not in the direction of Nemery and Mohdek.

"Do *we* try to stop them?" Mohdek whispered.

Nemery shook her head. "They'll be Moonsick, but that's not on our conscience."

The eight new volunteers were ready now, lined up at the

perimeter of the Transformation cloud. None of them were children this time, but Nemery had moved past that moral quandary.

"Enter," Garifus said from the heart of the detonation. "Come unto the Homeland."

Nemery had seen enough. She needed to put a swift end to this. With the dragons so close on the summit, she expected to see one within a few minutes of her Call . . . if one chose to respond at all.

Leaning forward, she pressed her lips to the instrument and sounded the *Trespassing Sow*. The vibrant Call seemed to freeze all movement on the mountainside, sending fear into the cultist crowd. Then two of the Glassminds whirled on her position. Nemery didn't know if they actually spotted the instrument through the trees, or just traced the sound to its origin with surprising accuracy. Either way, it sent her stumbling away from the horn, Mohdek pulling her up.

"I guess I'll only get one shot," she said as they sprinted through the trees.

"Sounded good," Mohdek replied.

It *had* been a solid performance; she just wished the Glassminds hadn't noticed them so quickly. With no choice but to leave the instrument behind, what would they do if the Call didn't . . .

The mighty cry of a dragon sent goose bumps down Nemery's arms. Against her better judgment, she skidded to a halt in the wet underbrush, gazing skyward through a gap in the leafy canopy.

There were two dragons—no, three!—dropping from the sky like raptors on their prey. In this lighting, Nemery couldn't identify them, and they were out of her sight as quickly as she'd glimpsed them.

Then the screams started. Nemery Baggish found her mind transported to the grassy plateau of Wilder Far. Only this time, the terror was magnified by greater numbers.

She stood rooted to the ground, a wet branch dripping steadily on her shoulder. *Drop. Drop.* Like the spattering of blood on the slope above. The horrific cries persisted for seconds that stretched like hours. Then a new sound filled the air.

"That's a dragon in distress," Nemery whispered. Her foot seemed to uproot from the ground and she took a step back toward the massacre.

"Nem." Mohdek caught her arm, shaking his head.

"But the dragons…" By the sounds of it, the nine Glassminds were already overpowering them.

"We can't help the others if we die today." Mohdek's vibrating eyes were full of pleading. "This is just the beginning of our fight."

Nemery swallowed against the lump in her throat. Then the two of them were off, branches whipping past them as they fled deeper into the woods.

~

*I have never let the odds shake me. Some might find strength in numbers, but I find it in the sharp collection of my thoughts.*

# CHAPTER

# 31

Ard must have dozed off in the *Be'Igoth*, but his eyes snapped open as the door swung wide. He sprang to his feet through sheer instinct, but the figure in the doorway was no enemy.

"Raek!" Ard raced through the debris on the floor to reach his friend. "You're alive! Thank the Homeland. You look fine. Why haven't you..."

He trailed off now that he was closer. Raek *didn't* look fine. His face was covered in sweat and his jaw trembled as if he were freezing cold. Ard had seen that kind of Heg withdrawal on him before. But what was really unsettling were his eyes.

The brown irises seemed to have a milky haze over them, and the whites had discolored to a uniform pink. The skin around them was slightly puffy and swollen, with little veins bulging like streaks of blue lightning.

Moonsick.

His best friend was dying. Stricken by a plague that had always seemed so foreign and unimaginable when they'd been younger. It was a horrible reality now, and Ard felt the weight of responsibility crash onto his shoulders. Getting Moonsick had been his idea. Would Raek have attempted it if Ard hadn't seeded the thought? If he hadn't been so sure that there was a way to cheat the sickness with a glorious transformation?

Looking at him now, Ardor Benn wasn't so sure. Something must have gone wrong. Why hadn't he used the Metamorphosis Grit yet?

"He hasn't had a granule of Heg since yesterday." San Green pushed past Raek and charged into the *Be'Igoth*. The lad was noticeably thinner than when he'd left, and he moved with more confidence. How quickly Pekal could turn a boy into a man. "He told me where he kept his stash. It was..." He trailed off, studying the ransacked room. "Homeland! What happened here?"

"Why..." Ard stammered. "Why didn't he transform?"

"It's not too late," San said, drawing a knife. "He entered the second phase this morning. We've got time before he starts tearing into people."

Raek... He was talking about *Raek*! Not some wild Bloodeye monster.

The young man cut into the padded arm of the couch, withdrawing a paper roll of Compounded Health Grit. Ard wanted to feel shocked that his friend had kept a stash right under his nose, but it wasn't the first time this had happened. And Ard was in no position to be judgmental. He was just grateful to have them back alive for the moment. Three days since the Moon Passing meant they'd made excellent time coming down from the summit. He'd been expecting them in another day or two...but not like *this*!

"What happened up there, San?" Ard asked. But the scholar ignored him, holding the paper roll out to Raek. The big man squinted at it, his eyesight obviously failing. Then he reached out and pushed San's offering aside. He looked back at Ard and nodded resolutely.

"What's going on, Raek? What are you..." Ard trailed off as he saw the glass vial in his friend's hand. He stepped forward, taking it for his own inspection. "Metamorphosis Grit? But if you had it up there, why didn't you—"

"He wouldn't let me," San explained. "I tried to detonate it for him, but he said he had an Urging not to."

"Raek?" Ard said. "Raekon Dorrel said he had an *Urging*? Oh, he must be farther along in Moonsickness than I thought. Already gone insane." He turned to look at the sick man. Raek flipped him an offensive hand gesture.

"He felt really strongly that we needed to bring the vial back to you," San went on. "What happened here?"

The motivation behind Raek's supposed Urging suddenly struck Ard like a Void detonation. There was only one vial of Metamorphosis and two Moonsick creatures that needed it. Luckily, the Mixing experts had returned. They could make more.

"Hedge went off-script," Ard explained. "He followed us to Motherwatch, but she finished him off."

"She's awake?" San cried.

"Only for a moment," replied Ard. "Quarrah's with her now,

keeping her in Stasis. But we haven't been able to try to transform her yet because we were waiting for the two people that know how to make more Metamorphosis Grit."

"We gave Quarrah the formula—" San began.

Ard cut him off with a wide swipe of his hand across the trashed room. "We need the experts to identify the source material."

San rubbed his chin, an overwhelmed look on his face as he turned to examine the littered space. "How would we even—"

"Just figure it out, San!" Ard snapped, tucking the vial into his pocket. He took a deep breath. There was a lot riding on this. Too much. "Let me get more light." He crossed to a rack on the wall by the door, picking out eight pots and detonating them at various spots across the room. In moments, the inside of the *Be'Igoth* matched the bright morning sunlight that slanted through the half-open door.

By the time Ard finished, San had located the empty canister of processed dragon tooth and was trying to trace its path from the overturned table. Judging by the look on his face, he didn't have much confidence in what he was discovering.

Raek stood by awkwardly, a silent monolith that occasionally squinted his bleary eyes at the messy floor.

"Well, you did it, Raek," Ard said to him. He waited, willing his friend to reply, but knowing that he couldn't. The first phase of Moonsickness had stolen his voice, and with it, any chance they might have had for a redeeming conversation. But at least this way, Ard could say his peace without Raek interrupting.

"It took me a while to come around, but I understand why you went," Ard said. "I guess I owe you a thanks."

Looking at him now, Ard was grateful he wasn't the Moonsick one. Although he probably wouldn't have let it progress so far. He would have transformed on the summit, like Garifus and the cultists. The fact that Raek hadn't done that made Ard feel even more responsible.

"This is going to work." Ard pointed at the three books on the desk. "I wrote up everything you'll need to know. The big one has all the information we need to convey to Hedge. I've got notes for Baroness Lavfa, too. And Moroy Peng. Oh, and there are a couple of miscellaneous folks who might need some coaxing. It's hard to know what things people did naturally, and what we inspired them to do..."

Ard trailed off. His rambling was falling on deaf ears. Not literally. In fact, Moonsickness sharpened hearing and smell. But Raek didn't care about what Ard had written in the books right now. He was going blind! There was probably only one question on his mind...

*What are you going to do with that single vial of Grit?*

Ard felt a pang of guilt at the unasked question. They'd go through with the transformation soon enough. He just needed to make sure they had the ability to make more Metamorphosis Grit first.

"This is..." San grunted in frustration. "This is impossible. Even if I could tell which pile was the dragon tooth, it would be so contaminated—"

"It has to be there." Ard dropped to his knees, scouring the piles of loose Grit as if his untrained eye would be of any assistance. "I didn't touch a thing in here since Hedge trashed the place. We *need* to find it."

"There's enough in the vial for Raek," San said.

"*And* for Motherwatch?" Ard didn't want to talk about it so openly in front of Raek. But the big man was so silent, it almost seemed as if someone else were in the room. "What if we divide what we've got?"

"I don't know." San sat back on his knees. "That wouldn't be a very big detonation."

"But it would be enough to cover his head, right?" said Ard. "That's how Stasis Grit works..."

"We've never tested Transformation Grit like that," said San. "It would be better to make sure he's completely enveloped."

"Maybe they could share the space." Ard glanced nervously at Raek. "We can be at the Pale Tors by early afternoon. Raek can stand right next to Motherwatch. We catch them in the same Transformation cloud."

San looked skeptical. "I wouldn't risk exposing Motherwatch to the Grit while she's in Stasis."

"You're saying we have to wake her up for the transformation?" Ard exhaled. San was right, but the risks were woefully apparent. Motherwatch had eaten Hedge the moment she'd awakened. He couldn't expect Raek to share a cloud with her. "Can't you just start making the Transformation solution using every pile you find on the floor?"

"That's a possibility," said San skeptically. "But it would take days to sift through all of this. Maybe weeks."

So it was down to that awful question Ard had been avoiding. One detonation of Transformation Grit. Two Moonsick beings.

Save Raek. Or save Motherwatch.

Ard wouldn't voice his options aloud. Putting the choice into words sounded so cold and heartless. Raek was practically family, but Ard needed to remain purely objective about this.

What could Raek provide them that Motherwatch couldn't? He needed to become a Glassmind to travel back in time and make sure their plans came to fruition.

But Motherwatch had the potential to become a *god*. If she became something greater than a Glassmind—something beyond Perfection—couldn't *she* travel back in time to plant the clues? She was the final hope. Possibly the only thing that could save the world from its impending doom.

Slowly, Ard drew the vial from his pocket. He stared at it for a moment, his heart hammering. So much depended on this little drib of liquid, and no matter how difficult the choice, Ardor Benn knew what he had to do.

He moved toward the exit. Raek's reddening eyes were boring into him, but his friend made no move to stop him in a silent test of their brotherhood.

Ard reached out and pushed the door shut.

Behind him, San sighed in obvious relief. "Oh...I thought you were going to—"

"What?" Ard swiveled around to face the young man. "Thought I was going to leave? What do you think you know about me? Yeah, I make the hard calls that other people won't even look at. I'll sell out my friends if my ambitions direct it. Sparks, I'll even gamble with the fate of the world if I think I have a better plan. But when it comes to Raekon Dorrel..." He swallowed against the sudden emotion in his throat. "Well, I'd let all of time and space burn out of existence before turning my back on him."

Ard looked at his friend. Raek's pink eyes shimmered in the bright Light Grit. His blanched face looked especially haggard, moistened with the sweat from his withdrawals. A lifetime of memories passed between their gaze—joys and sorrows, laughs and squabbles, elaborate plans, harebrained escapes...

Ard held up the vial of Transformation Grit. "Are you ready?"

Raek nodded solemnly, moving into the center of the room.

"Okay," Ard said. "We'll need to act fast. Give Garifus less of a chance to connect you to his hive mind." If he didn't link up immediately. "How do you think I should do it?"

"We were going to use a rock on the summit," San suggested.

"Sparks! We need to crack it, not shatter it." Ard felt strange that he was talking about his best friend's head. "San. Go ask Geppel for a hammer."

"A hammer?" said San. "You're just going to take a blazing swing at his skull with a hammer?"

Ard shrugged. "Better than a rock, isn't it?" Raek didn't look overly worried. There was an inherent trust between them. Trust to get the job done right, even when it was Raek's own head on the line.

San grumbled as he pulled open the door to the *Be'Igoth* and disappeared outside.

"Maybe you should sit," Ard said after a moment of silence between him and Raek. "I'll want to make sure I can reach the top of your head, and the Glassminds we've seen have all been on the tall side."

Raek picked up a wooden chair that had toppled to its side in Hedge's raid. Placing it squarely on the floor, he dropped into it, his breathing laborious. Through his dirty gray shirt, Ard could see the distinct outline of the metal pipe forming a circle on his chest. If this worked, his friend would soon be free of it.

Ard remembered the night of that wound with vivid clarity. Raek, aflame in a sunflare cloak, trying to pass himself off as a glorious Paladin Visitant. It had been Ard's plan within an overly complicated ruse. Ard's fault that Raek had ended up with King Pethredote's sword in his chest. Ard's fault that the subsequent years had come with such a terrible cost for his friend.

That night, Ard had only been able to disguise his partner as a pretended Paladin Visitant, but today he could transform him into something real. Something even more powerful than a fiery Paladin. Mortal aches and pains would be little more than unpleasant memories for Raek. He would be able to absorb and manipulate Grit. To move though time itself.

This was a life-altering transformation for Raek. But for Ardor Benn, it felt like redemption.

San stepped back into the *Be'Igoth* holding the small hammer that Ard had seen Geppel using to pound loose nails in the boardwalks.

"Will this do?" San handed the tool to Ard. Gesturing for the young man to stand back, Ard moved into position behind Raek's chair. Ceremoniously, he passed the vial of Transformation Grit over his partner's shoulder.

"I'll let you do the honors," Ard said as Raek took the small item in his trembling hand. Without a moment's delay, he brought it down, smashing the glass against the floor between his feet.

The detonation cloud looked just like any other, slightly hazy, even vaporous as it surrounded Ard and Raek. The former felt nothing, his grip tightening around the handle of the hammer, waiting for the change.

In front of him, Raek looked frozen in his chair. So still, that even his shaking had ceased. Then there was a wet ripping sound, like the tearing of soggy fabric.

Something red and shiny was emerging through Raek's scalp— a new head that rose up as his skin shed away like the husk of dragon.

The emergence of Raek's new form seemed to deny possibility. He stretched upward, shoulders and arms ripping free, the new ones pale blue and even more muscular than before.

In a way, it looked as if this grander form had always been inside him, cooped up in a substandard shell. Raek couldn't remain seated, rising to his new height as he stepped out of his old legs. A few shreds of cloth clung to him, but he was mostly naked, towering almost to the ceiling.

The first sound he made was a low moan of satisfaction, as if he had just awoken from a great slumber and stood to stretch. Then he turned sharply and Ard caught the first glimpse of his face.

It was still unmistakably Raekon Dorrel, though his crooked nose was straight and his abundance of old scars was gone. But his eyes were completely unrecognizable. They looked like detonations of Light Grit in his head, but they glowed with an intense crimson like the Red Moon.

As Ard stared in a blend of awe and dread, his friend raised a blue hand to his chest, feeling the smoothness of his new sternum. A smile crossed his face at the assurance that the awful pipe was gone. But Raek's moment of celebration was short lived.

He gasped, fiery eyes squinting shut as his hand flew to the side of his head.

"They've found me," he whispered, his new voice filling the

*Be'Igoth* with its multi-resonant timbre. He fell to his knees in front of Ard, head lowered as if in worshipful reverence.

"Hang in there, Raek." Ard stepped forward, raising the hammer. He brought it down with a tentative blow directly on the crown of Raek's new skull. The tool glanced off without so much as a mark.

"Hit me!" Raek bellowed. Ard thought he saw a flicker of light beneath the red glass where his brain should be. Ard raised the hammer again for a more deliberate strike, but Raek suddenly lurched forward, his large body spasming in pain. He knocked into Ard, sending him staggering backward to collide with the wooden chair.

The hammer slipped from Ard's grasp, clattering to the floor as he tried to keep his footing. Sparks shot from Raek's fingertips, but not in the controlled way that he'd seen from Gloristar and Garifus. In fact, sparks were sizzling across his entire body as he convulsed like a person struck by lightning from above.

As Ard turned for the hammer, one of Raek's involuntary sparks found a loose pile of Grit on the *Be'Igoth* floor. A small Barrier cloud detonated around them, Ard jamming his fingers against the impenetrable shell as he reached for the fallen tool.

*No!* This couldn't be happening. He spun to find something else he could use. An inch or two of the chair leg stuck into the Barrier cloud, but it wasn't enough to break off. Raek was only partially contained inside the dome, the perimeter passing right around his middle.

"San!" Ard screamed. "Get Null Grit!" The shocked young man sprang into action, sprinting across the room and practically pulling a cabinet door off its hinges. But Ard knew he wouldn't find anything in there. Hedge Marsool's raid had been too thorough.

"Ard…" Raek groaned.

Ard turned to his friend, who was lying facedown, one arm outstretched into the pile of old skin he had just shed. His blue hand lifted through the heap of cloth and discarded flesh.

Raek was holding a length of metal pipe.

Ard snatched it by one end and brought it down on the back of Raek's head with a merciless blow. He saw a scuff on the smooth glass where it had struck. He swung again, landing it in the exact same place.

It cracked. A single hairline fracture that Ard could barely see in his panic. A third blow split it longer, and a forth sent a spiderweb of cracks from ear to ear. Ard was bringing his arm down for another blow when Raek's hand shot out, catching him by the wrist. He raised his face from the *Be'Igoth* floor, glowing eyes fixing on Ard.

"Let's not overdo it," Raek said.

Ard managed to sigh and laugh at the same time. His grip went limp and the metal pipe clattered to the floor between them.

"That could have gone better." Ard rocked back on his knees. "What was all that sparking?"

"Glassminds can do that," Raek said defensively.

"Not like *that*," said Ard. "Looked like you lost all control of your bodily functions."

"Oh, forgive me for trying to figure out my new abilities while fifty-six Glassminds tried to blow up my brain with their mind powers."

"What were you trying to do?" Ard asked.

Raek held up his hand. Suddenly, the Barrier dome and the Metamorphosis detonation began to dissipate, the clouds absorbing into Raek's palm until the air in the *Be'Igoth* was clear and calm.

"I thought you were big before," San muttered as Raek and Ard rose to their feet. The lad's back was against the wall, still empty-handed from his search.

"Do you still hear their thoughts?" Ard asked.

Raek shook his head, gingerly reaching up to touch his cracked scalp. "I'd say you did the trick."

"Does Garifus know you transformed?" Ard followed up.

Raek shrugged. "I'm guessing so."

It was strange to talk to him. Raek was so much the same in speech and personality, but his body was impossibly different and alien.

"We better prepare ourselves, then," said Ard. "In case the other Glassminds come after you."

"I don't think they will," said Raek. "They're all on Pekal, killing the dragons. I didn't share my location with the hive mind, which was probably the first thing that tipped them off."

"Good work," Ard said. "I wouldn't want people poking around in my thoughts, either. Makes a fellow feel downright violated."

"They could only see what I showed them," Raek said.

"Which was...?" questioned Ard.

"Nothing," he replied. "But they weren't so stingy with their thoughts. They told me all of their plans. Probably as a test to see how I'd respond."

"Perfect." Ard rubbed his hands together. "You know their plans."

"I mean, it wasn't anything new or groundbreaking," said Raek. "Kill all the dragons. Then wait for the next Moon Passing to get everyone in the Greater Chain good and sick. They'll transform anyone willing to share their ideals."

"Did they provide some more clarification on what those ideals are?"

"They believe that the ideas of the majority will always dominate over the few," he answered. "That *unity* means we're all the same, and there's no room for anyone who thinks or feels differently."

"Sounds like the Homeland, sure enough." As Ard stepped forward, his foot hit the metal pipe. It rolled across the floor, stopping against Raek's bare toes.

The Glassmind stooped and picked it up, holding the piece of scrap thoughtfully in one hand. "Feels like I haven't really taken a breath in years."

"You're finally free," Ard whispered.

Taking the pipe in both hands, Raek bent it in half and cast it aside.

"You couldn't do that before," Ard pointed out.

Raek grinned. "I'm full of new tricks."

"Spherical Time?"

"I'm ready for it."

"Might I recommend putting on some clothes first," said Ard.

Chuckling, Raek picked up a fallen tablecloth and tied it around his waist. "I'm going to need some Visitant Grit to access the Sphere. Garifus and his buddies probably used up all the Islehood fragments. That means we'll have to find a piece on Pekal and feed it to one of the dragons before the Glassminds kill them all."

"Let's skip that step." Ard crossed the room and produced a lock box from one of the cabinets. Pulling the key from his pocket, he opened it, proudly retrieving the keg that was lying inside.

"Is that...?" San stepped toward it, squinting in disbelief.

"Pure, processed Visitant Grit," Ard declared. "Ready for your detonation and absorption."

"Where did you get that?" Raek asked.

"We have Hedge Marsool to thank for that," said Ard. "He left it hidden in a secure location in the Char. I sent Geppel to pick it up for me a few days ago."

"How did you know where it was?" San asked.

"Because we told him exactly where to hide it." Ard crossed back to the desk, setting down the keg and picking up one of the books. "It's all right here. Everything we need to get where we are today. Let's start at the beginning. Remember the treasury convoy that Forton Spel told us about last year? The one that got robbed outside of Midway?"

"Oh, I remember," said Raek. "There were one thousand four hundred and three Ashings being transported in the second wagon from the end. What does that have to do with Hedge Marsool?"

"He's the one who stole them," said Ard. "Based on the information we learned when Spel recounted the incident for us."

"And why are we starting there?" Raek asked. "Why do we want to help our enemy earn a thousand Ashings?"

"Think about it," said Ard. "A man like Hedge Marsool isn't going to trust the Urgings right away. We need him to gain our trust. Feed him a couple of quick moneymaking jobs. Once he starts following his gut without question, we'll let him know it's time to hire us for the dragon heist."

"You have more jobs than the Midway convoy?" Raek asked.

"Just another small one."

Raek put a fist on his hip disapprovingly. "What is it, Ard?"

"We need to give him a roundabout way to steal our safe box in Teffelton."

"What?" Raek roared. "That was Hedge?"

"Sorry," Ard said. "I had to give him something."

"You said you didn't know who got to that box."

"I didn't," admitted Ard, "until I really thought about it this week. It had to be Hedge. The Teffelton box was too secure. The only way someone could have found it was if we had told him about it."

"But wait..." said San. "You're going to give Hedge instructions based on what you heard that Hedge had already done?"

"Spherical Time, kid," said Raek. "It'll break your brain if you think too hard about it."

"I think that ought to do it," said Ard. "Prove the Urgings that Hedge is receiving are more than common feelings." He held out the book he was holding. "Next, I've detailed the Urgings he'll need to hire us for the dragon job—writing the note in the Char ruins, Quarrah's note in Lord Dulith's vase, the events of our first encounter with Hedge at the *Be'Igoth*." Ard wiggled the book at him. "Maybe you should just read it."

Raek accepted the journal, thumbing through the pages as if he were fanning himself. "Got it."

"No time for funny business, Raek. I spent a lot of time writing these."

"I said I got it." He shoved the journal back at Ard.

"You barely even looked at it."

"I have perfect recall, Ard. I read what you wrote. And besides, I remember everything you ever said, word for word."

"Flames," Ard muttered. "That can't be a good thing."

Raek nodded his head in agreement. "Surprisingly unpleasant."

Trying not to think about what offensive things he might have said over the last fifteen years, Ard turned to collect the books for Raek to speed-read.

"You really thought through everything, didn't you?" Raek said.

"The best I could."

"I might be the Glassmind." Raek quickly thumbed through the remaining books. "But you..." He handed them back to Ard. "You're always the mastermind." Striding past, he picked up the keg of Visitant Grit and popped open the lid. "Spherical Time... Let's find out what all this hype is really about."

Extending one blue finger into the opening, Raek ignited the Grit with a controlled spark. Instead of filling the room, the detonation funneled straight into his pale blue hand, absorbed until only a small orb of haze hung in the air in front of him.

Raek's eyes peered into the sphere with unmatched intensity. Ard saw nothing unusual, even moving around the room to view it from different angles.

"Fascinating," Raek muttered.

"What is it?" San asked.

"All of time and space."

"Could you be less cryptic?" Ard said.

"The past, the future, and countless possible alternatives are flickering past my vision," he explained. "It's like the view from a carriage window at full gallop. Only now I can see every passing blade of grass in perfect clarity. And as long as I stay connected to the Visitant cloud, I can use my mind to refine the search."

"What are you looking for?" San asked.

"Not what," Raek said. "*When*." He pulled back his hand and the detonation cloud grew, stretching into a tall oval. It hovered before him like a doorway into time.

"Well, well…there you are." Raek stepped forward, passing into the Visitant cloud. His body shimmered at the perimeter, then vanished completely.

San took a startled step toward the lingering cloud, but Ard caught his arm. "What happened?" the lad asked.

"He's doing it." Ard squinted into the haze, but there was nothing to see.

Then, all at once, Raekon Dorrel reappeared. He stepped out of the cloud, drawing the detonation back into his hand as he looked at Ard and San with a big grin.

"You're still here," said Raek, dusting his big hands together. "I'm guessing that means we didn't screw anything up?"

"Not yet," said Ard. "But there's a lot more information to pass."

Raek shook his head. "I did it already."

"*All* of it?" he cried. "Sparks, you were only gone a couple of seconds!"

"Seconds, hours, days…" Raek mused. "They mean nothing to the Sphere. All I had to do was step into one of the alternate timelines and travel to wherever—*whenever*—I needed to go."

"What did you do when you got there?"

"I sifted through those shadow timelines until I found Hedge feeling something, or saying something…Then I drew that emotion or that whisper and applied it to him in the Material Time. He had the words 'Treasury convoy outside Midway. Second wagon from the end' running through his head for weeks."

"But he took the bait?"

"Actually, no."

"What?" Ard shrieked. "It didn't work?"

"Hedge didn't steal the money from that convoy," explained

Raek. "But when he heard about the theft, he cursed aplenty and decided to start trusting his gut."

"So he still did what we wanted." Ard grinned. "All of the other Urgings go smoothly?"

Raek nodded. "Like clockwork. Speaking of which...Our jail guard—the one you called Hal—wasn't being very open to the Urgings, so I had to convince someone else to stash that mantel clock loaded with Heg under my cot."

"Really?" Ard said. "Who?"

"The one guy who seems to obey every Urging without question."

"Prime Isle Trable?" Ard cried. That almost felt like dishonest manipulation, abusing a man of such faith.

Raek chuckled. "He couldn't get the thought out of his head. He whined about it when he came to *Be'Igoth*. Poor guy didn't want to do it, but he's just too blazing faithful!"

"Out of curiosity," said Ard, "you didn't tinker with me, right? I mean, beyond the Urgings I'd written about in the journals."

Raek smiled, clapping his hands together. "San! Let's get some water boiling."

"Excuse me?" The lad scratched his head.

"You feel like a cup of tea?" Ard questioned.

Raek stooped, picking up a handful of spilled Grit from one of the piles on the floor. "I feel like making Transformation Grit."

"Is that the dragon tooth?" San asked. "But it's so contaminated..."

"Then I'll pick through it by hand." Raek opened his fingers, studying the small pile of powder. "It's time to create a god."

~

*Do broken things always need repair? I wish I were better at accepting the beauty in the cracks and the holes.*

# CHAPTER

# 32

Nemery sprang backward, the tip of the dragon's tail missing her by mere inches.

"Blazes, Timberhide!" she screamed, slipping in the mud and landing flat on her back. "I'm on *your* side!"

The yearling dragon paid no attention to her words, craning his neck to snap at one of the Glassminds racing toward him.

They were in a lush draw, a small ravine cutting down the middle with a gurgling brook at its bottom. Grasses and underbrush stood waist high, with a scattering of short trees leading to a thick forest that rambled up a steep slope.

A Glassmind woman reached the dragon, bringing down her axe in a two-handed swing. Under enhanced arms, the blade cut through Timberhide's scales, biting into his nose.

The dragon yowled, pulling back his head with such force that the axe slipped from the Glassmind's hands. It dislodged from his nose, hurtling across the clearing.

From the corner of her eye, Nemery saw a spurt of flames. That would be Preen, a hatchling of just six cycles. The small dragon was facing off against five Glassminds, their pale blue skin impervious to her flames.

But there was no time to help Preen right now. Nemery scrambled backward through the mud as a Glassmind sprinted toward her, those long legs covering more ground than should be possible.

She felt a recent wound pop open, her left side suddenly hot and wet from the fresh blood. That had been from yesterday's failed attempt to save Rassar. No, that had been a hole in her shoulder two days ago. The one in her side had been from trying to save Cloudeye.

Grunting against the pain, Nemery rolled aside as the Glassmind reached her, his short sword squelching into the mud where she had just been. Mohdek came out of nowhere, leaping onto the Glassmind's back with a battle cry. With his legs wrapped around his enemy's torso, he raised an arm and Nemery saw a large rock in his hand. He brought it down with a well-placed blow, the Glassmind dropping to his knees in an attempt to shake off his assailant. Mohdek clung tightly, striking again and again until the red skull finally shattered and the Glassmind slumped lifeless onto the soggy ground.

Mohdek rose slowly, a painful grimace on his face. He dropped the rock, and Nemery saw that his hand was dripping with blood. His own blood, the skin probably having shredded when he broke through the glass. And that wasn't his only wound. The front of his shirt lay open in tatters, his dark blue chest covered in lacerations. There was a massive bruise on the side of his face, and his left eye was swollen shut.

"They got Lucho," Mohdek reported. "He didn't stand a chance against so many of them."

He was talking about another hatchling. They had found Lucho first, struggling against a pair of Glassminds just downhill from their current position. Only moments after reaching him, Timberhide and Preen had started making a racket. In a rare decision to split up, Nemery had come uphill to assess the situation while Mohdek stayed with little Lucho.

"I only counted two Glassminds down there when I left you." Nemery put a hand to her bleeding side.

"Seven more showed up right after you left," he replied. "I killed one of them, but it wasn't enough."

She pointed at the Glassmind man lying facedown in the mud. "How many is that for you, Moh?"

"Maybe six," he said.

"Well, that's five more than Timberhide," Nemery commented. She pointed at the yearling dragon. He was a spunky one, his name coming from the distinct brownish hue of his scales.

As if he had heard and resented Nemery's comment, Timberhide pounced forward, his jaws closing around the nearest Glassmind. Shimmering golden blood sprayed in a wide arc as he thrashed his victim back and forth.

"*Four* more than Timberhide," Nemery corrected her statement.

Still, the dent they were making in the Glassmind population was insufficient. A return to the site of transformation below Goldred's Scramble had revealed a number of things. The three dragons that had so quickly responded to her Call were Jahdu, Bors, and Sleekback. Nemery and Mohdek had found their carcasses, along with the remains of about sixty cultists.

After that hit to their numbers, combined with the deserters and Garifus's own purge of those whose ideals didn't fit the hive mind, Nemery guessed there were about eighty Glassminds on the island. Probably closer to sixty now, with Mohdek's six kills, her even ten, and however many the dragons managed to destroy in their self-defense.

According to the tracks below Goldred's Scramble, the newly transformed Glassminds had divided into groups to cover more area. Nemery and Mohdek had already counted sixteen dead dragons, and they had encountered enough Glassminds in the last three days to realize one important thing.

They were out of Grit.

Probably never even had enough to go around. And without Grit to absorb and manipulate, the Glassminds were little more than overgrown thugs.

Nemery liked to think that their raids of the caravans had given them this advantage. By this point, the Glassminds were even out of Blast cartridges, so most of them had ditched their useless guns for hand-to-hand weapons, tools, or clubs they were shaping out of hardwood tree limbs.

Timberhide bellowed, drawing Nemery's attention. The dragon was downhill, his attempt to flee cut off by a new group of eight Glassminds. They were probably the ones who had just killed Lucho, but Nemery wouldn't have been surprised to find out that they were another party altogether. That was the problem in fighting a group that was mentally interconnected. They could share their location and call for help across any distance.

Preen shrieked. The Glassminds had driven the outnumbered hatchling across the small ravine, their spears puncturing her developing scales. She was bleeding profusely, spurts of black gore flowing down the side of the ravine and mingling with the clear stream water.

Nemery recognized the sound she was making—*Hatchling in Distress.* It was the same Call she had once imitated to counter Tanalin's attack, summoning a second dragon to the spot where they'd been Harvesting the Slagstone that contained the Royal Regalia. Hearing it now made Nemery realize that she'd never truly performed it correctly. The panicked chip that echoed across the mountainside carried a heart-wrenching fear and desperation that no horn could ever hope to imitate.

Nemery dug her hand into the leather pouch Raek had left them, withdrawing a small paper roll. It wasn't full of Health Grit anymore; they'd used all of that to heal their myriad wounds. Wounds that should have left them bleeding out on Pekal's slopes. She regretted having none left for Preen. But to be honest, the hatchling was probably already past the point of saving.

Nemery set aside the paper roll and bit off a length of string she kept on a spool in the pouch. She felt for her quiver. Four arrows left, and only two of them had been altered with those special Slagstone arrowheads.

She pulled one out, the handmade Slagstone tip sparking as it bumped against the shafts of the other arrows. Quickly, she tied a slipknot in the thread, cinching a paper roll of Blast Grit against it.

By the time she was finished, Preen's cry of distress had been silenced forever. The young dragon lay in a heap at the edge of the ravine, her tail hanging limply into the water.

A familiar anger filled Nemery as she nocked the arrow onto her bowstring. She drew, sighting at one of the Glassminds who still had his back to her. The transformed man was making an unnecessary jab at the dead dragon with the tip of his blood-blackened spear. Nemery exhaled coolly, releasing her anger with the arrow.

It soared true, striking him at the base of the skull. Her Slagstone arrowhead sparked on impact, and her parcel of crude Blast Grit detonated. She saw chunks of red glass fly, glinting in the morning sunlight as her target went down.

One less Glassmind. But the others had already moved on to Timberhide.

Nemery nocked a regular arrow, but it was more out of habit, born of her wooziness. Where would she even shoot the point-less weapon? She knew the limestone arrowhead couldn't pene-trate Glassmind flesh. She took a staggering step in the yearling's direction, but Mohdek caught her arm.

"What can we do for him?" he whispered. She felt dizzy, pain-fully aware of the stream of her own blood that pumped down her side with every heartbeat.

Already, two of the Glassminds had managed to climb onto Timberhide's back, stabbing repeatedly with swords and daggers. Screeching in pain, he tried to take flight, his leathery wings unfold-ing. But they had already been cut to tatters, now sorely unable to bear his weight.

Timberhide's once-grand cry had been reduced to an awful gur-gling from deep within, his huge body limp on the mountainside.

"We need to recover," Mohdek said. "Once we bind our wounds, we can—"

A new cry pealed through the trees, long grasses bending at the flap of giant wings. Nemery turned, leaning on Mohdek's arm for support.

Cochorin, the father of all dragons, descended upon the clearing with a breath of air hot enough to peel the bark off a tree. He landed, angry and proud, a father responding to the cry of his progeny.

Two of the Glassminds were instantly trapped under his mighty forelegs, and he snapped at a third, severing her arm in a gush of golden blood.

"No," Nemery whispered. "Get out of here." The fact that she wasn't cheering for the dragon's arrival only proved how much she feared the Glassminds. And how much she had learned not to underestimate them.

One of them threw a spear with tremendous force, but the wooden tip was not enough to pierce the bull's scales. The impact reduced the weapon to splinters. Cochorin shifted his weight to snap at another enemy. The moment he did, Nemery saw one of the pinned Glassminds wriggle out from beneath his long talons, stabbing a knife into the dragon's foot.

Cochorin snarled. His tail whipped around, leveling three more enemies and impaling a forth with one of the spikes at the tip. Of all the fights Nemery had witnessed, this one was perhaps the most evenly matched.

The Glassminds suddenly withdrew a little, taking turns leaping forward to taunt the dragon, calling to him in a language Nemery had never heard before. It sounded elegant and flowing even as they barked at their outnumbered foe.

"What are they doing?" Mohdek whispered.

"Stalling," Nemery answered. "They're trying to keep him here."

"They must be calling for reinforcements."

Just then, something passed in front of the sun, a flickering shadow that Nemery had only ever known to be a dragon. But as she turned her gaze skyward, she realized it was something different.

A Glassmind woman. Nemery recognized her from the original group that had transformed with Garifus Floc. Raek had called her Alumay.

And she was flying.

Nemery felt a tangible despair. It would seem not *all* of them were out of Grit. Hands down to her sides, the woman pushed columns of Void Grit, propelling herself off the ground as the grasses splayed beneath her. She dropped, landing in a crouch just uphill from Cochorin.

Instantly, and without any verbal command, all of the Glassminds made a hasty retreat, moving past the dragon to stand at Alumay's side.

Instead of taking his one chance to flee, the angry bull whirled around. Alumay raised her hand, a twirling ribbon of detonated Grit streaming from her sparking fingertips. The moment it touched Cochorin's head, he collapsed in a heap, his form as still as a statue.

"Stasis Grit," Nemery hissed. It was the exact same tactic Gloristar had used to capture Motherwatch. Except this time Nemery had a feeling that these Glassminds weren't going to take Cochorin peacefully.

Alumay dropped her hand, the Grit cloud detaching and instantly taking a spherical shape around the dragon's head. With a nod, Alumay granted permission to the rest of the Glassminds. They raced forward, weapons drawn. They fell upon Cochorin's helpless form, stabbing and hacking with a deranged frenzy.

Her eyes full of tears, Nemery reached out and found Mohdek's bloody hand. She pressed her palm against his, and she suddenly thought of the first time they had measured hands like this.

Namsum had been dead three cycles, and though Mohdek had practiced steadily with his brother's bow, Nemery had quickly proven to be the more skilled archer. Mohdek had said it was because of her thin fingers, so they had measured one evening at their isolated campsite in the Dronodanian wilderness.

She had melted into his arms that night, and their lips had touched for the first time in a forbidden kiss, the pop and crackle of their low fire carrying them away into the night.

She longed to lie against him now, to pretend like everything would be all right. Mohdek looked over at her, his battered face as steady and constant as ever.

"We have to do something," she whispered.

"What can we do, Nem?"

"I don't know. We have to try. Something. *Anything*. Please. It's Cochorin..." She saw him soften under her pleading gaze. His vibrating eyes were always so anxious to please her. Nemery didn't know what she expected him to do, but she could see that he wanted nothing more than to try. For her.

Mohdek held out his other hand and Nemery saw a piece of Slagstone roughed into a point, the beginnings of another arrowhead he was making for her. "You know I love you, Salafan."

Then he stepped away, suddenly gripping the Blast Grit pouch at her belt and tugging it free. She reached out to stop him, but her side gushed in protest. He moved into the open at a labored sprint, Alumay's head turning as she saw him come. But he wasn't headed for the Glassmind.

Some sixty feet away from Cochorin, Mohdek hurled the parcel of Blast Grit. He must have slipped his Slagstone arrowhead into the pouch because the moment it hit the ground, it detonated into a gush of flames and smoke.

The force knocked Mohdek back, and it took a second for the smoke to clear before Nemery saw what he had done. The explosion had pushed Cochorin's head sideways, just far enough to exit the stationary Stasis cloud.

The great dragon reared up, shrieking against the sudden pain of his injuries. He took flight, but made it no more than twenty feet off the ground before Alumay reacted, manipulating another Grit cloud. This one seemed to catch the dragon by the underbelly, holding him in place despite the frantic flapping of his tremendous wings.

Mohdek rose, an effort that seemed to expend all his energy. With his back turned, Nemery didn't think he saw it coming. And it happened so quickly, she didn't even have a chance to shout.

Alumay slammed the hovering dragon directly down onto Mohdek, more than ten thousand panweights crushing him instantly.

Nemery felt a spear of grief, more acute than any feeling she'd ever experienced, stab through her heart. It passed through her with a violent shock, and then her senses suddenly numbed, and she was sprinting toward Alumay.

Nemery passed the still form of Timberhide, her eye catching the glint of metal in the grass. Without breaking stride, she reached down, scooping up the axe that had injured the yearling. A dozen more steps and she was there, springing off a rock and bringing the axe down with everything she had.

The blade cleaved into the back of Alumay's skull. It shattered the glass, but didn't stop there, slicing down into her neck. Nemery's momentum carried her into the dead woman, toppling them both to the gold blood–stained soil.

Nemery felt no satisfaction in her accomplishment. Just a hollow emptiness.

With the Grit cloud released, Cochorin tried to rise again. Nemery glimpsed Mohdek's lifeless body pressed into the flattened grass. She knelt there, feeling the first sob rise within her as the dragon staggered across the draw, too injured now to take flight. She knelt there, her entire world falling apart around her.

Mohdek was gone. The dragons were dying. Moonsickness

would spread across the Greater Chain. She felt detached from her surroundings, like an outsider gazing upon the ruins of her own life. Watching with a numb disconnection as the Glassminds brought Cochorin lower and lower until his mighty chin lay upon the ground.

The world spun around her, whether from her own loss of blood or her overwhelming sorrow. It was time to get up. If she couldn't save Cochorin, she would save the next one. Or the next one. She couldn't stop. Not while she had breath to give and blood to bleed.

Nemery heard a shout from across the field. She looked up as one of the Glassminds hurled his spear. The long shaft of wood sailed toward her as if time itself had slowed to a crawl. She should have been able to move. To roll aside. But her head was spinning and her heart was broken.

The spear took her in the stomach, lodging itself halfway through her body. She looked down at it, stunned, and yet somehow unsurprised.

It was all right. She didn't want to live in a world where a singular mindset ruled supreme. A world without the majestic creatures that had called to her from such a young age.

A world without Mohdek.

She rolled forward, reaching out for him. Wayfarist doctrine claimed that the soul of a body who died on Pekal would never reach the Homeland, but the Agrodites believed something far more beautiful—that those who perished here were taken up by the Moon, their souls kept bright to shine down every thirty days.

How would she find Mohdek in the Moon? She tried to crawl toward him, her fingers clawing in the soft dirt.

*It is the name of a bird that digs in the sand of the Trothian islets.*

She felt herself dying, vision darkening. The weight of the spear through her middle was too heavy.

*To hear one sing is a good omen. It means that your enemy can look you in the eye and you'll feel no remorse about the way you treated them.*

She closed her eyes, unsure if she had actually reached Mohdek, or if it was happening only in her head. She felt no remorse. She had done enough.

Nemery Baggish, the Terror of Wilder Far.

*Salafan.*

~

*Could there be anything more powerful than a man's final words?*

# CHAPTER

# 33

Quarrah stood rooted in place at the sight of Raekon Dorrel. She'd glimpsed the transformed man from a distance, Ardor Benn struggling to keep up as the duo crossed the Pale Tors. But standing face-to-face with him as a Glassmind was downright shocking.

"Raek…" Quarrah recognized his face only if she blocked out the glowing red eyes. He smiled at her, probably hoping it would ease the shock of his appearance. Then he reached out with one sky-blue hand and pressed a metal Ashlit into her palm.

"What's this?" she asked.

"You overpaid me on a delivery of liquid Grit seven cycles, one week, and two days ago," he answered.

*Seven cycles ago?* "What, so becoming a Glassmind suddenly made you honest?"

"Not at all," he replied. "I just didn't realize the error until the hike up. And it's bad form to take advantage of a repeat customer."

She passed the Ashlit back to Raek. "Consider it a tip." The least she could do for the risks he'd taken to hide liquid Grit for her around the city.

"Quarrah!" Ard's voice was winded as he crested the landing behind his overgrown partner. "Thank the Homeland you're all right." He looked at the dragon, whose long body was still spilling out of the cave mouth in her days-old attempt to escape. "Everything go all right here?"

"Fine," she answered. "Running low on Stasis Grit, so it's a blazing good thing you got here when you did. By my calculations we wouldn't have made it through the night."

"But how are *you*?" Ard said. "Nearly a week alone in the Pale Tors would take a toll on anyone."

But waiting with a purpose was something Quarrah Khai excelled at. "You know I don't mind the silence."

"Ha," Ard said. "Something I can't seem to offer."

She hadn't meant for that to be a jab at him, but it *had* been rather peaceful. Tajis and Basgid had even taken the night shifts, so she felt plenty rested.

"Any change in Motherwatch?" Ard asked, stepping closer to where her head rested, still as a statue without the natural breathing of slumber.

"She's Moonsick," answered Raek, squinting his glowing eyes at the beast. "I can see the energy coming off her."

"That's what Tajis said, too," replied Quarrah. But Raek's Glassmind eyes had to be superior, even to those of a Trothian. After all, the latter was a corrupt descendant of the former, having lost the most powerful Glassmind traits.

"The question is *how* Moonsick?" Quarrah turned to Ard. "The Bloodeye I kept in Stasis seemed to progress slower than normal.

And your entire hypothesis was based on Grotenisk, but he lived in Beripent peacefully for three years before he snapped."

Quarrah felt like it was a rare opportunity for her to point out something that Ard hadn't already thought of—or at least *claimed* to have thought of. But this was one of those moments. She could see it on his face.

"What are you saying?" Ard quietly asked.

"It takes a person between five and seven days to reach the final phase of Moonsickness, right?" she checked. "Well, what if it takes cycles, or even *years*, for a dragon to get there?"

Ard pondered it for a moment before shaking his head. "It doesn't really matter *how* Moonsick she is, as long as it's started. In fact, the last thing we want is for Motherwatch to be *too* sick and past the point of transformation. I say we detonate the Grit immediately."

"You found more?" Quarrah asked.

Ard glanced at Raek. "He salvaged enough pulverized dragon tooth from the mess in the *Be'Igoth* to concoct a couple of vials. And we convinced San to stay behind and get the place looking ship-shape. Between us, I think the kid's had his fill of dragons."

Quarrah glanced back at the hourglass under the canopy. "That Stasis Grit is going to wear off in about six minutes. We should probably hit her with the Transformation before she wakes up."

"On the contrary," Ard said, his tone leaning toward the annoying side. "Just because the Moon rays penetrate a Stasis cloud doesn't mean the Transformation will."

"Oh, you *want* to wake her up?" Quarrah said. "Like last time? She's not even chained down anymore."

"Not that those chains did much," Ard admitted.

"Even if this *does* work," continued Quarrah, "you'll be transforming her into something potentially even more powerful. How do we know she'll be on our side?"

"Flames, Quarrah. You've had too much time to sit and worry

out here." Ard pulled something from his pocket. It was a glass Grit vial tucked into a hardened leather sleeve to keep it safe.

"Maybe there are some unknowns," he said, "but the idea is solid, and that's what I'm good for." Reaching out, he handed the vial to Raek. "I'll leave the actual procedure up to our Grit expert."

"I see that nothing has changed between us," Raek said flatly. It was strange to hear him talk, his new voice both familiar and yet foreign.

Raek slipped the vial from the sleeve and dashed it against the rocks between his bare feet. What was he doing? Had that been an accident? But as quickly as the detonation could form, it was sucked into his outstretched hand.

"I suggest you both stand back." Raek stepped up to the still dragon's nose.

Quarrah didn't need to be told twice. She retreated, sheltering under the canvas awning next to their dwindling supply of Stasis Grit. But Ardor Benn...The man remained at Raek's elbow like an annoying tagalong child.

The big Glassmind reached out his pale blue hand, fingertips touching the hazy detonation that surrounded Motherwatch's muzzle. He absorbed the Stasis Grit in a single draw and the dragon's eyes popped open. Quarrah gasped. She'd been expecting the clear glassiness of those emerald orbs, but now they looked coated in a milky substance, raw pink edging in from the sides.

The creature raised her head slowly, nostrils flaring with twin trails of vapor. She didn't make a sound, but opened her mouth as if drawing a massive breath. Raek reacted with a new detonation from his sparking fingertips. The cloud instantly enclosed the dragon's head, and Motherwatch went still. It wasn't the same kind of stillness induced by the Stasis Grit that Quarrah had been using all week. This seemed to freeze the dragon in place, sickly eyes wide and mouth half open.

Then without warning, her scaly face ripped right down the

middle, a split forming from the tip of her nose to the first spine on her elegant neck. Quarrah flinched at the dry tearing sound, but nothing happened.

Silent seconds passed, Quarrah not daring to breathe. "Come on," she heard Ard mutter.

Anticipation.

Quarrah Khai usually thrived on it. That moment when she heard footsteps idly drawing toward her hiding place. That first glimpse of a locked box begging to be opened. But in that moment, with the fate of the world hanging in the silence, Quarrah realized she had never truly experienced anticipation at all.

Something burst out of Motherwatch's torn face, streaming straight up into the afternoon sky. Quarrah staggered in surprise, eyes turning upward only to find that she'd lost it in the sun. Then there was a dark blur—something coming down with as much speed as it had gone up. It landed on the stone platform between Ard and Quarrah, breaking rocks with the force of arrival.

It was a woman, easily standing the height of a Glassmind. She was unclothed, but her entire body was covered in shimmering green scales. Not the rough, separable scales of a dragon, but something smooth and interconnected unlike anything Quarrah had ever seen. Her hands were somehow graceful and bestial at the same time, each of her fingers ending in an inch-long talon of deepest black.

From between her shoulder blades, a pair of wings extended, spanning at least twenty feet in breathtaking plumage. The feathers looked to be dipped in liquid gold, but they rustled in the breeze with the delicacy of a gosling's down.

Her face was at once both human and dragon, the blend striking Quarrah as more beautiful than frightful. Her hair was a weave of gold and blue, flowing freely as it spilled nearly to her waist. But those eyes...

They glowed with the same terrifying red light as the Glassminds.

She opened her mouth to speak and the words rolled out in a language so beautiful that Quarrah found herself transfixed, wishing it would go on forever. The creature's voice was melancholy and indescribably rich. As her sentence ended, the unknown words hung over the cave's opening like the final notes of a song.

Quarrah expected Ardor Benn to impose some sort of overwrought introduction, but another voice beat him to it. From somewhere behind the woman, Raek replied in the same flowing language.

Her huge wings folded along her back and she turned to find Raek standing near the cave's mouth. They exchanged a few more sentences before she stretched out her taloned hand. Her palm was facing up and she stared at it as if studying something there. Suddenly, sparks sizzled across her talons and a small orb of hazy Grit appeared. It hung suspended, the strange woman gazing into it.

"She doesn't speak our languages," Raek explained, stepping toward Quarrah and Ard.

"And you?" Ard sputtered. "Since when did you learn to speak... *Dragon God*?"

"It came with the upgrade to Glassmind," he answered.

"Then why doesn't she know Landerian?" Ard asked. "I mean, if she is what we think she is..."

"I am one of the Drothans," said the winged woman, the ball of Grit drawing back into her hand. She turned to Ard. "When the mind of a simple *toogsa* like yourself evolves to perfection, it learns the True Speech, while still retaining a perfect remembrance of its former language. In my previous form, I had no method of verbal communication, beyond rudimentary needs."

Ard stared at her unblinking. "Quick learner," he finally squeaked out.

"The Sphere has been complete." She lowered her taloned hand. "Great knowledge can be found within time and space. Perhaps even the answer to existence itself."

"I didn't know existence was a question," said Ard. Was he seriously bantering with a goddess?

"Sooner or later it becomes a question for everyone," she said. "Even you, Ardor Benn."

"I knew it," Ard whispered, taking an anxious step forward. "You know me."

"I recognize your scent from my son's shell. You were with the egg at the time of fertilization. But that would have been over two hundred years ago. How are you still alive?"

"I was a Paladin Visitant," Ard explained. "I hid myself in a cloud of Visitant Grit, and Grotenisk never knew that the egg and I were there. It probably helped that he was blind from the Moon-sickness, but nobody actually knew that handy fact."

The woman nodded. "He was the only dragon to grow Moon-sick. But in our degenerate form, we did not understand that he was thus one step closer to transforming back into what we once were."

"Well, his condition certainly helped," continued Ard. "Old Grotenisk basically blasted fire across the entire city. He almost couldn't miss torching that egg."

"And you returned to the present day after the fertilization?" she said.

He nodded. "The egg and I came back as soon as the Visitant cloud burned out."

"That would have been the moment I sensed its fertilization," she said. "You must have stayed by the egg until I came to retrieve it at the palace."

Ard cast a glance at Quarrah. Hadn't that been the decision that had driven them apart?

"More or less," Ard replied. "And I suppose I should thank you for eating King Pethredote that night."

"He drenched himself in a potent scent that triggered a primal response within my beastly form," she said.

"The real question is, how did he taste?" asked Ard.

The dragon woman seemed to find no amusement in his statement. "I am not a monster," she said. "I find no delight in having done all I did in my lesser form."

"I'm sorry." Ard took an earnest step toward her, formulating a delicate question in his mind. "You could have killed me that night. I would have been completely helpless against you." He paused. "So...why didn't you?"

"I am not a monster," she said again. "I knew what you had done for that egg. And though I could not voice my gratitude, I expressed it in another way."

Ard cleared his throat. "You mean...by not eating me?"

A smile tugged at the corner of her mouth. "Perhaps the highest level of respect in the wild animal kingdom of Pekal."

"Thank you..." They'd been referring to her as Vethrey, but Ard wasn't sure if he should call her that now. "We don't even know your name."

Suddenly, a detonation appeared in her hand. At once, Ard saw sparks falling like rain through a forest of blossoming fruit trees. His senses were filled with the rich aroma of damp soil after a storm and he felt a lazy sleepiness overtake him. Then, just when he thought he might drift off to sleep, the sparks began to kiss the soft pink blossoms with the chime of a distant bell, the pale petals instantly transforming into wisps of multicolored light.

It was over as quickly as it had started.

Ard pawed over his own body, making sure he was still intact and actually present.

"Where was that place?" Quarrah whispered, proving that she'd just experienced the same vision.

The dragon woman smiled. "It is my true name."

"You are..." Ard stammered. "How exactly do you say that?"

"*You* don't," she answered. "The Drothans communicate on a higher level."

"How should we address you, then?" asked Ard.

"You call him Raekon Dorrel?" She pointed at their companion. "The same as before his transformation?"

"That's right," answered Raek.

"Then you may call me as you did before mine," she responded.

"Motherwatch," Ard said.

She rustled her feathers in obvious distaste. "Actually, maybe we could think of something better."

"Yeah," replied Ard. "That wasn't my idea. You actually got named by a teenage girl."

"Vethrey," Quarrah blurted out.

"Isn't that just a translation of the same name?" Ard asked. Although he had to admit it sounded grander in Trothian.

"*Vethrey* is a Trothian word," said the woman. "And I see its derivation from the True Speech—*Evetherey*."

"And what does that mean?" asked Quarrah.

"One who saves."

"Evetherey it is, then." Ard made a sweeping bow, dropping to one knee before her. "We are humbled to be at your service."

Her glowing eyes dimmed as she gazed across the Pale Tors. "I have awakened, as it were, from a deep slumber. The world is not what it once was, and the race of the Drothans is no more."

"That's one way to look at it," Ard said. "Or we could say that you're just the first to transform. If we hurry to Pekal, we might—"

"The dragons are dead," she said. "All of them."

A detonation flickered in her hand, and Ard felt his heart sink. He saw the mighty corpses of the dragons strewn across the island, the mountainside stained with their black blood. Just when the despair threatened to overtake him, it ended.

"Sparks." Ard gasped. "How do you do that?"

"Garifus was successful, then?" whispered Quarrah.

"The one you speak of calls himself Centrum," said Evetherey. "He has set things into motion that cannot be undone."

"But the Sphere..." Ard said. "We can change things. We already have."

"Your understanding of the Sphere is sorely limited," she said.

"Then help us understand."

Another detonation appeared in Evetherey's hand, instantly accompanied by a flood of knowledge and understanding directly into Ard's mind.

The Glassminds suddenly seemed weak, compared to what the dragon goddess could do with Spherical Time. The former could reach sideways through time to draw emotions and thoughts from alternate timelines.

But the Drothans could draw *life*.

*"Is there anything you can do for him?"* Quarrah had asked Gloristar as young Shad Agaul lay dying on the throne.

*"Not until the Sphere is complete. For now, there is an order to life and a time for death."*

Evetherey's new vision made Gloristar's words as clear as thin glass. There were an infinite number of Shad Agauls scattered through alternate timelines. They were immaterial. Mere shadows. But a Drothan could scour those shadow timelines to find a version of Shad Agaul that was basically indistinguishable from the one they'd known—same look, same experiences, same memories. Perhaps the only difference might be the size of the mole on the boy's cheek.

The Glassminds could see this boy, imposing his thoughts and emotions onto people in the real world, but the Drothans could actually bring this replica boy into the Material time. Bring him into reality as a near-identical replacement of the one who was killed.

"Garifus knew about this," Ard whispered. "He knew what a Drothan could do with the Sphere, and he tempted Gloristar to use it to save the prince."

"It was not a lie," she said, the detonation in her hand snuffing out. "The Sphere could have saved the boy—a version of him, at least. But Centrum wouldn't have been able to bring anyone into the Material Time. A Drothan would have to detonate the Visitant Grit in order to draw a replica person from a shadow timeline. Nor would Centrum have been willing to accept the price."

"Price?" Quarrah asked.

"The Final Era of Utmost Perfection," said Evetherey. "It is supposed to be a time when humankind has struck the balance to live in peaceful harmony with the gods."

Ard shook his head. "You really think such an era could exist? There will always be someone who won't follow the rules." He shared a subtle glance with Raek.

"That is the sole purpose of the Glassminds," she said. "If such a rabble-rouser is creating trouble, he should swiftly be transformed into an Othian."

"Oh, good," Ard muttered sarcastically. "Give the troublemakers *more* power."

"Once evolved," continued Evetherey, "the gods could see the true intent of their glass minds. If there was evil therein, the individual could be sent into the Sphere in exchange for a more compliant version of themselves from an alternate timeline."

"So the price to bring someone out of the Sphere is the life of a Glassmind," Quarrah summarized.

Would the gods just keep shuffling people around until they had their perfect civilization? Ardor Benn shuddered. Was that any better than what Garifus was doing? "Doesn't sound like Perfection to me."

"It is the very purpose of existence," explained Evetherey. "The gods intended to create Spherical Time to usher in the Final Era of Utmost Perfection. Garifus initiated it prematurely, likely to assure his existence as an Othian. Now time cannot be changed or reset. It can be nudged toward this end, but if anything in the linear past were to change what has happened, all of time and space would collapse upon itself. It would literally be the end of everything."

People kept saying that, but what did it really mean? *Something* would surely live on. And in the end, Ard couldn't decide which was preferable—Garifus's utopia, or utter nonexistence. There had to be a third option. Why wasn't Ard seeing it?

"I can see Centrum's mind," said Evetherey. "He is honest in his beliefs."

"Sparks," Ard swore. "Can he see yours?"

Evetherey turned to him, eyes flaring in indignation. "I am their god! My mind is not open to the perusal of my inferiors."

"Great." Ard clapped his hands together. "Then they don't know you're here?"

"To their knowledge, they have slain the last of the dragons." Her voice was soft. "Even my son . . ."

"Cochorin," whispered Ard.

"Cochorin?" Evetherey questioned.

"Your son," said Ard. "The new bull. The girl that named you called him Cochorin."

The dragon goddess smiled. "A Trothian word meaning *Big Hope*. I had not seen him for many centuries."

"Your son?" Ard clarified. "You'd seen him *before*?"

"When one of my kind dies, we are not gone forever," explained Evetherey. "Eventually, we are born again. Born of our ancestors who are our progeny."

"Bet that makes for a tumbleweed of a family tree," Raek muttered.

"There are a fixed number of Drothans." She pressed on, ignoring the interruption. "Before we brought your kind into existence, all of the gods existed together and Time was Spherical."

Without warning, Evetherey ignited another detonation in her hand. Ard was suddenly far above the world, but it wasn't covered in nearly as much water as the one they lived on. Like before, he understood exactly what he was seeing. Evetherey's rich voice resonated clearly in his mind.

*"We drew our power from the Red Moon, but it was not always so potent.*

*When we founded this world, the orbit of our moon was in perfect alignment with the planet."*

Ard saw the world spinning, the Red Moon always hanging on the far side of their world, never cycling past.

*"We lived far below,"* Evetherey's narration continued, *"on what you now know as the bed of the InterIsland Waters."*

"We heard a little about this." Ard spoke aloud, pleased to discover that it didn't disrupt the vision. "We discovered a spire of red glass down there. It told us the history of the Glassminds."

*"The Othians have no history other than this one,"* said Evetherey.

Then it unfolded before Ard's eyes. It was complex and involved, yet he seemed to perceive it all in the space of a few moments.

The gods—the Drothans—ruled over mankind in benevolence, using powers drawn from the Red Moon to ease the lives of the mortals. Humans could bring raw materials before the Drothans, who could alter them with a simple exhalation. The gods breathed power into the materials, which could then be ground to powder and detonated as Grit.

*That's certainly a lot more hygienic than the way we've been doing it,* Ard thought.

The gods knew that the Moon's rays would be too intense for mortal life-forms, so they imposed boundaries. Half of the planet was available to their subjects, but some people wanted more. Eventually, a portion of the humans ignored the rules and broke past the perimeter where the gods stood watch. Those humans exposed themselves to the red rays, but the Moon's distance meant that the sickness didn't set in for many weeks. Before the madness took them, they were able to kill one of the Drothans and transform themselves with their teeth.

"Hold on," Ard interrupted again. "I thought the Transformation Grit was derived from the teeth of a *dragon*."

*"Gods and dragons…"* Evetherey's speech resumed in his mind. *"The two words have always been synonymous."*

Ard's vision continued. He saw the changed Glassminds wage war against the gods, demanding that all humankind undergo the process and join their collective mind. It was just like Garifus. Did power *always* do this to people?

The gods lamented all this death and devised a plan to save the humans while sparing the rebellious Othians. With unfathomably Compounded detonations of Grit—Drift, Gather, Void, Weight—they pulled great amounts of soil and rock together, piling them miles high during the night to create five towers of safety for the surviving humans.

Pekal and the Greater Chain.

Before sunrise, the Drothans lifted the humans to the tops of the towers in long clouds of Drift Grit. With concentrated detonations of Heat Grit, the gods melted the great caps of ice that bookended the planet, drowning the world in a mighty flood.

This wasn't a merciless execution, and a way was prepared for the Othians to live forever in massive pockets of air on the seabed. The gods used Barrier Grit, Prolonged to such an extent that the detonation would hold back the water for centuries.

And while the Othians could have easily absorbed the detonation, they must have realized that the rush of water through the collapsing Barrier could have crushed their glass skulls. So they waited below, their enhanced forms needing no light to see, and no food or water to sustain them. Their race could bear no offspring, but they could live forever in the depths.

But far above, Ard saw that something had changed. With a sudden rearrangement of so much mass, the planet was thrown from its regular orbit. In turn, the Moon was sent into a counterorbit, no longer hidden safely on the dark side.

That first Moon Passing took everyone by surprise. And the Moon's proximity gave it a much more potent effect on the unsuspecting humans. Many fell sick, reaching the brink of violent insanity within a short week. The gods absorbed as much of the Moon rays as possible, but their efforts were sorely insufficient. There simply weren't enough Drothans to make an effective shield. Something had to be done before the next Passing.

*"We altered ourselves."* Evetherey's voice rang into Ard's mind. *"With a detonation of Visitant Grit, we accessed the Sphere, scouring alternate timelines until we found a version of ourselves that was more effective in absorbing the dangerous Moon rays."*

A new vision flashed before Ard's eyes, and he understood what Evetherey was talking about. He saw the dragons—alternate versions of the Drothans, trading elegant feathers for leathery wings, smooth glistening flesh for coarse scales. Keen minds for bestial instincts. They lumbered on four legs, and instead of their gentle breath that imbued materials with power, they breathed fire and vaporous heat. Their ability to spontaneously create Grit was lost, the process degenerating to the point that the dragons were required to ingest source materials. The dragons would dither away in this depraved existence, only vaguely aware that they had once been something greater.

Ard saw the Drothans enter the Sphere, exchanging themselves for these new creatures in a selfless sacrifice. In so doing, Spherical Time collapsed, the Material Time becoming wholly linear, unless reset with a detonation of Visitant Grit.

But there were three who were afraid to make the sacrifice.

The god-brothers, afraid to give up their power. Afraid to change. Afraid that time would make the humans forget that these hulking beasts were once their gods, who had sacrificed themselves to shield the world from the dangerous Moon. The god-brothers were afraid that the humans would treat them like a base resource, mining their bodies for valuable materials until they drove the dragons to extinction.

*They weren't wrong*, Ard thought. He knew the disposition of the common citizen toward the dragons. The beasts, and their powerful by-products, existed solely for the taking.

Ard saw the god-brothers meet in secret, forming a pact to control the dragon population by destroying the other male Drothans. In time, the three would die. But as each one met death he would be reincarnated, vowing to ignore the other males and find only his brother's egg so he could bring him back to life with fertilizing fire.

They entered the Sphere with the others, but they exchanged themselves for another version—one with just enough intelligence to hold on to the memory of their pact.

Ard drew in a slow breath. Evetherey was showing them the Bull Dragon Patriarchy. The same three males, being born over and over again to manipulate the dragon population, making sure it was an insufficient number to provide total coverage against the Moon rays. It was an attempt to create a safe space, making Pekal impossible for human colonization.

"The Bull Patriarchy was evil." Quarrah's voice cut through Ard's vision.

*"Were they?"* replied Evetherey. *"The rest of the Drothans had faith that humans would understand and respect what we were doing for them. Instead, you baited and tracked us. You harvested our bodies for your monetary system and built your throne atop our bones."*

"You're right," Ard said. "We didn't understand. Humankind forgot what you were. They replaced you with a meaningless torch. But you're back now. We can make everyone understand the truth."

Evetherey lowered her hand, extinguishing the Visitant cloud she had been using to create the visions.

"In my experience, no one can be *made* to understand the truth," she said. "Even the Othians, with whom we could share thoughts, rebelled against us. Time alone on the seabed did not soften their hearts. Once the potency of the Barrier Grit had decayed enough, the Othians pressed through. They swam up from the depths, full of vengeance against their gods. But when they could not find us, they began a great slaughter of your people. Yet even the mighty Othians could not withstand the new proximity to the Moon. Over the course of a single generation, they devolved into the race you know as Trothians."

"So *altitude* created the Trothian race?" said Raek.

Evetherey nodded. "And in a sense, the dragons. From Pekal, we oversaw everything without understanding. The god-brothers' pact, though its true purpose had been forgotten with their bestial degeneration, had been engrained into the three male dragons and they upheld it instinctually." She turned to Ard with a half smile. "Until Cochorin."

"He wasn't one of the three god-brothers?" Ard asked.

"No," said the majestic woman. "As a result, he was sworn to no pact. From the moment he reached fertility, he strove to restore the dragon population to full capacity so even Pekal would be free of Moonsickness during the Passings. The Patriarchy would never have allowed him to hatch, but the dragon who fertilized my son's egg did not do so knowingly."

"Because Grotenisk never realized I was there." Ard grinned. That whole event had turned out to be even more clever than he'd intended.

"Why did it take Grotenisk so long?" Quarrah asked. "The history books state that he hatched in Beripent, but it took three years before he got Moonsick enough to raze the city."

"Maturity," Evetherey answered. "Our young dragons do not need the Moon rays until they reach an age of fertility—usually around three years."

"Ha!" Ard clapped his hands. "That's why Hedge specified that we steal a *mature* dragon from Pekal. If we'd taken one of the hatchlings, the Moonsickness wouldn't have taken and we wouldn't have been able to transform it."

"Makes sense," said Raek. "But we're just learning that now. I've already communicated all the information to Hedge in the past."

"It's all right," Ard replied. "You can go back into the Sphere and tell him what we need. An update, of sorts."

"You must cease in your efforts to manipulate the past," commanded Evetherey. "You have taken too many risks already. Should anything jeopardize the creation of the Othians—"

"Yeah, yeah," Ard cut her off. "All of time and space will collapse on itself and existence will come to an abrupt end. But aren't we safe to go back in time and give Hedge one more little nudge? I mean, hasn't it happened already? After all, the information about an adult sow was what brought you back. It would have been easier to steal a hatchling."

Evetherey sighed like a weary mother talking to a disobedient child. "I suppose I could allow it."

"How very nice of you," Raek replied. "Pretty sure Ard was going to make me do it either way."

"You do not understand," she said. "Now that I have accessed the Sphere, the Othians can only use it with my permission."

"Wait," Quarrah cut in. "You mean, Garifus and the other Glassminds can no longer access Spherical Time?"

"Only if I allow them to," Evetherey said. "The Othians exist only to serve the Drothans."

"Except when they revolt and start slaughtering everyone," Raek pointed out.

"There were never meant to be so many Othians," said Evetherey. "Centrum, like the Othians of old, has gone against the true purpose of the transformation."

"To be a token for exchanging life," Ard clarified. "To make sure that only the best versions of people are living in the Final Era of Utmost Perfection."

"Precisely."

"So now that the Glassminds have gone off their rocker again," said Raek, "how do we stop them?"

Evetherey looked wistfully up at the sky, the breeze playing in her silky white hair. "We don't."

"Wait...what?" Ard cried. "You're the most powerful being ever to exist. There has to be something you can do."

"There is but one of me," she said. "With the other dragons gone, the Moonsickness is coming."

*The Great Egress*, Ard thought again. It was prophesied in *Wayfarist Voyage*. Did that make it truly inevitable?

"You mentioned that the dragon version of yourself was better at absorbing the Moon rays." Quarrah pointed toward the corpse in the cave's mouth. "But can you do it as a Drothan?"

"To some extent."

"How many people could you shield?" Quarrah asked.

Evetherey tilted her head in thought. "It is not the number of people so much as the geographical space. If I was elevated to a certain height, I would be able to hold a shield over approximately one square mile of terrain."

"About the size of the Char," Ard mused. "I guess it's time to find out how many people we can squeeze into a square mile."

"The rest of the world—millions of people—will either be Moonsick, or transformed into a unified force of Othians," said Evetherey. "To what end would we shelter a relative few?"

"To keep humanity alive," Ard stated.

"We will pose little threat to such a mass of enemies," she said.

"Clearly, you don't know us very well," said Ard. "Standing right here we have a legendary ruse artist, a master thief, a cracked Glassmind, and a dragon goddess. And we've got a college dropout holding down the fort at Tofar's Salts."

"We'll find a densely populated area and make it defensible," Raek backed him up.

"We have just over three weeks before the Moon Passing," said Evetherey.

Ardor Benn cracked his knuckles. "Then we'd better get started."

~

*In generations, the stories of our exploits will become legend. Then scripture, I'll wager.*

# PART V

---

Every soul desires perfection. Some erect facades, feigning flawlessness when viewed from the front. But there is deception there. True perfection is a sphere, seen the same from every angle.

—Wayfarist Voyage, *vol. 3*

Sing! Sing a ceaseless song. One whose end is just a new beginning.

—*Ancient Agrodite song*

# CHAPTER
# 34

A rd inspected the floor of the council chamber for bloodstains. There was a one-in-three chance that this was the room where King Remium Agaul's hours-long rule had come to an abrupt end. The death of Abeth's beloved husband had been a shame, but assassinations and secret organizations like the Realm seemed like small potatoes compared to what they were facing now.

"She's not coming," Quarrah said, her eyes fixed on the closed door that led to the hallway. "I should have stayed with San at Tofar's Salts."

"She'll come." Ard turned away from the open window and the horizon tinged with the paint strokes of sunset. "I brought doughnuts." He gestured to the greasy bag on the long rectangular council table.

"Ah, yes. Doughnuts'll do the trick." Raek was seated in one of the stout wooden chairs, his huge cloaked form making it look like it was built for a child. "In case the Glassmind and the dragon goddess weren't enough to get the queen's attention."

He gestured at himself and Evetherey, who was leaning against the wall. She had agreed to keep a black cloak draped around her shoulders even though her wings had ripped through during their brief conflict with the Reggies on the palace grounds.

"Oh, you certainly got *everyone's* attention, throwing that iron gate halfway across the grounds," said Ard. "Pretty sure half of Beripent heard you coming."

"You're going to lecture *me* about making a dramatic entrance?" Raek retorted.

"Killing the palace guards and literally flying through the front door was a little much," said Ard. "Even for me."

"It was not my intent to kill anyone." Evetherey's voice was calm. "I was merely moving those guards aside in the most efficient way possible. If they died, it was due to the frailty of their mortal forms."

"Isn't that *always* the cause of death?" Ard muttered.

With Raek and Evetherey, their little group seemed nearly invincible. The two enhanced beings had manipulated walls of Barrier Grit to shield their entrance from Roller balls, while Ard had shouted for the Reggies to bear a message to the queen, telling her to meet them in the council chamber.

They had made it to the room with little resistance, and even now, Evetherey was holding a Barrier over the doorway and the exterior window, sealing off the council chamber from any kind of attack while they awaited Queen Abeth.

The gunshots from the hallway had ceased about fifteen minutes ago, but every time Ard had peeked out the door, he'd seen the corridor choked with uniforms. According to the limited understanding of the Regulators, the Barrier Grit had to burn out *sometime*. Little did they know that the one manipulating this cloud was, herself, an endless well of Grit.

Evetherey suddenly stepped away from the wall, head cocking to one side in a distinctly reptilian way. "Someone new is at the door. A woman. The others are addressing her as queen."

"About time..." muttered Quarrah.

Without another word, Evetherey raised a hand, disappearing into a cloud of impenetrable darkness that filled the corner of the dim room.

Ard sprang toward the door, but paused as he passed Raek. "You might want to follow suit." He gestured back toward Evetherey's hiding spot.

"What?" Raek cried in mock upset. "You're ashamed of me now?" He snapped his fingers and a spark appeared. "It's because of my crack, isn't it." A Shadow cloud formed around him, concealing his huge form. "Just remember...I can still see you."

Ard reached the door, feeling more anxious than he was afraid. To be honest, it was hard to feel very scared when flanked by a Glassmind and a Drothan. He'd have to keep his feelings of invincibility in check. A knife could still cut him the same way it always had.

He yanked the door open, stepping back as it swung inward. Evetherey's shimmering Barrier wall held immutably across the threshold, but the Regulators in red had fallen back.

Queen Abeth Ostel Agaul stood with her hands clasped in front of her, pale blue dress simple yet elevated to an almost elegant appearance due to her poise and demeanor. Behind her, Ard could see shadowy figures that were nevertheless unmistakable as the seven members of the royal council.

"Ah, Your Majesty!" Ard swept into a respectful bow. "Thank you so much for responding to our—"

"You didn't leave me any other choice," Queen Abeth cut him off.

"With respect, we weren't anticipating the council." He lowered his voice. "Frankly, that kind of paperwork and politics will only slow us down."

"You have somewhere to be?" the queen asked.

"We all do," Ard replied. "And less than a cycle to get there."

Queen Abeth lifted one eyebrow quizzically. "Even if that were true, you can't possibly think I will let you walk out of here. After everything you've done—"

Ard held up his hands. "Once the council hears what I have to say, you'll be clearing out a guest room in the palace's west wing for us to stay."

Abeth laughed, but there was no mirth in it. "You are in no position to say what the council will decide."

Ah. So that was the real reason Abeth had assembled the other royals. The council would demand punishment, and her final words to Ard had been very clear. Abeth owed him nothing, and now she knew it was time to follow through with her threat. But could she really execute the man who had been responsible for giving her another day with her son?

Queen Abeth had summoned the council to shield her conscience. If Evetherey was not convincing, Ard had little doubt that the other royals would cry for his swift execution. Having them here would give Abeth a chance to hide behind their decision.

"Would you like to come in?" Ard's tone was cordial, as if inviting the queen for tea. He studied her through the Barrier, reading her expression, trying to peer into her soul. The queen seemed distrusting and uneasy, the look of a woman manipulated into a difficult position. Well, Ard would just have to manipulate her out of it...

"Ard!" Quarrah warned. "Who's to say that the Regulators in the hallway won't fill us with Roller balls the moment that Barrier drops?"

*"It's all right,"* Evetherey's voice sounded in Ard's mind. Quarrah must have heard it, too, because she turned her attention to the cloud of Shadow where the dragon goddess was hidden. *"I can admit them with no risk of that."*

Ard nodded. "That would be wonderful."

"Getting filled with Roller balls?" replied the queen.

"Sorry," Ard said. "I was talking to the dragon in my head."

Queen Abeth peered at him through squinted eyes. "What the blazes are you talking about?"

Ard gestured to the council table. "Why don't you come in and find out."

From the hallway, Ard heard the voice of a Regulator chief. "Your Majesty, I must discourage you from entering the chamber."

"The doorway is sealed." She reached out to touch it.

Still concealed from view inside her Shadow cloud, Evetherey spoke aloud. "Step forward, Queen."

The timbre of her voice sent a visible tremble through Abeth Agaul.

"Your Majesty, please," counseled the Regulator in the hallway. But Abeth sucked in a deep breath as Ard moved out of her way. In what was sure to be called a leap of faith, Queen Abeth stepped forward.

Ard watched the Barrier wall part around the woman's leg first, and then her torso as she moved forward. The Drothan gatekeeper masterfully kept the rest of the Barrier intact, resealing over Abeth's outline the moment she had passed through.

Clearly puzzled by the behavior of the Grit, Queen Abeth turned back, gesturing for the council members to follow. One by one, they came through, the queen introducing them as they staggered through the transparent Barrier in amazement.

"Lord Owers and Lady Volen, representing Espar." The former was a short man with dark skin and a glittering diamond earring. The second was a pale young woman who looked to be just out of her teens.

"Lord Kinter of Dronodan." He was tall, his bald head slightly lumpy. "Lady Heel"—with a noticeable lazy eye—"and Lord Ment of Strind." He was a feeble old man whose name rang a bell. Likely a cousin to the late queen dowager, Fabra Ment.

"And from Talumon, Lady Werner and Lord Blindle." The woman was well dressed, while the man wore mostly black, doing no favors to his harsh frown under a large beak of a nose.

Ard offered a polite bow, reaching past Blindle to swing the door shut for privacy. He felt the air of self-importance that instantly bloated the room as the *noble council* took seats around the table. After seeing Evetherey, Ard realized that there was nothing noble about this group. In fact, these were the same people who had decided not to authorize any kind of rescue when Ard had been doomed to die on Ra Ennoth.

Well, they looked even *less* impressed with him now. "A pleasure to meet you all," Ard said. "My name is Ardor Benn—"

"Stow it, ruse artist." Lord Owers seated himself beside Quarrah with a *hrumph*. "Your time is up. If anyone here opposes the swift execution of this man at sunrise, let them speak now."

"I object." The voice was Raek's, his Shadow cloud slowly dispersing, making it seem as if he were shimmering into view from another plane of existence. "Why does the execution have to be *swift?*"

The room erupted into fear as Raek stood slowly, red eyes shining. Lord Kinter drew a Singler, but a gesture from Raek sent it spiraling out of his hand.

"So you're working with them now?" the queen asked, her voice tight.

"This?" Ard pointed at his partner. "Sparks, no! This isn't one of Garifus Floc's goons. It's just Raek! He's not one of them."

"Sure looks like one," said Lord Kinter.

"Yes, he's a Glassmind," Ard explained. "But I hit him over the head with a pipe. He's on our side now."

Raek nodded. "That's how it works, kids."

"And he's not our only visitor this evening." Ard gestured to the Shadow cloud in the corner. "Everyone try to remain calm."

The cloud dropped in the blink of an eye and Evetherey was plainly visible. Someone in the room screamed. In response, shots were fired from the hallway, but the Barrier Grit still blocked the way.

"My friends!" Ard tried to regain order in the room. "Meet Evetherey, formerly known as Motherwatch, formerly known as the dragon who ate King Pethredote."

"Dragon?" someone stammered.

"No longer," Evetherey said. "I am one of the Drothans. I am the pure and original form of the creatures you now call dragons."

"It's a trick!" shouted one of the ladies. "Like those golden Homelanders who visited King Termain!"

"I assure you this is no trick," Ard said. "And if you would calm down long enough for me to explain—"

*"Would you like me to convince them of the truth?"* Evetherey's voice sounded in his head.

"Yes, please," Ard replied.

*"How much would you like them to know?"*

Ard took a deep breath. "Everything."

Quarrah Khai sat in a veritable hailstorm of words as the noble lords and ladies unpacked the mess of information and emotions that Evetherey had just put into their minds. In the aftermath, Ard was fielding questions and managing countless interruptions.

At last, some of the most influential people in the Greater Chain knew the truth! Everything from Ard's time as a time-traveling Paladin Visitant, to Evetherey's evolution. To be honest, Quarrah couldn't decide how she felt about the knowledge becoming public after she'd kept it secret for so many years. In a way, it felt like a betrayal, instilling in her a sudden sense of vulnerability.

The queen and council didn't question this new information. Evetherey's unique method of transmitting it had left little room for doubt. But there was still plenty of doubt being thrown at Ardor Benn as the conversation turned to the most pressing matter.

"What do we do about it?" Lady Werner asked for the third time. "If the dragons are gone and Moonsickness is coming, what are you suggesting we do to avoid it?"

Evetherey stepped forward. "In this form, my ability to absorb the Moon's rays is limited. If I am lifted up to a sufficient height, I should be able to cover a square mile."

"Don't you have wings?" asked Lady Heel. "Why can't you fly up to the Moon and absorb it all?"

"That is certainly not how it works," Evetherey answered. "The Moon's rays have a deeply calming effect on my species. I will need a spot to perch and roost while my mind slips into a catatonic state."

"Surely, the palace turrets are high enough," said Lord Owers. He leaned across the table to address the queen. "We need to shield the palace and grounds."

"No," Ard cut in.

"Excuse me?" cried Lord Owers. But the queen held up her hand to allow Ard to continue.

"We need to choose a location with the highest population density," Ard explained. "That way we have the best chance of saving the largest number of people."

"That would be Beripent's Southern Quarter, then," Raek chimed in.

"I should think we would not choose slums and taverns over Beripent's royal palace," protested Lord Owers.

"Your statement is incorrect anyhow," said Lady Werner. "Talumon has the highest population density. We may have fewer overall citizens there, but they are stacked upon one another like fleas on a dog's back. Take Grisn's Mercantile District—"

"What does it matter how many we save?" asked Lady Heel. "Shouldn't we be thinking about the *quality* of people? My relatives populate a good portion of the Reaching Ward in northern Trasken."

"She makes a valid point," said Lord Kinter. "Not about Trasken, but regarding the quality of people who should be shielded. After all, we must think of the ramifications of this coming Moon Passing. The precious few who survive will be facing a whole new world. It will be a land filled with Bloodeyes hungering for violence, and an interconnected web of Glassminds intent upon the extinction of the human race. My relatives are a hardy stock—survivors. It's not merely land we control, but an entire infrastructure of workers and equipment to adequately farm and ranch it. If we were to extend this shield over the rural farmlands of central Dronodan, we could assure adequate food for the long-term survival of those who make it through."

"Protect your *farmlands*?" cried Lady Werner. "The students at the Music Conservatory in Octowyn are among the brightest minds. We should extend the shield over that great city and assure that the arts live on."

"Oh, yes," Lord Kinter replied. "When the Bloodeyes come thrashing at their doorstep, the last survivors of the human race can be sure to serenade them with Marsten's Concerto in D."

Ard circled around and dropped into an empty chair next to Quarrah. "This is why I didn't want to assemble the council," he whispered under the ongoing bickering.

"Look on the bright side," Quarrah replied. "They're not crying for your swift execution anymore. Not that it really matters. We'll all be dead in less than a cycle anyway."

"Not if we keep hanging around the Drothan." Ard pointed across the room to where Evetherey stood as a silent observer.

"Great," said Quarrah. "The four of us against the world."

"Sounds about right. Maybe the queen and the Prime Isle will join us."

"Oh, please," she replied. "Trable wouldn't even show up to this meeting."

"Maybe he didn't hear about it."

She gave him a deadpan look. "Abeth said she was talking to him when she heard about our arrival. Face it. Trable's ignoring you, Ard." And after the way he'd lied to the Prime Isle, Quarrah didn't blame him.

Ard grunted, clearly bothered by the thought. "The thing is, I've figured out a solution to their problem." He jabbed a thumb at the arguing nobles, changing the subject.

"I'm sure you have," Quarrah said.

"It's quantity versus quality, right?" Ard said. "They all want Evetherey to shield their own people, so..."

When he didn't finish the sentence, Quarrah felt a pang of nervousness. "You're not going to tell me what you have in mind, are you?"

He shot her a look that she couldn't quite interpret. It seemed... apologetic? "You're not going to like my plan."

"Oh? Why not?"

He took a deep breath. "You'll see." Then he slammed both hands on the table and stood up. The arguments quieted and the focus in the room shifted back to Ardor Benn. Beside him, Quarrah started to get a familiar woozy feeling that came whenever he roped her into his plans unwillingly. What would it be this time?

"It's only natural that you want to protect your families and loyal subjects," Ard began. "And all the points that have been raised are valid. We're talking about the survival of our species. We need numbers, yes, but we also need good people who are willing to work to stay alive."

"What are you talking about, boy?" asked Lord Ment. Quarrah thought he seemed so deaf he probably really didn't know. But Ard pressed on as though his comment had been a prompt.

"The Char."

"That would be an utter waste!" cried Lady Volen. "The only residents of the Char are squatters and vagrants."

"We don't need residents," said Ard. "Just visitors. The Char is almost exactly the right size. And it has enough open space to cram people as tightly as sand on a Trothian islet. Anyone in the Char would be safe and the perimeter of the historic area would be the new Redeye line."

"An interesting proposal," said Lord Blindle. "I believe many would come from Talumon if we explained what was at stake."

"Now, hold on," said Ard. "We can't exactly go shouting from the rooftops that the world is ending."

"And why not?" Lady Heel fixed one eye on Ard, the other wandering.

"Can you imagine the panic that would cause?" Raek stepped in. "Evetherey can't shield everyone. If we draw too much attention to what we're doing, it'll spark chaos."

"Not to mention it might tip off Garifus and the Glassminds to our plan," added Ard. "This has to be done on the sly. We protect a group of people, but they don't even know it until the next morning when the rest of the world wakes up Moonsick."

"You're asking us to keep this a *secret*?" shouted Lady Heel. "Everything we've just learned?"

"Yes," Ard said. "Our survival may depend on it."

"As much as I see protecting the Char as a healthy compromise," said Lady Werner, "I must point out one obvious flaw. The Char's open space has great potential, but in the current season, the vast majority of visitors would be from Espar. Not a fair cross-section of the islands."

"One exception comes to mind," said Ard. "During the Grotenisk Festival, the Char sees tens of thousands of people from all over the Greater Chain."

"That's not until the spring," said Lord Kinter. "If the dragons really are extinct, we have less than a cycle."

Ard smiled, clapping his hands together. "Which is why I'm proposing a new festival to be held over this coming Moon Passing. You thought the Grotenisk Festival was big, well, wait until you see this one. It'll make the spring event look like a neighborhood potluck."

"This is absurd!" shouted Lord Owers. "Do you have any idea how much cost goes in to the spring festival?"

"I wouldn't worry about the money, pal," said Raek. "Ashings won't mean much when a Bloodeye is ripping your arms and legs off. And last I checked, you need dragon scales to make Ashings, so I'd say our whole monetary system is about to fold on itself."

"It's not just the cost," seconded Lady Werner. "The Grotenisk Festival is a time-honored tradition that brings in the masses because of its reputation. We would have only a few weeks to spread the word about this new gathering."

"Then you'd better get your ships prepped," said Ard. "If there is any group of people capable of spreading gossip at the speed of a falcon's dive, it's you lot."

"What are we supposed to say?" asked Lady Heel.

"Whatever it takes to entice people to come," said Ard. "It's going to be big. Bigger than anything else. Arial Light Grit displays like no one has ever witnessed. Food, games, contests. And of course, the Royal Orchestra will play a free concert for the public. Don't you remember the last concert under King Pethredote?"

A murmur of approval went around the table, and Quarrah felt a social noose drop around her neck.

"Nothing will top it," someone said.

"This will," replied Ard. Quarrah swallowed. The noose tightened.

"How can you make such a claim?" asked Lady Volen.

"Do you remember the soprano soloist for that concert?" Ard asked.

"Azania Fyse," said Lord Owers, causing Quarrah's breath to catch. "I believe Lord Kinter can tell you more about her."

Quarrah's heart picked up its pace. Did they know she was still alive? Did they know she was in this very room?

"Owers," hissed Kinter, eyes downcast.

Ard threw a puzzled glance at Quarrah, but she felt just as confused by this sudden turn in the conversation.

"Do tell," encouraged Ard. Was he trying to blow her cover? Why did Ard seem so relaxed about this? "If you know something about Azania Fyse…"

"Oh, he knows," continued Owers with a grin.

"That's enough." Lord Kinter raised a hand.

"Now you must go on," Ard insisted. "Our curiosity is piqued."

The man cleared his throat, a sudden sheen of sweat on his smooth head. "The soprano and I were…romantically involved for a short time."

"What?" Ard's eyes snapped to Quarrah.

She stood up, mouth open, unable to find words. That was a blatant lie! She had only just met Lord Kinter at the council meeting a few cycles ago.

"I have endeavored to keep it quiet out of respect for the late King Pethredote," Kinter continued.

Ard tilted his head. "What do you mean?"

"You were probably unaware because you're not a member of high society," said Lady Heel, "but everyone knows that King Pethredote and Azania Fyse were illicitly *involved*."

"That's not true!" Quarrah finally found the words and they came out as a shout.

"Of course it is!" continued the lady. "Why, even on the night of her murder, she was seen climbing into the king's *personal* carriage as she exited the Char."

"But the king wasn't even in there," snapped Quarrah.

"I should say not!" she replied. "His Majesty had to maintain some level of propriety. After all, as crusader monarch, he was under the jurisdiction of the Islehood and forbidden to produce an heir."

"There was no producing of anything," Quarrah said, flustered. She felt sick, as though her name had been dragged through the mud. And with a man like Pethredote! Had he started these rumors? Or had they spread after his death?

"I wasn't going to say this," continued Lady Heel, with her voice low. "But that woman once made overtures toward me, as well."

Lord Owers chuckled. "Sounds like nearly everyone had a stint with the ginger soprano."

"Stop!" Quarrah shouted. The room fell silent and she looked to Ard, her eyes pleading with him to bail her out of this awkward situation.

"I"—Ard stood slowly—"did not." He fixed his gaze on Quarrah. "But I haven't given up hope yet."

"Hah!" cried Owers. "Let us know how that goes for you."

"I will," said Ard.

"But..." stammered Lady Heel. "She's dead."

Ard held up a finger. "Only as dead as we need her to be."

"Ard..." Quarrah tried to make her voice sound threatening.

"I don't completely understand what you're saying," said Lady Werner. "But if you could get that soprano to come back from the dead and perform again, people would flock from far and wide to see her."

Ard smiled at Quarrah. "That is the plan."

~

*Everything is a performance. Some performers are just more honest than others.*

# CHAPTER

# 35

A rd knew it was bad form to invite two women to dinner at the same time and place. But Quarrah understood what was going on, and Ard had no romantic interest in Kercha Gant whatsoever, despite the fact that the brunette soprano clinging to his arm looked gorgeous and smelled like honey and bergamot.

He paid the doorman a couple of Ashings and led his companion into the fine establishment. Loren's was busy tonight, and the buzz of conversation was punctuated by the clink of expensive cutlery on painted china plates.

"Have you eaten here before?" Kercha asked. She had a way

of maintaining a bored expression regardless of what was happening around them. The carriage ride from her Northern Quarter apartment had been less than stimulating, even though Ard could tell she was bubbling with excitement beneath that put-upon exterior.

"It came highly recommended," Ard replied. "A dining experience that is worth the price, if one would like to make an indelible impression."

"Well, would you?" Kercha asked. "Like to make an impression tonight?"

"Let's just see if it comes naturally."

Ard led Kercha past the table where Quarrah sat with her face downcast. She was in fancier clothes than her usual black, but her sandy hair was pulled back in a plain ponytail. Ard didn't miss the fact that her placement in the room provided her a clear path to the back door.

Casting Kercha Gant a debonaire smile, Ard pulled out a chair at a table just arm's reach from Quarrah's.

"Tell me more about yourself, Mister Nordesh," Kercha said once they were settled. "You hardly said a word in the carriage."

"I wasn't sure if you were interested," he replied. "I try not to be the kind of man who says more than is wanted." From the next table, Ard thought he heard Quarrah spew her drink. "And please, call me Erdon."

"Your looks have interested me enough," Kercha said flatly. "What you have to say might help me *stay* interested."

"I'm afraid most of what I'd like to say is about you." Ard reached across the table to take her gloved hand.

"Yes," she said. "You made that clear in your letter of invitation. I hope you understand how uncharacteristic it is of me to entertain an offer from a total stranger."

On the contrary. In the week and a half since meeting with the queen and council, Ard had done plenty of research on Kercha

Gant. The woman was basically starved for attention—a far cry from her peak of popularity, cut down by the rise of Azania Fyse.

"I hardly feel like we're strangers," Ard whispered. "You made me feel something that night. Something I cannot forget."

She looked down her nose at him. "I'm sorry... Have we met?"

"Coastal Concert Hall, Octowyn, five years ago. The moment I heard you sing, I knew I had to meet you." Ard could see how susceptible she was to his fawning. "The Royal Concert Hall, the Glower Street Promenade, Boulevac's Plaza... I watched you sing at all of them. But I lost track of you during the war. Many of the halls closed down. Performances were scarce. I only recently caught wind of you again from a mutual friend—Dale Hizror."

"Hizror?" She drew back her hand. "Wasn't he...?"

"An imposter?" said Ard.

"I was going to say *engaged*," she replied. "To that redheaded brat... *Fyse*."

"I'm glad you mentioned her," Ard said. "I'm sure a woman of your social standing has heard the news by now."

"That she's alive?" droned Kercha. "I should hope she's scarred enough that the crowds at the festival will be repulsed by her face."

*Scarring*, Ard thought. *That would be a nice touch. Garner some sympathy from the crowd.* He'd add it to the costume list for the big night.

"I've yet to hear what piece she's singing, though," continued the soprano. "Not that people even care. I've heard that citizens are flocking from every island of the Greater Chain to be a part of this historic Moonwatch Festival. Personally, I find the whole thing to be in poor taste. Upstaging the longstanding tradition of the Grotenisk Festival... and over a Moon Passing, no less! It hardly seems fitting for a crusader monarch to have authorized such an event."

"Then you wouldn't perform in it if they asked you?" Ard dropped the line that would really get this conversation going.

"Well, I wouldn't say that, but..."

Ard leaned across the table, lowering his voice to a whisper.

"The queen has put me in charge of recruiting for the festivities. I would like you to join us as the premier soloist."

"Me?" Kercha gasped, but quickly recovered her level of disdain. "I don't think I'd like to share the stage with Azania Fyse."

"Oh, you won't," Ard assured. "You'll be *under* the stage."

Kercha's eyebrow raised in puzzlement. "I'm afraid I don't follow."

"No, I wouldn't expect you to, dull as you are." Ard cleared his throat. "Let me explain things clearly...Quarrah!"

At the sound of her name, Quarrah abruptly turned her chair around, tucking it up to Ard's table right beside a startled Kercha Gant.

"Miss Gant," Ard began. "May I introduce you to Azania Fyse."

Kercha studied Quarrah with a mix of confusion and contempt, like a rich noblewoman who couldn't figure out how a mangy dog got inside the house. "*You?*" she finally squeaked out. "But you aren't—"

"Redheaded?" Quarrah cut her off.

"Pretty," replied Kercha.

"You're right," said Ard. "Her beauty transcends such simple words. As does your idiocy. See, my name is not Erdon Nordesh. In truth, I am Ardor Benn."

"The ruse artist?" said Kercha.

"Good, you've heard of me," he went on. "Actually, we spoke once before in the palace reception hall before Noet Farasse's concert. Of course, at the time I was dressed as the composer Dale Hizror. You paid me little attention. So little, in fact, that my associate"—he gestured to Quarrah—"had no trouble dosing you with Furybeth extract so you'd be in no condition to sing that upcoming concert."

Kercha's expression lost every drib of propriety and she spun on Quarrah, raising a hand. Ard didn't know if the soprano planned to slap her, or go straight for the eyes with those long painted fingernails. Either way, she was too slow. Quarrah had her by the wrist in a blink, Kercha's arm twisted painfully and pinned against the tabletop.

"We're going to let you in on another secret." Ard tossed a cloth napkin over their gripped hands, keeping his voice low. "Azania Fyse is no singer. The voice that everyone adored belonged to another woman, who sang from a concealed position beneath the stage. She happens to be unavailable for the upcoming Moonwatch Festival, so we thought we'd extend the offer to you. What do you say?"

"You can rot in the Settled depths," Kercha hissed, her face now wholly twisted in anger. "You ruined my career. My entire life!"

"Has your life really been so bad?" Ard patronized her. "We've just given you more time to spend with Natanial. Your boy must be five years old by now—Oh, wait. It's hard to spend time with him when he's at the boarding house in Midway. A hundred Ashings a cycle for a room there, isn't it? Good thing Lord Eaves covers that exorbitant fee. Why has he taken such an interest in your child, I wonder? I suppose if you're not cooperative, we could talk to him about it."

"You're a monster," Kercha whispered.

"I've been called worse on a first date," replied Ard. "Now, what piece would you like to sing? Something by Sender, perhaps? Or Agrico?"

She glowered. "I haven't performed in years."

"Then we'll need to dig deep into your old repertoire," continued Ard. "Give us a crowd pleaser. Nothing too academic, as this will be a public concert for the common citizen."

Kercha seemed to think about it for a moment. "The third song cycle, by Rous Kenette?"

"I'm unfamiliar with it," Ard admitted.

"Eleven short songs in a sequence," she explained. "The entire work lasts about forty minutes."

"What's the topic of the text?" asked Ard.

"It's a comedy," she replied. "Strong, independent woman sings a series of anecdotes about life in the home. Only, the listener is never sure if the male she is singing about is her husband or her dog."

"I think I can learn those lyrics in a hurry." Quarrah smirked at Ard.

"Woof," he replied in a deadpan tone.

"This won't work," said Kercha. "You might have gotten away with it when Lorstan Grale was on the podium. That man was a buffoon. Swayla Tham will see right through your ruse."

"Which is why Swayla Tham will not be conducting the song cycle at the Moonwatch Festival," said Ard. "Conques Fabley will be the guest conductor. He's already been approved by the queen."

"Never heard of him," Kercha spit.

"No one has," replied Ard. "But I hear he's a frightfully handsome fellow. Imagine this face"—he put a hand to his own chin—"but with a mustache and hair the color of ripe wheat."

"*You?*" Kercha Gant chuckled in angry disbelief. "*You're* going to conduct the orchestra?"

Ard smiled and shrugged. "How hard can it be? Just have to stand up there and write my name in the air with a pointy little stick."

The serving maid suddenly appeared at Ard's elbow, causing him to turn. Unlike a common tavern barmaid, this young woman was buttoned up in clothes made of fine fabrics.

"Sorry about the delay," she said. "As you can see, we are quite busy tonight. What would the three of you like to eat this evening?"

"You know . . . I just remembered." Ard stood up abruptly. "Food does not agree with me." He dropped two five-mark Ashings on the table in front of Kercha. "But get our star vocalist anything she'd like. Surely, you recognize the elegant Kercha Gant? Or are you too young to remember the darling of bygone concerts?"

Kercha huffed and Ard glanced down at her. "We'll be in touch about how to proceed. In the meantime, best not to say a word about this to anyone. They say Lord Eaves's wife is a jealous one." Ard stepped past the serving maid, sauntering for the exit.

"Well, she's as sour as I remembered," Quarrah whispered, following him outside. The darkness was touched with the coolness of autumn's first cycle, and it felt like a storm was brewing. Quarrah tucked a short strand of jewels into her pocket.

"Her bracelet?" Ard assumed, seeing it out of the corner of his eye.

"I needed to get *something* out of this," Quarrah replied. "Even Kercha got a free meal. Besides, you were kind enough to throw that napkin over our hands. Nabbed her ring, too."

"We're already stealing her voice." Ard scanned the dark street. "Isn't that enough?" He spotted their carriage waiting by the corner. It had to be the one, the suspended cab leaning slightly to the left under the great weight of its hidden passenger.

"You really think we can pull this off without Cinza and Elbrig?" Quarrah followed him in the direction of the vehicle.

"Hey. They made the mistake of teaching us all their tricks. Besides, we bought the character of Azania Fyse fair and square. We can do with her what we please."

"I'm just thinking maybe her name would be enough," Quarrah continued. "It's the hype of her return that's going to bring people to the Moonwatch Festival. And once they arrive, isn't that all we need? What if I don't have to get in costume? And we wouldn't have to use Kercha..."

They had reached the carriage, but Ard didn't open the door. Instead, he turned and put a steadying hand on Quarrah's shoulder. He understood where her ramblings originated—from fear and uneasiness. Not wanting to step back into a role that had stretched her out of her comfort zone and nearly taken her to death's door.

"I know this isn't easy for you, but you'll do great. Azania's name will bring people to the Char, but we need them to stay all night. The entertainment has to be good enough to keep them happy."

Before she could say another word, he pulled open the carriage door. The darkness of the cab's interior was broken only by two eyes glowing red.

"Only Ardor Benn could pull that off," Raek's enhanced voice greeted them.

"What are you talking about?" He climbed in, seating himself across from his slouching partner, Raek's glass scalp touching the cab roof.

"Only you could go to dinner with one woman and go home with another," clarified Raek.

"I'm not going home with—" Quarrah started, but Ard cut her off to put an end to the awkward conversation.

"Where's San?"

"He was just finishing up at Oriar's Square," Raek answered as the carriage ambled up the street.

"Where are we with the outdoor stage?"

"San said the workers have started bringing the lumber into the Char," he reported. "Should start assembling by middle of next week."

"Good," said Ard. "Once they're done, that'll give us a few days to rehearse. The builders know about the modifications we need?"

"They're using the same plans from the year Quarrah sang at the Grotenisk Festival," said Raek. "The stage will have a grate on the front so our soprano can stay beneath the stage and bellow unseen."

"But I shouldn't need a trapdoor this time," said Quarrah.

"Right," Ard agreed. "We should have them take it out. The last thing we need is for Kercha Gant to pop up and take credit during the applause."

"At least she won't be singing between my legs like Cinza did," Quarrah muttered. "That dress was too breezy anyway."

"Speaking of dresses..." said Raek. "I gave your measurements to the tailor."

"How do you know my measurements?" she retorted.

Raek merely waved his large blue hand. "The same guy's getting us a red wig and some beefy spectacles to complete the look. But you'll have to apply your own makeup."

"Well, that's going to be a disaster," admitted Quarrah.

"You've got time to practice," said Ard.

She shifted in her seat. "When's our first rehearsal?"

"Ten days from now," Ard replied. "Unless I'm not back yet. Then you can cancel that rehearsal."

"Back?" Quarrah cried. "Where are you going?"

Ard glanced across the carriage at Raek's glowing eyes, then he turned his whole attention to her. "There's something I need to take care of."

"Something so important you can't tell me about it?"

"I don't want to trouble you."

"Ah. Just the fate of the world at stake and you're afraid I'll mess it up if I know too much?"

"It's not like that."

"How many times have you said there'd be no more secrets—"

"It's a personal matter!" Ard silenced her, his tone rising faster than he'd meant. "It's not about Glassminds or dragons. It's... personal."

The comment clearly surprised her, but Ard could see that Quarrah was still hesitant to believe him. He supposed that was the price he had to pay for deceiving her so many times.

But he was being honest now. This was something he had to deal with on his own.

Ard reached behind him and pounded on the wall of the carriage, the driver bringing it to a quick halt.

"What are you doing?" Raek asked.

"I could use some fresh air." Ard pushed open the door.

"See you back at the palace later?" Raek checked. "The carpenters have been working all day to heighten the doorway into my room so I don't have to duck anymore." He turned his glowing eyes to Quarrah. "See what you're missing out on?"

"Well, I hope the perks of living at the palace outweigh the risks," said Quarrah.

"No risks so far," Raek said.

"Just wait until someone slits the three of your throats in your sleep."

"Ha. But I don't actually sleep anymore," Raek pointed out. "And I don't think a knife could hurt me or Evetherey. Besides, they're not going to kill us. They think they're *sheltering* us at the palace. Homeland knows there are enough people out there who want Ard dead."

Ard moved past Raek's obtrusive knees, dropping down to the packed dirt street. "I don't know if I'll be back to the palace tonight, Raek. I'm heading over to the harbor to see if they have a late ship sailing out."

His friend nodded respectfully. "You're doing the right thing, Ard. Tell them hello from me."

Ard forced a smile onto his face. "I will."

He ended the conversation on his terms, swinging the carriage door shut. Then he tugged at his jacket and headed into the night.

~

*The thrill is in the convincing. To transform a stalwart no into an eager yes is unrivaled satisfaction.*

# CHAPTER

# 36

Life moved at a different pace here. Ard had felt it even before entering the village of Sunden Springs. The houses were spaced thinly across the hilly green landscape. The residents, in their simple woven clothing, seemed to be in no rush, despite the fact that most of them looked actively engaged in some kind of work.

Many were scattered across sprawling farmlands. Others were weeding in the yard or making simple repairs to their plain homes. Children played in the dirt and Ard saw several adults take goods without any noticeable exchange of money. Even Ard's horse seemed to respond to the atmosphere, slowing to a lazy saunter.

But the strangest thing—the biggest difference from his life in Beripent—were the smiles. Nearly every man, woman, and child greeted him with a friendly grin or a wave. Some even called out a midday, "How do you do!"

*Looks like you picked a good spot for them, Raek,* Ard thought as he followed his friend's directions, winding up the road toward the taller of two hills.

His coat hung open, the fall weather noticeably warmer this far to the south of Espar. Dust motes hung in the still air, shimmering in rays of direct sunlight like detonated Grit. It was always drier on the leeward side. Not a barren desert, but a pleasant aridity that felt refreshing compared to the mold-growing dampness of Beripent.

Despite his abrupt departure from Raek and Quarrah, Ardor Benn hadn't rushed his journey. The ship on which he'd booked passage had been anything but express, stopping for a full day at every harbor along Espar's western coast. Contrary to his usual nature, Ard wanted the time alone, feeling no need to speak or be spoken to. Time to wander Espar's other cities as a mere observer.

The world had felt bigger to him over the last week. In a new way, he'd noticed people living full and complex lives, each life intertwining with countless others until the world seemed like one inexplicably connected hive. Not akin to Centrum's Glassminds, but a web of individuality and agency. People did right. People did wrong.

And all these people were going to die.

Ard had been painfully aware how word of the Moonwatch Festival decreased the farther south he traveled. It stung him with an overwhelming feeling of despair. Even if everyone knew the truth—even if every woman, man, and child were flocking to the Char, Evetherey could never hope to shield them all.

A small leather-wrapped ball rolled onto the path—Ard could hardly call it a *road*, this far on the fringe of the rural village. His horse stopped as a young boy raced out to collect the object. Waiting beside a rocky outcropping were two friends, none of the kids looking older than ten.

"Sorry about that, mister." The shaggy-haired lad's accent was more country than Ard was used to hearing. As the boy stood there covered in dust, holding that ball, Ard's thoughts suddenly turned to Tobey. Would his little gang of street orphans go to the Char during the coming Passing? Did anyone know the real extent of the danger?

These kids in Sunden Springs were certainly going to die of Moonsickness. This far off the beaten path, it seemed unlikely that the Glassminds would find them in time to see them through the transformation—not that anyone in Sunden Springs would meet Garifus's mob-mentality criteria for joining.

Instinctively, Ard reached into his jacket and plucked a single mark Ashing from his pocket. He flicked it off his thumb, watching the large coin make revolutions through the sunlight. The little boy caught it without flinching, a smile on his face as he opened his hand and studied it.

"What's this, mister?"

Ard stared down from the saddle in disbelief. Had this kid never seen an Ashing before? Maybe Ard shouldn't have been so shocked. It had taken him two full days of riding just to reach Sunden Springs. The small community seemed wholly self-sufficient, with trade, barter, and borrow being enough for these humble people.

"It's a dragon scale," Ard decided to say.

"Goff stars, mister!" exclaimed the kid, his friends racing to his side to inspect the gift. "You seen a dragon?"

Ard chuckled. "Seen them, tracked them...spoken with them."

"Bet you's got some tales to tell," said one of the other boys.

"Like the man on the hill," said the other.

His comment sent a chill of nerves down Ard's spine, causing him to glance up the path. At this distance, he could barely make out the large house set into a grassy divot in the hillside.

"You know him?" Ard asked. But when he turned back, the three boys were racing through the field, tossing the ball and whooping gleefully.

Ard nudged his horse forward again, the anxiety of his visit building as he drew so close to his destination. Once again, he found himself rehearsing his opening lines for the conversation ahead, all the time knowing that when it came time to say them, even the verbose Ardor Benn would be rendered speechless.

His horse splashed through a small creek that flowed across the path, a telltale sign of the plentiful freshwaters springs that originated higher in the hills. From here, the trail climbed just two hundred feet before it reached the house that Raek had told him about.

Ard swung down from the saddle, leaving his mount by the clear water and continuing upward on foot. He paced his steps by the pounding of his heart, two beats per footfall, and finding that he was there all too soon.

It was a quaint residence, but noticeably more elaborate than the rest of the village below. Nestled into the hillside, it had a steeply pitched roof with clay shingles and a wide covered porch that wrapped around three sides. Open barrels were positioned below the eaves, hopeful to catch any rain that might break over the hills. A lazy black-and-white cat lounged on the front steps, its twitching tail the only indicator that it was even alive.

Much of the hillside property was dedicated to a flourishing garden, which brought a smile to Ard's face. Ripe, red tomatoes, peppers, squash, and gourds. Ard recognized the tops of carrots, onions, and garlic. Twisting grape vines along a white trellis. A swatch of corn with mature ears bowing for harvest.

Movement inside the house caught his eye, just a flash of something passing inside the window. His stomach in his throat, Ard moved up the porch steps, finally inspiring the cat to leap up and disappear into the garden. Removing his brimmed riding hat, Ard dropped it onto a bench beside the door.

He had planned to knock, but the thought of waiting those brief moments for the door to open seemed like unnecessary torture. Casting aside all his inhibitions, Ardor Benn threw open the door and barged into his parents' home.

Not two steps past the threshold, he ground to a halt. A dark-haired girl of seven or eight years was cross-legged on the floor of the small sitting room, a collection of wooden dolls seated in a semi-circle around her. She leapt up at Ard's intrusion calling, "Papa! Papa!" as she ran into the next room.

As Ard stood rooted in confusion, a man rounded the corner, his hands white with flour. "Can I help you?" He looked roughly Ard's age, with a similar height and build. His hair was black and his skin was two shades darker. The look on his face was more curious than concerned.

"Yes," Ard replied. "Is this not the Castenac home?"

"It was."

"*Was?*" repeated Ard. "Did they...move?"

The man's expression softened almost to the point of tears. "They...They passed on, Homeland keep them."

Ard felt the wooden floor reel beneath him. His emotions tangled inside his chest until he didn't know what he was feeling. Was it sadness? Anger? Or just an overwhelming sense of regret?

"When did..." he stammered, trying to regain control. Trying not to have a total breakdown in front of this stranger. "What happened?"

"It was just...their time."

*Time.* What was *time*? What right did it have to take his parents when Garifus Floc had cheated time and lived for centuries?

"Arelia went first," the man explained. "About a year ago. Just laid down for bed one night and didn't wake up. Sidon hung on for another eight cycles or so, but it was just too much for his heart. We buried him at the start of summer."

Ard felt tears running down his face, but they barely felt like his. They were the tears of his past, the version of himself that had loved his parents enough to do anything to free them from their debts.

"How did you know them?" the man asked, his own eyes starting to glisten.

"They were..." started Ard. "I knew them a long time ago."

A woman suddenly appeared at the man's elbow. She was petite and fair, with light brown hair pulled into a braid. Plain features, but beautiful in her simplicity.

"Would you like to come in?" She gestured behind her.

Ard didn't reply, but his feet must have moved on their own. By the time the room stopped spinning, he was seated at a rustic dining table, the woman placing a steaming cup of tea and a buttery biscuit in front of him.

"The Castenacs didn't have many callers from out of town," she said. "Where did you say you were from?"

Ard stared at the curls of steam rising in front of his face. "Who are you?" he whispered. *And what are you doing in my parents' home?*

"Sorry," the man said. "We're the Akers. Thomps"—he gestured to himself—"Juna"—to his wife—"and our daughter Guidance."

"Guidance," Ard repeated. "A Wayfarist name."

"Yes," said Thomps. "That's how we first connected with the Castenacs when they came to Sunden Springs, what...over a decade ago. We don't have Holy Isles out here, but Arelia was as close as they come."

Ard heard his mother's voice—not as clearly as Evetherey's telepathy, but much more meaningful, trickling down the dried-up riverbed of his memory.

*"Never Settle, Ardor. Trust in the Homeland and it will give you strength to rise above."*

What would his mother say now? The Homeland was a group of enhanced beings determined to exterminate anyone who didn't join them. And as for his religious name...well, now he had made it infamous as a criminal and a liar.

"We shared many dinners around this table with them." Juna ran her hand along its wooden edge. "Sidon was quite the craftsman. Fixed up a lot of homes before his body grew too weak. Even then, the kids will tell you they loved to hear his stories of the big city."

"The man on the hill," Ard muttered. His dad's smiling face unexpectedly imprinted itself on Ard's mind. Father had been so positive. So affable. Ard had his dad to thank for the Castenac charisma.

Ardor Benn glanced around the room, overwhelmed with a mix of helplessness and foolishness. His parents were dead. And he hadn't been here for them.

"Sidon left us the house," said Thomps.

"And Arelia's beautiful garden," Juna added.

"Didn't they...have any family?" Ard asked.

Thomps and Juna shared a sad look. "Just us."

Thomps might as well have reached across the table and punched him in the stomach. These two simpletons sitting in his parents' home were not family. This felt like a ruse gone wrong. Like the Akers had stolen from Ard while his guard was down.

"They had a son." Juna's comment seemed like an afterthought.

Ard felt his mind clear, his entire focus keying into her words. "Oh?"

Thomps nodded. "They didn't speak of him much. Except at the end. Sidon told the kids that his son had been a Harvester on Pekal. That he had chased dragons and brought Grit to the cities."

Ard swallowed. "What happened to him?"

"He met a Harvester's end," answered Thomps. "His body was never recovered."

As if on cue, Guidance ran into the room. Her mother caught her in passing and pulled her into a tight hug. "I can't imagine what they felt all those years."

Grief. Despair. He had brought that upon his parents. And when the grief had grown too strong, his parents had simply replaced him. Another version of himself. One that had stayed true to his religious upbringing. Married a wholesome woman. Had a child...

In a very real way, Tomps Aker was living the life that could have been his. Ard acknowledged the envy bubbling up inside him. He let it stew for a time before shoving it back down. These people hadn't done anything wrong. On the contrary. They had been here when Ard hadn't.

Something struck him. An idea. A thought. It rolled around his head, gaining momentum until he felt sure of it. With perfect clarity, Ardor Benn saw how things needed to end. Not for the world, or for civilization, but how things needed to end *for him*.

He had ruined everything he'd once had in this life—his parents had died in grief over him, and he'd destroyed almost every relationship he'd ever had. All for the sake of the ruse. Only Raek had remained constant, but even his partner had changed beyond compare. There was no place for Ardor Benn anymore.

No *need* for him.

Ard stood up, his biscuit and tea untouched. "I have to go." It had been a mistake to come here. He had meant to take his parents back to Beripent so Evetherey could shield them from the Moon rays. Now he was all the way across Espar for nothing. If he left now, he might make it back to the Char in time for the first orchestra rehearsal with Azania Fyse.

"We didn't catch your name." Thomps rose, following Ard back into the sitting room.

"It doesn't matter." Ard pushed open the front door and moved onto the porch. The cat had returned, and the animal stared at him with eyes that bored into his soul.

"I can see you're hurting," Thomps persisted. "They must have meant a lot to you. They were special to a lot of people."

*But not like they were to me*, Ard wanted to say. But how could he measure another's grief?

"We like to think Si and Arelia are watching over us," Thomps said quietly. "Even now."

Ard paused, not turning. "What do you mean?"

"They're buried at the top of the hill," the man answered. "Sidon's request. So they could look down on all of Sunden Springs and make sure we're taking care of each other. You're welcome to spend a while up there before you leave town."

"I don't have the time," Ard said. But the moment the door shut, he changed directions, his feet finding a well-worn trail that carried him up the hill. He knew he wouldn't leave Sunden Springs today if he saw his parents' resting place. He knew a potent sorrow and remorse would claim him, holding him captive through the remainder of the day. Probably into the night. If he went up there, he wouldn't make it back to Beripent in time for the first rehearsal with the orchestra. His delay could complicate the job and jeopardize the ruse.

But for once, Ardor Benn didn't care.

~

*I'm feeling heavy tonight, yet there is a strange freedom in this weight upon my shoulders.*

# CHAPTER

# 37

Quarrah stared at her reflection in the tall easel mirror propped in the corner of the staging tent. In a way, it was like looking at her past. Thick-rimmed spectacles, ringlets in her red wig, and makeup caked so thick that her skin looked like it was sculpted out of wax.

Stepping back into the heeled shoes of Azania Fyse came with a wide array of emotions. But hidden among the anxiety and uneasiness, Quarrah couldn't help but recognize a significant dose of nostalgia. Being Azania Fyse had never been comfortable, but the last time she'd been onstage, the world hadn't been so complicated. She hadn't worried about time travel or evolved human transformations. It had been a simple game of staying ahead of the Regulators and fooling the king to steal his Regalia.

"I'm surprised the mirror hasn't cracked, the way you're glowering at it," Kercha Gant said from behind her.

Without turning around, Quarrah looked at the woman through the mirror. Kercha was lounging on a padded chair, both legs draped over one arm. Quarrah wasn't wearing a gown for this rehearsal, but her green dress was much finer than the black shirt and pants Kercha was wearing. Their apparent uniform swap left Quarrah with a twinge of envy toward the soprano's role. Quarrah would much rather be the one lurking under the stage, just as she was sure Kercha would rather be posing on it.

"I'm not glowering." Quarrah leaned toward the mirror, scraping at the red line of her lipstick. "Just concentrating."

"Don't touch your lips," said Kercha. "You'll only make it worse." The woman swung her legs down and stood up, crossing the tent with a lackadaisical gait. She grabbed Quarrah's shoulder and yanked her away from the easel mirror.

"Ugh. What did you do?" Kercha pinched the hem of her black sleeve and used the edge of the fabric to wipe the smear. "I told you not to bite your lips. Teeth?" Kercha bared hers, prompting Quarrah to do the same. There must have been a smear there, too, because Kercha promptly gave them a scrub.

Quarrah had developed an interesting relationship with Kercha Gant in the last ten days. The two women had seen each other every single day, rehearsing in the privacy of the *Be'Igoth* so Kercha's voice would line up with the movement of Quarrah's mouth.

As teachers went, Quarrah actually preferred Kercha Gant over Cinza Ortemion. Obviously more passionate about music than anything else in her life, Kercha had started her coaching with tips about rhythm and timing. Eventually, it had turned to diction, expression, and physical poise. And when the snooty woman had seen Quarrah's first attempt at applying her own makeup, Kercha had been compelled to intervene.

Quarrah had been pleased by how quickly the mannerisms of Azania Fyse had come back to her. It was a good thing, too. She'd had half a year to master it the first time, but this concert had given her less than a cycle.

"And I don't know why you were concentrating so hard," Kercha said, stepping back to examine Quarrah's makeup. "Looking glum comes naturally to you."

The insults were the constant, regardless of the teacher. Kercha made it continually apparent that she and Quarrah were not to consider themselves allies, let alone colleagues, or friends. The soprano was helping her out of a sense of loyalty to music and her son. That was all fine with Quarrah Khai. She certainly wasn't looking for a friend at such a critical time as this.

In a few moments, she would walk onto that stage for Azania Fyse's first public reappearance. In Ardor Benn's absence, she'd been forced to come up with a story about what had happened to Azania in her years-long disappearance. To be honest, Quarrah was having a hard time keeping those details straight. Hopefully, Ard would bail her out of any verbal corner into which she might paint herself.

But that was only if Ard decided to return from whatever *personal* outing had taken him away from their world-saving ruse. The fact that she hadn't seen him tonight was unnerving, but Quarrah didn't lose hope. Ard was notorious for being late, but he always made it work. His new conductor persona—Conques Fabley—would probably show up in the nick of time, leaping onto the podium with a smile that would charm everyone.

"I was concentrating on the lyrics," Quarrah replied. "I've been stumbling over the fourth song in the cycle. Can we go over the second stanza?"

Kercha cleared her throat and began to sing, the tempo quick and the melody bouncy.

I despise when he's out in the rain,
All my patience I try to maintain,

When he drips and he shakes,

I point out his mistakes,

Then he whines to break free of his chain.

Quarrah waved her hand. "I've got that one. I guess it's the next verse."

She didn't find the lyrics overly humorous or clever, playing for cheap laughs more often than not. Kercha had told her that, as the performer, the song would come across more sincere if Quarrah secretly decided which she was singing about—a husband or a dog. Quarrah couldn't imagine having either in real life, so she had come to terms with the fact that her performance might be seen as insincere. What did it matter anyway? The morning after the concert, the world would wake up Moonsick and no one would be talking about Azania's song.

"I'm talking about the verse with the nonsense words," said Quarrah.

"Ah." Kercha launched into it without hesitation.

Bow wow biddy boo biddy ruff-ruff,

He thinks he is so very tough-tough,

His logic is patchy,

His kisses are scratchy,

And he cries when I tell him enough-nough.

The tent flap parted and Wysar Stone appeared. The stage manager was notably young for such a prestigious position. Quarrah had only just met him two hours ago, when her private carriage had delivered her and Kercha directly into the dressing tent at the edge of the stage. The young man had already popped in a dozen times to update Azania about the progress of the rehearsal. But this time he seemed more anxious than usual, his left eye visibly twitching.

"Swayla Tham has gone home," he reported with a degree of finality in his voice.

"Wasn't she going to rehearse the orchestra on the instrumental pieces?" said Quarrah.

"She did," squeaked Wysar, "for the last hour and a half. She could not be persuaded to stay any longer, considering that she already feels insulted for not being allowed to conduct the song cycle with you."

"You know it is customary for the soloist to bring her own conductor," replied Quarrah.

"With all due respect," said Wysar, "that seems to be a custom only you observe, Miss Fyse."

"Maestro Fabley will be here," Quarrah assured him.

"Eventually, I'm sure," said Wysar. "But how long can we make the orchestra wait? Sixty of the most respected musicians in the Greater Chain are sitting on that stage out there, waiting for instruction."

"Then give them some," Kercha interjected. "You are the stage manager, are you not? Why don't you manage the stage?"

"Yes. I'm happy to relay any message you would like, Miss Azania," said Wysar. "Or you could deliver it yourself. I believe your appearance would go a long way toward keeping everyone content. Despite my assurances, I have heard murmurs among the musicians. Some think it possible that your name is merely being used as a publicity scam to draw a large number of people to the Moonwatch Festival."

"Ha!" Kercha laughed, dropping into the padded chair again. "Imagine that! Some people don't believe Azania Fyse could possibly be back from the dead."

Quarrah stiffened awkwardly. "Well, I'm not going to parade myself across the stage just to satisfy their curiosity. They'll see I'm alive when we begin our rehearsals."

Wysar cleared his throat. "And when will that be, exactly?"

"You can tell them I am quite exhausted after my travel from Dronodan—"

"You told Wysar you'd been in Talumon," Kercha interjected.

Quarrah squirmed. She couldn't even remember where Azania had supposedly come from, let alone all she'd done in the last four and a half years. Quarrah felt a sizzle of indignation rise in her chest. This was Ard's stupid ruse. If he didn't care enough to be here for it, then Quarrah wasn't going to put her neck on the line and cover for him.

"You know what," she exclaimed hotly, "send the blazing orchestra home. Conques Fabley can reassemble them whenever he chooses to show up."

Wysar Stone swallowed the bad news, nodding reluctantly as he escaped through the tent flap.

"Well, that was a bit out of character for Azania, wouldn't you say?" Kercha remarked.

"What do you know about it?" snapped Quarrah.

"I know enough to say that you're going to get swarmed by curious musicians the moment you step out of this tent."

"Then I'll wait them out," said Quarrah. "I can dress down and slip out after the excitement has died."

Kercha Gant stood. "I hope you're not expecting me to wait with you…"

Quarrah flicked her wrist in Kercha's direction. "Get out of here. You can take my carriage. That might draw some of them away."

"You're a gem," Kercha droned, helping herself to a shot of liquor on the side table before ducking outside.

Finally alone, Quarrah let out a long sigh and plopped herself down on the soft chair, feeling one of the wig pins prick her scalp as she leaned her head back. What did dressing up provide a woman, besides making her easier to notice? Ha. The very thing Quarrah Khai always tried to avoid.

She found a comfortable position and closed her eyes. If Ard really wasn't back, she might have to drop by the palace to bother Raek about it tonight. Or maybe she'd check the *Be'Igoth*. Raek was there most afternoons, helping San keep his Grit supply stocked.

*Sparks.* Knowing Ard, he was probably getting himself into trouble. Strange that he hadn't taken Raek. Didn't Ard know better than to wander off by himself where no one could watch his back?

For the first time, Quarrah wondered if Ard might not come back at all. What if the Moonwatch Festival ruse was exactly that— a trick to keep her and Raek busy while he slipped away on his own? She knew Ard had a penchant for starting his life over. The number of times he had faked his own death was proof of that. What if he had decided that their fight against the Glassminds and Moonsickness was beyond hope? Maybe he had a plan of his own that didn't involve even his closest companions.

The rustle of the tent flap caused Quarrah to sit up swiftly. A gray-haired woman wearing servant clothes startled at the sudden movement, the canvas falling closed behind her.

"My apologies," the woman said, bowing her head and wringing a damp rag in both hands. "I was asked to tidy up in here. The carriage wasn't outside, so I'd assumed you'd gone. I'll come back at a more convenient time."

"Thank you," Quarrah said dismissively. But the servant didn't go.

"You're the singer everyone is talking about…" She ventured an admiring step closer. "Asinine Fyse?"

"*Azania*," Quarrah corrected, grateful that she hadn't been in the process of taking off her wig during the intrusion.

"Such an honor," the servant exclaimed. "I used to clean the dressing rooms at the Conservatory of Music in Octowyn. I left in '28, but everyone there spoke so highly of you."

"That's good to hear." Something about this woman made Quarrah's skin crawl. Her steady approach seemed more predatory than adulatory, and the twinkle in her eye wasn't altogether friendly.

"I'm surprised to hear you say that," the woman continued, the wringing of the rag growing more intense. "Because Azania Fyse was not at the Conservatory of Music until '29."

All at once, Quarrah realized what was happening. She tried to sidestep, springing for the exit, but the woman's rag was suddenly replaced with a thin gold knife. She caught a fistful of Quarrah's dress and pulled her off balance. With the gracefulness of a trained fighter, the servant spun Quarrah around, restraining both arms and dropping her to a knee on the tent floor. The cold blade touched her throat, its razor edge held with a determined steadiness.

"Cinza," Quarrah hissed through clenched teeth. She should have seen it coming.

"You may be a fine thief, Quarrah Khai," the woman whispered, "but nobody steals from me."

Really? She was worried about a theft? Maybe this was all just a big misunderstanding. "I don't know what you're talking about," said Quarrah. "I haven't seen you since—"

"You have stolen my soprano!"

"Kercha Gant?"

"No, you idiot!" cried Cinza. "I'm talking about *this*." She reached up and yanked off Quarrah's red wig, the pins and clips ripping free with chunks of her own sandy hair. Quarrah held in a howl, trying to wrench free. Somehow Cinza managed to regain her grip and the knife pressed even tighter.

"Azania Fyse is not yours to flaunt and display as you see fit," Cinza continued. "She is the property of Elbrig Taut and Cinza Ortemion, professional disguise management. And I demand that she be discontinued and returned immediately."

"You accuse *me* of theft," said Quarrah. "We bought Azania five years ago."

"Incorrect," Cinza cried. "You bought the exclusive rights to impersonate Azania Fyse for the period of two years. Didn't you read our agreement?"

"I did..." Quarrah muttered. "I think."

"Oh, that's good," said Cinza. "At least you've started thinking. If you care to dig up the signed papers and read the fine lettering, you'll see that there was an option to buy the rights to the persona at the end of the lease period. I don't recall you paying that."

"Azania was dead!" Quarrah cried. "And I didn't think I'd ever use her name again. Sparks, you think I *want* to be here? This was Ard's idea."

"Elbrig and I are well aware of his fingerprints all over your face," she said. "Which is the only reason I have not put this blade into your windpipe." Cinza's breath over Quarrah's shoulder smelled faintly of citrus. "Where is he?"

"If I answer, what's to stop you from killing me?"

"Ardor betrayed us!" Cinza's spittle flecked across Quarrah's cheek.

"That was a decision he made alone," she answered. "Raek and I tried to stop him."

"After everything we've done for him!"

"You're angry," said Quarrah. "I get it. If you put down the knife, maybe we can talk about it."

"Where is he?" shouted Cinza, not any closer to relinquishing her position.

"I don't know," said Quarrah.

"If you lie—"

"I'm telling the truth," she insisted. "He left in the middle of the night. Ten days ago. He was supposed to be back for the rehearsal tonight, but... he's not here."

"Why have you brought back Azania?"

"For the festival," Quarrah said. "We're trying to draw as many people into the Char as possible."

"Why?"

"To protect them from Moonsickness," Quarrah answered. "The dragons are dead."

Cinza finally let go. Quarrah dropped forward, catching herself with both hands on the rug.

"When you see Ardy," Cinza said, "tell him we're going to kill him."

Quarrah stood up, rubbing her neck. "You'll have to get in line. The Trothians have it out for him, too."

"We will also kill you," continued Cinza, "if you insist on going through with Azania Fyse at the concert."

That certainly added some unnecessary pressure. "What if we pay you the final amount?"

"I'm afraid bribery is out of the question." She picked up her fallen rag and moved toward the tent flap. "This is a matter of principle now."

"Cinza," Quarrah said as the old woman reached the exit. "Three days until the Passing…Ard's not going to stop."

Cinza Ortemion smiled, her false teeth crooked and discolored. "He never does."

Ardor Benn pressed through the crowded Char, mindful of the orange hues of sunset that clung to the broken storm clouds to the west. There was a crisp coolness in the autumn air—slightly offset by the warmth of so many gathered bodies.

Ard was pleased with the turnout for the festival, especially considering the day's poor weather. People seemed to be camped in every available open space, regardless of mud or puddles. Ard wished he could say that everyone had come unsuspectingly, merely hoping to be entertained by the concert and festivities. But the truth was abuzz through the congregation, almost louder than the music itself.

People had come in fear.

Ard didn't waste time wondering who had leaked the information about the coming Moonsickness. Each one of the council members was an equal suspect. Despite his warnings to keep the truth under wraps, someone had likely spilled it to convince a hesitant relative to come to the Char. From there, the gossip would spiral out of control until it swept every island.

Citizens and nobles had arrived as early as five days ago, pitching tents and trying to make themselves at home in the last safe place on earth. By dawn this morning, all roads leading into the Char had been utterly clogged, a perimeter of Regulators working tirelessly to dispel rumors and keep the peace.

From the snippets of conversation Ard had picked up, the people didn't really understand what was going to happen. Some said the Moon would be more powerful tonight and the Islehood would be burning a special torch in the Char. Others claimed a dragon would arrive in the nick of time to shield them. In a way, they were both right. Evetherey was both dragon and Holy Torch, and tonight she was the only hope for humankind.

Ard ducked around the back of the grand outdoor stage, the orchestra swelling in a dissonant chord. Swayla Tham's instrumental portion of the concert seemed lackluster, but hopefully it would hold people's attention until the main event.

Ard spotted San Green and a troop of Regulators standing by a Trans-Island Carriage anchored to the muddy ground, its sailcloth balloon straining upward. Instead of the usual large carriage designed to carry multiple passengers, a pilot, and plenty of equipment, this balloon would only be hauling a small basket with room for one.

Ard was almost to the carriage when a cloaked figure appeared from a cluster of trees where night's shadows had already taken root.

"Sparks, Evetherey!" Ard grabbed his chest, reeling back a step. "We need to hang a bell around your neck."

"You are startled?" Her glowing eyes narrowed under a hairless brow furrowed in confusion. "Did we not agree to meet here at sunset?"

"Sure, we did, but…" Hadn't Evetherey ever felt startled? Wasn't the pressure of tonight prickling her nerves? "Never mind." Ard glanced around the quickly darkening area. "Where's Raek?"

"I grow faint," she said. "The Moon is near. I will be quite incapacitated until sunrise."

"I know," Ard replied. "We'll try to get along without you. How much time do we have?"

"It will rise in twenty minutes," she answered. "At that time, the sickness will begin outside my reach."

"Then you'd better get to your perch." Ard moved toward the anchored basket, Evetherey following close behind. Her figure looked strangely shapeless with her broad wings confined under that cloak. In the twilight, it reminded Ard of the shrouding cloaks worn by the Faceless in the Realm.

"Ardor!" San stepped away from the line of Regulators and waved him over anxiously. "Everything's ready." The young man couldn't pull his eyes from Evetherey.

"Good work." Ard proudly slapped a hand on the wicker basket secured beneath the balloon. "This is it."

Evetherey studied the vessel, obviously unconvinced. "I am trusting your people to keep me aloft…in *this*?"

"San and Raek ran all the calculations," Ard assured her. "These Reggies know their jobs. And they have plenty of Heat Grit to keep it up."

One of the Regulators stepped forward, eyes glued to Evetherey's unique face. "Our orders come directly from Her Majesty, Queen Abeth Agaul. We will protect this vessel with our lives."

In silent response, Evetherey shrugged out of her long cloak, feathered wings suddenly unfolding as the black cloth fell to the damp earth. The Reggie swallowed visibly, a look of underqualification displayed as plainly as if she'd written it on her forehead.

San opened a little woven door on the side of the basket. "Whenever you're ready, Madam Drothan."

Evetherey stepped into the basket, San latching the door behind her. Ard thought her perch looked just large enough for her to lie down for the night. He nodded to the reptilian woman as San moved away, shouting commands at the Reggies to begin the ascent.

"Thank you, Evetherey."

The Drothan goddess turned her glowing eyes on Ard. "The real work will begin in the morning."

He nodded in understanding, suddenly hit with a measure of fatigue equal to his coming responsibility. Keeping the survivors separate from those who would be inflicted by the Moon, fighting off the growing number of Glassminds... In the morning, they might look back on this night and consider it quite relaxing.

Ard watched as the balloon rose straight upward, tethered to the earth by nothing but a thick rope. Evetherey would sail to the optimal height of three hundred feet, hovering there all night as the Regulators used strings and a simple pulley system to administer more Heat Grit into the balloon as needed.

By the look of it, Evetherey would have no problem getting to altitude before the Moon rose. Good thing, since every inch counted. Any lower and the effective perimeter of her shield would shrink. Any higher and the spot directly beneath her would be compromised.

"This isn't meant to be a reptile pun," Raek's voice chimed from behind Ard, "but I feel like we're putting all our eggs in one basket."

Ard spun around to find his enhanced friend standing a few yards away, red eyes watching the balloon rise.

"You're late," Ard said.

"Hey. That's usually my line for you," replied Raek. "There was a little kerfuffle at the southern entrance. Had to give the Reggies a hand."

"Everything okay?"

"Depends on who you ask," Raek said, sobering. "Some lord and lady from Strind showed up with half their property in a caravan of wagons."

Ard shook his head. They knew the truth, obviously. "Let me guess," said Ard. "They threw a fit because the Regulators wouldn't let them bring it all in."

"It was the opposite problem," said Raek. "They *did* let them."

Ard grunted in frustration. "They had orders! No more than a night's possessions per family. A tent and some blankets is one thing, but...we don't have the space!"

It was a limitation they had instigated this morning when it became clear that the turnout was going to explode. They needed *people* to survive the Moon Passing. Goods and possessions, even livestock, would weather the Moon rays with no effect. And the queen had ordered enough rations for everyone inside the radius to survive for a week. By then, it would be terribly obvious who was Moonsick and who wasn't.

"I know." Raek rubbed his chin. "But the goods were already inside by the time I caught wind of it. When I got to the entrance, the Reggies were turning away a working family who looked like they'd brought everything they owned in a pair of handcarts."

"Sparks," Ard cursed. "Does *everyone* know what's really going on tonight?"

"I don't think anybody *really* knows," said Raek. "But the hearsay almost makes it worse. Things are getting pretty bad on the edge of the Char."

Ard steepled his fingers against his forehead, sighing. "It's time, Raek."

"You want me to go through with it, then?"

Ard nodded sullenly. "There's no way the Regulators can keep everyone out once the Moon comes up. Sounds wrong to say it, but I guess I was hoping the festival wouldn't be quite so popular."

"It's the right thing to do," said Raek.

"It's going to cause a panic."

"We're getting close to one out there anyway."

Ard glanced up at the darkening sky. "Where do you need to be?"

"The eastern entrance is closest," said Raek. "Once I get it started, I should be able to control it from anywhere along the edge."

"We should hurry." Ard checked to make sure that San Green had everything under control with the carriage. Then he struck off, quickly realizing that he was turned around and unsure which way was east.

"Don't you have a song to conduct?" Raek asked.

Ard waved his hand. "I've got time. Quarrah might be stuck in that tent, smothered in makeup, but all I have to do is slap on a wig and mustache. Besides, they're not going to start without me."

"I'll lead," Raek said.

Ard had to jog every few steps to keep up with his partner's gait, but he wouldn't have wanted to go any slower, with mere minutes remaining. They moved down a small overgrown path, passing throngs of pedestrians. Ahead, a crimson glow was creeping into view on the eastern horizon, not warm like the rising sun, but a sickly scarlet that bled into a blackness awakening with stars.

The Char's eastern entrance was a wide plaza with a single road leading from the neighborhood beyond. The Reggies were doing exactly what they'd been told, closing the Char the moment the sunset faded. They had squared off, holding their position in front of the tall archway entrance, wooden shields raised and helmeted heads bowed. Little did the Reggies know they were guarding the new Redeye line. Most of them were likely to escape the sickness tonight, but beyond that point...

The crowd stretched into every intersecting street—hundreds of citizens still pushing to get in. Ard could sense that the situation was on the verge of hostility. If the citizens decided to charge, the Regulators wouldn't stand a chance.

That was why Raek needed to do this. As definitive and absolute as it seemed, it was their only real shot at containing the situation.

Ard was close enough now to hear what the Reggies were shouting.

"Return to your homes!"

"The Char is closed!"

"You are trespassing!"

Ard flinched as a gunshot punctuated the returning shouts from the citizens. One of the Regulators staggered backward, the line suddenly breached.

"Raek!" Ard shouted. "Now!"

Raekon Dorrel reached out his pale blue hands, the ends of his long fingers sparking. A stream of detonated Grit flowed from him, rushing out to form a Barrier wall between the Regulators and the advancing mob. But it didn't stop there. He pushed his hands to both sides, and the Barrier Grit continued to stream out, racing along the perimeter to encircle the entire Char, just as Raek had planned it. The wall stretched upward, doming in a gentle inward curve until it met at the top, the whole area safely sealed beneath.

Ard looked at his friend, eyes wide at the power he exuded. A detonation this size was unprecedented! Raek's hands remained outstretched, coaxing and manipulating the massive Barrier.

"Evetherey?" Ard asked.

"She's enclosed," he answered. "As are all the Regulators at each entrance point. They're all safe."

*But no one outside.* Ard stared through the transparent wall at the countless faces they had just doomed to Moonsickness. The Reggies were backing away in confusion, but the excluded citizens were hopelessly assaulting the Barrier with anything they had.

In just a few days, those same attackers would be voiceless, blind...their fury driven beyond anything they could now muster.

Or they'd be Glassminds.

"The bad news is," Raek said, his concentration remaining on the wall, "I'm going to miss the rest of the concert."

"The dome won't hold itself?" Ard asked.

"It might look like a perfect dome from where you are," he replied, "but this thing's as dimpled as an old lady's backside. I had to weave around people and plants. Even now, I can sense somebody on the north side trying to dig under." He flexed his hands, the result seeming to send an extra burst of Barrier Grit to patch the weak spot.

Raek glanced over his shoulder at Ard. "Tell the crazies hello from me."

"Too soon, Raek," Ard muttered. Quarrah had told him about the threat. Cinza and Elbrig were a complication, yes, but he'd planned for those.

"Just remember," Raek added, "you're the dog in Quarrah's song."

But Ard barely heard his friend's jibe. A face had caught his eye. A face on the other side of the Barrier.

"Lyndel," he whispered.

Flanked by a group of Trothians, the priestess was pounding her fist against the Barrier wall, screaming something into the face of the nearest Regulator.

Ard stepped forward, touching Raek's elbow to get his attention. "Raek. It's her."

"Lyndel. I see her."

"She's going to die out there." The realization was like a knife of guilt. Lyndel had been at the beginning of everything. She and Isle Halavend had taken the first steps toward knowledge that had forever changed the world. How was it that she was now standing on the wrong side of the wall?

"Drop the Barrier," Ard said.

"What?"

"You have to drop the Barrier and let her in." Ard's eyes flicked to the eastern sky. It was redder now, and significantly brighter. But from where he stood, it didn't look like the Moon had crested the horizon yet.

"Ard," snapped Raek, "she's been trying to kill you for cycles."

"I know," he replied. "But she won't see me. By the time she gets her bearing, I'll be back in Oriar's Square dressed like Conques Fabley. You can do it, right? Let them through the Barrier like Evetherey did in the council chamber?"

"I mean, yeah, but…" Raek shook his glass head. "This isn't right, Ard."

"How can it not be right?" he cried. "It's thanks to Lyndel that we're here!"

"She didn't make it into the Char in time," said Raek.

"You're afraid she's already Moonsick?"

"The Moon isn't up just yet."

"Then what?" Ard shouted above the tumult of the panicked mob.

"How do we decide who lives and who dies?" Raek said.

"We already did," he insisted. "That's what this whole plan is about."

"But we didn't handpick them," said Raek. "They came, or they didn't come. It wasn't up to us."

"Well, now it is." Ard's voice was low and serious. "And I'm telling you to let her through."

"She's going to kill you, Ard."

Ardor Benn sniffed. "*Someone* has to."

Raek studied him for a moment with his glowing red eyes. Then a portion of the Barrier wall seemed to blink. Lyndel stumbled through, the detonation quickly resealing behind her.

"You might want to run," Raek said.

Without another word, Ard sprinted toward Oriar's Square.

*　　*　　*

Under the great orb of the Red Moon, Azania Fyse walked onto the stage to thunderous applause. Quarrah had forgotten about the thrill that came from the roar of approval. She'd remembered the nerves and the discomfort—and what she was feeling tonight certainly lived up to those memories.

At the moment, her mind was totally blank, lyrics and phrasing blanched from her thoughts. But the sudden boost of adrenaline from the massive crowd was like a long-forgotten friend. Her body was ready to spring into action at the first sign of trouble. With this gift from the spectators, she felt like she could outrun any foe and jump to impossible heights without the aid of Drift Grit.

*Walk to your mark without looking down.* Cinza's coaching from years past rattled through Quarrah's thoughts. She kept her chin up, striding across the stage with confidence while silently cursing the uselessness of her high-heeled shoes.

Ard was approaching from the other side of the stage, a smile pasted beneath that hideous drooping blond mustache. She was sure he was reveling in the applause, despite knowing it wasn't intended for him. Conques Fabley had already received numerous complaints from the musicians about his confusing conducting patterns and inability to cue entrances. He was a no-name conductor with a shallow past—nothing like the rich complexity that had accompanied Dale Hizror's character.

The thought only made Quarrah more aware of the reach and power of the disguise managers. A new wave of fear rose in her throat. Suddenly, the precautions they'd taken against Cinza's threat seemed wholly insufficient, though it was too late to do anything about it now.

Quarrah and Ard met in the middle of the stage, just in front of the conductor's podium.

"Here we are again," he whispered.

She didn't reply, too afraid that she'd lose containment of the small detonation of Silence Grit that she'd already ignited in her mouth.

Ard winked at her in understanding. "I can think of nothing better to keep twenty thousand eyes focused than your poise and beauty, my dear."

She didn't blush under his praise like she once had, even knowing that his words were sincere. Quarrah couldn't think of anything *worse* than having ten thousand people staring at her, but she understood the need to keep the citizens happy and distracted.

Ard's quick report before changing into his conductor's costume had been worrisome. The way he'd made it sound, the rest of Beripent was pounding at the Barrier wall surrounding the Char. Raek would be able to hold them, but that meant she and Ard would have no backup if things went wrong onstage.

Cinza and Elbrig hadn't shot them from the crowd yet, so that was a good sign. Still, why was Ard taking so long to offer his hand?

She stuck out hers instead, adjusting her thin, lacy glove. Ard took it in a gesture of respect and acknowledgment, but Quarrah squeezed with a firmness that Cinza would have deemed very unladylike. At the impact of their hands, Quarrah felt the Slagstone spark in Ard's palm, a slight tingling singe. At once, the Grit in her white glove detonated, rushing around them and encompassing the entire stage.

They were doubly protected now. Raek's outer wall had drawn the Redeye line, but the stage was now enclosed in its own protective Barrier—a dome within a dome.

Ard released her hand and turned to the crowd, the applause quickly dying to hear what he had to say. Quarrah saw Queen Abeth's tent prominently placed at the edge of the stage along with several that belonged to members of the noble council.

"Ladies and gentlemen from across the Greater Chain!" Ard was affecting his voice with a slight Talumonian accent. One more thing to get people to dissociate him from Dale Hizror. "On this historic night, the Royal Orchestra is proud to present Rous Kenette's comedic Song Cycle Number Three, sung for you by our inimitable, transcendent, unparalleled soloist. A woman of mystery and allure who some claim cheated death itself. I give you...the beautiful Lady Azania Fyse!"

Ard stepped back and the crowd cheered louder than before. Quarrah tried not to wriggle under the praise, gaining no additional adrenaline from this round. Doing her best to maintain elegant poise, she glided a few steps to the side as Ard took the podium.

His baton came up and the crowd quieted even faster than before. It was almost an eerie silence, following so shortly after cacophony. As the first notes rolled out of the orchestra, Quarrah dared part her lips just a little. The tiniest bit of the contained detonation in her mouth leaked out, and not even her breath made a sound.

The first short song in the group was set to a fast tempo, but Quarrah was confident in her entrance. She counted the beats, the lyrics coming back to her in the heat of the moment.

She opened her mouth and began to sing at full volume, trusting in the Silence Grit to mask her lackluster voice.

> My troubles began on the first day of fall.
> I found him curled up at the base of a wall...

Not a sound.

The Silence Grit was doing its job perfectly, but Kercha Gant wasn't! What the blazes? Quarrah had seen her crawl beneath the stage not fifteen minutes ago. The soprano had missed her entrance!

With a wave of his baton, Ard cut off the confused orchestra. Without stepping down from the podium, he turned to Quarrah, who silently widened her eyes to show that she didn't know what was happening. He put on a confident smile and spoke to her loudly so the bated crowd could easily overhear.

"My dear Azania, the song is a comedy, not a prank. Must you toy with me when you know this is the biggest concert of my life?"

His words got a chuckle from the front rows of the crowd, but the musicians were shooting him glares, murmuring about the unprofessionalism of being cut off mere measures into a piece.

"Now," Ard continued, tapping his baton on the podium stand, "let us start again from the top."

He marked the downbeat and the brisk tempo resumed in what felt like a loop in time. Every passing note raised Quarrah's anxiety, but when her entrance came, she hit it with full voice, her mouth clearly articulating the words. This time a beautiful soprano tone pealed forth from beneath the stage. But it wasn't Kercha Gant.

That voice belonged to Cinza Ortemion.

Keeping her chin up, Quarrah flicked her eyes to the podium. Ard was staring back at her, obviously coming to the same chilling conclusion. With Ard's attention turned away from the orchestra, Quarrah saw one of the cellists suddenly rise from his seat. The man was pale, with a round face and a head of curly black hair. He let the expensive instrument fall to the side and she saw the glint of a blade—a thin knife fixed to the tip of his horsehair string bow.

"Ard!" Quarrah shouted, abandoning her lyrics for a warning. But any sound that would have escaped her throat was muted by Silence Grit.

At the same time, the stage beneath Quarrah's feet heaved upward. She staggered backward, rolling an ankle on those blazing heels and tumbling into the violin section.

A trapdoor in the floor banged open. Hadn't they removed the trapdoor from the plans for this stage? As Quarrah righted herself, Cinza Ortemion sprang through the opening, her jump clearly assisted by Drift Grit as she landed squarely on the stage.

She was in a physical state like Quarrah had seen her in only once before—hairless, toothless, wearing tan long underwear that was splattered in fresh blood. Cinza clutched a long knife in one hand and a Roller in the other.

Without hesitation, she snapped off a shot. The lead ball ripped through the puffy sleeve of Quarrah's red gown, grazing her shoulder, but finding a deadlier mark in the violinist behind her.

The musician slumped from his chair with a groan, instrument clattering to the floor as the rest of the players erupted into screams and chaos. Quarrah dove forward, snatching up the fallen violin and pouncing at Cinza, who was cocking the Slagstone hammer for a second shot.

Quarrah brought the violin around like a club, slamming it into the side of Cinza's bald head. It exploded into scraps, splinters of wood floating lazily through the cloud of weightlessness that mushroomed up from beneath the stage.

The panicked musicians had retreated as far as possible, abandoning instruments in their haste, only to realize that they were trapped onstage by the detonation of Barrier Grit. Outside the protective dome, citizens and nobles were screaming and retreating from the sudden violence. A few Regulators had fired on the Barrier dome before taking to a more sensible plan and scouring the perimeter for some way in. Beyond the stage, the audience stumbled away from the danger like a crashing wave of fear and confusion.

From the corner of Quarrah's eye she saw Ard and the man grappling on the podium, the bayonetted cello bow on the ground at their feet. At some point in the fight, the man's hair had come loose, revealing it as a wig with an artificial forehead attached. The rubbery skin was folded grotesquely back as if his face had melted in a hot blast. It was clearly Elbrig Taut, and he was screaming in Ard's face.

"You sold us out, Ardor Benn! You were a trusted client, and you sent the queen's own Reggies hunting for us!"

Ard began to articulate a response, but Quarrah's attention was stolen by Cinza, who was coming around with the Roller, a trickle of blood dripping down her pasty forehead.

Quarrah jumped backward, catching the pocket of Drift Grit and sending her higher than Cinza had expected as the second shot sounded. This time the ball ricocheted off the inside of the Barrier dome, chipping into the stage.

Glancing through the trapdoor as she passed over, Quarrah saw the dead figure of Kercha Gant lying facedown in the mud. The responsibility for her death struck Quarrah like a Roller ball. She and Ard had taken precautions for themselves, but they hadn't considered for a moment that Kercha would be in danger. And their precautions were turning out to be more of a detriment since Cinza and Elbrig had managed to get themselves *inside* the Barrier.

Quarrah landed adroitly on the edge of the stage, her spacious gown swishing around her legs. She lunged forward, only to find that her right heel had come down between two boards, wedging itself impossibly tight from the extra weight of her landing.

"You thought a simple detonation of Barrier Grit would keep us from fulfilling our word?" Cinza squawked, moving toward her with dread determination. "We warned you, Quarrah. You didn't have to throw in your lot with *him*. Now you'll die unarmed, dressed like the lady you could never hope to be."

But Cinza was wrong. Quarrah wasn't unarmed. Whipping up the front of her gown, she plucked a mesh teabag of Grit from a strap around her thigh. She pitched it as Cinza raised the Roller.

Sparks flared on impact and the Void Grit erupted at Cinza's feet, throwing the woman forcefully backward. The gun went off in a harmless direction as it left her hand, half its balls now spent.

"Elbrig!" Ard shouted. "It doesn't have to end like this!"

The two men were standing ten feet apart among toppled chairs and music stands. Elbrig was holding his bow knife, but Ard had something in his outstretched hand as well. A small glass Grit vial.

"Our kind of trust cannot be rebuilt," Elbrig said.

"And that's worth dying over?" Ard asked. "If I drop this vial, it'll snuff out the Barrier. You'll have two dozen Regulators swarming you and Cinza in seconds."

"I only need half that time to kill you," he sneered.

Ard hurled the vial at the stage, thin glass shattering as a flash cloud erupted from the sparks. At the same moment, the Barrier around the stage was extinguished.

Elbrig thrust, but Quarrah was faster, throwing a small bag of Drift Grit in his path. He lost his balance in the unexpected weightlessness, kicking helplessly as he floated forward. He exited into the arms of two Regulators, one of them breaking the bow as they wrested it from his grasp.

"There was another," Ard informed the Reggies. "A woman." He moved to Quarrah's side, breathing heavily, but otherwise looking uninjured. His mustache had fallen off, but that unflattering blond wig was still intact.

Quarrah scanned across the stage. "Where did she—"

Cinza leapt up from behind the podium, rushing Elbrig's captors in what looked like a hopeless rescue.

"Look out!" Ard shouted.

The Regulator with the knife bow whirled, bringing up the broken weapon in self-defense. The sharp tip skewered Cinza's neck, drawing along a string of bloody horsehair as it passed through.

The bald woman reached up, gasping, gurgling. The Reggie let go and she staggered backward, pawing at the fatal wound. Cinza stumbled into a music stand and fell to her knees, the life fading from her eyes.

Quarrah felt her own breath stolen away by the gory shock of it. Her gaze turned to Elbrig, who stood in horrified silence with both arms pinned behind his back. He stared at Cinza—his mysterious other half. His face shone with a look of unspeakable sadness, twinged with visible disappointment. Then he nodded resolutely to

Cinza, his curly wig accentuating the gesture. Straining against his captors, he kicked something across the stage.

Cinza's Roller skidded directly to her. With one bloody hand, she picked it up, her thumb pulling back the hammer. One of the Regulators shouted, "Gun!" and then the shot sounded.

The ball took Elbrig through his wrinkled false forehead, the curly wig slumping off as he fell against the Regulator holding him. Everyone stood rigid, but by Quarrah's count, there were still two more shots in that gun. Just enough to carry out what Cinza had threatened.

The dying woman clicked back the hammer, turning the barrel toward Quarrah. There was a puff of smoke and a loud crack. Quarrah flinched, but the shot had come from the Reggie behind her. Cinza Ortemion fell backward with a hole in her chest. Her gun went skyward, lifeless finger pulling the trigger.

Then everything was still.

Ard reached out for Quarrah's hand and she felt him trembling. She was having a hard time comprehending what had just happened. For some strange reason, the next lines from the blazing song cycle were stuck in her head.

> *He looked at me helplessly, big eyes imploring,*
> *And I thought his life looked pathetic and boring.*

The man standing beside her was certainly neither. She clung to his hand, wondering how she had gotten here again. Wondering why she was *still* beside him. Then someone shouted a warning and all eyes turned upward.

The Trans-Island Carriage was coming down.

The thick rope that was supposed to be keeping it tethered had gone slack and the whole thing was dropping steadily toward the stage.

"Sparks." Ard released her hand, eyes to the sky.

Quarrah saw what Cinza's final shot had done. The ball had struck one of the curved wooden slats that formed the balloon's frame. It had splintered, rending a long tear in the side of the sailcloth.

"Keep it up!" Ard bellowed, sprinting across the stage. Quarrah took off after him, ducking around the acoustic shell to the area where the flying carriage was tethered.

San was standing as still as a statue, the limp rope in his hands, a coil of it at his feet. Around him, the Regulators were in full panic, some of them hopelessly hurling clay pots of Heat Grit at the falling balloon.

"We've got to keep her up!" Ard screamed.

"There's nothing…" San muttered, staring upward. "We can't do anything for her, sir! She's coming down."

"The trees…" Quarrah muttered, an idea coming to her. She raced to San, ripping the rope from his shocked hands without an explanation. Throwing it over one shoulder, she sprinted in the direction of the tall trees that bordered the area like walls of shadow.

Ard was at her side in a heartbeat, dragging against the weight of the settling balloon. In moments, Evetherey's basket caught the treetop and nestled out of sight into the darkness of the upper branches, the sailcloth balloon collapsing over the top. Quarrah and Ard eased off the rope, hoping the tree would hold the basket's precious life-saving cargo.

"I'm guessing you didn't finish the song?" Raek's voice cut through the darkness. Quarrah turned to see his glowing eyes drawing toward them at a run.

"She's dropped too far," Ard cried. "The outer edge of the Char won't be protected. Flames! We're lost, Raek!"

"Not yet." The Glassmind slid to a halt in the mud, his eyes flashing upward at the tree. "Every foot counts, and she's not on the ground. The population is most dense in front of the stage, and the basket is secure at a height of fifty-three feet. Considering the maximum range of her absorption at three hundred feet, we're looking at an eighty-two percent decrease…" He trailed off, sprinting away from them.

"Where are you going?" Ard shouted. "We need to get her back up there!"

"Too late for that," replied Raek's booming voice. "The Moon has touched too much of the Char now. Redeye line is much closer. It's time to cut our losses and put up a new Barrier."

Quarrah felt her stomach sink. A single shot fired in senseless revenge had reduced humanity's sole chance at survival from a square mile to...what? Mere yards?

"Well," Ard said with a weary sigh. "I guess this means you don't have to sing that stupid song."

Quarrah scoffed at how trivial it all sounded now. What would the morning bring? The world wouldn't know for sure about the spread of Moonsickness until the symptoms started showing up. That gave people most of tomorrow to worry and stress.

Then their voices would be silenced.

Then their sight would fade.

Then the world would tear itself apart in a mindless rage.

~

*When the music swells around me, I am nearly deafened by the choices I've made.*

# CHAPTER

# 38

Afternoon sunlight angled through the tavern's broken window, spilling across empty tables and overturned chairs. It was the quiet that Quarrah found most unnerving—an eerie silence that pervaded places that should have been teaming with liveliness.

She squeezed through the open door, a pot of protective Barrier Grit clutched in one hand. The place smelled of mold and spilled ale, and a dozen rats scurried away at her arrival.

A mere three days since the Moon Passing and Quarrah Khai could clearly see that the world was dying. Her boots crunched over broken glass as she crept for the stairs. This place had been ransacked, just like the rest of what she'd seen in the Northern Quarter. Not by Bloodeyes; they weren't ripe yet. This place had been torn apart by desperate people. What could they have possibly wanted? Ashings? Ale? Neither would protect them from what had already infected their bodies.

She rounded the bar, a cloud of flies buzzing up from a corpse on the ground. Quarrah drew back, surprised to recognize the man in the bloodstained apron. Folks at the tavern had called him Jingles, probably for the large ring of keys he often wore. The bartender's throat was slit and his right hand still clutched a spent Singler. Jingle's glazed eyes were fixed open in a death stare, and Quarrah could tell by the whites that he had been killed before the second phase of Moonsickness had taken him.

Feeling her stomach churn, Quarrah moved up the stairs toward the third floor. Beripent wore the consequences of the Moon Passing on its damp sleeve, the city so quickly devolved into a cesspool of lawless fear. From what she'd seen since leaving the Char on her secret mission, slums stood abandoned while wealthy neighborhoods like the Northern Quarter were completely pilfered. Outside, bodies littered the streets, murdered like Jingles without so much as a scream to offer.

Sliding a key from her pocket, she headed down the hallway. Numbered doors lined both sides, leading to simple, single-room apartments. Most were broken open, some of the doors knocked completely to the floor.

The hallway came to a T and she rounded the corner, nearly crashing into a man who stood with a broken board tucked under one arm.

"Sparks!" She reared back, raising her Grit pot. The man also readied for action, bringing up the wooden slat like a club. They faced off for just a moment, the man's swollen eyes a pinkish hue as he squinted against his fading vision.

Quarrah recognized him, too. Didn't know his name, but she'd seen him plenty of times on her way to and from her apartment here.

He lowered the board, taking a curious step toward her. The man tried to say something, but not a sound escaped. He tried again, mouthing the words with more emphasis so she could read his lips.

*You speak?* There was hope in his sickened gaze.

Quarrah shook her head, stepping sideways to move around him. The man blocked her, holding the board in front of him like a shield. His reddening eyes were fixed on hers, a desperation shining through.

*Help. Help us!*

He might have said more, but Quarrah looked away so she wouldn't see his lips moving. The door behind him cracked open and a woman's face peered out. Ragged, Moonsick. She rapped softly on the doorframe to get the man's attention.

He spun, gesturing to Quarrah and pointing at his eyes. He mouthed something more. A child's face appeared in the open door. A little girl of maybe five years, who looked even farther along in the Moonsickness than the adults. She was holding a handful of nails and a hammer, offering them to the man.

*She can help us,* Quarrah saw the man mouth to the others in the room.

"No." Quarrah decided to break her silence. "There's nothing I can do for any of you." Her words sounded strange in the hollow corridor, and the woman shuddered at the sound. "I'm sorry."

*Are there more of you?* the man mouthed.

Quarrah thought of that recent night, Evetherey's perch crash-landing in a tree top, silhouetted by the Red Moon.

Eight thousand four hundred and forty-eight survivors.

There should have been ten times that number, but Elbrig and Cinza had crippled humanity with their oath of vengeance.

"Not enough," Quarrah answered the man.

He nodded in solemn understanding, tears welling in his rotting eyes. Then he held up the board and mimed an action toward the apartment door.

"It's a good idea." Quarrah found it surprisingly easy to lie. What good would it do to barricade his door against the inevitable violence ahead, when that same violence would soon awaken within his own family?

In a rush of pity, Quarrah reached out and offered him the clay pot. "Barrier Grit," she said. "It'll only last ten minutes, but..."

The man accepted it, his quivering lips mouthing a sincere *thank you*.

She stepped past him, wishing she could have done more. There were additional Grit pots on her belt, but nothing would actually save this family.

Quarrah reached her room at the end of the hallway. As it turned out, there was no need for her key. The lock was broken and the door was ajar like all the others. She pushed it a few more inches, slipping inside.

Of the many apartments Quarrah kept across the city, she had always liked the location of this one. The respectable neighborhood meant she had never worried as much about the things she'd stashed here. Now the bureau in the corner was toppled and ransacked, even the mattress torn open and slid off its frame.

*Amateur hiding spots*, Quarrah thought, flipping back the rug and taking a knee on the wooden floor. Poking her finger through a knothole in one board, she pried it up with ease, revealing the things she'd hidden between the floor joists.

A sack of a hundred Ashings, a diamond ring, a ruby broach...

Noises from the street outside brought her to her feet. The glass window was smashed, white bird droppings spattered across the sill and floor, but the view was still the same.

From the height of the third floor, she could see across the broad intersection of five major roads below. Normally, the confluence was bustling with carriages and pedestrians at nearly all hours of the day and night. The usual bustle of business might have been lacking today, but the intersection was not empty.

Glassminds were coming down Pole Avenue. At least half a dozen of them, the afternoon sunlight glinting on their glass skulls. Behind them marched a massive group of citizens, several hundred strong, their faces weary but eager.

Even from this distance, Quarrah could hear the words the Glassminds were calling, their voices sounding in an unnerving unison, like a choral recitation.

"Come unto the Homeland! Your salvation awaits you with a mind of clarity and a body perfected. Do not fear us, but rather join us. Your willingness is the cure you so desperately seek."

She'd seen a similar gathering at the edge of the Central Quarter this morning. That mass transformation had resulted in at least another hundred Glassminds, and a heap of dead ones whose minds did not live up to Garifus's standards.

Quarrah imagined that these kinds of gatherings were happening all over the Greater Chain. The Glassminds rounded people up with a great deal of efficiency, but the clock was ticking, even for them. Once the people hit the third phase of Moonsickness, their minds would be too far gone to undergo the transformation. That meant the Glassminds would reach their maximum population in the next three or four days. After that, Garifus's only concern would be the paltry clump of human survivors.

"Stand close together!" called the Glassminds in the intersection below. "You shall all receive the cure at once."

*Everyone at once?* Quarrah studied the crowd more closely. There had to be close to four hundred speechless followers down there! The implication was terrifying. She knew that Garifus relied on a majority mindset to keep control of his hive. He wouldn't risk transforming more people than there were faithful Glassminds for fear of tipping the balance. Even with this method, their numbers would grow exponentially. Four hundred would become eight hundred, would become sixteen hundred...

Telepathically, they could communicate their exact numbers across any distance, maintaining the integrity of the group while scouring every inch of the Greater Chain.

Directly below, Quarrah saw three figures exiting her building. It was the family from down the hall, and the man was waving his arms as if begging the Glassminds to wait for them.

In Quarrah's limited interactions with them, they had always seemed like respectable people, not prone to extremes or radicalism. She knew they were simply desperate for a cure, and what harm was there in trying the transformation, since they would soon lose their minds to Moonsickness anyway? Of course, Garifus and his team would have a peek into their thoughts and memories first to see if—

"Oh, flames," Quarrah whispered, suddenly realizing what this could mean. The Glassminds wouldn't have to pry very deep to see that the family had just spoken with her. *Spoken.* They would know she was close by, and they'd want to know how she'd escaped the Moon's rays.

Quarrah backed away from the window, her mind already tracing through the fastest route to exit on the opposite side of the tavern. Her foot caught on the edge of the rug and she glanced down at her concealed treasures.

Was this all she had to show for her life? Expensive jewelry and money? It suddenly seemed almost comical in its unimportance and she stepped over the stash. She hadn't really come into the city to gather these treasures anyway. What did they matter?

She had come to spy. Because sitting inside their bubble of safety in the Char was driving her mad. Because she couldn't stand to wait and wonder about the fate of the outside world.

Because sneaking around Beripent felt right when nothing else in the world did.

Through the window, red lights caught her eye in the intersection below. The skulls of the Glassminds were glowing, preparing for swift and merciless assessment of those who were about to transform. It was happening so quickly. On the road, hundreds of civilians of all ages and sizes were literally crawling out of their skin, emerging as something new. But Quarrah couldn't afford to wait around and see how many of them survived Centrum's judgment.

She turned, sprinting out the open door and down the hallway. Past the partially barricaded door of the family that had just turned themselves over to a different fate. Past the corpse of the bartender and out the back door.

She was a long ways from the Char, but she would reach it well before sundown if she didn't run into trouble. Raek would let her through the Barrier, just as he'd let her out earlier that morning.

But Quarrah would have to be extra careful to avoid any Glassminds. If that man, woman, or little girl had joined their ranks, Quarrah's face would be shared among every connected mind in the city. And if they caught her, they might uncover details about the survivors... about Evetherey.

Things out here were every bit as bad as she'd imagined. And it was only a matter of time—probably short—before the Glassminds turned their attention to the Char.

What chance did eight thousand four hundred and forty-eight frightened humans have against an unstoppable force like that?

*          *          *

"Of course we've got a chance!" Ard slammed his hand on the table. "It's not over until it's over. And it's not over."

He didn't appreciate the glum looks that surrounded their make-shift council table. Only five of the seven council members had survived the rearrangement of Raek's Barrier wall when Evetherey had crash-landed. Apparently, Lady Volen of Espar and the aged Lord Ment of Strind had pitched their royal camps farther from Oriar's Square and hadn't joined the others for the concert.

By now, Ard imagined that they either had undergone the transformation into Glassminds, or were shredding their fingers to the bone in a senseless desire to tear apart any manmade structure in Beripent. By the sound of Quarrah's report, most of the city had been ransacked before the Bloodeyes had even gotten ripe in the sickness. Now it had been almost a week since the Passing, and things were sure to be downright apocalyptic outside the little Barrier where the eight thousand survivors huddled.

Queen Abeth Ostel Agaul sighed deeply, rubbing her forehead. Her hair was down and her face untouched by makeup. She had exchanged her gown for a pair of sensible trousers and a loose-fitting blouse, which was now smudged with soot from their campfires.

Ard thought she looked more war general than queen. Fitting, since most of the commanding officers of the Regulation had been cut off in the realignment. Now Abeth had given up her palace for this single-story historic site, one of the only Char ruins with something that resembled a roof overhead.

"We can't keep *saying* we'll put up a fight," said the queen. "We need actionable strategies. Any day now, the Bloodeyes will be at our border."

"It's not the Bloodeyes we should be worried about," said Raek. "They'll never get through the Barrier wall."

Their defenses hadn't dropped in a week. Even now, Evetherey was outside, taking her turn to maintain the small dome of Barrier Grit that surrounded the last of humanity.

"It's the Glassminds that should scare your pants off," Raek finished.

"I'm not so sure," said Lord Blindle. "It's been six days and we haven't seen a single one of them! We have to consider the possibility that the Glassminds are simply not interested in us."

"Don't fool yourself," Ard said. "Garifus Floc won't stop until his Glassminds have sole occupancy of this world."

"Then why haven't they come yet?" barked Blindle.

"They will." Quarrah leaned forward, resting her forearms on the edge of the table. "The Glassminds know exactly where we are. Up until now, they've had to focus all their attention on rounding up the Moonsick people and transforming them before the sickness got too advanced. That'll be winding down today. The people out there are entering the third stage. Once the Glassminds see that there's no one else to transform, they'll have their numbers. Then they'll deal with the next problem on their list." She sat back. "Us."

Ard smiled at her boldness. There was even a touch of drama to her monologue. "Tell them how many we're dealing with, Quarrah."

Lady Werner scoffed. "How would she know?"

"I've been sneaking out into the city every day," Quarrah said.

"What? How?" The council members all began to murmur.

"Did you visit my estate in the Southern Quarter?" asked Lord Owers. "What is the condition of my manor?"

"I'd say you can count on all your valuables to be scattered and lost," she reported. "But that's not our problem. It's impossible to know for sure, but I'd say there are thousands of Glassminds by now. Probably more like *tens* of thousands when you consider that Beripent is just a small percentage of what's happening all over the Greater Chain. The Glassminds aren't forcing anyone to join them, but the people are desperate for a cure from Moonsickness."

"I thought only those who shared Centrum's ideals were allowed into his hive mind," said the queen.

Quarrah nodded. "If you think the number of living Glassminds is worrisome, I can assure you that you'll find ten times that number of rejects, their glass skulls blown out in the streets."

There was an uncomfortable silence as the queen and the noble council shifted in their chairs.

"Anyway, we're safe here," Lady Heel finally declared. "Veth... Eveth... the dragon woman said she can create all the Barrier Grit we need to—"

"The Glassminds can manipulate a Barrier wall," Raek cut off her optimism. "Any one of them could absorb our defenses. And with their numbers, Evetherey and I won't have a chance of keeping a Barrier intact."

"We should start mandatory military training with all the survivors," said Lord Blindle.

"With what?" said Lord Owers. "We have no weapons!"

"There is plenty of available vegetation here," said Raek. "Evetherey and I can shape tree limbs into spears and clubs—"

"We need guns!" Lady Werner cut him off.

"Why?" said Quarrah. "The balls won't pierce the skin of the Glassminds. We're better off trying to club them over the head."

Quarrah had been more talkative than usual in these meetings. Ard was grateful for her input since she was the only person who had seen what things were really like out there.

"A soldier isn't defined by his weapon," continued Blindle. "Training would at least give the people some hope. The Regulators who survived may be few, but they should be teaching the citizens to fight. After all, even if we survive the outside threats, I do not think any of us feel completely safe *within*."

"You're referring to the Trothian group?" said Lord Owers. "They have not been hostile—"

"Six hundred Trothians—even their children show more

combat discipline than our Reggies," Lord Blindle went on. "You can't tell me that the Trothians aren't already posturing. I hate to think what will happen when they decide to make their move."

"The Trothian *posturing*, as you put it, is in regards to Ardor Benn." This came from a new voice at the doorway.

Ard whirled to see Prime Isle Trable standing rigid. Unlike the queen, he still looked every part the Prime Isle, his purple robes as clean as could be expected. All week long, he had busied himself among the people, speaking calming words and reading passages from *Wayfarist Voyage*. But he still hadn't said one word to Ardor Benn. In fact, this was the first time Ard remembered standing within speaking distance of the Prime Isle.

Ard took it harder than he'd expected. He had filled his life with people who were willing to forgive him. Raek had done it countless times. And regardless of his many offenses toward Quarrah, she kept coming back, too. But Ard had finally given up hope that Olstad Trable might find forgiveness—sparks, he'd settle for *understanding*.

Ard stood by what he'd done in the Mooring. Trable had his family—Gaevala and the girls. And if Ard's actions had in some small measure kept them safe, then it was worth the death of their friendship.

"Regardless of everything that has happened," Trable continued impassively, "the Trothian priestess is still determined to exact justice on Ardor for his crimes against her nation."

"Exactly!" cried Blindle. "And despite his crimes, our Regulators are spending all their time guarding him."

"I assure you that not a single Regulator has received orders to protect Ardor Benn," Queen Abeth said in a voice of steel. "They guard this building and the royal section of Oriar's Square."

The segregation seemed uncalled for, and Ard realized that the queen had authorized it only to appease the other nobles. She herself was often out among the citizen section with Prime Isle Trable.

But Ard didn't dare venture out to where Lyndel and the Trothians were *posturing* for justice against him.

"This man doesn't have a drop of noble blood in his veins," said Lord Kinter. "If he's causing an upset, we should force him to leave the royal section."

Ard held up his hands. How had this turned from a plan against the Glassminds to sacrificing Ard to the Trothians so quickly? "I don't see how that is going to help us with the real problem."

"You are the real problem!" shouted Trable. "I don't know why—call it an Urging from the Homeland—but I can't shake the feeling that you're responsible for all of this . . . the Glassminds, the Moonsickness . . ."

Ard cleared his throat. "Everything I've done has been Urged by the Homeland."

"You arrogant little son of a gun!" Trable laughed, but there was no mirth in it. "The Homeland would never speak to *you*. You manipulated me, Ardor! You used your connections with the Islehood for your own gain."

"I didn't gain anything," protested Ard. "Yes, I knew the location of the Islehood's shell storage. But I didn't take any of it!"

Ard's eyes flicked to Raek, quickly realizing just how hot the water of this conversation was becoming. Downplaying his knowledge of the shell location would only dig into a sore spot with Raek.

"It doesn't matter what I knew, or when I knew it," Ard settled on saying. "What matters is what I did with that information. I saw an opportunity to lure Garifus and his Glassminds out of the Mooring, and I took it."

"And I suppose you'd like me to thank you for that?"

"It was nothing really," said Ard. "Just putting my life on the line for the Islehood I had sworn to serve."

"We have protocols for violent trespassers in the Mooring," barked Trable. "I had tripped a silent alarm. A sizable Regulation platoon was on its way."

"And you think they would have arrived before Garifus plucked your arms off?"

"I was stalling them," Trable said. "It was a risk I was willing to take."

"Gaevala and the girls need you, Ols—"

"Do not speak of my family!" he bellowed, silencing Ard with an upraised hand. Then he took a deep breath and seemed to compose himself. "Our friendship might have been nothing more than a ruse to you, but it meant something to me." He clenched his jaw. "But unlike your other ruses, this one isn't going to end favorably for you, Ardor Benn."

Ard lowered his gaze. "I know." The defeat in his voice was palpable. "And I've come to peace with that."

Another bout of awkward silence filled the run-down building. Then Prime Isle Trable tugged at the front of his purple robes. "I came to report that the rations were raided again. Even if we cut back to the bare minimum, we'll be lucky to last three more days."

"We won't last that long anyway," said Quarrah. "The Glassminds will get to us before then. They're an unstoppable force that can't be run from, beaten, or deceived."

Ardor Benn cleared his throat. The bleak picture Quarrah was painting set him up nicely. "I have an idea."

He tried to smile coolly as all heads turned to him. Ard's plan was the very reason he had asked the queen to call this morning's meeting. Quarrah's report last night had sealed it for him. He'd barely slept a wink, running his plan through the gauntlet of his mind, testing it for weaknesses and preparing himself for naysayers.

"Quarrah is right." Ard slowly rose from his seat. "Things *are* hopeless. There's no recovering from this. If it were possible, I'd say our only chance at survival would be a Paladin Visitant. But that doesn't work anymore. The advent of Spherical Time makes it impossible to re*set* the Material Time. But what if we could re*start* it?"

"What are you talking about?" Prime Isle Trable's voice was full of distrust.

"Glassminds exist, but to what end?" Ard asked.

"To cause all of humankind to evolve or be destroyed," said the queen.

Ard held up a finger. "That's Centrum's plan. But Evetherey told us the real reason Glassminds were supposed to exist."

"To be used in exchange," said Quarrah. "Send a Glassmind into the Sphere and bring a human life into the Material Time."

"Any point in the Material Time," Ard clarified. He had double-checked that detail with Evetherey just this morning.

"What's the point of this?" asked Lord Owers.

"Don't you see?" Ard clapped his hands. "Evetherey opens a cloud of Visitant Grit and we all go into the Sphere—"

"We can't," Quarrah cut in. "On the docks, Garifus threw that Regulator into the cloud. He was erased from existence."

"Erased, or trapped?" Ard said. "Garifus said we can go *in*. We just can't get out."

"Sounds like a great plan." Raek's comment dripped with sarcasm.

"We can't get out of the Sphere...on our own," Ard added. "But Evetherey has the power to bring us out in exchange for Glassminds."

The idea lingered in the room, striking the noble council with varying expressions. Whether or not they were really comprehending it remained to be seen.

"Let's say this wild theory could actually work," said Kinter. "At what point in the past would we all reappear?"

"How would that be any different than becoming a Paladin Visitant?" asked Prime Isle Trable. "If we could get out, we'd make a huge impact on whatever point we appear, inevitably changing the course of history and erasing all existence. You can't possibly think to hide eight thousand four hundred and forty-eight of us."

"He's right. We can't alter the timeline," Quarrah said again. "Completing the Sphere locked everything down so the Glassminds couldn't be undone."

"I'm not suggesting we *change* anything," said Ard. "I'm suggesting we go back to a time when there was nothing *to* change."

The queen leaned forward. "I'm afraid I don't follow."

"The beginning of time," said Ard. "The *very* beginning, even before the gods brought humans to walk on this earth."

"How are we supposed to know when that was?" asked Lord Blindle.

"Evetherey will know," said Ard. "We'll become immaterial—lost in a state of limbo. Our existence will be scrubbed from every alternate timeline. But we'll still exist—just completely removed from time. Evetherey can guide everyone through the Sphere and we'll exit at the dawn of time itself."

"And *he's* our bargaining chip?" Lady Werner gestured at Raek. "He'll remain in the Sphere as an exchange, so the rest of us can exit?"

Raek shook his head. "I'm afraid that's not how it works. The exchange rate is one to one."

"Hold on," said Trable. "You're saying we'll need *eight thousand four hundred and forty-eight* Glassminds to enter the Sphere with us?"

"That's the idea," said Ard. "And by the sound of it, we'll have no shortage of them when they come knocking at our proverbial door."

"How exactly will this happen?" asked Queen Abeth.

"Evetherey can create a detonation of Visitant Grit," Ard began. "All the survivors step in and we vanish into the Sphere. Before the Glassminds can wonder what happened, Evetherey will expand the Visitant cloud to engulf about nine thousand of the enemy. Then the Drothan guides us the rest of the way."

Ard knew he'd gone off track somewhere. Raek was shaking his head. "It won't be that simple. Evetherey won't be able to push a Visitant cloud on the Glassminds. They'll absorb it faster than the detonation could catch them."

"What if they were distracted?" Ard said.

"All of them?" Quarrah questioned. "One of them is bound to be paying attention, and since they have a collective mind—"

"There may be one way," Raek interrupted. "The Glassminds can't absorb or manipulate Grit when they are carrying out mental judgment."

"Mental judgment?" the queen asked.

"It's what they do when they're evaluating the ideals and thoughts of a new member of their race," Raek continued. "It's not a long process, but that would probably be the only time they'd leave themselves vulnerable."

Ard nodded. "We saw them do it on Pekal. Their glass skulls glow for a moment and then anyone who doesn't qualify gets their brains blown out."

"So we just need to catch them in the middle of this act?" said Lady Werner. "When will it be happening?"

"It's been going on all around the Greater Chain for the last week," said Quarrah. "Just check the streets of Beripent."

"Then we need to go out there," said Lord Kinter. "Hope we can come upon a group of them while they're evaluating the newly transformed."

"No," said Ard. "Quarrah's reports tell us that the transformations are winding down as the Moonsickness becomes more severe. Besides, it's too risky to hope that we'll stumble upon nine thousand Glassminds in the same place. And our massive group of humans isn't going to be stealthy."

"Then what are you suggesting?"

"We wait," Ard said. "Let them come to us."

"I hate to point out the big flaw," said Raek, "but isn't the point to catch them with their skulls glowing? By the time they get to us, the Bloodeyes will be too ripe to transform."

"But that's not the *only* time their heads light up in judgment," said Ard.

"Oh?" Raek questioned. "It's not?"

"Technically, they could judge each other in the same way, right?"

"Well...I guess?" He scratched his chin. "But everyone who is part of the group has already been screened and accepted."

Ard grinned. "Doesn't mean they can't change their minds."

"Ha!" Olstad Trable folded his arms. "You're suggesting that we get the Glassminds to use their fatal judgment system on *each other*?"

"Now you're getting it!" Ard cried. "And the moment they're distracted by it, Evetherey manipulates a Visitant cloud, surrounding all the human survivors and netting nine thousand unsuspecting Glassminds at the same time."

"Well, color me curious." Prime Isle Trable let out a disapproving chortle. "How exactly do you expect us to turn the Glassminds against each other?"

That was it! Ard interlaced his fingers tightly as if to hold the idea captive before it escaped. He nodded slowly. "Leave that to the ruse artist."

~

*I hope you'll grant me that one last arrogance. It's something you won't have to put up with any longer.*

# CHAPTER

# 39

The autumn morning was clear and bright, white clouds billowing across the sky like distant detonations. Ahead, on the wide path leading into the forested acreage of the Char, Quarrah saw the Glassminds gathering. It was impossible to tell how many there were, but the red glint of the sun's rays stretched out of sight toward the Central Quarter.

A raw anxiety was thick among the eight and a half thousand survivors assembled in Oriar's Square. Humans of all ages and social standing, mixed with a cluster of Trothians. The children, the elderly, and other noncombatants were huddled in front of the orchestra stage while the more able-bodied citizens were still stumbling to form ranks. Poor souls. Those men and women would be the first line of defense against the enemies. Their lines bristled with wooden spears and clubs, the best they could shape from the trees surrounding the square.

Quarrah breathed deeply, trying to keep herself steady and focused, standing between Ard and Raek on the outdoor stage. The former was muttering something under his breath, as if rehearsing a memorized script. The latter had his hands outstretched, maintaining his latest Barrier dome—a reduced detonation shielding only the square. Quarrah could see a flicker in his eye. The man was itching for a fight.

But Ard had promised that there wouldn't be one today. At least not a fight between the survivors and the Glassminds. The outcome of such a conflict was obvious anyway. No. Ardor Benn was planning to smooth talk their way to salvation...

Naturally, Quarrah had her concerns.

"What are they waiting for?" Prime Isle Trable whispered.

Quarrah glanced over her shoulder at the holy man. He looked blanched with fear, his body stiff under those purple robes. Beside him, Queen Abeth was cool and resolved, wearing trousers and a brown tunic like a common citizen, a Roller clutched in either hand. A dozen of her finest Regulators flanked them, their helmets strapped tightly, dirty uniforms buttoned up.

*"They're still gathering."* Evetherey's voice sounded in Quarrah's head.

The others must have heard it, too, because the queen replied. "How many are there?"

*"Just under a million,"* she replied.

"Here?" San Green cried, the lad fidgeting behind Ard.

*"I sense their numbers across all of the islands,"* Evetherey answered. *"Today we will face only fifty thousand."*

Raek chuckled sarcastically. "Oh, good. Only fifty thousand."

Quarrah glanced up at the Drothan. She was perched on the acoustical shell that rose twenty feet up the back of the stage like a freestanding wall. The reptilian goddess peered forward, her feathered wings spread to counterbalance herself. Could she actually see all fifty thousand Glassminds in the Char, or was she perceiving them as she had with their total numbers?

*"They are surrounding the square from all sides,"* Evetherey continued. *"As are the ones too sick to transform."*

"Bloodeyes?" Prime Isle Trable clarified.

*"Yes,"* came the answer. *"They sense the survivors and desire to tear the life from their healthy bodies."*

"Why don't they tear into the Glassminds?" Quarrah asked.

*"Even in their madness, their minds can sense the superiority of the Othians,"* said Evetherey.

"Well, that's not fair," muttered Ard.

"At least they'll have to wade through fifty thousand Glassminds to get to us," said Queen Abeth.

"I rue our odds if that statement gives us any comfort," said Prime Isle Trable.

"Evetherey!" Ard called, watching the survivors nervously shuffle on the pavers in front of the stage. "Where is Garifus Floc?"

She must have responded, but only to him. He nodded, tugging at the white cuffs of his billowy sleeves, which extended beyond the length of his long leather jacket. Of course he was dressed nicely on the last day of existence. He'd probably swindled that shirt right off Lord Kinter's back.

"Where is he?" Quarrah asked him.

Ard pointed far ahead, where the main gathering of Glass-minds had congregated on the road leading into the square. "He's here."

"Ard," she whispered. "What if he doesn't listen to you?"

He turned sharply to face her. "You're here, Quarrah."

She wrinkled her forehead in confusion. "Of course I'm—"

"I don't fool myself anymore," he pressed. "I understand that you'll never see me like you once did. And that's on me. I've been dishonest with you so many times. Tricked and lied. So I understand that things can never be what I wanted them to be between us. But you're here now. Why?"

His intense gaze forced hers away. She glanced at the pot of Blast Grit she was clutching. She had a few explosives and a knife, but she felt totally unarmed for this kind of conversation.

"I didn't have a choice," Quarrah finally answered. "First with the Realm, then with Hedge Marsool—"

"I've seen you squeeze out of tighter spaces," Ard cut her off. She could tell he was still looking at her, even though she had glanced away.

Quarrah swallowed. How could she answer him truthfully? She honestly didn't love him now, though she once had. The flame was dead, and any spark she might feel was for the thought of what this man *could* have been . . . if only he had listened to her.

"You always know what to do," she stammered out a response. "When everyone else is retreating, you advance." She dared to look at him again. "You're the man with the answers. Whether you really have them, or not."

Ard smiled—puckish, yet backed by a twinge of sadness. "That's why the Glassminds will stop to listen. Because if someone as clever and strong as you keeps coming back to hear what I have to say, what chance does Garifus Floc have in resisting my speech?"

Quarrah felt a strange sense of calm wash over her—a tribute to his way with words. Surely, in a collective mind of a million souls, *someone* would recognize the power behind the name *Ardor Benn*.

"Quarrah," he whispered. "I know I've apologized before, but I'm sorry I couldn't value you the way you deserve. I'm going to change. I'm going to be a better man."

Was he seriously saying this *now*? She glanced self-consciously at the others on the stage, but each seemed preoccupied by their own thoughts and the tangible fear of the inevitable conflict.

"They are coming!" Evetherey's voice called from her perch. The audible warning washed across the stage and rattled through the human throng, energizing the survivors with a sudden panic.

Quarrah squinted across Oriar's Square, but the distance was too great. Especially without her spectacles. Instead, her attention turned back to Raek. The big man was grunting, hands outstretched as his fingertips sizzled with sparks.

"I can't..." he muttered. "They're taking it in as quickly as I can ignite it."

Ard reached out and placed a hand on his best friend's shoulder. "It's all right, Raek. Let them come." Raekon Dorrel lowered his massive arms and Ard took a deep breath. "Thanks, brother."

"This better work," whispered Raek.

Ard chuckled, but Quarrah sensed an unusual melancholy buried shallowly beneath it. "Oh, I'm betting my life on it." He squared his shoulders and strode toward the steps at the edge of the stage.

"Where are you going?" Quarrah called, all the panicky feelings of anticipation returning like a detonation of its own.

"I need to have a word with Garifus Floc," he replied.

"I thought you'd say it from here," she said.

"And let these poor civilians be the first line of defense against a wave of Glassminds and Bloodeyes?" Ard turned back to her in a fleeting glance, his brown eyes alight with an intensity that matched his religious name. "I have to make sure Garifus doesn't miss a word."

*     *     *

Ard stood on the grass with both hands raised in an innocent gesture. Behind him, the human survivors were making an undisciplined clamor, their knees knocking together in justifiable fear.

*It's just a ruse,* he told himself. *Just another ruse.* The thought calmed his nerves, even though he knew this would be different than anything he'd done before.

*"Are you sure of this, Ardor Benn?"* Evetherey's voice spoke into his mind. He sensed that the message was for him alone, but he didn't know how to respond. He settled for a firm nod, trusting that Evetherey's superior eyes could pick up the gesture from her perch.

The task ahead terrified him in a way that nothing ever had. But the fear didn't make him unsure of the plan. In fact, he would've considered something to be very wrong with him if he hadn't been shaking at the thought. No, his fear was his conviction today.

The enemy was close enough that Ard could see their glowing eyes. Their advance had been steady, and notably without haste. If there was any good news to be had, it was that the density of the Glassminds was obviously slowing the Bloodeyes. Gratefully, Ard hadn't glimpsed any of those mindless creatures yet.

"Centrum!" Ard shouted. "I know you to be a man of understanding... one who respects the ideals of the masses. Today, I speak for this mass." He pointed at the disarray behind him. "Will you step forward and speak for yours?"

The entire Glassmind processional came to a unified halt. Then one broke ranks and tromped across the grass toward Ard. Garifus Floc's perfect lips were curled up in a winning sneer. Well, it would be fun to see how long *that* lasted.

"Ardor Benn." His enhanced voice pealed with much greater ease and clarity than Ard's practiced projection. That didn't matter. Ard had the man here. And what he said to one Glassmind, he said to all of them.

He was counting on that.

"My people stand ready to fight. Ready to die," said Ard. "But I have to ask…Are we such a threat to your race that we cannot coexist?"

"Your question shows a fundamental lack of understanding of the word *perfection*," answered Centrum. "The simplicity of humans is fraught with flaws. This earth cannot attain its true potential with your people floundering upon its surface. We can only rise together."

This comment sparked a chorus of approval from the Glassmind host behind him.

"And the Bloodeyes?" Ard asked. "They don't upset your perfect world?"

"They are easily dealt with," said Garifus. "But I do not think your people will find them so. Even now, thousands are clamoring for you, though I have ordered my people to hold them back while we speak. It is not my wish that you be torn to shreds. Of course, I would rather you join me."

"That's just not possible," said Ard.

"Which leads me to ask," Garifus replied. "How did you all escape the Moonsickness?"

"We had a little help." Ard pointed to the top of the distant stage behind him. Centrum's gaze narrowed on the spot, and Ard wondered if he could actually see Evetherey with his superior eyes.

"For a being who can see all of time as a Sphere, you didn't pay attention to your history, Centrum." Ard folded his arms. "The first Glassminds—I'm talking the *very* first—were imprisoned beneath miles of water. Who do you think did that?"

"You speak of the Drothans?"

"Yeah," said Ard. "We got ourselves one."

Ard sensed a little ripple of upset pass through the Glassmind ranks, but that was just the beginning. A tasteless appetizer, compared to what he had to say.

"Lies!" Garifus bellowed. "You see, this is why we must all be of one mind. This kind of corruption and deceit sows only chaos and destruction. Already, I grow tired of your words."

"That's fine," said Ard. "I only need one."

"One . . . *what*?"

"A single word," he continued. "It's really that simple."

"What are you talking about?"

"It's something Prime Isle Trable said to me recently. I've just been waiting for the right time to say it. The right time to convince you all of this word's merit."

Ard didn't speak, letting the silence and anticipation brew until the pressure blew the lid off.

"Say it!" Garifus demanded.

Ard sighed. "Time."

"That's your word?" Garifus scoffed. "Time?"

"Flames, no," Ard said, pretending to be aghast at the misunderstanding. "Time is just something I've been contemplating lately. Side thought—You see, most of us waste it while we have it, yet in the end, don't we all beg for more? *Time is the great challenger, for idly it can defeat. Yet if we win but a short battle, it leaves a mark upon its pride.*"

Ard saw the look of recognition cross Garifus's large features—knowing the verse from his own experience or drawing it from the memories of another Wayfarist-turned-Glassmind.

"I didn't understand what that meant when my mother read that verse to me as a child," Ard said. "She might have been a simple gardener, but Arelia Castenac knew. She knew that none of us really *win* against time. That it's not about the outcome, but the journey. And when our *time* comes, will we have done enough? Will we have left a mark upon time's pride and shown those who come after—I was here, and I did *not* stand idly by. My soul did not Settle!"

This time, a cry of support went up from the survivors who were close enough to hear.

"You preach outdated doctrines," answered Garifus. "Your

weak minds cannot recognize the perfected Homeland, even when we loom before you! What we have become will withstand time. Its passage, so ravenous to you, has no effect upon our bodies or minds."

"Yet you still won't win," said Ard. "At best, you'll be locked in an eternal standoff with time. And what will you have to show for it? You can't learn anything new because your perfect minds already know it all. You can't relish in the sweetness of victory, because you can't taste defeat. Who is really winning, Centrum? The runner who sprints forever and never sees the finish line? Or the one who just wants to make it to the top of the hill?'"

Garifus glanced across the human survivors, their meager weapons of defense clanking in woeful lack of discipline. He chuckled.

"You're wrong, Ardor. The Glassminds are superior in every way. Time is our servant and we will remain long after you are gone."

"But I will have left a mark, because you'll remember me." A smirk touched Ard's face. "With your perfect memory, you'll never be able to forget what I did here today. You'll never forget the *word*."

"What is this blazing word you speak of?" cried Garifus.

"A word that'll change everything," he said. "A word that'll change the minds of your followers. That's what Trable said to me. Don't you get it?"

Garifus scowled. "We are united in thought. Nothing you can say will change that."

"Because you'll kill them?" Ard said. "If anyone in your hive begins to think differently, you'll just blow out their skulls. Isn't that right? Because uncertainty is too much of a risk. *Individuality* is too dangerous."

Garifus huffed, teeth clenched in his broad jaw. "I believe you misunderstand our collectivity. It is not my mind alone that rules us, but the thoughts of the majority."

"Oh, I understand perfectly," said Ard. "As long as fifty-one percent of your people think the same way, you don't have anything to worry about."

"We are united!" Garifus bellowed, truly losing his temper for the first time. "We have scoured the world for the right minds. And the ones you see before you now represent the true and the faithful. Not some majority rule, but one hundred percent."

"And the Glassminds in Dronodan? Talumon? Strind?" Ard questioned.

"It is as if they are with us even now." Garifus touched his middle finger to his glass forehead in the old cultist sign of loyalty.

"Good," Ard said. "Then I can change their minds, too."

Out of the corner of his eye, he glimpsed a jostle of commotion among the human ranks nearest him. Someone was pushing through to get to him. His heart slammed against his chest, but he couldn't pull his eyes from Garifus. He was so close! And the ruse demanded every last drib of his focus.

"Ha!" Garifus snorted. "With your lies? And your antiquated doctrines? Go ahead. Tell us this *word* that you claim has so much power. Change our minds."

Ard took a deep, steadying breath. "If you insist."

From the line of humans behind, Ard saw a blur of dark blue skin, forearms wrapped in religious red cloth. Lyndel's voice sounded in his ear and he felt the tip of a blade entering his rib cage from behind.

"Justice," she whispered. "Justice for my people."

Ardor Benn sputtered, choked. He glanced down to see the point of the long knife protruding from his chest.

Red.

Deepest red.

"The word..." he muttered, "word is—"

With one swift motion, Lyndel whisked the knife from his heart and drew it across his throat.

Blood sprayed. *His* blood. And all at once, the world grew dim. He thought he heard a woman shout his name.

Ardor Benn hoped it was Quarrah.

~

*It has the power to drive people to do things.*

# CHAPTER

# 40

Quarrah's mind was numb, but her legs carried her out of the crowd.

"Ard!" she screamed again. At least, she assumed it was her voice grating through her throat. It felt like someone else's. Like the scene she had just witnessed was the final moments of a terrible dream. She would wake up. She would wake up soon.

Lyndel released Ard's body and it slumped to the grass, motionless. Open eyes already glazed. Quarrah landed on her knees beside him, reaching out. But her hand hovered just above his bloodstained shoulder.

Touching him would make it real. Touching his corpse would affirm that this hadn't been some kind of ruse performed under Illusion Grit.

Warm. His blood felt almost *hot* as her hand finally rested upon his shoulder. He was dead. Ardor Benn. Dead. Not a trick or a scheme. Not a clever ruse.

Dead.

Quarrah looked up to see that time, as it were, had stopped. Glassminds and humans alike were frozen in shock and confusion. Only Lyndel seemed able to move, wiping the flat of the knife on her cloth-wrapped forearm.

That knife!

The blade, Quarrah now saw, was not metal or stone. It was thick red glass, unmistakably crafted from the shard that had broken from the Moon Glass in the *Ucru* that night. Identical to the one she'd seen in her vision, the handle was wrapped in rawhide, now forever stained with the lifeblood of the ruse artist.

Quarrah felt a hopeless rage overtake her. Had her vision in the *Ucru* tried to warn her about this? Why hadn't she stopped Lyndel? She'd seen someone moving through the crowd. Quarrah had been so close, hidden among the ranks to hear Ard's words. A moment ago, she'd found his speech flowery and melodramatic, but suddenly his final words struck her as poignant.

Quarrah didn't need to run forever to win. She just needed to make it to the top of the hill.

She sprang from Ard's side like a pouncing cat, a savage cry escaping her lips as she drew her own knife. She would kill Lyndel for this. Stab her through the heart. Slit her throat.

But her knife never found its mark.

Garifus, startling at her sudden movement, raised his hands. Quarrah felt the rush of Void Grit strike her, hurtling her haphazardly across Oriar's Square. Lyndel was caught in the same detonation, but her trajectory threw her elsewhere.

Quarrah tumbled painfully across the grass, knife flying from her grasp. The impact must have detonated the little bag of Barrier Grit at her side, because her head suddenly slammed into an impenetrable shimmering wall.

Fighting to remain conscious inside her accidental protective dome, she pushed herself up, blinking away the stars that crowded the edge of her vision.

She had landed in the open space between forces, perhaps closer to the Glassminds than the survivors. But neither side was charging. In fact, the army of enhanced beings seemed to be in the middle of a telepathic argument. She saw their heads moving, expressions changing—all happening without an audible word exchanged.

Twenty yards away, Garifus's face twisted with concentration. Raising both fists, he ignited a light within his skull.

"Do not move!" His cry was as thunderous as a great bass drum in a small concert hall. Beside him, a few more Glassminds began to ignite, the red light as bright as a welder's forge, even in the morning sun.

*"The dissension has begun."* Evetherey's voice startled Quarrah, seeming suddenly invasive in her rattled mind.

"Over what?" Quarrah muttered aloud, knowing that Evetherey couldn't possibly hear her from that distance. "He never said it."

*"Some believe that Prime Isle Trable knows the word Ardor Benn spoke of,"* she continued, as if perceiving Quarrah's question. *"They are curious enough to interrogate him, while Centrum is convinced that no word could hold such power. He doesn't want them pursuing this avenue any further."*

"He's scared," Quarrah whispered. Because, what if there really *was* a way to change the mindset of the majority?

Quarrah stared at the group. Maybe a thousand skulls were lit now, a visible statement that they stood with Garifus. But it wasn't nearly enough. They needed nine times that number before Evetherey would dare smother them with a Visitant cloud and drag them into the Sphere.

Along the straight row of Glassminds, one of them stepped forward, putting herself equal with Garifus. Her smooth skull was dark, but Quarrah could see a bold expression.

"Stay!" Garifus shouted at her. "Stay where you are, Sorama!"

But the woman strode forward with her head raised high in defiance. Behind her, Garifus grunted, his face strained so severely that the golden veins on his neck bulged.

*He can't kill her*, Quarrah realized. Too few of the Glassminds had weighed in on this matter. Without the majority's consensus, he couldn't extinguish her mind.

The woman, Sorama, paused before the wall of humans who raised their clubs at her, bravely holding the line.

"I desire to speak to the Prime Isle," she said. "Stand aside or I will destroy you."

"Sparks!" Garifus screamed, his skull suddenly going dark. Then his hand came up, a wave of Barrier Grit flowing from his fingertips. It ripped through Sorama from behind, spattering the front row of fighters with gold blood as her headless body toppled sideways.

At once, skulls across the field began to ignite, spurred into mental judgment by Garifus's bold execution. Quarrah couldn't count them from inside her Barrier. And it occurred to her that the glowing glass didn't necessarily mean they were siding with Garifus. Represented, too, would be those *opposing* him.

Quarrah's face felt numb and tingly, wracked with sobs she hadn't even been aware of. But in a moment, she stilled, a single thought breaking through the cloud of grief.

*He did it.*

Ard had been so sure that he could convince the Glassminds to turn on each other, and that was exactly what was happening. Surely, not in the way he had expected, but it was working nevertheless.

Ardor Benn, running a ruse, even from beyond the grave.

*"There is something else,"* Evetherey's voice interrupted Quarrah's thoughts. *"The Othians are no longer blocking the Moonsick ones."*

No sooner had the words entered Quarrah's mind than a human figure came hurtling through the Glassmind ranks. With horrifying speed, it launched itself across the space between armies and tore into the front line of unsuspecting citizens.

Screams rippled through the crowd of survivors. Before Quarrah could see the outcome of the attack, a dozen more Blood-eyes appeared through the line of Glassminds. They closed the gap to the human side with jerky movements, as if their madness compelled them to run at a speed at which their rotting bodies could not quite manage.

They clashed with the humans, with no concern for their own bodily harm. Their tough, leathery skin turned the primitive wooden weapons, but a few metal spearheads found their marks. Blood flecked the faces of the unprepared fighters. Several of the Blood-eyes broke past the untrained line, the screams of fear turning to pain as the first citizens fell dying.

From the helpless confines of her Barrier dome, Quarrah's shock over Ard's death compounded with the horror of the attack and she felt like she might never be able to draw another full breath. More Bloodeyes were breaking through the Glassmind ranks, passing the enhanced beings as if they were nothing more than trees in a forest.

But *another* fight was just beginning.

Two Glassminds, both of their heads glowing, had broken their unified line to face one another. They were shouting in the flowing language of the Othians, but there was nothing elegant about their exchange. Beyond them, Quarrah saw the same dissension manifesting itself throughout the entire group. Glass skulls glimmered. Some merely flickered, as if the individual could not decide which side of the argument deserved their lethal vote.

Within seconds, it came to blows.

Heavy fists striking with merciless precision. Quarrah saw a skull shatter, the light from within leaking out like a wisp of steam.

In moments, the entire area around Oriar's Square had turned into a mighty hand-to-hand brawl, the Glassminds unable to manipulate their internal Grit while ignited in judgment.

Still, it was an elegant and complex combat, the scope of which made the human survivors struggling against the Bloodeyes look like Karvan lizards scratching at each other in the ring.

Something slammed against the side of Quarrah's Barrier. She turned with a startled yelp, adrenaline piercing through her grief, snuffing out her tears like a detonation of Null Grit.

A Bloodeye was pounding against the transparent shell, clearly puzzled by why it could not reach the human it sensed. The creature had been a noblewoman, by the looks of it. Chunks of her dark hair had been ripped out, leaving scabby yellow pockmarks in her head. The fine dress she had been wearing was mere strips of dirty silk now, her mangled feet bare. Her jaw looked broken, unhinged. And her left arm was completely missing. But through it all, she'd somehow managed to keep a string of bloodstained pearls around her neck.

Quarrah stared at her sightless crimson eyes, momentarily wondering what kind of person she'd been in life. Had she refused Garifus's offer to transform? Or had the Glassminds not found her until it was too late?

A human fighter sprinted past, and his fresh wounds must have drawn the attention of the Bloodeye woman. She leapt away from Quarrah, latching on to the man's back and dragging him out of sight.

Before Quarrah could catch her breath, a Glassmind man, his head glowing brightly, slammed against the outside of her Barrier. His opponent loomed over him, an Othian woman with her fingertips sparking. At once, she extinguished the light in her red skull, desperate to harness the full range of her Grit manipulation.

Visibly panicking, the Glassmind man extinguished his own light, reaching back with one hand. His fingers pressed against Quarrah's shell and he absorbed the detonation, throwing it in front of him, formed like a flat shield as the woman brought down a great blade of manipulated Barrier Grit.

Without any protection, Quarrah rolled away from the fighting duo. She scanned the line of humans, hoping for an opening to duck into the crowd without getting skewered by a spear in the untrained hands of a frightened youth. But her eyes caught something else...

Lyndel.

She was surrounded by a cluster of her Trothian warriors, standing as a bulge in the human line of defense, facing a trio of Bloodeyes with much more precision than the Lander citizens.

A great fury boiled up inside her again. Quarrah had almost lost it for a moment, drowning in grief, shock, and the need for survival. But now that she saw the Agrodite priestess once more, her conviction to avenge Ardor Benn redoubled.

One step into Quarrah's path of vengeance, the noblewoman Bloodeye appeared out of nowhere, single arm flailing in dread fury, unhinged mouth dangling in a silent scream. Quarrah reeled, hand darting to her thigh pocket out of pure instinct. Her final tea-bag of Grit formed a Drift detonation around her. Quarrah sprang upward, using the weightlessness to aid her jump as the Bloodeye tumbled into the cloud.

The noblewoman lost her footing, turning head over feet in an uncontrolled tumble, while Quarrah exited the Drift cloud near the top, a height of about twelve feet. Quarrah dropped to the grass, landing in a crouch not three yards from where the Bloodeye rolled out.

In the distance, one voice had risen above the rest of the chaos. Quarrah knew it was Garifus, but he was screaming something in the Othian language.

*"Our moment is almost at hand."* Evetherey spoke into her mind. *"Centrum calls for a show of loyalty. He instructs his true followers to cease fighting and cast their final votes in judgment. He believes that the majority will rule in his favor and they can smite this insurrection with the power of their unity."*

Quarrah heard the uneven shuffle of the Bloodeye's footsteps from behind, but something glittered in a patch of tall grass in front of her, a flash of red catching the morning sun. Leaning forward, her heart caught in her throat as she saw what it was.

Lyndel's Moon Glass knife. The blade that had taken Ard's life. Probably thrown to this spot in Garifus's first cloud of Void Grit.

Quarrah grabbed the wrapped handle, the rawhide still wet from the ruse artist's blood. She spun, catching a glimpse of the world through the flat of the wide blade. Seeing like a Trothian— the energies of every living soul.

She saw the powerful aura of the Glassmind army, each being

exuding the exact same vibration and hue. Then she saw the darkness of death overcoming the human survivors. But there was an array of color there, too. A multi-prismatic show of frailty and strength, cowardice and bravery.

*Individuality.*

Quarrah brought the knife around and plunged it into the Bloodeye's throat. It slid through the tough skin with surprising ease, and through its lens, she saw the corrupted life drain from the noblewoman's ruined body.

She pulled out the glass blade and let the woman's corpse fall to the ground. Stepping away, Quarrah gasped for breath. The knife dripped in her right hand, and her left clutched the string of stained pearls.

*Old habits*, she thought, pocketing the jewelry.

Behind her, the Glassmind conflict had changed. She couldn't spot Garifus, but a large group of the Othians were retreating to a tactical position where they could execute the rebels with their thoughts alone. There were thousands of them...at least, it was a number well beyond Quarrah's count. Certainly enough to exchange for the human survivors if Evetherey could net them into a Visitant cloud.

But Quarrah had one more thing to take care of.

Turning, she glimpsed Lyndel again. A few of her Trothian warriors had fallen, but the group had managed to kill two of the attacking Bloodeyes.

*Good*, Quarrah thought. They were just clearing the way for her to reach the priestess. Tucking the glass knife into her leather belt, she set off at a sprint, hoping the element of surprise would be enough.

She was almost there, feet touching down on the first stone pavers of Oriar's Square, when Lyndel vanished.

Not just her, but the entire army of human survivors, along with the number of Bloodeyes they were fighting...All gone in a wink.

Oriar's Square was suddenly empty, an eerie quiet replacing the chaos of battle. In front of her, the haziness of a Grit detonation filled the entire area.

*Oh, flames.* Quarrah had been left behind.

She glanced over her shoulder to see that the congregation of glowing Glassminds had also disappeared into the Visitant cloud, its manipulated shape carefully encompassing them while leaving behind those who hadn't lit their skulls.

*"Make haste!"* Evetherey's voice spoke in her mind. *"I cannot extend to your position for fear of the unlit Othians at your flank."*

With her heart squirming up her throat, Quarrah scanned the distant empty stage for any sign of the dragon goddess. Too far to see. Maybe Evetherey was speaking from within the Sphere.

Shaking aside the panic, Quarrah resumed her sprint. She was arm's reach from the edge of the cloud when a powerful force seized her from behind. The familiar pull of Gather Grit dragged her legs out from under her, throwing her facedown on the ground. Yanked backward, she felt the skin peel off her chin as she tumbled across the stones, hands clawing for any kind of hold.

With a scream of defiance, Quarrah managed to dig her fingers between two flagstone pavers, holding fast against the draw. Dry leaves whipped past her, and her eyes watered from the dust and wind.

Turning her head, Quarrah saw the source of her struggle. A face she recognized.

Garifus Floc's arms were outstretched toward her, making himself the center of the Gather detonation, inevitably drawing everything toward him. To use Grit like this, his skull was dark. He hadn't been taken by the Visitant cloud like the others. His loyal followers had risked everything for him, and Evetherey had stolen them away. But he was still here.

"Coward!" she screamed, her voice instantly whisked in his direction.

"You don't understand, child," he said. "Your Drothan goddess has taken the majority." His face tightened in a grimace. "But they were not mine."

*What?*

So Centrum had lost the battle, after all! His announcement to cease the fighting and ignite their minds had caused the opposing side to do so as well. And when Evetherey saw that *their* numbers were greater, she had taken them instead of Garifus's loyalists!

"*Haste!*" Evetherey urged again in her mind. "*One of them is approaching the cloud.*"

Quarrah's fingers were scraped and bleeding, the flat paver stone beginning to pull loose from the ground. Her clothes were plastered to her body, the glass knife digging into her side.

"But all is right again," Garifus chimed behind her. "Your Drothan has done us the favor of purging the gangrenous limb of disunity. Those that remain have now been tested and proven. Our minds are one. There is no defense against the transparency of our red glass."

*Red glass …*

Her mother's voice came racing back to her, hallucinated words from inside the *Ucru* that suddenly made sense after so much time.

Sucking in a deep breath, Quarrah risked letting go of the flat stone with one hand. She didn't have to focus or aim—Garifus was doing that for her. All she had to do was rip off her belt. Her knuckles raked across the buckle, loosening it just enough for Lyndel's glass knife to come free. Instantly, the weapon was caught in Centrum's Gather, whisked toward him before he could stop it.

The blade passed his outstretched hands, its momentum driving the tip home through Garifus Floc's right eye. Quarrah heard the shattering of glass as the knifepoint smashed through the back of his skull.

"*Point into the Homeland.*"

At once, the detonation of Gather Grit lost its hold and she tumbled forward. Getting her feet down, Quarrah Khai ran the final distance and leapt into the Sphere as it closed behind her.

~

*still, it doesn't make it easy to say goodbye.*

# EPILOGUE

*This* was the treasure?

Five cycles of planning to get past eighteen temple guards, six flights of stairs, nine locks, and a Void Grit trap that had nearly blown her halfway back to the old timeline. And *this* was all Evetherey had been hiding?

A book.

Quarrah really didn't have time to read anything right now. Raek was at the temple entrance, distracting the guards with some great hullabaloo. Probably another doctrinal tiff with Isle Halavend. Six stories up in Evetherey's Drothan temple and Quarrah could easily hear the big man's voice. If he'd still been a Glassmind, Raek's shouting probably would have deafened everyone within a quarter mile.

She took a cautious step forward and lifted the book from the little stone table in the center of the room. Particles of dust swirled in the glow of her Light Grit detonation. No matter the treasure, it felt *good* to be thieving again! It scratched an itch that had been bothering her for more than half a year now. Sure, she'd swiped a few goods in the last cycles, but it barely satisfied. Most of the people weren't even protecting the common things she'd nabbed.

But in this windowless stone room, she could almost pretend like she was back in Beripent—the old city, with its noises and smells. Its bustling crowds and an energy that filled its labyrinthine streets all the way up to a damp smoky sky.

Not enough places to hide in this new world.

And not nearly enough things to steal.

Turning toward the doorway, Quarrah cracked open the book. Might as well have a peek at the first page. She stopped, frozen as if in Stasis, except for the pounding of her heart, which suddenly increased tenfold.

That was Ard's handwriting.

She snapped the book shut. Sparks, did she even *want* to read this? Time was softening the pain. Would reading something he'd written only dig it up? And what was it doing here at the top of the Drothan temple? Evetherey was guarding Ard's words?

Never mind. She could talk it over with Raek. They could read it together.

She had taken only one more step when her hands opened the book of their own accord. And once she saw her name written there, she couldn't help but read on.

*My dear Quarrah Khai,*

*You deserve the truth, so I'll do my best to lay it all out for you. Consider this <u>my</u> glass mind. No tricks. No lies. All my barest intentions made plain even to the simplest of human minds.*

*Just to clarify, I am in no way calling <u>you</u> simpleminded. Sparks. One paragraph in and I'm already making a mess of things. I never could keep my silver tongue around you.*

*I'm feeling heavy tonight, yet there is a strange freedom in this weight upon my shoulders. Centrum and his Glassminds will probably strike in the morning—if not sooner. I have made every necessary arrangement and I believe we will succeed.*

*By the time you read this, you'll either be safely settled into your new world, or . . . Or I guess you'll be erased along with all of existence. I sure as sparks hope my plan works. Evetherey seems confident. She already peered through the Sphere and found the place—and time—where all the survivors can exit.*

*You've actually been there before. You'll find yourselves back on the bottom of the InterIsland Waters in a time long before the islands and the seas. It'll be a sweeping, expansive landscape, safe from the Red Moon, which will have returned to its original position on the dark side of the world. Evetherey has told me that civilization will be protected as long as people don't go beyond the sea to the east, and the mountains to the west.*

*But isn't that what was said before, thousands of years ago when the first Othians rebelled? Evetherey will take you to a time that predates even that. A time before life even existed on this planet.*

*Which only begs the question ... Is all of time nothing but a great loop? Wayfarist doctrine implies that humans came into this world from a "place beyond time." Sounds like being lost in the Sphere to me.*

*See? It's just a big circle. In generations, the stories of our exploits will become legend. Then scripture, I'll wager. Why else would Gloristar and Portsend find their names in the same verse? And why would the word <u>Ardor</u> appear so many times, ultimately driving me to do the very things I did?*

*I hope you'll grant me that one last arrogance. It's something you won't have to put up with any longer. I'm going to change. I'm going to be a better man.*

*I've been thinking of that night often—The night I became a Paladin Visitant and returned to our time with a fertilized dragon egg. I wonder how things might have turned out differently if I'd listened to you then. If I hadn't sent the egg into the palace to rescue Raek and lure out Pethredote.*

*I still see your face sometimes, pleading with me not to risk the egg for vengeance. But I didn't listen. I fired my Roller into the air to alert the Regulators of the egg's position. Those same shots sent you away, and no matter how hard I've tried, I understand that there's no getting you back.*

*And that's okay. You deserve someone better. Someone kinder. Someone who is able to see your complexities and appreciate your passions—not just as a supplement to his own, but as an independent entity with no limitations or restrictions. As much as I wanted to be that man, I found myself sorely lacking.*

*By now, you've probably thumbed through this journal to see how longwinded I'm going to be. Yes, I filled every page. When you finish reading this foreword, I won't be offended if you toss this book. But if you choose to read on, you can consider this an official letter of apology, like the ones I wrote for the queen when I accepted her pardon. Only, I'm not expecting a pardon from you, Quarrah. More than anything, I'm writing this to clear my conscience. To acknowledge my vast shortcomings and misbehaviors over the years.*

*You know I was always swept away by the job. My need to outthink and outplan everyone was like dragonfire consuming the forest of my soul. But I only ever bit off what I knew I could chew. I only ever tackled the enemies I knew would go down.*

*So you see, it was all planned. There never was a single word that could change the world. Words are my favorite weapons, and yet I knew all along that there was nothing I could say to get the Glassminds to turn on each other.*

*<u>Curiosity</u> changes minds. It has the power to drive people to do things. Why do you need to know what treasures are hiding on the other side of a locked door? Why did I ruse my way into all kinds of situations?*

*Curiosity.*

*And if it's such a driving force for flawed humans like you and me, imagine what effect it might have on an enhanced, perfected mind. I know that the best chance I have of dividing the Glassminds is by piquing their curiosity. But in order for this to happen, I know I need to die. Could there be anything more powerful than a man's final words?*

*I went to Lyndel last night and negotiated the terms of my execution. It really is the only way. The Trothians will get their justice for my crimes, the Glassminds will erode into disunity, and Evetherey will be able to capture them in the Visitant cloud so the survivors can exit and restart all of time from the beginning.*

*But there is one more ruse you don't know about. I thought it up on my way back from Sunden Springs. I found something there in the absence of my parents. I found another person living my life. A different version of my life. And as I sat on the hill between the headstones of my mother and father, my own fate became terribly clear to me.*

*Still, it doesn't make it easy to say goodbye.*

*But what is "goodbye" when all of time and space has been perfected in a single Sphere? If all goes according to plan, Evetherey will exchange the lives of the Glassminds for our meager group of survivors, and I have asked her to net a few more of Centrum's people than necessary. Once she has them, she will scan through alternate timelines until she finds a near-identical version of a few friends we lost along the way. I've given her the names and she can bring them back to life—Shad Agaul, Lomaya Vans, Prime Isless Gloristar, Portsend Wal, Isle Halavend…*

*But not me.*

*And therein lies my final ruse. Unfortunately, I'll be dead, so I'm counting on Evetherey to carry it out for me. I have asked her to sift through the timelines to find a version of Ardor Benn that is* better*. A version that didn't fire those shots into the empty night. Assuming there is one—and with an infinite number of possibilities, I'm surely hoping I'm not always an idiot—Evetherey has agreed to bring my alternate into the new world under a cloud of Stasis Grit.*

*I see no reason why he should ever wake up if you don't wish to meet him. But if you do, I told Evetherey to keep him buried at the foothills of the western mountains. She will keep the Stasis Grit burning over my alternate body for a year, which I hope will be enough time for you to decide. Of course, when the Grit runs out, New Ard will suffocate…and supposedly, he's a really nice guy, so I don't think you want that on your conscience.*

*All jesting aside, there would be no death in that. Because, technically, he was never supposed to exist in the Material Time. The choice is yours, Quarrah, but I'm hoping you'll give him a chance.*

*One more thing… We can't have Raek running around with a cracked glass skull and sparking fingertips, so I told Evetherey to swap him for the old Raek. He'll get an upgrade, though, because she'll pick a version of him that didn't get stabbed through the heart. And for all our sakes, I'm hoping he gets a better-looking face.*

*Evetherey's going to keep this book well guarded and locked securely away. I figure that'll draw you and Raek right to it. And if you thought it was hard to get this book, wait until you see what traps and safeguards Evetherey placed around my alternate body. I'm sure you and Raek are itching for a challenge, so . . .*

Quarrah read the last line aloud.

"Come steal me."

# ACKNOWLEDGMENTS

The first inklings of a magic system based on dragon dung came to me as a teenage boy (sounds about right, huh?). It wasn't until some fifteen years later that I found a character who I felt was capable of pulling off such an *unusual* magic system.

I recorded and dictated most of Nemery's chapters while hiking the mountains of northern Utah. Pekal felt very real and majestic at times, and I could almost see the dragons through the aspen trees.

Big thanks to my family—my wife and two boys who live with a man every bit as intense and driven as Ard. Thanks to my parents and siblings and nieces and nephews for their huge support in my writing career.

As always, thanks to my dedicated agent, Ammi-Joan Paquette, for her support in this project. I'd like to thank my editor, Bradley Englert, and the great team at Orbit. Thanks to Lauren Panepinto for the art direction, Ben Zweifel for the amazing cover art, and Serena Malyon for the map.

And thank YOU, reader! I loved writing this trilogy and the characters meant a lot to me. Linear time is valuable and I'm grateful for every minute you spent reading my books!

# extras

www.orbitbooks.net

# about the author

**Tyler Whitesides** is the author of bestselling children's series Janitors and The Wishmakers. *The Thousand Deaths of Ardor Benn* is his adult debut. When he's not writing, Tyler enjoys playing percussion, hiking, fly-fishing, cooking, and the theater. He lives in the mountains of northern Utah with his wife and two sons.

Find out more about Tyler Whitesides and other Orbit authors by registering for the free monthly newsletter at www.orbitbooks.net.

# if you enjoyed

# THE LAST LIES OF ARDOR BENN

### look out for

# THE RAGE OF DRAGONS

## The Burning: Book One

### by

# Evan Winter

*IN A WORLD CONSUMED BY ENDLESS WAR, ONE YOUNG MAN WILL BECOME HIS PEOPLE'S ONLY HOPE FOR SURVIVAL.*

*The Omehi people have been fighting an unwinnable war for generations. The lucky ones are born gifted: some have the power to call down dragons, others can be magically transformed into bigger, stronger, faster killing machines.*

*Everyone else is fodder, destined to fight and die in the endless war. Tau Tafari wants more than this, but his plans of escape are destroyed when those closest to him are brutally murdered.*

*With too few gifted left, the Omehi are facing genocide, but Tau cares only for revenge. Following an unthinkable path, he will strive to become the greatest swordsman to ever live, willing to die a hundred thousand times for the chance to kill three of his own people.*

# LANDFALL

Queen Taifa stood at the bow of *Targon*, her beached warship, and looked out at the massacre on the sands. Her other ships were empty. The fighting men and women of the Chosen were already onshore, were already killing and dying. Their screams, not so different from the cries of those they fought, washed over her in waves.

She looked to the sun. It burned high overhead and the killing would not stop until well past nightfall, which meant too many more would die. She heard footsteps on the deck behind her and tried to take comfort in the sounds of Tsiory's gait.

'My queen,' he said.

Taifa nodded, permitting him to speak, but did not turn away from the slaughter on the shore. If this was to be the end of her people, she would bear witness. She could do that much.

'We cannot hold the beach,' he told her. 'We have to retreat to the ships. We have to relaunch them.'

'No, I won't go back on the water. The rest of the fleet will be here soon.'

'Families, children, the old and infirm. Not fighters. Not Gifted.'

Taifa hadn't turned. She couldn't face him, not yet. 'It's beautiful here,' she told him. 'Hotter than Osonte, but beautiful. Look.' She pointed to the mountains in the distance. 'We landed on a peninsula bordered and bisected by mountains. It's defensible, arable. We could make a home here. Couldn't we? A home for my people.'

She faced him. His presence comforted her. Champion Tsiory, so strong and loyal. He made her feel safe, loved. She wished she could do the same for him.

His brows were knitted and sweat beaded on his shaved head. He had been near the front lines, fighting. She hated that, but he was her champion and she could not ask him to stay with her on a beached ship while her people, his soldiers, died.

He shifted and made to speak. She didn't want to hear it. No more reports, no more talk of the strange gifts these savages wielded against her kind.

'The *Malawa* arrived a few sun spans ago,' she told him. 'My old nursemaid was on board. She went to the Goddess before it made ground.'

'Sanura's gone? My queen . . . I'm so—'

'Do you remember how she'd tell the story of the dog that bit me when I was a child?'

'I remember hearing you bit it back and wouldn't let go. Sanura had to call the Queen's Guard to pull you off the poor thing.'

Taifa turned back to the beach, filled with the dead and dying in their thousands. 'Sanura went to the Goddess on that ship, never knowing we found land, never knowing we escaped the Cull. They couldn't even burn her properly.' The battle seemed louder. 'I won't go back on the water.'

'Then we die on this beach.'

The moment had arrived. She wished she had the courage to face him for it. 'The Gifted, the ones with the forward scouts, sent word. They found the rage.' Taifa pointed to the horizon, past the slaughter, steeling herself. 'They're nested in the Central Mountains, the ones dividing the peninsula, and one of the dragons has just given birth. There is a youngling and I will form a coterie.'

'No,' he said. 'Not this. Taifa . . .'

She could hear his desperation. She would not let it sway her.

'The savages, how can we make peace if we do this to them?' Tsiory said, but the argument wasn't enough to change her mind, and he must have sensed that. 'We were only to follow them,' he said. 'If we use the dragons, we'll destroy this land. If we use the dragons, the Cull will find us.'

That sent a chill through her. Taifa was desperate to forget what they'd run from and aware that, could she live a thousand cycles, she never would. 'Can you hold this land for me, my champion?' she asked, hating herself for making this seem his fault, his shortcoming.

'I cannot.'

'Then,' she said, turning to him, 'the dragons will.'

Tsiory wouldn't meet her eyes. That was how much she'd hurt him, how much she'd disappointed him. 'Only for a little while,' she said, trying to bring him back to her. 'Too little for the Cull to notice and just long enough to survive.'

'Taifa—'

'A short while.' She reached up and touched his face. 'I swear it on my love for you.' She needed him and felt fragile enough to break, but she was determined to see her people safe first. 'Can you give us enough time for the coterie to do their work?'

Tsiory took her hand and raised it to his lips. 'You know I will.'

# CHAMPION TSIORY

Tsiory stared at the incomplete maps laid out on the command tent's only table. He tried to stand tall, wanting to project an image of strength for the military leaders with him, but he swayed slightly, a blade of grass in an imperceptible breeze. He needed rest and was unlikely to get it.

It'd been three days since he'd last gone to the ships to see Taifa. He didn't want to think he was punishing her. He told himself he had to be here, where the fighting was thickest. She wanted him to hold the beach and push into the territory beyond it, and that was what he was doing.

The last of the twenty-five hundred ships had arrived, and every woman, man, and child who was left of the Chosen was now on this hostile land. Most of the ships had been scavenged for resources, broken to pieces, so the Omehi could survive. There would be no retreat. Losing against the savages would mean the end of his people, and that Tsiory could not permit.

The last few days had been filled with fighting, but his soldiers had beaten back the natives. More than that, Tsiory had taken the beach, pushed into the tree line, and marched the bulk of his army deeper into the peninsula. He couldn't hold the ground he'd taken, but he'd given her time. He'd done as his queen had asked.

Still, he couldn't pretend he wasn't angry with her. He loved Taifa, the Goddess knew he did, but she was playing a suicidal game. Capturing the peninsula with dragons wouldn't mean much if they brought the Cull down on themselves.

'Champion!' An Indlovu soldier entered the command tent, taking Tsiory from his thoughts. 'Major Ojore is being overrun. He's asking for reinforcements.'

'Tell him to hold.' Tsiory knew the young soldier wanted to say more. He didn't give him the chance. 'Tell Major Ojore to hold.'

'Yes, Champion!'

Harun spat some of the calla leaf he was always chewing. 'He can't hold,' the colonel told Tsiory and the rest of the assembled Guardian Council. The men were huddled in their makeshift tent beyond the beach. They were off the hot sands and sheltered by the desiccated trees that bordered them. 'He's out of arrows. It's all that kept the savages off him, and Goddess knows, the wood in this forsaken land is too brittle to make more.'

Tsiory looked over his shoulder at the barrel-chested colonel. Harun was standing close enough for him to smell the man's sour breath. Returning his attention to the hand-drawn maps their scouts had made of the peninsula, Tsiory shook his head. 'There are no reinforcements.'

'You're condemning Ojore and his fighters to death.'

Tsiory waited, and, as expected, Colonel Dayo Okello chimed in. 'Harun is right. Ojore will fall and our flank will collapse. You need to speak with the queen. Make her see sense. We're outnumbered and the savages have gifts we've never encountered before. We can't win.'

'We don't need to,' Tsiory said. 'We just need to give her time.'

'How long? How long until we have the dragons?' Tahir

asked, pacing. He didn't look like the man Tsiory remembered from home. Tahir Oni came from one of the Chosen's wealthiest families and was renowned for his intelligence and precision. He was a man who took intense pride in his appearance.

Back on Osonte, every time Tsiory had seen Tahir, the man's head was freshly shaved, his dark skin oiled to a sheen, and his colonel's uniform sculpted to his muscular frame. The man before him now was a stranger to that memory.

Tahir's head was stubbly, his skin dry, and his uniform hung off a wasted body. Worse, it was difficult for Tsiory to keep his eyes from the stump of Tahir's right arm, which was bleeding through its bandages.

Tsiory needed to calm these men. He was their leader, their inkokeli, and they needed to believe in their mission and queen. He caught Tahir's attention, tried to hold it and speak confidently, but the soldier's eyes twitched like a prey animal's.

'The savages won't last against dragons,' Tsiory said. 'We'll break them. Once we have firm footing, we can defend the whole of the valley and peninsula indefinitely.'

'Your lips to the Goddess's ears, Tsiory,' Tahir muttered, without using either of his honorifics.

'Escaping the Cull,' Dayo said, echoing Tsiory's unvoiced thoughts, 'won't mean anything if we all die here. I say we go back to the ships and find somewhere a little less . . . occupied.'

'What ships, Dayo? There aren't enough for all of us, and we don't have the resources to travel farther. We're lucky the dragons led us here,' Tsiory said. 'It was a gamble, hoping they'd find land before we starved. Even if we could take to the water again, without them leading us, we'd have no hope.'

Harun waved his arms at their surroundings. 'Does this look like hope to you, Tsiory?'

'You'd rather die on the water?'

'I'd rather not die at all.'

Tsiory knew where the conversation would head next, and it would be close to treason. These were hard men, good men, but the voyage had made them as brittle as this strange land's wood. He tried to find the words to calm them, when the shouting outside their tent began.

'What in the Goddess's name—' said Harun, opening the tent's flap and looking out. He couldn't have seen the hatchet that took his life. It happened too fast.

Tahir cursed, scrambling back as Harun's severed head fell to the ground at his feet.

'Swords out!' Tsiory said, drawing his weapon and slicing a cut through the rear of the tent to avoid the brunt of whatever was out front.

Tsiory was first through the new exit, blinking under the sun's blinding light, and all around him was chaos. Somehow, impossibly, a massive force of savages had made their way past the distant front lines, and his lightly defended command camp was under assault.

He had just enough time to absorb this when a savage, spear in hand, leapt for him. Tsiory, inkokeli of the Omehi military and champion to Queen Taifa, slipped to the side of the man's downward thrust and swung hard for his neck. His blade bit deep and the man fell, his life's blood spilling onto the white sands.

He turned to his colonels. 'Back to the ships!'

It was the only choice. The majority of their soldiers were on the front lines, far beyond the trees, but the enemy was between Tsiory and his army. Back on the beach, camped in the shadows of their scavenged ships, there were fighters and Gifted, held in reserve to protect the Omehi people. Tsiory, the colonels, the men assigned to the command camp, they had to get back there if they hoped to survive and repel the ambush.

Tsiory cursed himself for a fool. His colonels had wanted the command tent pitched inside the tree line, to shelter the leadership from the punishing sun, and though it didn't feel right, he'd been unable to make any arguments against the decision. The tree line ended well back from the front lines, and he'd believed they had enough soldiers to ensure they were protected. He was wrong.

'Run!' Tsiory shouted, pulling Tahir along.

They made it three steps before their escape was blocked by another savage. Tahir fumbled for his sword, forgetting for a moment that he'd lost his fighting hand. He called out for help and reached for his blade with his left. His fingers hadn't even touched the sword's hilt when the savage cut him down.

Tsiory lunged at the half-naked aggressor, blade out in front, skewering the tattooed man who'd killed Tahir. He stepped back from the impaled savage, seeking to shake him off the sword, but the heathen, blood bubbling in his mouth, tried to stab him with a dagger made of bone.

Tsiory's bronze-plated leathers turned the blow and he grabbed the man's wrist, breaking it across his knee. The dagger fell to the sand and Tsiory crashed his forehead into his opponent's nose, snapping the man's head back. With his enemy stunned, Tsiory shoved all his weight forward, forcing the rest of his sword into the man's guts, drawing an open-mouthed howl from him that spattered Tsiory with blood and phlegm.

He yanked his weapon away, pulling it clear of the dying native, and swung round to rally his men. He saw Dayo fighting off five savages with the help of a soldier and ran toward them as more of the enemy emerged from the trees.

They were outnumbered, badly, and they'd all die if they didn't disengage. He kept running but couldn't get to his colonel before Dayo took the point of a long-hafted spear to the side and went down. The closest soldier killed the native who had dealt the blow, and Tsiory, running full tilt, slammed into two others, sending them to the ground.

On top of them, he pulled his dagger from his belt and rammed it into the closest man's eye. The other one, struggling beneath him, reached for a trapped weapon, but Tsiory shoved his sword hilt against the man's throat, using his weight to press it down. He heard the bones in the man's neck crack, and the savage went still.

Tsiory got to his feet and grabbed Dayo, 'Go!'

Dayo, bleeding everywhere, went.

'Back to the beach!' Tsiory ordered the soldiers near him. 'Back to the ships!'

Tsiory ran with his men, looking back to see how they'd been undone. The savages were using gifts to mask themselves in broad daylight. As he ran, he saw more and more of them stepping out of what his eyes told him were empty spaces among the trees. The trick had allowed them to move an attacking force past the front lines and right up to Tsiory's command tent.

Tsiory forced himself to move faster. He had to get to the reserves and order a defensive posture. His heart hammered in his chest and it wasn't from running. If the savages had a large enough force, this surprise attack could kill everyone. They'd still have the front-line army, but the women, men, and children they were meant to protect would be dead.

Tsiory heard galloping. It was an Ingonyama, riding double with his Gifted, on one of the few horses put on the ships when they fled Osonte. The Ingonyama spotted Tsiory and rode for him.

'Champion,' the man said, dismounting with his Gifted. 'Take the horse. I will allow the others to escape.'

Tsiory mounted, saluted before galloping away, and looked back. The Gifted, a young woman, little more than a girl, closed her eyes and focused, and the Ingonyama began to change, slowly at first, but with increasing speed.

The warrior grew taller. His skin, deep black, darkened further, and, moving like a million worms writhing beneath his flesh, the man's muscles re-formed thicker and stronger. The soldier, a Greater Noble of the Omehi, was already powerful and deadly, but now that his Gifted's powers flowed through him, he was a colossus.

The Ingonyama let out a spine-chilling howl and launched himself at his enemies. The savages tried to hold, but there was little any man, no matter how skilled, could do against an Enraged Ingonyama.

The Ingonyama shattered a man's skull with his sword pommel, and in the same swing, he split another from collarbone to waist. Grabbing a third heathen by the arm, he threw him ten strides.

Strain evident on her face, the Gifted did all she could to maintain her Ingonyama's transformation. 'The champion has called a retreat,' she shouted to the Omehi soldiers within earshot. 'Get back to the ships!'

The girl – she was too young for Tsiory to think of her as much else – gritted her teeth, pouring energy into the enraged warrior, struggling as six more savages descended on him.

The first of the savages staggered back, his chest collapsed inward by the Ingonyama's fist. The second, third, and fourth leapt on him together, stabbing at him in concert. Tsiory could see the Gifted staggering with each blow her Ingonyama took. She held on, though, brave thing, as the target of her powers fought and killed.

It's enough, thought Tsiory, leave. It's enough.

The Ingonyama didn't. They almost never did. The colossus was surrounded, swarmed, mobbed, and the savages did so much damage to him that he had to end his connection to the Gifted or kill her too.

The severing was visible as two flashes of light emanating from the bodies of both the Ingonyama and the Gifted. It was difficult to watch what happened next. Unpowered, the Ingonyama's body shrank and his strength faded. The next blow cut into his flesh and, given time, would have killed him.

The savages gave it no time. They tore him to pieces and ran for the Gifted. She pulled a knife from her tunic and slit her own throat before they could get to her. That didn't dissuade them. They fell on her and stabbed her repeatedly, hooting as they did.

Tsiory, having seen enough, looked away from the butchery, urging the horse to run faster. He'd make it to the ships and the reserves of the Chosen army. The Ingonyama and Gifted had given him that with their lives. It was hard to think it mattered.

Too many savages had poured out from the tree line. They'd come in force and the Chosen could not hold. The upcoming battle would be his last.